PENGUIN C

WAVERLE

WALTER SCOTT was born in Edinburgh in 1771, educated at the High School and University there, and admitted to the Scottish Bar in 1792. From 1799 until his death he was Sheriff-Depute of Selkirkshire, and from 1806 to 1830 he held a well-paid office as a principal clerk to the Court of Session in Edinburgh, the supreme Scottish court. From 1805, too, Scott was secretly an investor in, and increasingly controller of, the printing and publishing business of his associates, the Ballantyne brothers.

Despite suffering crippling polio in infancy, conflict with his Calvinist lawyer father in adolescence, rejection by the woman he loved in his twenties and financial ruin in his fifties, Scott displayed an amazingly productive energy, and his personal warmth was attested by almost everybody he met. His first literary efforts, in the late 1790s, were translations of romantic and historical German poems and plays. In 1805 Scott's first considerable original work, *The Lay of the Last Minstrel*, began a series of narrative poems that popularized key incidents and settings of early Scottish history, and brought him fame and fortune.

In 1813 Scott, having declined the Poet Laureateship and recommended Southey instead, moved towards fiction and devised a new form that was to dominate the early-nineteenth-century novel. *Waverley* (1814) and its successors draw on the social and cultural contrasts and the religious and political conflicts of recent Scottish history to illustrate the nature and cost of political and cultural change and the relationship between the historical process and the individual. *Waverley* was published anonymously and, although many people guessed, Scott did not acknowledge authorship of the Waverley Novels until 1827. Many of the novels from *Ivanhoe* (1819) on extended their range to the England and Europe of the Middle Ages and Renaissance. Across the English-speaking world, and by means of innumerable translations throughout Europe, the Waverley Novels changed for ever the way people constructed their personal and national identities.

Scott was created a baronet in 1820. During the financial crisis of 1825-6, Scott, his printer Ballantyne and his publishers Constable and their London partner became insolvent. Scott chose not to be declared bankrupt, determining instead to work to generate funds to pay his creditors. Despite his failing health he continued to write new novels, to revise and annotate earlier ones for a new edition, and to write a nine-volume *Life of Napoleon* and a history of Scotland under the title *Tales of a Grandfather*. His private thoughts during and after his financial crash are set down in a revealing and moving *Journal*. Scott died in September 1832; his creditors were finally paid in full in 1833 from the proceeds of his writing.

PETER GARSIDE is a Professorial Fellow at the University of Edinburgh. He has edited a number of volumes for both the Edinburgh Edition of the Waverley Novels and the Stirling/South Carolina Edition of the Collected Works of James Hogg, and was also one of the general editors of *The English Novel, 1770–1829: A Bibliographical Survey of Prose Fiction Published in the British Isles* (2 vols, 2000). He has also written widely on aspects of Romantic fiction, Scottish literature and publishing history.

IAN DUNCAN is Professor of English at the University of California, Berkeley. He is the author of *Scott's Shadow: The Novel in Romantic Edinburgh* (2007) and *Modern Romance and Transformations of the Novel* (1992), and a co-editor of *Scotland and the Borders of Romanticism* (2004), *Travel Writing 1700–1830* (2005), *Approaches to Teaching Scott's Waverley Novels* (2009) and the forthcoming *Edinburgh Companion to James Hogg*. He has edited Scott's *Rob Roy* and *Ivanhoe*, as well as Hogg's *Winter Evening Tales* and *Private Memoirs and Confessions of a Justified Sinner*.

Emeritus Professor DAVID HEWITT held the Regius Chalmers Chair in English Literature at the University of Aberdeen until his retirement. He is the editor-in-chief of the Edinburgh Edition of the Waverley Novels, and a Director of Aberdeen's Walter Scott Research Centre. He edited Scott's *The Antiquary* and *Rob Roy* and co-edited *The Heart of Midlothian* and *Redgauntlet* for the Edinburgh Edition and has published widely on nineteenth-century and modern Scottish literature

CLAIRE LAMONT is Emeritus Professor of English Romantic Literature at Newcastle University. She specializes in the study of English and Scottish poets and novelists of the late eighteenth and early nineteenth centuries, in particular Austen, Scott and Wordsworth. She edited Scott's *Chronicles of the Canongate* for the Edinburgh Edition of the Waverley Novels and is the Advisory Editor for the novels of that edition published in paperback by Penguin.

WALTER SCOTT

WAVERLEY

Edited by
P. D. GARSIDE
with an introduction by
IAN DUNCAN

PENGUIN BOOKS

PENGUIN CLASSICS

Published by the Penguin Group
Penguin Books Ltd 80 Strand, London WC2R ORL, England
Penguin Group (USA) Inc., 375 Hudson Street, New York, New York 10014, USA
Penguin Group (Canada), 90 Eglinton Avenue East, Suite 700, Toronto, Ontario,
Canada M4P 2Y3 (a division of Pearson Penguin Canada Inc.)
Penguin Ireland, 25 St Stephen's Green, Dublin 2, Ireland (a division of Penguin Books Ltd)
Penguin Group (Australia), 250 Camberwell Road, Camberwell, Victoria 3124, Australia
(a division of Pearson Australia Group Pty Ltd)
Penguin Books India Pvt Ltd, 11 Community Centre, Panchsheel Park, New Delhi – 110 017, India
Penguin Group (NZ), 67 Apollo Drive, Rosedale, Auckland 0632, New Zealand
(a division of Pearson New Zealand Ltd)
Penguin Books (South Africa) (Pty) Ltd, 24 Sturdee Avenue, Rosebank, Johannesburg 2196, South Africa

Penguin Books Ltd, Registered Offices: 80 Strand, London WC2R ORL, England

www.penguin.com

First published 1814
Published in the Edinburgh Edition of the Waverley Novels by the Edinburgh University Press 2007
Published with revised critical apparatus in Penguin Classics 2011

021

Text, historical note, explanatory notes and glossary
© The University Court of the University of Edinburgh, 2007
Editor-in-chief's Preface and Chronology © David Hewitt, 1998
Introduction © Ian Duncan, 2011
Note on the Text © Peter Garside, 2011
All rights reserved

The moral right of the editors and authors of the introduction and editorial material has been asserted

Set in 10.25/10.75pt Postscript Ehrhardt MT
Typeset by Jouve (UK), Milton Keynes
Printed in England by Clays Ltd, Elcograf S.p.A

ISBN: 978-0-140-43660-0

www.greenpenguin.co.uk

CONTENTS

ACKNOWLEDGEMENTS

The editors of a critical edition incur many debts, and the indebtedness of the editors of the Edinburgh Edition of the Waverley Novels and of its paperback progeny in the Penguin Scott is particularly heavy. The universities which employ editors have, in practice, provided the most substantial assistance; but in addition the Universities of Edinburgh and of Aberdeen have been particularly generous with their grants towards the cost of editorial preparation, and it has been the support of the British Academy and the Arts and Humanities Research Council that has allowed the Edition to employ a research fellow.

The Edinburgh Edition of the Waverley Novels has been most fortunate in having as its principal financial sponsor the Bank of Scotland, which has continued its long and fruitful involvement with the affairs of Walter Scott. The P. F. Charitable Trust and the Robertson Trust have also given generous grants.

Scott's manuscripts are widely distributed, but the greatest concentrations are in the National Library of Scotland in Edinburgh and the Pierpont Morgan Library in New York, which between them hold the bulk of the surviving manuscript of *Waverley*. Without their preparedness to make manuscripts readily accessible, and to provide support beyond the ordinary, this edition would not have been feasible.

The editors have, perforce, had to seek specialist advice on many matters, and they are most grateful to their consultants, Professor John Cairns, Professor Thomas Craik, Caroline Jackson-Houlston, Professor David Nordloh, Professor Donald Meek, Roy Pinkerton and Professor David Stevenson. They owe much to their research fellows, Mairi Robinson and Gerard Carruthers. They have asked many colleagues far and wide for information. They have continuously sought advice from the members of the Scott Advisory Board, and are particularly grateful for the support of Professor Jane Millgate and the late Sir Kenneth Alexander, Professor David Daiches, Professor Douglas Mack and Dr Archie Turnbull.

Additionally, the editor of *Waverley* would like to thank the following for specific advice, information or assistance: Professor Ian Campbell, Professor Claire Connolly, Professor Douglas Gifford, Professor Andrew Hook, Richard J. Jackson, Lindsay Levy,

Dr Anthony Mandal, Professor Silvia Mergenthal, Professor Murray Pittock, Dr Colm Ó Baoill and Dr Sharon Ragaz.

To all of these the editors express their thanks, and acknowledge that the production of the Edinburgh Edition of the Waverley Novels and the Penguin Scott has involved a collective effort to which all those mentioned by name, and very many others, have contributed generously and with enthusiasm.

David Hewitt
Editor-in-chief

Claire Lamont
Advisory editor, the Penguin Scott

J. H. Alexander
P. D. Garside
Alison Lumsden
G. A. M. Wood
General editors

The novels of Walter Scott published in Penguin are based on the volumes of the Edinburgh Edition of the Waverley Novels (EEWN). This series, which started publication in 1993 and runs to thirty volumes, is published in hardback by Edinburgh University Press. The Penguin edition of *Waverley* reproduces the text of the novel, Historical Note, Explanatory Notes and Glossary unaltered from the EEWN volume. It does not reproduce the substantial amount of textual information in the Edinburgh Edition but instead provides, in the following paragraphs, a summary of general issues common to all Scott's novels and, in the Note on the Text, a succinct statement of the textual history of *Waverley*. A new critical introduction has been written specifically for the paperback, as well as a Chronology of Scott's life and a list of recommended further reading.

The most important aspect of the EEWN is that the text of the novels is based on the first editions, corrected so as to present what may be termed an 'ideal first edition'. Normally Scott's novels gestated over a long period: for instance, the historical works on which he drew for *The Tale of Old Mortality* (1816) had all been read by 1800. By contrast the process of committing a novel to paper, and of converting the manuscript into print, was in most cases extremely rapid. Scott wrote on only one side of his paper, and he used the blank back of the preceding leaf for additions and corrections, made both as he wrote and as he read over what he had written the previous day. Scott's novels were published anonymously—hence the title 'the Waverley Novels', named after the first of them— which meant that only a few people could be allowed to see his handwritten manuscript. Before delivery to the printing-house, therefore, the manuscript was copied and it was the copy that went to the compositor. The person who oversaw the printing of Scott's novels was his friend and business partner James Ballantyne, with whom he jointly owned the printing firm of James Ballantyne & Co. from 1805 (except for the period 1816–22 when Scott was sole partner) until they both became insolvent in 1826.

The compositors in the printing-house set the novels as copy arrived, and while doing so they inserted the great majority of the punctuation marks, normalised and regularised the spelling without standardising it, and corrected many small errors. It was in the printing-house that the presentation of the texts of the novels was changed from the conventions appropriate to manuscript to those of a printed novel of the early nineteenth century. Proofs were corrected in-house, and then a new set of proofs was given to Ballantyne, who annotated them prior to sending them to the author. Scott did not read his proofs against his manuscript or against the printer's copy; he read for sense and, making full use of the prerogatives of ownership, he took the opportunity of revising, amplifying, and even introducing new ideas. Thus for Scott reading proofs was a creative rather than just a corrective engagement with his texts. The proofs went back to Ballantyne, who oversaw the copying of Scott's new material on to a clean set of proofs and its incorporation into the printed text. Only occasionally did Scott see revised proofs. Two points in particular might be noted about the above procedures. First, Scott delivered his manuscript in batches as he wrote it, and the result was that the first part of a novel was set in type, and proofs corrected, before the end was written. And secondly, in the business of turning a rapidly written text from manuscript to print Scott was indebted to a series of people, copyist, printer, proof-reader, whom Scott editors have come to refer to as 'the intermediaries'.

The business of producing a Waverley novel was so pressurised that mistakes were inevitable. The manuscript was sometimes misread or misunderstood (Scott's handwriting is neat but his letters poorly differentiated); punctuation was often inserted in a mechanical way and the implication of Scott's light manuscript punctuation lost; period words were sometimes not recognised and more obvious, modern terms were substituted for them. The EEWN has examined every aspect of the first-edition texts in the light of the manuscript and the full textual history of the novel. This has enabled the editors to correct the text where Scott's intentions were clearly not fulfilled in the first edition. The EEWN corrects errors, but it does so conservatively bearing in mind that the production of the printed text was a collective effort to which Scott had given his sanction.

Most of the Waverley Novels went through many editions in Scott's lifetime; Scott was not normally involved in the later editions although very occasionally he did see proofs. But in 1827, after his insolvency the previous year, it was decided to issue the first full collected edition of the Waverley Novels, and much of Scott's time in the last years of his life was committed to writing introductions and notes, and to reviewing his text for what he

called his 'Magnum Opus' ('Great Work'), or Magnum for short.
Scott had acknowledged his authorship of the novels in 1827, and
this enabled him to describe the origins of his novels in the introductions to the Magnum edition in a way which was impossible to
an author seeking anonymity. The Magnum (48 vols, Edinburgh,
1829–33) has formed the basis of every edition of the Waverley
Novels published from Scott's death in 1832 until the EEWN chose
the first editions as its base-text. In the EEWN the additions made
for the Magnum will be published in two volumes at the end of
the series. In the volumes published in Penguin, passages from
the Magnum Introduction relating to the genesis of the novel are
included in the new editorial material produced for the paperback
edition.

This edition of Scott in Penguin offers the reader a text which
is not only closer to what the author actually wrote and intended
but is also new in that it uses for the first time material recovered
from manuscripts and proof-sheets, revealing to fuller view the
flair and precision of Scott's writing. In addition it supplies the
editorial assistance necessary for a modern reader to interpret and
enjoy the novel.

David Hewitt
Editor-in-chief
The Edinburgh Edition of the Waverley Novels

I

Waverley has a strong claim to be the most influential work in the modern history of the novel. With it Walter Scott founded 'the classical form of the historical novel'[1] and made the novel itself historical, ensuring its global ascendancy as a representation of national life. *Waverley* also established the phenomenon of the international best-seller. Published in July 1814, by the end of the year it had gone through three printings and four thousand copies. Two dozen more 'Waverley Novels' – as they came to be known – poured from the press in multiple editions and formats over the next couple of decades, outselling all other novels by 'all the other novelists of the time put together'.[2] That popularity, undiminished throughout the nineteenth century, brought Scott wealth, honours and critical prestige. The Victorians revered him as the paragon of authors, the last of the classics and the first of the moderns one who had reinvented the traditional forms of ballad, folktale, epic and romance for an industrial reading public. His success was not confined to the English-speaking world or even to literature. Translations of *Waverley* appeared in Danish, Dutch, French, German, Italian, Polish, Russian, Spanish and Swedish in Scott's lifetime.[3] Re-tellings and adaptations of his novels cascaded across the genres of print into the theatrical, pictorial, musical, touristic, architectural, ceremonial and other media and practices that made up the nineteenth-century public sphere.

Waverley itself, interestingly, proved not to be an especially popular source for paintings and dramatizations – certainly not on the scale of Scott's later mega-hits *Rob Roy* and *Ivanhoe*.[4] It shaped the collective imagination at a deeper level, where it shapes it today, even as Scott's writings have sunk out of popular consciousness, so thoroughly have they been absorbed. *Waverley* provided a fable and an arrangement of topics that structure the stories we are still telling about the relations between past and present, tradition and progress, and the lives of nations and individuals. A naïve young man ventures into remote frontier territory, encounters outlaws and wild tribes, and gets caught up in a historic struggle between the civilization he represents and an older, 'organic' world of honour and loyalty. In *Waverley* the frontier is the Highlands of Scotland, the haunt of Gaelic-speaking clans. The historic struggle is the Jacobite rising of 1745, the last attempt of the exiled Stuart dynasty to regain the British throne. The 1745 rising makes a double-edged topic for the first historical novel. On the one hand it frames Scott's story with an inevitable outcome. Our knowledge that the Jacobite cause is lost, and that its loss will speed the destruction of the clans, overcasts Waverley's adventure with a fatal cloud. On the other hand, the character of the rising as not simply a power-grab but an attempt to reverse the current of history – to restore a past regime and preserve vanishing worlds of life – charges the tale with the utopian pathos of a crisis in which things might, at least imaginably, have turned out otherwise. The historical novel, committed to the pathway of the present, draws its energy from deviations along roads not taken, tracks not even charted.

Scott followed Shakespeare in making civil war the occasion of historical fiction, as his title-page epigraph proclaims: 'Under which King, Bezonian? speak, or die!' 'History' becomes visible in the clash of rival regimes, thus of alternative histories, and in the catastrophic breach of everyday life. Scott departed from Shakespeare in making the fate of cultures – ways of life and values – at stake in the collision, more than of dynasties or parties; and in giving the losing side the bias of human interest and feeling. Major European novelists in Scott's wake, among them Victor Hugo, Alessandro Manzoni and Lev Tolstoy, transformed his achievement in their own historical novels. Others – Alexandre Dumas, Robert Louis Stevenson – turned the form further in the direction of romantic adventure. Still others, from Honoré de Balzac to George Eliot, applied Scott's insights and techniques to represent modern life as an historically evolving, complex social totality. Scott's impact reverberated across the frontiers and satellites of imperial Europe, where – with Fenimore Cooper in New York, Bankim Chatterjee in Bengal, Ivan Vazov in Bulgaria – the historical novel became the main literary genre for reckoning the struggles of modernization and nation-making. After the heyday of the novel, Scott's fiction would supply a template for the epic ambitions of the next global story-telling medium, from *Birth of a Nation* to *Avatar*.[5]

Scott's popularity and critical standing declined throughout the twentieth century. Standing on its far shore, we may find it difficult to imagine what it was like to be immersed in that living flood. 'People don't read Scott any more', one of Virginia Woolf's characters sneers in *To the Lighthouse* (1927). The aesthetic revolutions of Modernism cast Sir Walter as the Victorians' dreary forefather; the rise of new media, such as film, made his story-telling techniques seem too ponderous – too *literary* – for an electric-age mass public; while academic canons of moral and formal realism sidelined him from the 'great tradition' of the English novel. Even in Scotland, many more people today know Waverley as the name of a railway station than of a masterpiece of world literature. While a revival of scholarly interest in Scott has gathered momentum over the past two decades, buoyed by the new Edinburgh Edition of the Waverley Novels, it is probably safe to predict that his works will never regain their once universal currency. But to have forgotten to read Scott makes it possible to discover him afresh, unencumbered by nineteenth-century imperial pieties. Peter Garside's Edinburgh Edition of *Waverley*, reprinted in this Penguin Classics volume, assists that discovery by bringing us the novel as Scott intended it (or as close to that state as it is possible to get): a rougher, quirkier, more audacious text than the polished and elaborated version of 1829, which became the official *Waverley* for modern readers.

We can read *Waverley*, then, not as one of a set of 'Waverley Novels' (gathering dust in second-hand bookshops) but as a brilliant, mercurial experiment, the product – like *Lyrical Ballads* or *Frankenstein* – of an era rich in literary experiments: hesitantly begun in 1808 and then laid aside, resumed in 1810–11, and rushed to completion in the heady aftermath of the allied victory over Napoleon. Already famous as one of Europe's leading poets – the first volume of *Waverley* was drafted while *Marmion* (1808) and *The Lady of the Lake* (1810) were breaking sales records – Scott decided to try out the ascendant, still barely respectable genre of the novel. He himself promoted the legend that he turned to prose fiction after Byron overtook him with *Childe Harold's Pilgrimage* in 1812, although the evidence indicates that Scott's poems continued to outsell Byron's. It is likely that Scott sensed he had reached the limits of what he could achieve in verse, and took up prose as a more flexible and capacious medium for combining fiction with history, especially recent history. His experiment was spurred by dissatisfaction with the antiquarian heaviness of Joseph Strutt's unfinished medieval romance *Queenhoo-Hall* (1808), for which he had supplied the closing chapters. The opening of *Waverley* shows Scott paying keen attention to the field he is entering (pretending that he is entering it in 1805), as he takes care to distinguish his work – 'neither a romance of chivalry, nor a tale of modern manners' – from the brands of Gothic, sentimental and fashionable-life fiction that crowded the early nineteenth-century market.[6] These negative definitions clear space for his own attempt: 'It is from the great book of Nature, the same through a thousand editions . . . that I have venturously essayed to read a chapter to the public'. In what will become a characteristic gesture, Scott cloaks the innovative force of his experiment in the pretence that it is something well-established – and that the author is only another reader. Scott also hides his famous name. Like most novels of the period, *Waverley* was published anonymously. As his second literary career took off, soaring to altitudes scarcely anyone could have imagined, he held fast to that anonymity. Not 'Sir Walter Scott' but 'the Author of Waverley' blazed across the firmament of late Romanticism.

To get a feel for the scene in which the Author of Waverley made his debut we could do worse than turn to Jane Austen's last completed novel, *Persuasion*, the early chapters of which are set in the late summer and autumn of 1814. In a series of literary discussions, Anne Elliot and Captain Benwick compare the merits of Mr Scott and Lord Byron, the pre-eminent poets of the day. They make no mention of the new novel that was at that moment sweeping up thousands of readers, one of whom was Jane Austen herself. Like many of those readers, Austen saw through the mask of anonymity. 'Walter Scott has no business to write novels, especially good ones,' she complained, several weeks before the mid-November conversation between Anne and Captain Benwick is supposed to take place: 'I do not like him, & do not mean to like Waverley if I can help it – but fear I must.'[7] It is as though she recognized, already, something compulsive or addictive in the new kind of enjoyment offered by Scott's fiction.

Early in *Persuasion*, Austen's narrator reflects on the history of the heroine, Anne Elliot:

> She had been forced into prudence in her youth, she learned romance as she grew older – the natural sequel of an unnatural beginning.
>
> With all these circumstances, recollections and feelings, she could not hear that Captain Wentworth's sister was likely to live at Kellynch, without a revival of former pain; and many a stroll and many a sigh were necessary to dispel the agitation of the idea.[8]

The narrator remarks Anne's turn to 'romance' as the poignant consequence of a thwarted development: 'the natural sequel of an unnatural beginning'. The passage carries a delicate yet unmistakable echo of an analogous episode late in *Waverley*, in which Scott's

narrator considers his hero's progress (also involving 'many a . . .
walk' and 'sigh'). But this reflection brings a disavowal of romance:

> [I]t was in many a winter walk by the shores of Ulswater, that he
> acquired a more complete mastery of a spirit tamed by adversity, than
> his former experience had given him; and that he felt himself entitled
> to say firmly, though perhaps with a sigh, that the romance of his life
> was ended, and that its real history had now commenced. (301)

Edward Waverley's initiation into his life's 'real history' obeys (or
so it seems) the conventional sentence of a banishment of romance
by experience. Inverting that sentence at the beginning of her tale,
Austen admits a subtle affinity with Scott's art, rather than a rebut-
tal of it. *Waverley* and *Persuasion* both close with a modified triumph
of romance, in which the hero and heroine are compensated – more
than compensated – for the disappointments they have endured.
Both novels teach their readers to 'learn romance' through a
renunciation of it, modelled by the characters' arrival at the happy
ending through the winter walk of loss. Austen's echo of Scott also
acknowledges the status of *Persuasion* as her own essay in the
national historical novel: one in which she recalibrates Scott's past
setting, 'sixty years since', to a more recent and far greater national
crisis – not the least momentous product of which is *Waverley*
itself.[9]

II

Waverley sprang into the world without literary forebears, according to Georg Lukács in his classic study of the historical novel.
New historical conditions, the vistas of mass experience and
national consciousness opened by the French Revolution and
Napoleonic Wars, made the new form of representation possible.
Earlier attempts at historical fiction, lacking those conditions,
were not authentically 'historical'.[10] In recent years scholars have
brought to light prior works and traditions eclipsed by Scott's
worldwide triumph, notably a long genealogy of French historical
fiction, reaching back into the seventeenth century, which
developed a fatal tension between love-intrigues of fictional protagonists and the public realm of dynastic and military events.[11]
Scott's own ground-clearing declarations swept some of his local
forerunners from cultural memory. Characters called 'Waverley'
had appeared in novels by Charlotte Smith (*Desmond*, 1792) and

Jane West (*The Loyalists*, 1812), despite Scott's claim to have given his hero 'an uncontaminated name'; Smith's dithering Waverley reads like a parody of Scott's, *avant la lettre* – an effect Scott surely intended. And while Scott acknowledges Anglo-Irish novelist Maria Edgeworth as a model for his depictions of regional life and manners, he neglects to mention Edgeworth's more controversial compatriot, Sydney Owenson, whose 'national tale' *The Wild Irish Girl* (1806) pioneered the plot of a young Englishman's journey to the Celtic hinterland, his love affair with a harp-playing heiress, and a final marriage which recapitulates (and reforms) the political union between their nations. (Scott's Anglo-Scottish version divides the 'national' heroine into two figures, douce Rose Bradwardine and fiery Flora Mac-Ivor.)[12] Most of Scott's local forerunners were women, who dominated the early nineteenth-century British fiction market. The influential periodicals that sought to regulate that market dismissed the novel, accordingly, as a feminine genre, mere 'romance', unworthy of serious attention. By combining fiction with history, the most prestigious of the late-Enlightenment human sciences, Scott raised the novel to something like classical dignity – and in doing so (as such promotions tend to) he reclaimed novel-reading, as well as novel-writing, as a properly masculine business.[13]

Knowledge of his antecedents brings a keener appreciation of Scott's artistic achievement rather than otherwise. The historical novel means something more than the insertion of a fictional protagonist's adventures into a narrative of historical events. *Waverley* and its successors imagine the 'inundation' of ordinary life by the great tides of social and economic change upon which historical events are borne: the breakup of clan and feudal societies, the decay of traditional moral ecologies, the large-scale, complex transformations that we sum up with such words as 'progress', 'development', 'modernization'.[14] Scott's novels render the whole of human life – institutions, customs, manners, morals, beliefs, feelings – as historically saturated, dynamic and interwoven. Especially in the great series of novels of the making of modern Scotland that *Waverley* inaugurated, Scott disclosed the past as 'the prehistory of the present', in Lukács' phrase, 'giving poetic life to those historical, social and human forces which, in the course of a long evolution, have made our present-day life what it is and as we experience it'.[15] The past is historical because the present is. And history determines more than the outcome of the novel's plot. It comes to bear, with an unprecedented force and precision, on the details of setting and character. Scott distinguishes the variety and complexity of motives impelling his Jacobite loyalists, and analyzes (in a notable set piece) the 'mixed and peculiar tone' of the 'acuteness, fire, and ambition' infusing the Highland chief Fergus Mac-Ivor, 'which could only have been acquired Sixty Years since' (98). Had he lived sixty years earlier, observes the narrator, Fergus 'would, in all probability, have wanted the polished manner and knowledge of the world which he now possessed'; sixty years later, 'his ambition and love of rule would have lacked the fuel which his situation now afforded' (98).

The catchphrase 'sixty years since' locates the prehistory of the present at the shifting border between living memory and the written record. Scott drew on reminiscences by witnesses of the 1745 rising he had met in his youth, as well as on manuscript and printed chronicles, memoirs, travelogues and newspaper reports, not just for the record of party intrigues and military campaigns but for the ethnographic and antiquarian details of ordinary life. Trained in the tenets of the Scottish Enlightenment, Scott brought a method to this matter. While a student he had attended the lectures of Dugald Stewart, Professor of Moral Philosophy at Edinburgh University; one of his lifelong friends was the son of Stewart's teacher, Adam Ferguson, whose *History of Civil Society* (1767) developed the sociological and anthropological mode of 'philosophical history' pioneered in the jurisprudence lectures of Adam Smith and taken up by other influential Scottish thinkers, notably William Robertson (Principal of the University of Edinburgh until 1793). Philosophical history held that human societies develop through a succession of increasingly complex economic formations, from hunting through herding and agriculture to commerce. 'Commercial society' is the order of modernity, exemplified by the metropolitan centres of late eighteenth-century Great Britain. The logic of development is universal. It applies not only to past and present stages of a particular nation but to different nations existing at the same time in different parts of the world, sorting them along a chronological axis. The indigenous societies of America or the South Pacific – or the Scottish Highlands – represent primitive, ancestral stages of civilization, superseded in modern life.[16]

Scott invokes this imperial logic of inexorable if uneven development in the last chapter of *Waverley*, called 'A Postscript, which should have been a Preface':

There is no European nation which, within the course of half a century, or little more, has undergone so complete a change as this

kingdom of Scotland. The effects of the insurrection of 1745 ...
commenced this innovation. The gradual influx of wealth, and
extension of commerce, have since united to render the present
people of Scotland a class of beings as different from their grandfathers, as the existing English are from those of Queen Elizabeth's
time ... But the change, though steadily and rapidly progressive,
has, nevertheless, been gradual; and, like those who drift down the
stream of a deep and smooth river, we are not aware of the progress
we have made until we fix our eye on the now-distant point from
which we set out. (363)

Looking back across his story, the narrator views the Highland
clans and Jacobite nobility as archaic tribal and feudal remnants,
surviving in the hinterlands of a modernizing nation until shaken
into oblivion by the convulsion of civil war. This temporal scheme
underwrites the map of Edward Waverley's adventures. The first
volume of the novel tracks our hero's extended journey north, from
the quiet backwater of his uncle's estate to the more emphatically
old-fashioned Scottish manor of Tully-Veolan and thence deep into
the Perthshire Highlands. The sequence of settings articulates a
receding sequence of anthropological and historical stages, increasingly remote from modern life. More than a matter of miles, roads
and mountain-passes, the difference between London and Tully-
Veolan or Glennaquoich becomes a matter of time: the sixty years
it will take, in a violent acceleration of two hundred years of English history, for the Scots to become British. The exotic scenes
visited by Waverley have sunk into the past – into memory and the
imagination – by the end of the story. Tully-Veolan still stands, as a
museum-like restoration or facsimile; but the clans are long gone.

III

The fusion of fiction with the new scientific history calls for a new
kind of hero. Waverley, an English gentleman and an army officer,
is a representative of the regime that will shortly destroy the worlds
he enters as a guest. However – and this is one of Scott's great
coups – he does not know that. Indeed, far from wishing harm
upon the ecology of 'old Scottish faith, hospitality, worth, and
honour' (363), Waverley abandons his allegiance and takes sides
with it. He does so (again) largely unwittingly. By the time he
makes a choice and kneels in homage to a rival prince, midway
through the tale, it is no choice at all; or rather, the act of choice has

been emptied by the sequence of causes leading up to it. Until now Waverley has been swept along by a combination of circumstance, accident and other people's intrigues. He remains a blank figure, the 'white shield' of Scott's opening metaphor (3), onto whom others project their wishes and intentions. At the end of the novel he floats free of his entanglement in the rebellion almost as lightly as he has drifted into it. In a far-reaching irony, the 'wavering and unsettled habit of mind' for which the narrator has mocked the protagonist (34) ends up saving him. Since his will and knowledge have never quite meshed into a morally authentic commitment to the Jacobite cause, Waverley can be released from the charge of treason that sends his friends to the scaffold.[17]

The cognitive dissociation of the hero from the history through which he moves is one of Scott's powerful innovations. That dissociation rests not on a lack of feeling or imagination but on an excess of it. Waverley's objective status as a cipher in his own story stems from the undisciplined luxuriance of his inner life. If Waverley's descendants are the vague, ineffectual, superfluous protagonists of the nineteenth-century novel, disengaged from a historical role, his forebears include eighteenth-century types of extreme sensibility, the 'man of feeling' and the 'female Quixote', filtered through the beleaguered heroine of Ann Radcliffe's Gothic romances, whose refined imagination supports her amid wild mountain perils. More like a Gothic heroine than a hero, Waverley finds himself accused of deeds he has no knowledge of having committed, made a prisoner and carried off bodily, in a series of extreme realizations of the passivity that has always characterized his relation to events: beginning with the all-but-motiveless drift of his journey into the north. He falls into a tremendous national crisis through no epic ambition of military prowess but 'a curiosity to know something more of Scotland' (34). The hero of the historical novel, then, has a third notable characteristic. He changes sides; he is unconscious of the history he takes part in; and he is a tourist.

To be a tourist is to go on leave from one's own time and place; to take a vacation from historical reality. The industrial development of tourism, beginning in the late eighteenth century, promoted a new kind of aesthetic attention to scenery detached from history: 'picturesque' natural landscapes, adorned with ruins of an extinct civilization or figures from a timeless, far-off past. The village girls in Tully-Veolan remind Waverley, 'a lover of the picturesque', of 'Italian forms of landscape' (35). He listens to Rose Bradwardine's account of her father's feud with the Mac-Ivors:

Waverley could not help starting at a story which bore so much resemblance to one of his own day-dreams. Here was a girl . . . who had witnessed with her own eyes such a scene as he had used to conjure up in his imagination, as only occurring in ancient times. He felt at once the impulse of curiosity, and that slight sense of danger which only serves to heighten its interest. (77)

He follows the impulse:

He had now time to give himself up to the full romance of his situation. Here he sate on the banks of an unknown lake, under the guidance of a wild native, whose language was unknown to him, on a visit to the den of some renowned outlaw, a second Robin Hood, perhaps, or Adam o' Gordon . . . The only circumstance which assorted ill with the rest was the cause of his journey – the Baron's milk cows! this degrading incident he kept in the back-ground. (84)

Waverley embraces the 'romance of his situation' by suppressing the situation's historical content, screening it with aesthetic associations.[18]

The 'renowned outlaw', Donald Bean Lean, turns out to be a pale, slight, unprepossessing person, clad in an old French uniform instead of his Highland dress – far from the 'stern, gigantic, ferocious figure, such as Salvator would have chosen to be the central object of a group of banditti' that Waverley is expecting (86). The substitution of costume sums up the historical meaning of the adventure, if only Waverley could read it: no titanic upsurge of autochthonous forces but an inadequately backed intrigue in the great game between Britain and France that will only just have reached geopolitical resolution in 1814. As Waverley goes on to encounter more sophisticated agents, the ironical dissonance between his aesthetic framing of the scene and its historical content fades to an overtone – still audible, however, to the alert reader. Waverley falls into raptures at Flora Mac-Ivor's recital of Gaelic song, ignorant that it is a Jacobite call to arms. He sees only a stag-hunt, not the mobilization of rebel militias.

In the 'Highland minstrelsy' that closes the first volume, Flora and Waverley collaborate in setting up 'the romance of the scene', she with her spectacle and song and he with his expectations (114). Their romantic designs are at odds with one another as well as with historical reality. Flora intends her rhapsody to inspire Waverley to join the rebellion, not fall in love with her. He mistakes it for a purely artistic performance, the evocation of a lost world of ancient heroes, like 'Fingal' and the other 'Poems of Ossian' that James Macpherson will unleash on the world some fifteen years later. Contending romanticisms yield contending ironies. Although she speaks to the present crisis, Flora's impulse is backward-looking, inauthentic, 'Ossianic' – deluded in its literal attempt to revive the past. Waverley's dissociation from the present, in contrast, looks forward to a genuine 'romantic movement' – genuine because it finds its expression not in military action but in poetry:

> Indeed the wild feeling of romantic delight, with which he heard the few first notes she drew from her instrument, amounted almost to a sense of pain. He would not for worlds have quitted his place by her side; yet he almost longed for solitude, that he might decypher and examine at leisure the complication of emotions which now agitated his bosom. (115)

The impulse to refine a complex aesthetic experience through 'recollection in tranquillity' reaches beyond Macpherson's dubious translations of Gaelic epic to the more rigorously experimental art of Scott's friend, William Wordsworth.

Waverley's aesthetic eye and ear predict the world to come, just as they are products of modern life, detached from a historical struggle that belongs in the past. The political and juridical dismantling of the clan system that followed the defeat of the 1745 rising made the Highlands safe for tourism. 'There was perhaps never any change of national manners so quick, so great, and so general, as that which has operated in the Highlands, by the last conquest, and the subsequent laws,' wrote Samuel Johnson (in words echoed at the end of *Waverley*) on the occasion of his 1773 tour: 'We came thither too late to see what we expected, a people of peculiar appearance, and a system of antiquated life.'[19] Waves of emigration, driven by economic collapse, cleared the ground for visitors' appreciation of 'wild' scenery. Domestic tourism was boosted by the long wars with France, which closed the Continent to British travellers. *The Lady of the Lake*, *Waverley* and *Rob Roy* ensured that the Highlands would remain one of Europe's, indeed the world's, premier romantic destinations. Waverley's untimely relation to history, then, expresses his synchronization with the future – with Scott's day, if not our own – rather than with the past. All this has encouraged some critics and (especially) historians to arraign Scott's novels for promoting an imperialist historiography in which regret for the vanished clans softens pride in British progress with a tone of aesthetic refinement, a luxurious aura of melancholy. *Waverley* is one of the highlights of an 'invention of Scotland' – tartan-clad, retro-Jacobite, drained of real history – that begins with Macpherson's 'Ossian' and runs through Scott to Balmoral and *Brigadoon*.[20]

This critique has made the novel's last scene notorious. The happy survivors gather before a memento of Waverley's adventure:

> It was a large and animated painting, representing Fergus Mac-Ivor and Waverley in their Highland dress, the scene a wild, rocky, and mountainous pass, down which the clan were descending in the back-ground. It was taken from a spirited sketch, drawn while they were in Edinburgh by a man of high genius, and had been painted on a full length scale by an eminent London artist. Raeburn himself, (whose Highland Chiefs do all but walk out of the canvas) could not have done more justice to the subject; and the ardent, fiery, and impetuous character of the unfortunate Chief of Glennaquoich was finely contrasted with the contemplative, fanciful, and enthusiastic expression of his happier friend. Beside this painting were hung the arms which Waverley had borne in the unfortunate civil war. The whole piece was generally admired. (361)

The technical name for this is an *ecphrasis*, a literary description of a work of art. A well-established epic convention, associated with the arming of the hero to return to war, it calls for sophisticated attention – not least because Scott makes it commemorate his hero's definitive exit from the field. (Waverley's arms, hung up with the painting, have become aesthetic objects, part of 'the whole piece'.) Rather than installing a phony vision of Scotland, Scott invites his reader to consider the dynamics of historical memory in which his novel traffics. The narrator tells us that the painting is an artificial, sentimental production, assembled, like the novel itself, in Edinburgh and London – far from the scene it represents. If we compare the painting's version of Waverley's adventures with the story we have been reading, we recall the absence of any such idyllic brotherhood from its pages. Mockery lightens Waverley's kitting out with Highland dress (214–15), while intrigue and resentment spoil his friendship with Fergus (until the rising is defeated). The difference between the dreaming hero and the knowing narrator prompts critical reflection as part of our work of reading. Only a heroic self-forgetfulness on his own part, confusing the work with its protagonist, can have prompted Henry James to call *Waverley* 'the first novel which was self-forgetful'.[21]

IV

Almost nothing Waverley encounters is what at first he imagines it to be. The patriarchal community of the Mac-Ivors is an artificial rather than natural system, kept up by the French-born chief for reasons which blend devotion to the Stuarts with a more sordid ambition. Waverley's first view of Tully-Veolan bears a satirical indictment of the estate's poverty and squalor; by the end of the story the experience of civil war has disclosed it as the ground of a genuine 'organic society', as faithful tenants rally around their hunted lord. Shy Rose Bradwardine emerges as the novel's wiliest character, stage-managing the plot when Waverley is most lost in it. The closer we look at the novel – not just the more attentively we read it, but the better we remember reading it – the more equivocal its certainties become. In the concluding 'Postscript', the narrator's assumption of the sober style of the Enlightenment historian follows his facetious impersonation of a coach-driver hanging about at the end of the journey in hope of a tip: which of these is the true voice of the Author of Waverley? What kind of a story is this?

Scott makes play throughout *Waverley* with the well-worn metaphor of the narrative as vehicle, most conspicuously at the end of the fifth chapter, where he likens his story – laden with the baggage of history, 'old-fashioned politics' and 'the feelings, prejudices, and parties, of the times' – to 'a humble English post-chaise, drawn upon four wheels, and keeping his Majesty's high-way', as opposed to the marvellous flying machines of Arabian and Italian romance (26). Yet the narrative that follows gains imaginative energy the further it strays from 'his Majesty's high-way' – the more it veers like a flying carpet or hippogriff. The author (no longer a mere narrator) opens the second volume by characterizing his 'natural style of composition' as 'what scholars call the periphrastic and ambagitory, and the vulgar the circumbendibus' (122) – joyously pompous, roundabout, off the beaten track. He has made a similarly exuberant boast several chapters earlier:

> I . . . hold it the most useful quality of my pen, that it can speedily change from grave to gay, and from description and dialogue to narrative and character. So that if my quill displays no other properties of its mother-goose than her mutability, truly I shall be well pleased; and I conceive that you, my worthy friend, will have no occasion for discontent. (97)

Where other novelists have felt bound to apologize to their readers, the Author of Waverley revels in the mixed, inconstant, 'wavering' character of his art. What is vagueness in his hero is in him virtuosity.

Waverley glitters with such authorial punctuations, not only of the action but of the historian's decorum. Scott's subdivision of the narrative into short chapters, bracketed with titles, epigraphs, rhetorical flourishes and gear-shifts, keeps nudging the reader awake from the dream of the hero's life. (Waverley falls asleep at the end of no fewer than ten chapters.) These devices can jolt us in and out of the scene, as in the wonderfully tense build-up to the battle of Prestonpans: 'The vapours rose like a curtain, and shewed the two armies in the act of closing,' Scott writes, enthralling us in the counterpoint of opening and closing – only to pull back: 'The rest is well known' (240). Or they are exquisitely modulated, as in the vernacular Scots elegies that fold several chapters in the second half of the book: the outcry of the village children as Waverley is marched off to prison ('Eh! see to the Southland gentleman, that's gaun to be hanged for shooting lang Johnie Micklewrath the smith', 185); the obsequies spoken over the Laird of Balmawhapple (242) and over Fergus and Evan Dhu ('It's a great pity of Evan Dhu, who was a very weel-meaning and good-natured man, to be a Hielandman; and indeed so was the Laird o' Glennaquoich, for that matter, when he was na in ane o' his tirrivies', 351). Such cadences, shifting without loss of pathos from a 'high', heroic or tragic register to tones of irony and burlesque, do not merely relieve tension. Admitting the viewpoints and verdicts of 'ordinary daily life',[22] they affirm the irreducibly mixed, complex, fluctuating quality of human experience – and justify the novel as the literary form best equipped to represent it.

Scott overlays classical and popular styles in the most moving of these elegies. On the eve of the march from Edinburgh – the beginning of the end of the Jacobite adventure – Charles Edward Stuart bids his followers good night:

> When the Baron of Bradwardine afterwards mentioned this adieu of the Chevalier, he never failed to repeat, in a melancholy tone,
>
> > 'Audiit, et voti Phœbus succedere partem
> > Mente dedit; partem volucres dispersit in auras;
>
> which,' as he added, 'is weel rendered into English metre by my friend Bangour;
>
> > Ae half the prayer wi' Phœbus grace did find,
> > The t'other half he whistled down the wind.' (224–25)

William Hamilton of Bangour translated part of the *Aeneid*, but not (so far as we know) these particular verses; and his translations maintain a stately Augustan English. The Baron's version, warming Virgil's sonorous Latin into familiar Scots, is almost certainly Scott's own. The historical novelist makes his claim (covertly, as usual) to be an author of modern epic.

At the same time, Scott aligns his art with the Baron's pedantry: an aesthetic commitment that today's readers may want to resist, although to do so would mean missing much of the novel's delight. We are introduced to the Baron, early on, through the English stranger's eyes, and like Waverley we at first take his gusts of erudition to express nothing more than his 'humour', the grotesque tic (as in a novel by Smollett) of a secondary comic character. Gaining dignity and pathos as the story proceeds, Bradwardine takes over as its true hero. His adventures, hiding out on his estate, outshine Waverley's, and he literally – grammatically – displaces Waverley from the role of protagonist in the final pages. The Baron guides our reading of the novel as what Peter Garside has called a 'bibliomaniacal romance'. We learn to adjust our view of his pedantry, and recognize in it the expression of a distinctive Scots Humanist literary tradition – the cultural roots of a Jacobite movement that the novel elsewhere shows to be compromised if not corrupt.[23] The translation of Virgil affiliates the Baron, and Scott, to the distinguished lineage of Scots versions of the *Aeneid*, going back to Gavin Douglas in 1513. '*Fuimus Troes* – and there's the end of an auld sang' (323): Bradwardine transmutes Lord Seafield's sarcastic epitaph for an independent Scotland into Virgilian elegy, the only remaining genuine epic note.

The reader's education accompanies the hero's, and reading is its theme.[24] The early chapters establish Waverley as a masculine version of the Female Quixote (the heroine of Charlotte Lennox's 1752 novel) rather than a modern Don Quixote – reading purely, passively, for pleasure, not for action, in a narcissistic trance. His unchecked imagination turns every scenario he encounters, in life as well as in books, into 'romance'. The novel's curriculum of literary allusion endows romance with an increasingly specific literary-historical gravity as the story unfolds – and we are meant to take note. The term is persistently associated with the Italian Renaissance poets Boiardo, Ariosto and Tasso, whose tales narrate the distraction of epic ambition by enchantment, even as they themselves are decadent (if enchanting) romantic substitutes for classical epic. Their relation to the Jacobite rising becomes clear in the latter part of the novel, where Scott's chapter title 'The

Confusion of King Agramant's Camp' (285) confirms the dour English patriot Talbot's jibe at the Chevalier as an 'Italian knight-errant' (257). Unfit to claim the dignity of British epic, the Jacobite dream of national restoration wears the literary guise not just of Ossianic false translation but of Italian courtly romance: a shimmering, delusive fabric of marvellous adventure wrapped around the worn-out politics of Catholic absolutism.[25]

In *Waverley*, then, Scott synchronizes three kinds or levels of history to create the effect of a grand, complex, overdetermined historical process: the public history of national formation, in which the final defeat of an old regime heralds Scotland's full assimilation into the modern British state; the sentimental history of a fictional protagonist, who grows up from dreamy adolescence into sober adulthood; and a literary history, in which the ancient narrative forms of epic and romance give way to the novel as the genre of modern life, exemplified by the historical novel we are reading. The three levels converge on the scene (discussed earlier) in which Waverley 'felt himself entitled to say firmly, though perhaps with a sigh, that the romance of his life was ended, and that its real history had now commenced'. Some critics have mistaken the narrator's phrase (carefully hedged and indirect) for Scott's own gloss on his novel – as though the reader is meant to share the hero's awakening from romance to real history. Such a progression characterizes neither the final outcome of Waverley's adventures, however, nor the work that relates them. Waverley is set free – as improbably as in any Italian romance – from the historical consequences of involvement in rebellion and rewarded with a home and bride. Flora's advice to him – 'you seek, or ought to seek, in the object of your attachment, a heart whose principal delight should be in augmenting your domestic felicity, and returning your affection, even to the height of romance' (143) – bears a prophetic force. The story delivers its hero to the romance of domestic felicity which is the proper end of modern novels, and the ideal condition of our reading.

V

Like *Persuasion*, *Waverley* narrates a redemption of romance, not a rejection of it. The redemption takes place through the fusion of romance and history in the new genre of modern life, the novel. To be sure, eighteenth-century English novels – citing *Don Quixote* as their model – had made the rejection of romance a founding ritual.

Lacking a classical genealogy, tainted by association with the market, with unregulated fantasy, and with popular and female literacy, novels called themselves 'histories' in a bid for respectability and laid claim to a 'realistic', morally responsible account of human nature – vehemently disavowing that other, licentious, outmoded kind of fiction called 'romance'. *Waverley* recapitulates but also outpaces this literary history. The disavowal of romance may be true to a setting in 1745, the chronological horizon of 'the rise of the novel' in the work of Henry Fielding (*The History of the Adventures of Joseph Andrews*; *The History of Tom Jones*) and Samuel Richardson (*Clarissa, or The History of a Young Lady*; *The History of Sir Charles Grandison*). In 1814, however, at the close of the long historical arc of modernization, Scott reinvents the form through a synthesis of its opposing terms. 'History' becomes an internal, essential ingredient of the novel, not just a gentrifying title.[26]

At the same time as he completes the rise of the novel by making it historical, Scott affirms – no less consequentially – its alternative principle: romance, or fiction. The combination of history and fiction does not dissolve one category into the other but releases both into autonomous cultural life. Opening the Victorian era of the novel as well as of historiography, *Waverley* makes fiction the medium through which modern readers imaginatively inhabit their own history. It does so not just through the technical means by which a novel 'brings the past to life', but through the complex interplay of distance and attachment, identification and reflection, sympathy and irony, that constitutes the aesthetic of fiction, and through which novels 'may be said to activate a fundamental practice of modern ideology – acquiescence without belief, crediting without credulousness'.[27] We know that what we are reading is only a story, an invention – and yet we imaginatively assent to it; indeed, our knowledge that it is a fiction is the condition of our assent to it. *Waverley* – constantly ruffling the illusion of historical reality with reminders that it is a fiction – cultivates in the reader the quintessentially secular, liberal relation to historical being which is proper to the occupants of modern civil society, who have outlived archaic ('superstitious', 'fanatical') modes of adherence to a religious or political cause. Our flickeringly sceptical awareness of our condition, tempering enjoyment of the benefits of modernity with the melancholy remembrance of worlds extinguished in its making, differentiates us from the unwitting Waverley (until, perhaps, the novel's closing chapters). Double consciousness, not false consciousness, is the novel's gift to its reader, the characteristic mode of the imagination in modern life.

Here, too, as in the case of philosophical history, Scott's achievement has intellectual roots in the Scottish Enlightenment, this time in the work of David Hume. Hume (writing in the age of Richardson and Fielding) reclaims fiction and the imagination from their traditional opposition to canons of religious truth or scientific reality. The argument of his major philosophical work, *A Treatise of Human Nature* (1740), dissolves the metaphysical foundations of reality and covers the resulting 'abyss of scepticism' with an instinctual, sentimental commitment to 'common life', everyday social intercourse: in which the philosopher cannot help being a participant, even as he intermittently recognizes common life to be an imaginary construction of reality stabilized by custom. The connections and continuities that knit together our world and our identities in it are an ongoing, largely unconscious work of fiction, sustained by repetition, habit and social consensus. As well as historical, psychological and literary histories, then, *Waverley* rehearses a philosophical history, a Humean dialectic of Enlightenment, in which romantic illusion gives way to bleak disenchantment ('the romance of his life was over') which gives way, in turn, to a reattachment – at once ironical and sentimental – to common life: the 'domestic felicity' that awaits the hero at the end of the adventure, but that his readers look upon with a more alienated eye, aware even as they are enjoying it that this is another fiction.[28]

We do not know what Waverley is thinking or feeling at the end of the story, and we do not need to. Scott's unremarkable hero fades into the picture of his late adventure (framed at last) while we contemplate the scene through the Baron's tear-blurred eyes. Pathos and irony, melancholy and delight, naïve excitement and connoisseurial relish: these make up the complex enjoyment with which Scott layered his first novel. No less potent than it was in the summer of 1814, that enjoyment lies in store for the adventurous reader today.

NOTES

1   Georg Lukács, *The Historical Novel*, trans. H. and S. Mitchell (Lincoln, NE, 1983), p. 19.
2   See William St Clair, *The Reading Nation in the Romantic Period* (Cambridge, 2004), pp. 221, 418–20; Philip Waller, *Writers, Readers and Reputations: Literary Life in Britain, 1870–1918* (Oxford, 2006), pp. 177–82.

3   See Murray Pittock, ed., *The Reception of Sir Walter Scott in Europe*
    (London, 2006).
4   On this, and the larger topic of nineteenth-century Scott adaptations,
    see Ann Rigney, *Portable Monuments: The Afterlives of Walter Scott*
    (Oxford: forthcoming).
5   See James Chandler, 'The Historical Novel Goes to Hollywood:
    Scott, Griffith and the Film Epic Today', in Robert Lang, ed., *The
    Birth of a Nation: D. W. Griffith, Director* (New Brunswick, NJ, 1994),
    pp. 225–49.
6   See Peter Garside, 'Walter Scott and the "Common" Novel, 1808–
    1819', *Cardiff Corvey: Reading the Romantic Text* 3 (1999): http://
    www.cardiff.ac.uk/encap/journals/corvey/articles/cc03_no2.html;
    and Michael Gamer, '*Waverley* and the Object of (Literary) History',
    Modern Language Quarterly 70:4 (2009), 495–525.
7   Jane Austen to Anna Austen, 28 September 1814, *Jane Austen's Let-*
    ters, ed. Deirdre Le Faye (Oxford, 1995), p. 277.
8   Jane Austen, *Persuasion*, ed. James Kinsley, with a new introduction
    by Deidre Lynch (Oxford, 2004), p. 30.
9   On *Persuasion, Waverley* and historical fiction see Lynch, ibid., pp.
    xv–xxi; Jocelyn Harris, *A Revolution Almost Beyond Expression: Jane*
    Austen's Persuasion (Wilmington, DE, 2007), pp. 109–18.
10 Lukács, *The Historical Novel*, pp. 23–25.
11 Richard Maxwell, *The Historical Novel in Europe, 1650–1950* (Cam-
    bridge, 2009), pp. 11–58.
12 See Peter Garside, 'Popular Fiction and National Tale: Hidden Ori-
    gins of Scott's *Waverley*', *Nineteenth-Century Literature* 46 (1991),
    30–53; Ina Ferris, *The Achievement of Literary Authority: Gender,*
    History, and the Waverley Novels (Ithaca, 1991), pp. 105–33; Katie
    Trumpener, *Bardic Nationalism: The Romantic Novel and the British*
    Empire (Princeton, 1997), pp. 128–57.
13 See Ferris, *The Achievement of Literary Authority*, pp. 79–104.
14 For a recent discussion see Maxwell, *The Historical Novel in Europe*,
    pp. 75–82.
15 Lukács, *The Historical Novel*, p. 53.
16 On Scott and philosophical history see, e.g., Peter D. Garside, 'Scott
    and the "Philosophical Historians"', *Journal of the History of Ideas*,
    36 (1975), 497–512; Graham McMaster, *Scott and Society* (Cam-
    bridge, 1981), pp. 49–77; James Chandler, *England in 1819: The*
    Politics of Literary Culture and the Case of Romantic Historicism (Chi-
    cago, 1998), pp. 127–35.
17 The classic study of Scott's passive hero is Alexander Welsh, *The*
    Hero of the Waverley Novels (Princeton, NJ, 1992).
18 On *Waverley*, tourism and the picturesque, see P. D. Garside, '*Waver-*
    ley's Pictures of the Past', *ELH* 44 (1977), 659–82; Jane Millgate,
    Walter Scott: The Making of the Novelist (Edinburgh, 1984), pp. 41–
    52; James Buzard, *Disorienting Fiction: The Autoethnographic Work of*
    Nineteenth-Century British Novels (Princeton, 2005), pp. 68–100; and

George Dekker, *The Fictions of Romantic Tourism: Radcliffe, Scott and Mary Shelley* (Stanford, 2005), pp. 129–41.

19 Samuel Johnson, *A Journey to the Western Islands of Scotland*, ed. J. D. Fleeman (Oxford, 1985), p. 46.

20 See, e.g., H. Trevor-Roper, 'The Invention of Tradition: The Highland Tradition of Scotland', in E. Hobsbawm and T. Ranger (eds.), *The Invention of Tradition* (Cambridge, 1983), pp. 15–42; Murray G. H. Pittock, *The Invention of Scotland: The Stuart Myth and the Scottish Identity, 1638 to the Present* (London, 1991), pp. 84–90; Colin Kidd, *Subverting Scotland's Past: Scottish Whig Historians and the Creation of an Anglo-British Identity, 1689–c. 1830* (Cambridge, 1993), pp. 256–67; Saree Makdisi, *Romantic Imperialism: Universal Empire and the Culture of Modernity* (Cambridge, 1998), pp. 70–99.

21 Henry James, *Literary Criticism*, Vol. 1: *Essays on Literature, American Writers, English Writers*, ed. Leon Edel and Mark Wilson (New York, 1984), p. 1202.

22 See David Daiches, 'Scott's Achievement as a Novelist', *Nineteenth-Century Fiction* 6:2 (1951), 94–95.

23 See Peter Garside, 'The Baron's Books: Scott's *Waverley* as a Bibliomaniacal Romance', *Romanticism* 14:3 (2008), 245–58. See also Chris Ann Matteo, '*Spolia* from Troy: Classical Epic Allusion in Walter Scott's *Waverley*', *Literary Imagination* 9:3 (2007), 250–69.

24 The richest discussion of 'romance as education' in *Waverley* remains Jane Millgate's, in *Walter Scott: The Making of the Novelist*, pp. 35–57.

25 For a fuller discussion see Ian Duncan, *Modern Romance and Transformations of the Novel: The Gothic, Scott, Dickens* (Cambridge, 1992), pp. 79–105.

26 See Everett Zimmerman, *The Boundaries of Fiction: History and the Eighteenth-Century British Novel* (Ithaca, NY, 1996), pp. 220–22.

27 Catherine Gallagher and Stephen Greenblatt, *Practicing New Historicism* (Chicago, 2000), p. 169.

28 See Ian Duncan, *Scott's Shadow: The Novel in Romantic Edinburgh* (Princeton, NJ, 2007), pp. 119–38.

1771	*15 August.* Born in College Wynd, Edinburgh. His father, Walter (1729–99), son of a sheep-farmer at Sandyknowe, near Smailholm Tower, Roxburghshire, was a lawyer. His mother, Anne Rutherford (1732–1819), was daughter of Dr John Rutherford, Professor of Medicine at the University of Edinburgh. His parents married in April 1758; Walter was their ninth child. The siblings who survived were Robert (1767–87), John (1769–1816), Anne (1772–1801), Thomas (1774–1823), and Daniel (?1776–1806).
1772–73	*Winter.* Contracted what is now termed poliomyelitis, and became permanently lame in his right leg. His grandfather Rutherford advised that he be sent to Sandyknowe to benefit from country air, and, apart from a period of 'about a year' in 1775 spent in Bath, a spell in 1776 with his family in their new home on the west side of George Square, Edinburgh, and a time in 1777 at Prestonpans, near Edinburgh, he lived there until 1778. From his grandmother and his aunt Janet he heard many ballads and stories of the Border past, and these narratives were crucial to his intellectual and imaginative development.
1779–83	Attended the High School of Edinburgh; he was particularly influenced by the Rector, Dr Alexander Adam, and his teaching of literature in Latin. After the High School, he spent 'half a year' with his aunt Janet in Kelso, where he attended the grammar school, and read for the first time Thomas Percy's *Reliques of Ancient English Poetry*.
1783–86	Attended classes at Edinburgh University, including Humanity (Latin), Greek, Logic and Metaphysics, and Moral Philosophy.
1786	Studies terminated by serious illness; convalescence in Kelso. Apprenticed as a lawyer to his father.
1787	Met Robert Burns at the house of the historian and philosopher, Adam Ferguson.
1789	Decided to prepare for the Bar.

1789–92   Attended classes at Edinburgh University, including History, Moral Philosophy, Scots Law, and Civil Law.

1792   *11 July.* Admitted to the Faculty of Advocates.

           Autumn. First visit to Liddesdale, in the extreme south of Scotland, with Robert Shortreed, in search of ballads and ballad-singers. Seven such 'raids' followed over seven years. Shortreed later commented: 'He was makin' himsell a' the time'. His tours took him into many parts of Scotland and the north of England: e.g. in 1793 to Perthshire and the Trossachs; in 1796 to the north-east of Scotland; and in 1797 to Cumberland and the Lake District.

1794   In April involved in a brawl with some political radicals and bound to keep the peace. In September attended the trials of the radicals Watt and Downie, and in November Watt's execution.

*c.*1794–96 In love with Williamina Belsches, culminating in April 1796 with an invitation to her home, Fettercairn House, Kincardineshire.

1796   Anonymous publication of *The Chase and William and Helen*, Scott's translations of two of Bürger's poems.

           October. Announcement of the engagement of Williamina Belsches to William Forbes.

1797   Volunteered for the new volunteer cavalry regiment, the Royal Edinburgh Light Dragoons, and appointed quartermaster.

           September. Met Charlotte Carpenter (1770–1826), at Gilsland, Cumberland, and within three weeks proposed marriage. Charlotte's parents were Jean François Charpentier and Margaret Charlotte Volère (d. 1788), of Lyons. Some time after the break-up of the marriage around 1780, her mother brought Charlotte and her brother Charles (1772–1818) to England; Charlotte and Charles later became the wards of the 2nd Marquess of Downshire, and changed their name to Carpenter.

           24 December. Married Charlotte in Carlisle, and set up house at 50 George Street, Edinburgh.

1798   Met Matthew Gregory ('Monk') Lewis, and agreed to contribute to *Tales of Wonder* (published 1801).

           Rented cottage in Lasswade near Edinburgh for the summer, and made many political and literary contacts, including Lady Louisa Stuart, who proved to be one of the most acute and trusted of his friends and critics.

Moved to 19 Castle Street, Edinburgh.

October. Birth and death of first son.

1799   Publication of *Goetz of Berlichingen*, Scott's translation of Goethe's tragedy.

April. Death of Scott's father.

Met John Leyden and the publisher Archibald Constable, and had his first discussion with the printer James Ballantyne about undertaking book-printing: Ballantyne brought out Scott's anthology *An Apology for Tales of Terror* in 1800.

October. Birth of daughter, Charlotte Sophia Scott.

December. Appointed Sheriff-Depute of Selkirkshire.

1801   *October.* Birth of son, Walter Scott.

Moved to 39 Castle Street, Edinburgh.

1802   Publication of *Minstrelsy of the Scottish Border*, Vols 1 and 2. The *Minstrelsy* was the first publication in a lifetime of scholarly editing, and it shows both the strengths and weaknesses of Scott as editor. He found new texts (of the 72 ballads he published, 38 had not appeared in print before), and his literary, historical, and anthropological essays and notes are always illuminating; but, following the editorial practice of the time, he had no settled methods or principles for choosing or establishing a text.

Met James Hogg.

1803   *February.* Birth of daughter, Anne Scott.

Second edition of *Minstrelsy of the Scottish Border*, Vols 1 and 2, and first edition of Vol. 3.

Began to contribute reviews to the *Edinburgh Review*. Scott was an acute reviewer, in the expansive manner characteristic of heavyweight reviews in the early nineteenth century, and was particularly perceptive about such contemporaries as Jane Austen, Byron, and Mary Shelley.

September. Visit from William and Dorothy Wordsworth.

1804   Took the lease of Ashestiel near Selkirk as his country house in place of the cottage in Lasswade.

Publication of Scott's edition of the medieval metrical romance, *Sir Tristrem*.

1805   Publication of *The Lay of the Last Minstrel*, the first of a series of verse romances which established his fame as a poet.

Entered into partnership with James Ballantyne in the printing business of James Ballantyne & Co. Until the financial crash in 1826, the partnership was not just a financial arrangement, but a unique collaboration: Ballantyne managed the business, but also acted as Scott's editor; Scott seems to have been responsible for much of the financial planning, and it was a standard part of his contracts with publishers that his works should be printed by James Ballantyne & Co.

December. Birth of son, Charles Scott.

1806   Hurried to London to secure his appointment as one of the Principal Clerks to the Court of Session, a position which had been under negotiation for much of the previous year but which was imperilled by the advent of a new government after the death of William Pitt on 23 January. The appointment was announced on 8 March. Scott took the place of an elderly Clerk, but, as there was no retirement and pension scheme, allowed his predecessor to keep the salary of £800 per annum for life. While in London Scott was 'taken up' by high society.

1807   Brother Tom bankrupt. It also emerged that Tom, a lawyer who had inherited his father's practice, and who had been retained as agent for the Duddingston estate of the Marquess of Abercorn, had misappropriated some of his client's money. Scott felt financially and morally endangered by his brother's breach of trust, and extended efforts were required over several years to protect his own financial credit and provide for his brother and his family.

1808   Publication of poem *Marmion* (the rights of which the publisher Archibald Constable had bought for £1050 in 1807).

Appointed secretary to the Parliamentary Commission to Inquire into the Administration of Justice in Scotland. The Commission ended its work in 1810.

Publication of *The Works of John Dryden . . . with Notes . . . and a Life of the Author*, 18 vols.

Cancelled his subscription to the *Edinburgh Review* because of its 'defeatist' view of the war in Spain, and began (with others) planning the *Quarterly Review* and the *Edinburgh Annual Register*, launched in 1809 and 1810. The political disagreement developed into a quarrel with Archibald Constable & Co., and Scott and the Ballantyne brothers, James and John, set up and became the partners in a rival publishing business, John Ballantyne & Co. Scott entrusted his own works to the new business and whenever possible directed other writers and new ventures to it, but Constable withdrew printing work from James Ballantyne & Co., and the printing firm stopped making significant profits.

1809   Publication of *A Collection of Scarce and Valuable Tracts* (Somers Tracts), Vols 1–3; completed in 13 vols 1815.

1810   Publication of *The Lady of the Lake*, his most commercially successful poem.

1811   Scott's predecessor as Clerk of Session agreed to apply for a pension, and from 1812 Scott was paid a salary of £1300 per annum.
Publication of poem *The Vision of Don Roderick*.
Purchase of Cartley Hole, the nucleus of the Abbotsford Estate, between Galashiels and Melrose.

1812   Byron began correspondence with Scott.
Removal from Ashestiel to Abbotsford, and plans for rebuilding the small farmhouse there.

1813   Publication of poems *Rokeby* and *The Bridal of Triermain*. First financial crisis. It became apparent in 1812 that the publishing firm of John Ballantyne & Co. was making losses on every publication except Scott's poetry, and that the *Edinburgh Annual Register* was losing £1000 per issue. The firm was undercapitalised, and depended overmuch on bank credit. The national financial crisis of 1812–14 led to reduced orders for books from retailers, late payments, and the bankruptcy of many companies whose debts to John Ballantyne & Co. were either not paid or paid in part. John Ballantyne & Co. found itself unable to pay its own bills and repay the banks on time, and *Rokeby*, greatly profitable though it was, failed to generate enough ready money to meet obligations. Protracted negotiations with Constable over much of 1813 led to the purchase of Ballantyne stock, on the condition that John Ballantyne & Co. ceased to be an active publisher, to the sale of a share in *Rokeby*, and later to the advance sale to Constable of rights for the publication of the long poem *The Lord of the Isles*. Scott had to ask the Duke of Buccleuch to guarantee a bank loan of £4000, and many friends gave small loans. All the personal loans were repaid in 1814, and the publishing business was eventually wound up profitably in 1817, largely through Scott's efforts. As part of the reconciliation Constable commissioned essays on Chivalry and the Drama for the Supplement to the *Encyclopaedia Britannica* (published 1818 and 1819 respectively). Offered and declined the Poet Laureateship.

1814   Publication of his first novel, *Waverley*. The novel was probably begun in 1808 (the date '1st November, 1805' in the first chapter is part of the fiction), resumed in 1810 and completed 1813–14; it was first advertised in 1810, and again in January 1814. The early parts (up to the beginning of Chapter 5, and Chapters 5–7) were probably written in parallel with Scott's autobiography (first published at the beginning of Lockhart's *Life of Scott* in 1837).

Publication of *The Works of Jonathan Swift . . . with Notes and a Life of the Author*, 19 vols.

Toured the northern and western isles of Scotland with the Lighthouse Commissioners. His diary of the voyage is published in Lockhart's *Life of Scott* (1837).

1815   Publication of poem *The Lord of the Isles* and *Guy Mannering*, his second novel.

First visit to the Continent, including Waterloo and Paris, where he was lionised.

1816   Publication of *Paul's Letters to his Kinsfolk*, *The Antiquary*, and *Tales of my Landlord* (*The Black Dwarf* and *The Tale of Old Mortality*).

1817   Publication of *Harold the Dauntless* (Scott's last long poem) and *Rob Roy* (1818 on title page).

1817–19   First phase of the building of Abbotsford.

1818   Publication of *Tales of my Landlord*, second series (*The Heart of Mid-Lothian*).

Offered and accepted a baronetcy (announced March 1820).

1819   Seriously ill, probably from gallstones. From 1817 Scott had been suffering stomach cramps, but in the spring and early summer of 1819 he was thought to be dying. Nonetheless he continued to work, dictating to an amanuensis when he was too ill to write. He completed *The Bride of Lammermoor* in April (the greater part of the manuscript is in his own hand) but the latter part of the novel and most of *A Legend of the Wars of Montrose* must have been dictated. The two tales constitute *Tales of my Landlord*, third series, and were published in June 1819.

Purchase by Constable of the copyrights of the 'Scotch novels' and publication of the first collection of Scott's fiction as *Novels and Tales of the Author of Waverley*, 16 vols. All the novels eventually appeared in collected editions in three formats: 8vo, 12mo, and 18mo. Publication of three articles in the *Edinburgh Weekly Journal*, later issued as a pamphlet entitled *The Visionary*, which was in essence political propaganda for the constitutional status quo in the period after Peterloo, when there was a real possibility of a radical rising in the west of Scotland.

December. Death of Scott's mother.

Publication of *Ivanhoe* (1820 on title-page).

1820	Publication of *The Monastery* and *The Abbot*.
	Marriage of daughter Sophia to John Gibson Lockhart.
	Elected president of the Royal Society of Edinburgh.
1821	Publication of *Kenilworth* and *The Pirate* (1822 on title-page).
1821–24	Publication of *Ballantyne's Novelist's Library*, for which Scott wrote the lives of the novelists.
1822	Publication of *The Fortunes of Nigel*.
	Visit of King George IV to Edinburgh.
1822–25	Demolition of the original house and second phase of the building of Abbotsford.
1823	Publication of *Peveril of the Peak* (1822 on title-page).
	Bannatyne Club founded and Scott made first president.
	Publication of *Quentin Durward* and *St Ronan's Well* (1824 on title-page).
1824	Publication of *Redgauntlet*.
1825	Marriage of son Walter to Jane Jobson.
	Publication of *Tales of the Crusaders* (*The Betrothed* and *The Talisman*).
	Began his journal.
1826	*January.* Scott insolvent. There was a severe economic recession in the winter of 1825–26 and many companies and individuals became bankrupt. Scott's princi-

pal publishers, Archibald Constable & Co., and the printers James Ballantyne & Co., in which he was co-partner, had always been undercapitalised, and relied on bank borrowings for working capital. In paying for goods and services, including such things as paper, printing, and publication rights, all parties used promissory bills, a system in which the drawer promised to pay stated sums on stated dates, and which the acceptor 'discounted' at the banks, i.e. got the money in advance of the date less the amount the banks charged in interest for what was in fact a loan. Both Constable's and Ballantyne's hoped that the money coming in from the sale of books when they were published would be sufficient to pay off the money due to the banks, but in practice both firms too often borrowed more money to pay off debts when they were due, and acted as guarantors for each other's loans. In December 1825 it was realised that they were unable to get further credit from the banks; and in January the bankruptcy of the London publishers of Scott's works, Hurst, Robinson & Co., precipitated the collapse of Constable's, then Ballantyne's, and the ruin of all the partners. Scott, the only one of those involved with a capacity to generate a large income, signed a trust deed undertaking to repay his own private debts (£35,000), all the debts of the printing business for which he and James Ballantyne were jointly liable (£41,000), the debts of Archibald Constable & Co. for which he was legally liable (£40,000), and a mortgage on Abbotsford (£10,000), amounting in all to over £126,000. Such were the profits from works like *Woodstock*, *The Life of Napoleon Buonaparte*, and above all the Magnum Opus, the collected edition of the Waverley Novels with introductions and notes specially written by Scott, and issued in monthly parts from 1829–33, that by Scott's death in 1832 more than £53,000 had been repaid, and the remaining debts were paid in 1833.

Publication of three letters in the *Edinburgh Weekly Journal*, later issued as *The Letters of Malachi Malagrowther*, in which Scott attacked a government proposal to restrict the rights of the Scottish banks to issue their own banknotes; Scott was so effective that the government withdrew its proposal.

Sale of 39 Castle Street, Edinburgh, on behalf of creditors.

15 May. Death of wife, Charlotte Scott.

Publication of *Woodstock*.

Autumn. Visit to Paris.

1827 Public acknowledgement of the authorship of the Waverley Novels.

Publication of *The Life of Napoleon Buonaparte*, 9 vols, *Chronicles of the Canongate* (Chrystal Croftangry's Narrative, 'The Highland Widow', 'The Two Drovers', and 'The Surgeon's Daughter'), and *Tales of a Grandfather* (Scotland to 1603).

1828 Publication of *Chronicles of the Canongate*, second series (*The Fair Maid of Perth*), and *Tales of a Grandfather*, second series (Scotland 1603–1707).

1829 Publication of *Anne of Geierstein*, *History of Scotland*, Vol. 1, and *Tales of a Grandfather*, third series (Scotland 1707–45). The first volume of the Magnum Opus, completed in 48 vols in 1833, appeared on 1 June.

1830 *February.* First stroke.

November. Retired as Clerk to the Court of Session with pension of £864 per annum. Second stroke.

Publication of *Letters on Demonology and Witchcraft*, *Tales of a Grandfather* (France), and *History of Scotland*, Vol. 2.

1831 *April.* Third stroke.

Publication of *Tales of my Landlord*, fourth series (*Count Robert of Paris* and *Castle Dangerous*).

October. Departure on HMS *Barham* to the Mediterranean, Malta and Naples.

1832 Overland journey home, via Rome, Florence, Venice, Verona, the Brenner Pass, Augsburg, Mainz, and down the Rhine, but had his fourth stroke at Nijmegen. Travelling by sea to London and then Edinburgh, he reached Abbotsford on 11 July.

21 September. Death at Abbotsford.

THE WORKS OF SCOTT

The Journal of Sir Walter Scott, ed. W. E. K. Anderson (Oxford, 1972).

The Letters of Sir Walter Scott, ed. H. J. C. Grierson and others, 12 vols (London, 1932–37). The index to this edition is by James C. Corson, *Notes and Index to Sir Herbert Grierson's Edition of the Letters of Sir Walter Scott* (Oxford, 1979).

'Memoirs', in *Scott on Himself: A Selection of the Autobiographical Writings of Sir Walter Scott*, ed. David Hewitt (Edinburgh, 1981).

The Poetical Works of Sir Walter Scott, ed. J. Logie Robertson (Oxford, 1904; frequently reprinted).

The Poetical Works of Sir Walter Scott, Bart. [ed. J. G. Lockhart], 12 vols (Edinburgh, 1833–34).

The Prose Works of Sir Walter Scott, Bart., 28 vols (Edinburgh, 1834–36).

Waverley Novels, 48 vols (Edinburgh, 1829–33), known as the 'Magnum Opus'.

The Waverley Novels were among the most frequently reprinted works of the nineteenth century, and all editions after Scott's death were based upon the edition of 1829–33. Of these, the best are the Centenary Edition, 25 vols (London, 1871), the Dryburgh Edition, 25 vols (London, 1892–94), and the Border Edition, ed. Andrew Lang, 24 vols (London, 1892–94). The first critical edition of the novels is the Edinburgh Edition of the Waverley Novels (1993–2012), on which the volumes of the new Penguin Scott are based.

The most complete listing of the works of Scott is in:

William B. Todd and Ann Bowden, *Sir Walter Scott: A Bibliographical History 1796–1832* (New Castle, DE, 1998).

There are two simpler listings:

J. G. Lockhart, 'Chronological List of the Publications of Sir Walter Scott', in *Memoirs of the Life of Sir Walter Scott, Bart.*, 7 vols (Edinburgh, 1837–38; many times republished), 7, 433–39.

J. H. Alexander, 'Sir Walter Scott', in *The Cambridge Bibliography of English Literature, Volume 4: 1800–1900*, 3rd edn, ed. Joanne Shattock (Cambridge, 1999), 992–1063.

BIOGRAPHY

There are very many biographies of Scott. The most important still is by J. G. Lockhart, for, although it is unreliable in some of its detail, it is the work of someone who knew Scott and his circle intimately. The most comprehensive of the modern works is by Edgar Johnson; it is generally reliable. John Buchan's one-volume life is the most sympathetic of all the studies of Scott, while John Sutherland takes a harsher view of the way in which Scott used those in his circle for his own advantage.

James Hogg, *Anecdotes of Scott*, ed. Jill Rubinstein (Edinburgh, 1999).

J. G. Lockhart, *Memoirs of the Life of Sir Walter Scott, Bart.*, 7 vols (Edinburgh, 1837–38; many times republished).

John Buchan, *Sir Walter Scott* (London, 1932).

Sir Herbert Grierson, *Sir Walter Scott, Bart.: A New Life supplementary to, and corrective of, Lockhart's Biography* (London, 1938).

Arthur Melville Clark, *Sir Walter Scott: The Formative Years* (Edinburgh, 1969).

Edgar Johnson, *Sir Walter Scott: The Great Unknown*, 2 vols (London, 1970).

John Sutherland, *The Life of Walter Scott* (Oxford, 1995).

CRITICISM

Complete listings of critical works on Scott are to be found in:

James C. Corson, *A Bibliography of Sir Walter Scott: A Classified and Annotated List of Books and Articles relating to his Life and Works 1797–1940* (Edinburgh, 1943).

Jill Rubenstein, *Sir Walter Scott: A Reference Guide* (Boston, MA, 1978) (covers the period 1932–77).

Jill Rubenstein, *Sir Walter Scott: An Annotated Bibliography of Scholarship and Criticism 1975–1990* (Aberdeen, 1994).

Paul Barnaby, 'Recent Publications', *Scott Digital Archive* (http://www.walterscott.lib.ed.ac.uk/publications.html) (includes coverage of criticism since January 2000).

THE FOLLOWING ARE USEFUL FOR THE STUDY OF
WAVERLEY

David Daiches, 'Scott's Achievement as a Novelist', *Nineteenth-Century Fiction*, 6:2 (1951), 81–95.

Georg Lukács, *The Historical Novel*, trans. H. and S. Mitchell (London, 1962; repr. Lincoln, NE, 1983), Chapter 1.

Alexander Welsh, *The Hero of the Waverley Novels* (New Haven, 1963; new edn, with additional essays on Scott, Princeton, NJ, 1992).

Francis Russell Hart, *Scott's Novels: The Plotting of Historic Survival* (Charlottesville, 1966), Section 1, Chapter 1.

P. D. Garside, '*Waverley*'s Pictures of the Past', *ELH* 44 (1977), 659–82.

Graham McMaster, *Scott and Society* (Cambridge, 1981), Part 1.

Jane Millgate, *Walter Scott: The Making of the Novelist* (Edinburgh, 1984), Chapter 3.

Judith Wilt, *Secret Leaves: The Novels of Walter Scott* (Chicago, 1985), Chapter 1.

Joseph Valente, ' "Upon the Braes": History and Hermeneutics in *Waverley*', *Studies in Romanticism*, 25 (1986), 251–76.

James Kerr, *Fiction Against History: Scott as Storyteller* (Cambridge, 1989), Chapter 1.

Ina Ferris, *The Achievement of Literary Authority: Gender, History, and the Waverley Novels* (Ithaca, 1991), Chapters 3–4.

Peter Garside, 'Popular Fiction and National Tale: Hidden Origins of Scott's *Waverley*', *Nineteenth-Century Literature*, 46 (1991), 30–53.

Bruce Beiderwell, *Power and Punishment in Scott's Novels* (Athens, GA, and London, 1992), Chapter 1.

Robert Crawford, *Devolving English Literature* (Oxford, 1992; repr. Edinburgh, 2001), Chapter 3.

Ian Duncan, *Modern Romance and Transformations of the Novel: The Gothic, Scott, Dickens* (Cambridge, 1992), Chapter 2.

Alexander Welsh, *Strong Representations: Narrative and Circumstantial Evidence in England* (Baltimore, 1992), Chapter 2.

Cairns Craig, *Out of History: Narrative Paradigms in Scottish and English Culture* (Edinburgh, 1996), Chapter 3.

Homer Obed Brown, *Institutions of the English Novel: From Defoe to Scott* (Philadelphia, 1997), Chapter 5.

Ina Ferris, 'Translation from the Borders: Encounter and Recalcitrance in *Waverley* and *Clan-Albin*', *Eighteenth-Century Fiction*, 9:2 (1997), 203–22.

Katie Trumpener, *Bardic Nationalism: The Romantic Novel and the British Empire* (Princeton, NJ, 1997), Chapter 3.

Saree Makdisi, *Romantic Imperialism: Universal Empire and the Culture of Modernity* (Cambridge, 1998), Chapter 4.

Franco Moretti, *Atlas of the European Novel 1800–1900* (London, 1998), Chapter 1.

Peter Garside, 'Walter Scott and the "Common" Novel, 1808–1819', *Cardiff Corvey: Reading the Romantic Text* 3 (no pagination), September 1999. Electronic publication: <http://www.cardiff.ac.uk/encap/journals/corvey/articles/cc03_no2.html>.

Jerome Christensen, *Romanticism at the End of History* (Baltimore, 2000), Chapter 6.

Wolfram Schmidgen, *Eighteenth-Century Fiction and the Law of Property* (Cambridge, 2002), Chapter 6.

Joan Garden Cooper, 'Scott's Critique of the English Treason Law in *Waverley*', *Scottish Studies Review*, 4:2 (Autumn 2003), 17–36.

Paul Hamilton, *Metaromanticism: Aesthetics, Literature, Theory* (Chicago, 2003), Chapter 5.

Yoon Sun Lee, *Nationalism and Irony: Burke, Scott, Carlyle* (New York, 2004), Chapter 1.

Nancy Armstrong, *How Novels Think: The Limits of Individualism from 1719–1900* (New York, 2005), Chapter 2.

James Buzard, *Disorienting Fiction: The Autoethnographic Work of Nineteenth-Century British Novels* (Princeton, 2005), Chapter 4.

Julian Meldon D'Arcy, *Subversive Scott: The Waverley Novels and Scottish Nationalism* (Reykjavik, 2005), Chapter 1.

George Dekker, *The Fictions of Romantic Tourism: Radcliffe, Scott, and Mary Shelley* (Stanford, 2005), Chapter 5.

Caroline McCracken-Flesher, *Possible Scotlands: Walter Scott and the Story of Tomorrow* (New York, 2005), Chapter 1.

Michael Simpson, 'Wavering on Europe: Walter Scott and the Equilibrium of the Empires', *Romanticism*, 11:2 (2005), 127–42.

Douglas Mack, *Scottish Fiction and the British Empire* (Edinburgh, 2006), Chapter 4.

Margaret Bruzelius, *Romancing the Novel: Adventure from Scott to Sebald* (Lewisburg, PA, 2007), Chapter 2.

Ian Duncan, *Scott's Shadow: The Novel in Romantic Edinburgh* (Princeton, NJ, 2007), Chapter 5.

Peter Garside, '*Waverley* and the National Fiction Revolution', in *The Edinburgh History of the Book in Scotland, Volume 3: Ambition and Industry 1800–1880*, ed. Bill Bell (Edinburgh, 2007), 222–31.

Evan Gottlieb, *Feeling British: Sympathy and National Identity in Scottish and English Writing, 1707–1832* (Lewisburg, PA, 2007), Chapter 5.

Andrew Lincoln, *Walter Scott and Modernity* (Edinburgh, 2007).

Kenneth McNeil, *Scotland, Britain, Empire: Writing the Highlands, 1760–1860* (Columbus, OH, 2007), Chapter 5.

Peter Garside, 'The Baron's Books: Scott's *Waverley* as a Bibliomaniacal Romance', *Romanticism* 14:3 (2008), 245–58.

Michael Gamer, '*Waverley* and the Object of (Literary) History', *Modern Language Quarterly*, 70:4 (2009), 495–525.

Richard Maxwell, *The Historical Novel in Europe, 1650–1950* (Cambridge, 2009), Chapters 1-2.

This text is based on the first edition of *Waverley*, published in three volumes early in July 1814, but incorporates readings from Scott's original manuscript which were lost through accident, error or misunderstanding. It also includes a number of readings from later printed editions in Scott's lifetime which correct manifest error, as well as several changes in the earliest of these which appear to be authorial in origin.

According to traditional accounts, following Scott's own testimony in the 'General Preface' (1829) to the Magnum Opus edition of the Waverley Novels, *Waverley* was written in two main phases, this involving the laying aside of the first seven ('English') chapters drafted in 1805 after the negative response of a 'critical friend', their rediscovery during a search for fishing tackle at Abbotsford, followed by a rapid completion in 1814. More recent investigation, however, has pointed towards a probable starting point in 1808, as well as a significant re-engagement in 1810–11, when the work was first advertised and possibly extended towards the end of its first volume.[1] Not only are Scott's references to an 1805 starting date in his secondary accounts often qualified, but the sequence of events given in the 'General Preface' is riddled with inconsistencies, chief among which is the claim that the inception occurred in the direct wake of the runaway success of Scott's poem *The Lady of the Lake*, which was first published in May 1810. Even the temporal focus provided by the first chapter, where the narrator talks of 'fixing then the date of my story Sixty Years before this present 1st November, 1805' (4.38–39) is interpretable as a fictional device, carrying among other things a special historical poignancy, 1 November 1745 being the date when Prince Charles Edward and his small Jacobite army set out from Edinburgh on their ill-fated campaign into England. Stretching to a broader 1805–6, when Scott's attention was engaged by issues relating to the Highlands on a number of fronts, there is still little support either in his career or the literary background for a composition at this point. Conversely, the earliest chapters contain a number of clear echoes of Scott's situation after the completion of *Marmion* (1808), and more particularly Francis Jeffrey's unexpectedly sharp critique of the poem in the *Edinburgh Review* for April 1808, to which at points Scott appears to be responding. In a similar way, Scott's parody of available modes in the first chapter matches closely the state of novel production during 1808: a field which then occupied his attention closely as a result of plans to produce a multi-volume collection of past fiction in association with the publisher John Murray.

The first surviving record of *Waverley*'s existence comes in a letter to Scott from his printer, James Ballantyne, dated 15 September 1810, in response to an unspecified portion sent for evaluation.[2] Evidence from the letter suggests that this comprised the first four chapters while a number of elements in the present Chapter 5 appear to be reacting to Ballantyne's particular criticisms, his general advice being that Scott should proceed with the project. Scott had recently returned from an extensive tour of the Highlands and Western Isles, his confidence to take on the depiction of Highland 'manners' heightened by the experience. On 29 September he was anticipating a visit from William Erskine, his closest literary adviser, during which *Waverley* was to be discussed;[3] a number of advertisements by the publisher John Ballantyne have also been discovered, anticipating publication in Spring 1811. How far Scott might have continued writing in this phase is a moot point: Claire Lamont has proposed at least as far as the Highland scenes with the Mac-Ivors at Glennaquoich,[4] though it is also possible that negative advice from Erskine proved a deterrent before that stage had been reached. Whatever the exact circumstances, the project was unlikely to survive the disruption caused by the move to Abbotsford in Spring 1812, and Scott's need to generate secure funds for his building plans, most achievable by the undertaking of *Rokeby* (1813).

The resumption of the novel after the disappointing reception of that poem is relatively well-documented. According to J. G. Lockhart, Scott had assembled 'the greater part of the first volume' by the close of his Christmas vacation at Abbotsford, having by that stage secured Erskine's approval.[5] According to two letters from Scott to his friend J. B. S. Morritt, the last two volumes were completed after his return to Edinburgh for the Summer legal term in 1814, in 'three weeks' and 'between the 4th June & the 1st July'.[6] Accepting the last date, it would seem Scott continued writing virtually to the point of publication. On 2 July Archibald Constable was able to send a presentation copy to Henry Mackenzie, as the dedicatee, as well as an inspection copy to his London associates, Longman and Co., formally offering them 700 of the 1000 impression.[7] The novel was first advertised as 'this day published' in the *Edinburgh Evening Courant* on 7 July 1814, which can be taken as the date of its public release in Edinburgh.

The evidence of the manuscript, the largest portions of which are held by the National Library of Scotland and the Pierpont Morgan Library, New York, tends to support the idea of an uneven composition. As a whole some 60 per cent of the first edition printed text is covered by surviving manuscript. These parts include Waverley's choice of profession and early stay at Tully-Veolan; his adventures after leaving Glennaquoich for the south, leading up to his first meeting with Charles Edward; and nearly all the sequence from the battle of Prestonpans to the 'Postscript' (but not the end dedication to Henry Mackenzie). Three different kinds of paper are in evidence. The first main surviving sequence, covering Chapters 5–11, is written on two kinds of quarto-sized paper, both of which can also be found in use in Scott's fragmentary Ashestiel 'Memoirs': a record of his upbringing paralleling in several respects the novel's account of Waverley's desultory education, and which may well have been written in tandem with the earlier parts of the novel. This is dated at the head 26 April 1808, but the later stages have been identified as belonging to 1810–11.[8] When the surviving manuscript resumes near the beginning of Volume 2, Chapter 6, midstream in the narrative (at 'That will not be very pleasant Callum': see 155.4), Scott is still using the second kind of 'quarto' paper, though a fresh sequence of foliation begins at this point. He continues to write for nine more leaves on the same paper, before transferring to a larger, folio-sized paper, bearing an 1813 watermark, on which the remaining parts of the manuscript are written. It is tempting to associate this change with Scott's removal to Edinburgh in 1814, though the possibility that he had stored up a supply of the earlier kind of paper for later use should also be borne in mind. Certainly Scott at this stage seems to be writing with a new fluidity, the extra space allowing him to include as many as 550 words on a page, as well as facilitating his use of the facing versos in his gatherings for larger corrections and additions. During this period Scott must have been engaged in the demanding process of handling proofs while driving forward his narrative, an interchange that is likely to have intensified as publication loomed.

While there are some reasons for believing that the first two sheets (48 pages) of the first edition, incorporating the bulk of Chapters 1–4, were set experimentally in 1810/11,[9] the earliest evidence of an intention to print in numbers is found in a note from James Ballantyne to Constable on 4 February 1814: 'Will you

have the goodness to order paper for Waverley? Is it to be 750 or
1000?'[10] There is also strong anecdotal evidence that printed
pages from the first volume were handed out among members of
the Edinburgh *literati* in early Spring 1814, presumably in an
effort to convince Constable of its saleability. Negotiations over
terms were concluded with the publishers early in April, after an
inspection of the first volume, Scott through Ballantyne resisting
an outright purchase of copyright, and insisting on strict anonymity. According to Lockhart the transcript of *Waverley* (thought
necessary to preserve that anonymity in the printing house, and
which no longer survives) was made by John Ballantyne, a possibility strengthened by signs of John's writing as well as James's on
the manuscript itself. No proofs either have apparently survived,
though some 300 instances of verbal sharpening and embellish-
ment between the manuscript and the first edition indicate a fertile
engagement by Scott through this medium. At the same time, a
large body of more routine changes were undoubtedly the work of
intermediaries, including James Ballantyne, the compositors and
house-readers, whose acknowledged brief was to transform the
manuscript into a formal published text. Changes originating from
this source are likely to have included the application of a full
punctuation system, replacing Scott's system of dashes with more
conventional marks; replacement of Scott's older and personally
idiosyncratic spellings with more orthodox forms; the standardi-
sation of proper names, where the manuscript is inconsistent (only
partially achieved by the first edition); and the transference of
some seventy English words into Scots forms in the mouths of
Scottish speakers. In addition over 1400 verbal changes took place
between the manuscript and the first edition, these varying
between improvements which are almost certainly authorial, routine corrections of syntax and grammar which could be by either
Scott or an intermediary, and palpable misreadings or misinterpre-
tations. Signs of the hectic completion of the first edition can be
found in a number of areas, including a confusion in chapter num-
bering in the later stages of the final volume, and the adoption,
presumably unintentional, of the same title ('The March') for two
chapters.[11]

The main aim of the present text is to provide a version of *Waverley* comparable to the first edition that might have been produced
if conditions had been less pressurised and if the intermediaries
had carried out all their functions correctly. In all some 1600
emendations have been made to the first-edition base text, a large
proportion of these involving restoration of the manuscript read-

ing where it had been lost through error or misunderstanding. The first edition's punctuation has been mostly accepted, one exception here being a few cases where the intermediaries failed to unpick the original syntactical structure of Scott's sentences in direct narrative. The present text also omits some forty commas added by the first edition, as significantly impeding rhetorical flow and/or deflecting from Scott's meaning; it also restores around eighty of Scott's original dashes, especially in cases where the mood or tone of a speaker is affected. Initial capitals are altered from the manuscript on more than eighty occasions, cases of raising including character descriptors such as 'the Baillie', or where a public institution or sobriquet is involved as in 'Church of England' (27.21) and 'the Good Town' (214.14), the latter signifying Edinburgh. The first edition's orthography is generally accepted, even though this means retaining a number of internal inconsistencies; spellings are however brought back from the manuscript in cases where Scott's knowledge of specialist terminology exceeded that of the intermediaries. The present text also restores some forty Scots forms which were either deliberately or inadvertently anglicised by the first edition, most of these occurring in the mouths of consistent speakers of Scots, though a number are also restored to the Baron of Bradwardine, in moments of heightened emotion or when he is addressing social subordinates. The following proper names have been standardised throughout on the authority of Scott's preferred usage as deduced from the manuscript: Ballenkeiroch; Brere-wood Lodge; Gellatley; Gilfillan; Inch-Grubbit; Mellville; Micklewrath; Rubrick; Ruffen; Saunders Saunderson; Tims; Tully-Veolan; Waverley Chace. At the same time, the present text reverses the first edition's imposition of Waverley-Honour as a single place name, by restoring several instances of 'Waverley Hall', as used by the manuscript to differentiate the family residence from the estate at large.

Overall, nearly 750 verbal changes, ranging from single-word substitutions to more substantial alterations, have been adopted on the manuscript's authority. As a result of emendations made on the grounds of misreading, Sir Everard Waverley's feelings are now 'sorely' not 'severely' jarred at 23.21; the mysterious 'pedlar' declaims against 'mumming' not 'murmuring' in churches (187.19); and the slain after the skirmish at Clifton are found in a 'knot' rather than on a 'knoll' at 300.19. In the case of misunderstanding, where the intermediaries have provided wrong or less precise alternatives, restorations include 'Cavaliero' (174.42) for 'Cavalier', 'symptomatic' (190.41) for 'sympathetic', and 'Sesamum'

(347.30) for '*Sesame*'. Other areas of restoration, involving wrong
insertions, omissions and rearrangements, are especially evident in
dialogue where the intermediaries applied grammatical and stylis-
tic conventions more appropriate to formal narrative. The present
text also brings in several larger areas of text apparently overlooked
by the intermediaries, mainly from facing versos, these omissions
having accelerated in the final stages of the novel. In a few instances
alternative readings are offered in cases where the intermediaries,
faced with instability in the manuscript, appear to have opted for a
wrong or inadequate solution. One such case occurs at 285.18–20,
where, as Evan Dhu gives Waverley a warning prior to his ambush,
the manuscript reads: 'as he passd him he only approachd his stirrup and said in Gaelic [space] that is Beware and then walkd
swiftly on'. Here the hiatus is physically obvious, and the intention
evidently was that it would be filled in later with an appropriate
Gaelic equivalent of 'Beware'. In the event, the first edition effectively avoided the problem in supplying: 'as he passed him, he only
approached his stirrup, and pronounced the single word, Beware!
and then walked swiftly on'. As an alternative, the present text
conjecturally supplements the original manuscript reading with
'*'N aire!*', signifying in Gaelic 'Careful!'

Additionally, the present text introduces some 270 emendations (eighty-five of them verbal) from subsequent British editions
in Scott's lifetime, which in all amounted to twelve, including collected sets. This amount is boosted by evidence of interventions by
Scott himself in both the second and third editions, which
appeared fairly rapidly after the first, in August and October 1814
respectively. Changes in the second edition which bear the mark of
Scott, and which are now adopted by the present text, include the
addition of 'savour or' to produce 'without ony sense or savour or
life' at 185.28, and the substitution of 'a deacon of his craft' for 'his
craft's master' at 237.29. Clearer evidence of involvement by Scott
is found in the third edition through the inclusion there of a handful of changes recommended by his friend Morritt, the most
obvious of which is the replacement at 114.4 of Claude [Lorraine]
by Poussin, which the present text rejects as misinterpreting
Scott's original design. The present text also adopts a number of
more routine changes from these two editions, including substitutions to avoid close repetition, of a kind that ideally should have
been made by the first edition. Another major overhaul of the text,
including several embellishments that are almost certainly authorial, can be found in the sixth edition, published in June 1816; but
by then Scott was re-engaging with his text at a distance of two

years and after two other of his novels had intervened, and these changes are generally not adopted. Nor, apart from two adjustments from the third edition, are any alterations made to the first edition's Gaelic, notwithstanding an overhaul in the 1819 octavo edition of *Novels and Tales of the Author of Waverley*, the first collected set in which *Waverley* appeared.

The Magnum Opus text, published in two volumes in June 1829, contains some 4600 variants compared with the first edition of 1814, an accumulation boosted during the intervening years by the practice in the printing house of using immediately preceding editions as copy texts. Of these over 360 (mostly verbal) changes can be identified as stemming from the Interleaved Set, in which Scott made textual alterations and annotations for the Magnum project. Scott here, however, was working not only at a considerable distance from the initial creative process but also with a base text irretrievably altered through the accretions of different printings; and while, in some instances, a creative re-engagement with the original narrative can be sensed, other interventions have a routine feel to them, as in the introduction of nearly 115 indicators identifying speakers. The Magnum also originates approximately 1525 variants (430 verbal) on its own, a large majority of which are unlikely to have involved Scott. The present text does however follow the Magnum in supplying accents to French words in nearly thirty instances, a procedure no doubt initially curtailed by the limitations of Ballantyne's types.

Compared with the much-reprinted Magnum Opus version, the Penguin edition of *Waverley* offers a more vibrant, if superficially less cohesive, representation of the creative and experimental energies which went into Scott's first entry into prose fiction, dazzling the novel's first generation of readers as if by 'an electric shock of delight'.[12] A more extensive explanation of emendations and a full listing are to be found in the Edinburgh Edition: EEWN 1, ed. P. D. Garside (Edinburgh, 2007), 367–494.

NOTES

1   See, e.g., P. D. Garside, 'Dating *Waverley*'s Early Chapters', *The Bibliotheck*, 13:3 (1986), 61–81.
2   National Library of Scotland (henceforth NLS), MS 3879, ff. 189–90.
3   See Scott's letter to Erskine of that date: 'I want to consult you about Waverley and a thousand things' (NLS, MS 23141, f. 131).

4 'A History of the Text of *Waverley*', in *Waverley; or 'Tis Sixty Years Since*, ed. Claire Lamont (Oxford, 1981), xxiv–xxv.

5 J. G. Lockhart, *Memoirs of the Life of Sir Walter Scott, Bart.*, 7 vols (Edinburgh, 1837–38), 3.124.

6 *The Letters of Sir Walter Scott*, ed. H. J. C. Grierson and others, 12 vols (London, 1932–37), 3.457, 479.

7 NLS MS 789, pp. 85, 86–87.

8 See *Scott on Himself*, ed. David Hewitt (Edinburgh, 1981), xxiv–xxv.

9 The setting in type of 'a sheet or two' in 1811 is noted by Robert Pearce Gillies in his *Recollections of Sir Walter Scott* (London, 1837), 204.

10 NLS, MS 23230, f. 54r.

11 Vol. 2, Ch. 21; and Vol. 3, Ch. 10. The repetition was followed by subsequent printings, and is accepted into the present text, in the absence of any authority for an alternative.

12 The expression was used to describe the contemporary reaction by Henry Cockburn, in *Memorials of His Time* (Edinburgh, 1856), 281.

WAVERLEY;

OR,

'TIS SIXTY YEARS SINCE.

IN THREE VOLUMES.

Under which King, Bezonian? speak, or die!
Henry IV. Part II.

VOL. I.

EDINBURGH:

Printed by James Ballantyne and Co.

FOR ARCHIBALD CONSTABLE AND CO. EDINBURGH; AND
LONGMAN, HURST, REES, ORME, AND BROWN,
LONDON.

1814.

WAVERLEY

OR,

'TIS SIXTY YEARS SINCE

VOLUME I

Chapter One

INTRODUCTORY

THE TITLE of this work has not been chosen without the grave and
solid deliberation which matters of importance demand from the prudent. Even its first, or general denomination, was the result of no
common research or selection, although, according to the example of
my predecessors, I had only to seize upon the most sounding and
euphonic surname that English history or topography affords, and
elect it at once as the title of my work, and the name of my hero. But,
alas! what could my readers have expected from the chivalrous epi-
thets of Howard, Mordaunt, Mortimer, or Stanley, or from the softer
and more sentimental sounds of Belmour, Belville, Belfield, and Belgrave, but pages of inanity, similar to those which have been so chris-
tened for half a century past? I must modestly admit I am too diffident
of my own merit to place it in unnecessary opposition to preconceived
associations: I have therefore, like a maiden knight with his white
shield, assumed for my hero, WAVERLEY, an uncontaminated name,
bearing with its sound little of good or evil, excepting what the reader
shall be hereafter pleased to affix to it. But my second or supplemental
title was a matter of much more difficult election, since that, short as it
is, may be held as pledging the author to some special mode of laying
his scene, drawing his characters, and managing his adventures. Had
I, for example, announced in my frontispiece, "Waverley, a Tale of
other Days," must not every novel-reader have anticipated a castle

scarce less than that of Udolpho, of which the eastern wing had been long uninhabited, and the keys either lost or consigned to the care of some aged butler or housekeeper, whose trembling steps, about the middle of the second volume, were doomed to guide the hero, or heroine, to the ruinous precincts? Would not the owl have shrieked and the cricket cried in my very title-page? and could it have been possible for me, with a moderate attention to decorum, to introduce any scene more lively than might be produced by the jocularity of a clownish but faithful valet, or the garrulous narrative of the heroine's fille-de-chambre, when rehearsing the stories of blood and horror which she had heard in the servants' hall? Again, had my title borne, "Waverley, a Romance from the German," what head so obtuse as not to image forth a profligate abbot, an oppressive duke, a secret and mysterious association of Rosycrucians and illuminati, with all their properties of black cowls, caverns, daggers, electrical machines, trap-doors, and dark lanterns? Or if I had rather chosen to call my work a "Sentimental Tale," would it not have been a sufficient presage of a heroine with a profusion of auburn hair, and a harp, the soft solace of her solitary hours, which she fortunately finds always the means of transporting from castle to cottage, although she herself be sometimes obliged to jump out of a two-pair-of-stairs window, and is more than once bewildered on her journey, alone and on foot, without any guide but a blowzy peasant girl, whose jargon she hardly can understand? Or again, if my Waverley had been entitled "A Tale of the Times," wouldst thou not, gentle reader, have demanded from me a dashing sketch of the fashionable world, a few anecdotes of private scandal thinly veiled, and if lusciously painted so much the better; a heroine from Grosvenor Square, and a hero from the Barouche Club or the Four-in-Hand, with a set of subordinate characters from the elegantes of Queen Anne Street East, or the knowing heroes of the Bow-Street Office? I could proceed in proving the importance of a title-page, and displaying at the same time my own intimate knowledge of the particular ingredients necessary to the composition of romances and novels of various descriptions. But it is enough, and I scorn to tyrannize longer over the impatience of my reader, who is doubtless already anxious to know the choice made by an author so profoundly versed in the different branches of his art.

By fixing then the date of my story Sixty Years before this present 1st November, 1805, I would have my readers understand that they will meet in the following pages neither a romance of chivalry, nor a tale of modern manners; that my hero will neither have iron on his shoulders, as of yore, nor on the heels of his boots, as is the present fashion of Bond Street; and that my damsels will neither be clothed "in purple and in pall," like the Lady Alice of an old ballad, nor reduced to the primitive nakedness of a modern fashionable at a route. From this my choice of an æra the understanding critic may farther presage, that the object of my tale is more a description of men than manners. A tale of manners, to be interesting, must either refer to antiquity so great as to have become venerable, or it must bear a vivid reflection of those scenes which are passing daily before our eyes, and are interesting from their novelty. Thus the coat-of-mail of our ancestors, and the triple-furred pelisse of our modern beaux, may, though for very different reasons, be equally fit for the array of a fictitious character; but who, meaning the costume of his hero to be impressive, would willingly attire him in the court dress of George the Second's reign, with its no collar, large sleeves, and low pocket-holes? The same may be urged, with equal truth, of the Gothic hall, which, with its darkened and tinted windows, its elevated and gloomy roof, and massive oaken table garnished with boar's-head and rosemary, pheasants and peacocks, cranes and cygnets, has an excellent effect in fictitious description. Much may also be gained by a lively display of a modern fête, such as we have daily recorded in that part of a newspaper entitled the Mirror of Fashion. But if we contrast these, or either of them, with the splendid formality of an entertainment given Sixty Years since, it will be readily seen how much the painter of antique or of fashionable manners gains over him who delineates those of the last generation.

Considering the disadvantages inseparable from this part of my subject, I must be understood to have resolved to avoid them as much as possible, by throwing the force of my narrative upon the characters and passions of the actors;—those passions common to men in all stages of society, and which have alike agitated the human heart, whether it throbbed under the steel corslet of the fifteenth century, the brocaded coat of the eighteenth, or the blue frock and white dimity waistcoat of the present day. Upon these passions it is no doubt true that the state of manners and laws casts a necessary colouring; but the bearings, to use the language of heraldry, remain the same, though the tincture may be not only different, but opposed in strong contradis-tinction. The wrath of our ancestors, for example, was coloured *gules;* it broke forth in acts of open and sanguinary violence against the objects of its fury: our malignant feelings, which must seek gratifica-tion through more indirect channels, and undermine the obstacles which they cannot openly bear down, may be rather said to be tinc-tured *sable*. But the deep ruling impulse is the same in both cases; and the proud peer, who can now only ruin his neighbour according to law, by protracted suits, is the genuine descendant of the baron who wrapped the castle of his competitor in flames, and knocked him on the head as he endeavoured to escape from the conflagration. It is from the great book of Nature, the same through a thousand editions, whether of black letter or wire-wove and hot-pressed, that I have venturously essayed to read a chapter to the public. Some favourable opportunities of contrast have been afforded me, by the state of society in the northern part of the island at the period of my history, and may serve at once to vary and to illustrate the moral lessons which I would willingly consider as the most important part of my plan, although I am sensible how short these will fall of their aim, if I shall be found unable to mix them with amusement,—a task not quite so easy in this critical generation as it was "Sixty Years since."

Chapter Two

WAVERLEY-HONOUR.——A RETROSPECT

IT IS THEN Sixty Years since Edward Waverley, the hero of the following pages, took leave of his family to join the regiment of dragoons in which he had lately obtained a commission. It was a melancholy day at Waverley-Honour when the young officer parted with Sir Everard, the affectionate old uncle to whose title and estate he was presumptive heir. A difference in political opinions had early separated the Baronet from his younger brother, Richard Waverley, the father of our hero. Sir Everard had inherited from his sires the whole train of tory or high-church predilections and prejudices, which had distinguished the house of Waverley since the great civil war. Richard, on the contrary, who was ten years younger, beheld himself born to the fortune of a second brother, and anticipated neither dignity nor entertainment in sustaining the character of Will Wimble. He saw early, that to succeed in the race of life, it was necessary he should carry as little weight as possible. Painters talk of the difficulty of expressing the existence of compound passions in the same features at the same moment: It would be no less difficult for the moralist to analyze the mixed motives which unite to form the impulse of our actions. Richard Waverley read and satisfied himself from history and sound argument, that in the words of the old song,

> Passive obedience was a jest,
> And pshaw! was non-resistance.

Yet reason would have probably been unable to remove hereditary prejudice, could Richard have anticipated that Sir Everard, taking to heart an early disappointment, would have remained a bachelor at seventy-two. The prospect of succession, however remote, might in that case, have led him to endure dragging through the greater part of his life as "Master Richard at the Hall, the baronet's brother," in hopes that ere its conclusion he should be distinguished as Sir Richard Waverley of Waverley-Honour, successor to a princely estate, and to extended political connections as head of the country interest. But this was a consummation of things not to be expected at Richard's outset, when Sir Everard was in the prime of life, and certain to be an acceptable suitor in almost any family, whether wealth or beauty should be the object of his pursuit, and when, indeed, his speedy marriage was a report which regularly amused the neighbourhood once a year. His brother therefore saw no road to independence save that of relying upon his own exertions, and adopting a political creed more consonant both to reason and his own interest than the hereditary faith of Sir Everard in high church and the house of Stuart. He therefore read his recantation at the beginning of his career, and entered life as an avowed whig, and friend of the Hanover succession.

The ministry of the period were prudently anxious to diminish the phalanx of opposition. The tory nobility, depending for their reflected lustre upon the sunshine of a court, had for some time been gradually reconciling themselves to the new dynasty. But the wealthy country gentlemen of England, a rank which retained, with much of ancient manners and primitive integrity, a great proportion of obstinate and unyielding prejudice, stood aloof in haughty and sullen opposition, and cast many a look of mingled regret and hope to Bar le Duc, Avignon, and Italy. The accession of the near relation of one of these steady and inflexible opponents was considered as a means of bringing over more converts, and therefore Richard Waverley met with a share of ministerial favour more than proportioned to his talents or his political importance. It was, however, discovered that he had respectable parts for public business, and the first admittance to the minister's levee being negociated, his success became rapid. Sir Everard learned from the public News Letter, first, that Richard Waverley, Esquire, was returned for the ministerial borough of Barterfaith; next, that Richard Waverley, Esquire, had taken a distinguished part in the debate upon the Excise Bill in the support of government; and, lastly, that Richard Waverley, Esquire, had been honoured with a seat at one of those boards where the pleasure of serving the country is combined with other important gratifications, which, to render them the more acceptable, occur regularly once a quarter.

Although these events followed each other so closely that the sagacity of the editor of a modern newspaper would have presaged the two last even while he announced the first, yet they came upon Sir Everard gradually, and drop by drop, as it were, distilled through the cool and procrastinating alembic of Dyer's Weekly Letter. For it may be observed in passing, that instead of those mail-coaches, by means of which every mechanic at his six-penny club may nightly learn from twenty contradictory channels the yesterday's news of the capital, a weekly post brought, in those days, to Waverley-Honour, a Weekly Intelligencer, which, after it had gratified Sir Everard's curiosity, his sister's, and that of his aged butler, was regularly transferred from the hall to the rectory, from the rectory to Squire Stubbs at the Grange, from the Squire to the Baronet's steward at his neat white house on the heath, from the steward to the bailiff, and from him through a huge circle of honest dames and gaffers, by whose hard and horny hands it was generally worn to pieces in about a month after its arrival.

This slow succession of intelligence was of some advantage to Richard Waverley in the case before us. For had the sum total of his enormities reached the ears of Sir Everard at once, there can be no doubt the new commissioner would have had little reason to pique himself on the success of his politics. The Baronet, although the mildest of human beings, was not without sensitive points in his character; his brother's conduct had wounded these deeply; the Waverley estate was fettered by no entail, (for it had never entered into the head of any of its former possessors that one of their progeny could be guilty of the atrocities laid by Dyer's Letter to the door of Richard,) and if it had, the marriage of the proprietor might have been fatal to a collateral heir. These various ideas floated through the brain of Sir Everard, without, however, producing any determinate conclusion.

He examined the tree of his genealogy, which, emblazoned with many an emblematic mark of honour and heroic achievement, hung upon the well-varnished wainscot of his hall. The nearest descendants of Sir Hildebrand Waverley, failing those of his eldest son Wilfred, of whom Sir Everard and his brother were the only representatives, were, as this honoured register informed him, (and indeed as he himself well knew) the Waverleys of Highley Park, com. Hants; with whom the main branch, or rather stock, of the house had renounced all connection since the great law-suit in 1670. This scion had committed a further offence against the head and source of their gentility, by the intermarriage of their representative with Judith, heiress of Oliver Bradshawe, of Highley Park, whose arms, the same with those of Bradshawe the regicide, they had quartered with the ancient coat of Waverley. These offences, however, had vanished from Sir Everard's recollection in the heat of his resentment, and had Lawyer Clippurse, for whom his groom was dispatched express, arrived but an hour earlier, he might have had the benefit of drawing a new settlement of the lordship and manor of Waverley-Honour, with all its dependencies. But an hour of cool reflection is a great matter, when employed in weighing the comparative evils of two measures, to neither of which we are internally partial. Lawyer Clippurse found his patron involved in a deep study, which he was too respectful to disturb, otherwise than by producing his paper and leathern ink-case, as prepared to minute his honour's commands. Even this slight manœuvre was embarrassing to Sir Everard, who felt it as a reproach to his indecision. He looked at the attorney with some desire to issue his fiat, when the sun, emerging from behind a cloud, poured at once its chequered light through the stained window of the gloomy cabinet in which they were seated. The Baronet's eye, as he raised it to the splendour, fell right upon the central scutcheon, impressed with the same device which his ancestor was said to have borne in the field of Hastings; three ermines passant, argent, in a field azure, with its appropriate motto, *sans tache*. "May our name rather perish," thought Sir Everard, "than that ancient and loyal symbol should be blended with the dishonoured insignia of a traitorous round-head!"

All this was the effect of the glimpse of a sun-beam just sufficient to light Lawyer Clippurse to mend his pen. The pen was mended in vain. The attorney was dismissed, with directions to hold himself in readiness on the first summons.

The apparition of Lawyer Clippurse at the Hall occasioned much speculation in that portion of the world of which Waverley-Honour formed the centre: But the more judicious politicians of this microcosm augured yet worse consequences to Richard Waverley from a movement which shortly followed his apostacy. This was no less than an excursion of the Baronet in his coach and six, with four attendants in rich liveries, to make a visit of some duration to a noble peer on the confines of the shire, of untainted descent, steady tory principles, and the happy father of six unmarried and accomplished daughters. Sir Everard's reception in this family was, as it may be easily conceived, sufficiently favourable; but of the six young ladies, his taste unfortunately determined him in favour of Lady Emily, the youngest, who received his attentions with an embarrassment which shewed at once that she durst not decline them, and that they afforded her any thing but pleasure. Sir Everard could not but perceive something uncommon in the restrained emotions which she testified at the advances he hazarded; but assured by the prudent countess that they were the natural effects of a retired education, the sacrifice might have been completed, as doubtless has happened in many similar instances, had it not been for the courage of an elder sister, who revealed to the wealthy suitor that Lady Emily's affections were fixed upon a young soldier of fortune, a near relation of her own. Sir Everard manifested great emotion on receiving this intelligence, which was confirmed to him, in a private interview, by the young lady herself, although under the most dreadful apprehensions of her father's indignation. Honour and generosity were hereditary attributes of the house of Waverley. With a grace and delicacy worthy the hero of a romance, Sir Everard withdrew his claim to the hand of Lady Emily. He had even, before leaving Blandeville Castle, the address to extort from her father a consent to her union with the object of her choice. What arguments he used on this point cannot exactly be known; but the young officer immediately after this transaction rose in the army with a rapidity far surpassing the usual pace of unpatronized professional merit, although, to outward appearance, that was all he had to depend upon.

The shock which Sir Everard encountered upon this occasion, although diminished by the consciousness of having acted virtuously and generously, had its effect upon his future life. His resolution of marriage had been adopted in a fit of indignation; the labour of courtship did not quite suit the dignified indolence of his habits; he had but just escaped the risk of marrying a woman who could never love him, and his pride could not be greatly flattered by the termination of his amour, even if his heart had not suffered. The result of the whole matter was his return to Waverley-Honour without any transfer of his affections, notwithstanding the sighs and languishments of the fair tell-tale, who had revealed, in mere sisterly affection, the secret of Lady Emily's attachment, and in despite of the nods, winks, and inuendoes of the officious lady mother, and the grave eulogiums which the earl pronounced successively on the prudence, and good sense, and admirable disposition of his first, second, third, fourth, and fifth daughters. The memory of his unsuccessful amour was with Sir Everard, as with many more of his temper, at once shy, proud, sensitive, and indolent, a beacon against exposing himself to similar mortification, pain, and fruitless exertion for the time to come. He continued to live at Waverley-Honour in the style of an old English gentleman, of ancient descent and opulent fortune. His sister, Miss Rachael Waverley, presided at his table, and they became by degrees an old bachelor and an ancient maiden lady, the gentlest and kindest of the votaries of celibacy.

The vehemence of Sir Everard's resentment against his brother was but short-lived; yet his dislike to the whig and the placeman, though unable to stimulate him to resume any active measures prejudicial to Richard's interest, continued to maintain the coldness between them. Accident at length occasioned a renewal of their inter- course. Richard had married a young woman of rank, by whose family interest and private fortune he hoped to advance his career. In her right he became possessor of a manor of some value, at the distance of a few miles from Waverley-Honour.

Little Edward, the hero of our tale, then in his fifth year, was their only child. It chanced that the child with his keeper had strayed one morning to a mile's distance from the avenue of Brere-wood Lodge, his father's seat. Their attention was attracted by a carriage drawn by six stately black long-tailed horses, and with as much carving and gilding as would have done honour to my lord mayor's. It was waiting for the owner, who was at a little distance inspecting the progress of a half-built farm-house. I know not whether the boy's nurse had been a Welch-woman or a Scotch-woman, or in what manner he associated a shield emblazoned with three ermines with the idea of personal property, but he no sooner beheld this family emblem than he stoutly determined on vindicating his right to the splendid vehicle on which it was displayed. The Baronet arrived while the boy's maid was in vain endeavouring to make him desist from his determination to appropriate the gilded coach and six. The rencontre was at a happy moment for Edward, as his uncle had been just eyeing wistfully, with something of a feeling like envy, the chubby boys of the stout yeoman whose mansion was building by his direction. In the round-faced rosy cherub before him, bearing his eye and his name, and vindicating a hereditary title to his family, affection, and patronage, by means of a tie which Sir Everard held as sacred as either Garter or Blue-mantle, Providence seemed to have granted to him the very object best calculated to fill up the void in his hopes and his affections. The child and his attendant were sent home in the carriage to Brere-wood Lodge, with such a message as opened to Richard Waverley a door of reconciliation with his elder brother. Their intercourse, however, continued to be rather formal and civil, than partaking of brotherly cordiality; yet it was sufficient to the wishes of both parties. Sir Everard obtained, in the frequent society of his little nephew, something on which his hereditary pride might found the anticipated pleasure of a continuation of his lineage, and on which his kind and gentle affections could at the same time fully exercise themselves. For Richard Waverley, he beheld in the growing attachment between the uncle and nephew, the means of securing his son's, if not his own, succession to the hereditary estate, which he felt would be rather endangered than promoted by any attempt on his own part towards a more intimate commerce with a man of Sir Everard's habits and opinions.

Thus, by a sort of tacit compromise, little Edward was permitted to pass the greater part of the year at the Hall, and appeared to stand in the same intimate relation to both families, although their intercourse was otherwise limited to formal messages and more formal visits. The education of the youth was regulated alternately by the taste and opinions of his uncle and of his father. But more of this in a subsequent chapter.

Chapter Three

EDUCATION

THE EDUCATION of our hero, Edward Waverley, was of a nature somewhat desultory. In infancy his health suffered, or was supposed to suffer, (which is quite the same thing) by the air of London. As soon, therefore, as official duties, attendance on parliament, or the prosecution of any of his plans of interest or ambition, called his father to town, which was his usual residence for eight months in the year, Edward was transferred to Waverley-Honour, and experienced a change of instructors and of lessons, as well as of residence. This might have been remedied had his father placed him under the super-intendance of a permanent tutor. But he considered that one of his chusing would probably have been unacceptable at Waverley-Honour, and that such a selection as Sir Everard might have made, were the matter left to him, would have burdened him with a disagreeable inmate, if not a political spy, in his family. He therefore prevailed upon his private secretary, a young man of taste and accomplishment, to bestow an hour or two on Edward's education while at Brere-wood Lodge, and left his uncle answerable for his improvement in literature while an inmate at the Hall.

This was in some degree respectably provided for. Sir Everard's chaplain, an Oxonian, who had lost his fellowship for declining to take the oaths at the accession of George I., was not only an excellent classical scholar, but reasonably skilled in science, and master of most modern languages. He was, however, old and indulgent, and the recurring interregnum, during which Edward was entirely freed from his discipline, occasioned such a relaxation of authority, that the youth was permitted, in a great measure, to learn as he pleased, what he pleased, and when he pleased. This looseness of rule would have been ruinous to a boy of slow understanding, who, feeling labour in the acquisition of knowledge, would have altogether neglected it, save for the command of a task-master; and it might have proved equally dangerous to a youth whose animal spirits were more powerful than his imagination or his feelings, and whom the irresistible influence of Alma, when seated in his arms and legs, would have engaged in field sports from morning till night. But the character of Edward Waverley was remote from either of these. His powers of apprehension were so uncommonly quick, as almost to resemble intuition, and the chief care of his preceptor was to prevent him, as a sportsman would phrase it, from over-running his game, that is, from acquiring his knowledge in a slight, flimsy, and inadequate manner. And here the instructor had to combat another propensity too often united with brilliancy of fancy and vivacity of talent,—that indolence, namely, of disposition, which can only be stirred by some strong motive of gratification, and which renounces study so soon as curiosity is gratified, the pleasure of conquering the first difficulties exhausted, and the novelty of pursuit at an end. Edward would throw himself with spirit upon any classical author of which his preceptor proposed the perusal, make himself master of the style so far as to understand the story, and if that pleased or interested him, he finished the volume. But it was in vain to attempt fixing his attention on critical distinctions of philology, upon the difference of idiom, the beauty of felicitous expression, or the artificial combinations of syntax. "I can read and understand a Latin author," said young Edward, with the self-confidence and rash reasoning of fifteen, "and Scaliger or Bentley could not do much more." Alas! while he was thus permitted to read only for the gratification of his own amusement, he foresaw not that he was losing for ever the opportunity of acquiring habits of firm and incumbent application, of gaining the art of controuling, directing, and concentrating the powers of his own mind for earnest investigation,—an art far more essential than even that learning which is the primary object of study.

I am aware I may be here reminded of the necessity of rendering instruction agreeable to youth, and of Tasso's infusion of honey into the medicine prepared for a child; but an age in which children are taught the driest doctrines by the insinuating method of instructive games, has little reason to dread the consequences of study being rendered too serious or severe. The history of England is now reduced to a game at cards, the problems of mathematics to puzzles and riddles, and the doctrines of arithmetic may, we are assured, be sufficiently acquired by spending a few hours a-week at a new and complicated edition of the Royal Game of the Goose. There wants but one step further, and the Creed and Ten Commandments may be taught in the same manner, without the necessity of the grave face, deliberate tone of recital, and devout attention hitherto exacted from the well-governed childhood of this realm. It may in the mean time be subject of serious consideration, whether those who are accustomed only to acquire instruction through the medium of amusement, may not be brought to reject that which approaches under the aspect of study; whether those who learn history by the cards, may not be led to prefer the means to the end; and whether, were we to teach religion in the way of sport, our pupils might not thereby be gradually induced to make sport of their religion. To our young hero, who was permitted to seek his instruction only according to the bent of his own mind, and who, of consequence, only sought it so long as it afforded him amusement, the indulgence of his tutors was attended with evil consequences, which long continued to influence his character, happiness, and utility. Edward's power of imagination and love of literature, although the former was vivid, and the latter ardent, were so far from affording a remedy to this peculiar evil, that they rather inflamed and increased its violence. The library at Waverley Hall, a large Gothic room, with double arches and a gallery, contained that miscellaneous and extensive collection of volumes usually assembled together, during the course of two hundred years, by a family which have been always wealthy, and inclined of course, as a mark of splendour, to furnish their shelves with the current literature of the day, without much scrutiny or nicety of discrimination. Through this ample realm Edward was permitted to roam at large. His tutor had his own studies; and church politics and controversial divinity, together with a love of learned ease, though they did not withdraw his attention at stated times from the progress of his patron's presumptive heir, induced him readily to grasp at any apology for not extending a strict and regulated survey towards his general studies. Sir Everard had never been himself a student, and, like his sister Miss Rachael Waverley, held the vulgar doctrine, that idleness is incompatible with reading of any kind, and that the mere tracing the alphabetical characters with the eye, is in itself a useful and meritorious task, without scrupulously considering what ideas or doctrines they may happen to convey. With a desire of amusement therefore, which better discipline might soon have converted into a thirst for knowledge, young Waverley drove through the sea of books, like a vessel without a pilot or a rudder. Nothing perhaps increases by indulgence more than a desultory habit of reading, especially under such opportunities of gratifying it. I believe one reason why such numerous instances of erudition occur among the lower ranks is, that, with the same powers of mind, the poor student is limited to a narrow circle for indulging his passion for books, and must necessarily make himself master of the few he possesses ere he can acquire more. Edward, on the contrary, like the epicure who only deigned to take a single morsel from the sunny side of a peach, read no volume a moment after it ceased to excite his curiosity or interest; and it necessarily happened, that the habit of seeking only this sort of gratification rendered it daily more difficult of attainment, till the passion for reading, like other strong appetites, produced by indulgence a sort of satiety.

Ere he attained this indifference, however, he had read over, and stored in a memory of uncommon tenacity, much curious, though ill-arranged and miscellaneous information. In English literature he was master of Shakspeare and Milton, of our earlier dramatic authors, of many picturesque and interesting passages from our old historical chronicles, and particularly of Spenser, Drayton, and other poets who have exercised themselves on romantic fiction, of all themes the most fascinating to a youthful imagination, before the passions have roused themselves, and demand poetry of a more sentimental description. In this respect his acquaintance with the Italian opened him yet a wider range. He had perused the numerous romantic poems which, from the days of Pulci, have been a favourite exercise of the wits of Italy, and had sought gratification in the numerous collections of *novelle* which were brought forth by the genius of that elegant though luxurious nation, in emulation of the Decameron. In classical literature, Waverley had made the usual progress, and read the usual authors; and the French had afforded him an almost exhaustless collection of memoirs, scarcely more faithful than romances, and of romances so well written as hardly to be distinguished from memoirs. The splendid pages of Froissart, with his heart-stirring and eye-dazzling descriptions of war and of tournaments, were among his chief favourites; and from those of Brantome and De la Noue he learned to compare the wild and loose, yet superstitious character of the nobles of the League, with the stern, rigid, and sometimes turbulent disposition of the Huguenot party. The Spanish had contributed to his stock of chivalrous and romantic lore. The earlier literature of the northern nations did not escape the study of one who read, rather to awaken the imagination than to benefit the understanding. And yet, knowing much that is known but to few, Edward Waverley might justly be considered as ignorant, since he knew little of what adds dignity to man, and qualifies him to support and adorn an elevated situation in society.

The occasional attention of his parents might indeed have been of service to prevent the dissipation of mind incidental to such a desultory course of reading. But Mrs Richard Waverley died in the seventh year after the reconciliation between the brothers, and Waverley himself, who after this event resided more constantly in London, was too much interested in his own plans of wealth and ambition, to notice more respecting Edward than that he was of a very bookish turn, and probably destined to be a bishop. If he could have discovered and analyzed his son's waking dreams, he would have formed a very different conclusion.

Chapter Four

CASTLE-BUILDING

I HAVE ALREADY hinted that the dainty, squeamish, and fastidious taste acquired by a surfeit of idle reading, had not only rendered our hero unfit for serious and sober study, but had even disgusted him in some degree with that in which he had hitherto indulged. He was in his sixteenth year when his habits of abstraction and love of solitude became so much marked as to excite Sir Everard's affectionate apprehension. He tried to counterbalance these propensities, by engaging his nephew in field-sports, which had been the chief pleasure of his own youth. But although Edward eagerly carried the gun for one season, yet when practice had given him some dexterity, the pastime ceased to afford him amusement. In the succeeding spring, the perusal of old Isaac Walton's fascinating volume determined Edward to become "a brother of the angle." But of all diversions which ingenuity ever devised for the relief of idleness, fishing is the worst qualified to amuse a man who is at once indolent and impatient, and our hero's rod was speedily flung aside. Society and example, which, more than any other motives, master and sway the natural bent of our passions, might have had their usual effect upon our youthful visionary. But the neighbourhood was thinly inhabited, and the home-bred young squires whom it afforded, were not of a class fit to form Edward's usual companions, far less to excite him to emulate them in the practice of those pastimes which composed the serious business of their lives. Sir Everard had, upon the death of Queen Anne, resigned his seat in parliament, and, as his age increased and the number of his contemporaries diminished, gradually withdrawn himself from society; so that, when upon any particular occasion Edward mingled with accomplished and well-educated young men of his own rank and expectations, he felt an inferiority in their society, not so much from deficiency of information, as from the want of the skill to command and to arrange that which he possessed. A deep and increasing sensibility added to this dislike of society. The idea of having committed the slightest solecism in politeness, whether real or imaginary, was agony to him; for perhaps even guilt itself does not impose upon some minds so keen a sense of shame and remorse as a modest, sensitive, and inexperienced youth feels from the consciousness of having neglected etiquette, or excited ridicule. Where we are not at ease, we cannot be happy; and therefore it is not surprising, that Edward

Waverley supposed that he disliked and was unfitted for society, merely because he had not yet acquired the habit of living in it with ease and comfort, and of reciprocally giving and receiving pleasure.

The hours he spent with his uncle and aunt were exhausted in listening to the oft-repeated tale of narrative old age. Yet even there his imagination, the predominant faculty of his mind, was frequently excited. Family tradition and genealogical history, upon which much of Sir Everard's discourse turned, is the very reverse of amber, which, itself a valuable substance, usually includes flies, straws, and other trifles, whereas these studies, being themselves very insignificant and trifling, do nevertheless serve to perpetuate a great deal of what is rare and valuable in ancient manners, and to record many curious and minute facts which could have been preserved and conveyed through no other medium. If, therefore, Edward Waverley yawned at times over the dry deduction of his line of ancestors, with their various intermarriages, and inwardly deprecated the remorseless and protracted accuracy with which the worthy Sir Everard rehearsed the various degrees of propinquity between the house of Waverley-Honour and the doughty barons, knights, and squires, to whom they stood allied; if (notwithstanding his obligations to the three ermines passant) he sometimes cursed in his heart the jargon of heraldry, its griffins, its moldwarps, its wyverns, and its dragons, with all the bitterness of Hotspur himself, there were moments when these communications interested his fancy and rewarded his attention. The deeds of Wilibert of Waverley in the Holy Land, his long absence and perilous adventures, his supposed death, and his return on the evening when the betrothed of his heart had wedded the hero who had protected her from insult and oppression during his absence; the generosity with which the crusader relinquished his claims, and sought in a neighbouring cloister that peace which passeth not away; to these and similar tales he would hearken till his heart glowed and his eye glistened. Nor was he less affected, when his aunt Mrs Rachael narrated the sufferings and fortitude of Lady Alice Waverley during the great civil war. The benevolent features of the venerable spinster kindled into more majestic expression as she told how Charles had, after the field of Worcester, found a day's refuge at Waverley-Honour, and how, when a troop of cavalry were approaching to search the mansion, Lady Alice dismissed her youngest son with a handful of domestics, charging them to make good with their lives an hour's diversion, that the king might have that space for escape. "And, God help her," would Mrs Rachael continue, fixing her eyes upon the heroine's portrait as she spoke, "full dearly did she purchase the safety of her prince with the life of her darling child. They brought him here a prisoner,

mortally wounded, and you may trace the drops of his blood from the
great hall-door, along the little gallery, and up to the saloon, where
they laid him down to die at his mother's feet. But there was comfort
exchanged between them; for he knew from the glance of his mother's
eye that the purpose of his desperate defence was attained—Ah! I
remember," she continued, "I remember well to have seen one that
knew and loved him. Miss Lucy St Aubin lived and died a maid for his
sake, though one of the most beautiful and wealthy matches in this
country; all the country ran after her, but she wore widow's mourning
all her life for poor William, for they were betrothed though not
married, and died in——I cannot think of the date; but I remember,
in the November of that very year, when she found herself sinking, she
desired to be brought to Waverley-Honour once more, and visited all
the places where she had been with my grand-uncle, and caused the
carpets to be raised that she might trace the impression of his blood,
and if tears could have washed it out, it had not been there now; for
there was not a dry eye in the house. You would have thought, Edward,
that the very trees mourned for her, for their leaves dropt around her
without a gust of wind; and indeed she looked like one that would
never see them green again."

From such legends our hero would steal away to indulge the fancies
they excited. In the corner of the large and sombre library, with no
other light than was afforded by the decaying brands on its ponderous
and ample hearth, he would exercise for hours that internal sorcery by
which past or imaginary events are presented in action, as it were, to
the eye of the muser. Then arose in long and fair array the splendour
of the bridal feast at Waverley-Castle; the tall and emaciated form of
its real lord, as he stood in his pilgrim weeds, an unnoticed spectator
of the festivities of his supposed heir and intended bride; the electrical
shock occasioned by the discovery; the springing of the vassals to
arms; the astonishment of the bridegroom; the terror and confusion
of the bride; the agony with which Wilibert observed, that her heart as
well as consent was in these nuptials; the air of dignity, yet of deep
feeling, with which he flung down the half-drawn sword, and turned
away for ever from the house of his ancestors. Then would he change
the scene, and fancy would at his wish represent Aunt Rachael's
tragedy. He saw the Lady Waverley seated in her bower, her ear
strained to every sound, her heart throbbing with double agony; now
listening to the decaying echo of the hoofs of the king's horse, and
when that had died away, hearing in every breeze that shook the trees
of the park, the noise of the remote skirmish. A distant sound is heard
like the rushing of a swoln stream; it comes nearer, and Edward can
plainly distinguish the galloping of horses, the cries and shouts of

men, with straggling pistol-shots between, rolling forwards to the hall. The lady starts up—a terrified menial rushes in—But why pursue such a description.

As living in this ideal world became daily more delectable to our hero, interruption was disagreeable in proportion. The extensive domain that surrounded the Hall, which, far exceeding the dimensions of a park, was usually termed Waverley Chace, had originally been forest ground, and still, though broken by extensive glades in which the young deer were sporting, retained its pristine and savage character. It was traversed by broad avenues, in many places half-grown up with brushwood, where the beauties of former days used to take their stand to see the stag coursed with greyhounds, or to gain an aim at him with the cross-bow. In one spot distinguished by a moss-grown gothic monument, which retained the name of Queen's Standing, Elizabeth herself was said to have pierced seven bucks with her own arrows. This was a favourite haunt of Edward Waverley. At other times, with his gun and his spaniel, which served as an apology to others, and with a book in his pocket, which perhaps served as an apology to himself, he used to pursue one of these long avenues, which, after an ascending sweep of four miles, gradually narrowed into a rude and contracted path through the cliffy and wooded pass called Mirkwood Dingle, and opened suddenly upon a deep, dark, and small lake, named from the same cause, Mirkwood-Mere. There stood in former times a solitary tower upon a rock almost surrounded by the water, which had acquired the name of the Strength of Waverley, because in perilous times it had often been the refuge of the family. There in the wars of York and Lancaster, the last adherents of the Red Rose who dared to maintain her cause, carried on a harassing and predatory warfare, till the strong-hold was reduced by the celebrated Richard of Gloucester. Here too a party of cavaliers long maintained themselves under Nigel Waverley, elder brother of that William, whose fate Aunt Rachael commemorated. Through these scenes it was that Edward loved to "chew the cud of sweet and bitter fancy," and, like a child amongst his toys, culled and arranged, from the splendid yet useless imagery and emblems with which his imagination was stored, visions as brilliant and as fading as those of an evening sky. The effect of this indulgence upon his temper and character will appear in the next chapter.

Chapter Five

CHOICE OF A PROFESSION

FROM THE minuteness with which I have traced Waverley's pursuits, and the bias which they unavoidably communicated to his imagination, the reader may perhaps anticipate, in the following tale, an imitation of the romance of Cervantes. But he will do my prudence injustice in the supposition. My intention is not to follow the steps of that inimitable author, in describing such total perversion of intellect as misconstrues objects actually presented to the senses, but that more common aberration from sound judgment, which apprehends indeed occurrences in their reality, but communicates to them a tincture of its own romantic tone and colouring. So far was Edward Waverley from expecting general sympathy with his own feeling, or concluding that the present state of things was calculated to exhibit the reality of those visions in which he loved to indulge, that he dreaded nothing more than the detection of such sentiments as were dictated by his musing. He neither had nor wished to have a confidant, with whom to communicate his reveries; and so sensible was he of the ridicule attached to them, that had he been to chuse between any punishment short of ignominy, and the necessity of giving a cold and composed account of the ideal world in which he lived the better part of his day, I think he would not have hesitated to chuse the former infliction. This secrecy became doubly precious as he felt in advancing life the influence of the awakening passions. Female forms of exquisite grace and beauty began to mingle in his mental adventures; nor was he long without looking abroad to compare the creatures of his own imagination with the females of actual life. The list of the beauties who displayed their hebdomadal finery at the parish church of Waverley, was neither numerous nor select. By far the most passable was Miss Sissly, or, as she rather chose to be called, Miss Cæcilia Stubbs, daughter of Squire Stubbs at the Grange. I know not whether it was by the "merest accident in the world," a phrase which from female lips does not always exclude *malice prepense*, or whether it was from a conformity of taste, that Miss Cæcilia more than once crossed Edward in his favourite walks through Waverley Chace. He had not as yet assumed courage to accost her on these occasions; but the meeting was not without its effect. A romantic lover is a strange idolater, who sometimes cares not out of what log he frames the object of his adoration; at least, if nature has given that object any passable proportion of personal charms, he

can easily play the Jeweller and Dervise in the oriental tale,* and
supply her richly out of the stores of his own imagination with supernatural beauty, and all the properties of intellectual wealth. But ere the
charms of Miss Cæcilia Stubbs had erected her into a positive goddess, or elevated her at least to a level with the saint her namesake,
Mrs Rachael Waverley gained some intimation which determined her
to prevent the approaching apotheosis. Even the most simple and
unsuspicious of the female sex have (God bless them!) an instinctive
sharpness of perception in such matters, which sometimes goes the
length of observing partialities that never existed, but rarely misses to
detect such as pass actually under their observation. Mrs Rachael
applied herself, with great prudence, not to combat, but to elude, the
approaching danger, and suggested to her brother the necessity that
the heir of his house should see something more of the world, than
was consistent with constant residence at Waverley Hall. Sir Everard
would not at first listen to a proposal which went to separate his
nephew from him. Edward was a little bookish, he admitted; but
youth, he had always heard, was the season for learning, and no doubt,
when his rage for letters was abated, and his head fully stocked with
knowledge, his nephew would take to field-sports and county business. He had often, he said, himself regretted that he had not spent
some time in study during his youth: he would neither have shot nor
hunted with less skill, and he might have made the roof of St Stephen's
echo to longer orations than were comprised in those zealous Noes,
with which, when a member of the House during Godolphin's administration, he encountered every measure of government.

Aunt Rachael's anxiety, however, lent her address to carry her
point. Every representative of their house had visited foreign parts, or
served his country in the army, before he settled for life at Waverley
Hall, and she appealed for the truth of her assertion to the great
genealogical pedigree, an authority which Sir Everard was never
known to contradict. In short, a proposal was made to Mr Richard
Waverley that his son should travel, under the direction of his present
tutor, Mr Pembroke, with a suitable allowance from the Baronet's
liberality. He saw no objection to this overture; but upon mentioning
it casually at the table of the minister, the great man looked grave. The
reason was explained in private. The unhappy turn of Sir Everard's
politics, the minister observed, was such as would render it highly
improper that a young gentleman of such hopeful prospects should
travel on the continent with a tutor doubtless of his uncle's chusing,
and directing his course by his injunctions. What might Mr Edward
Waverley's society be at Paris, what at Rome, where all manner of

* See Hoppner's tale of the Seven Lovers.

snares were spread by the Pretender and his sons; these were points for Mr Waverley to consider. This he could himself say, that he knew his Majesty had such a just sense of Mr Richard Waverley's merits, that if his son adopted the army for a few years, a troop, he believed, might be reckoned upon in one of the dragoon regiments lately returned from Flanders. A hint thus conveyed and enforced, was not to be neglected with impunity; and Richard Waverley, though with great dread of shocking his brother's prejudices, deemed he could not avoid accepting the commission thus offered him for his son. The truth is, he calculated much, and justly, upon Sir Everard's fondness for Edward, which was unlikely to resent any step that he might take in due submission to parental authority. Two letters announced this determination to the Baronet and his nephew. The latter barely communicated the fact, and pointed out the necessary preparations for joining his regiment. To his brother, Richard was more diffuse and circuitous. He coincided with him in the most flattering manner in the propriety of his son's seeing a little more of the world, and was even humble in expressions of gratitude for his proposed assistance; was, however, deeply concerned that it was now, unfortunately, not in Edward's power exactly to comply with the plan which had been chalked out by his best friend and benefactor. He himself had thought with pain on the boy's inactivity, at an age when all his ancestors had borne arms; even Royalty himself had deigned to enquire whether young Waverley was not now in Flanders, at an age when his grandfather was already bleeding for his king, in the great Civil War. This was accompanied by an offer of a troop of horse. What could he do? There was no time to consult his brother's inclinations, even if he could have conceived there might be objections on his part to his nephew's following the glorious career of his predecessors. And in short, that Edward was now (the intermediate steps of cornet and lieutenant being overleapt with great agility) Captain Waverley, of the —— regiment of dragoons, which he must join in their quarters at D—— in Scotland, in the course of a month.

Sir Everard Waverley received this intimation with a mixture of feelings. At the period of the Hanoverian accession he had withdrawn from parliament, and his conduct, in the memorable year 1715, had not been altogether unsuspected. There were reports of private musters of tenants and horses in Waverley Chace by moonlight, and of cases of carabines and pistols purchased in Holland, and addressed to the Baronet, but intercepted by the vigilance of a riding officer of the excise, who was afterwards tossed in a blanket on a moonless night, by an association of stout yeomen, for his officiousness. Nay, it was even said that at the arrest of Sir W—— W——, the leader of the tory party, a letter from Sir Everard was found in the pocket of his night-gown. But there was no overt act to be founded on, and government, contented with suppressing the insurrection of 1715, felt it neither prudent nor safe to push their vengeance farther than against those who actually took up arms. Nor did Sir Everard's apprehensions of personal consequences seem to correspond with the reports spread among his whig neighbours. It was well known that he supplied with money several of the distressed Northumbrians and Scotchmen, who, after being made prisoners at Preston in Lancashire, were imprisoned in Newgate and the Marshalsea, and it was his solicitor and ordinary counsel who conducted the defence of some of these unfortunate gentlemen at their trial. It was generally supposed, that had ministers possessed any real proof of Sir Everard's accession to the rebellion, he either would not have ventured thus to brave the existing government, or at least would not have done so with impunity. The feelings, how-ever, which then dictated his proceedings, were those of a young man, and at an agitating period. Since that time Sir Everard's jacobitism had been gradually decaying, like a fire which burns out for want of fuel. His tory and high-church principles were kept up by some occa-sional exercise at elections and quarter-sessions; but those respecting hereditary right were fallen into a sort of abeyance. Yet it jarred sorely upon his feelings, that his nephew should go into the army under the Brunswick dynasty; and the more so as, independent of his high and conscientious ideas of paternal authority, it was impossible, or at least highly imprudent, to interfere authoritatively to prevent it. This sup-pressed vexation gave rise to many poohs and pshaws, which were placed to the account of an incipient fit of gout, until, having sent for the Army List, the worthy baronet consoled himself with reckoning up the descendants of the houses of genuine loyalty, Mordaunts, Gran-villes, and Stanleys, whose names were to be found in that military record; and calling up all his feelings of family grandeur and warlike glory, he concluded, with logic something like Falstaff's, that when war was at hand, although it were shame to be on any side but one, it were worse shame to be idle than to be on the worst side, though blacker than rebellion could make it. As for Aunt Rachael, her scheme had not exactly terminated according to her wishes, but she was under the necessity of submitting to circumstances; and her mortification was diverted by the employment she found in fitting out her nephew for the campaign, and greatly consoled by the prospect of beholding him blaze in complete uniform.

Edward Waverley himself received with animated and undefined surprise this most unexpected intelligence. It was, as a fine old poem expresses it, "like a fire to heather set," that covers a solitary hill with smoke, and illumines it at the same time with dusky fire. His tutor, or, I should say, Mr Pembroke, for he scarce assumed the name of tutor, picked up about Edward's room some fragments of irregular verse, which he appeared to have composed under the influence of the agitating feelings occasioned by this sudden page being turned up to him in the book of life. The doctor, who was a believer in all poetry which was composed by his friends, and written out in fair straight lines, with a capital at the beginning of each, communicated this treasure to Aunt Rachael, who, with her spectacles dimmed with tears, transferred them to her common-place book, among choice receipts for cookery and medicine, favourite texts, and portions from high-church divines, and a few songs, amatory and jacobitical, which she had caroll'd in her younger days. From thence they were extracted when the volume itself, with other authentic records of the Waverley family, were exposed to the inspection of the unworthy editor of this memorable history. If they afford the reader no higher amusement, they will serve at least, better than narrative of any kind, to acquaint him with the wild and irregular spirit of our hero.

Late, when the Autumn evening fell
On Mirkwood-Mere's romantic dell,
The lake return'd, in chasten'd gleam,
The purple cloud, the golden beam:
Reflected in the crystal pool,
Headland and bank lay fair and cool;
The weather-tinted rock and tower,
Each drooping tree, each fairy flower,
So true, so soft, the mirror gave,
As if there lay beneath the wave,
Secure from trouble, toil, and care,
A world than earthly world more fair.

But distant winds began to wake,
And roused the Genius of the Lake!
He heard the groaning of the oak,
And donn'd at once his sable cloak,
As warrior, at the battle-cry,
Invests him with his panoply;
Then, as the whirlwind nearer press'd,
He 'gan to shake his foamy crest
O'er furrow'd brow and blacken'd cheek,
And bade his surge in thunder speak.
In wild and broken eddies whirl'd,
Flitted that fond ideal world,
And to the shore in tumult tost,
The realms of fairy bliss were lost.

Yet, with a stern delight and strange,
I saw the spirit-stirring change.
As warr'd the wind with wave and wood,
Upon the ruin'd tower I stood,
And felt my heart more strongly bound,

Responsive to the lofty sound,
While, joying in the mighty roar,
I mourn'd that tranquil scene no more.
    So, on the idle dreams of youth,
Breaks the loud trumpet-call of Truth,
Bids each fair vision pass away,
Like landscape on the lake that lay,
As fair, as flitting, and as frail,
As that which fled the Autumn gale—
For ever dead to fancy's eye
Be each gay form that glided by,
While dreams of love and lady's charms
Give place to honour and to arms!

In sober prose, as perhaps these verses intimate less decidedly, the transient idea of Miss Cæcilia Stubbs passed from Captain Waverley's heart amid the turmoil which his new destinies excited. She appeared indeed in full splendour in her father's pew upon the Sunday when he attended service for the last time at the old parish church, upon which occasion, at the request of his uncle and Aunt Rachael, he was induced (nothing loth, if the truth must be told) to present himself in full uniform.

There is no better antidote against entertaining too high an opinion of others, than having an excellent one of ourselves at the very same time. Miss Stubbs had indeed summoned up every assistance which art could afford to beauty; but, alas! hoop, patches, frizzled locks, and a new mantua of genuine French silk, were lost upon a young officer of dragoons, who wore for the first time his gold-laced hat, boots, and broad sword. I know not whether, like the champion of an old ballad,

His heart was all on honour bent,
He could not stoop to love;
No lady in the land had power
His frozen heart to move;—

or whether the deep and flaming bars of embroidered gold, which now fenced his breast, defied the artillery of Cæcilia's eyes, but every arrow was launched at him in vain.

Yet did I mark where Cupid's shaft did light:
It lighted not on little western flower,
But on a yeoman, flower of all the west,
Hight Jonas Culbertfield, the steward's son.

Craving pardon for my heroics, (which I am unable in certain cases to resist giving way to) it is a melancholy fact, that my history must here take leave of the fair Cæcilia, who, like many a daughter of Eve, after the departure of Edward, and the dissipation of certain idle visions which she had adopted, quietly contented herself with a *pis-aller*, and gave her hand, at the distance of six months, to the aforesaid Jonas, son of the Baronet's steward, and heir (no unfertile prospect)

to a steward's fortune; besides the snug probability of succeeding to
his father's office. All these advantages moved Squire Stubbs, as
much as the ruddy brow and manly form of the suitor influenced his
daughter, to abate somewhat in the article of their gentry, and
so the match was concluded. None seemed more gratified than Aunt
Rachael, who had hitherto looked rather askaunce upon the presump-
tuous damsel, (as much so peradventure as her nature would permit)
but who, on the first appearance of the new-married pair at church,
honoured the bride with a smile and profound courtesy, in presence of
the rector, the curate, the clerk, and the whole congregation of the
united parishes of Waverley *cum* Beverley.

I beg pardon, once and for all, of those readers who take up novels
merely for amusement, for plaguing them so long with old-fashioned
politics, and Whig and Tory, and Hanoverians and Jacobites. The
truth is, I cannot promise them that this story shall be intelligible, not
to say probable, without it. My plan requires that I should explain the
motives on which its action proceeded; and these motives necessarily
arose from the feelings, prejudices, and parties, of the times. I do not
invite my fair readers, whose sex and impatience give them greatest
right to complain of these circumstances, into a flying chariot drawn
by hippogriffs, or moved by enchantment. Mine is a humble English
post-chaise, drawn upon four wheels, and keeping his Majesty's high-
way. Those who dislike the vehicle may leave it at the next halt, and
wait for the conveyance of Prince Hussein's tapestry, or Malek the
Weaver's flying sentry-box. Those who are contented to remain with
me will be occasionally exposed to the dulness inseparable from heavy
roads, steep hills, sloughs, and other terrestrial retardations; but, with
tolerable horses, and a civil driver, (as the advertisements have it) I
also engage to get as soon as possible into a more picturesque and
romantic country, if my passengers incline to have some patience with
me during my first stages.

Chapter Six

THE ADIEUS OF WAVERLEY

IT WAS UPON the evening of this memorable Sunday that Sir Everard entered the library, where he narrowly missed surprising our
young hero as he went through the guards of the broad-sword with the
ancient brand of old Sir Hildebrand, which, being preserved as an
heir-loom, usually hung over the chimney in the library, beneath a
picture of the knight and his horse, where the features were almost

entirely hidden by the knight's profusion of curled hair, and the Bucephalus which he bestrode concealed by the voluminous robes of the
Bath with which he was decorated. Sir Everard entered, and after a
glance at the picture and another at his nephew, began a little speech,
which, however, soon dropt into the natural simplicity of his common
manner, agitated upon the present occasion by no common feeling.

"Nephew," he said; and then, as mending his phrase, "My dear
Edward—it is God's will, and also the will of your father, whom,
under God, it is your duty to obey, that you should leave us to take up
the profession of arms, in which so many of your ancestors have been
distinguished. I have made such arrangements as will enable you to
take the field as their descendant, and as the probable heir of the
house of Waverley—And, sir, in the field of battle you will remember
what name you bear—and, Edward, my dear boy, remember also that
you are the last of that race, and the only hope of its revival depends
upon you; therefore, as far as duty and honour permit, avoid danger—
I mean unnecessary danger—And keep no company with rakes, gam-
blers, and whigs, of whom, it is to be feared, there are but too many in
the service into which you are going. Your colonel, as I am informed,
is an excellent man—for a presbyterian; but you will remember your
duty to God, the Church of England, and the —— (this breach ought
to have been supplied, according to the rubrick, with the word *king;*
but as, unfortunately, that word conveyed a double and embarrassing
sense, one meaning *de facto*, and the other *de jure*, the knight filled up
the blank otherwise)—the Church of England, and all constituted
authorities." Then, not trusting himself with any farther oratory, he
carried his nephew to his stables to see the horses he destined for his
campaign. Two were black, (the regimental colour) superb chargers
both; the other three were stout active hacks, designed for the road, or
for his domestics, of whom two were to attend him from the Hall; an
additional groom, if necessary, might be picked up in Scotland. "You
will depart with but a small retinue," quoth the Baronet, "compared to
Sir Hildebrand, when he mustered before the gate of the Hall a larger
body of horse than your whole regiment consists of. I could have
wished that these twenty young fellows from my estate, who have
enlisted in your troop, had been to march with you on your journey to
Scotland. It would have been something at least; but I am told their
attendance would be thought unusual in these days, when every new
and foolish fashion is introduced to break the natural dependance of
the people upon their landlords." Sir Everard had done his best to
correct this unnatural disposition of the times; for he had brightened
the chain of attachment between the recruits and their young captain,
not only by a copious repast of beef and ale, by way of a parting feast,

but by such a pecuniary donative to each individual, as tended rather to improve the conviviality than the discipline of their march.

After inspecting the cavalry, Sir Everard again conducted his nephew to the library, where he produced a letter, carefully folded, surrounded by a little stripe of flox-silk, according to an ancient form, and sealed with an accurate impression of the Waverley coat-of-arms. It was addressed, with great formality, "For Cosmo Comyne Bradwardine, Esq. of Bradwardine, at his principal mansion of Tully-Veolan, in Perthshire, North Britain. These—By the hands of Captain Edward Waverley, nephew of Sir Everard Waverley of Waverley-Honour, Bart." The gentleman to whom this ceremonious greeting was addressed, of whom we shall have more to say in the sequel, had been in arms for the exiled family of Stuart in the year 1715, and was made prisoner at Preston, in Lancashire. He was a man of very ancient family and somewhat embarrassed fortune; a scholar, according to the scholarship of Scotchmen, that is, his learning was more diffuse than accurate, and he was rather a reader than a grammarian. Of his zeal for one classic author, he is said to have given an uncommon instance. On the road between Preston and London, he made his escape from his guards; but being afterwards found loitering near the place where they had lodged the former night, he was recognized and again arrested. His companions, and even his escort, were surprised at his infatuation, and could not help enquiring, why, being once at liberty, he had not made the best of his way to a place of safety; to which he replied, that he had intended to do so, but, in good faith, he had returned to seek his Titus Livius, which he had forgot in the hurry of his escape. The simplicity of this anecdote struck the gentleman, who, as we before observed, had managed the defence of some of those unfortunate persons, at the expence of Sir Everard, and perhaps some others of the party. He was besides a special admirer of the old Patavinian, and though probably his own zeal might not have carried him such extravagant lengths, even to recover the edition of Sweynheim and Pannartz, (supposed to be the princeps) he did not the less estimate the devotion of the North Briton, and so exerted himself to remove and soften evidence, detect legal flaws, et cetera, that he accomplished the final discharge and deliverance of Cosmo Comyne Bradwardine from certain very awkward consequences of a plea before our sovereign lord the king in Westminster. The Baron of Bradwardine, for he was generally so called in Scotland, (although his intimates, from his place of residence, used to denominate him Tully-Veolan, or, more familiarly, Tully) no sooner stood rectus in curia, than he posted down to pay his respects and make his acknowledgments at Waverley Hall. A congenial passion for field sports, and a general coincidence

in political opinions, cemented his friendship with Sir Everard, notwithstanding the difference in their habits and studies in other particulars; and having spent several weeks at Waverley Hall, he departed
with many expressions of regard, warmly pressing the Baronet to
return his visit, and partake of the diversion of grouse-shooting upon
his moors in Perthshire next season. Shortly after, Mr Bradwardine
remitted from Scotland a sum in reimbursement of expences incurred
in the King's High Court of Westminster, which, although not quite so
formidable when reduced to the English denomination of pounds,
shillings, and pence, had, in its original form of pounds Scotch, such
a formidable effect upon the frame of Duncan Macwheeble, the
laird's confidential factor, baron baillie, and man of resource, that he
had a fit of the cholic which lasted for five days, occasioned, he said,
solely and utterly by becoming the unhappy instrument of conveying
such a serious sum of money out of his native country into the hands of
the false English. But patriotism, as it is the fairest, so it is often the
most suspicious mask of other feelings; and many who knew Baillie
Macwheeble, concluded that his professions of regret were not altogether disinterested, and that he would have grudged the monies paid
to the *loons* at Westminster much less had they not come from the
Bradwardine estate, a fund which he considered as more peculiarly
his own. But the Baillie protested he was absolutely disinterested—

Woe, woe for Scotland, not a whit for me!

The laird was only rejoiced that his worthy friend, Sir Everard
Waverley of Waverley-Honour, was reimbursed of the expenditure
which he had outlaid on account of the house of Bradwardine. It
concerned, he said, the credit of his own family, and of the kingdom of
Scotland at large, that these debursements should be repaid forthwith,
and if delayed, it would be a matter of national reproach. Sir Everard,
accustomed to treat much larger sums with indifference, received the
remittance of L.297:13:6, without being aware that the payment was
an international concern, and indeed would probably have forgot the
circumstance altogether, if Baillie Macwheeble had thought of com-
forting his cholic by intercepting the subsidy. His habits of opulent
indolence interfered with his wish to pay a visit to Perthshire, but there
was still maintained a yearly intercourse of a short letter, and a hamper
or cask or two between Waverley Hall and Tully-Veolan, the English
exports consisting of mighty cheeses and mightier ale, pheasants, and
venison, and the Scottish returns being vested in grouse, white hares,
pickled salmon, and usquebaugh. All which were meant and received
as pledges of constant friendship and amity between these two important houses. It followed as a matter of course, that the heir-apparent of

Waverley-Honour could not with propriety visit Scotland without being furnished with credentials to the Baron of Bradwardine.

When this matter was explained and settled, Mr Pembroke expressed his wish to take a private and particular leave of his dear pupil. The good man's exhortations to Edward to preserve an unblemished life and morals, to hold fast the principles of the Christian religion, and to eschew the idle and profane company of scoffers and latitudinarians, too much abounding in the army, were not unmingled with his political prejudices. It had pleased Heaven, he said, to place Scotland (doubtless for the sins of their ancestors in 1642) in a more deplorable state of darkness than even this unhappy kingdom of England. Here, at least, although the candlestick of the Church of England had been in some degree removed from its place, it yet afforded a glimmering light; there *was* a hierarchy, though schismatical and fallen from the principles maintained by those great fathers of the church, Sancroft and his brethren; there *was* a liturgy, though woefully perverted in some of the principal petitions. But in Scotland it was utter darkness, and, excepting a sorrowful, scattered, and persecuted remnant, the pulpits were abandoned to presbyterians, and, he feared, to sectaries of every description. It should be his duty to fortify his dear pupil to resist such unhallowed and pernicious doctrines in church and state, as must necessarily be forced at times upon his unwilling ears.—Here he produced two immense folded packets, which appeared each to contain a whole ream of closely-written manuscript. They had been the labour of the worthy man's whole life; and never were labour and zeal more absurdly wasted. He had at one time gone to London, with the intention of giving them to the world, by the medium of a bookseller in Little Britain, well known to deal in such commodities, and to whom he was instructed to address himself in a particular phrase, and with a certain sign, which, it seems, passed at that time current among the initiated Jacobites. The moment Mr Pembroke had uttered the Shibboleth with the appropriated gesture, the bibliopolist greeted him, notwithstanding every disclamation, by the title of Doctor, and conveying him into his back shop, after inspecting every possible and impossible place of concealment, he commenced: "Eh, doctor!—Well—all under the rose—snug—I keep no holes here even for a Hanoverian rat to hide in—and what eh—any good news from our friends over the water?—and how does the worthy King of France?—Or perhaps you are more lately from Rome? it must be Rome will do it at last—the church must light its candle at the old lamp—eh—What, cautious? I like you the better; but no fear." Here Mr Pembroke with some difficulty stopt a torrent of interrogations, eked out with signs, nods, and winks; and, having convinced the bookseller that he did him too much honour in supposing him an emissary of exiled royalty, he explained his real business. The man of books with a much more composed air proceeded to examine the manuscripts. The title of the first was, "A Dissent from Dissenters, or the Comprehension Confuted; shewing the impossibility of any composition between the Church and Puritans, Presbyterians, or Sectaries of any description; illustrated from the Scriptures, the Fathers of the Church, and the soundest controversial Divines." To this work the bookseller positively demurred. "Well meant," he said, "and learned, doubtless; but the time had gone by. Printed on small pica it would run to eight hundred pages, and could never pay. Begged therefore to be excused—Loved and honoured the true church from his soul, and, had it been a sermon on the martyrdom, or any twelve-penny touch— why I would venture something for the honour of the cloth—But come, let's see the other. 'Right Hereditary righted!'—Ay! there's some sense in this. Hum—hum—hum—pages so many, paper so much, letter-press——Ay—I'll tell you, though, doctor, you must knock out some of the Latin and Greek; heavy, doctor, damn'd heavy —(beg pardon) and if you throw in a few grains more pepper—I am he that never peached my author—I have published for Drake and Charlwood Lawton, and poor Amhurst—Ah, Caleb! Caleb! Well, it was a shame to let poor Caleb starve, and so many fat rectors and squires among us. I gave him a dinner once a-week; but, Lord love you, what's once a-week, when a man does not know where to go the other six days?—Well, but I must shew the manuscript to little Tom Alibi the solicitor, who manages all my law affairs—must keep on the windy side—the mob were very uncivil the last time in Old Palace Yard—all whigs and roundheads every man of them, Williamites and Hanoverian rats."

The next day Mr Pembroke again called on the publisher, but found Tom Alibi's advice had determined him against undertaking the work. "Not but what I would go to—(what was I going to say?) to the plantations for the church with pleasure—but, dear doctor, I have a wife and family; but, to show my zeal, I'll recommend the job to my neighbour Trimnel—he is a bachelor, and leaving off business, so a voyage in a western barge would not inconvenience him." But Mr Trimnel was also obdurate, and Mr Pembroke, fortunately perchance for himself, was compelled to return to Waverley Hall with his treatises in vindication of the real fundamental principles of church and state safely packed in his saddle-bags.

As the public was thus likely to be deprived of the benefit arising from his lucubrations by the selfish cowardice of the trade, Mr Pembroke resolved to make two copies of these tremendous manuscripts for the use of his pupil. He felt he had been indolent as a tutor, and besides his conscience checked him for complying with the request of Mr Richard Waverley, that he would impress no sentiments upon Edward's mind inconsistent with the present settlement in church and state. "But now," thought he, "I may without breach of my word, since he is no longer under my tuition, afford the youth the means of judging for himself, and have only to dread his reproaches for so long concealing the light which the perusal will flash upon his mind." While he thus indulged the reveries of an author and a politician, his destined proselyte, seeing nothing very inviting in the title of the tracts, and appalled by the bulk and compact lines of the manuscript, quietly consigned them to a corner of his travelling trunk.

Aunt Rachael's farewell was brief and affectionate. She only cautioned her dear Edward, whom she probably deemed somewhat susceptible, against the fascination of Scottish beauty. She allowed that the northern part of the island contained some ancient families, but they were all whigs and presbyterians except the Highlanders; and respecting them she must needs say, there could be no great delicacy among the ladies, where the gentlemen's usual attire was, as she had been assured, to say the least, very singular, and not at all decorous. She concluded her farewell with a kind and moving benediction, and gave the young officer, as a pledge of her regard, a valuable diamond ring, (frequently worn by the male sex at that time) and a purse of broad gold pieces, which also were more common Sixty Years since than they have been of late.

Chapter Seven

A HORSE-QUARTER IN SCOTLAND

THE NEXT morning, amid varied feelings, the chief of which was a predominant, anxious, and even solemn impression, that he was now in a great measure abandoned to his own guidance and direction, Edward Waverley departed from the Hall amid the blessings, and tears also, of the old domestics and the inhabitants of the village, mingled with some sly petitions for serjeantcies and corporal-ships, and so forth, on the part of those who professed that they never thoft to ha' seen Jacob, and Giles, and Jonathan, go off for soldiers, save to attend his onnor, as in duty bound. Edward, as in duty bound, extricated himself from the supplicants with the pledge of fewer promises than might have been expected from a young man so little accustomed to the world. After a short visit at London, he proceeded on horseback, then the general mode of conveyance, to Edinburgh, and from thence to ——, a sea-port town on the eastern coast of Angus-shire, where his regiment was then quartered.

He now entered on a new world, where, for a time, all was beautiful because all was new. Colonel G——, the commanding officer of the regiment, was himself a study for a romantic, and at the same time an inquisitive youth. In person he was tall, handsome, and active, though somewhat advanced in life. In his early years, he had been what is called, by manner of palliative, a very gay young man, and strange stories were circulated about his sudden conversion from doubt, if not infidelity, to a serious and even enthusiastic turn of mind. It was whispered that a supernatural communication, of a nature obvious even to the exterior senses, had produced this wonderful change; and though some mentioned the proselyte as an enthusiast, none hinted at his being a hypocrite. This singular and mystical circumstance gave Colonel G—— a peculiar and solemn interest in the eyes of the young captain. It may be easily imagined that the officers of a regiment, commanded by so remarkable a person, composed a society more sedate and orderly than a military mess always exhibits; and that Waverley escaped some temptations to which he might otherwise have been exposed.

Meantime his military education proceeded. Already a good horseman, he was now initiated into the arts of the manege, which, when carried to perfection, almost realize the fable of the Centaur, the guidance of the horse appearing to proceed from the rider's mere volition, rather than from the use of any external and apparent signal of motion. He received also instructions in his field duty; but I must own, that when his first ardour was passed, his progress fell short in the latter particular of what he wished and expected. The duty of an officer, the most imposing of all others to the unexperienced mind, because accompanied with so much outward pomp and circumstance, is in its essence a very dry and abstract study, depending chiefly upon arithmetical combinations, requiring much attention, and a cool and reasoning head to bring them into action. Our hero was liable to fits of absence, in which his blunders excited some mirth, and called down some reproof. This circumstance impressed him with a painful sense of inferiority in those qualities which appeared most to deserve and obtain regard in his new profession. He asked himself in vain, why his eye could not judge of distance or space so well as those of his companions; why his head was not always successful in disentangling the various partial movements necessary to execute a particular evolution; and why his memory, so alert upon most occasions, did not always retain technical phrases, and minute points of etiquette or field discipline. Waverley was naturally modest, and therefore did not fall into the egregious mistake of supposing such minuter rules of military duty beneath his notice, or conceiting himself to be born a general because he made an indifferent subaltern. The truth was, that the vague and unsatisfactory course of reading which he had pursued, working upon a temper naturally retired and abstracted, had given him that wavering and unsettled habit of mind which is most averse to steady and rivetted attention. Time, in the mean while, hung heavy on his hands. The gentry of the neighbourhood were disaffected, and shewed little hospitality to the military guests; and the people of the town, chiefly engaged in mercantile pursuits, were not such as Waverley chose to associate with. The arrival of summer, and a curiosity to know something more of Scotland than he could see in a ride from his quarters, determined him to request leave of absence for a few weeks. He resolved first to visit his uncle's ancient friend and correspondent, with a purpose of extending or shortening the term of his residence according to circumstances. He travelled of course on horseback, and with a single attendant, and passed his first night at a miserable inn, where the landlady had neither shoes nor stockings, and the landlord, who called himself a gentleman, was disposed to be rude to his guest, because he had not bespoke the pleasure of his society to supper. The next day, traversing an open and uninclosed country, Edward gradually approached the Highlands of Perthshire, which at first had appeared a blue outline in the horizon, but now swelled into huge gigantic masses, which frowned defiance over the more level country that lay beneath them. Near the bottom of this stupendous barrier, but still in champaign country, dwelt Cosmo Comyne Bradwardine of Bradwardine; and if grey-haired eld can be in aught believed, there had dwelt his ancestors, with all their heritage, since the days of the gracious King Duncan.

Chapter Eight

A SCOTTISH MANOR HOUSE SIXTY YEARS SINCE

IT WAS ABOUT noon when Captain Waverley entered the straggling village, or rather hamlet, of Tully-Veolan, close to which was situated the mansion of the proprietor. The houses seemed miserable in the extreme, especially to an eye accustomed to the smiling neatness of English cottages. They stood, without any respect for regularity, on each side of a straggling kind of unpaved street, where children, almost in a primitive state of nakedness, lay sprawling, as if to be crushed by the hoofs of the first passing horse. Occasionally, indeed, when such a consummation seemed inevitable, a watchful old grandame, with her close cap, distaff, and spindle, rushed like a sybil in frenzy out of one of these miserable cells, dashed into the midst of the path, and snatching up her own charge from among the sun-burned loiterers, saluted him with a sound cuff, and transported him back to his dungeon, the little white-headed varlet screaming all the while from the very top of his lungs a shrilly treble to the growling remonstrances of the enraged matron. Another part in this concert was sustained by the incessant yelping of a score of idle useless curs, which followed, snarling, barking, howling, and snapping at the horses' heels: a nuisance at that time so common in Scotland, that a French tourist, who, like other travellers, longed to find a good and rational reason for every thing he saw, has recorded, as one of the memorabilia of Caledonia, that the state maintained in each village a relay of curs, called *collies*, whose duty it was to chase the *chevaux de poste* (too starved and exhausted to move without such a stimulus) from one hamlet to another, till their annoying convoy drove them to the end of their stage. The evil and remedy (such as it is) still exist: But this is remote from our present purpose, and is only thrown out for consideration of the collectors of Mr Dent's dog-taxes.

As Waverley moved on, here and there an old man, bent as much by toil as years, his eyes bleared with age and smoke, tottered to the door of his hut, to gaze on the dress of the stranger and the form and motions of the horses, and then assembled, with his neighbours, in a little groupe at the smithy, to discuss the probabilities of whence the stranger came, and where he might be going. Three or four village girls, returning from the well or brook with pitchers and pails upon their heads, formed more pleasing objects, and with their thin short-gowns and single petticoats, bare arms, legs, and feet, uncovered heads and braided hair, somewhat resembled Italian forms of landscape. Nor could a lover of the picturesque have challenged either the elegance of their costume, or the symmetry of their shape, although, to say the truth, a mere Englishman, in search of the *comfortable*, a word peculiar to his native tongue, might have wished the clothes less scanty, the feet and legs somewhat protected from the weather, the head and complexion shrouded from the sun, or perhaps might even have thought the whole person and dress considerably improved by a plentiful application of spring water, with a *quantum sufficit* of soap. The whole scene was depressing, for it argued, at the first glance, at least a stagnation of industry, and perhaps of intellect. Even curiosity, the busiest passion of the idle, seemed of a listless cast in the village of Tully-Veolan: the curs aforesaid alone shewed any part of its activity;

36   WAVERLEY   Vol. 1, ch. 8

with the villagers it was passive. They stood and gazed at the handsome young officer and his attendant, but without any of those quick motions and eager looks that indicate the earnestness with which those who live in monotonous ease at home look out for amusement abroad. Yet the physiognomy of the people, when more closely examined, was far from exhibiting the indifference of stupidity; their features were rough but remarkably intelligent, grave but the very reverse of stupid; and from among the young women, an artist might have chosen more than one model whose features and form resembled those of Minerva. The children also, though their skins were burned black, and their hair bleached white, by the influence of the sun, had a look and manner of life and interest. It seemed, upon the whole, as if poverty, and indolence, its too frequent companion, were combining to depress the natural genius and acquired information of a hardy, intelligent, and reflecting peasantry.

Some such thoughts crossed Waverley's mind as he paced his horse slowly through the rugged and flinty street of Tully-Veolan, interrupted only in his meditations by the occasional cabrioles which his charger exhibited at the reiterated assaults of these canine Cossacks, the *collies* before mentioned. The village was more than half a mile long, the cottages being irregularly divided from each other by gardens, or yards, as the inhabitants called them, of different sizes, where (for it is Sixty Years since) the now universal potatoe was unknown, but which were stored with gigantic plants of *kale* or colewort, encircled with groves of nettles, and exhibited here and there a huge hemlock, or the national thistle, overshadowing a quarter of the petty inclosure. The broken ground on which the village was built had never been levelled, so that these inclosures presented declivities of every degree, here rising like terraces, there sinking like tan-pits. Dry stone walls which fenced, or seemed to fence, (for they were sorely breached) these hanging gardens of Tully-Veolan, were intersected by narrow lanes leading to the common field, where the joint labour of the villagers cultivated alternate ridges and patches of rye, oats, barley, and pease, each of such minute extent, that at a little distance the unprofitable variety of the surface resembled a tailor's book of patterns. In a few favoured instances, there appeared behind the cottages a miserable wigwam, compiled of earth, loose stones, and turf, where the wealthy might perhaps shelter a starved cow or sorely galled horse. But almost every hut was fenced in front by a huge black stack of turf on one side of the door, while on the other the family dunghill ascended in noble emulation.

About a bow-shot from the end of the village appeared the inclosures proudly denominated the parks of Tully-Veolan, being certain square fields, surrounded and divided by stone walls five feet in height. In the centre of the exterior barrier was the upper gate of the avenue, opening under an archway, battled on the top, and ornamented with two large weather-beaten mutilated masses of upright stone, which, if the tradition of the hamlet could be trusted, had once represented, at least had been once designed to represent, two rampant bears, the supporters of the family of Bradwardine. The avenue was straight, and of moderate length, running between a double row of very ancient horse-chesnuts, planted alternately with sycamores, which rose to such huge height, and flourished so luxuriantly, that their boughs completely over-arched the broad road beneath. Beyond these venerable ranks, and parallel to them, were two walls, of apparently the like antiquity, overgrown with ivy, honey-suckle, and other climbing plants. The avenue seemed little trodden, and chiefly by foot passengers; so that being very broad, it was clothed with grass, which enjoying a constant shade was of a very deep and rich verdure, excepting where a foot-path, worn by occasional passengers, tracked with a natural sweep the way from the upper to the lower gate. This nether portal, like the former, opened in front of a wall ornamented with some rude sculpture, and battlemented on the top, over which were seen, half-hidden by the trees of the avenue, the high steep roof and narrow gables of the mansion, with ascending lines cut into steps, and corners decorated with small turrets. One of the folding leaves of the lower gate was open, and as the sun shone full into the court behind, a long line of brilliancy was flung from the aperture up the dark and sombre avenue. It was one of those effects which a painter loves to represent, and mingled well with the struggling light which found its way between the boughs of the shady arch that vaulted the broad green alley.

The solitude and repose of the whole scene seemed almost monastic, and Waverley, who had given his horse to his servant on entering the first gate, walked slowly down the avenue, enjoying the grateful and cooling shade, and so much pleased with the placid ideas of rest and seclusion excited by this confined and quiet scene, that he forgot the misery and dirt of the hamlet he had left behind him. The opening into the paved court-yard corresponded with the rest of the scene. The house, which seemed to consist of two or three high, narrow, and steep-roofed buildings, projecting from each other at right angles, formed one side of the inclosure. It had been built at a period when castles were no longer necessary, and when the Scottish architects had not yet acquired the art of designing a domestic residence. The windows were numberless, but very small; the roof had some nondescript kind of projections called bartizans, and displayed at each frequent angle, a small turret, rather resembling a pepper-box than a Gothic watch-tower. Neither did the front indicate absolute security from danger. There were loop-holes for musquetry, and iron stancheons on the lower windows, probably to repel any roving band of gipsies, or resist a predatory visit from the caterans of the neighbouring Highlands. Stables and other offices occupied another side of the square. The former were low vaults, with narrow slits instead of windows, resembling, as Edward's groom observed, "rather a prison for murderers and larceners, and such like as are tried at sizes, than a place for any Christian cattle." Above these dungeon-looking stables were granaries, called girnels, and other offices, to which there was access by outside stairs of heavy masonry. Two battlemented walls, one of which faced the avenue and the other divided the court from the garden, completed the inclosure. It was not without its ornaments. In one corner was a tun-bellied pigeon-house, of great size and rotundity, resembling in figure and proportions the curious edifice called Arthur's Oven, which would have turned the brains of all the antiquaries in England, had not the worthy proprietor pulled it down for the sake of mending a neighbouring dam-dyke. This dove-cote, or *columbarium*, as the owner called it, was no small resource to a Scottish laird of the period, whose scanty rents were eked out by the contributions levied upon the farms by these light foragers, and the conscriptions exacted from the latter for the benefit of the table.

Another corner of the court displayed a fountain, where a huge bear, carved in stone, predominated over a large stone bason, into which he disgorged the water. This work of art was the wonder of the country for ten miles round. It must not be forgotten, that all sorts of bears, small and large, demi or in full proportion, were carved over the windows, upon the ends of the gables, terminated the spouts, and supported the turrets, with the ancient family motto, "𝔅𝔢𝔴𝔞𝔯 𝔱𝔥𝔢 𝔅𝔞𝔯," cut under each hyperborean form. The court was spacious, well paved, and perfectly clean, there being probably another entrance behind the stables for removing the litter. Every thing around appeared solitary, and would have been silent, but for the continued splashing of the fountain; and the whole scene still maintained the monastic illusion which the fancy of Waverley had conjured up.—And here we beg permission to close a chapter of still life.

Chapter Nine

MORE OF THE MANOR HOUSE AND ITS ENVIRONS

AFTER HAVING satisfied his curiosity by gazing around him for a
few minutes, Waverley applied himself to the massive knocker of the
hall-door, the architrave of which bore the date 1594. But no answer
was returned, though the peal resounded through a number of apartments, and was echoed from the court-yard walls without the house,
startling the pigeons in clouds from the venerable rotunda which they
occupied, and alarming anew even the distant village curs, which had
retired to sleep upon their respective dunghills. Tired of the din which
he created, and the unprofitable responses which it excited, Waverley
began to think he had reached the castle of Orgoglio, as entered by the
victorious Prince Arthur,

> When 'gan he loudly through the house to call,
> But no man cared to answer to his cry,
> There reign'd a solemn silence over all,
> Nor voice was heard, nor wight was seen in bower or hall.

Filled almost with expectation of beholding some "old, old man,
with beard as white as snow," whom he might question concerning
this deserted mansion, our hero turned to a little oaken wicket-door,
well clenched with iron nails, which opened in the court-yard wall at
its angle with the house. It was only latched, notwithstanding its fortified appearance, and when opened, admitted him into the garden,
which presented a pleasing scene. The southern side of the house,
clothed with fruit trees, and having many evergreens trained upon its
walls, extended its irregular yet venerable front, along a terrace,
partly paved, partly gravelled, partly bordered with flowers and choice
shrubs. This elevation descended by three several flights of steps,
placed in its centre and at the extremities, into what might be called
the garden proper, and was fenced along the top by a stone parapet,
with a heavy balustrade, ornamented from space to space with
huge grotesque figures of animals seated upon their haunches, among
which the favourite bear was repeatedly introduced. Placed in the
middle of the terrace, between a sashed-door opening from the house
and the central flight of steps, a huge animal of the same species
supported on his head and fore paws a sun-dial of large circumfer-
ence, inscribed with more diagrams than Edward's mathematics
enabled him to decypher.

The garden, which seemed to be kept with great accuracy,
abounded in fruit trees, and exhibited a profusion of flowers and

evergreens, cut into grotesque forms. It was laid out in terraces, which descended rank by rank from the western wall to a large brook, which had a tranquil and smooth appearance where it served as a boundary to the garden; but near the extremity, leaped in tumult over a strong dam, or wear-head, the cause of its temporary tranquillity, and there forming a cascade, was overlooked by an octangular summer-house, with a gilded bear on the top by way of vane. After this feat, the brook, assuming its natural rapid and fierce character, escaped from the eye down a deep and wooded dell, from the copse of which arose a massive but ruinous tower, the former habitation of the Barons of Bradwardine. The margin of the brook, opposite to the garden, displayed a narrow meadow, or *haugh*, as it was called, which formed a small washing-green; the bank, which retired behind it, was covered by ancient trees.

The scene, though pleasing, was not quite equal to the gardens of Alcina; yet it wanted not the "*due donzelette garrule*" of that enchanted paradise, for upon the green aforesaid two bare-legged damsels, each standing in a spacious tub, performed with their feet the office of a patent washing-machine. These did not, however, like the maidens of Armida, remain to greet with their harmony the approaching guest, but, alarmed at the appearance of a handsome stranger on the opposite side, hastily dropped their garments (I should say garment, to be quite correct) over the limbs which their occupation exposed somewhat too freely, and, with a shrill exclamation of "Eh sirs!" uttered with an accent between modesty and coquetry, sprung off like deer in different directions.

Waverley began to despair of gaining entrance into this solitary and seemingly enchanted mansion, when a figure advanced up one of the garden alleys towards the terrace, where he still retained his station. Trusting it might be a gardener, or some domestic belonging to the house, Edward descended the steps in order to meet him; but as the being approached, and long before he could descry its features, he was struck with the oddity of its appearance and gestures. Sometimes this "mister wight" held his hands clasped over his head, like an Indian Jogue in the attitude of penance; sometimes he swung them perpendicularly, like a pendulum, on each side; and anon he flapped them swiftly and repeatedly across his breast, like a hackney coachman, as a substitute for his usual flogging exercise, when his carriage and cattle are idle on the stand in a clear frosty day. His gait was as singular as his gestures, for at times he hopp'd with great perseverance on the right foot, then exchanged that supporter to advance in the same manner on the left, and then putting his feet close together, he hopp'd upon both at once. His dress also was antiquated and extravagant. It consisted in a sort of grey jerkin, with scarlet cuffs and slash'd sleeves, shewing a scarlet lining; the other parts of the dress corresponded in colour, not forgetting a pair of scarlet stockings, and a scarlet bonnet, proudly surmounted with a turkey's feather. Edward, whom he did not seem to observe, now perceived confirmation in his features of what the mien and gestures had already announced. It was apparently neither idiocy nor insanity which gave that wild, unsettled, irregular expression to a face which was naturally rather handsome, but something resembling a compound of both, where the simplicity of the fool was mixed with the extravagance of a crazed imagination. He sung with great earnestness, and not without some taste, a fragment of an old Scotch ditty:

> False love, and hast thou play'd me this
>   In summer among the flowers?
> I will repay thee back again
>   In winter among the showers.
> Unless again, again, my love,
>   Unless you turn again,
> As you with other maidens rove,
>   I'll smile on other men.

Here lifting up his eyes, which had hitherto been fixed in observing how his feet kept time to the tune, he beheld Waverley, and instantly doff'd his cap, with many grotesque signals of surprise, respect, and salutation. Edward, though with little hope of receiving answer to any constant question, requested to know whether Mr Bradwardine were at home, or where he could find any of the domestics. The questioned party replied, and like the witch of Thalaba, "still his speech was song,"—

> The Knight's to the mountain
>   His bugle to wind;
> The Lady's to greenwood
>   Her garland to bind.
> The bower of Burd Ellen
>   Has moss on the floor,
> That the step of Lord William
>   Be silent and sure.

This conveyed no information. Edward repeated his queries and received a rapid answer, in which, from the haste and the peculiarity of the dialect, the word "butler" alone was intelligible. Waverley then requested to see the butler; upon which the fellow, with a knowing look and nod of intelligence, made a signal to Edward to follow, and began to dance and caper down the alley up which he had made his approaches. "A strange guide this," thought Edward, "and not much unlike one of Shakspeare's roynish clowns. I am not over prudent to trust to his pilotage; but wiser men have been led by fools." By this time he reached the bottom of the alley, where, turning short on a little parterre of flowers, shrouded from the east and north by a close yew hedge, he found an old man at work without his coat, whose appearance hovered between that of an upper servant and gardener; his red nose and ruffled shirt belonging to the former profession, his hale and sun-burned visage, with his green apron, appearing to indicate

Old Adam's likeness, set to dress this garden.

The major domo, for such he was, and indisputably the second officer of state in the barony, (nay, as chief minister of the interior, superior even to Baillie Macwheeble in his own department of the kitchen and cellar)—the major domo laid down his spade, slipped on his coat in haste, and, with a wrathful look at Edward's guide, probably excited by his having introduced a stranger while he was engaged in this laborious, and, as he might suppose it, degrading office, requested to know the gentleman's commands. Being informed that he wished to pay his respects to his master, that his name was Waverley, and so forth, the old man's countenance assumed a great deal of respectful importance. "He could take it upon his conscience to say, his honour would have exceeding pleasure in seeing him. Would not Mr Waverley chuse some refreshment after his journey? His honour was with the folk who were getting doon the dark hag; the two gardener lads (an emphasis on the word *two*) had been ordered to attend him; and he himself had been just amusing the time with dressing up Miss Rose's flower-bed, that he might be near to receive his honour's orders, if need were: he was very fond of a garden, but had little time for such divertisements."

"He canna get it wrought in above twa days in the week, at no rate whatever," said Edward's fantastic conductor. A grim look from the butler chastised his interference, and he commanded him, by the name of Davie Gellatley, in a tone which admitted no discussion, to go look for his honour at the dark hag, and tell him there was a gentleman from the south had arrived at the Ha'. "Can this poor fellow deliver a letter?" asked Edward. "With all fidelity, sir, to any one whom he respects. I would hardly trust him with a long message by word of mouth—though he is more knave than fool."

Waverley delivered his credentials to Mr Gellatley, who seemed to confirm the butler's last observation, by twisting his features at him, when he was looking another way, into the resemblance of the grotesque face on the bole of a German tobacco-pipe; after which, with an odd congé to Waverley, he danced off to discharge his errand. "He is an *innocent*, sir," said the butler; "there is one such in almost every laird's house in this country, but ours is brought far ben. He used to work a day's turn well enough; but he help'd Miss Rose when she was flemit with the Laird of Killancureit's new English bull, and since that time we call him Davie Do-little; indeed we might call him Davie Do-nothing, for since he got that gay clothing, to please his honour and my young mistress, (great folks will have their fancies) he has done nothing but dance up and down about the *town*, without doing a single turn, unless trimming the laird's fishing-wand or busking his flies, or may be catching a dish of trouts at an orra time. But here comes Miss Rose, who, I take burden upon me for her, will be especial glad to see one of the house of Waverley at her father's mansion of Tully-Veolan."

But Rose Bradwardine deserves better of her unworthy historian, than to be introduced at the end of a chapter.

In the mean while it may be noticed, that Waverley learned two things from this colloquy; that in Scotland a single house was called a *town*, and a natural fool an *innocent*.

Chapter Ten

ROSE BRADWARDINE AND HER FATHER

MISS BRADWARDINE was but seventeen; yet, at the last races of the county town of ——, upon her health being proposed among a round of beauties, the Laird of Bumperquaigh, permanent toast-master and croupier of the Bauther-whillery Club, not only said *More* to the pledge in a pint bumper of Bourdeaux, but, ere pouring forth the libation, denominated the divinity to whom it was dedicated the Rose of Tully-Veolan. Upon which festive occasion, three cheers were given by all the sitting members of that respectable society, whose throats the wine had left capable of such exertion. Nay, I am well assured that the sleeping partners of the company snorted applause, and that although strong bumpers and weak brains had consigned two or three to the floor, yet even these, fallen as they were from their high estate, and weltering—I will carry the parody no farther—uttered divers inarticulate sounds intimating their assent to the motion.

Such unanimous applause could not be extorted but by acknow-ledged merit, and Rose Bradwardine not only deserved it, but also the approbation of much more rational persons than the Bauther-whillery Club could have mustered, even before discussion of the first *magnum*. She was indeed a very pretty girl of the Scotch cast of beauty, that is, with a profusion of hair of paley gold, and a skin like the snow of her own mountains in whiteness. Yet she had not a pallid or pensive cast of countenance; her features, as well as her temper, had a lively expression; her complexion, though not florid, was so pure as to seem transparent, and the slightest cause sent her blood at once to her whole face and neck. Her form, though under the common size, was remarkably elegant, and her motions light, easy, and unembarrassed. She came from another part of the garden to receive Captain Waverley, with a manner that hovered between bashfulness and courtesy.

The first greetings past, Edward learned from her that the *dark hag*, which had somewhat puzzled him in the butler's account of his master's avocations, had nothing to do either with a black cat or a broomstick, but was simply a portion of oak copse which was to be felled that day. She offered, with embarrassed civility, to shew the stranger the way to the spot, which, it seems, was not distant; but they were prevented by the appearance of the Baron of Bradwardine in person, who, summoned by David Gellatley, now appeared, "on hospitable thoughts intent," clearing the ground at a prodigious rate with swift and long strides, which reminded Waverley of the seven-leagued boots of the nursery fable. He was a tall, thin, athletic figure, old indeed and grey-haired, but with every muscle rendered as tough as whip-cord by constant exercise. He was dressed carelessly, and more like a Frenchman than an Englishman of the period, while, from his hard features and perpendicular rigidity of stature, he bore some resemblance to a Swiss officer of the guards, who had resided some time at Paris, and caught the *costume*, but not the ease or manner of its inhabitants. The truth was, that his language and habits were as heterogeneous as his external appearance.

Owing to his natural disposition to study, or perhaps to a very general Scottish fashion of giving young men of rank a legal education, he had been bred with a view to the bar. But the politics of his family precluding the hope of his rising in that profession, Mr Bradwardine travelled with high reputation for several years, and made some campaigns in foreign service. After his démêlée with the law of high treason in 1715, he had lived in retirement, conversing almost entirely with those of his own principles in the vicinage. The pedantry of the lawyer, superinduced upon the military pride of the soldier, might remind a modern of the days of the zealous volunteer service, when the bar-gown of our pleaders was often flung over a blazing uniform. To this must be added the prejudices of ancient birth and jacobite politics, greatly strengthened by habits of solitary and secluded authority, which, though exercised only within the bounds of his half-cultivated estate, was there indisputable and undisputed. For, as he used to observe, "the lands of Bradwardine, Tully-Veolan, and others, had been erected into a free barony by a charter from David the First, *cum liberali potest. habendi curias et justicias, cum fossa et furca* (LIE pit and gallows) *et saka et soka, et thol et theam, et infang thief et outfang thief, sive hand-habend. sive bak-barand.*" The peculiar meaning of all these cabalistical words few or none could explain; but they implied, upon the whole, that the Baron of Bradwardine might imprison, try, and execute his vassals and tenants at his pleasure. Like James the First, however, the present possessor of this authority was more pleased in talking about prerogative than in exercising it; and excepting that he imprisoned two poachers in the dungeon of the old tower of Tully-Veolan, where they were sorely frightened by ghosts, and almost eaten by rats, and that he set an old woman in the *jougs* (or Scottish pillory) for saying "there were mair fules in the laird's ha' house than Davie Gellatley," I do not learn that he was accused of abusing his high powers. Still, however, the conscious pride of possessing them gave additional importance to his language and deportment.

At his first address to Waverley, it would seem that the hearty pleasure he felt to behold the nephew of his friend had somewhat discomposed the stiff and upright dignity of the Baron of Bradwardine's demeanour, for the tears stood in the old gentleman's eyes, when, having first shaken Edward heartily by the hand in the English fashion, he embraced him *à-la-mode Françoise*, and kissed him on both sides of the face; while the hardness of his gripe, and the quantity of Scotch snuff which his *accolade* communicated, called corresponding drops of moisture to the eyes of his guest. "Upon the honour of a gentleman," he said, "but it makes me young again to see you here, Mr Waverley! A worthy scion of the old stock of Waverley-Honour—*spes altera*, as Maro hath it—and you have the look of the old line, Captain Waverley; not so portly yet as my old friend Sir Everard—*mais cela viendra avec le tems*, as my Dutch acquaintance, Baron Kikkitbroeck, said of the *sagesse de Madame son epouse.*—And so ye have mounted the cockade? right, right—though I could have wished the colour different, and so I would ha' deemed might Sir Everard. But no more of that; I am old, and times are changed.—And how does the worthy knight baronet and the fair Mrs Rachael?—Ah, ye laugh, young man; but she was the fair Mrs Rachael in the year of grace seventeen hundred and sixteen; but time passes—*et singula prædantur anni*—that is most certain. But, once again, ye are most heartily welcome to my poor house of Tully-Veolan!—Hie to the house, Rose, and see that Alexander Saunderson looks out the old Chateau Margoux, which I sent from Bourdeaux to Dundee in the year 1713."

Rose tripped off demurely enough till she turned the first corner, and then ran with the speed of a fairy, that she might gain leisure, after discharging her father's commission, to put her own dress in order, and produce all her little finery, an occupation for which the approaching dinner-hour left but little time. "We cannot rival the luxuries of your English table, Captain Waverley, or give you the *epulæ lautiores* of Waverley-Honour—I say *epulæ* rather than *prandium*, because the latter phrase is popular; *Epulæ ad senatum, prandium vero ad populum attinet*, says Suetonius Tranquillus. But I trust ye will applaud my Bourdeaux; *c'est des deux oreilles*, as Captain Vinsauf used to say— *Vinum primæ notæ*, the Principal of St Andrews denominated it. And, once more, Captain Waverley, right glad am I that ye are here to drink the best my cellar can make forthcoming." This speech, with the necessary interjectional answers, continued from the lower alley where they met, up to the door of the house, where four or five servants in old-fashioned liveries, headed by Alexander Saunderson the butler, who now bore no token of the sable stains of the garden, received them in grand *costume*,

> In an old hall hung round with pikes and with bows,
> With old bucklers and corslets that had borne many shrewd blows.

With much ceremony, and still more real kindness, the Baron, without stopping in any intermediate apartment, conducted his guest through several into the great dining parlour, wainscotted with black oak, and hung round with the pictures of his ancestry, where a table was set forth in form for six persons, and an old-fashioned beaufet displayed all the ancient and massive plate of the Bradwardine family. A bell was now heard at the head of the avenue; for an old man, who acted as porter upon gala days, had caught the alarm given by Waverley's arrival, and, repairing to his post, announced the arrival of other guests.

These, as the Baron assured his young friend, were very estimable persons. "There was the young Laird of Balmawhapple, a Falconer by surname, of the house of Glenfarquhar, given right much to field-sports—*gaudet equis et canibus*—but a very discreet and well-principled young gentleman. Then there was the Laird of Killancureit, who had devoted his leisure *untill* tillage and agriculture, and boasted himself to be possessed of a bull of matchless merit, brought from the county of Devon (the Damnonia of the Romans, if we can trust Robert of Cirencester.) He is, as ye may well suppose from such a tendency, but of yeoman extraction—*servabit odorem testa diu*—and I believe, between ourselves, his grandsire was from the wrong side of the Border—one Bullsegg, who came hither as a steward, or bailiff, or ground officer, or something in that department, to the last Girnigo of Killancureit, who died of an atrophy. After his master's death, sir,—ye would hardly believe such a scandal,—but this Bullsegg, being portly

and comely of aspect, intermarried with the lady dowager, who
was young and amorous, and possessed himself of the estate, which
devolved on this unhappy woman by a settlement of her umwhile
husband, in direct contravention of an unrecorded taillie, and to the
prejudice of the disponer's own flesh and blood, in the person of his
natural heir and seventh cousin, Girnigo of Tipperhewit, whose family
was so reduced by the ensuing law-suit, that his representative is now
serving as a private gentleman-centinel in the Highland Black Watch.
But this gentleman, Mr Bullsegg of Killancureit that now is, has good
blood in his veins by the mother and grandmother, who were both of
the family of Pickletillim, and he is well liked and looked upon, and
knows his own place. And God forbid, Captain Waverley, that we of
irreproachable lineage should exult over him, when it may be, that in
the eighth, ninth, or tenth generation, his progeny may rank, in a
manner, with the old gentry of the country. Rank and ancestry, sir,
should be the last words in the mouth of us men of unblemished race
—*vix ea nostra voco*, as Naso saith.—There is, besides, a clergyman of
the true (though suffering) episcopal church of Scotland. He was a
confessor in her cause after the year 1715, when a whiggish mob
destroyed his meeting-house, tore his surplice, and plundered his
dwelling-place of four silver spoons, intromitting also with his mart
and his meal-ark, and with two barrels, one of single and one of
double ale, besides three bottles of brandy. My baron-baillie and
doer, Mr Duncan Macwheeble, is the fourth of our list. There is a
question, owing to the incertitude of ancient orthography, whether he
belongs to the clan of Wheedle or of Quibble, but both have produced
persons eminent in the law."

As thus he described them by person and name,
They enter'd, and dinner was served as they came.

Chapter Eleven

THE BANQUET

THE ENTERTAINMENT was ample, and handsome according to
the Scotch ideas of the period, and the guests did great honour to it.
The Baron eat like a famished soldier, the Laird of Balmawhapple like
a sportsman, Bullsegg of Killancureit like a farmer, Waverley himself
like a traveller, and Baillie Macwheeble like all four together, though,
either out of more respect, or in order to preserve that proper declina-
tion of person which shewed his sense that he was in the presence of
his patron, he sat upon the edge of his chair, placed at three feet

distance from the table, and atchieved a communication with his plate by projecting his person towards it in a line which obliqued from the bottom of his spine, so that the person who sat opposite to him could only see the foretop of his riding periwig.

This stooping position might have been inconvenient to another person, but long habit made it, whether seated or walking, perfectly easy to the worthy Baillie. In the latter posture, it occasioned, to be sure, an unseemly projection of the person towards those who happened to walk behind; but those being at all times his inferiors, for Mr Macwheeble was very scrupulous in giving place to all others, he cared very little what inference of contempt or slight regard *they* might derive from the circumstance. Hence, when he waddled across the court to and from his old grey poney, he somewhat resembled a turnspit walking upon its hind legs.

The nonjuring clergyman was a pensive and interesting old man, with much the air of a sufferer for conscience sake. A gentleman by birth and education, a distant relation indeed of the Baron, he was one of those,

Who, undeprived, their benefice forsook.

For this whim, when the Baron was out of hearing, the Baillie used sometimes gently to rally Mr Rubrick, upbraiding him with the nicety of his scruples. Indeed, it must be owned, that he himself, though at heart a keen partizan of the exiled family, had kept pretty fair with all the different turns of state in his time; so that Davie Gellatley once described him as a particular good man, who had a very good and peaceful conscience, that *never did him any harm*.

When the dinner was removed, the Baron announced the health of the king, politely leaving to the consciences of his guests to drink to the sovereign *de facto* or *de jure*, as their politics inclined. The conversation now became general; and, shortly afterwards, Miss Bradwardine, who had done the honours with natural grace and simplicity, retired, and was soon followed by the clergyman. Among the rest of the party, the wine, which fully justified the encomium of the landlord, flowed freely round, although Waverley, with some difficulty, obtained the privilege of sometimes neglecting his glass. At length, as the evening grew more late, the Baron made a private signal to Mr Saunders Saunderson, or, as he facetiously denominated him, *Alexander ab Alexandro*, who left the room with a nod, and soon after returned, his grave countenance mantling with a solemn and mysterious smile, and placed before his master a small oaken casket, mounted with brass ornaments of curious form. The Baron, drawing out a private key, unlocked the casket, raised the lid, and produced a golden goblet of a singular and antique appearance, moulded into the shape of a rampant bear, which the owner regarded with a look of mingled reverence, pride, and delight, that irresistibly reminded Waverley of Ben Jonson's Tom Otter, with his Bull, Horse, and Dog, as that wag wittily denominated his chief carousing cups. But Mr Bradwardine, turning toward him with complacence, requested him to observe this curious relique of the olden time. "It represents," he said, "the chosen crest of our family, a bear, as ye observe, and *rampant;* because a good herald will depict every animal in its noblest posture, as a horse *salient*, a greyhound *currant*, and, as may be inferred, a ravenous animal *in actu ferociori*, or in a voracious, lacerating, and devouring posture. Now, sir, we hold this most honourable atchievement by the wappen-brief, or concession of arms of Frederick Red-beard, Emperor of Germany, to my predecessor Godmund Bradwardine, being the crest of a gigantic Dane, whom he slew in the lists in the Holy Land, on a quarrel touching the chastity of the emperor's spouse or daughter, tradition saith not precisely which. And thus, as Virgilius hath it—

> Mutemus clypeos, Danaumque insignia nobis
> Aptemus.*

"Then for the cup, Captain Waverley, it was wrought by the command of Saint Duthac, abbot of Aberbrothock, for behoof of another baron of the house of Bradwardine, who had valiantly defended the patrimony of that monastery against certain encroaching nobles. It is properly termed the Blessed Bear of Bradwardine, (though old Dr Doubleit used jocosely to call it Ursa Major,) and was supposed, in old and catholic times, to be invested with certain properties of a mystical and supernatural quality. And though I give not in to such *anilia*, it is certain it has always been esteemed a solemn standard cup and heirloom of our house; nor is it ever used but upon seasons of high festival, and such I hold to be the arrival of the heir of Sir Everard under my roof; and I devote this draught to the health and prosperity of the ancient and highly-to-be-honoured house of Waverley." During this long harangue, he carefully decanted a cobwebbed bottle of claret into the goblet, which held nearly an English pint; and, at the conclusion, delivering the bottle to the butler, to be held carefully in the same angle with the horizon, he devoutly quaffed of the contents of the Blessed Bear of Bradwardine.

Edward, with horror and alarm, beheld the animal making his rounds, and thought with great anxiety upon the appropriate motto, "Beware the bear;" but plainly foresaw, that, as none of the guests scrupled to do him this extraordinary honour, a refusal on his part to pledge their courtesy would be extremely ill received. Resolving,

---

* 'Then change we shields and their devices bear.' Dryden.

therefore, to submit to this last piece of tyranny, and then to quit the
table, if possible, and confiding in the strength of his constitution, he
did justice to the company in the contents of the Blessed Bear, and felt
less inconvenience from the draught than he could possibly have
expected. The others, whose time had been more actively employed,
began to show symptoms of innovation,—"the good wine did its good
office." The frost of etiquette, and pride of birth, began to give way
before the genial blessings of this benign constellation, and the formal
appellatives with which the three dignitaries addressed each other,
were now familiarly abbreviated into Tully, Bally, and Killie. When a
few rounds had passed, the two latter, after whispering together,
craved permission (a joyful hearing for Edward) to ask the grace cup.
This, after some delays, was at length produced, and Waverley concluded the orgies of Bacchus were terminated for the evening. He was
never more mistaken in his life.

As the guests had left their horses at the small inn, or *change-house*,
as it was called, of the village, the Baron could but in politeness walk
with them up the avenue, and Waverley, from the same motive, and to
enjoy, after this feverish revel, the cool summer evening, attended the
party. But when they arrived at Luckie Macleary's, the Lairds of
Balmawhapple and Killancureit declared their determination to
acknowledge their sense of the hospitality of Tully-Veolan, by partaking, with their entertainer and his guest, Captain Waverley, what they
technically called *doch an dorroch*, a stirrup-cup, to the honour of the
Baron's roof tree.

It must be noticed, that the Baillie, knowing by experience that the
day's joviality, which had been hitherto sustained at the expence
of his patron, might terminate partly at his own, had mounted his
spavined grey poney, and, between gaiety of heart, and alarm for
being hooked into a reckoning, spurred him into a hobbling canter,
(a trot was out of the question,) and had already cleared the village.
The others entered the change-house, leading Edward in unresisting
submission; for his landlord whispered him that to demur to such an
overture would be construed into a high misdemeanour against the
leges conviviales, or regulations of genial compotation. Widow Macleary
seemed to have expected this visit, as well she might, for it was the
usual consummation of merry bout, not only at Tully-Veolan, but at
most other gentlemen's houses in Scotland, Sixty Years since. The
guests thereby at once acquitted themselves of their burden of
gratitude to their entertainer's kindness, encouraged the trade of his
change-house, did honour to the place which afforded harbour to
their horses, and indemnified themselves for the previous restraints
imposed by private hospitality, by spending what Falstaff calls the

sweet of the night, in the general licence of a tavern.

Accordingly, in full expectation of these distinguished guests, Luckie Macleary had swept her house for the first time this fortnight, tempered her turf fire to such a heat as the season required in her damp hovel even at Midsummer, set forth her deal table newly washed, propped its lame foot with a fragment of turf, arranged four or five stools of huge and clumsy form, upon the sites which best suited the inequalities of her clay floor; and having, moreover, put on her clean toy, rokelay, and scarlet plaid, gravely awaited the arrival of the company, in full hope of custom and profit. When they were seated under the sooty rafters of Luckie Macleary's only apartment, thickly tapestried with cobwebs, their hostess, who had already taken her cue from the Laird of Balmawhapple, appeared with a huge pewter measuring-pot, containing at least three English quarts, familiarly denominated a *tappit hen*, and which, in the language of the hostess, reamed (*i. e.* mantled) with excellent claret just drawn from the cask.

It was soon plain that what crumbs of reason the Bear had not devoured, were to be picked up by the Hen; but the confusion which appeared to prevail favoured Edward's resolution to evade the gaily circling glass. The rest began to talk thick and at once, each performing his own turn, without the least respect to his neighbour. The Baron of Bradwardine sung French *chansons-à-boire*, and spouted pieces of Latin; Killancureit talked in a steady unalterable dull key, of top-dressing and bottom-dressing, and year-olds, and gimmers, and dinmonts, and stots, and runts, and kyloes, and a proposed turnpike-act; while Balmawhapple, in notes exalted above both, extolled his horse, his hawks, and a greyhound called Whistler. In the middle of this din, the Baron repeatedly implored silence; and when at length the instinct of polite discipline so far prevailed, that for a moment he obtained it, he hastened to beseech their attention "unto a military ariette, which was a particular favourite of the Marechal Duc de Berwick;" then, imitating as well as he could, the manner and tone of a French mousquetaire, he immediately commenced,—

> Mon coeur volage, dit elle,
>> N'est pas pour vous garçon,
> Est pour un homme de guerre,
>> Qui a barbe au menton.
>>> Lon, Lon, Laridon.

> Qui port chapeau à plume,
>> Souliers à rouge talon,
> Qui joue de la flute,
>> Aussi de violon.
>>> Lon, Lon, Laridon.

Balmawhapple could hold no longer, but broke in with what he

called a d——d good song, composed by Gibby Gaethrowi't, the
piper o' Cupar, and without wasting more time struck up,—

> It's up Glenbarchan's braes I gaed,
> And ower the bent of Killiebraid,
> And mony a weary cast I made,
>   To cuittle the moor-fowl's tail.

The Baron, whose voice was drowned in the louder and more
obstreperous strains of Balmawhapple, now dropped the competition,
but continued to hum, Lon, Lon, Laridon, and to regard the successful candidate for the attention of the company with an eye of disdain,
while Balmawhapple proceeded,—

> If up a bonny black-cock should spring,
> To whistle him down wi' a slug in his wing,
> And strap him on to my lunzie string,
>   Right seldom wad I fail.

After an ineffectual attempt to recover the second verse, he sung the
first over again; and, in prosecution of his triumph, declared there was
"more sense in that than in all the *derry-dongs* of France, and Fifeshire
to the boot of it." The Baron only answered with a long pinch of snuff
and a glance of infinite contempt. But those noble allies, the Bear and
the Hen, had emancipated the young laird from the habitual reverence
in which he held Bradwardine at other times. He pronounced the
claret *shilpit*, and demanded brandy with great vociferation. It was
brought; and now the Dæmon of Politics envied even the harmony
arising from this Dutch concert, merely because there was not a
wrathful note in the strange compound of sounds which it produced.
Inspired by her, the Laird of Balmawhapple, now superior to the
nods and winks with which the Baron of Bradwardine, in delicacy
to Edward, had checked his entering upon political discussion,
demanded a bumper with the lungs of a Stentor, "to the little gentleman in black velvet who did such service in 1702, and may the white
horse break his neck over a mound of his making."

Edward was not at that moment clear-headed enough to remember
that King William's fall, which occasioned his death, was said to be
owing to his horse stumbling at a mole-hill, yet he felt inclined to take
umbrage at a toast which seemed, from the glance of Balmawhapple's
eye, to have a peculiar and uncivil reference to the government that he
served. But ere he could interfere, the Baron of Bradwardine had
taken up the quarrel. "Sir, whatever my sentiments, *tanquam privatus*,
may be in such matters, I shall not tamely endure your saying any thing
that may impinge upon the honourable feeling of a gentleman under
my roof. Sir, if you have no respect for the laws of urbanity, do ye not
respect the military oath, the *sacramentum militare*, by which every
officer is bound to the standards under whilk he is enrolled? Look at

Titus Livius, what he says of those Roman soldiers who were so unhappy as *exuere sacramentum*,—to renounce their legionary oath; but ye are ignorant, sir, alike of ancient history and modern courtesy."

"No so ignorant as ye would pronounce me," roared Balmawhapple. "I ken well that you mean the solemn league and covenant, but if all the whigs in hell had taken the"——

Here the Baron and Waverley spoke both at once, the former calling out, "Be silent, sir! ye only show your ignorance and disgrace your native country before a stranger and an Englishman;" and Waverley, at the same moment, entreating Mr Bradwardine to permit him to reply to an affront which seemed levelled at him personally. But the Baron was exalted by wine, wrath, and scorn, above all sublunary considerations.

"I crave you to be hushed, Captain Waverley; you are elsewhere, peradventure, *sui juris*, being foris-familiated and entitled, it may be, to think and resent for yourself; but in my domain, in this poor barony of Bradwardine, and under this roof, which is *quasi* mine, being held by tacit relocation by a tenant at will, I am *in loco parentis* to you, and bound to see you scathless.—And for you, Mr Falconer of Balmawhapple, I warn ye let me see no more aberrations from the paths of good manners."

"And I tell you, Mr Cosmo Comyne Bradwardine of Bradwardine and Tully-Veolan," retorted the sportsman, in huge disdain, "that I'll make a moor-cock of the man that refuses my toast, whether it be a crop-eared English whig with a black ribband at his lug, or ane who deserts his own friends to claw favour with the rats of Hanover."

In an instant both rapiers were brandished, and some desperate passes exchanged. Balmawhapple was young, stout, and active; but the Baron, infinitely more master of his weapon, would, like Sir Toby Belch, have tickled his opponent other gates than he did, had he not been under the influence of Ursa Major.

Edward rushed forward to interfere between the combatants, but the prostrate bulk of the Laird of Killancureit, over which he tumbled, intercepted his passage. How Killancureit happened to be in this recumbent posture, at so interesting a moment, was never accurately known. Some thought he was about to ensconce himself under the table; he himself alleged that he stumbled in the act of lifting a joint-stool, to prevent mischief, by knocking down Balmawhapple. Be that as it may, if readier aid than either his or Waverley's had not interposed, there would certainly have been bloodshed. But the well-known clash of swords, which was no great stranger to her dwelling, aroused Luckie Macleary as she sat quietly beyond the hallan, or earthen partition of the cottage, with eyes employed on Boston's

Crook of the Lot, while her ideas were engaged in summing up the reckoning. She boldly rushed in, with the shrill expostulation, "Wad their honours slay each other there, and bring discredit on an honest widow-woman's house, when there was a' the lea-land in the country to fight upon?" a remonstrance which she seconded by flinging her plaid with great dexterity over the weapons of the combatants. The servants by this time rushed in, and being, by great chance, tolerably sober, separated the incensed opponents, with the assistance of Edward and Killancureit. The latter led off Balmawhapple, cursing, swearing, and vowing revenge against every whig, presbyterian, and fanatic from John-o'-Groat's to Land's End, and with difficulty got him to horse. Our hero, with the assistance of Saunders Saunderson, escorted the Baron of Bradwardine to his own dwelling, but could not prevail upon him to retire to bed until he had made a long and learned apology for the events of the evening, of which, however, there was not a word intelligible, except something about the Centaurs and the Lapithæ.

Chapter Twelve

REPENTANCE, AND A RECONCILIATION

WAVERLEY was unaccustomed to the use of wine, excepting with great temperance. He slept therefore soundly till late in the succeeding morning, and then awakened to a painful recollection of the scene of the preceding evening. He had received a personal affront,—he, a gentleman, a soldier, and a Waverley. True, the person who offered it was not, at the time it was given, possessed of the moderate share of sense which nature had allotted him; true also, in resenting this insult, he would break the laws of Heaven, as well as of his country; true, in doing so, he might take the life of a young man who perhaps respectably discharged the social duties, and render his family miserable; or he might lose his own, no pleasant alternative even to the bravest, when it is debated coolly and in private.

All this pressed on his mind; yet the original statement recurred with the same irresistible force. He had received a personal insult; he was of the house of Waverley; and he bore a commission. There was no alternative; and he descended to the breakfast parlour with the intention of taking leave of the family, and writing to one of his brother officers to meet him at the inn mid-way between Tully-Veolan and the town where they were quartered, in order that he might convey such a message to the Laird of Balmawhapple as the circumstances seemed to demand. He found Miss Bradwardine presiding over the tea and coffee, the table loaded with warm bread, both of flour and barley, in the shape of loaves, cakes, biscuits, and other varieties, together with eggs, rein-deer ham, mutton and beef ditto, smoked salmon, marmalade, and all the other delicacies which induced even Johnson himself to extol the luxury of a Scotch breakfast above that of all other countries. A mess of oat-meal porridge, flanked by a silver jug, which held an equal mixture of cream and butter-milk, was placed for the Baron's share of this repast; but Rose observed he had walked out early in the morning, after giving orders that his guest should not be disturbed.

Waverley sat down almost in silence, and with an air of absence and abstraction which could not give Miss Bradwardine a favourable opinion of his talents for conversation. He answered at random one or two observations which she ventured to make upon ordinary topics; so that feeling herself almost repulsed in her efforts at entertaining him, and secretly wondering that a scarlet coat should cover no better breeding, she left him to his mental amusement of cursing Dr Double-it's favourite constellation of Ursa Major, as the cause of all the mischief which had already happened, and was likely to ensue. At once he started, and his colour heightened, as looking towards the window he beheld the Baron and young Balmawhapple pass arm in arm, apparently in deep conversation. "Did Mr Falconer sleep here last night?" Rose, not much pleased with the abruptness of the first question which the young stranger addressed to her, answered drily in the negative, and the conversation again sunk into silence.

At this moment Mr Saunderson appeared, with a message from his master, requesting to speak with Captain Waverley in another apartment. With a heart which beat a little quicker, not indeed from fear, but from uncertainty and anxiety, Edward obeyed the summons. He found the two gentlemen standing together, an air of complacent dignity on the brow of the Baron, while something like sullenness or shame, or both, blanked the bold visage of Balmawhapple. The former slipped his arm through that of the latter, and thus seeming to walk with him, while in reality he led him, advanced to meet Waverley, and, stopping in the midst of the apartment, made in great state the following oration: "Captain Waverley,—my young and esteemed friend, Mr Falconer of Balmawhapple, has craved of my age and experience, as of one not wholly unskilled in the dependancies and punctilios of the duello or monomachia, to be his interlocutor in expressing to you the regret with which he calls to remembrance certain passages of our symposion last night, which could not but be highly displeasing to you, as serving for the time under this present existing government. He craves you, sir, to drown in oblivion the memory of such solecisms against the laws of politeness, as being what his better reason disavows, and to receive the hand which he offers you in amity; and I must needs assure you, that nothing less than a sense of being *dans son tort*, as a gallant French chevalier, Mons. Le Bretailleur, once said to me on such an occasion, and an opinion also of your peculiar merit, could have extorted such concessions; for he and all his family are, and have been, time out of mind, *mavortia pectora*, as Buchanan saith, a bold and warlike sept or people."

Edward immediately, and with natural politeness, accepted the hand which Balmawhapple, or rather the Baron in his character of mediator, extended towards him. "It was impossible," he said, "for him to remember what a gentleman expressed his wish he had not uttered; and he willingly imputed what had passed to the exuberant festivity of the day."

"That is very handsomely said," answered the Baron; "for, undoubtedly, if a man be *ebrius*, or intoxicated, an incident which on solemn and festive occasions may and will take place in the life of a man of honour; and if the same gentleman, being fresh and sober, recants the contumelies which he hath spoken in his liquor, it must be held *vinum locutum est;* the words cease to be his own. Yet would I not find this exculpation relevant in the case of one who was *ebriosus*, or a habitual drunkard; because, if such person chuse to pass the greater part of his time in the predicament of intoxication, he hath no title to be exeemed from the obligations of the code of politeness, but should learn to deport himself peaceably and courteously when under influence of the vinous stimulus. And now let us proceed to breakfast, and think no more of this daft business."

I must confess, whatever inference may be drawn from the circumstance, that Edward, after so satisfactory an explanation, did much greater honour to the delicacies of Miss Bradwardine's breakfast-table than his commencement had promised. Balmawhapple, on the contrary, seemed embarrassed and dejected; and Waverley now, for the first time, observed that his arm was in a sling, which seemed to account for the awkward and embarrassed manner with which he had presented his hand. To a question from Miss Bradwardine, he muttered, in answer, something about his horse having fallen; and, seeming desirous to escape both from the subject and the company, he arose as soon as breakfast was over, made his bow to the party, and, declining the Baron's invitation to tarry till after dinner, mounted his horse and returned to his own home.

Waverley now announced his purpose of leaving Tully-Veolan early enough after dinner to gain the stage at which he meant to sleep; but the unaffected and deep mortification with which the good-natured and affectionate old gentleman heard the proposal, quite deprived him of courage to persist in it. No sooner had he gained Waverley's consent to lengthen his visit for a few days, than he laboured to remove the grounds upon which he conceived he was meditating a more early retreat. "I would not have you opine, Captain Waverley, that I am by practice or precept an advocate of ebriety, though it may be that, in our festivity of last night, some of our friends, if not perchance altogether *ebrii*, or drunken, were, to say the least, *ebrioli*, by which the ancients designed those who were fuddled, or, as your English vernacular and metaphorical phrase goes, half-seas over. Not that I would so insinuate respecting you, Captain Waverley, who, like a prudent youth, did rather abstain from potation; nor can it be truly said of myself, who, having assisted at the tables of many great generals and marechals at their solemn carousals, have the art to carry my wine discreetly, and did not, during the whole evening, as ye must have doubtless observed, exceed the bounds of a modest hilarity."

There was no refusing assent to a proposition so decidedly laid down by him, who undoubtedly was the best judge; although, had Edward formed his opinion from his own recollections, he would have pronounced that the Baron was not only *ebriolus*, but verging to become *ebrius;* or, in plain English, was incomparably the most drunk of the party, except perhaps his antagonist, the Laird of Balma-whapple. However, having received the expected, or rather the required compliment on his sobriety, the Baron proceeded—"No, sir, though I am myself of a strong temperament, I abhor ebriety, and detest those who swallow wine *gulæ causa*, for the oblectation of the gullet. Albeit I might deprecate the law of Pittacus of Mitylene, who punished doubly a crime committed under the influence of *Liber Pater;* nor utterly accede to the objurgation of the younger Plinius, in the fourteenth book of his 'Historia Naturalis.' No, sir, I distinguish, I discriminate, and approve of wine so far as it maketh glad the face, or, in the language of Flaccus, *recepto amico*."

Thus terminated the apology which the Baron of Bradwardine thought it necessary to make for the superabundance of his hospitality; and it may be easily believed that he was neither interrupted by dissent, or any expression of incredulity.

He then invited his guest to a morning's ride, and ordered that Davie Gellatley should meet them at the *dern path* with Ban and Buscar. "For, until the shooting season commence, I would willingly shew you some sport; and we may, God willing, meet with a roe. The roe, Captain Waverley, may be hunted at all times alike; for never being in what is called *pride of grease*, he is also never out of season, though it be a truth that his venison is not equal to that of either the red or fallow-deer. But he will serve to shew how my dogs run; and therefore they shall attend us with David Gellatley."

Waverley expressed his surprise that his friend Davie was capable of such trust; but the Baron gave him to understand, that this poor simpleton was neither fatuous, *nec naturaliter idiota*, as is expressed in the brieves of furiosity, but simply a crack-brained knave, who could execute very well any commission which jumped with his own humour, and made his folly a plea for avoiding every other. "He has made an interest with us," continued the Baron, "by saving Rose from a great danger with his own proper peril; and the roguish *loon* must therefore eat of our bread and drink of our cup, and do what he can, or what he will; which, if the suspicions of Saunderson and the Baillie are well founded, may perchance in his case be commensurate terms."

Miss Bradwardine then gave Waverley to understand, that this poor simpleton was doatingly fond of music, deeply affected by that which was melancholy, and transported into extravagant gaiety by light and lively tunes. He had in this respect a prodigious memory, stored with miscellaneous snatches and fragments of all tunes and songs, which he sometimes applied, with considerable address, as the vehicles of remonstrance, explanation, or satire. Davie was much attached to the few who shewed him kindness; and both aware of any slight or ill usage which he happened to receive, and sufficiently apt, where he saw opportunity, to revenge it. The common people, who often judge hardly of each other, as well as of their betters, although they had expressed great compassion for the poor *innocent* while suffered to wander in rags about the village, no sooner beheld him decently clothed, provided for, and even a sort of favourite, than they called up all the instances of sharpness and ingenuity, in action and repartee, which his annals afforded, and charitably bottomed thereupon a hypothesis, that David Gellatley was no farther fool than was necessary to avoid hard labour. This opinion was not better founded than that of the Negroes, who, from the acute and mischievous pranks of the monkies, suppose that they have the gift of speech, and only suppress their powers of elocution to escape being set to work. David Gellatley was in good earnest the half-crazed simpleton which he appeared, and was incapable of any constant and steady exertion. He had just so much solidity as kept on the windy side of insanity; so much wild wit as saved him from the imputation of idiocy; some dexterity in field-sports, (in which we have known as great fools excel;) great kindness and humanity in the treatment of animals entrusted to him, warm affections, a prodigious memory, and an ear for music.

The stamping of horses was now heard in the court, and Davie's voice singing to the two large deer greyhounds,

> Hie away, hie away,
> Over bank and over brae,
> Where the copsewood is the greenest,
> Where the fountains glisten sheenest,
> Where the lady fern grows strongest,
> Where the morning dew lies longest,
> Where the black-cock sweetest sips it,
> Where the fairy latest trips it;
> Hie to haunts right seldom seen,
> Lovely, lonesome, cool and green,
> Over bank and over brae,
> Hie away, hie away.

"Do the verses he sings belong to old Scottish poetry, Miss Bradwardine?"

"I believe not," she replied. "This poor creature had a brother, and Heaven, as if to compensate to the family Davie's deficiencies, had given him what the hamlet thought uncommon talents. An uncle contrived to educate him for the Scottish kirk, but he could not get preferment because he came from our *ground*. He returned from college hopeless and broken-hearted, and fell into a decline. My father supported him till his death, which happened before he was nineteen. He played beautifully on the flute, and was supposed to have a great turn for poetry. He was affectionate and compassionate to his brother, who followed him like his shadow, and we think that from him Davie gathered many fragments of songs and music unlike those of this country. But if we ask him where he got such a fragment as he is now singing, he either answers with wild and long fits of laughter, or else breaks into tears of lamentation; but was never heard to give any explanation, or mention his brother's name since his death."

"Surely," said Edward, who was readily interested by a tale bordering on the romantic, "more might be learned by more particular enquiry."

"Perhaps so," answered Rose; "but my father will not permit any one to practise on his feelings on this subject."

By this time the Baron, with the help of Mr Saunderson, had indued a pair of jack-boots of large dimension, and now invited our hero to follow him as he stalked clattering down the ample staircase, tapping each huge balustrade as he passed with the butt of his massive horse-whip, and humming, with the air of a chasseur of Louis Quatorze,

> Pour la chasse ordonnée il faut preparer tout,
> Ho la ho! Vite! vite debout.

Chapter Thirteen

A MORE RATIONAL DAY THAN THE LAST

THE BARON of Bradwardine, mounted on an active and well-managed horse, and seated on a demi-pique saddle, with deep housings to agree with his livery, was no bad representation of the old school. His light-coloured embroidered coat, and superbly barred waistcoat, his brigadier wig, surmounted by a small gold-laced cocked hat, completed his personal costume; but he was attended by two well-mounted servants on horseback, armed with holster-pistols.

In this guise he ambled forth over hill and valley, the admiration of every farm-yard which they passed in their progress; till, "low down in a grassy vale," they found David Gellatley leading two very tall deer greyhounds, and presiding over half a dozen curs, and about as many bare-legged and bare-headed boys, who, to procure the chosen distinction of attending on the chase, had not failed to tickle his ears with the dulcet appellation of *Maister Gellatley*, though probably all and each had hooted him on former occasions in the character of *daft Davie*. But this is no uncommon strain of flattery to persons in office, nor altogether confined to the bare-legged villagers of Tully-Veolan; it was in fashion Sixty Years since, is now, and will be six hundred years hence, if this admirable compound of folly and knavery, called the world, should be then in existence.

These *gillie-white-foots*, as they were called, were destined to beat the bushes, which they performed with so much success, that after half an hour's search a roe was started, coursed, and killed; the Baron following on his white horse, like Earl Percy of yore, and magnanimously flaying and disembowelling the slain animal (which, he observed, was called by the French chasseurs, *faire la curée*) with his own baronial couteau de chasse. After this ceremony, he conducted his guest homeward by a pleasant and circuitous route, commanding an extensive prospect of different villages and houses, to each of which Mr Bradwardine attached some anecdote of history or genealogy, told in language whimsical from prejudice and pedantry, but often respectable for the good sense and honourable feeling which his narratives displayed, and almost always curious, if not valuable, for the information they contained.

The truth is, the ride seemed agreeable to both gentlemen, because they found amusement in each other's conversation, although their characters and habits of thinking were in many respects totally oppos-

ite. Edward, we have informed the reader, was warm in his feelings,
wild and romantic in his ideas and in his taste of reading, with a strong
disposition towards poetry. Mr Bradwardine was the reverse of all
this, and piqued himself upon stalking through life with the same
upright, starched, stoical gravity which distinguished his evening
promenade upon the terrace of Tully-Veolan, where for hours
together—the very model of old Hardyknute—

> Stately stepp'd he east the wa',
> And stately stepp'd he west.

As for literature, he read the classic poets, to be sure, and the
Epithalamium of Georgius Buchanan, and Arthur Johnstoun's
Psalms, of a Sunday; and the Deliciæ Poetarum, and Sir David
Lindsay's Works, and Barbour's Bruce, and Blind Harry's Wallace,
and the Gentle Shepherd, and the Cherry and the Slae. But though he
thus far sacrificed his time to the muses, he would, if the truth must be
spoken, have been much better pleased had the pious or sapient
apothegms, as well as the historical narratives which these various
works contained, been presented to him in the form of simple prose.
And he sometimes could not refrain from expressing contempt of the
"vain and unprofitable art of poem-making," in which he said, "the
only one who had excelled in his time was Allan Ramsay the periwig
maker."

But although Edward and he differed *toto cœlo*, as the Baron would
have said, upon this subject, yet they met upon history as on a neutral
ground, in which each claimed an interest. The Baron, indeed, only
cumbered his memory with matters of fact; the cold, dry, hard outlines
which history delineates. Edward, on the contrary, loved to fill up and
round the sketch with the colouring of a warm and vivid imagination,
which gives light and life to the actors and speakers in the drama of
past ages. Yet with tastes so opposite, they contributed greatly to each
other's amusement. Mr Bradwardine's minute narratives and powerful memory supplied to Waverley fresh subjects of the kind upon
which his fancy loved to labour, and opened to him a new mine of
incident and of character. And he repaid the pleasure thus communicated, by an earnest attention, valuable to all story-tellers, more especially to the Baron, who felt his habits of self-respect flattered by it;
and sometimes also by reciprocal communications, which interested
Mr Bradwardine, as confirming or illustrating his own favourite anecdotes. Besides, Mr Bradwardine loved to talk of the scenes of his
youth, which had been spent in camps and foreign lands, and had
many interesting particulars to tell of the generals under whom he had
served, and the actions he had witnessed.

Both parties returned to Tully-Veolan in great good humour with each other; Waverley, desirous of studying more attentively what he considered as a singular and interesting character, gifted with a memory containing a curious register of ancient and modern anecdotes; and Bradwardine disposed to regard Edward as *puer* (or rather *juvenis*) *bonæ spei et magnæ indolis*, a youth devoid of that petulant volatility, which is impatient of, or vilipends, the conversation and advice of his seniors, from which he predicted great things of his future success and deportment in life. There was no other guest except Mr Rubrick, whose information and discourse, as a clergyman and a scholar, harmonized very well with that of the Baron and his guest.

Shortly after dinner, the Baron, as if to shew that his temperance was not entirely theoretical, proposed a visit to Rose's apartment, or, as he termed it, her *Troisieme Etage*. Waverley was accordingly conducted through one or two of those long awkward passages with which ancient architects studied to puzzle the inhabitants of the houses which they planned, at the end of which Mr Bradwardine began to ascend, by two steps at once, a very steep, narrow, and winding stair, leaving Mr Rubrick and Waverley to follow at more leisure, while he should announce their approach to his daughter.

After having climbed this perpendicular cork-screw until their brains were almost giddy, they arrived in a little matted lobby, which served as an anti-room to Rose's *sanctum sanctorum*, and through which they entered her parlour. It was a small, but pleasant apartment, opening to the south, and hung with tapestry; adorned besides with two pictures, one of her mother, in the dress of a shepherdess, with a bell-hoop; the other of the Baron, in his tenth year, in a blue coat, embroidered waistcoat, laced hat, and bag-wig, with a bow in his hand. Edward could not help smiling at the costume, and at the odd resemblance between the round, smooth, red-cheeked, staring visage in the portrait, and the gaunt, bearded, hollow-eyed, swarthy features which travelling, fatigues of war, and advanced age, had bestowed on the original. The Baron joined in the laugh. "Truly," he said, "that picture was a woman's fantasy of my good mother's, (a daughter of the Laird of Tulliellum, Captain Waverley; I indicated the house to you when we were on the top of the Shinny-heuch; it was burned by the Dutch auxiliaries brought in by the government in 1715;) I never sate for my pourtraicture but once since that was painted, and it was at the special and reiterated request of the Marechal Duke of Berwick."

The good old gentleman did not mention, what Mr Rubrick afterwards told Edward, that the Duke had done him this honour on account of his being the first to mount the breach of a fort in Savoy during the memorable campaign of 1709, and having there defended himself with his half-pike for nearly ten minutes before any support reached him. To do the Baron justice, although sufficiently prone to exaggerate his family dignity and consequence, he was too much a man of real courage ever to dwell upon such personal acts of merit as he had himself manifested.

Miss Rose now appeared from the interior room of her apartment to welcome her father and his friends. The little labours in which she had been employed obviously shewed a natural taste, which required only cultivation. Her father had taught her French and Italian, and a few of the ordinary authors in those languages ornamented her shelves. He had endeavoured also to be her preceptor in music; but as he began with the more abstruse doctrines of the science, and was not perhaps master of them himself, she had made no proficiency further than to be able to accompany her voice with the harpsichord: but even this was not very common in Scotland at that period. To make amends, she sung with great taste and feeling, and with a respect to the sense of what she uttered that might be proposed in example to ladies of much superior musical talent. Her natural good sense taught her, that if, as we are assured by high authority, music be "married to immortal verse," they are very often divorced by the performer in a most shameful manner. It was perhaps owing to this sensibility to poetry, and power of combining its expression with those of the musical notes, that her singing gave more pleasure to all the unlearned in music, and even to many of the learned, than could have been extracted by a much finer voice and more brilliant execution, unguided by the same delicacy of feeling.

A bartizan, or projecting gallery, before the windows of her parlour, served to illustrate another of Rose's pursuits, for it was crowded with flowers of different kinds, which she had taken under her special protection. A projecting turret gave access to this Gothic balcony, which commanded a most beautiful prospect. The formal garden, with its high bounding walls, lay below, contracted, as it seemed, to a mere parterre; while the view extended beyond them down a wooded glen, where the small river was sometimes visible, sometimes hidden in copse. The eye might be delayed by a desire to rest on the rocks, which here and there rose from the dell with massive or spiry fronts, or it might dwell on the noble, though ruined tower, which was here seen in all its dignity, frowning from a promontory over the river. To the left were seen two or three cottages, a part of the village; the brow of a hill concealed the others. The glen, or dell, was terminated by a sheet of water, called Loch Veolan, into which the brook discharged itself, and which now glistened in the western sun. The distant country seemed open and varied in surface, though not wooded; and there was nothing to interrupt the view until the scene was bounded by a ridge of distant and blue hills, which formed the southern boundary of the strath or valley. To this pleasant station Miss Bradwardine had ordered coffee.

The view of the old tower, or fortalice, introduced some family anecdotes and tales of Scottish chivalry, which the Baron told with great enthusiasm. The projecting peak of an impending crag which rose near it, had acquired the name of St Swithin's Chair. It was the scene of a peculiar superstition, of which Mr Rubrick mentioned some curious particulars, which reminded Waverley of a rhyme quoted by Edgar in King Lear; and Rose was called upon to sing a little legend, in which they had been interwoven by some village poet,

> Who, noteless as the race from which he sprung,
> Saved others' names, but left his own unsung.

The sweetness of her voice, and the simple beauty of her music, gave all the advantage which the minstrel could have desired, and which his poetry so much wanted. I almost doubt if it can be read with patience, destitute of those advantages; although I conjecture the following copy to have been somewhat corrected by Waverley, to suit the taste of those who might not relish pure antiquity.

St Swithin's Chair

On Hallow-Mass Eve, ere you boune ye to rest,
Ever beware that your couch be bless'd;
Sign it with cross, and sain it with bead,
Sing the Ave, and say the Creed.

For on Hallow-Mass Eve the Night-Hag will ride,
All her nine-fold sweeping on by her side,
Whether the wind sing lowly or loud,
Sailing through moonshine or swath'd in the cloud.

The Lady she sate in St Swithin's Chair,
The dew of the night has damp'd her hair;
Her cheek was pale—but resolved and high
Was the word of her lip and the glance of her eye.

She mutter'd the spell of St Swithin bold,
When his naked foot traced the midnight wold,
When he stopp'd the Hag as she rode the night,
And bade her descend, and her promise plight.

He that dare sit in St Swithin's Chair,
When the Night-Hag wings the troubled air,
Questions three, when he speaks the spell,
He may ask, and she must tell.

The Baron has been with King Robert his liege,
These three long years in battle and siege;
News are there none of his weal or his woe,
And fain the Lady his fate would know.

She shudders and stops, as the charm she speaks;
Is it the moody owl that shrieks?
Or is that sound, betwixt laughter and scream,
The voice of the Demon who haunts the stream?

The moan of the wind sunk silent and low,
And the roaring torrent has ceased to flow;
The calm was more dreadful than raging storm,
When the cold grey mist brought the ghastly Form!

*　　*　　*　　*　　*

"I am sorry to disappoint the company, especially Captain Waverley, who listens with such laudable gravity; it is but a fragment, although I think there are other verses, describing the return of the Baron from the wars, and how the lady was found 'clay-cold upon the grounsill ledge.'"

"It is one of those figments," observed Mr Bradwardine, "with which the early history of distinguished families was deformed in the times of superstition; as that of Rome, and other ancient nations, had their prodigies, sir, the which you may read in ancient histories, or in the little work compiled by Julius Obsequens, and inscribed by the learned Scheffer, the editor, to his patron, Benedictus Skytte, Baron of Dudershoff."

"My father has a strange defiance of the marvellous, Captain Waverley, and once stood firm when a whole synod of presbyterian divines were put to the rout, by a sudden apparition of the foul fiend."

Waverley looked as if desirous to hear more.

"Must I tell my story as well as sing my song?—Well—Once upon a time there lived an old woman, called Janet Gellatley, who was suspected to be a witch, on the infallible grounds that she was very old, very ugly, very poor, and had two sons, one of whom was a poet, and the other a fool, which visitation, all the neighbourhood agreed, had come upon her for the sin of witchcraft. And she was imprisoned for a week in the steeple of the parish-church, and sparely supplied with food, and not permitted to sleep, until she herself became as much persuaded of her being a witch as her accusers; and in this lucid and happy state of mind was brought forth to make a clean breast, that is, to make open confession of her sorceries before all the whig gentry and ministers in the vicinity, who were no conjurors themselves. My father went to see fair play between the witch and the clergy; for the witch had been born on his estate. And while the witch was confessing that the enemy appeared, and made his addresses to her as a handsome black man,—which, if you could have seen poor old blear-eyed Janet, reflected little honour on Apollyon's taste,—and while the auditors listened with astonished ears, and the clerk recorded with a trembling

hand, she, all of a sudden, changed the low mumbling tone with which
she spoke into a shrill yell, and exclaimed, 'Look to yourselves! look to
yourselves! I see the Evil One seated in the midst of ye.' The surprise
was general, and terror and flight its immediate consequence. Happy
were those who were next the door; and many were the disasters that
befel hats, bands, cuffs, and wigs, before they could get out of the
church, where they left the obstinate prelatist to settle matters with the
witch and her admirer, at his own peril or pleasure."

"*Risu solvuntur tabulæ*," said the Baron; "when they recovered their
panic trepidation, they were too much ashamed to bring any wakening
of the process against Janet Gellatley."

This anecdote led into a long discussion of

> All those idle thoughts and phantasies,
>   Devices, dreams, opinions unsound,
> Shows, visions, soothsays, and prophecies,
>   And all that feigned is, as leasings, tales, and lies.

With such conversation, and the romantic legends which it introduced, closed our hero's second evening in the house of Tully-
Veolan .

Chapter Fourteen

A DISCOVERY—WAVERLEY BECOMES DOMESTICATED
AT TULLY-VEOLAN

THE NEXT day Edward arose betimes, and in a morning walk around
the house and its vicinity, came suddenly upon a small court in front of
the dog-kennel, where his friend Davie was employed about his four-
footed charge. One quick glance of his eye recognised Waverley,
when, instantly turning his back, as if he had not observed him, he
began to sing part of an old ballad:

> Young men will love thee more fair and more fast;
>   *Heard ye so merry the little bird sing?*
> Old men's love the longest will last,
>   *And the throstle-cock's head is under his wing.*
>
> The young man's wrath is like light straw on fire;
>   *Heard ye so merry the little bird sing?*
> But like red-hot steel is the old man's ire,
>   *And the throstle-cock's head is under his wing.*
>
> The young man will brawl at the evening board;
>   *Heard ye so merry the little bird sing?*
> But the old man will draw at the dawning the sword,
>   *And the throstle-cock's head is under his wing.*

Waverley could not avoid observing that Davie laid something like a satirical emphasis on these lines. He therefore approached, and endeavoured, by sundry queries, to elicit from him what the inuendo might mean; but Davie had no mind to explain, and had wit enough to make his folly cloak his knavery. Edward could collect nothing from him excepting that the Laird of Balmawhapple had gone home "wi' his boots full o' bluid." In the garden, however, he met the old butler, who no longer attempted to conceal, that, having been bred in the nursery line with Sumack and Co. of Newcastle, he sometimes wrought a turn in the flower-borders to oblige the laird and Miss Rose. By a series of queries, Edward at length discovered, with a painful feeling of surprise and shame, that Balmawhapple's submission and apology had been the consequence of a rencontre with the Baron before he had quitted his pillow, in which the younger combatant had been disarmed and wounded in the sword arm.

Greatly mortified at this information, Edward sought out his friendly host, and anxiously expostulated with him upon the injustice he had done him in anticipating his meeting with Mr Falconer, a circumstance, which, considering his youth and the profession of arms which he had just adopted, was capable of being represented much to his prejudice. The Baron justified himself at greater length than I chuse to report. He urged, that the quarrel was common to them, and that Balmawhapple could not, by the code of honour, *evite* giving satisfaction to both, which he had done in his case by an honourable meeting, and in that of Edward by such a *palinode* as rendered the use of the sword unnecessary, and which, being made and accepted, must necessarily *sopite* the whole affair. With this excuse or explanation Waverley was silenced, if not satisfied, but he could not help testifying some displeasure against the Blessed Bear which had given rise to the quarrel, nor refrain from hinting, that the sanctified epithet was hardly appropriate. The Baron observed, he could not deny that "the Bear, though allowed by heralds as a most honourable ordinary, had, nevertheless, somewhat fierce, churlish, and morose in his disposition, (as might be read in Archibald Simson pastor of Dalkeith's *Hierogliphica Animalium*) and had thus been the type of many quarrels and dissensions which had occurred in the house of Bradwardine; of which," he continued, "I might commemorate mine own unfortunate dissension with my third cousin by the mother's side, Sir Hew Halbert, who was so unthinking as to deride my family name, as if it had been *quasi Bear-warden;* a most uncivil jest, since it not only insinuated that the founder of our house occupied such a mean situation as to be a custodier of wild beasts, a charge which ye must have observed is only entrusted to the very basest plebeians; but, moreover, seemed to infer that our coat-armour had not been achieved by honourable actions in war, but bestowed by way of *paranomasia*, or pun, upon our family appellation,—a sort of bearing which the French call *armoiries parlantes;* the Latins, *arma cantantia;* and your English authorities, canting heraldry; being indeed a species of emblazoning more befitting canters, gaberlunzies, and such like mendicants, whose gibberish is formed upon playing on the word, than the noble, honourable, and useful science of heraldry, which assigns armorial bearings as the reward of noble and generous actions, and not to tickle the ear with vain quodlibets, such as are found in jest-books." Of his quarrel with Sir Hew, he said nothing more than that it was settled in a fitting manner.

Having been so minute with respect to the diversions of Tully-Veolan, on the first days of Edward's arrival, for the purpose of introducing its inmates to the reader's acquaintance, it becomes less necessary to trace the progress of his intercourse with the same accuracy. It is probable that a young man, accustomed to more cheerful society, would have tired of the conversation of so violent an asserter of the "boast of heraldry" as the Baron; but Edward found an agreeable variety in that of Miss Bradwardine, who listened with eagerness to his remarks upon literature, and shewed great justness of taste in her answers. The sweetness of her disposition had made her submit with complacency, and even pleasure, to the course of reading prescribed by her father, although it not only comprehended several heavy folios of history, but certain gigantic tomes in high-church polemics. In heraldry he was fortunately contented to give her only such a slight tincture as might be acquired by perusal of the two folio volumes of Nisbett. Rose was indeed the very apple of her father's eye; her constant liveliness, her attention to all those little observances most gratifying to those who would never think of exacting them, her beauty, in which he recalled the features of his beloved wife, her unfeigned piety, and the noble generosity of her disposition, would have justified the affection of the most doating father.

His anxiety on her behalf did not, however, seem to extend itself in that quarter where, according to the general opinion, it is most efficiently displayed, in labouring, namely, to establish her in life, either by a large dowry or a wealthy marriage. By an old settlement, almost all the landed estates of the Baron went, after his death, to a distant relation; and it was supposed that Miss Bradwardine would remain but slenderly provided for, as the good gentleman's cash-matters had been too long under the exclusive charge of Baillie Macwheeble, to admit of any great expectations from his personal succession. It is true, the said Baillie loved his patron and his patron's daughter next (though at an incomparable distance) to himself. He thought it was possible to set aside the settlement on the male line, and had actually procured an opinion to that effect (and, as he boasted, without a fee) from an eminent Scottish counsel, under whose notice he contrived to bring the point while consulting him regularly on some other business. But the Baron would not listen to such a proposal for an instant. On the contrary, he used to have a perverse pleasure in boasting that the barony of Bradwardine was a male fief, the first charter having been given at that early period when women were not deemed capable to hold a feudal grant; because, according to *Les coustusmes de Normandie*, *C'est L'Homme ki se bast et ki conseille;* or, as is yet more ungallantly expressed by other authorities, all of whose barbarous names he delighted to quote at full length, because a woman could not serve the superior, or feudal lord, in war, on account of the decorum of her sex, nor assist him with advice, because of her limited intellect, nor keep his counsel, owing to the infirmity of her disposition. He would triumphantly ask, how it would become a female, and that female a Bradwardine, to be seen employed *in servitio exuendi seu detrahendi caligas regis post battaliam?* that is, in pulling off the king's boots after an engagement, which was the feudal service by which he held the barony of Bradwardine. "No," he said, "beyond hesitation, *procul dubio*, many females, as worthy as Rose, had been excluded, in order to make way for my own succession, and Heaven forbid that I should do aught that might contravene the destination of my forefathers, or impinge upon the right of my kinsman, Malcolm Bradwardine of Inch-Grubbit, an honourable, though decayed branch of my own family."

The Baillie, as prime minister, having received this decisive communication from his sovereign, durst not press his own opinion any farther, but contented himself with deploring, on all suitable occasions, to Saunderson, the minister of the interior, the laird's self-willedness, and with laying plans for uniting Rose with the young Laird of Balmawhapple, who had a fine estate, only moderately burthened, and was a faultless young gentleman, being as sober as a saint —if you kept brandy from him, and him from brandy—and who, in brief, had no imperfection but that of keeping light company at a time; such as Jinker, the horse-couper, and Gibby Gaethrowi't, the piper o' Cupar; "o' whilk follies, Mr Saunderson, he'll mend, he'll mend,"— pronounced the Baillie.

"Like sour ale in summer," added Davie Gellatley, who happened to be nearer the conclave than they were aware of.

Miss Bradwardine, such as we have described her, with all the

simplicity and curiosity of a recluse, attached herself to the opportunities of increasing her store of literature which Edward's visit afforded
her. He sent for some of his books from his quarters, and they opened
to her sources of delight of which she had hitherto had no idea. The
best English poets, of every description, and other works on belles
lettres, made a part of this precious cargo. Her music, even her
flowers, were neglected, and Saunders not only mourned over, but
began to mutiny against the labour for which he now scarce received
thanks. These new pleasures became gradually enhanced by sharing
them with one of a kindred taste. Edward's readiness to comment, to
recite, to explain difficult passages, rendered his assistance invaluable; and the wild romance of his spirit delighted a character too
young and inexperienced to observe its deficiencies. Upon subjects
which interested him, and when quite at ease, he possessed that flow
of natural, and somewhat florid eloquence, which has been supposed
as powerful as figure, fashion, fame, or fortune, in winning the female
heart. There was, therefore, an increasing danger in this constant
intercourse, to poor Rose's peace of mind, which was the more immin-
ent, as her father was greatly too much abstracted in his studies, and
wrapped up in his own dignity, to dream of his daughter's incurring it.
The daughters of the house of Bradwardine were, in his opinion, like
those of the house of Bourbon or Austria, placed high above the
clouds of passion which might obfuscate the intellects of meaner
females; they moved in another sphere, were governed by other feelings, and amenable to other rules than those of idle and fantastic
affection. In short, he shut his eyes so resolutely to the natural consequences of Edward's intimacy with Miss Bradwardine, that the
whole neighbourhood concluded that he had opened them to the
advantages of a match between his daughter and the wealthy young
Englishman, and pronounced him much less a fool than he had generally shown himself in cases where his own interest was concerned.

If the Baron, however, had really meditated such an alliance, the
indifference of Waverley would have been an insuperable bar to
his project. Our hero, since mixing more freely with the world, had
learned to think with great shame and confusion upon his mental
legend of Saint Cecilia, and the vexation of these reflections was
likely, for some time at least, to counterbalance the natural susceptibil-
ity of his disposition. Besides, Rose Bradwardine, beautiful and amiable as we have described her, had not precisely the sort of beauty or
merit which captivates a romantic imagination in early youth. She was
too frank, too confiding, too kind; amiable qualities undoubtedly,
but destructive of the marvellous with which a youth of imagination
delights to dress the empress of his affections. Was it possible to bow,

to tremble, and to adore before the timid, yet playful little girl, who now asked Edward to mend her pen, now to construe a stanza in Tasso, and now how to spell a very—very long word in her version of it? All these incidents have their fascination on the mind at a certain period in life, but not when a youth is entering it, and rather looking out for some object whose affection may dignify him in his own eyes, than stooping to one who looks up to him for such distinction.— Hence, though there can be no rule in so capricious a passion, early love is frequently ambitious in chusing its object; or, which comes to the same, selects her (as in the case of Saint Cecilia aforesaid) from a situation that gives fair scope for *le beau ideal*, which the reality of intimate and familiar life rather tends to limit and impair. I knew a very accomplished and sensible young man cured of a violent passion for a pretty woman, whose talents were not equal to her face and figure, by being permitted to bear her company for a whole afternoon. Thus, it is certain, that had Edward enjoyed such an opportunity of conversing with Miss Stubbs, Aunt Rachael's precaution would have been unnecessary, for he would as soon have fallen in love with the dairy-maid. And although Miss Bradwardine was a very different character, it seems probable that the very intimacy of their intercourse prevented his feeling for her other sentiments than those of a brother for an amiable and accomplished sister, while the sentiments of poor Rose were gradually, and without her being conscious, assuming a shade of warmer affection.

I ought to have mentioned that Edward had applied for, and received permission, extending his leave of absence. But the letter of his commanding-officer contained a friendly recommendation to him, not to spend his time exclusively with persons, who, estimable as they might be in a general sense, could not be supposed well affected to a government which they declined to acknowledge by taking the oath of allegiance. The letter further insinuated, though with great delicacy, that although some family connections might be supposed to render it necessary for Captain Waverley to communicate with gentlemen who were in this unpleasant state of suspicion, yet his father's situation and wishes ought to prevent his prolonging those attentions into exclusive intimacy. And it was intimated, that while his political principles were endangered by communicating with laymen of this description, he might also receive erroneous impressions in religion from the prelatic clergy, who so perversely laboured to set up the royal prerogative in things sacred.

This last insinuation probably induced Waverley to set both down to the prejudices of his commanding-officer. He was sensible that Mr Bradwardine had acted with the most scrupulous delicacy in never entering upon any discussion that had the most remote tendency to bias his mind in political opinions, although he was himself not only a decided partizan of the exiled family, but had been trusted at different times with important commissions for their service. Sensible, therefore, that there was no risque of his being perverted from his allegiance, Edward felt as if he should do his uncle's old friend injustice in removing from a house where he gave and received pleasure and amusement, merely to gratify a prejudiced and ill-judged suspicion. He therefore wrote a very general answer, assuring his commanding-officer that his loyalty was not in the most distant danger of contamination, and continued an honoured guest and inmate of the house of Tully-Veolan.

Chapter Fifteen

A CREAGH, AND ITS CONSEQUENCES

WHEN EDWARD had been a guest at Tully-Veolan nearly six weeks, he descried, one morning as he took his usual walk before the breakfast hour, signs of unusual perturbation in the family. Four bare-legged dairy-maids, with each an empty milk-pail in her hand, ran about with frantic gestures, and uttering loud exclamations of surprise, grief, and resentment. From their appearance, a pagan might have conceived them a detachment of the celebrated Belides, just come from their baleing penance. As nothing was to be got from this distracted chorus, excepting "Lord guide us!" and "Eh sirs!" ejaculations which threw no light upon the cause of their dismay, Waverley repaired to the fore-court, as it was called, where he beheld Baillie Macwheeble cantering his white poney down the avenue with all the speed it could muster. He had arrived, it would seem, upon a hasty summons, and was followed by half a score of peasants from the village, who had no great difficulty in keeping pace with him.

The Baillie, greatly too busy, and too important, to enter into explanations with Edward, summoned forth Mr Saunderson, who appeared with a countenance in which dismay was mingled with solemnity, and they immediately entered into close conference. Davie Gellatley was also seen in the group, idle as Diogenes at Sinope, while his countrymen were preparing for a siege. His spirits always rose with any thing, good or bad, which occasioned tumult, and he continued frisking, hopping, dancing, and singing the burden of an old ballad,—

> "Our gear's a' gane,"

until, happening to pass too near the Baillie, he received an admonitory hint from his horse-whip, which converted his songs into lamentation.

Passing from thence towards the garden, Waverley beheld the Baron in person, measuring and re-measuring, with swift and tremendous strides, the length of the terrace; his countenance clouded with offended pride and indignation, and the whole of his demeanour such as seemed to indicate, that any enquiry concerning the cause of his discomposure would give pain at least, if not offence. Waverley therefore glided into the house, without addressing him, and took his way to the breakfast parlour, where he found his young friend Rose, who, though she neither exhibited the resentment of her father, the turbid importance of Baillie Macwheeble, nor the despair of the handmaidens, seemed vexed and thoughtful. A single word explained the mystery. "Your breakfast will be a disturbed one, Captain Waverley. A party of catherans have come down upon us last night, and driven off all our milk cows."

"A party of catherans?"

"Yes; robbers from the neighbouring Highlands. We used to be quite free from them while we paid *black-mail* to Fergus Mac-Ivor Vich Ian Vohr; but my father thought it unworthy of his rank and birth to pay it any longer, and so this disaster has happened. It is not the value of the cattle, Captain Waverley, that vexes me; but my father is so much hurt at the affront, and is so bold and hot, that I fear he will try to recover them by the strong hand; and then, if he is not hurt himself, he will hurt some of these wild people, and there will be no peace between them and us perhaps for our lifetime; and we cannot defend ourselves as in old times, for the government have taken all our arms; and my dear father is so rash—O what will become of us!"——Here poor Rose lost heart altogether, and burst into a flood of tears.

The Baron entered at this moment, and rebuked her with more asperity than Waverley had ever heard him use to any one. "Was it not a shame," he said, "that she should exhibit herself before any gentleman in such a light, as if she shed tears for a drove of horned nolt and milch kine, like the daughter of a Cheshire yeoman!—Captain Waverley, I must request your favourable construction of her grief, which may, or ought to proceed solely from seeing her father's estate exposed to *spuilzie* and depredation from common thieves and *sornars*, while we are not allowed to keep a half score of muskets, whether for defence or rescue."

Baillie Macwheeble entered immediately afterwards, and, by his report of arms and ammunition, confirmed this statement, informing the Baron, in a melancholy voice, that though the people would certainly obey his honour's orders, yet was there no chance of their following the *gear* to any guid purpose, in respect there were only his honour's body servants who had swords and pistols, and the depredators were twelve Highlanders, completely armed after the manner of their country.—Having delivered this doleful annunciation, he assumed a posture of silent dejection, shaking his head slowly with the motion of a pendulum when it is ceasing to vibrate, and then remained stationary, his body stooping at a more acute angle than usual, and the latter part of his person projected in proportion.

The Baron, meanwhile, paced the room in silent indignation, and at length fixing his eye upon an old portrait, whose person was clad in armour, and whose features glared grimly out of a huge bush of hair, part of which descended from his head to his shoulders, and part from his chin and upper lip to his breast-plate,—"That gentleman, Captain Waverley, my grandsire, with two hundred horse, whom he levied within his own bounds, discomfited and put to the rout more than five hundred of these Highland *reivers*, who have been ever *lapis offensionis, et petra scandali*, a stumbling-block and a rock of offence to the Lowland vicinage—He discomfited them, I say, when they had the temerity to descend to *harry* this country, in the time of the civil dissensions, in the year of grace sixteen hundred forty and two. And now, sir, I, his grandson, am thus used at such unworthy hands."

Here there was an awful pause; after which all the company, as is usual in cases of difficulty, began to give separate and inconsistent counsel. Alexander ab Alexandro proposed they should send some one to compound with the catherans, who would readily, he said, give up their prey for a dollar a-head. The Baillie opined that this transaction would amount to *theft-boot*, or composition of felony; and he recommended that some *canny hand* should be sent up to the glens to make the best bargain he could, as it were for himself, so that the Laird might not be seen in such a transaction. Edward proposed to send off to the nearest garrison for a party of soldiers and a magistrate's warrant; and Rose, as far as she dared, endeavoured to insinuate the course of paying the arrears of tribute-money to Fergus Mac-Ivor Vich Ian Vohr, who, they all knew, could easily procure restoration of the cattle, if he was properly propitiated.

None of these proposals met the Baron's approbation. The idea of composition, direct or implied, was absolutely ignominious; that of Waverley only shewed that he did not understand the state of the country, and of the political parties which divided it; and, standing matters as they did with Fergus Mac-Ivor Vich Ian Vohr, the Baron would make no concession to him, were it, he said, "to procure restitution *in integrum* of every stirk and stot that his clan had stolen since the days of Malcolm Canmore."

In fact, his voice was still for war, and he proposed to send expresses to Balmawhapple, Killancureit, Tulliellum, and other lairds, who were exposed to similar depredations, inviting them to join in the pursuit; "and then, sir, shall these *nebulones nequissimi*, as Leslæus calls them, be brought to the fate of their predecessor Cacus,

> Elisos oculos, et siccum sanguine guttur."

The Baillie, who by no means relished these warlike councils, here pulled forth an immense watch, of the colour, and nearly of the size, of a pewter warming-pan, and observed it was now past noon, and that the catherans had been seen in the pass of Bally-Brough soon after sun-rise; so that before the allied forces could assemble, they and their prey would be far beyond the reach of the most active pursuit, and sheltered in those pathless deserts, where it was neither advisable to follow, nor indeed possible to trace them.

This proposition was undeniable. The council therefore broke up without coming to any conclusion, as has occurred to councils of more importance; only it was determined that the Baillie should send his own three milk cows down to the Mains for the use of the Baron's family, and brew small ale as a substitute for milk in his own. To this arrangement, which was suggested by Saunderson, the Baillie readily assented, both from habitual deference to the family, and an internal consciousness that his courtesy would, in some mode or other, be repaid tenfold.

The Baron having also retired to give some necessary directions, Waverley seized the opportunity to ask, whether this Fergus, with the unpronounceable name, were the chief thief-taker of the district?

"Thief-taker!" answered Rose, laughing; "he is a gentleman of great honour and consequence; the chieftain of an independent branch of a powerful Highland clan, and is much respected, both for his own power, and that of his *kith*, *kin*, and *allies*."

"And what has he to do with the thieves then? Is he a magistrate, or in the commission of peace?"

"The commission of war rather, if there be such a thing," said Rose; "for he is a very unquiet neighbour to his *un-friends*, and keeps a greater *following* on foot than many that have thrice his estate. As to his connection with the thieves, that I cannot well explain; but the boldest of them will never steal a hoof from any one that pays *black-mail* to Vich Ian Vohr."

"And what is *black-mail?*"

"A sort of protection-money that low-country gentlemen and her-itors, lying near the Highlands, pay to some Highland chief, that he may neither do them harm himself, nor suffer it to be done to them by others; and then if your cattle are stole, you have only to send him word, and he will recover them; or it may be, he will drive away cows from some distant place, where he has a quarrel, and give them to you to make up your loss."

"And is this sort of Highland Jonathan Wild admitted into society, and called a gentleman?"

"So much so, that the quarrel between my father and Fergus Mac-Ivor began at a county meeting, where he wanted to take precedence of all the Lowland gentlemen then present, only my father would not suffer it. And then he upbraided my father that he was under his banner, and paid him tribute; and my father was in a towering passion, for Baillie Macwheeble, who manages such things his own way, had contrived to keep this *black-mail* a secret from him, and passed it in his account for cess-money. And they would have fought; but Fergus Mac-Ivor said, very gallantly, he would never raise his hand against a grey head that was so much respected as my father's.—O I wish, I wish they had continued friends!"

"And did you ever see this Mr Mac-Ivor, if that be his name, Miss Bradwardine?"

"No, that is not his name; and he would consider *master* as a sort of affront, only that you are an Englishman, and know no better. But the Lowlanders call him, like other gentlemen, by the name of his estate, Glennaquoich; and the Highlanders call him Vich Ian Vohr, that is, the Son of John the Great; and we upon the *braes* here call him by both names indifferently."

"I am afraid I shall never bring my English tongue to call him by either one or other."

"But he is a very polite, handsome man," continued Rose; "and his sister Flora is one of the most beautiful and accomplished young ladies in this country: she was bred in a convent in France, and was a great friend of mine before this unhappy dispute. Dear Captain Waverley, try your influence with my father to make matters up. I am sure this is but the beginning of our troubles; for Tully-Veolan has never been a safe or quiet residence when we have been at feud with the Highlanders. When I was a girl about ten, there was a skirmish fought between a party of twenty of them, and my father and his servants, behind the Mains; and the bullets broke several panes in the north windows, they were so near. Three of the Highlanders were killed, and they brought them in, wrapped in their plaids, and laid them on the stone floor of the hall; and next morning their wives and daughters came, clapping their hands, and crying the coronach and shrieking, and carried away the dead bodies, with the pipes playing before them. I could not sleep for six weeks without starting, and thinking I heard these terrible cries, and saw the bodies lying on the steps, all stiff and swathed up in their bloody tartans. But since that time there came a party from the garrison at Stirling, with a warrant from the Lord Justice Clerk, or some such great man, and took away all our arms; and now, how are we to protect ourselves if they come down in any strength?"

Waverley could not help starting at a story which bore so much resemblance to one of his own day-dreams. Here was a girl scarce seventeen, the gentlest of her sex, both in temper and appearance, who had witnessed with her own eyes such a scene as he had used to conjure up in his imagination, as only occurring in ancient times. He felt at once the impulse of curiosity, and that slight sense of danger which only serves to heighten its interest. He might have said with Malvolio, "'I do not now fool myself, to let imagination jade me.' I am actually in the land of military and romantic adventures, and it only remains to be seen what will be my own share in them."

The whole circumstances now detailed concerning the state of the country, seemed equally novel and extraordinary. He had indeed often heard of Highland thieves, but had no idea of the systematic mode in which their depredations were conducted; and that the practice was connived at, and even encouraged, by many of the Highland chieftains, who not only found these *creaghs*, or forays, useful for the purpose of training individuals of their clans to the practice of arms, but also of maintaining a wholesome terror among their Lowland neighbours, and levying, as we have seen, a tribute from them, under colour of protection-money.

Baillie Macwheeble, who soon afterwards entered, expatiated still more at length upon the same topic. This honest gentleman's conversation was so formed upon his professional practice, that Davie Gellatley once said his discourse was like a "charge of horning." He assured our hero, that "from the maist ancient times of record, the lawless thieves, *limmers*, and broken men of the Highlands, had been in fellowship together, by reason of their surnames, for the committing of divers thefts, *reifs*, and *herships* upon the honest men of the low country, when they not only intromitted with their whole goods and gear, corn, cattle, horse, nolt, sheep, outsight and insight plenishing, at their wicked pleasure, but moreover made prisoners, ransomed them, or concussed them into giving borrows (pledges,) to enter into captivity again: All which was directly prohibited in divers parts of the Statute Book, both by the act one thousand five hundred and sixty-seven, and various others; the whilk statutes, with all that had followed and might follow thereupon, were shamefully broken and vilipended by the said sorners, limmers, and broken men, associated into fellowships for the aforesaid purposes of theft, stouth-reef, fire-raising, murther, *raptus mulierum*, or forcible abduction of women, and such like as aforesaid."

It seemed like a dream to Waverley that these deeds of violence should be familiar to men's minds, and currently talked of, as falling within the common order of things, and happening daily in the imme-diate neighbourhood, without his having crossed the seas, and while he was yet in the otherwise well-ordered island of Great Britain.

Chapter Sixteen

AN UNEXPECTED ALLY APPEARS

THE BARON returned at the dinner hour, and had in a great measure recovered his composure and good humour. He not only confirmed the stories which Edward had heard from Rose and Baillie Mac-wheeble, but added many anecdotes from his own experience, con-cerning the state of the Highlands and their inhabitants. The chiefs, he pronounced to be, in general, gentlemen of great honour and high pedigree, whose word was accounted as a law by all those of their own sept or clan. "It did not indeed," he said, "become them, as had occurred in late instances, to propone their *prosapia*, a lineage which rested for the most part on the vain and fond rhimes of their *Sean-nachies* or *Bhairds*, as æquiponderant with the evidence of ancient charters and royal grants of antiquity, conferred upon distinguished houses in the low country by divers Scotish monarchs; nevertheless, such was their *outrecuidance* and presumption, as to undervalue those who possessed such evidents, as if they held their lands in a sheep's skin."

This, by the way, pretty well explained the cause of quarrel between the Baron and his Highland ally. But he went on to state so many curious particulars concerning the manners, customs, and habits, of this patriarchal race, that Edward's curiosity became highly interested, and he enquired whether it were possible to make with safety an excursion into the neighbouring Highlands, whose dusky barrier of mountains had already excited his wish to penetrate beyond them. The Baron assured his guest that nothing would be more easy, provid-ing this quarrel were first made up, since he could himself give him letters to many of the distinguished chiefs, who would receive him with the utmost courtesy and hospitality.

While they were on this topic, the door suddenly opened, and, ushered by Saunders Saunderson, a Highlander, fully armed and equipped, entered the apartment. Had it not been that Saunders acted the part of master of the ceremonies to this martial apparition, without appearing to deviate from his usual composure, and that neither Mr Bradwardine nor Rose exhibited any emotion, Edward would certainly have thought the intrusion hostile. As it was, he started at the sight of what he had not yet happened to see, a mountaineer in his full national costume. The individual Gael was a stout dark man of low stature, the ample folds of whose plaid added to the appearance of strength which his person exhibited. The short kilt, or petticoat, showed his sinewy and clean-made limbs; the goat-skin purse, flanked by the usual defences, a dirk and steel-wrought pistol, hung before him; his bonnet had a short feather, which indicated his claim to be treated as a Duinhé-Wassell, or sort of gentleman; a broad sword dangled by his side, a target hung upon his shoulder, and a long Spanish fowling-piece occupied one of his hands. With the other hand he pulled off his bonnet, and the Baron, who well knew their customs, and the proper mode of addressing them, immediately said, with an air of dignity, but without rising, and much, as Edward thought, in the manner of a prince receiving an embassy, "Welcome, Evan Dhu Maccombich, what news from Fergus Mac-Ivor Vich Ian Vohr?"

"Fergus Mac-Ivor Vich Ian Vohr," said the ambassador, in good English, "greets you well, Baron of Bradwardine and Tully-Veolan, and is sorry there has been a thick cloud interposed between you and him, which has kept you from seeing and considering the friendship and alliances that have been between your houses and forbears of old; and he prays you that the cloud may pass away, and that things may be as they have been heretofore between the clan Ivor and the house of Bradwardine, when there was an egg between them for a flint, and a knife for a sword. And he expects you will also say, you are sorry for the cloud, and no man shall hereafter ask whether it descended from the hill to the valley, or rose from the valley to the hill; for they never struck with the scabbard who did not receive with the sword, and woe to him who would lose his friend for the stormy cloud of a spring morning."

To this the Baron of Bradwardine answered with suitable dignity, that he knew the chief of clan Ivor to be a well-wisher to the *King*, and he was sorry there should have been a cloud between him and any gentleman of such sound principles, "for when folks are banding together, feeble is he who hath no brother."

This appearing perfectly satisfactory, that the peace between these august persons might be duly solemnized, the Baron ordered a stoup of usquebaugh, and, filling a glass, drank to the health and prosperity of Mac-Ivor of Glennaquoich; upon which the Celtic ambassador, to requite his politeness, turned down a mighty bumper of the same generous liquor, seasoned with his good wishes to the house of Bradwardine.

Having thus ratified the preliminaries of the general treaty of pacification, the envoy retired to adjust with Mr Macwheeble some subordinate articles, with which it was not thought necessary to trouble the Baron. These probably referred to the discontinuance of the subsidy, and apparently the Baillie found means to satisfy their ally without suffering his master to suppose that his dignity was compromised. At least, it is certain, that after the plenipotentiaries had drunk a bottle of brandy in single drams, which seemed to have no more effect upon such seasoned vessels, than if it had been poured upon the two bears at the top of the avenue, Evan Dhu Maccombich having possessed himself of all the information which he could procure respecting the robbery of the preceding night, declared his intention to set off immediately in pursuit of the cattle, which he pronounced to be "no that far off;—they have broken the bone," he observed, "but have had no time to suck the marrow."

Our hero, who had attended Evan Dhu during his perquisitions, was much struck with the ingenuity which he displayed in collecting information, and the precise and pointed conclusions which he drew from it. Evan Dhu, on his part, was obviously flattered with the attention of Waverley, the interest he seemed to take in his enquiries, and his curiosity about the customs and scenery of the Highlands. Without much ceremony he invited Edward to accompany him on a short walk of ten or fifteen miles into the mountains, and see the place where the cattle were conveyed to; adding, "If it be as I suppose, you never saw such a place in your life, nor ever will, unless you go with me or the like of me."

Our hero, feeling his curiosity considerably excited by the idea of visiting the den of a Highland Cacus, took however the precaution to enquire if his guide might be trusted. He was assured, that the invitation would on no account have been given had there been the least danger, and that all he had to apprehend was a little fatigue; and as Evan proposed he should pass a day at his chieftain's house in returning, where he would be sure of good accommodation and an excellent welcome, there seemed nothing very formidable in the task he undertook. Rose, indeed, turned pale when she heard of it; but her father, who loved the spirited curiosity of his young friend, did not attempt to damp it by an alarm of danger which really did not exist, and a knapsack, with a few necessaries, being bound on the shoulders of a sort of deputy gamekeeper, our hero set forth with a fowling-piece in his hand, accompanied by his new friend Evan Dhu, and followed by the gamekeeper aforesaid, and by two wild Highlanders, the attendants of Evan, one of whom had upon his shoulder a hatchet at the end of a pole, called a Lochaber axe, and the other a long ducking gun. Evan, upon Edward's enquiry, gave him to understand, that this martial escort was by no means necessary as a guard, but merely, as he said, drawing up and adjusting his plaid with an air of dignity, that he might appear decently at Tully-Veolan, and as Vich Ian Vohr's foster-brother ought to do. "Ah! if you Saxon Duinhé-wassal (English gentleman) saw but the chief himself with his tail on!"

"With his tail on?" echoed Edward in some surprise.

"Yes—that is, with all his usual followers, when he visits those of the same rank. There is," he continued, stopping and drawing himself proudly up, while he counted upon his fingers the several officers of his chief's retinue; "there is his *hanchman*, or right-hand man, then his *bhaird*, or poet; then his *bladier*, or orator, to make harangues to the great folks whom he visits; then his *gilly-more*, or armour-bearer, to carry his sword, and target, and his gun; then his *gilly-casflue*, who carries him on his back through the sikes and brooks; then his *gilly-comstraine*, to lead his horse by the bridle in steep and difficult paths; then his *gillie-trusharnish*, to carry his knap-sack; and the piper and the piper's man, and it may be a dozen young lads beside, that have no business, but are just boys of the belt to follow the laird, and do his honour's bidding."

"And does your Chief regularly maintain all these men?"

"All these? aye, and many a fair head beside, that would not ken where to lay itself, but for the mickle barn at Glennaquoich."

With similar tales of the grandeur of the chief in peace and war, Evan Dhu beguiled the way till they approached more closely those huge mountains which Edward had hitherto only seen at a distance. It was towards evening as they entered one of the tremendous passes which afford communication between the high and low country; the path, which was extremely steep and rugged, winded up a chasm between two tremendous rocks, following the passage which a foaming stream, that brawled far below, appeared to have worn for itself in the course of ages. A few slanting beams of the sun, which was now setting, reached the water in its darksome bed, and shewed it partially, chafed by an hundred rocks, and broken by an hundred falls. The descent from the path to the stream was a mere precipice, with here and there a projecting fragment of granite, or a scathed tree, which had warped its twisted roots into the fissures of the rock. On the right hand, the mountain rose above the path with almost equal inaccessibility; but the hill on the opposite side displayed a shroud of copsewood, with which some pines were intermingled.

"This," said Evan, "is the pass of Bally-Brough, which was kept in former times by ten of the clan Donnochie against a hundred of the low country carls. The graves of the slain are still to be seen in that little corri, or bottom, on the opposite side of the burn—if your eyes are good you may see the green specks among the heather.—See, there is an earn, which you southrons call an eagle—you have no such birds as that in England—he is going to fetch his supper from the Laird of Bradwardine's braes, but I'll send a slug after him."

He fired his piece accordingly, but missed the superb monarch of the feathered tribes, who, without noticing the attempt to annoy him, continued his majestic flight to the southward. A thousand birds of prey, hawks, kites, carrion crows, and ravens, disturbed from the lodgings which they had just taken up for the evening, rose at the report of the gun, and mingled their hoarse and discordant notes with the echoes which replied to it, and with the roar of the mountain cataracts. Evan, a little disconcerted at having missed his mark, when he meant to have displayed peculiar dexterity, covered his confusion by whistling part of a pibroch as he reloaded his piece, and proceeded in silence up the pass.

It issued in a narrow glen, between two mountains, both very lofty and covered with heath. The brook continued to be their companion, and they advanced up its mazes, crossing them occasionally, on which occasions Evan Dhu uniformly offered the assistance of his attendants to carry over Edward; but our hero, who had been always a tolerable pedestrian, declined the accommodation, and obviously rose in his guide's opinion, by shewing that he did not fear wetting his feet. Indeed he was anxious, so far as he could without affectation, to remove the opinion which Evan seemed to entertain of the effeminacy of the Lowlanders, and particularly of the English.

Through the gorge of this glen they found access to a black bog, of tremendous extent, full of large pit-holes, which they traversed with great difficulty and some danger, by tracks which no one but a High-lander could have followed. The path itself, or rather the portion of more solid ground on which the travellers half walked, half waded, was rough, broken, and in many places quaggy and unsound. Some-times the ground was so completely unsafe, that it was necessary to spring from one hillock to another, the space between being incapable of bearing the human weight. This was an easy matter to the High-landers, who wore thin-soled brogues fit for the purpose, and moved with a peculiar springing step; but Edward began to find the exercise, to which he was unaccustomed, more fatiguing than he expected. The lingering twilight served to shew them through this Serbonian bog, but deserted them almost totally at the bottom of a steep and very stony hill, which it was the travellers' next toilsome task to ascend. The night, however, was pleasant, and not dark; and Waverley, calling up mental energy to support personal fatigue, held on his march gallantly, though envying in his heart his Highland attendants, who continued, without a symptom of abated vigour, the rapid and swinging pace, or rather trot, which, according to his computation, had already brought them fifteen miles upon their journey.

After crossing the mountain, and descending on the other side towards a black wood, Evan Dhu held some conference with his Highland attendants, in consequence of which Edward's baggage was shifted from the shoulders of the gamekeeper to that of one of the *gillies*, and the former was sent off with the other mountaineer in a direction different from that of the three remaining travellers. On asking the meaning of this separation, Waverley was told that the Lowlander must go to a hamlet about three miles off for the night; for unless it was some very particular friend, Donald Bean Lean, the worthy person whom they supposed to be possessed of the cattle, did not much approve of strangers approaching his retreat. This seemed reasonable, and silenced a qualm of suspicion which came across Edward's mind, when he saw himself, at such a place and such an hour, deprived of his only Lowland companion. And Evan immediately afterwards added, "that indeed he himself had better get forward, and announce their approach to Donald Bean Lean, as the arrival of a *sidier roy* (red soldier) might otherwise be a disagreeable surprise." And without waiting for an answer, in jockey phrase, he trotted out, and putting himself to a very round pace, was out of sight in an instant.

Waverley was now left to his own meditations, for his attendant with the battle-axe spoke very little English. They were traversing a thick, and, as it seemed, an endless wood of pines, and consequently the path was altogether undiscernible in the murky darkness which surrounded them. The Highlander, however, seemed to trace it by instinct, without the hesitation of a moment, and Edward followed his footsteps as close as he could.

After journeying a considerable time in silence, he could not help asking, "Was it far to the end of their journey?"

"Ta cove was tree, four mile; but as Duinhé-wassal was a wee taiglit, Donald could, tat is, might—would—should send ta curragh."

This conveyed no information. The *curragh* which was promised might be a man, a horse, a cart, or chaise; and no more could be got from the man with the battle-axe but a repetition of "Aich aye! ta curragh."

But in a short time Edward began to conceive his meaning, when, issuing from the wood, he found himself on the banks of a large river or lake, where his conductor gave him to understand they must sit down for a little while. The moon, which now began to rise, shewed obscurely the expanse of water which spread before them, and the shapeless and indistinct forms of mountains, with which it seemed to be surrounded. The cool, and yet mild air of the summer night, refreshed Waverley after his rapid and toilsome walk; and the perfume which it wafted from the birch trees, bathed in the evening dew, was exquisitely fragrant.

He had now time to give himself up to the full romance of his situation. Here he sate on the banks of an unknown lake, under the guidance of a wild native, whose language was unknown to him, on a visit to the den of some renowned outlaw, a second Robin Hood perhaps, or Adam o' Gordon, and that at deep midnight, through scenes of difficulty and toil, separated from his attendant, left by his guide:—what a fund of circumstances for the exercise of a romantic imagination, and all enhanced by the solemn feeling of uncertainty at least, if not of danger! The only circumstance which assorted ill with the rest was the cause of his journey—the Baron's milk cows! this degrading incident he kept in the back-ground.

While wrapt in these dreams of imagination, his companion gently touched him, and, pointing in a direction nearly straight across the lake, said, "Yon's ta cove." A small point of light was seen to twinkle in the direction in which he pointed, and, gradually increasing in size and lustre, seemed to flicker like a meteor upon the verge of the horizon. While Edward watched this phenomenon, the distant dash of oars was heard. The measured splash arrived near and more near, and presently a loud whistle was heard in the same direction. His friend with the battle-axe immediately whistled clear and shrill, in reply to the signal, and a boat, manned with four or five Highlanders, pushed for a little inlet, near which Edward was seated. He advanced to meet them with his attendant, was immediately assisted into the boat by the officious attention of two stout mountaineers, and had no sooner seated himself than they resumed their oars, and began to row across the lake with great rapidity.

Chapter Seventeen

THE HOLD OF A HIGHLAND ROBBER

THE PARTY preserved silence, interrupted only by the monotonous and murmured chaunt of a Gaelic song, sung in a kind of low recitative by the steersman, and by the dash of the oars, which the notes seemed to regulate, as they dipped to them in cadence. The light, which they now approached more nearly, assumed a broader, redder, and more irregular splendour. It appeared plainly to be a large fire, but whether kindled upon an island or the main-land, Edward could not determine. As he saw it, the red glaring orb seemed to rest on the very surface of the lake itself, and resembled the fiery vehicle in which the Evil Genius of an oriental tale traverses land and sea. They approached nearer, and the light of the fire sufficed to shew that it was kindled at the bottom of a huge dark crag or rock, rising abruptly from the very edge of the water; its front, changed by the reflection to dusky red, formed a strange, and even awful contrast to the banks around, which were from time to time faintly and partially enlightened by pallid moonlight.

The boat now neared the shore, and Edward could discover that this large fire, amply supplied with branches of pine-wood by two figures, who, in the red reflection of its light, appeared like demons, was kindled in the jaws of a lofty cavern, into which an inlet from the lake seemed to advance; and he conjectured, which was indeed true, that the fire had been lighted as a beacon to the boatmen on their return. They rowed right for the mouth of the cave, and then shipping their oars, permitted the boat to enter with the impulse which it had received. The skiff passed the little point, or platform, of rock on which the fire was blazing, and running about two boats' length farther, stopped where the cavern, for it was already arched overhead, ascended from the water by five or six broad ledges of rock, so easy and regular that they might be termed natural steps. At this moment a quantity of water was suddenly flung upon the fire, which sunk with a hissing noise, and with it disappeared the light it had hitherto afforded. Four or five active arms lifted Waverley out of the boat, placed him on his feet, and almost carried him into the recesses of the cave. He made a few paces in darkness, guided in this manner; and advancing towards a hum of voices, which seemed to sound from the centre of the rock, at an acute turn Donald Bean Lean and his whole establishment were before his eyes.

The interior of the cave, which here rose very high, was illuminated by torches made of pine-tree, which emitted a bright and bickering light, attended by a strong, though not unpleasant odour. Their light was assisted by the red glare of a large charcoal fire, round which were seated five or six armed Highlanders, while others were indistinctly seen couched on their plaids, in the more remote recesses of the cavern. In one large aperture, which the robber facetiously called his *spence* (or pantry,) there hung by the heels the carcases of a sheep or ewe, and two cows, lately slaughtered. The principal inhabitant of this singular mansion, attended by Evan Dhu as master of ceremonies, came forward to meet his guest, totally different in appearance and manner from what his imagination had anticipated. The profession which he followed—the wilderness in which he dwelt—the wild warrior forms that surrounded him, were all calculated to inspire terror. From such accompaniments, Waverley prepared himself to meet a stern, gigantic, ferocious figure, such as Salvator would have chosen to be the central object of a group of banditti.

Donald Bean Lean was the very reverse of all these. He was thin in person and low in stature, with light sandy-coloured hair and small pale features, from which he derived his agnomen of *Bean*, or white; and although his form was light, well proportioned, and active, he appeared, on the whole, rather a diminutive and insignificant figure. He had served in some inferior capacity in the French army, and in order to receive his English visitor in great form, and probably meaning, in his way, to pay him a compliment, he had laid aside the Highland dress for the time, to put on an old blue and red uniform, and a feathered hat, in which he was far from showing to advantage, and indeed looked so incongruous, compared with all around him, that Waverley would have been tempted to laugh, had laughter been either civil or safe. He received Captain Waverley with a profusion of French politeness and Scottish hospitality, seemed perfectly to know his name and connections, and to be particularly acquainted with his uncle's political principles. On these he bestowed great applause, to which Waverley judged it prudent to make a very general reply.

Being placed at a convenient distance from the charcoal fire, the heat of which the season rendered oppressive, a strapping Highland damsel placed before Waverley, Evan, and Donald Bean, three cogues, or wooden vessels, composed of staves and hoops, containing *inrigh*, a sort of strong soup made out of a particular part of the inside of the beeves. After this refreshment, which, though coarse, fatigue and hunger rendered palatable, steaks, roasted on the coals, were supplied in liberal abundance, and disappeared before Evan Dhu and their host with a promptitude that seemed like magic, and astonished Waverley, who was much puzzled to reconcile their voracity with what he had heard of the abstemiousness of the Highlanders. He was ignorant that this abstinence was with the lower ranks only compulsory, and that, like some animals of prey, those who practise it were usually gifted with the power of indemnifying themselves to good purpose, when chance threw plenty in their way. The whisky came forth in abundance to crown the cheer. The Highlanders drank it copiously and undiluted; but Edward, having mixed a little with water, did not find it so palatable as to invite him to repeat the draught. Their host bewailed himself exceedingly that he could offer him no wine: "Had he but known four-and-twenty hours before, he would have had some had it been within the circle of forty miles round him. But no gentleman could do more to shew his sense of the honour of a visit from another, than to offer him the best cheer his house afforded. Where there are no bushes there can be no nuts, and the way of those you live with is that you must follow."

He went on regretting to Evan Dhu the death of an aged man, Donnacha an Amrigh, or Duncan with the Cap, "a gifted seer," who foretold, through the second sight, visitors of every description who haunted their dwelling, whether as friends or foes.

"Is not his son Malcolm *taishatr* (a seer)?" asked Evan.

"Nothing equal to his father," replied Donald Bean. "He told us the other day we were to see a great gentleman riding on a horse, and there came nobody that whole day but Shemus Beg, the blind harper, with his dog. Another time he advertised us of a wedding, and behold it proved a funeral; and on the creagh, when he foretold to us we should bring home a hundred head of horned cattle, we gripped nothing but a fat baillie of Perth."

From this discourse he passed to the political and military state of the country; and Waverley was astonished, and even alarmed, to find a person of this description so accurately acquainted with the strength of the various garrisons and regiments quartered north of the Tay. He even mentioned the exact number of recruits who had joined Waverley's troop from his uncle's estate, and observed they were *pretty men*, meaning not handsome, but stout warlike fellows. He put Waverley in mind of one or two minute circumstances which had happened at a general review of the regiment, which satisfied him that the robber had been an eye-witness of it; and Evan Dhu having by this time retired from the conversation, and wrapped himself up in his plaid to take some repose, Donald asked Edward in a very significant manner, whether he had nothing particular to say to him.

Waverley, surprised and somewhat startled at this question from such a character, answered he had no motive in visiting him but curiosity to see his extraordinary place of residence. Donald Bean Lean looked him steadily in the face for an instant, and then said, with a significant nod, "You might as well have confided in me; I am as much worthy of trust as either the Baron of Bradwardine or Vich Ian Vohr:—but you are equally welcome to my house."

Waverley felt an involuntary shudder creep over him at the mysterious language held by this outlawed and lawless bandit, which, in despite of his attempts to master it, deprived him of the power to ask the meaning of his insinuations. A heath pallet, with the flowers stuck uppermost, had been prepared for him in a recess of the cave, and here, covered with such spare plaids as could be mustered, he lay for some time watching the motions of the other inhabitants of the cavern. Small parties of two or three entered or left the place without any other ceremony than a few words in Gaelic to the principal outlaw, and when he fell asleep, to a tall Highlander who acted as his lieuten-ant, and seemed to keep watch during his repose. Those who entered, seemed to have returned from some excursion, of which they reported the success, and went without farther ceremony to the larder, where cutting with their dirks their rations from the carcases which were there suspended, they proceeded to broil and eat them at their own time and leisure. The liquor was under stricter regulation, being served out either by Donald himself, his lieutenant, or the strapping Highland girl aforesaid, who was the only female that appeared. The allowance of whisky, however, would have appeared prodigal to any but Highlanders, who, living entirely in the open air, and in a very moist climate, can consume great quantities of ardent spirits, without the usual baneful effects either upon the brain or constitution.

At length the fluctuating groupes began to swim before the eyes of our hero as they gradually closed; nor did he re-open them till the morning sun was high on the lake without, though there was but a faint and glimmering twilight in the recesses of Uaimh an Ri, or the King's cavern, as the abode of Donald Bean Lean was proudly denominated.

Chapter Eighteen

WAVERLEY PROCEEDS ON HIS JOURNEY

WHEN EDWARD had collected his scattered recollection, he was surprised to observe the cavern totally deserted. Having arisen and put his dress in some order, he looked more accurately around him, but all was still solitary. If it had not been for the decayed brands of the fire, now sunk into grey ashes, and the remnants of the festival, con-sisting of bones half burned and half gnawed, and an empty keg or two, there remained no traces of Donald and his band. When Waver-ley sallied forth to the entrance of the cave, he perceived that the point of rock, on which remained the mark of last night's beacon, was accessible by a small path, either natural, or roughly hewn in the rock, along the little inlet of water which ran a few yards up into the cavern, where, as in a wet-dock, the skiff which brought him there the night before, was still lying moored. When he reached the small projecting platform on which the beacon had been established, he would have believed his farther progress by land impossible, only that it was scarce probable that the inhabitants of the cavern had not some mode of issuing from it otherwise than by the lake. Accordingly, he soon observed one or two shelving steps, or ledges of rock, at the very extremity of the little platform; and making use of them as a staircase, he clambered by their means around the projecting shoulder of the crag on which the cavern opened, and, descending with some difficulty on the other side, he thus gained the wild and precipitous shores of a Highland loch, about four miles in length, and a mile and a half over, surrounded by heathy and savage mountains, on the crests of which the morning mist was still sleeping.

Looking back to the place from which he came, he could not help admiring the address which had adopted a retreat of such seclusion and secrecy. The rock, round the shoulder of which he had turned by a few imperceptible notches, that barely afforded place for the foot, seemed, in looking back upon it, a huge precipice, which barred all farther passage by the edge of the lake in that direction. There could be no possibility, the breadth of the lake considered, of descrying the entrance of the narrow and low-browed cave from the other side; so that unless the retreat had been sought for with boats upon the lake, or disclosed by treachery, it might be a safe and secret residence to its garrison so long as they were supplied with provisions. Having satisfied his curiosity in these particulars, Waverley looked around for Evan Dhu and his attendant, who, he rightly judged, would be at no great distance, whatever might have become of Donald Bean Lean and his party, whose mode of life was, of course, liable to sudden migrations of abode. Accordingly, at the distance of about half a mile, he beheld a Highlander (Evan apparently) angling in the lake, with another attending him, whom, from the weapon which he shouldered, he recognized for his friend with the battle-axe.

Much nearer to the mouth of the cave he heard the notes of a lively Gaelic song, guided by which, in a sunny recess, shaded by a glittering birch-tree, and carpeted with a bank of firm white sand, he found the damsel of the cavern, whose lay had already reached him, busy, to the best of her power, in arranging to advantage a morning repast of milk, eggs, barley bread, fresh butter, and honeycomb. The poor girl had made a circuit of four miles that morning in search of the eggs, of the meal which baked her cakes, and of the other materials of the breakfast, being all delicacies which she had to beg or borrow from distant cottagers. The followers of Donald Bean Lean used little food except the flesh of the animals which they drove away from the Lowlands; bread itself was a delicacy seldom thought of, because hard to be obtained, and all the domestic accommodations of milk,

poultry, butter, &c., were out of the question in this Scythian camp.
Yet it must not be omitted, that although Alice had occupied a part of
the morning in providing those accommodations for her guest which
the cavern did not afford, she had secured time also to arrange her
own person in her best trim. Her finery was very simple. A short
russet-coloured jacket, and a petticoat, of scanty longitude, was her
whole dress; but these were clean, and neatly arranged. A piece of
scarlet embroidered cloth, called the *snood*, confined her hair, which
fell over it in a profusion of rich dark curls. The scarlet plaid, which
formed part of her dress, was laid aside, that it might not impede her
activity in attending the stranger. I should forget Alice's proudest
ornament, were I to omit mentioning a pair of gold ear-rings, and a
golden rosary which her father (for she was the daughter of Donald
Bean Lean) had brought from France, the plunder probably of some
battle or storm.

Her form, though rather large for her years, was very well proportioned, and her demeanour had a natural and rustic grace, with nothing of the sheepishness of an ordinary peasant. The smiles, displaying
a row of teeth of exquisite whiteness, and the laughing eyes, with
which, in dumb show, she gave Waverley that morning greeting which
she wanted English words to express, might have been interpreted by
a coxcomb, or perhaps a young soldier, who, without being such, was
conscious of a handsome person, as meant to convey more than the
courtesy of a hostess. Nor do I take it upon me to say that the little wild
mountaineer would have welcomed any staid old gentleman advanced
in life, the Baron of Bradwardine, for example, with the cheerful pains
which she bestowed upon Edward's accommodation. She seemed
eager to place him by the meal which she had so sedulously arranged,
and to which she now added a few bunches of cran-berries, gathered
in an adjacent morass. Having had the satisfaction of seeing him
seated at his breakfast, she placed herself demurely upon a stone at a
few yards distance, and appeared to watch with great complacency for
some opportunity of serving him.

Evan and his attendant now returned slowly along the beach, the
latter bearing a large salmon-trout, the produce of the morning's
sport, together with the angling-rod, while Evan strolled forward with
an easy, self-satisfied, and important gait towards the spot where
Waverley was so agreeably employed at the breakfast-table. After
morning greetings had passed on both sides, and Evan, looking at
Waverley, had said something in Gaelic to Alice, which made her
laugh, yet colour up to the eyes, through a complexion well
embrowned by sun and wind, Evan intimated his commands that the
fish should be prepared for breakfast. A spark from the lock of his

pistol produced a light, and a few withered fir branches were quickly in flame, and as speedily reduced to hot embers, on which the trout was broiled in large slices. To crown the repast, Evan produced from the pocket of his short jerkin a large scallop shell, and from under the folds of his plaid, a ram's horn full of whisky. Of this he took a copious dram, observing, he had already taken his *morning* with Donald Bean Lean, before his departure; he offered the same cordial to Alice and to Edward, which they both declined. With the bounteous air of a lord, Evan then proffered the scallop to Dugald Mahony, his attendant, who, without waiting to be asked a second time, drank it off with great gusto. Evan then prepared to move towards the boat, inviting Waverley to attend him. Meanwhile Alice had made up in a small basket what she thought worth removing, and flinging her plaid around her, she advanced up to Edward, and, with the utmost simplicity, taking hold of his hand, offered her cheek to his salute, dropping, at the same time, her little courtesy. Evan, who was esteemed a wag among the mountain fair, advanced, as if to secure a similar favour, but Alice, snatching up her basket, escaped up the rocky bank as fleetly as a deer, and, turning round and laughing, called something out to him in Gaelic, which he answered in the same tone and language; then waving her hand to Edward, she resumed her road, and was soon lost among the thickets, though they continued for some time to hear her lively carrol, as she proceeded gaily on her solitary journey.

They now again entered the gorge of the cavern, and stepping into the boat, the Highlander pushed off, and taking advantage of the morning breeze, hoisted a clumsy sort of sail, while Evan assumed the helm, directing their course, as it appeared to Edward, rather higher up the lake than towards the place of his embarkation on the preceding night. As they glided along the silver mirror, Evan opened the conversation with a panegyrick upon Alice, who, he said, was both *canny* and *fendy;* and was, to the boot of all that, the best dancer of a strathspey in the whole strath. Edward assented to her praises so far as he understood them, yet could not help regretting that she was condemned to such a perilous and dismal life.

"Oich! for that," said Evan, "there is nothing in Perthshire that she need want, if she ask her father to fetch it, unless it is too hot or too heavy."

"But to be the daughter of a cattle-stealer,—a common thief!"

"Common thief!—No such thing; Donald Bean Lean never *lifted* less than a drove in his life."

"Do you call him an uncommon thief, then?"

"No—he that steals a cow from a poor widow, or a stirk from a cottar, is a thief; he that lifts a drove from a Sasenach laird is a gentleman-drover. And, besides, to take a tree from the forest, a salmon from the river, a deer from the hill, or a cow from a Lowland strath, is what no Highlander need ever think shame upon."

"But what can this end in, were he taken in such an appropriation?"

"To be sure, he would *die for the law*, as many a pretty man has done before him."

"Die for the law!"

"Ay; that is, with the law, or by the law; be strapped up on the *kind* gallows of Crieff, where his father died, and his goodsire died, and where, I hope, he'll live to die himsell, if he's not shot, or slashed, in a creagh."

"You hope such a death for your friend, Evan?"

"And that do I e'en; would you have me wish him to die on a bundle of wet straw in yon den of his, like a mangy tyke?"

"But what becomes of Alice, then?"

"Troth, if such an accident were to happen, as her father would not need her help any longer, I ken nought to hinder me to marry her mysell."

"Gallantly resolved," said Edward;—"but, in the meanwhile, Evan, what has your father-in-law (that shall be, if he have the good fortune to be hanged) done with the Baron's cattle?"

"Oich," answered Evan, "they were all trudging before your lad and Allan Kennedy, before the sun blinked ower Ben-Lawers this morning; and they'll be in the pass of Bally-Brough by this time, in their way back to the parks of Tully-Veolan, all but two, that were unhappily slaughtered before I got last night to Uaimh an Ri."

"And where are we going, Evan, if I may be so bold as to ask?" said Waverley.

"Where would ye be ganging, but to the laird's own house of Glennaquoich? Ye would not think to be in his country without going to see him. It would be as much as a man's life's worth."

"And are we far from Glennaquoich?"

"But five bits of miles; and Vich Ian Vohr will meet us."

In about half an hour they reached the upper end of the lake, where, after landing Waverley, the two Highlanders drew the boat into a little creek among thick flags and reeds, where it lay perfectly concealed. The oars they put in another place of concealment, both for the use of Donald Bean Lean probably, when his occasions should next bring him to that place.

The travellers followed for some time a delightful opening into the hills, down which a little brook found its way to the lake. When they had pursued their walk a short distance, Waverley renewed his questions about their host of the cavern.

"Does he always reside in that cave?"

"Out, no! it's past the skill of man to tell where he's to be found at all times: there's not a dern nook, or cove, or corri, in the whole country, that he's not acquainted with."

"And do others beside your master shelter him?"

"My master?—*My* master is in Heaven," answered Evan, haughtily; and then immediately assuming his usual civility of manner, "but you mean my chief; now he does not shelter Donald Bean Lean, nor any that are like him, he only allows him (with a smile) wood and water."

"No great boon, I should think, Evan, when both seem to be very plenty."

"Ah! but ye don't see through it. When I say wood and water, I mean the loch and the land; and I fancy Donald would be put till't if the laird were to look for him wi' threescore men in the wood of Kailychat yonder; and if our boats, with a score or two more, were to come down the loch to Uaimh an Ri, headed by mysell, or any other pretty man."

"But suppose a strong party came against him from the low country, would not your chief defend him?"

"Na, he would not ware the spark of a flint for him if they came with the law."

"And what must Donald do, then?"

"He behoved to rid this country of himsell, and fall back, it may be, over the mount upon Letter-Scriven."

"And if he were pursued to that place?"

"I'se warrant he would go to his cousin's at Rannoch."

"Well, but if they followed him to Rannoch?"

"That," quoth Evan, "is beyond all belief; and, indeed, to tell you the truth, there durst not a Lowlander in all Scotland follow the fray a gun-shot beyond Bally-Brough, unless he had the help of the *Sidier Dhu*."

"Whom do you call so?"

"The *Sidier Dhu?* the black soldier; that is what they called the independent companies that were raised to keep peace and law in the Highlands. Vich Ian Vohr commanded one of them for five years, and I was a serjeant mysell, I shall warrant ye. They call them *Sidier Dhu*, because they wear the tartans, as they call your men,—King George's men,—*Sidier Roy*, or red soldiers."

"Well, but when you were in King George's pay, Evan, you were surely King George's soldiers?"

"Troth, and you must ask Vich Ian Vohr about that; for we are for his king, and care not much which o' them it is. At any rate, nobody can say we are King George's men now, when we have not seen his pay this twelvemonth."

This last argument admitted of no reply, nor did Edward attempt any: he rather chose to bring back the discourse to Donald Bean Lean. "Does Donald confine himself to cattle, or does he *lift*, as you call it, any thing else that comes in his way?"

"Troth he's nae nice body, and he'll just take any thing, but most readily cattle, horse, or live Christians; for sheep are slow of travel, and inside plenishing is cumberous to carry, and not easy to put away for silver in this country."

"But does he carry off men and women?"

"Out aye. Did not ye hear him speak o' the Perth baillie? It cost him five hundred marks ere he got to the south o' Bally-Brough. And ance Donald played a pretty sport. There was to be a blythe bridal between the Lady Cramfeezer, in the howe o' the Mearns, (she was the auld laird's widow, and not so young as she had been hersell,) and young Gilliewhackit, who had spent his heirship and moveables, like a gentleman, at cock-matches, bull-baitings, horse-races, and the like. Now, Donald Bean Lean, being aware that the bridegroom was in request, and wanting to cleik the cunzie, (that is, to hook the silver,) he cannily carried off Gilliewhackit one night when he was riding *dovering* hame, (with the malt rather above the meal,) and with the help of his gillies he gat him into the hills with the speed of light, and the first place he wakened in was the cove of Uaimh an Ri. So there was old to do about ransoming the bridegroom; for Donald would not lower a farthing of a thousand pounds"——

"The devil!"

"Punds Scottish, ye shall understand. And the lady had not the silver if she had pawned her gown; and they applied to the governor o' Stirling castle, and to the major o' the Black Watch; and the governor said, it was too far to the northward, and out of his district; and the major said, his men were gane hame to the shearing, and he would not call them out before the victual was got in for all the Cramfeezers in Christendom, let alone the Mearns, for that it would prejudice the country. And in the meanwhile ye'll not hinder Gilliewhackit to take the small-pox. There was not the doctor in Perth or Stirling would look near the poor lad, and I cannot blame them; for Donald had been misgugled by one of these doctors about Paris, and he swore he would fling the first into the loch that he catched beyond the Pass. However, some cailliachs (that is, old women,) that were about Donald's hand, nursed Gilliewhackit so well, that between the free open air in the cove and the fresh whey, deil an he did not recover may be as well as if he had been closed in a glazed chamber and a bed with curtains, and fed with red wine and white meat. And Donald was so vexed about it, that when he was stout and well, he even sent him free hame, and said he would be pleased with any thing they would chuse to give him for the plague and trouble which he had about Gilliewhackit to an unkenn'd degree. And I cannot tell you precisely how they sorted; but they agreed so well that Donald was invited to dance at the wedding in his Highland trews, and they said there was never sae meikle silver clinked in his purse either before or since. And to the boot of all that, Gilliewhackit said, that, be the evidence what it liked, if he had the luck to be on Donald's inquest, he would bring him in guilty of nothing whatever, unless it were wilful arson, or murder under trust."

With such bald and disjointed chat Evan went on illustrating the existing state of the Highlands, more perhaps to the amusement of Waverley than that of our readers. At length, after having marched over bank and brae, moss and heather, Edward, though not unacquainted with the Scottish liberality in computing distance, began to think that Evan's five miles were nearly doubled. His observation on the large measure which the Scottish allowed of their land, in comparison to the computation of their money, was readily answered by Evan, with the old jest, "The deil take them who have the least pint stoup."

And now the report of a gun was heard, and a sportsman was seen, with his dogs and attendant, at the upper end of the glen. "Shogh," said Dugald Mahony, "tat's ta Chief."

"It is not," said Evan, imperiously. "Do ye think he would come to meet a Sasenach duinhé-wassel (English gentleman) in such a way as that?"

But as they approached a little nearer, he said, with an appearance of mortification, "And it is even he sure enough, and he has not his tail on after all;—there is no living creature with him but Callum Beg."

In fact, Fergus Mac-Ivor, of whom a Frenchman might have said, as truly as of any man in the Highlands, "*Qu'il connoit bien ses gens,*" had no idea of raising himself in the eyes of an English young man of fortune, by appearing with a retinue of idle Highlanders disproportioned to the occasion. He was well aware that such an unnecessary attendance would seem to Edward rather ludicrous than respectable; and while few men were more attached to ideas of chieftainship and feudal power, he was, for that very reason, cautious of exhibiting external marks of dignity, unless at the time and in the manner when they were most likely to produce an imposing effect. Therefore, although, had he been to receive a brother chieftain, he would probably have been attended by all that retinue which Evan had described with so much unction, he judged it more respectable to advance to meet Waverley with a single attendant, a very handsome Highland boy, who carried his master's shooting-pouch and his broad-sword, without which he seldom went abroad.

When Fergus and Waverley met, the latter was struck with the peculiar grace and dignity of the chieftain's figure. Above the middle size, and finely proportioned, the Highland dress, which he wore in its simplest mode, set off his person to great advantage. He wore the trews, or close trowsers, made of tartan, checked scarlet and white; in other particulars, his dress strictly resembled Evan's, excepting that he had no weapon save a dirk, very richly mounted with silver. His page, as we have said, carried his claymore, and the fowling-piece, which he held in his hand, seemed only designed for sport. He had shot in the course of his walk some young wild-ducks, as, though *close-time* was then unknown, the broods of grouse were yet too young for the sportsman. His countenance was decidedly Scotch, with all the peculiarities of the northern physiognomy, but had yet so little of its harshness and exaggeration, that it would have been pronounced in any country extremely handsome. The martial air of the bonnet, with a single eagle's feather as a distinction, added much to the manly appearance of his head, which was besides ornamented with a far more natural and graceful cluster of close black curls than ever were exposed to sale in Bond-Street.

An air of openness and affability increased the favourable impression derived from this handsome and dignified exterior. Yet a skilful physiognomist would have been less satisfied with the countenance on the second than on the first view. The eye-brow and upper-lip bespoke something of the habit of peremptory command and decisive superiority. Even his courtesy, though open, frank, and unconstrained, seemed to indicate a sense of personal importance; and upon any check or accidental excitation, a sudden, though transient lour of the eye, shewed a hasty, haughty, and vindictive temper, not less to be dreaded because it seemed much under its owner's command. In short, the countenance of the chieftain resembled a smiling summer's day, in which, notwithstanding, we are made sensible by certain, though slight signs, that it may thunder and lighten before the close of evening.

It was not, however, upon their first meeting that Edward had an opportunity of making these less favourable remarks. The Chief received him, as a friend of the Baron of Bradwardine, with the utmost expression of kindness and obligation for the visit; upbraided him gently with chusing so rude an abode as he had done the night before; and entered into a lively conversation with him about Donald Bean's housekeeping, but without the least hint as to his predatory habits, or the immediate occasion of Waverley's visit, a topic which, as the Chief did not introduce it, our hero also avoided. While they walked merrily on towards the house of Glennaquoich, Evan, who now fell respectfully into the rear, followed with Callum Beg and Dugald Mahony.

We will take the opportunity to introduce the reader to some particulars of Fergus Mac-Ivor's character and history, which were not completely known to Waverley till after a connection which, though arising from a circumstance so casual, had for a length of time the deepest influence upon his character, actions, and prospects. But this, being an important subject, must form the commencement of a new chapter.

Chapter Nineteen

THE CHIEF AND HIS MANSION

THE INGENIOUS licentiate Francisco de Ubeda, when he commenced his history of La Picara Justina Diez,—which, by the way, is one of the most rare books of Spanish literature,—complained of his pen having caught up a hair, and forthwith begins, with more eloquence than common sense, an affectionate expostulation with that useful implement, upbraiding it with being the quill of a goose,—a bird inconstant by nature, as frequenting the three elements of water, earth, and air indifferently, and being, of course, "to one thing constant never." Now I protest to thee, gentle reader, that I entirely dissent from Francisco de Ubeda in this matter, and hold it the most useful quality of my pen, that it can speedily change from grave to gay, and from description and dialogue to narrative and character. So that if my quill displays no other properties of its mother-goose than her mutability, truly I shall be well pleased; and I conceive that you, my worthy friend, will have no occasion for discontent. From the jargon, therefore, of the Highland gillies, I pass to the character of their Chief. It is an important examination, and therefore, like Dogberry, we must spare no wisdom.

The ancestor of Fergus Mac-Ivor, about three centuries before, had set up a claim to be recognized as chieftain of the numerous and powerful clan to which he belonged, the name of which it is unnecessary to mention. Being defeated by an opponent who had more justice, or at least more force, on his side, he moved southwards, with those who adhered to him, in quest of new settlements, like a second Æneas. The state of the Perthshire Highlands favoured his purpose. A great baron in that country had lately become traitor to the crown; Ian, which was the name of our adventurer, united himself with those who were commissioned by the king to chastise him, and did such good service that he obtained a grant of the property, upon which he and his posterity afterwards resided. He followed the king also in war to the fertile regions of England, where he employed his leisure hours so actively in raising subsidies among the boors of Northumberland and Durham, that upon his return he was enabled to erect a stone tower, or fortalice, so much admired by his dependants and neighbours, that he, who had hitherto been called Ian Mac-Ivor, or John the son of Ivor, was thereafter distinguished, both in song and genealogy, by the high title of *Ian nan Chaistel*, or John of the Tower. The descendants of this worthy were so proud of him, that the reigning chief always bore the patronymic title of Vich Ian Vohr, *i. e.* the son of John the Great; the clan at large, to distinguish them from that from which they had seceded, were denominated *Sliochd nan Ivor*, the race of Ivor.

The father of Fergus, the tenth in direct descent from John of the Tower, engaged heart and hand in the insurrection of 1715, and was forced to fly to France, after the attempt of that year in favour of the Stuarts had proved unsuccessful. More fortunate than other fugitives, he obtained employment in the French service, and married a lady of rank in that kingdom, by whom he had two children, Fergus and his sister Flora. The Scottish estate had been forfeited and exposed to sale, but was bought in for a small price in the name of the young proprietor, who in consequence came to reside upon his native domains. It was soon perceived that he was a character of uncommon acuteness, fire, and ambition, which, as he became acquainted with the state of the country, gradually assumed a mixed and peculiar tone, which could only have been acquired Sixty Years since.

Had Fergus Mac-Ivor lived Sixty Years sooner than he did, he would, in all probability, have wanted the polished manner and knowledge of the world which he now possessed; and had he lived Sixty Years later, his ambition and love of rule would have lacked the fuel which his situation now afforded. He was indeed, within his little circle, as perfect a politician as Castruccio Castrucani himself. He applied himself with great earnestness to appease all the feuds and dissensions which frequently arose among other clans in his neighbourhood, so that he became a frequent umpire in their quarrels. His own patriarchal power he strengthened at every expence which his fortune would permit, and indeed stretched his means to the uttermost to maintain the rude and plentiful hospitality, which was the most valued attribute of a chieftain. For the same reason, he crowded his estate with a tenantry, hardy indeed, and fit for the purposes of war, but greatly outnumbering what the soil was calculated to maintain.

These consisted chiefly of his own clan, not one of whom he suffered to quit his lands if he could possibly prevent it. But he maintained, besides, adventurers from the mother sept, who deserted a less war-like, though more wealthy chief, to do homage to Fergus Mac-Ivor. Other individuals, too, who had not even that apology, were neverthe-less received into his allegiance, which indeed was refused to none who were, like Poins, proper men of their hands, and were willing to assume the name of Mac-Ivor.

He was enabled to discipline these forces from having obtained command of one of the independent companies, raised by government to preserve the peace of the Highlands. While in this capacity, he acted with vigour and spirit, and preserved great order in the country under his charge. He caused his vassals to enter by rotation in his company, and serve for a certain space of time, which gave them all in turn a general notion of military discipline. In his campaigns against the banditti, it was observed that he assumed and exercised to the utmost the discretionary power, which, while the law had not free course in the Highlands, was conceived to belong to the military parties who were called in to support it. He acted, for example, with great and suspicious lenity to those freebooters who made restitution on his summons and offered personal submission to himself, while he rigorously pursued, apprehended, and sacrificed to justice, all such interlopers as dared to despise his admonitions or commands. On the other hand, if any officers of justice, military parties, or others, pre-sumed to pursue thieves or marauders through his territories, and without applying for his consent and concurrence, nothing was more certain than that they would meet with some notable foil or defeat; upon which occasions Fergus Mac-Ivor was the first to condole with them, and after gently blaming their rashness, never failed deeply to lament the lawless state of the country. These lamentations did not exclude suspicion, and matters were so represented to government, that our Chieftain was deprived of his military command.

Whatever he felt upon this occasion, he had the art of entirely suppressing every appearance of discontent; but in a short time the neighbouring country began to feel bad effects from his disgrace. Donald Bean Lean and others of his class, whose depredations had hitherto been confined to other districts, appear from henceforward to have made a settlement on this devoted border; and their ravages were carried on with little opposition, as the Lowland gentry were chiefly Jacobites, and disarmed. This forced many of the inhabitants into contracts of black-mail with Fergus Mac-Ivor, which not only established him their protector, and gave him great weight in all their consultations, but moreover supplied funds for the waste of his feudal hospitality, which the discontinuance of his pay might have otherwise essentially diminished.

In all this course of conduct, Fergus had a further object than merely being the great man of his neighbourhood, and ruling despotically over a small clan. From his infancy upward, he had devoted himself to the cause of the exiled family, and had persuaded himself, not only that their restoration to the crown of Britain would be speedy, but that those who assisted them would be raised to honour and rank. It was with this view that he laboured to reconcile the Highlanders among themselves, and augmented his own force to the utmost, to be prepared for the first favourable opportunity of rising. With this purpose also he conciliated the favour of such Lowland gentlemen in the vicinity as were friends to the good cause; and for the same reason, having incautiously quarrelled with Mr Bradwardine, who, notwithstanding his peculiarities, was much respected in the country, he took advantage of the foray of Donald Bean Lean to solder up the dispute in the manner we have mentioned. Some indeed surmised that he caused the enterprize to be suggested to Donald, on purpose to pave the way to a reconciliation, which, supposing that to be the case, cost the Laird of Bradwardine two good milch cows. This zeal in their behalf the house of Stuart repaid with a considerable share of their confidence, an occasional supply of louis-d'ors, abundance of fair words, and a parchment with a huge waxen seal appended, purporting to be an earl's patent, granted by no less a person than James the Third King of England, and Eighth King of Scotland, to his right feal, trusty, and well-beloved Fergus Mac-Ivor of Glennaquoich, in the county of Perth, and kingdom of Scotland.

With this future coronet glittering before his eyes, Fergus plunged deeply into the correspondences and plots of that unhappy period; and, like all such active agents, easily reconciled his conscience to going certain lengths in the service of his party, from which honour and pride would have deterred him had his sole object been the direct advancement of his own personal interest. With this insight into a bold, ambitious, ardent, yet artful and politic character, we resume the broken thread of our narrative.

The Chief and his guest had by this time reached the house of Glennaquoich, which consisted of Ian nan Chaistel's mansion, a high rude-looking square tower, with the addition of a *lofted* house, that is, a building of two stories, constructed by Fergus's grandfather when he returned from that memorable expedition, well remembered by the western shires, under the name of the Highland Host. Upon occasion of this crusade against the Ayrshire whigs and covenanters, the Vich Ian Vohr of the time had probably been as successful as his predecessor was in harrying Northumberland, and therefore left to his posterity a rival edifice, as a monument of his magnificence.

Around the house, which stood on an eminence in the midst of a narrow Highland valley, there appeared none of that attention to convenience, far less to ornament and decoration, which usually surrounds a gentleman's habitation. An inclosure or two, divided by dry stone walls, were the only part of the domain that was fenced; as to the rest, the narrow slips of level ground which lay by the side of the brook exhibited a scanty crop of barley, liable to constant depredations from the herds of wild ponies and black cattle that grazed upon the adjacent hills. These ever and anon made an incursion upon the arable ground, which was repelled by the loud, uncouth, and dissonant shouts of half a dozen Highland swains, all running as if they had been mad, and every one hallooing a half-starved dog to the rescue of the forage. At a little distance up the glen was a small and stunted wood of birch; the hills were high and heathy, but without any variety of surface; so that the whole view was wild and desolate, rather than grand and solitary. Yet such as it was, no genuine descendant of Ian nan Chaistel would have exchanged the domain for Stow or Blenheim.

There was a sight, however, before the gate, which perhaps would have afforded the first owner of Blenheim more pleasure than the finest view in the domain assigned to him by the gratitude of his country. This consisted of about an hundred Highlanders, in complete dress and arms; at sight of whom the Chieftain apologized to Waverley in a sort of negligent manner. "He had forgot," he said, "that he had ordered a few of his clan out, for the purpose of seeing that they were in a fit condition to protect the country, and prevent such accidents as, he was sorry to learn, had befallen the Baron of Bradwardine. Before they were dismissed, perhaps Captain Waverley might chuse to see them go through a part of their exercise."

Edward assented, and the men executed with agility and precision some of the ordinary military movements. They then practised individually at a mark, and shewed extraordinary dexterity in the management of the pistol and firelock. They took aim standing, sitting, leaning, or lying prostrate, as they were commanded, and always with effect upon the target. Next they paired off for the broad-sword exercise; and having manifested their individual skill and dexterity, united in two bodies, and exhibited a sort of mock encounter, in which the charge, the rally, the flight, the pursuit, and all the current of a heady fight, were exhibited to the sound of the great war bagpipe. On a signal made by the Chief, the skirmish was ended. Matches were then made for running, wrestling, leaping, pitching the bar, and other sports, in which this feudal militia displayed incredible swiftness, strength, and agility; and accomplished the purpose which their chieftain had at heart, by impressing on Waverley no light sense of their merit as soldiers, and of the power of him who commanded them by his nod.

"And what number of such gallant fellows have the happiness to call you leader?" asked Waverley.

"In a good cause, and under a chieftain whom they loved, the race of Ivor have seldom taken the field under five hundred claymores. But you are aware, Captain Waverley, that the disarming act, passed about twenty years ago, prevents their being in the complete state of preparation, as in former times; and I keep no more of my clan under arms than may defend my own or my friends' property, when the country is troubled with such men as your last night's landlord; and government, which has removed other means of defence, must connive at our protecting ourselves."

"But with your force you might soon destroy, or put down, such gangs as that of Donald Bean Lean."

"Yes, doubtless; and my reward would be a summons to deliver up to General Blakeney, at Stirling, the few broad-swords they have left us: there were little policy in that methinks.—But come, captain, the sound of the pipes informs me that dinner is prepared—Let me have the honour to shew you into my rude mansion."

Chapter Twenty

A HIGHLAND FEAST

ERE WAVERLEY entered the banquetting-hall, he was offered the patriarchal refreshment of a bath for the feet, which the sultry weather, and the morasses he had traversed, rendered highly acceptable. He was not indeed so luxuriously attended upon this occasion as the heroic travellers in the Odyssey; the task of ablution and abstersion being performed, not by a beautiful damsel trained

> To chafe the limbs and pour the fragrant oil,

but by a smoke-dried skinny old Highland woman, who did not seem to think herself much honoured by the duty imposed upon her, but muttered between her teeth, "Our fathers' herds did not feed so near together, that I should do you this service." A small donation, however, amply reconciled this ancient handmaiden to the supposed degradation; and, as Edward proceeded to the hall, she gave him her blessing, in the Gaelic proverb, "May the open hand be filled the fullest."

The hall, in which the feast was prepared, occupied all the first story of Ian nan Chaistel's original erection, and a huge oaken table extended through its whole length. The apparatus for dinner was simple, even to rudeness, and the company numerous, even to crowding. At the head of the table was the Chief himself, with Edward, and two or three Highland visitors of neighbouring clans; the elders of his own tribe, wadsetters and tacksmen, as they were called, who occupied portions of his estate as mortgagers or lessees, sat next in rank; beneath them, their sons and nephews, and foster-brethren; then the officers of the Chief's household, according to their order; and, lowest of all, the tenants who actually cultivated the ground. Even beyond this long perspective, Edward might see upon the green, to which a huge pair of folding doors opened, a multitude of Highlanders of a yet inferior description, who, nevertheless, were considered as guests, and had their share both of the countenance of the entertainer, and of the cheer of the day. In the distance, and fluctuating round this extreme verge of the banquet, was a changeful group of women, ragged boys and girls, beggars, young and old, large greyhounds, and terriers, and pointers, and curs of low degree; all of whom took some interest, more or less immediate, in the main action of the piece.

This hospitality, apparently unbounded, had yet its line of economy. Some pains had been bestowed in dressing the dishes of fish, game, &c., which were at the upper end of the table, and immediately under the eye of the English stranger. Lower down stood immense clumsy joints of mutton and beef, which, but for the absence of pork, abhorred in the Highlands, resembled the rude festivity of the banquet of Penelope's suitors. But the central dish was a yearling lamb, called "a hog in harst," roasted whole. It was set upon its legs, with a bunch of parsley in its mouth, and was probably exhibited in that form to gratify the pride of the cook, who piqued himself more on the plenty than the elegance of his master's table. The sides of this poor animal were fiercely attacked by the clans-men, some with dirks, others with the knives which were usually in the same sheath with the dagger, so that it was soon rendered a mangled and rueful spectacle. Lower down still, the victuals seemed of yet coarser quality, though sufficiently abundant. Broth, onions, cheese, and the fragments of the feast, regaled the sons of Ivor, who feasted in the open air.

The liquor was supplied in the same proportion, and under similar regulations. Excellent claret and champagne were liberally distributed among the Chief's immediate neighbours; whiskey, plain or diluted, and strong-beer, refreshed those who sat near the lower end. Nor did this inequality of distribution appear to give the least offence. Every one present understood that his taste was to be formed according to the rank which he held at table; and consequently the tacksmen and their dependants always professed the wine was too cold for their stomachs, and called, apparently out of choice, for the liquor which was assigned to them from economy. The bagpipers, three in number, screamed, during the whole time of dinner, a tremendous war-tune; and the echoing of the vaulted roof, and clang of the Celtic tongue, produced such a Babel of noises, that Waverley dreaded his ears would never recover it. Mac-Ivor, indeed, apologised for the confusion occasioned by so large a party, and pleaded the necessity of his situation, on which unlimited hospitality was imposed as a paramount duty. "These stout idle kinsmen of mine," he said, "account my estate as held in trust for their support; and I must find them beef and ale, while the rogues will do nothing for themselves but practise the broadsword, or wander about the hills shooting, fishing, hunting, drinking, and making love to the lasses of the strath. But what can I do, Captain Waverley? every thing will keep after its kind, whether it be a hawk or a Highlander." Edward made the expected answer, in a compliment upon his possessing so many bold and attached followers.

"Why, yes," replied the Chief, "were I disposed, like my father, to put myself in the way of getting one blow on the head, or two on the neck, I believe the loons would stand by me. But who thinks of that in the present day, when the maxim is,—'Better an old woman with a purse in her hand, than three men with belted brands.'" Then, turning to the company, he proposed the "Health of Captain Waverley, a worthy friend of his kind neighbour and ally, the Baron of Bradwardine."

"He is welcome hither," said one of the elders, "if he come from Cosmo Comyne Bradwardine."

"I say nay to that," said an old man, who apparently did not mean to pledge the toast. "I say nay to that;—while there is a green leaf in the forest, there will be fraud in a Comyne."

"There is nothing but honour in the Baron of Bradwardine," answered another ancient; "and the guest that comes hither from him should be welcome though he came with blood on his hand, unless it were blood of the race of Ivor."

The old man, whose cup remained full, replied, "There has been blood enough of the race of Ivor on the hand of Bradwardine."

"Ah! Ballenkeiroch," replied the first, "you think rather of the flash of the carbine at the Mains of Tully-Veolan, than the glance of the sword that fought for the cause at Proud Preston."

"And well I may," answered Ballenkeiroch, "the flash of the gun cost me a fair-haired son, and the glance of the sword has done but little for King James."

The Chieftain, in two words of French, explained to Waverley that the Baron had shot this old man's son in a fray near Tully-Veolan about seven years since; and then hastened to remove Ballen-keiroch's prejudice, by informing him that Waverley was an English-man, unconnected by birth or alliance with the family of Bradwardine; upon which the old gentleman raised the hitherto-untasted cup, and courteously drank to his health. This ceremony being requited in kind, the Chieftain made a signal for the pipes to cease, and said, aloud, "Where is the song hidden, my friends, that Mac-Murrough cannot find it?" Mac-Murrough, the family *bhairdh*, an aged man, immediately took the hint, and began to chaunt, with low and rapid utterance, a profusion of Celtic verses, which were received by the audience with all the applause of enthusiasm. As he advanced in his declamation, his ardour seemed to increase. He had at first spoken with his eyes fixed on the ground; he now cast them around as if beseeching, and anon as if commanding attention, and his tones rose into wild and impassioned notes, accompanied with appropriate ges-ture. He seemed to Edward, who attended to him with much interest, to recite many proper names, to lament the dead, to apostrophize the absent, to exhort and entreat and animate those who were present. Waverley thought he even discerned his own name, and was convinced his conjecture was right, from the eyes of the company being at that moment turned towards him simultaneously. The ardour of the poet appeared to communicate itself to the audience. Their wild and sun-burned countenances assumed a fiercer and more animated expres-sion; all bent forwards towards the reciter, many sprung up and waved their arms in ecstacy, and some laid their hands on their swords. When the song ceased, there was a deep pause, while the aroused feelings of the poet and of the hearers gradually subsided into their usual channel.

The Chieftain, who, during this scene, had appeared rather to watch the emotions which were excited, than to partake their high tone of enthusiasm, filled with claret a small silver cup which stood by him. "Give this," he said to an attendant, "to Mac-Murrough nan Fonn, (*i. e.* of the songs) and when he has drank the juice, bid him keep, for the sake of Vich Ian Vohr, the shell of the gourd which contained it." The gift was received by Mac-Murrough with profound gratitude; he drank the wine, and, kissing the cup, shrouded it with reverence in the plaid which was folded on his bosom. He then burst forth into what Edward justly supposed to be an extemporaneous effusion of thanks and praises of his chief. It was received with applause, but did not produce the effect of his first poem. It was obvious, however, that the clan regarded the generosity of their chief-tain with high approbation. Many approved Gaelic toasts were then proposed, of some of which the Chieftain gave his guest the following versions:

"To him that will not turn his back on friend or foe." "To him that never forsook a comrade." "To him that never bought or sold justice." "Hospitality to the exile, and broken bones to the tyrant." "The lads with the kilts." "Highlanders, shoulder to shoulder,"—with many other pithy sentiments of the like nature.

Edward was particularly solicitous to know the meaning of that song which appeared to produce such effect upon the passions of the company, and hinted his curiosity to his host. "As I observe," said the Chieftain, "that you have passed the bottle during the last three rounds, I was about to propose to you to retire to my sister's tea-table, who can explain these things to you better than I can. Although I cannot stint my clan in the usual current of their festivity, yet I neither am addicted myself to exceed in its amount, nor do I," added he, smiling, "keep a Bear to devour the intellects of such as can make good use of them."

Edward readily assented to this proposal, and the Chieftain, saying a few words to those around him, left the table, followed by Waverley. As the door closed behind them, Edward heard Vich Ian Vohr's health invoked with a wild and animated cheer, that expressed the satisfaction of the guests, and the depth of their devotion to his service.

Chapter Twenty-One

THE CHIEFTAIN'S SISTER

THE DRAWING-ROOM of Flora Mac-Ivor was furnished in the plainest and most simple manner; for at Glennaquoich every other sort of expenditure was retrenched as much as possible, for the purpose of maintaining, in its full dignity, the hospitality of the chieftain, and retaining and multiplying the number of his dependants and adherents. But there was no appearance of this parsimony in the dress of the lady herself, which was in texture elegant, and even rich, and arranged in a manner which partook partly of the Parisian fashion, and partly of the more simple dress of the Highlands, blended together with great taste. Her hair was not disfigured by the art of the friseur, but fell in jetty ringlets on her neck, confined only by a circlet, richly set with diamonds. This peculiarity she adopted in compliance with the Highland prejudices, which could not endure that a woman's head should be covered before wedlock.

Flora Mac-Ivor bore a most striking resemblance to her brother

Fergus; so much so, that they might have played Viola and Sebastian
with the same exquisite effect produced by the appearance of Mrs
Henry Siddons and her brother in those characters. They had the
same antique and regular correctness of profile; the same dark eyes,
eye-lashes, and eye-brows; the same clearness of complexion, excepting that Fergus's was embrowned by exercise, and Flora's possessed
the utmost feminine delicacy. But the haughty, and somewhat stern
regularity of Fergus's features, was beautifully softened in those of
Flora. Their voices were also similar in tone, though differing in the
key. That of Fergus, especially while issuing orders to his followers
during their military exercise, reminded Edward of a favourite passage
in the description of Emetrius:

> ——whose voice was heard around,
> Loud as a trumpet with a silver sound.

That of Flora, on the contrary, was soft and sweet, "an excellent thing
in woman;" yet in urging any favourite topic, which she often pursued
with natural eloquence, it possessed as well the tones which impress
awe and correction, as those of persuasive insinuation. The eager
glance of the keen black eye, which, in the Chieftain, seemed impatient even of the material obstacles it encountered, had, in his sister's,
acquired a gentle pensiveness. His looks seemed to seek glory, power,
all that could exalt him above others in the race of humanity; while
those of his sister, as if she was already conscious of mental superiority,
seemed to pity rather than envy those who were struggling for any
other distinction. Her sentiments corresponded with the expression
of her countenance. Early education had impressed upon her mind, as
well as on that of the Chieftain, the most devoted attachment to the
exiled family of Stuart. She believed it the duty of her brother, of his
clan, of every man in Britain, at whatever personal hazard, to contribute to that restoration which the partizans of the Chevalier St George
had not ceased to hope for. For this she was prepared to do all, to
suffer all, to sacrifice all. But her loyalty, as it exceeded her brother's
in fanaticism, excelled it also in purity. Accustomed to petty intrigue,
and necessarily involved in a thousand paltry and selfish discussions,
ambitious also by nature, his political faith was tinctured at least, if not
tainted, by the views of interest and advancement so easily combined
with it; and at the moment he should unsheathe his claymore, it might
be difficult to say whether it would be most with the view of making
James Stuart a king, or Fergus Mac-Ivor an earl. This, indeed, was a
mixture of feelings which he did not avow even to himself, but it
existed, nevertheless, in a powerful degree.

In Flora's bosom, on the contrary, the zeal of loyalty burned pure
and unmixed with any selfish feeling; she would have as soon made

religion the mask of ambitious and interested views, as have shrouded them under the opinions which she had been taught to think patriotism. Such instances of devotion were not uncommon among the followers of the unhappy race of Stuart, of which many memorable proofs will recur to the mind of most of my readers. But peculiar attention on the part of the Chevalier de St George and his princess to the parents of Fergus and his sister, and to themselves, when orphans, had rivetted their faith. Fergus, upon the death of his parents, had been for some time a page of honour in the train of the Chevalier's lady, and, from his beauty and sprightly temper, was uniformly treated by her with the utmost distinction. This was also extended to Flora, who was maintained for some time at a convent of the first order, at the princess's expence, and removed from thence into her own family, where she spent nearly two years, and both retained the deepest and most grateful sense of her kindness.

Having thus touched upon the leading principle of Flora's character, I may dismiss the rest more slightly. She was highly accomplished, and had acquired those elegant manners to be expected from one who, in early youth, had been the companion of a princess; yet she had not learned to substitute the gloss of politeness for the reality of feeling. When settled in the lonely regions of Glennaquoich, she found that her resources in French, English, and Italian literature, were likely to be few and interrupted; and, in order to fill up her vacant time, she bestowed a part of it upon the music and poetical traditions of the Highlanders, and began really to feel that pleasure in the pursuit, which her brother, whose perceptions of literary merit were more blunt, rather affected for the sake of popularity than actually experienced. Her resolution was strengthened in these researches, by the extreme delight which her enquiries seemed to afford those to whom she resorted for information.

Her love of her clan, an attachment which was almost hereditary in her bosom, was, like her loyalty, a more pure passion than that of her brother. He was too much a politician, regarded his patriarchal influence too much as the means of accomplishing his own aggrandisement, that we should term him the model of a Highland chieftain. Flora felt the same anxiety for cherishing and extending their patriarchal sway, but it was with the generous desire of vindicating from poverty, or at least from want and foreign oppression, those whom her brother was by birth, according to the notions of the time and country, entitled to govern. The savings of her income, for she had a small pension from the Princess Sobieski, were dedicated, not to add to the comforts of the peasantry, for that was a word which they neither knew nor apparently wished to know, but to relieve their absolute necessities, when in sickness or extreme old age. At every other period, they rather toiled to procure something which they might share with the Chief, as a proof of their attachment, than expected other assistance from him than was afforded by the rude hospitality of his castle, and the general division and subdivision of his estate among them. Flora was so much beloved by them, that when Mac-Murrough composed a song, in which he enumerated all the principal beauties of the district, and intimated her superiority by concluding, that "the fairest apple hung on the highest bough," he received, in donatives from the individuals of the clan, more seed-barley than would have sowed his Highland Parnassus, the *Bard's croft*, as it was called, ten times over.

From situation, as well as choice, Miss Mac-Ivor's society was extremely limited. Her most intimate friend had been Rose Bradwardine, to whom she was much attached; and when seen together, they would have afforded an artist two admirable subjects for the gay and the melancholy muse. Indeed Rose was so tenderly watched by her father, and her circle of wishes was so limited, that none arose but what he was willing to gratify, and scarce any which did not come within the compass of his power. With Flora it was otherwise. While almost a girl, she had undergone the most complete change of scene, from gaiety and splendour to absolute solitude and comparative poverty; and the ideas and wishes which she chiefly fostered, respected great national events and changes not to be brought round without both hazard and bloodshed, and therefore not to be thought of with levity. Her manner consequently was grave, though she readily contributed her talents to the amusement of society, and stood very high in the opinion of the old Baron, who used to sing along with her such French duets of Lindor and Cloris, &c. as were in fashion about the end of the reign of old Louis le Grand.

It was generally believed, though no one durst have hinted it to the Baron of Bradwardine, that Flora's entreaties had no small share in allaying the wrath of Fergus upon occasion of their quarrel. She took her brother on the assailable side, by dwelling first upon the Baron's age, and then representing the injury which the cause might sustain, and the damage which must arise to his own character in point of prudence, so necessary to a political agent, if he persisted in carrying it to extremity. Otherwise it is probable it would have terminated in a duel, both because the Baron had, on a former occasion, shed blood of the clan, though the matter had been timely accommodated, and on account of his high reputation for address at his weapon, which Fergus almost condescended to envy. For the same reason she had urged their reconciliation, which the Chieftain the more readily agreed to, as it favoured some ulterior projects of his own.

To this young lady, now presiding at the female empire of the tea-table, Fergus introduced Captain Waverley, whom she received with the usual forms of politeness.

Chapter Twenty-Two

HIGHLAND MINSTRELSY

WHEN THE first salutations had passed, Fergus said to his sister, "My dear Flora, before I return to the barbarous ritual of our fore-fathers, I must tell you that Captain Waverley is a worshipper of the Celtic muse, not the less so perhaps that he does not understand a word of her language. I have told him you are eminent as a translator of Highland poetry, and that Mac-Murrough admires your versions of his songs upon the same principle that Captain Waverley admires their original,—because he does not comprehend them. Will you have the goodness to read or recite to our guest in English, the extraordinary string of names which Mac-Murrough has tacked together in Gaelic? My life to a moor-fowl's feather, you are provided with a version; for I know you are in all the bard's councils, and acquainted with his songs long before he rehearses them in the hall."

"How can you say so, Fergus! You know how little these verses can possibly interest an English stranger, even if I could translate them as you pretend."

"Not less than they interest me, lady fair. To-day your joint com-position, for I insist you had a share in it, has cost me the last silver cup in the castle, and I suppose will cost me something else next time I hold *cour plénière*, if the muse descends on Mac-Murrough; for you know our proverb,—When the hand of the chief ceases to bestow, the breath of the bard is frozen in the utterance.—Well, I would it were even so: there are three things that are useless to a modern High-lander,—a sword which he must not draw,—a bard to sing of deeds which he dare not imitate,—and a large goat-skin purse without a louis-d'or to put into it."

"Well, brother, since you betray my secrets you cannot expect me to keep yours.—I assure you, Captain Waverley, that Fergus is too proud to exchange his sword for a marechal's baton; that he esteems Mac-Murrough a far greater poet than Homer, and would not give up his goat-skin purse for all the louis-d'ors which it could contain."

"Well pronounced, Flora; blow for blow, as Conan said to the devil. Now do you two talk of bards and poetry, if not of purses and clay-mores, while I return to do the final honours to the senators of the tribe of Ivor." So saying he left the room.

The conversation continued between Flora and Waverley; for two well-dressed young women, whose character seemed to hover between that of companions and dependants, took no share in it. They were both pretty girls, but served only as foils to the grace and beauty of their patroness. The discourse followed the turn which the Chieftain had given it, and Waverley was equally amused and surprised with the accounts which the lady gave him of Celtic poetry.

"The recitation," she said, "of poems, recording the feats of heroes, the complaints of lovers, and the wars of contending tribes, forms the chief amusement of a winter fire-side in the Highlands. Some of these are said to be very ancient, and, if they are ever translated into any of the languages of civilized Europe, cannot fail to produce a deep and general sensation. Others are more modern, the composition of those family bards whom the chieftains of more distinguished name and power retain as the poets and historians of their tribes. These, of course, possess various degrees of merit; but much of it must evaporate in translation, or be lost on those who do not sympathise with the feelings of the poet."

"And your bard, whose effusions seemed to produce such effect upon the company to-day, is he reckoned among the favourite poets of the mountains?"

"That is a trying question. His reputation is high among his countrymen, and you must not expect me to depreciate it."

"But the song, Miss Mac-Ivor, seemed to awaken all these warriors, both young and old."

"The song is little more than a catalogue of names of the Highland clans under their distinctive peculiarities, and an exhortation to them to remember and to emulate the actions of their forefathers."

"And am I wrong in conjecturing, however extraordinary the guess appears, that there was some allusion to me in the verses which he recited?"

"You have a quick observation, Captain Waverley, which in this instance has not deceived you. The Gaelic language, being uncommonly vocalic, is well adapted for sudden and extemporaneous poetry; and a bard seldom fails to augment the effect of a premeditated song, by throwing in any stanzas which may be suggested by the circumstances attending the recitation."

"I would give my best horse to know what the Highland bard could find to say of such an unworthy southern as myself."

"It shall not even cost you a lock of his mane.—Una, *Mavourneen!* (She spoke a few words to one of the young girls in attendance, who instantly curtsied and tripped out of the room.)—I have sent Una to

learn from the bard the expressions he used, and you shall command
my skill as Dragoman."

Una returned in a few minutes, and repeated to her mistress a few
lines in Gaelic. Flora seemed to think a moment, and then, slightly
colouring, she turned to Waverley—"It is impossible to gratify your
curiosity, Captain Waverley, without exposing my own presumption.
If you will give me a few moments for consideration, I will endeavour
to engraft the meaning of these lines upon a rude English translation,
which I have attempted of a part of the original. The duties of the tea-
table seem to be concluded, and, as the evening is delightful, Una will
shew you the way to one of my favourite haunts, and Cathleen and I
will join you there."

Una, having received instructions in her native language, conducted
Waverley out by a passage different from that through which he had
entered the apartment. At a distance he heard the hall of the Chief still
resounding with the clang of bagpipes and the high applause of the
guests. Having gained the open air by a postern door, they walked a
little way up the wild, bleak, and narrow valley in which the house was
situated, following the course of the stream that winded through it. In
a spot, about a quarter of a mile from the castle, two brooks, which
formed the little river, had their junction. The larger of the two came
down the long bare valley, which extended, apparently without any
change or elevation of character, as far as the hills which formed its
boundary permitted the eye to reach. But the other stream, which had
its source among the mountains on the left hand of the strath, seemed
to issue from a very narrow and dark opening betwixt two large rocks.
These streams were different also in character. The larger was placid,
and even sullen in its course, wheeling in deep eddies, or sleeping in
dark blue pools; but the motions of the lesser brook were rapid and
furious, issuing from between the precipices like a maniac from his
confinement, all foam and uproar.

It was up the course of this last stream that Waverley, like a knight of
romance, was conducted by the fair Highland damsel, his silent guide.
A small path, which had been rendered easy in many places for Flora's
accommodation, led him through scenery of a very different description from that which he had just quitted. Around the castle, all was
cold, bare, and desolate, yet tame even in desolation; but this narrow
glen, at so short a distance, seemed to open into the land of romance.
The rocks assumed a thousand peculiar and varied forms. In one
place, a crag of huge size presented its gigantic bulk, as if to forbid the
passenger's farther progress; and it was not until he approached its
very base, that Waverley discerned the sudden and acute turn by
which the pathway wheeled its course around this formidable obstacle.

In another spot, the projecting rocks from the opposite sides of the chasm had approached so near to each other, that two pine-trees laid across, and covered with turf, formed a rustic bridge at the height of at least one hundred and fifty feet. It had no ledges, and was barely three feet in breadth.

While gazing at this pass of peril, which crossed, like a single black line, the small portion of blue sky not intercepted by the projecting rocks on either side, it was with a sensation of horror that Waverley beheld Flora and her attendant appear, like inhabitants of another region, propped, as it were, in mid air, upon this trembling structure. She stopped upon observing him below, and, with an air of graceful ease which made him shudder, waved her handkerchief to him by way of signal. He was unable, from the sense of dizziness which her situation conveyed, to return the salute; and was never more relieved than when the fair apparition passed on from the precarious eminence which she seemed to occupy with so much indifference, and disappeared on the other side.

Advancing a few yards, and passing under the bridge which he had viewed with so much terror, the path ascended rapidly from the edge of the brook, and the glen widened into a sylvan amphitheatre, waving with birch, young oaks, and hazels, with here and there a scattered yew-tree. The rocks now receded, but still shewed their grey and shaggy crests rising among the copse-wood. Still higher, rose eminences and peaks, some bare, some clothed with wood, some round and purple with heath, and others splintered into rocks and crags. At a short turning, the path, which had for some furlongs lost sight of the brook, suddenly placed Waverley in front of a romantic water-fall. It was not so remarkable either for great height or quantity of water, as for the beautiful accompaniments which made the spot interesting. After a broken cataract of about twenty feet, the stream was received in a large natural basin, filled to the brim with water, which, where the bubbles of the fall subsided, was so exquisitely clear, that, although it was of great depth, the eye could discern each pebble at the bottom. Eddying round this reservoir, the brook found its way as if over a broken part of the ledge, and formed a second fall, which seemed to seek the very abyss; then wheeling out beneath, from among the smooth dark rocks, which it had polished for ages, it wandered murmuring down the glen, forming the stream up which Waverley had just ascended. The borders of this romantic reservoir corresponded in beauty; but it was beauty of a stern and commanding cast, as if in the act of expanding into grandeur. Mossy banks of turf were broken and interrupted by huge fragments of rock, and decorated with trees and shrubs, some of which had been planted under the direction of Flora, but so cautiously, that they added to the grace, without diminishing the romantic wildness of the scene.

Here, like one of those lovely forms which decorate the landscapes of Claude, Waverley found Flora gazing on the water-fall. Two paces farther back stood Cathleen, holding a small Scottish harp, the use of which had been taught to Flora by Rory Dall, one of the last harpers of the Western Highlands. The sun, now stooping in the west, gave a rich and varied tinge to all the objects which surrounded Waverley, and seemed to add more than human brilliancy to the full expressive darkness of Flora's eye, exalted the richness and purity of her complexion, and enhanced the dignity and grace of her beautiful form. Edward thought he had never, even in his wildest dreams, imagined a figure of such exquisite and interesting loveliness. The wild beauty of the retreat, bursting upon him as if by magic, augmented the mingled feeling of delight and awe with which he approached her, like a fair enchantress of Boiardo or Ariosto, by whose nod the scenery around seemed to have been created, an Eden in the wilderness.

Flora, like every beautiful woman, was conscious of her own power, and pleased with its effects, which she could easily discern from the respectful, yet confused address of the young soldier. But as she possessed excellent sense, she gave the romance of the scene, and other accidental circumstances, full weight in appreciating the feelings with which Waverley seemed obviously to be impressed; and, unacquainted with the fanciful and susceptible peculiarities of his character, considered his homage as the passing tribute which a woman of even inferior charms might have expected in such a situation. She therefore quietly led the way to a spot at such a distance from the cascade, that its sound should rather accompany than interrupt that of her voice and instrument, and, sitting down upon a mossy fragment of rock, she took the harp from Cathleen.

"I have given you the trouble of walking to this spot, Captain Waverley, both because I thought the scenery would interest you, and because a Highland song would suffer still more from my imperfect translation, were I to produce it without its own wild and appropriate accompaniments. To speak in the poetical language of my country, the seat of the Celtic Muse is in the mist of the secret and solitary hill, and her voice in the murmur of the mountain stream. He who woos her must love the barren rock more than the fertile valley, and the solitude of the desert better than the festivity of the hall."

Few could have heard this lovely woman make this declaration, with a voice where harmony was exalted by pathos, without exclaiming that the muse whom she invoked could never find a more appropriate representative. But Waverley, though the thought rushed on his mind, found no courage to utter it. Indeed the wild feeling of romantic delight, with which he heard the few first notes she drew from her instrument, amounted almost to a sense of pain. He would not for worlds have quitted his place by her side; yet he almost longed for solitude, that he might decypher and examine at leisure the complication of emotions which now agitated his bosom.

Flora had exchanged the measured and monotonous recitative of the bard for a lofty and uncommon Highland air, which had been a battle-song in former ages. A few irregular strains introduced a prelude of a wild and peculiar tone, which harmonized well with the distant water-fall, and the soft sigh of the evening breeze in the rustling leaves of an aspen which overhung the seat of the fair harpress. The following verses will convey but little idea of the feelings with which, so sung and accompanied, they were heard by Edward:

> Mist darkens the mountain, night darkens the vale,
> But more dark is the sleep of the sons of the Gael:
> A stranger commanded—it sunk on the land,
> It has frozen each heart, and benumb'd every hand!
>
> The dirk and the target lie sordid with dust,
> The bloodless claymore is but redden'd with rust;
> On the hill or the glen if a gun should appear,
> It is only to war with the heath-cock or deer.
>
> The deeds of our sires if our bards should rehearse,
> Let a blush or a blow be the meed of their verse!
> Be mute every string, and be hush'd every tone,
> That shall bid us remember the fame that is flown.
>
> But the dark hours of night and of slumber are past,
> The morn on our mountains is dawning at last;
> Glenaladale's peaks are illumed with the rays,
> And the streams of Glenfinnan leap bright in the blaze.
>
> O high-minded Moray!—the exiled—the dear!—
> In the blush of the dawning the STANDARD uprear!
> Wide, wide on the winds of the north let it fly,
> Like the sun's latest flash when the tempest is nigh!
>
> Ye sons of the strong, when the dawning shall break,
> Need the harp of the aged remind you to wake?
> That dawn never beam'd on your forefathers' eye,
> But it roused each high chieftain to vanquish or die.
>
> O sprung from the Kings who in Islay kept state,
> Proud chiefs of Clan Ranald, Glengary, and Sleat!
> Combine like three streams from one mountain of snow,
> And resistless in union rush down on the foe!

> True son of Sir Evan, undaunted Lochiel,
> Place thy targe on thy shoulder and burnish thy steel!
> Rough Keppoch, give breath to thy bugle's bold swell,
> Till far Coryarrick resound to the knell!
>
> Stern son of Lord Kenneth, high chief of Kintail,
> Let the stag in thy standard bound wild in the gale!
> May the race of Clan Gillean, the fearless and free,
> Remember Glenlivat, Harlaw, and Dundee!
>
> Let the clan of grey Fingon, whose offspring has given
> Such heroes to earth, and such martyrs to heaven,
> Unite with the race of renown'd Rorri More,
> To launch the long galley, and stretch to the oar!
>
> How Mac-Shimei will joy when their chief shall display
> The yew-crested bonnet o'er tresses of grey!
> How the race of wrong'd Alpin and murder'd Glencoe
> Shall shout for revenge when they pour on the foe!
>
> Ye sons of brown Dermid, who slew the wild boar,
> Resume the pure faith of the great Callain-More!
> Mac-Neil of the Islands, and Moy of the Lake,
> For honour, for freedom, for vengeance awake!—

Here a large greyhound, bounding up the glen, jumped upon Flora, and interrupted her music by his importunate caresses. At a distant whistle, he turned and shot down the path again with the rapidity of an arrow. "That is Fergus's faithful attendant, Captain Waverley, and that was his signal. He likes no poetry but what is humorous, and comes in good time to interrupt my long catalogue of the tribes, whom one of your saucy English poets calls

> Our bootless host of highborn beggars,
> Mac-Leans, Mac-Kenzies, and Mac-Gregors."

Waverley expressed his regret at the interruption.

"O you cannot guess how much you have lost! The bard, as in duty bound, has addressed three long stanzas to Vich Ian Vohr of the Banners, enumerating all his great properties, and not forgetting his being a cheerer of the harper and bard—'a giver of bounteous gifts.' Besides, you should have heard a practical admonition to the fair-haired son of the stranger, who lives in the land where the grass is always green—the rider on the shining pampered steed, whose hue is like the raven, and whose neigh is like the scream of the eagle for battle. This valiant horseman is affectionately conjured to remember that his ancestors were distinguished by their loyalty, as well as by their courage.—All this you have lost; but since your curiosity is not satisfied, I judge, from the distant sound of my brother's whistle, I may have time to sing the concluding stanzas before he comes to laugh at my translation.

> Awake on your hills, on your islands awake,
> Brave sons of the mountain, the frith, and the lake!
> 'Tis the bugle—but not for the chase is the call;
> 'Tis the pibroch's shrill summons—but not to the hall.
>
> 'Tis the summons of heroes for conquest or death,
> When the banners are blazing on mountain and heath;
> They call to the dirk, the claymore, and the targe,
> To the march and the muster, the line and the charge.
>
> Be the brand of each chieftain like Fin's in his ire!
> May the blood through his veins flow like currents of fire!
> Burst the base foreign yoke as your sires did of yore,
> Or die like your sires, and endure it no more!"

Chapter Twenty-Three

WAVERLEY CONTINUES AT GLENNAQUOICH

As Flora concluded her song, Fergus stood before them. "I knew I should find you here, even without the assistance of my friend Bran. A simple and unsublimed taste now, like my own, would prefer the jet d'eau at Versailles to this cascade, with all its accompaniments of rock and roar; but this is Flora's Parnassus, Captain Waverley, and that fountain her Helicon. It would be greatly for the benefit of my cellar if she could teach her coadjutor, Mac-Murrough, the value of its influence: he has just drank a pint of usquebaugh to correct, he said, the coldness of the claret—Let me try its virtues." He sipped a little water in the hollow of his hand, and immediately commenced, with a theatrical air,—

> "O Lady of the desert, hail!
> That lovest the harping of the Gael,
> Through fair and fertile regions borne,
> Where never yet grew grass or corn.

But English poetry will never succeed under the influence of a Highland Helicon—*Allons, courage*—

> O vous, qui buvez à tasse pleine,
> A cette heureuse fontaine,
>   Ou on ne voit sur le rivage,
>   Que quelques vilains troupeaux,
>   Suivis de nymphes de village,
>   Qui les escortent sans sabots"—

"A truce, dear Fergus! spare us those most tedious and insipid persons of all Arcadia. Do not, for Heaven's sake, bring down Coridon and Lindor upon us."

"Nay, if you cannot relish *la houlette et le chalumeau*, have with you in heroic strains."

"Dear Fergus, you have certainly partaken of the inspiration of Mac-Murrough's cup, rather than of mine."

"I disclaim it, *ma belle demoiselle*, although I protest it would be the more congenial of the two. Which of your crack-brained Italian romancers is it that says,

> Io d'Elicona niente
> Mi curo, in fe de Dio, che'l bere d'acque
> (Bea chi ber ne vuol) sempre mi spiacque!*

But if you prefer the Gaelic, Captain Waverley, here is little Cathleen shall sing you Drimmindhu.—Come, Cathleen, *astore*, (*i. e.* my dear,) begin; no apologies to the *Cean-kinné*."

Cathleen sung with much liveliness a little Gaelic song, the burlesque elegy of a countryman upon the loss of his cow, the comic tones of which, though he did not understand the language, made Waverley laugh more than once.

"Admirable, Cathleen!" cried the Chieftain; "I must find you a handsome husband among the clansmen one of these days."

Cathleen laughed, blushed, and sheltered herself behind her companion.

In the progress of their return to the castle, the Chieftain warmly pressed Waverley to stay for a week or two, in order to see a grand hunting party, in which he and some other Highland gentlemen proposed to join. The charms of melody and beauty were too strongly impressed in Edward's breast to permit his declining an invitation so pleasing. It was agreed, therefore, that he should write a note to the Baron of Bradwardine, expressing his intention to stay a fortnight at Glennaquoich, and requesting him to forward by the bearer (a *gilly* of the Chieftain) any letters which might have arrived for him.

This turned the discourse upon the Baron, whom Fergus highly extolled as a gentleman and soldier. His character was touched with yet more discrimination by Flora, who observed he was the very model of the old Scottish cavalier, with all his excellencies and peculiarities. "It is a character, Captain Waverley, which is fast disappearing; for its best point was a self-respect which was never lost sight of till now. But now, in the present time, the gentlemen whose principles do not permit them to pay court to the present government, are neglected and degraded, and many conduct themselves accordingly; and, like some of the persons you have seen at Tully-Veolan, adopt habits and companions inconsistent with their birth and breeding. The ruthless proscription of party seems to degrade the victims whom it brands, however unjustly. But let us hope a brighter day is approaching, when

---

* Good sooth, I reck nought of your Helicon;
  Drink water whoso will, in faith I will drink none.

a Scottish country-gentleman may be a scholar without the pedantry of our friend the Baron, a sportsman without the low habits of Mr Falconer, and a judicious improver of his property without becoming a boorish two-legged steer like Killancureit."

Thus did Flora prophesy a revolution, which time indeed has produced, but in a manner very different from what she had in her mind.

The amiable Rose was next mentioned, with the warmest encomium on her person, manners, and mind. "That man," said Flora, "will find an inestimable treasure in the affections of Rose Bradwardine, who shall be so fortunate as to become their object. Her very soul is in home, and in the discharge of all those quiet virtues of which home is the centre. Her husband will be to her what her father now is, the object of all her care, solicitude, and affection. She will see nothing, and connect herself with nothing, but by him and through him. If he is a man of sense and virtue, she will sympathise in his sorrows, divert his fatigue, and share his pleasures. If she becomes the property of a churlish or negligent husband, she will suit his taste also, for she will not long survive his unkindness. And, alas! how great is the chance that some such unworthy lot may be that of my poor friend!— O that I were a queen this moment, and could command the most amiable and worthy youth of my kingdom to accept happiness with the hand of Rose Bradwardine!"

"I wish you would command her to accept mine *en attendant*," said Fergus, laughing.

I don't know by what caprice it was that this wish, however jocularly expressed, rather jarred on Edward's feelings, notwithstanding his growing inclination to Flora, and his indifference to Miss Bradwardine. This is one of the inexplicabilities of human nature, which we leave without comment.

"Yours, brother?" answered Flora, regarding him steadily. "No; you have another bride—Honour; and the dangers you must run in pursuit of her rival would break poor Rose's heart."

With this discourse they reached the castle, and Waverley soon prepared his dispatches for Tully-Veolan. As he knew the Baron was punctilious in such matters, he was about to impress his billet with a seal on which his armorial bearings were engraved, but he did not find it at his watch. He mentioned his loss, borrowing at the same time the family seal of the Chieftain. He thought he must have left it at Tully-Veolan.

"Surely," said Miss Mac-Ivor, "Donald Bean Lean would not"——

"My life for him, in such circumstances," answered her brother; "besides, he would never have left the watch behind."

"After all, Fergus," said Flora, "and with every allowance, I am surprised you can countenance that man."

"I countenance him?—This kind sister of mine would persuade you, Captain Waverley, that I take what the people of old used to call a 'steak-raid,' that is, a 'collop of the foray,' or, in plainer words, a portion of the robber's booty, paid by him to the laird, or chief, through whose grounds he drove his prey. O it is certain that unless I can find some way to charm Flora's tongue, General Blakeney will send a serjeant's party from Stirling (this he said with haughty and emphatic irony) to seize Vich Ian Vohr, as they nickname me, in his own castle."

"Now, Fergus, must not our guest be sensible that all this is folly and affectation? You have men enough to serve you without enlisting banditti, and your own honour is above taint—Why don't you send this Donald Bean Lean, whom I hate for his smoothness and duplicity, even more than for his rapine, out of your country at once? No cause should induce me to tolerate such a character."

"*No* cause, Flora?" said the Chieftain, significantly.

"No cause, Fergus! not even that which is nearest to my heart. Spare it the omen of such evil supporters!"

"O but, sister," rejoined the Chief, gaily, "you don't consider my respect for *la belle passion*. Evan Dhu Maccombich is in love with Donald's daughter Alice, and you cannot expect me to disturb him in his amours. Why the whole clan would cry shame on me. You know it is one of their wise sayings, that a kinsman is part of a man's body, but a foster-brother is a piece of his heart."

"Well, Fergus, there is no disputing with you; but I would all this may end well."

"Devoutly prayed, my dear and prophetic sister, and the best way in the world to close a dubious argument.—But hear ye not the pipes, Captain Waverley? Perhaps you will like better to dance to them in the hall, than to be deafened with their harmony without taking part in the exercise they invite us to."

Waverley took Flora's hand. The dance, song, and merry-making proceeded, and closed the day's entertainment at the castle of Vich Ian Vohr. Edward at length retired, his mind agitated by a variety of new and conflicting feelings, which detained him from rest for some time, in that not unpleasing state of mind in which fancy takes the helm, and the soul rather drifts passively along with the rapid and confused tide of reflections, than exerts itself to encounter, systematize, or examine them. At a late hour he fell asleep, and dreamed of Flora Mac-Ivor.

END OF VOLUME FIRST

WAVERLEY

OR,

'TIS SIXTY YEARS SINCE

VOLUME II

Chapter One

A STAG-HUNTING AND ITS CONSEQUENCES

SHALL THIS be a short or a long chapter?—This is a question in which you, gentle reader, have no vote, however much you may be interested in the consequences; just as probably you may (like myself) have nothing to do with the imposing a new tax, excepting the trifling circumstance of being obliged to pay it. More happy surely in the present case, since, though it lies within my arbitrary power to extend my materials as I think proper, I cannot call you into Exchequer if you do not think proper to read my narrative. Let me therefore consider. It is true, that the annals and documents in my hands say but little of this Highland chase; but then I can find copious materials for description elsewhere. There is old Lindsay of Pitscottie ready at my elbow, with his Athole hunting, and his "lofted and joisted palace of green timber; with all kind of drink to be had in burgh and land, as ale, beer, wine, muscadel, malvasie, hippocras, and aquavitæ; with wheat-bread, main-bread, ginge-bread, beef, mutton, lamb, veal, venison, goose, grice, capon, coney, crane, swan, partridge, plover, duck, drake, brissell-cock, pawnies, black-cock, muir-fowl, and caper-cailzies;" not forgetting the "costly bedding, vaiselle, and napry," and least of all the "excelling stewards, cunning baxters, excellent cooks, and pottingars, with confections and drugs for the deserts." Besides the particulars which may be thence gleaned from this Highland feast, (the splendour of which induced the pope's legate to dissent from an

opinion which he had hitherto held, that Scotland namely was the—
the—the latter end of the world)—besides these, might I not illumin-
ate my pages with Taylor the Water Poet's hunting in the braes of
Mar, where,

> Through heather, mosse, mong frogs, and bogs, and fogs,
>   Mongst craggy cliffs and thunder-battered hills,
> Hares, hinds, bucks, roes, are chased by men and dogs,
>   Where two hours hunting fourscore fat deer kills.
> Lowland, your sports are low as is your seat;
> The Highland games and minds are high and great.

But without further tyranny over my readers, or display of the extent
of my own reading, I will content myself with borrowing a single
incident from the memorable hunting at Lude, commemorated in the
ingenious Mr Gunn's Essay on the Caledonian Harp, and so proceed
in my story with all the brevity that my natural style of composition,
partaking of what scholars call the periphrastic and ambagitory, and
the vulgar the circumbendibus, will permit me.

The solemn hunting was delayed, from various causes, for about
three weeks. The interval was spent by Waverley with great satisfaction at Glennaquoich; for the impression which Flora had made on
his mind at their first meeting, grew daily stronger. She was precisely
the character to fascinate a youth of romantic imagination. Her manners, her language, her talents for poetry and music, gave additional
and varied influence to her eminent personal charms. Even in her
hours of gaiety, she was in his fancy exalted above the ordinary daughters of Eve, and seemed only to stoop for an instant to those topics of
amusement and gallantry which others seem to live for. In the neighbourhood of this enchantress, while sport consumed the morning, and
music and the dance led on the hours of evening, Waverley became
daily more delighted with his hospitable landlord, and more enam-
oured of his bewitching sister.

At length, the period fixed for the grand hunting arrived, and Waverley and the Chieftain departed for the place of rendezvous, which
was a day's journey to the northward of Glennaquoich. Fergus was
attended on this occasion by about three hundred of his clan, well
armed, and accoutred in their best fashion. Waverley complied so far
with the custom of the country as to adopt the trews, (he could not be
reconciled to the kilt,) brogues, and bonnet, as the fittest dress for the
exercise in which he was to be engaged, and which less exposed him to
be stared at as a stranger when they should reach the place of rendezvous. They found, on the spot appointed, several distinguished Chiefs,
to all of whom Waverley was formally presented, and by all cordially
received. Their vassals and clans-men, a part of whose feudal duty
it was to attend upon such parties, appeared in such numbers as

amounted to a small army. These active assistants spread through the country far and near, forming a circle, technically called the *tinchel*, which, gradually closing, drove the deer in herds together towards the glen where the Chiefs and principal sportsmen lay in wait for them. In the meanwhile, these distinguished personages *bivouacked* among the flowery heath, wrapped up in their plaids; a mode of passing a summer's night which Waverley found by no means unpleasant.

For many hours after sun-rise, the mountain ridges and passes retained their ordinary appearance of silence and solitude, and the Chiefs, with their followers, amused themselves with various pastimes, in which the joys of the shell, as Ossian has it, were not forgotten. "Others apart sate on a hill retired;" probably as deeply engaged in the discussion of politics and news, as Milton's spirits in metaphysical disquisition. At length signals of the approach of the game were descried and heard. Distant shouts resounded from valley to valley, as the various parties of Highlanders, climbing rocks, struggling through copses, wading brooks, and traversing thickets, approached more and more near to each other, and compelled the astonished deer, with the other wild animals that fled before them, into a narrower circuit. Every now and then the report of muskets was heard, repeated by a thousand echoes. The baying of the dogs was soon added to the chorus, which grew ever louder and more loud. At length the advanced parties of the deer began to shew themselves, and as the stragglers came bounding down the pass by two or three at a time, the Chiefs shewed their skill by distinguishing the fattest deer, and their dexterity in bringing them down with their guns. Fergus exhibited remarkable address, and Edward was also so fortunate as to attract the notice and applause of the sportsmen.

But now the main body of the deer appeared at the head of the glen, compelled into a very narrow compass, and presenting a most formidable phalanx, their antlers appearing at a distance over the ridge of the steep pass like a leafless grove. Their number was very great, and, from a desperate stand which they made, with the tallest of the red-deer stags arranged in front, in a sort of battle array, gazing on the group which barred their passage down the glen, the more experienced sportsmen began to augur danger. The work of destruction, however, now commenced on all sides. Dogs and hunters were at work, and muskets and fusees resounded from every quarter. The deer, driven to desperation, made at length a fearful charge right upon the spot where the more distinguished sportsmen had taken their stand. The word was given in Gaelic to fling themselves upon their faces; but Waverley, upon whose English ears the signal was lost, had almost fallen a sacrifice to his ignorance of the ancient language in which it was communicated. Fergus, observing his danger, sprung up and pulled him with violence to the ground just as the whole herd broke down upon them. The tide being absolutely irresistible, and wounds from a stag's horn highly dangerous, the activity of the Chieftain may be considered, on this occasion, as having saved his guest's life. He detained him with a firm grasp until the whole herd of deer had fairly run over them. Waverley then attempted to rise, but found that he had suffered several severe contusions, and upon a further examination discovered that he had sprained his ancle violently.

This checked the mirth of the meeting, although the Highlanders, accustomed to such incidents, and prepared for them, had suffered no harm themselves. A wigwam was erected almost in an instant, where Edward was deposited on a couch of heather. The surgeon, or he who assumed the office, appeared to unite the characters of a leach and a conjuror. He was an old smoke-dried Highlander, wearing a venerable grey beard, and having for his sole garment a tartan frock, the skirts of which descended to the knee, and, being undivided in front, made the vestment serve at once for doublet and breeches. He observed great ceremony in approaching Edward; and though our hero was writhing with pain, would not proceed to any operation which would assuage it until he had perambulated his couch three times, moving from east to west, according to the course of the sun. This, which was called making the *deasil*, both the leach and the assistants seemed to consider as a matter of the last importance to the accomplishment of a cure; and Edward, whom pain rendered incapable of expostulation, and who indeed saw no chance of its being attended to, submitted in silence.

After this ceremony was duly performed, the old Esculapius let Edward blood with a cupping-glass with great dexterity, and proceeded, muttering all the while to himself in Gaelic, to boil upon the fire certain herbs, with which he compounded an embrocation. He then fomented the parts which had sustained injury, never failing to murmur prayers or spells, which of the two Waverley could not distinguish, as his ear only caught the words *Gaspar-Melchior-Balthazar-max-prax-fax*, and similar gibberish. The fomentation had a speedy effect in alleviating the pain and swelling, which our hero imputed to the virtue of the herbs, or the effect of the chafing, but which was by the by-standers unanimously ascribed to the spells with which the operation had been accompanied. Edward was given to understand, that not one of the ingredients had been gathered except during the full moon, and that the herbalist had, while collecting them, uniformly recited a charm, which, in English, run thus;

Hail to thee, thou holy herb,
That sprung on holy ground!
All in the Mount Olivet
First wert thou found:
Thou art boot for many a bruise,
And healest many a wound;
In our Lady's blessed name,
I take thee from the ground.

Edward observed, with some surprise, that even Fergus, notwith-standing his knowledge and education, seemed to fall in with the superstitious ideas of his countrymen, either because he deemed it impolitic to affect scepticism on a matter of general belief, or more probably because, like most men who do not think deeply or accurately on such subjects, he had in his mind a reserve of superstition which balanced the freedom of his expressions and practice upon other occasions. Waverley made no commentary, therefore, on the manner of the treatment, but rewarded the professor of medicine with a liber-ality beyond the very conception of his wildest hopes. He uttered, on the occasion, so many incoherent blessings in Gaelic and English, that Mac-Ivor, rather scandalized at the excess of his acknowledgments, cut them short, by exclaiming, *ceade millia molighiart*, i. e. "A hundred thousand curses be with you," and so pushed the helper of men out of the cabin.

After Waverley was left alone, the exhaustion of pain and fatigue, for the whole day's exercise had been severe, threw him into a pro-found, but yet a feverish sleep, which he owed partly also to an opiate draught which the old Highlander had administered, from some decoction of herbs in his pharmacopeia.

Early the next morning, the purpose of their meeting being over, and their sports blanked by the untoward accident, in which Fergus and all his friends expressed the greatest sympathy, it became a ques-tion how to dispose of the disabled sportsman. This was settled by Mac-Ivor, who had a litter prepared, of "birch and hazel grey," which was borne by his people with such caution and dexterity as renders it not improbable that they may have been the ancestors of some of those sturdy Gael who have now the happiness to transport the belles of Edinburgh in their sedan-chairs, to ten routes in one evening. When Edward was elevated upon their shoulders, he could not help being gratified with the romantic effect produced by the breaking up of this sylvan camp.

The various tribes assembled, each at the pibroch of his native clan, and each headed by their patriarchal ruler. Some, who had already begun to retire, were seen winding up the hills, or descending the passes which led to the scene of action, the sound of their bagpipes dying away upon the ear. Others made still a moving picture upon the narrow plain, forming various changeful groups, their feathers and loose plaids waving in the morning breeze, and their arms glittering to the rising sun. Most of their chiefs came to take farewell of Waverley, and to express their anxious hope they might again, and speedily, meet, but the care of Fergus abridged the ceremonies of taking leave. At length, his own men being completely assembled and mustered, Mac-Ivor commenced his march, but not towards the quarter from which they had come. He gave Waverley to understand, that the greater part of his followers, now on the field, were bound upon a distant expedition, and that when he had deposited Waverley in the house of a gentleman, who he was sure would pay him every attention, he himself would be under the necessity of accompanying them the greater part of the way, but would lose no time in rejoining his friend.

Waverley was rather surprised that Fergus had not mentioned this ulterior destination when they set out upon the hunting-party; but his situation did not admit of many interrogations. The greater part of the clansmen went forward under the guidance of old Ballenkeiroch, and Evan Dhu Maccombich, apparently in high spirits. A few remained for the purpose of escorting the Chieftain, who walked by the side of Edward's litter, and attended him with the most affectionate assiduity. About noon, after a journey which the nature of the conveyance, the pain of his bruises, and the roughness of the way, rendered inexpressibly painful, Waverley was hospitably received in the house of a gentleman related to Fergus, who had prepared for him every accommodation which the simple habits of living then universal in the Highlands, put in his power. In this person, an old man about seventy, Edward admired a relic of primitive simplicity. He wore no dress but what his estate afforded; the cloth was the fleeces of his own sheep, woven by his own servants, and stained into tartan by the dyes produced from the herbs and lichens of the hills around him. His linen was spun by his daughters and maid-servants, from his own flax; nor did his table, though plentiful, and varied with game and fish, offer an article but what was of native produce.

Claiming himself no rights of clanship or vassalage, he was fortunate in the alliance and protection of Vich Ian Vohr, and other bold and enterprising chieftains, who protected him in the quiet unambitious life he loved. It is true, the youth born on his grounds were often enticed to leave him for the service of his more active friends; but a few old servants and tenants used to shake their grey locks when they heard their master censured for want of spirit, and observed, "When the wind is still, the shower falls soft." This good old man, whose charity and hospitality were unbounded, would have received Waverley with kindness, had he been the meanest Saxon peasant, since his situation required assistance. But his attention to a friend and guest of Vich Ian Vohr was anxious and unremitted. Other embrocations were applied to the injured limb, and new spells were put in practice. At length, after more solicitude than was perhaps for the advantage of his health, Fergus took farewell of Waverley for a few days, when, he said, he would return to Tomanrait, and hoped by that time Waverley would be able to ride one of the Highland ponies of his host, and in that manner return to Glennaquoich.

The next day, when his good old host appeared, Edward learned that his friend had departed with dawn, leaving none of his attendants except Callum Beg, the sort of foot-page who used to attend his person, and who had now in charge to wait upon Waverley. On asking his host, if he knew where the Chieftain was gone? the old man looked fixedly at him, with something mysterious and sad in the smile, which was his only reply. Waverley repeated his question, to which his host answered in a proverb,—

> "What sent the messengers to hell,
> Was asking what they knew full well."

He was about to proceed, but Callum Beg said, rather pertly as Edward thought, that "Ta Tighearnach (i. e. the Chief) did not like ta Sassenagh Duinhé-wassal to be pingled wi' mickle speaking, as she was na tat weel." From this Waverley concluded he should disoblige his friend by enquiring at a stranger the object of a journey which he himself had not communicated.

It is unnecessary to trace the progress of his recovery. The sixth morning had arrived, and he was able to walk about with a staff, when Fergus returned with about a score of his men. He seemed in the highest spirits, congratulated Waverley on his progress towards recovery, and finding he was able to sit upon horseback, proposed their immediate return to Glennaquoich; Waverley joyfully acceded, for the form of its fair mistress had lived in his dreams during all the time of his confinement.

> Now he has ridden o'er moor and moss,
> O'er hill and many a glen,

Fergus all the while, with his myrmidons, striding stoutly by his side, or diverging to get a shot at a roe or a heath-cock. Waverley's bosom beat thick when they approached the old tower of Ian nan Chaistel, and could distinguish the fair form of its mistress advancing to meet them.

Fergus began immediately, with his usual high spirits, to exclaim, "Open your gates, incomparable princess, to the wounded Moor

Abindarez, whom Rodrigo de Narvaez, constable of Antiquera, con-
veys to your castle; or open them, if you like it better, to the renowned
Marquis of Mantua, the sad attendant of his half-slain friend, Baldo-
vinos of the mountain.—Ah, long rest to thy soul, Cervantes! without
quoting thy romaunts, how should I frame my language to befit
romantic ears!"

Flora now advanced, and welcoming Waverley with much kindness,
expressed her regret for his accident, of which she had already heard
particulars, and her surprise that her brother should not have taken
better care to put a stranger on his guard against the perils of the sport
in which he engaged him. Edward readily exculpated the Chieftain,
who, indeed, at his own personal risk, had probably saved his life.

This greeting over, Fergus said three or four words to his sister in
Gaelic. The tears instantly sprung to her eyes, but they seemed to be
tears of devotion or joy, for she looked up to heaven, and folded her
hands as in a solemn expression of prayer or gratitude. After the pause
of a minute, she presented to Edward some letters which had been
forwarded from Tully-Veolan during his absence, and, at the same
time, delivered some to her brother. To the latter she likewise gave
three or four numbers of the Caledonian Mercury, the only newspaper
which was then published to the north of the Tweed.

Both gentlemen retired to examine their dispatches, and Edward
speedily found that those which he had received contained matters of
very deep interest.

Chapter Two

NEWS FROM ENGLAND

THE LETTERS which Waverley had hitherto received from his relations in England, were not such as required any particular notice in
this narrative. His father usually wrote to him with the pompous
affectation of one who was too much oppressed by public affairs to
find leisure to attend to those of his own family. Now and then he
mentioned persons of rank in Scotland to whom he could wish his son
should pay some attention; but Waverley, hitherto occupied by the
amusements which he had found at Tully-Veolan and Glennaquoich,
dispensed with paying any attention to hints so coldly thrown out,
especially as distance, shortness of leave of absence, and so forth,
furnished a ready apology. But, latterly, the burthen of Mr Richard
Waverley's paternal epistles consisted in certain mysterious hints of
greatness and influence which he was speedily to attain, and which

would insure his son's obtaining the most rapid promotion, should he
remain in the military service. Sir Everard's letters were of a different
tenor. They were short; for the good Baronet was none of your illimit-
able correspondents whose manuscript overflows the folds of their
large post paper, and leaves no room for the seal; but they were kind
and affectionate, and seldom concluded without some allusion to our
hero's stud, some question about the state of his purse, and a special
enquiry after such of his recruits as had preceded him from Waverley-
Honour. Aunt Rachael charged him to remember his principles of
religion, to take care of his health, to beware of Scotch mists, which,
she had heard, would wet an Englishman to the skin; never to go out at
night without his great-coat; and, above all, to wear flannel near his
skin.

Mr Pembroke only wrote to our hero one letter, but it was of the bulk
of six epistles of these degenerate days, containing, in the moderate
compass of ten folio pages, closely written, a precis of a supplementary
quarto manuscript of *addenda*, *delenda*, *et corrigenda*, in reference to
the two tracts with which he had presented Waverley. This he
considered as a mere sop in the pan to stay the appetite of Edward's
curiosity, until he should find an opportunity of sending down the
volume itself, which was much too heavy for the post, and which he
proposed to accompany with certain interesting pamphlets, lately
published by his friend in Little Britain, with whom he had kept up a
sort of literary correspondence, in virtue of which the library shelves
of Waverley Hall were loaded with much trash, and a good round bill,
seldom summed in fewer than three figures, was yearly transmitted, in
which Sir Everard Waverley of Waverley-Honour, Bart., was marked
Dr. to Jonathan Grubbet, bookseller and stationer, Little Britain.
Such had hitherto been the style of the letters which Edward had
received from England; but the packet delivered to him at Glennaquoich was of a different and more interesting complexion. It would be
impossible for the reader, even were I to insert the letters at full length,
to comprehend the real cause of their being written, without a glance
into the interior of the British Cabinet at the period in question.

The ministers of the day happened (no very singular event) to be
divided into two parties; the weakest of which, making up by assiduity
of intrigue their inferiority in real consequence, had of late acquired
some new proselytes, and with them the hope of superseding their
rivals in the favour of the sovereign, and overpowering them in the
House of Commons. Amongst others, they had thought it worth while
to practise upon Richard Waverley. This honest gentleman, by a grave
mysterious demeanour, an attention to the etiquette of business, as
well as to its essence, a facility in making long dull speeches, consisting

of truisms and common-places, hashed up with a technical jargon of office, which prevented the inanity of his orations from being discovered, acquired a certain name and credit in public life, and even established, with many, the character of a profound politician; none of your shining orators, indeed, whose talents evaporate in tropes of rhetoric and flashes of wit, but one possessed of steady parts for business, which would wear well, as the ladies say in chusing their silks, and ought in all reason to be good for common and every-day use, since they were confessedly formed of no holiday texture.

This faith had become so general, that the party in the cabinet of which we have made mention, after sounding Mr Richard Waverley, were so satisfied with his sentiments and abilities, as to propose, that, in case of a certain revolution in the ministry, he should take an ostensible place in the new order of things, not indeed of the first rank, but greatly higher in point both of emolument and influence, than that which he now enjoyed. There was no resisting so tempting a proposal, notwithstanding that the Great Man, under whose patronage he had enlisted, and by whose banner he had hitherto stood firm, was the principal object of the proposed attack by the new allies. Unfortunately, this fair scheme of ambition was blighted in the very bud, by a premature movement. All the official gentlemen concerned in it, who hesitated to take the part of a voluntary resignation, were informed that the king had no farther occasion for their services; and, in Richard Waverley's case, which the minister considered as aggravated by ingratitude, dismissal was accompanied by something like personal contempt and contumely. The public, and even the party of whom he shared the fall, sympathised little in the disappointment of this selfish and interested statesman, and he retired to the country under the comfortable reflection, that he had lost, at the same time, character, credit, and, what he at least equally deplored,—emolument.

Richard Waverley's letter to his son upon this occasion was a masterpiece of its kind. Aristides himself could not have made out a harder case. An unjust monarch, and an ungrateful country, were the burthen of each rounded paragraph. He spoke of long services, and unrequited sacrifices, though the former had been overpaid by his salary, and nobody could guess in what the latter consisted, unless it were in his deserting, not from conviction, but for the lucre of gain, the tory principles of his family. In the conclusion, his resentment was wrought to such an excess by the force of his own oratory, that he could not repress some threats of vengeance, however vague and impotent, and finally acquainted his son with his pleasure that he should testify his sense of the ill treatment he had sustained, by throwing up his commission as soon as the letter reached him. This, he said, was also his uncle's desire, as he would himself intimate in due course.

Accordingly, the next letter which Edward opened was from Sir Everard. His brother's disgrace seemed to have removed from his well-natured bosom all recollection of their differences; and, remote as he was from every means of learning that Richard's disgrace was in reality only the just, as well as natural consequence of his own unsuccessful intrigues, the good, but credulous baronet, at once set it down as a new and enormous instance of the injustice of the existing government. It was true, he said, and he must not disguise it even from Edward, that his father could not have sustained such an insult as was now, for the first time, offered to one of his house, unless he had subjected himself to it by accepting of an employment under the present system. Sir Everard had no doubt that he now both saw and felt the magnitude of this error, and it should be his (Sir Everard's) business, to take care that the cause of his regret should not extend itself to pecuniary consequences. It was enough for a Waverley to have sustained the public disgrace; the patrimonial injury could easily be obviated by the head of their family. But it was both the opinion of Mr Richard Waverley and his own, that Edward, the representative of the family of Waverley-Honour, should not remain in a situation which subjected him also to such treatment as that with which his father had been stigmatized. He requested his nephew therefore to take the fittest, and, at the same time, the most speedy opportunity, of transmitting his resignation to the War Office, and hinted, moreover, that little ceremony was necessary where so little had been used to his father. He sent multitudinous greetings to the Baron of Bradwardine.

A letter from Aunt Rachael spoke out even more plainly. She considered the disgrace of brother Richard as the just reward of his forfeiting his allegiance to a lawful, though exiled sovereign, and taking the oaths to an alien; a concession which her grandfather, Sir Nigel Waverley, refused to make, either to the roundhead parliament or to Cromwell, when his life and fortune stood in the utmost extremity. She hoped her dear Edward would follow the footsteps of his ancestors, and as speedily as possible get rid of the badge of servitude to the usurping family, and regard the wrongs sustained by his father as an admonition from Heaven, that every desertion of the line of loyalty becomes its own punishment. She also concluded with her respects to Mr Bradwardine, and begged Waverley would inform her whether his daughter, Miss Rose, was old enough to wear a pair of very handsome ear-rings, which she proposed to send as a token of her affection. The good lady also desired to be informed whether Mr Bradwardine took as much Scotch snuff, and danced as unweariedly, as he did when he was at Waverley-Honour about thirty years ago.

These letters, as might have been expected, highly excited Waverley's indignation. From the desultory style of his studies, he had not any fixed political opinion to place in opposition to the movements of indignation which he felt at his father's supposed wrongs. Of the real cause of his disgrace, Edward was totally ignorant; nor had his habits at all led him to investigate the politics of the period in which he lived, or remark the intrigues in which his father had been so actively engaged. Indeed, any impressions which he had accidentally adopted concerning the parties of the times, were (owing to the society in which he had lived at Waverley-Honour,) of a nature rather unfavourable to the existing government and dynasty. He entered, therefore, without hesitation, into the resentful feeling of the relations who had the best title to dictate his conduct; and not perhaps the less willingly when he remembered the tædium of his quarters, and the inferior figure which he had made among the officers of his regiment. If he could have had any doubt upon the subject, it would have been decided by the following letter from his commanding officer, which, as it is very short, shall be inserted verbatim:

"SIR,

"Having carried somewhat beyond the line of my duty, an indulgence which even the lights of nature, and much more those of Christianity, direct towards errors which may arise from youth and inexperience, and that altogether without effect, I am reluctantly compelled, at the present crisis, to use the only remaining remedy which is in my power. You are, therefore, hereby commanded to repair to ——, the head-quarters of the regiment, within three days after the date of this letter. If you shall fail to do so, I must report you to the War Office as absent without leave, and also take other steps, which will be disagreeable to you, as well as to,

"Sir,
"Your obedient Servant,
"J. G——, Lieut. Col.
"Commanding the —— Regt. Dragoons."

Edward's blood boiled within him as he read this letter. He had been accustomed from his very infancy to possess, in a great measure, the disposal of his own time, and had thus acquired habits which rendered the rules of military discipline as unpleasing to him in this as they were in some other respects. An idea that in his own case they would not be enforced in a very rigid manner, had also obtained full possession of his mind, and had hitherto been sanctioned by the indulgent conduct of his lieutenant-colonel. Neither had any thing occurred, to his knowledge, that should have induced his commanding officer, without any other warning than the hints we noticed at the end of the fourteenth chapter of the last volume, so suddenly to assume a harsh, and, as Edward deemed it, so insolent a tone of dictatorial authority. Connecting it with the letters he had just received from his family, he could not but suppose, that it was designed to make him feel, in his present situation, the same pressure of authority which had been exercised in his father's case, and that the whole was a concerted scheme to depress and degrade every member of the Waverley family.

Without a pause, therefore, Edward wrote a few cold lines, thanking his lieutenant-colonel for past civilities, and expressing regret that he should have chosen to efface the remembrance of them, by assuming a different tone towards him. The strain of his letter, as well as what he (Edward) conceived to be his duty, in the present crisis, called upon him to lay down his commission; and he therefore inclosed the formal resignation of a situation which subjected him to so unpleasant a correspondence, and requested Colonel G—— would have the goodness to forward it to the proper authorities.

Having finished this magnanimous epistle, he felt somewhat uncertain concerning the terms in which his resignation ought to be expressed, upon which subject he resolved to consult Fergus Mac-Ivor. It may be observed in passing, that the bold and prompt habits of thinking, acting, and speaking, which distinguished this young Chieftain, had given him a considerable ascendancy over the mind of Waverley. Endowed with at least equal powers of understanding, and with much finer genius, Edward yet stooped to the bold and decisive activity of an intellect which was sharpened by the habit of acting on a preconceived and regular system, as well as by extensive knowledge of the world.

When Edward found his friend, the latter had still in his hand the newspaper which he had perused, and advanced to meet him with the embarrassment of one who has unpleasing news to communicate. "Do your letters, Captain Waverley, confirm the unpleasing information which I find in this paper?"

He put the paper into his hand, where his father's disgrace was registered in the most bitter terms, transferred probably from some London journal. At the end of the paragraph was this remarkable inuendo:

"We understand that this same Richard who hath done all this, is not the only example of the *Wavering Honour* of W–v–rl–y H–n–r. See the Gazette of this day."

With hurried and feverish apprehension our hero turned to the place referred to, and found therein recorded, "Edward Waverley, captain in —— regiment dragoons, superseded for absence without leave;" and in the list of military promotions, referring to the same regiment, he discovered this farther article, "Lieut. Julius Butler to be captain, *vice* Edward Waverley superseded."

Our hero's bosom glowed with the resentment which undeserved and apparently premeditated insult was calculated to excite in the bosom of one who had aspired after honour, and was thus wantonly held up to public scorn and disgrace. Upon comparing the date of his colonel's letter with that of the article in the Gazette, he perceived that his threat of making a report upon his absence had been literally complied with, and without enquiry, as it seemed, whether Edward had either received his summons, or was disposed to comply with it. The whole, therefore, appeared a formed plan to degrade him in the eyes of the public; and the idea of its having succeeded filled him with such bitter emotions, that, after various attempts to conceal them, he at length threw himself into Mac-Ivor's arms, and gave vent to tears of shame and indignation.

It was none of this Chieftain's faults to be indifferent to the wrongs of his friends; and for Edward, independent of certain plans with which he was connected, he felt a deep and sincere interest. The proceeding appeared as extraordinary to him as it had done to Edward. He indeed knew of more motives than Waverley was privy to for the peremptory order that he should join his regiment. But that, without farther enquiry into the circumstances of a necessary delay, the commanding officer, in contradiction to his known and established character, should have proceeded in so harsh and unusual a manner, was a mystery which he could not penetrate. He soothed our hero, however, to the best of his power, and began to turn his thoughts on revenge for his insulted honour.

Edward eagerly grasped at the idea. "Will you carry a message for me to Colonel G——, my dear Fergus, and oblige me for ever?"

Fergus paused, "It is an act of friendship which you should command, could it be useful, or lead to the righting your honour; but in the present case, I doubt if your commanding officer would give you the meeting, on account of his having taken measures which, however harsh and exasperating, were still within the strict bounds of his duty. Besides, G—— is a precise Huguenot, and has adopted certain ideas about the sinfulness of such rencontres, from which it would be impossible to make him depart, especially as his courage is beyond all suspicion. And besides, I—I—to say the truth—I dare not at this moment, for some very weighty reasons, go near any of the military quarters or garrisons belonging to this government."

"And am I to sit down quiet and contented under the injury I have received?"

"That will I never advise, my friend. But I would have vengeance to fall on the head, not on the hand; on the tyrannical and oppressive government which designed and directed these premeditated and reiterated insults, not on the tools of office which they employed in the execution of the injuries they designed you."

"Upon the government!"

"Yes, upon the usurping house of Hanover, whom your grandfather would no more have served than he would have taken wages of red-hot gold from the great fiend of hell!"

"But since the time of my grandfather two generations of this dynasty have possessed the throne."

"True;—and because we have passively given them so long an opportunity of shewing their native character,—because both you and I myself have lived in quiet submission, have even truckled to the times so far as to accept commissions under them, and thus have given them an opportunity of disgracing us publicly by resuming them, are we not on that account to resent injuries which our fathers only apprehended, but which we have actually sustained?—Or is the cause of the unfortunate Stuart family become less just, because their title has devolved upon an heir who is innocent of the charges of misgovernment brought against his father?—Do you remember the lines of your favourite poet,—

> Had Richard unconstrain'd resign'd the throne,
> A king can give no more than is his own;
> The title stood entail'd had Richard had a son.

You see, my dear Waverley, I can quote poetry as well as Flora and you. But come, clear your moody brow, and trust to me to shew you an honourable road to a speedy and glorious revenge. Let us seek Flora, who, perhaps, has more news to tell us of what has occurred during our absence. She will rejoice to hear that you are relieved of your servitude. But first add a postscript to your letter, marking the time when you received this Calvinistical colonel's first summons, and express your regret that the hastiness of his proceedings prevented your anticipating them by sending your resignation. Then let him blush for his injustice."

The letter was sealed accordingly, covering a formal resignation of the commission, and Mac-Ivor dispatched it with some letters of his own by a special messenger, with charge to put them into the nearest post-office in the Lowlands.

Chapter Three

AN ECLAIRCISSEMENT

THE HINT which the Chieftain had thrown out respecting Flora was not unpremeditated. He had observed with great satisfaction the growing attachment of Waverley to his sister, nor did he see any bar to their union, excepting the situation which Waverley's father held in the ministry, and Edward's own commission in the army of George II. These obstacles were now removed, and in a manner which apparently paved the way for the son's at least becoming reconciled to another allegiance. In every other respect the match would be most eligible. The safety, happiness, and honourable provision of his sister, whom he dearly loved, appeared to be insured by the proposed union. And his heart swelled when he considered how his own interest would be exalted in the eyes of the ex-monarch, to whom he had dedicated his services, by an alliance with one of those ancient, powerful, and wealthy English families of the ancient cavalier faith, to awaken whose decayed attachment to the Stuart family was now a matter of such vital importance to their cause. Nor could Fergus perceive any obstacle to such a scheme. Waverley's attachment was evident; and as his person was handsome, and his taste apparently coincided with her own, he anticipated no opposition on the part of Flora. Indeed, between his ideas of patriarchal power, and those which he had acquired in France respecting the disposal of females in marriage, any opposition from his sister, dear as she was to him, would have been the last obstacle on which he would have calculated, even had the union been less eligible.

Influenced by these feelings, the Chief now led Waverley in quest of Miss Mac-Ivor, not without the hope that the present agitation of his guest's spirits might give him courage to cut short what Fergus termed the romance of the courtship. They found Flora, with her faithful attendants, Una and Cathleen, busied in preparing what appeared to Waverley to be white bridal favours. Disguising as well as he could the agitation of his mind, Waverley asked for what joyful occasion Miss Mac-Ivor made such ample preparation.

"It is for Fergus's bridal," said she, smiling.

"Indeed!—he has kept his secret well. I hope he will allow me to be his bride's-man."

"That is a man's office, but not yours, as Beatrice says."

"And who is the fair lady?"

"Did I not tell you long since that Fergus wooed no bride but Honour?"

"And am I then incapable of being his assistant and counsellor in the pursuit of Honour, Miss Mac-Ivor?" said our hero, colouring deeply. "Do I rank so low in your opinion?"

"Far from it, Captain Waverley. I would to God you were of our determination! and made use of the expression which displeased you, solely

> Because you are not of our quality,
> But stand against us as an enemy."

"That time is passed, sister; and you may wish Edward Waverley (no longer captain) joy of being freed from the slavery to an usurper, implied in this sable and ill-omened emblem."

"Yes," said Waverley, undoing the cockade from his hat, "it has pleased the king who bestowed this badge upon me, to resume it in a manner which leaves me little reason to regret his service."

"Thank God for that!" cried the enthusiast; "and O that they may be blind enough to treat every man of honour who serves them, with the same indignity, that I may have less to sigh for when the struggle approaches!"

"And now, sister, replace his cockade with one of a more lively colour. I think it was the fashion of the ladies of yore to arm and send forth their knights to high atchievement."

"Not till the knight-adventurer had well weighed the justice and the danger of the cause, Fergus. Mr Waverley is just now too much agitated by feelings of recent emotion for me to press him upon a resolution of consequence."

Waverley felt half-alarmed at the thought of adopting the badge of what was esteemed rebellion by the majority of the kingdom, yet he could not disguise his chagrin at the coldness with which Flora parried her brother's hint. "Miss Mac-Ivor, I perceive, thinks the knight unworthy of her encouragement and favour," said he, somewhat bitterly.

"Not so, Mr Waverley," she replied, with great sweetness. "Why should I refuse my brother's valued friend a boon which I am distributing to his whole clan? Most willingly would I enlist every man of honour in the cause to which my brother has devoted himself. But he has taken his measures with his eyes open. His life has been devoted to this cause from his cradle; with him its call is sacred, were it even a summons to the tomb. But how can I wish you, Mr Waverley, so new to the world, so far from every friend who might advise and ought to influence you,—in a moment too of sudden pique and indignation,—

how can I wish you to plunge yourself at once into so desperate an enterprize?"

Fergus, who did not understand these delicacies, strode through the apartment biting his lip, and then, with a constrained smile, said, "Well, sister, I leave you to act your new character of mediator between the Elector of Hanover and the subjects of your lawful sovereign and benefactor," and left the room.

There was a painful pause, which was at length broken by Miss Mac-Ivor. "My brother is unjust," she said, "because he can bear no interruption that seems to thwart his loyal zeal."

"And do you not share his ardour?"

"Do I not?—God knows mine exceeds his, if that be possible. But I am not, like him, rapt by the bustle of military preparation, and the infinite detail necessary to the present undertaking, beyond consideration of the grand principles of justice and truth, on which our enterprize is grounded; and these, I am certain, can only be furthered by measures in themselves true and just. To operate upon your present feelings, my dear Mr Waverley, to induce you to an irretrievable step, of which you have not considered either the justice or the danger, is, in my poor judgment, neither the one nor the other."

"Incomparable Flora!" said Edward, taking her hand; "how much do I need such a monitor!"

"A better one by far," said Flora, gently withdrawing her hand, "Mr Waverley will always find in his own bosom, when he will give its small still voice leisure to be heard."

"No, Miss Mac-Ivor, I dare not hope it; a thousand circumstances of fatal self-indulgence have made me the creature rather of imagination than reason. Durst I but hope—could I but think—that you would deign to be to me that affectionate, that condescending friend, who would strengthen me to redeem my errors, my future life"——

"Hush, my dear sir! you now carry your joy at escaping the hands of a jacobite recruiting officer to an unparalleled excess of gratitude."

"Nay, dear Flora, trifle with me no longer; you cannot mistake the meaning of those feelings which I have almost involuntarily expressed; and, since I have broke the barrier of silence, let me profit by my audacity—Or may I, with your permission, mention to your brother"——

"Not for the world, Mr Waverley."

"What am I to understand? Is there any fatal bar—has any prepossession"——

"None, sir. I owe it to myself to say, that I never yet saw the person on whom I thought, with reference to the present subject."

"The shortness of our acquaintance perhaps—If Miss Mac-Ivor will deign to give me time"——

"I have not even that excuse. Captain Waverley's character is so open—is, in short, of that nature that it cannot be misconstrued, either in its strength or its weakness."

"And for that weakness you despise me?"

"Forgive me, Mr Waverley—and remember it is but within this half hour that there existed between us a barrier of a nature to me insurmountable, since I never could think of an officer in the service of the Elector of Hanover in any other light than as a casual acquaintance. Permit me then to arrange my ideas upon so unexpected a topic, and in less than an hour I will be ready to give you such reasons for the resolution I shall express, as may be satisfactory at least, if not pleasing to you." So saying, Flora withdrew, leaving Waverley to meditate upon the manner in which she had received his addresses.

Ere he could make up his mind whether his suit had been acceptable or no, Fergus re-entered the apartment. "What, *a la mort*, Waverley?" he cried. "Come down with me to the court, and you shall see a sight worth all the tirades of your romances. An hundred firelocks, my friend, and as many broad-swords, just arrived from good friends; and two or three hundred stout fellows almost fighting which shall first possess them.—But let me look at you closer—Why, a true Highlander would say you had been blighted by an evil eye.—Or can it be this silly girl that has thus blanked your spirit?—Never mind her, dear Edward; the wisest of her sex are fools in what regards the business of life."

"Indeed, my good friend," answered Waverley, "all that I can charge against your sister is, that she is too sensible, too reasonable."

"If that be all, I insure you for a louis-d'or against the mood lasting four-and-twenty hours. No woman was ever steadily sensible for that period; and I will engage, if that will please you, Flora shall be as unreasonable to-morrow as any of her sex. You must learn, my dear Edward, to consider women *en mousquetaire*." So saying, he seized Waverley's arm, and dragged him off to review his military preparations.

Chapter Four

UPON THE SAME SUBJECT

FERGUS MAC-IVOR had too much tact and delicacy to renew the subject which he had interrupted. His head was, or appeared to be, so full of guns, broad-swords, bonnets, cantines, and tartan hose, that Waverley could not for some time draw his attention to any other topic.

"Are you to take the field so soon, Fergus, that you are making all these martial preparations?"

"When we have settled that you go with me, you shall know all; but otherwise the knowledge might rather be prejudicial to you."

"But are you serious in your purpose, with such inferior forces, to rise against an established government? It is mere frenzy."

"*Laissez faire à Don Antoine*—I shall take good care of myself. We shall at least use the compliment of Conan, who never got a stroke but he gave one. I would not, however, have you think me mad enough to stir till a favourable opportunity: I will not slip my dog before the game's a-foot.—But, once more, will you join with us, and you shall know all?"

"How can I? I, who have so lately held that commission which is now posting back to those that gave it. My accepting it implied a promise of fidelity, and an acknowledgment of the legality of the government."

"A rash promise is not a steel handcuff; it may be shaken off, especially when it was given under deception, and has been repaid by insult. But if you cannot immediately make up your mind to a glorious revenge, go to England, and ere you cross the Tweed you will hear tidings that will make the world ring; and if Sir Everard be the gallant old cavalier I have heard him described by some of our *honest* gentlemen of the year one thousand seven hundred and fifteen, he will find you a better horse-troop and a better cause than you have lost."

"But your sister, Fergus?"

"Out, hyperbolical fiend! how vexest thou this man!—Speakest thou of nothing but of ladies?"

"Nay, be serious, my dear friend; I feel that the happiness of my future life must depend upon the answer which Miss Mac-Ivor shall make to what I ventured to tell her this morning."

"And is this your very sober earnest, or are we in the land of romance and fiction?"

"My earnest, undoubtedly. How could you suppose me jesting on such a subject?"

"Then, in very sober earnest, I am very glad to hear of it; and so highly do I think of Flora, that you are the only man in England for whom I would say so much.—But before you shake my hand so warmly, there is more to be considered—Your own family, will they approve your connecting yourself with the sister of a high-born Highland beggar?"

"My uncle's situation, his general opinions, and his uniform indulgence, entitle me to say, that birth and personal qualities are all he would look to in such a connection. And where can I find both united in such excellence as in your sister?"

"O no where!—*cela va sans dire*. But your father will expect a father's prerogative in being consulted."

"Surely; but his late breach with the ruling powers removes all apprehension of objection on his part, especially as I am convinced that my uncle will be warm in my cause."

"Religion perhaps—though we are not bigotted Catholics."

"My grandmother was of the church of Rome, and her religion was never objected to by my family.—Do not think of my friends, dear Fergus; let me rather have your influence where it may be more necessary to remove obstacles—I mean with your lovely sister."

"My lovely sister, like her loving brother, is very apt to have a pretty decisive will of her own, by which, in this case, you must be ruled; but you shall not want my interest, nor my counsel. And, in the first place, I will give you one hint—Loyalty is her ruling passion; and since she could spell an English book, she has been in love with the memory of the gallant Captain Wogan, who renounced the service of the usurper Cromwell to join the standard of Charles II., marched a handful of cavalry from London to the Highlands to join Middleton, then in arms for the king, and at length died gloriously in the royal cause. Ask her to shew you some verses she made on his history and fate; they have been much admired, I assure you. The next point is—I think I saw Flora go up towards the water-fall a short time since—follow, man, follow!—don't allow the garrison time to strengthen its purposes of resistance—*Alerte à la muraille!* Seek Flora out, and learn her decision as soon as you can, and Cupid go with you, while I go to look over belts and cartouch-boxes."

Waverley ascended the glen with an anxious and throbbing heart. Love, with all its romantic train of hopes, fears, and wishes, was mingled with other feelings of a nature less easily defined. He could not but remember how much this morning had changed his fate, and into what a complication of perplexity it was likely to plunge him. Sunrise had seen him possessed of an esteemed rank in the honourable profession of arms, his father to all appearance rapidly rising in the favour of his sovereign;—all this had passed away like a dream—he himself was dishonoured, his father disgraced, and he had become involuntarily the confidant at least, if not the accomplice, of plans, dark, deep, and dangerous, which must infer either the subversion of the government he had so lately served, or the destruction of all who had participated in them. Should Flora even listen to his suit favourably, what prospect was there of its being brought to a happy termination amid the tumult of an impending insurrection? Or how could he make the selfish request that she should leave Fergus, to whom she was so much attached, and, retiring with him to England, wait, as a distant spectator, the success of her brother's undertaking, or the ruin of all his hopes and fortunes?—Or, on the other hand, to engage himself, with no other aid than his single arm, in the dangerous and precipitate councils of the Chieftain,—to be whirled along by him, the partaker of all his desperate and impetuous motions, renouncing almost the power of judging, or deciding upon the rectitude or prudence of his actions,—this was no pleasing prospect for the secret pride of Waverley to stoop to. And yet what other conclusion remained, saving the rejection of his addresses by Flora, an alternative not to be thought of, in the present high-wrought state of his feelings, with any thing short of mental agony. Pondering the doubtful and dangerous prospect before him, he at length arrived near the cascade, where, as Fergus had augured, he found Flora seated.

She was quite alone, and as soon as she observed his approach, she rose and came to meet him. Edward attempted to say something within the verge of ordinary compliment and conversation, but found himself unequal to the task. Flora seemed at first equally embarrassed, but recovered herself more speedily, and (an unfavourable augury for Waverley's suit) was the first to enter upon the subject of their last interview. "It is too important, in every point of view, Mr Waverley, to permit me to leave you in doubt upon my sentiments."

"Do not speak them speedily, unless they are such as I fear, from your manner, I must not dare to anticipate. Let time—let my future conduct—let your brother's influence"——

"Forgive me, Mr Waverley. I should incur my own heavy censure did I delay expressing my sincere conviction that I can never regard you otherwise than as a valued friend. I should do you the highest injustice did I conceal my sentiments for a moment—I see I distress you, and I grieve for it, but better now than later; and O better a thousand times, Mr Waverley, that you should feel a present momentary disappointment, than the long and heart-sickening griefs which attend a rash and ill-assorted marriage!"

"Good God! But why should you anticipate such consequences from an union where birth is equal, where fortune is favourable, where, if I may venture to say so, the taste is similar, where you allege no preference, where you even express a favourable opinion of him whom you reject?"

"Mr Waverley, I have that favourable opinion, and so strongly, that though I would rather have been silent upon the grounds of my resolution, you shall command them, if you exact such a mark of my esteem and confidence."

She sat down upon the fragment of a rock, and Waverley, placing himself near her, anxiously pressed for the explanation she offered.

"I dare hardly," she said, "tell you the situation of my feelings, they are so different from those usually ascribed to young women at my period of life; and I dare hardly touch upon what I think the nature of yours, lest I should give offence where I would willingly administer consolation. For myself, from my infancy till this day, I have had but one wish—the restoration of my royal benefactors to their rightful throne. It is impossible to express to you the devotion of my feelings on this single subject, and I will frankly confess, that it has so occupied my mind as to exclude every thought respecting what is called my own settlement in life. Let me but live to see the day of that happy restoration, and a Highland cottage, a French convent, or an English palace, will be alike indifferent to me."

"But, dearest Flora, how is your enthusiastic zeal for the exiled family inconsistent with my happiness?"

"Because you seek, or ought to seek, in the object of your attachment, a heart whose principal delight should be in augmenting your domestic felicity, and returning your affection, even to the height of romance. To a man of less keen sensibility, and less romantic tenderness of disposition, Flora Mac-Ivor might give content, if not happiness; for, were the irrevocable words spoken, never would she be deficient in the duties which she vowed."

"And why,—why, Miss Mac-Ivor, should you think yourself a more valuable treasure to one who is less capable of loving, of admiring you, than to me?"

"Simply because the tone of our affections would be more in unison, and because his more blunted sensibility would not require the return of enthusiasm which I have not to bestow. But you, Mr Waverley, would for ever refer to the idea of domestic happiness which your imagination is capable of painting, and whatever fell short of that ideal representation would be construed into coldness and indifference, while you might consider the enthusiasm with which I regarded the success of the royal family, as defrauding your affection of its due return."

"In other words, Miss Mac-Ivor, you cannot love me."

"I could esteem you, Mr Waverley, as much, perhaps more, than any man I have ever seen; but I cannot love you as you ought to be loved. O! do not, for your own sake, desire so hazardous an experiment. The woman whom you marry ought to have affections and opinions moulded upon yours. Her studies ought to be your studies; —her wishes, her feelings, her hopes, her fears, should all mingle with yours. She should enhance your pleasures, share your sorrows, and cheer your melancholy."

"And why will not you, Miss Mac-Ivor, who can so well describe a happy union, why will not you be yourself the person you describe?'"

"Is it possible you do not yet comprehend me? Have I not told you, that every keener sensation of my mind is bent exclusively towards an event, upon which indeed I have no power but those of my earnest prayers?'"

"And might not the granting the suit I solicit, even advance the interest to which you have devoted yourself? My family is wealthy and powerful, inclined in principles to the Stuart race, and should a favourable opportunity"——

"A favourable opportunity!—Inclined in principles!—Can such lukewarm adherence be honourable to yourselves, or gratifying to your lawful sovereign?—Think, from my present feelings, what I should suffer when I held the place of member in a family, where the rights which I hold most sacred are subjected to cold discussion, and only deemed worthy of support when they shall appear on the point of triumphing without it!"

"Your doubts," quickly replied Waverley, "are unjust so far as concerns myself. The cause that I shall assert, I dare support through every danger, as undauntedly as the boldest who draws sword in it."

"Of that," answered Flora, "I cannot doubt for a moment. But consult your own good sense and reason rather than a prepossession hastily adopted, probably only because you have met a young woman possessed of the usual accomplishments, in a sequestered and romantic situation. Let your part in this great and perilous drama rest upon conviction, and not upon a hurried, and probably a temporary feeling."

Waverley attempted to reply, but his words failed him. Every sentiment that Flora had uttered vindicated the strength of his attachment; for even her loyalty, although wildly enthusiastic, was generous and noble, and disdained to avail itself of any indirect means of supporting the cause to which she was devoted.

After walking a little way in silence down the path, Flora thus resumed the conversation.—"One word more, Mr Waverley, ere we bid farewell to this topic for ever; and forgive my boldness if that word have the air of advice. My brother Fergus is anxious that you should join him in his present enterprise. But do not consent to this;—you could not, by your single exertions, further his success, and you would inevitably share his fall, if it be God's pleasure that fall he must. Your character also would suffer irretrievably. Let me beg you will return to your own country; and, having publicly freed yourself from every tie to the usurping government, I trust you will see cause, and find opportunity, to serve your injured sovereign with effect, and stand forth, as your loyal ancestors, at the head of your natural followers and adherents, a worthy representative of the house of Waverley."

"And should I be so happy as thus to distinguish myself, might I not hope"——

"Forgive my interruption. The present time only is ours, and I can but explain to you with candour the feelings which I now entertain; how they might be altered by a train of events too favourable perhaps to be hoped for, it were in vain even to conjecture: Only be assured, Mr Waverley, that, after my brother's honour and happiness, there is none which I shall more sincerely pray for than for yours."

With these words she parted from him, for they were now arrived where two paths separated. Waverley reached the castle amidst a medley of conflicting passions. He avoided any private interview with Fergus, as he did not find himself able either to encounter his raillery, or reply to his solicitations. The wild revelry of the feast, for Mac-Ivor kept open table for his clan, served in some degree to stun reflection. When their festivity was ended, he began to consider how he should again meet Miss Mac-Ivor after the painful and interesting explanation of the morning. But Flora did not appear. Fergus, whose eyes flashed when he was told by Cathleen that her mistress designed to keep her apartment that evening, went himself in quest of her; but apparently his remonstrances were in vain, for he returned with a heightened complexion, and manifest symptoms of displeasure. The rest of the evening passed on without any allusion, on the part either of Fergus or Waverley, to the subject which engrossed the reflections of the latter, and perhaps of both.

When retired to his own apartment, Edward endeavoured to sum the business of the day. That the repulse he had received from Flora would be persisted in for the present, there was no doubt. But could he hope for ultimate success in case circumstances permitted the renewal of his suit? Would the enthusiastic loyalty, which at this animating moment left no room for a softer passion, survive, at least in its engrossing force, the success or the failure of the present political machinations? And if so, could he hope that the interest which she had acknowledged him to possess in her favour, might be improved into a warmer attachment? He taxed his memory to recall every word she had used, with the appropriate looks and gestures which had enforced them, and ended by finding himself in the same state of uncertainty. It was very late before sleep brought relief to the tumult of his mind, after the most painful and agitating day which he had ever passed.

Chapter Five

A LETTER FROM TULLY-VEOLAN

IN THE MORNING, when Waverley's troubled reflections had for
some time given way to repose, there came music to his dreams, but
not the voice of Selma. He imagined himself transported back to
Tully-Veolan, and that he heard David Gellatley singing in the court
those matins which used generally to be the first sounds that disturbed
his repose while a guest of the Baron of Bradwardine. The notes
which suggested this vision continued and waxed louder, until Edward
awaked in earnest. The illusion, however, did not seem entirely dispelled. The apartment was in the fortress of Ian nan Chaistel, but it
was still the voice of Davie Gellatley that made the following lines
resound under the window:—

> My heart's in the Highlands, my heart is not here,
> My heart's in the Highlands a-chasing the deer;
> A-chasing the wild-deer, and following the roe,
> My heart's in the Highlands wherever I go.

Curious to know what could have determined Mr Gellatley on an
excursion of such unwonted extent, Edward began to dress himself in
all haste, during which operation the minstrelsy of Davie changed its
tune more than once,—

> There's nought in the Highlands but syboes and leeks,
> And lang-leggit callans gaun wanting the breeks;
> Wanting the breeks, and without hose and shoon,
> But we'll a' win the breeks when King Jamie comes hame.

By the time Waverley was dressed and had issued forth, David had
associated himself with two or three of the numerous Highland loungers who always graced the gates of the castle with their presence, and
was capering and dancing full merrily in the doubles and full career of
a Scotch foursome reel, to the music of his own whistling. In this
double capacity of dancer and musician, he continued until an idle
piper, who observed his zeal, obeyed the unanimous call of *Seid suas*,
(*i.e.* blow up) and relieved him from the latter part of his trouble.
Young and old then mingled in the dance as they could find partners.
The appearance of Waverley did not interrupt David's exercise,
though he contrived, by grinning, nodding, and throwing one or two
inclinations of the body into the graces with which he performed the
Highland fling, to convey to our hero symptoms of recognition. Then,
while busily employed in setting, whooping all the while and snapping
his fingers over his head, he of a sudden prolonged his side-step until

it brought him to the place where Edward was standing, and, still keeping time to the music like Harlequin in a pantomime, he thrust a letter into our hero's hand, and continued his saltation without pause or intermission. Edward, who perceived that the address was in Rose's hand-writing, retired to peruse it, leaving the faithful bearer to continue his exercise until the piper or he should be tired out.

The contents of the letter greatly surprised him. It had originally commenced with, *Dear Sir*; but these words had been carefully erased, and the monosyllable, *Sir*, substituted in their place. The rest of the contents shall be given in Rose's own language.

"I fear I am using an improper freedom by intruding upon you, yet I cannot trust to any one else to let you know some things which have happened here, with which it seems necessary you should be acquainted. Forgive me, if I am wrong in what I am doing; for, alas! Mr Waverley, I have no better advice than that of my own feelings;—my dear father is gone from this place, and when he can return to my assistance and protection, God alone knows. You have probably heard, that, in consequence of some troublesome news from the Highlands, warrants were sent out for apprehending several gentlemen in these parts, and among others, my dear father. In spite of all my tears and entreaties that he would surrender himself to the government, he joined with Mr Falconer and some other gentlemen, and they have all gone northwards, with a body of about forty horsemen. So I am not so much anxious concerning his immediate safety, as about what may follow afterwards, for these troubles are only beginning. But all this is nothing to you, Mr Waverley, only I thought you would be glad to learn that my father had escaped, in case you happen to have heard that he was in danger.

"But the day after my father went off, there came a party of soldiers to Tully-Veolan, and behaved very rudely to Baillie Macwheeble; but the officer was very civil to me, only said his duty obliged him to search for arms and papers. My father had provided against this by taking away all the arms except the old useless things which hung in the hall, and he had put all his papers out of the way. But O! Mr Waverley, how shall I tell you that they made strict enquiry after you, and asked when you had been at Tully-Veolan, and where you now were. The officer is gone back with his party, but a non-commissioned officer and four men remain as a sort of garrison in the house. They have hitherto behaved very well, as we are forced to keep them in good humour. But these soldiers have hinted as if upon your falling into their hands you would be in great danger; I cannot prevail on myself to write what wicked falsehoods they said, for I am sure they are falsehoods; but you will best judge what you ought to do. The party that returned carried off your servant prisoner, with your two horses, and every thing that you left at Tully-Veolan. I hope God will protect you, and that you will get safe home to England, where you used to tell me there was no military violence nor fighting among clans permitted, but every thing was done according to an equal law that protected all who were harmless and innocent. I hope you will exert your indulgence as to my boldness in writing to you, where it seems to me, though perhaps erroneously, that your safety and honour are concerned. I am sure—at least I think, my father would approve of my writing; for Mr Rubrick is fled to his cousin's at the Duchran to be out of danger from the soldiers and the whigs, and Baillie Macwheeble does not like to meddle (he says) in other men's concerns, though I hope what may serve my father's friend at such a time as this, cannot be termed improper interference. Farewell, Captain Waverley, I shall probably never see you more; for it would be very improper to wish you to call at Tully-Veolan just now, even if these men were gone; but I will always remember with gratitude your kindness in assisting so poor a scholar as myself, and your attentions to my dear, dear father. I remain your obliged servant,

"ROSE COMYNE BRADWARDINE.

"P.S.—I hope you will send me a line by David Gellatley, just to say you have received this and will take care of yourself; and forgive me if I entreat you, for your own sake, to join none of these unhappy cabals, but escape, as fast as possible, to your own fortunate country. My compliments to my dear Flora and to Glennaquoich. Is she not as handsome and accomplished as I described her?"

Thus concluded the letter of Rose Bradwardine, the contents of which both surprised and affected Waverley. That the Baron should fall under the suspicion of government in consequence of the present stir among the partizans of the house of Stuart, seemed only the natural consequence of his political predilections; but how *he* should have been involved in such suspicions, conscious that until yesterday he had been free from harbouring a thought against the prosperity of the reigning family, seemed inexplicable. Both at Tully-Veolan and Glennaquoich his hosts had respected his engagements with the immediate government, and though enough passed by accidental inuendo that might induce him to reckon the Baron and the Chief among those disaffected gentlemen who were still numerous in Scotland, yet until his own connection with the army had been broken off by the resumption of his commission, he had no reason to suppose that they nourished any immediate or hostile attempts against the present establishment. Still he was aware that unless he meant at once to embrace the proposal of Fergus Mac-Ivor, it would deeply concern him to leave this suspicious neighbourhood without delay, and repair where his conduct might undergo a satisfactory examination. Upon this he the rather determined, as Flora's advice favoured his doing so, and because he felt inexpressible repugnance at the idea of being accessary to the plague of civil war. Whatever were the original rights of the Stuarts, calm reflection told him, that, omitting the question how far James the Second could forfeit those of his posterity, he had, according to the united voice of the whole nation, justly forfeited his own. Since that period, four monarchs had reigned in peace and glory over Britain, sustaining and exalting the character of the nation abroad, and its liberties at home. Reason asked, was it worth while to disturb a government so long settled and established, and to plunge a kingdom into all the miseries of civil war, to replace upon the throne the descendants of a monarch by whom it had been wilfully forfeited? If, on the other hand, his own final conviction of the goodness of their cause, or the commands of his father or uncle, should recommend to him allegiance to the Stuarts, still it was necessary to clear his own character by shewing that he had taken no step to this purpose, as seemed to be falsely insinuated, during his holding the commission of the reigning monarch.

The affectionate simplicity of Rose, and her anxiety for his safety, —his sense too of her unprotected state, and of the terror and actual dangers to which she might be exposed, made an impression upon his mind, and he instantly wrote to thank her in the kindest terms for her anxiety on his account, to express his earnest good wishes for her welfare and that of her father, and to assure her of his own safety. The feelings which this task excited were speedily lost in the necessity which he now saw of bidding farewell to Flora Mac-Ivor, perhaps for ever. The pang attending this reflection was inexpressible; for her high-minded elevation of character, her self-devotion to the cause which she had embraced, united to her scrupulous rectitude as to the means of serving it, had vindicated to his judgment the choice adopted by his passions. But time pressed, calumny was busy with his fame, and every hour's delay increased the power to injure it. His departure must be instant.

With this determination he sought out Fergus, and communicated to him the contents of Rose's letter, with his own resolution instantly to go to Edinburgh, and, seeking out some one or other of those persons of influence to whom he had letters from his father, to put into their hands his exculpation from any charge which might be preferred against him.

"You run your head into the lion's mouth," answered Mac-Ivor. "You do not know the severity of a government harassed by just apprehensions, and a consciousness of their own illegality and insecurity. I shall have to deliver you from some dungeon in Stirling or Edinburgh Castle."

"My innocence, my rank, my father's intimacy with Lord M——, General G——, &c. will be a sufficient protection."

"You will find the contrary: these gentlemen will have enough to do about their own matters. Once more, will you take the plaid, and stay a little while with me among the mists and the crows, in the bravest cause ever sword was drawn in?"

"For many reasons, my dear Fergus, you must hold me excused."

"Well then, I shall certainly find you exerting your poetical talents in elegies upon a prison, or your antiquarian researches in detecting the Oggam character, or some Punic hieroglyphic upon the keystones of a vault, curiously arched. Or what say you to *un petit pendement bien joli*, against which awkward ceremony I don't warrant you, should you meet a body of the armed west-country whigs."

"And why should they use me so?"

"For an hundred good reasons: First, you are an Englishman; secondly, a gentleman; thirdly, a prelatist abjured; and, fourthly, they have not had an opportunity to exercise their talents on such a subject this long while. But don't be cast down, beloved; all will be done in the fear of the Lord."

"Well, I must run my hazard."

"You are determined then?"

"I am."

"Wilful will do't;—but you cannot go on foot, and I shall want no horse, as I must march on foot at the head of the children of Ivor: you shall have brown Dermid."

"If you will sell him, I shall certainly be much obliged."

"If your proud English heart cannot be obliged by a gift or loan, I will not refuse money at the entrance of a campaign: his price is twenty guineas [Remember, reader, it was Sixty Years since.] And when do you propose to depart?"

"The sooner the better."

"You are right, since go you must, or rather, since go you will: I will take Flora's poney, and ride with you as far as Bally-Brough.—Callum Beg, see that our horses are ready, with a poney for yourself, to attend and carry Mr Waverley's baggage as far as —— (naming a small town,) where he can have a horse and guide to Edinburgh. Put on a Lowland dress, Callum, and see you keep your tongue close, if you would not have me cut it out: Mr Waverley rides Dermid." Then turning to Edward, "You will take leave of my sister?"

"Surely,——that is, if Miss Mac-Ivor will honour me so far."

"Cathleen, let my sister know Mr Waverley wishes to bid her fare-well before he leaves us.——But Rose Bradwardine, her situation must be thought of——I wish she were here——And why should she not?——There are but four red coats at Tully-Veolan, and their muskets would be very useful to us."

To these broken remarks Edward made no answer; his ear indeed received them, but his soul was intent upon the expected entrance of Flora. The door opened——It was but Cathleen, with her lady's excuse, and wishes for Captain Waverley's health and happiness.

Chapter Six

WAVERLEY'S RECEPTION IN THE LOWLANDS AFTER HIS HIGHLAND TOUR

IT WAS NOON when the two friends stood at the top of the pass of Bally-Brough. "I must go no farther," said Fergus Mac-Ivor, who during this journey had in vain endeavoured to raise his friend's spirits. "If my cross-grained sister has any share in your dejection, trust me she thinks highly of you, though her present anxiety about the public cause prevents her listening to any other subject. Confide your interest to me; I will not betray it, providing you do not again assume that vile cockade."

"No fear of that, considering the manner in which it has been recalled. Adieu, Fergus; do not permit your sister to forget me."

"And adieu, Waverley; you may soon hear of her with a prouder title. Get home, write letters, and make friends as many and as fast as you can; there will speedily be unexpected guests on the coast of Suffolk, or my news from France has deceived me."

Thus parted the friends; Fergus returning back to his castle, while Edward, followed by Callum Beg, the latter transformed from point to point into a Low-country groom, proceeded to the little town of ———.

Edward paced on under the painful, and yet not altogether em-bittered feelings, which separation and uncertainty produce in the mind of a youthful lover. I am not sure if the ladies understand the full value of the influence of absence, nor do I think it wise to teach it them, lest, like the Clelias and Mandanes of yore, they should resume the humour of sending their lovers to banishment. Distance, in truth, produces in idea the same effect as in real perspective. Objects are softened, and rounded, and rendered doubly graceful; the harsher and more ordinary points of character are melted down, and those by which it is remembered are the more striking outlines that mark sublimity, grace, or beauty. There are mists too in the mental, as well as the natural horizon, to conceal what is less pleasing in distant objects, and there are happy lights, to stream in full glory upon those points which can profit by brilliant illumination.

Waverley forgot Flora Mac-Ivor's prejudices in her magnanimity, and almost pardoned her indifference towards his affection, when he recollected the grand and decisive object which seemed to fill her whole soul. She, whose sense of duty so wholly engrossed her in the cause of a benefactor, what would be her feelings in favour of the happy individual who should be so fortunate as to awaken them? Then came the doubtful question, whether he might not be that happy man, —a question which fancy endeavoured to answer in the affirmative, by conjuring up all she had said in his praise, with the addition of a comment much more flattering than the text warranted. All that was common-place, all that belonged to the every-day world, was melted away and obliterated in these dreams of imagination, which only remembered with advantage the points of grace and dignity that distinguished Flora from the generality of her sex, not the particulars which she held in common with them. Edward was, in short, in the fair way of creating a goddess out of a high-spirited, accomplished, and beautiful young woman; and the time was wasted in castle-building until, at the descent of a steep hill, he saw beneath him the market town of ——.

The Highland politeness of Callum Beg—there are few nations, by the way, that can boast of so much natural politeness as the Highlanders—the Highland civility of his attendant had not permitted him to disturb the reveries of our hero. But, observing him rouse himself at the sight of the village, Callum pressed closer to his side, and hoped, "when they came to the public, his honour wad not say nothing about Vich Ian Vohr, for ta people were bitter whigs, deil burst tem."

Waverley assured the prudent page that he would be cautious; and as he now distinguished, not indeed the ringing of bells, but the tinkling of something like a hammer against the side of an old mossy, green, inverted porridge-pot, that hung in an open booth, of the size and shape of a parrot's cage, erected to grace the east end of a building resembling an old barn, he asked Callum Beg if it were Sunday.

"Could na say just preceesely—Sunday seldom came aboon the pass of Bally-Brough."

On entering the town, however, and advancing toward the most apparent public-house which presented itself, the numbers of old women, in tartan screens and red cloaks, who streamed from the barn-resembling building, debating as they went the comparative merits of the blessed youth Jabesh Rentowel, and that chosen vessel Maister Goukthrapple, induced Callum to assure his temporary master, "that it was either ta mickle Sunday hersell, or ta little government Sunday that they ca'd ta fast."

Upon alighting at the sign of the Seven-branched Golden Candlestick, which, for the further delectation of the guests, was graced with a short Hebrew motto, they were received by mine host, a tall thin puritanical figure, who seemed to debate with himself whether he ought to give shelter to those who travelled on such a day. Reflecting, however, in all probability, that he possessed the power of mulcting them for this irregularity, a penalty which they might escape by passing into Gregor Duncanson's, at the sign of the Highlander and the Hawick Gill, Mr Ebenezer Cruickshanks condescended to admit them into his dwelling.

To this sanctified person Waverley addressed his request, that he would procure him a guide, with a saddle-horse to carry his portmanteau to Edinburgh.

"And whare may ye be coming from?" demanded mine Host of the Candlestick.

"I have told you where I wish to go: I do not conceive any further information necessary either for the guide or his saddle-horse."

"Hem! Ahem!" returned he of the Candlestick, somewhat disconcerted at this rebuff. "It's the general fast, sir, and I cannot enter into ony carnal transactions on sick a day, when the people should be humbled, and the backsliders should return, as worthy Mr Goukthrapple said; and moreover when, as the precious Mr Jabesh Rentowel did well observe, the land was mourning for covenants burnt, broken, and buried."

"My good friend, if you cannot let me have a horse and a guide, my servant shall seek them elsewhere."

"A weel! Your servant?—and what for gangs he not forward with you himself?"

Waverley had but very little of a captain of horse's spirit within him —I mean of that sort of spirit which I have been obliged to, when I happened, in a mail-coach or diligence, to meet some military man who has kindly taken upon him the disciplining of the waiters, and the taxing of reckonings. Some of this useful talent our hero had, however, acquired during his military service, and on this gross provocation it began seriously to arise. "Look ye, sir, I came here for my own accommodation, and not to answer impertinent questions. Either say you can, or cannot, get me what I want; I shall pursue my course in either case."

Mr Ebenezer Cruickshanks left the room with some indistinct muttering, but whether negative or acquiescent, Edward could not well distinguish. The hostess, a civil, quiet, laborious drudge, came to take his orders for dinner, but declined to make answer upon the subject of the horse and guide, for the Salique law, it seems, extended to the stables of the Golden Candlestick.

From a window which overlooked the dark and narrow court in which Callum Beg dressed the horses after their journey, Waverley heard the following dialogue betwixt the subtle foot-page of Vich Ian Vohr and his landlord.

"Ye'll be frae the north, young man?" began the latter.

"And ye may say that," answered Callum.

"And ye'll hae ridden a lang way to-day, it may weel be?"

"Sae lang that I could weel tak a dram."

"Gudewife, bring the gill stoup."

Here some compliments passed fitting the occasion, when my Host of the Golden Candlestick, having, as he thought, opened his guest's heart by this hospitable propitiation, resumed his scrutiny.

"Ye'll no hae mickle better whisky than that aboon the pass?"

"I am nae from aboon the pass."

"Ye're a Highlandman by your tongue?"

"Na, I am but just Aberdeen-a-way."

"And did your master come from Aberdeen wi' you?"

"Ay—that's when I left it mysel," answered the cool and impenetrable Callum Beg.

"And what kind of a gentleman is he?"

"I believe he is ane o' King George's state officers; at least he's aye for ganging on to the south, and he has a hantle silver, and never grudges ony thing till a poor body, or in the way of lawing."

"He wants a guide and a horse from hence to Edinburgh?"

"Ay, and ye maun find it him forthwith."

"Ahem! It will be chargeable."

"He cares na for that a boddle."

"A weel, Duncan—Did ye say your name was Duncan, or Donald?"

"Na, man—Jamie—Jamie Steenson—I telt ye before."

This last undaunted parry altogether foiled Mr Cruickshanks, who, though not quite satisfied either with the reserve of the master, or the extreme readiness of the man, was contented to lay a tax upon the reckoning and horsehire, that might compound for his ungratified curiosity. The circumstance of its being the fast-day was not forgotten in the charge, which, upon the whole, did not, however, amount to much more than double what in fairness it should have been.

Callum Beg soon after announced in person the ratification of this treaty, adding, "Ta auld devil was ganging to ride wi' the Duinhé-wassal hersel."

"That will not be very pleasant, Callum, nor altogether safe, for our host seems a person of great curiosity; but a traveller must submit to these inconveniences. Meanwhile, my good lad, here is a trifle for you to drink Vich Ian Vohr's health."

The hawk's eye of Callum flashed delight upon a golden guinea, with which these last words were accompanied. He hastened, not without a curse upon the intricacies of a Saxon breeches pocket, or *spleuchan*, as he called it, to deposit the treasure in his fob; and then, as if he conceived the benevolence called for some requital on his part, he gathered close up to Edward, with an expression of countenance peculiarly knowing, and spoke in an under tone, "If his honour thought ta auld deevil whig carle was a bit dangerous, she could easily provide for him, and teil ane ta wiser."

"How, and in what manner?"

"Her ain sell," replied Callum, "could wait for him a wee bit frae the toun, and kittle his quarters wi' her *skene-occle*."

"Skene-occle? what's that?"

Callum unbuttoned his coat, raised his left arm, and, with an emphatic nod, pointed to the hilt of a small dirk, snugly deposited under it, in the lining of his jacket. Waverley thought he had misunderstood his meaning; he gazed in his face, and discovered in Callum's very handsome, though embrowned features, just the degree of roguish malice with which a lad of the same age in England would have brought forward a plan for robbing an orchard.

"Good God, Callum, would you take the man's life?"

"Indeed," answered the young desperado, "and I think he has had just a lang enough lease o't, when he's for betraying honest folk, that come to spend silver at his public."

Edward saw nothing was to be gained by argument, and therefore contented himself with enjoining Callum to lay aside all practices against the person of Mr Ebenezer Cruickshanks, in which injunction the page seemed to acquiesce with an air of great indifference.

"Ta Duinhé-wassal might please himsell; ta auld rudas loon had never done Callum nae ill. But here's a bit line frae ta Tighearnach, tat he bade me gie your honour ere I came back."

The letter from the Chief contained Flora's lines on the fate of Captain Wogan, whose enterprizing character is so well drawn by Clarendon. He had originally engaged in the service of the Parliament, but had abjured that party upon the execution of Charles I. and upon hearing that the royal standard was set up by the Earl of Glencairn and General Middleton, in the Highlands of Scotland, took leave of Charles II. who was then at Paris, passed into England, assembled a body of cavaliers in the neighbourhood of London, and traversed all the kingdom which had been so long under domination of the usurper, by marches conducted with such skill, dexterity, and speed, that he safely united his handful of horsemen with the body of Highlanders then in arms. After several months of desultory warfare, in which Wogan's skill and courage gained him the highest reputation, he had the misfortune to be wounded in a dangerous manner, and no surgical assistance being within reach, he terminated his short but glorious career.

There were obvious reasons why the politic Chieftain was desirous to place the example of this young hero under the eye of Waverley, with whose romantic disposition it coincided so peculiarly. But his letter turned chiefly upon some trifling commissions which Waverley had promised to execute for him in England, and it was only toward the conclusion that Edward found these words:—"I owe Flora a grudge for refusing us her company yesterday; and as I am giving you the trouble of reading these lines, in order to keep in your memory your promise to procure me the fishing-tackle and cross-bow from London, I will inclose her verses on the grave of Wogan. This I know will teaze her; for, to tell you the truth, I think her more in love with the memory of that dead hero, than she is likely to be with any living one, unless he shall tread a similar path. But English squires of our day keep their oak trees to shelter their deer parks, or repair the losses of an evening at White's, and neither invoke them to wreath their brows, or shelter their graves. Let me hope for one brilliant exception in a dear friend, to whom I would gladly give a dearer title."

The verses were inscribed,

TO AN OAK TREE,

In the Highlands of Scotland planted near the grave of a gallant English officer.

Emblem of England's ancient faith,
   Full proudly may thy branches wave,
Where loyalty lies low in death,
   And valour fills a timeless grave.

And thou, brave tenant of the tomb!
   Repine not if our clime deny,
Above thine honour'd sod to bloom,
   The flowerets of a milder sky.

These owe their birth to genial May;
   Beneath a fiercer sun they pine,

> Before the winter storm decay—
>   And can their worth be type of thine?
>
> No! for, mid storms of Fate opposing,
>   Still higher swell'd thy dauntless heart,
> And, while Despair the scene was closing,
>   Commenced thy brief but brilliant part.
>
> 'Twas then thou sought'st on Albyn's hill,
>   (When England's sons the strife resign'd,)
> A rugged race resisting still,
>   And unsubdued though unrefined.
>
> Thy death's-hour heard no kindred wail,
>   No holy knell thy requiem rung;
> Thy mourners were the plaided Gael,
>   Thy dirge the clamorous pibroch sung.
>
> Yet who, in Fortune's summer-shine
>   To waste life's longest term away,
> Would change that glorious dawn of thine,
>   Though darken'd ere its noontide day?
>
> Be thine the Tree whose dauntless boughs
>   Brave summer's drought and winter's gloom!
> Rome bound with oak her patriots' brows,
>   And Albyn shadows Wogan's tomb.

Whatever might be the real merit of Flora Mac-Ivor's poetry, the enthusiasm which it intimated was well calculated to make a corresponding impression upon her lover. The lines were read—read again—then deposited in Waverley's bosom—then again drawn out, and read line by line, in a low and smothered voice, and with frequent pauses which prolonged the mental treat, as an epicure protracts, by sipping slowly, the enjoyment of a delicious beverage. The entrance of Mrs Cruickshanks, with the sublunary articles of dinner and wine, hardly interrupted this pantomime of affectionate enthusiasm.

At length the tall ungainly figure and ungracious visage of Ebenezer presented themselves. The upper part of his form, notwithstanding the season required no such defence, was shrouded in a large great-coat, belted over his under habiliments, and crested with a huge cowl of the same stuff, which, when drawn over the head and hat, completely overshadowed both, and being buttoned beneath the chin, was called a *trot-cosy*. His hand grasped a huge jockey whip, garnished with brass mounting. His thin legs tenanted a pair of gambadoes, fastened at the sides with rusty clasps. Thus accoutred, he stalked into the midst of the apartment, and announced his errand in brief phrase, "Yere horses are ready."

"You go with me yourself then, landlord?"

"I do—as far as Perth; where ye may be supplied with a guide to Embro', as your occasions shall require."

Thus saying, he placed under Waverley's eye the bill which he held in his hand; and at the same time, self-invited, filled a glass of wine, and drank devoutly to a blessing on their journey. Waverley stared at the man's impudence, but, as their connection was to be short, and promised to be convenient, he made no observation upon it; and having paid his reckoning, expressed his intention to depart immediately. He mounted Dermid accordingly, and sallied forth from the Golden Candlestick, followed by the puritanical figure we have described, after he had, by the assistance of a "louping-on-stane," or structure of masonry erected for the traveller's convenience in front of his house, elevated his person, at the expence of some time and difficulty, to the back of a long-backed, raw-boned, thin-gutted phantom of a broken-down blood-horse, on which Waverley's portmanteau was deposited. Our hero, though not in a very gay humour, could hardly help laughing at the appearance of his new squire, and at imagining the astonishment which his person and equipage would have excited at Waverley-Honour.

Edward's tendency to mirth did not escape mine Host of the Candlestick, who, conscious of the cause, infused a double portion of souring into the pharisaical leaven of his countenance, and resolved internally that, in one way or other, the young *Englisher* should pay dearly for the contempt with which he seemed to regard him. Callum also stood at the gate, and enjoyed, with undissembled glee, the ridiculous figure of Mr Cruickshanks. As Waverley passed him, he pulled off his hat respectfully, and, approaching his stirrup, bade him "Tak heed the auld whig played him nae cantraip."

Waverley once more thanked, and bade him farewell, and then rode briskly onward, not sorry to be out of hearing of the shouts of the children, as they beheld old Ebenezer rise and sink in his stirrups, to avoid the concussions occasioned by a hard trot upon a half-paved street. The village of —— was soon several miles behind him.

Chapter Seven

SHOWS THAT THE LOSS OF A HORSE'S SHOE MAY BE A SERIOUS INCONVENIENCE

THE MANNER and air of Waverley—above all the glittering contents of his purse, and the indifference with which he seemed to regard them, somewhat overawed his companion, and deterred him from making any attempt to enter upon conversation. His own reflections were moreover agitated by various surmises, and by plans of self-interest, with which they were intimately connected. The travellers journeyed, therefore, in silence, until it was interrupted by the annunciation, on the part of the guide, that his "naig had lost a fore-foot shoe, which, doubtless, his honour would consider it was his part to replace." This was what lawyers call a *fishing question*, calculated to ascertain how far Waverley was disposed to submit to petty imposition. "My part to replace your horse's shoe, you rascal!" said Waverley, mistaking the purport of the intimation.

"Indubitably," answered Mr Cruickshanks, somewhat disconcerted and alarmed at the idea of having reached the goal of Edward's forbearance, "though there was no preceese clause to that effect, it canna be expected that I am to pay for the casualties whilk may befall the puir naig while in your honour's service—natheless if your honour"——

"O, you mean I am to pay the farrier; but where shall we find one?"

Rejoiced at discovering there would be no objection on the part of his temporary master, Mr Cruickshanks assured him that Cairnvreckan, a village which they were about to enter, was happy in an excellent blacksmith; "but as he was a *professor*, he wad drive a nail for no man on the Sabbath, or kirk fast, unless it were in a case of absolute necessity, for which he always charged sixpence each shoe." The most important part of this communication, in the opinion of the speaker, made a very slight impression on the hearer, who only internally wondered what college this veterinary professor belonged to; not aware that the word was used to denote any person who pretended to uncommon sanctity of faith and manner.

As they entered the village of Cairnvreckan, they speedily distinguished the smith's house. Being also a *public*, it was two stories high, and proudly reared its crest, covered with grey slate, above the thatched hovels by which it was surrounded. The adjoining smithy betokened none of the Sabbatical silence and repose which Ebenezer had augured from the sanctity of his friend. On the contrary, hammer clashed and anvil rang, the bellows groaned, and the whole apparatus of Vulcan appeared to be in full activity. Nor was the labour of a rural and pacific nature. The master smith, benempt, as his sign intimated, John Micklewrath, with two assistants, toiled busily in arranging, repairing, and furbishing old muskets, pistols, and swords, which lay scattered around his work-shop in military confusion. The open shed, containing the forge, was crowded with persons who came and went as if receiving and communicating important news; and a single glance at the aspect of the people who traversed the street in haste, or stood assembled in groups, with eyes elevated, and hands uplifted, announced that some extraordinary intelligence was agitating the public mind of the municipality of Cairnvreckan. "There is some news," said mine Host of the Candlestick, pushing his lanthorn-jawed visage and bare-boned nag rudely forward into the crowd—"there is some news, and if it please my Creator, I will forthwith obtain speerings thereof."

Waverley, with better regulated curiosity than his attendant, dismounted, and gave his horse to a boy who stood idling near. It arose, perhaps, from the shyness of his character in early youth, that he felt dislike at applying to a stranger even for casual information, without previously glancing at his physiognomy and appearance. While he looked about in order to select the person with whom he would most willingly hold communication, the buzz around saved him in some degree the trouble of interrogatories. The names of Lochiel, Clanronald, Glengary, and other distinguished Highland Chiefs, among whom Vich Ian Vohr was repeatedly mentioned, were familiar in men's mouths as household words; and from the alarm generally expressed, he easily conceived that their descent into the Lowlands, at the head of their armed tribes, had either already taken place, or was instantly apprehended.

Ere Waverley could ask particulars, a strong large-boned hardfeatured woman, about forty, dressed as if her clothes had been flung on with a pitchfork, her cheeks flushed with a scarlet red where they were not smutted with soot and lamp-black, jostled through the crowd, and, brandishing high a child of two years old, which she danced in her arms, without regard to its screams of terror, sang forth, with all her might,—

> "Charlie is my darling, my darling, my darling,
> Charlie is my darling,
> 　　　The young Chevalier.

D'ye hear what's come ower ye now, ye whingeing whig carles? D'ye hear wha's coming to cow yere cracks?

> Little wot ye wha's coming,
> Little wot ye wha's coming,
> 　　A' the wild Macraws' coming."

The Vulcan of Cairnvreckan, who acknowledged his Venus in this exulting Bacchanal, regarded her with a grim and ire-foreboding countenance, while some of the senators of the village hastened to interpose. "Whisht, gudewife; is this a time, or is *this* a day, to be singing your ranting fule-sangs in?—a time when the wine of wrath is poured out without mixture in the cup of indignation, and a day when the land should give testimony against popery and prelacy, and quakerism, and independency, and supremacy, and erastianism, and antinomianism, and a' the errors of the church."

"And that's a' your whiggery," re-echoed the virago; "that's a' your whiggery, and your presbytery, ye cut-lugged graning carles. What d'ye think the lads wi' the kilts will care for yere synods and yere presbyteries, and yere buttock-mail, and yere stool o' repentance? Vengeance on the black face o't! mony an honester woman's been set upon it than streeks doon beside ony whig in the country. I mysell"——

There John Micklewrath, who dreaded her entering upon a detail of personal experiences, interposed his matrimonial authority. "Get hame, and be d——, (that I should say sae) and put on the sowens for supper."

"And you, ye doil'd dotard," replied his gentle helpmate, her wrath, which had hitherto wandered abroad over the whole assembly, being at once and violently impelled into its natural channel, "ye stand there hammering dog-heads for fules that will never snap them at a High-landman, instead of winning bread for your family, and shoeing this winsome young gentleman's horse that's just come frae the north. I'se warrant him nane of your whingeing King George folk, but a gallant Gordon, at the least o' him."

The eyes of the assembly were now turned upon Waverley, who took the opportunity to beg the smith to shoe his guide's horse with all speed, as he wished to proceed on his journey, for he had heard enough to make him sensible that there would be danger in delaying long in this place. The smith's eyes rested on him with a look of displeasure and suspicion, not lessened by the eagerness with which his wife enforced Waverley's mandate. "D'ye hear what the weel-favoured young gentleman says, ye drunken ne'er-do-good?"

"And what may your name be, sir?" quoth Micklewrath.

"It is of no consequence to you, my friend, provided I pay your labour."

"But it may be o' consequence to the state, sir," replied an old farmer, smelling strongly of whisky and peat-smoke; "and I doubt we maun delay your journey till you have seen the laird."

"You certainly," said Waverley, haughtily, "will find it both difficult and dangerous to detain me, unless you can produce some proper authority."

There was a pause and a whisper among the crowd—"Secretary Murray;" "Lord Lewis Gordon;" "may be the Chevalier himsel;" such were the surmises that passed hurriedly among them, and there was obviously an increasing disposition to resist Waverley's departure.

He attempted to argue mildly with them, but his voluntary ally, Mrs Micklewrath, broke in upon and drowned his expostulations, taking his part with an abusive violence, which was all set down to Edward's account by those on whom it was bestowed. "Ye'll stop ony gentleman that's the Prince's friend?" for she too, though with other feelings, had adopted the general opinion respecting Waverley. "I dare ye to touch him," spreading abroad her long and muscular fingers, garnished with sable claws which a vulture might have envied. "I'll set my ten commandments in the face o' the first loon that lays a finger on him."

"Gae hame, gudewife," quoth the farmer aforesaid; "it wad better set you to be nursing the gudeman's bairns than to be deaving us here."

"His bairns!" retorted the Amazon, regarding her husband with a grin of ineffable contempt—"*His* bairns!—

> O gin ye were dead, gudeman,
> And a green turf on your head, gudeman,
> Then I wad ware my widowhood
> Upon a ranting Highlandman."

This canticle, which excited a suppressed titter among the younger part of the audience, totally overcame the patience of the taunted man of the anvil. "Deil be in me but I put this het gad down her throat," cried he, snatching a bar from the forge in a rhapsody of wrath; and he might have executed his threat, had he not been withheld by a part of the mob, while the rest endeavoured to force the termagant out of his presence.

Waverley meditated a retreat in the confusion, but his horse was nowhere to be seen. At length he observed, at some distance, his faithful attendant, Ebenezer, who, as soon as he had perceived the turn matters were likely to take, had withdrawn both horses from the press, and, mounted on the one, and holding the other, answered the loud and repeated call of Waverley for his horse, "Na, na! if ye are nae friend to kirk and the king, and are detained as siccan a person, ye maun answer to honest men of the country for breach o' contract; and I maun keep the nag and the walise for damage and expence, in respect my horse and mysell will lose to-morrow's day's-wark, besides the afternoon preaching."

Edward, out of patience, hemmed in and hustled by the rabble on every side, and every moment expecting personal violence, resolved to try measures of intimidation, and at length drew a pocket-pistol, threatening, on the one hand, to shoot whomsoever dared to stop him, and on the other menacing Ebenezer with a similar doom, if he stirred a foot with the horses. The sapient Partridge says, that one man with a

pistol is equal to an hundred unarmed, because, though he can shoot
but one of the multitude, yet no one knows but he himself may be that
luckless individual. The *levy en masse* of Cairnvreckan would therefore
probably have given way, nor would Ebenezer, whose natural paleness
had turned three shades more cadaverous, have ventured to dispute a
mandate so enforced, had not the Vulcan of the village, eager to
discharge upon some more worthy object the fury which his helpmate
had provoked, and not ill satisfied to find such an object in Waverley,
rushed at him with the red-hot bar of iron, with such determination, as
made the discharge of his pistol an act of self-defence. The unfortunate man fell; and while Edward, thrilled with a natural horror at the
incident, neither had presence of mind to unsheathe his sword, nor to
draw his remaining pistol, the populace threw themselves upon him,
disarmed him, and were about to use him with great violence, when
the appearance of a venerable clergyman, the pastor of the parish, put
a curb upon their fury.

This worthy man (none of the Goukthrapples or Rentowels) maintained his character with the common people, although he preached
the practical fruits of Christian faith, as well as its abstract tenets,
and was respected by the higher orders, notwithstanding he declined
soothing their speculative errors by converting the pulpit of the gospel
into a school of heathen morality. Perhaps it is owing to this mixture of
faith and practice, that, although his memory has formed a sort of era
in the annals of Cairnvreckan, so that the parishioners, to denote what
befell Sixty Years since, still say it happened "in good Mr Morton's
time," I have never been able to discover which he belonged to, the
evangelic or the moderate party in the kirk. Nor do I hold the circumstance of much moment, since, in my own remembrance, the one was
headed by an Erskine, the other by a Robertson.

Mr Morton had been alarmed by the discharge of the pistol, and the
increasing hubbub around the smithy. His first attention, after he had
directed the bye-standers to detain Waverley, but to abstain from
injuring him, was turned to the body of Micklewrath, over which his
wife, in a revulsion of feeling, was weeping, howling, and tearing her
elf locks, in a state little short of distraction. Upon raising up the
smith, the first discovery was, that he was alive; and the next, that he
was likely to live as long as if he had never heard the report of a pistol in
his life. He had made a narrow escape, however; the bullet had grazed
his head, and stunned him for a minute or two, which terror and
confusion of spirit had prolonged somewhat longer. He now arose to
demand vengeance on the person of Waverley, and with difficulty
acquiesced in the proposal of Mr Morton, that he should be carried
before the laird, as a justice of peace, and placed at his disposal. The

rest of the assistants unanimously agreed to the measure recommended; even Mrs Micklewrath, who had begun to recover from her hysterics, whimpered forth,—"She wadna say naething again what the minister proposed; he was e'en ower gude for his trade, and she hoped to see him wi' a dainty decent bishop's gown on his back; a comelier sight than your Geneva cloaks and bands, I wuss."

All controversy being thus laid aside, Waverley, escorted by the whole inhabitants of the village who were not bed-ridden, was conducted to the house of Cairnvreckan, which was about half a mile distant.

Chapter Eight

AN EXAMINATION

MAJOR MELLVILLE of Cairnvreckan, an elderly gentleman, who had spent his youth in the military service, received Mr Morton with great kindness, and our hero with civility, which the equivocal circumstances in which Edward was placed rendered constrained and distant.

The matter of the smith's hurt was enquired into, and as the actual injury was likely to prove trifling, and the circumstances in which it was received rendered it on Edward's part a natural act of self-defence, the Major conceived he might dismiss that matter, on Waverley's depositing in his hands a small sum for the benefit of the wounded person.

"I could wish, sir," continued the Major, "that my duty terminated here; but it is necessary that we should have some further enquiry into the cause of your journey through the country at this unfortunate and distracted time."

Mr Ebenezer Cruickshanks now stood forth, and communicated to the magistrate all he knew or suspected from the reserve of Waverley, and the evasions of Callum Beg. The horse upon which Edward rode, he said, he knew to belong to Vich Ian Vohr, though he dared not tax Edward's former attendant with the fact, lest he should have his house and stables burned over his head some night by that godless gang, the Mac-Ivors. He concluded by exaggerating his own services to kirk and state, as having been the means, under God, (as he modestly qualified the assertion) of attaching this suspicious and formidable delinquent. He intimated hopes of future reward, and of instant reimbursement for loss of time, and even of character, by travelling in the state business upon the fast-day.

To this Major Mellville answered, with great composure, that so far from claiming any merit in this affair, Mr Cruickshanks ought to deprecate the imposition of a very heavy fine for neglecting to lodge, in terms of the recent proclamation, an account with the nearest magistrate of any stranger who came to his inn; that as Mr Cruickshanks boasted so much of religion and loyalty, he should not impute this conduct to disaffection, but only suppose that his zeal for kirk and state had been lulled asleep by the opportunity of charging a stranger with double horse-hire; that, however, feeling himself incompetent to decide singly upon the conduct of a person of such importance, he should reserve it for consideration of the next quarter-sessions. Now our history for the present saith no more of Him of the Candlestick, who wended dolorous and mal-content back to his own dwelling.

Major Mellville then commanded the villagers to return to their homes, excepting two, who officiated as constables, and whom he directed to wait below. The apartment was thus cleared of every person but Mr Morton, whom the Major invited to remain; a sort of factor, who acted as clerk; and Waverley himself. There ensued a painful and embarrassed pause, till Major Mellville, looking upon Waverley with much compassion, and often consulting a paper or memorandum which he held in his hand, requested to know his name.—"Edward Waverley."

"I thought so; late of the —— dragoons, and nephew of Sir Everard Waverley of Waverley-Honour?"

"The same."

"Young gentleman, I am extremely sorry that this painful duty has fallen to my lot."

"Duty, Major Mellville, renders apologies superfluous."

"True, sir; permit me, therefore, to ask you how your time has been disposed of since you obtained leave of absence from your regiment, several weeks ago, until the present moment."

"My reply to so general a question must be guided by the nature of the charge which renders it necessary. I request to know what that charge is, and upon what authority I am forcibly detained to reply to it?"

"The charge, Mr Waverley, I grieve to say, is of a very high nature, and affects your character both as a soldier and a subject. In the former capacity, you are charged with spreading mutiny and rebellion among the men you commanded, and setting them the example of desertion, by prolonging your own absence from the regiment, contrary to the express orders of your commanding-officer. The civil crime of which you stand accused is that of high treason, and levying war against the king, the highest delinquency of which a subject can be guilty."

"And by what authority am I detained to reply to such heinous calumnies?"

"By one which you must not dispute, nor I disobey."

He handed to Waverley a warrant from the supreme criminal court of Scotland, in full form, for apprehending and securing the person of Edward Waverley, Esq. suspected of treasonable practices and other high crimes and misdemeanours.

The astonishment which Waverley expressed at this communication was imputed by Major Mellville to conscious guilt, while Mr Morton was rather disposed to construe it into the surprise of innocence unjustly suspected. There was something true in both conjectures; for although Edward's mind acquitted him of the crimes with which he was charged, yet a hasty review of his own conduct convinced him he might have great difficulty in establishing his innocence to the satisfaction of others.

"It is a very painful part of this painful business," said Major Mellville, after a pause, "that, under so grave a charge, I must necessarily request to see such papers as you have on your person."

"You shall, sir, without reserve," said Edward, throwing his pocketbook and memorandums upon the table; "there is but one with which I could wish you would dispense."

"I am afraid I can indulge you with no reservation."

"You shall see it then, sir; and as it can be of no service, I beg it may be returned."

He took from his bosom the lines he had that morning received, and presented them, with the envelope. The Major perused them in silence, and directed his clerk to make a copy of them. He then wrapped the copy in the envelope, and placing it on the table before him, returned the original to Waverley, with an air of melancholy gravity.

After indulging the prisoner, for such our hero must now be considered, with what he thought a reasonable time for reflection, Major Mellville resumed his examination, premising, that, as Mr Waverley seemed to object to general questions, his interrogatories should be as specific as his information permitted. He then proceeded in his investigation, dictating, as he went on, the import of the questions and answers to the amanuensis, by whom it was written down.

"Did Mr Waverley know one Humphrey Houghton, a non-commissioned officer in G——'s dragoons?"

"Certainly—he was serjeant of my troop, and son of a tenant of my uncle."

"Exactly,—and had a considerable share of your confidence, and an influence among his comrades?"

"I had never occasion to repose confidence in a person of his description. I favoured Serjeant Houghton as a clever, active young fellow, and I believe his fellow-soldiers respected him accordingly."

"But you used through this man to communicate with such of your troop as were recruited upon Waverley-Honour?"

"Certainly—the poor fellows, finding themselves in a regiment chiefly composed of Scotch or Irish, looked up to me in any of their little distresses, and naturally made their countryman, and serjeant, their spokesman on such occasions."

"His influence, then, extended particularly over those soldiers who followed you to the regiment from your uncle's estate?"

"Surely;—but what is that to the present purpose?"

"To that I am just coming, and I beseech your candid reply. Have you, since leaving the regiment, held any correspondence, direct or indirect, with this Serjeant Houghton?"

"I!—I hold correspondence with a man of his rank and situation!— How, or for what purpose?"

"That you are to explain;—but did you not, for example, send to him for some books?"

"You remind me of a trifling commission which I gave him, because my servant could not read. I do recollect I bade him, by letter, select some books, of which I sent him a list, and send them to me at Tully-Veolan."

"And of what description were those books?"

"They related almost entirely to elegant literature: they were designed for a lady's perusal."

"Were there not, Mr Waverley, treasonable tracts and pamphlets among them?"

"There were some political treatises, into which I hardly looked. They had been sent to me by the officiousness of a kind friend, whose heart is more to be esteemed than his prudence or political sagacity: they seemed to be dull compositions."

"That friend was a Mr Pembroke, a non-juring clergyman, the author of two treasonable works, of which the manuscripts were found among your baggage."

"But of which, I give you my honour as a gentleman, I never read six pages."

"I am not your judge, Mr Waverley; your examination will be transmitted elsewhere. And now to proceed—Do you know a person who passes by the name of Wily Will, or Will Ruthven?"

"I never heard of such a man till this moment."

"Did you never through such a person, or any other person, communicate with Serjeant Humphrey Houghton, instigating him to desert with as many of his comrades as he could seduce to join him, and unite with the Highlanders and other rebels now in arms, under the command of the young Pretender?"

"I assure you I am not only entirely guiltless of the plot you have laid to my charge, but I detest it from the very bottom of my soul, nor would I be guilty of such a treachery to gain a throne, either for myself or any other man alive."

"Yet when I consider this envelope, in the hand of one of those misguided gentlemen who are now in arms against this country, and the verses which it inclosed, I cannot but find some analogy between the enterprize I have mentioned and the exploit of Wogan, which the writer seems to expect you should imitate."

Waverley was struck with the coincidence, but denied that the wishes or expectations of the letter-writer were to be regarded as proofs of a charge otherwise chimerical.

"But, if I am rightly informed, your time was spent, during your absence from the regiment, between the house of this Highland Chieftain, and that of Mr Bradwardine of Bradwardine, also in arms for this unfortunate cause?"

"I do not mean to disguise it; but I do deny, most resolutely, being privy to any of their designs against the government."

"You do not, however, I presume, intend to deny, that you attended your host Glennaquoich to a rendezvous, where, under pretence of a general hunting-match, most of the accomplices of his treason were assembled to concert measures for taking arms?"

"I acknowledge having been at such a meeting; but I neither heard nor saw any thing which could give it the character you affix to it."

"From thence you proceeded, with Glennaquoich and a part of his clan, to join the army of the young Pretender, and returned, after having paid your homage to him, to discipline and arm the remainder, and unite them to his bands on their way southward."

"I never went with Glennaquoich on such an errand—I never so much as heard that the person whom you mention was in the country."

He then detailed the history of his misfortune at the hunting-match, and added, that on his return he found himself suddenly deprived of his commission, and did not deny that he then, for the first time, observed symptoms which indicated a disposition in the Highlanders to take arms; but added, that having no inclination to join their cause, and no longer any reason for remaining in Scotland, he was now on his return to his native country, to which he had been summoned by those who had a right to direct his motions, as Major Mellville would perceive from the letters on the table.

Major Mellville accordingly perused the letters of Richard Waverley, of Sir Everard, and of Aunt Rachael, but the inferences he drew from them were different from what Waverley expected. They held the language of discontent with government, threw out obscure hints of revenge, and that of poor Aunt Rachael, which plainly asserted the justice of the Stuart cause, was held to contain the open avowal of what the others only ventured to intimate.

"Permit me another question, Mr Waverley. Did you not receive repeated letters from your commanding officer, warning and commanding you to return to your post, and acquainting you with the use made of your name to spread discontent through your soldiers?"

"I never did, Major Mellville. One letter, indeed, I received from him, containing some civil intimation that I would employ my leave of absence otherwise than in constant residence at Bradwardine, as to which, I own, I thought he was not called upon to interfere; and, finally, I had, on the same day in which I observed myself superseded in the Gazette, a second letter from Colonel G——, commanding me to join the regiment, an order which, owing to my absence, already mentioned and accounted for, I received too late to be obeyed. If there were any intermediate letters, and certainly from Colonel G——'s high character I think it probable—they have never reached me."

"I have omitted, Mr Waverley, to enquire after a matter of less consequence, but which has nevertheless been publicly talked of to your disadvantage. It is said that a treasonable toast having been proposed in your hearing and presence, you, holding his Majesty's commission, suffered the task of resenting it to devolve upon another gentleman of the company. This, sir, cannot be charged against you in a court of justice; but if, as I am informed, the officers of your regiment requested an explanation of such a rumour, as a gentleman and soldier, I cannot but be surprised that you did not afford it to them."

This was too much. Beset and pressed on every hand by accusations, in which gross falsehoods were blended with such circumstances of truth as could not fail to procure them credit,—alone, unfriended, and in a strange land, Waverley almost gave up his life and honour for lost, and, leaning his head upon his hand, resolutely refused to answer any further questions, since the fair and candid statement he had already made had only served to furnish arms against him.

Without expressing either surprise or displeasure at this change in Waverley's manner, Major Mellville proceeded composedly to put several other queries to him. "What does it avail me to answer you?" said Edward, sullenly. "You appear convinced of my guilt, and wrest every reply I have made to support your own preconceived opinion. Enjoy it then, and torment me no further. If I am capable of the cowardice and treachery your charge burdens me with, I am not worthy to be believed in any reply I can make you. If I am not deserving of your suspicion—and God and my own conscience bear evidence with me that it is so—then I do not see why I should, by my candour, lend my accusers arms against my innocence. There is no reason I should answer a word more." And again he resumed his posture of sullen and determined silence.

"Allow me," said the magistrate, "to remind you of one reason that may suggest the propriety of a candid and open confession. The inexperience of youth, Mr Waverley, lays it open to the plans of the more designing and artful, and one of your friends at least—I mean Mac-Ivor of Glennaquoich—ranks high in the latter class, as, from your apparent ingenuity, youth, and unacquaintance with the manners of the Highlands, I should be disposed to place you among the former. In such a case, a false step, or error like yours, which I shall be happy to consider as involuntary, may be atoned, and I would willingly act as intercessor. But as you must necessarily be acquainted with the strength of the individuals in this country who have assumed arms, with their means, and with their plans, I must expect you will merit this mediation on my part by a frank and candid avowal of all that has come to your knowledge upon these heads. In which case, I think I can promise that a very short personal restraint will be the only ill consequence that can arise from your accession to these unhappy intrigues."

Waverley listened with great composure until the end of this exhortation, when, springing from his seat, with an energy he had not yet displayed, he replied, "Major Mellville, since that is your name, I have hitherto answered your questions with candour, or declined them with temper, because their import concerned myself alone. But as you presume to esteem me mean enough to commence informer against others, who received me—whatever may be their public misconduct—as a guest and friend, I declare to you that I consider your questions as an insult infinitely more offensive than your calumnious suspicions; and that, since my hard fortune permits me no other mode of resenting them than by defiance, you should sooner have my heart out of my bosom, than a single syllable of information upon subjects which I could only become acquainted with in the full confidence of unsuspecting hospitality."

Mr Morton and the Major looked at each other, and the former, who, in the course of the examination, had been repeatedly troubled with a sorry rheum, had recourse to his snuff-box and his handkerchief.

"Mr Waverley," said the Major, "my present situation prohibits me alike from giving or receiving offence, and I will not protract a discussion which approaches to either. I am afraid I must sign a warrant for detaining you in custody, but this house shall for the present be your prison. I fear I cannot persuade you to accept a share of our supper?—(Edward shook his head)—but I will order refreshments in your apartment."

Our hero bowed and withdrew, under guard of the officers of justice, to a handsome bed-room, where, declining all offers of food or wine, he flung himself on the bed, and, stupified by the harassing events and mental fatigue of this miserable day, he sunk into a deep and heavy slumber. This was more than he himself could have expected; but it is mentioned of the North-American Indians, when at the stake of torture, that on the least intermission of agony, they will sleep until the fire is applied to awaken them.

Chapter Nine

A CONFERENCE, AND THE CONSEQUENCES

MAJOR MELLVILLE had detained Mr Morton during his examination of Waverley, both because he thought he might derive assistance from his practical good sense and approved loyalty, and also because it was agreeable to have a witness of unimpeached candour and veracity to proceedings which touched the honour and life of a young Englishman of high rank and family, and the expectant heir of a large fortune. Every step he knew would be rigorously canvassed, and it was his business to place the justice and integrity of his own conduct beyond the limits of question.

When Waverley retired, the Laird and Clergyman of Cairnvreckan sat down in silence to their evening meal. While the servants were in attendance, neither chose to say any thing on the circumstances which occupied their minds, and neither felt it easy to speak upon any other. The youth and apparent frankness of Waverley stood in strong contrast to the shades of suspicion which darkened round him, and he had a sort of naiveté and openness of demeanour, that seemed to belong to one unhackneyed in the ways of intrigue, and pleaded highly in his favour.

Each mused over the particulars of the examination, and each viewed it through the medium of his own feelings. Both were men of ready and acute talent, and both were equally competent to combine various points of evidence, and to deduce from them the necessary conclusions. But the wide difference of their habits and education often occasioned a great discrepancy in their respective deductions from admitted premises.

Major Mellville had been versed in camps and cities; he was vigilant by profession, and cautious from experience, had met with much evil in the world, and therefore, though himself an upright magistrate and an honourable man, his opinions of others were always strict, and sometimes unjustly severe. Mr Morton, on the contrary, had passed from the literary pursuits of a college, where he was beloved by his companions and respected by his teachers, to the ease and simplicity of his present charge, where his opportunities of witnessing evil were few, and never dwelt upon, but in order to encourage repentance and amendment; and where the love and respect of his parishioners repaid his affectionate zeal in their behalf, by endeavouring to disguise from him what they knew would give him the most acute pain,—their own occasional transgressions, namely, of the duties which it was the business of his life to recommend. Thus it was a common saying in the neighbourhood, (though both were popular characters,) that the laird knew only the ill in the parish, and the minister only the good.

A love of letters, though kept in subordination to his clerical studies and duties, also distinguished the Pastor of Cairnvreckan, and had tinged his mind in earlier days with a slight feeling of romance, which no after incidents of real life had entirely dissipated. The early loss of an amiable young woman, whom he had married for love, and who was quickly followed to the grave by an only child, had also served, even after the lapse of many years, to soften and enhance a disposition naturally mild and contemplative. His feelings on the present occasion were therefore likely to differ from those of the severe disciplinarian, strict magistrate, and distrustful man of the world.

When the servants had withdrawn, the silence of both parties continued, until Major Mellville, filling his glass and pushing the bottle to Mr Morton, commenced.

"A distressing affair this, Mr Morton. I fear this youngster has brought himself within the compass of an halter."

"God forbid!" answered the clergyman.

"Marry and amen," said the temporal magistrate; "but I fear even your merciful logic will hardly deny the conclusion."

"Surely, Major, I should hope it might be averted, for aught we have heard to-night."

"Indeed!—But, my good parson, you are one of those who would communicate to every criminal the benefit of clergy."

"Unquestionably I would: Mercy and long-suffering are the grounds of the doctrine I am called to teach."

"True, religously speaking; but mercy to a criminal may be gross injustice to the community. I don't speak of this young fellow in particular, who I heartily wish may be able to clear himself, for I like both his modesty and his spirit. But I fear he has rushed upon his fate."

"And why?—Hundreds of misguided gentlemen are now in arms against the government, many, doubtless, upon principles which education and early prejudice have gilded with the names of patriotism and heroism;—Justice, when she selects her victims from such a multitude, (for surely all will not be destroyed,) must regard the moral motive. He whom ambition, or hope of personal advantage, has led to disturb the peace of a well-ordered government, let him fall a victim to the laws; but surely youth, misled by the wild visions of chivalry and imaginary loyalty, may plead for pardon."

"If visionary chivalry and imaginary loyalty come within the predicament of high treason, I know no court in Christendom, my dear Mr Morton, where they can sue out their Habeas Corpus."

"But I cannot see that this youth's guilt is at all established to my satisfaction."

"Because your good nature blinds your good sense. Observe now. This young man, descended of a family of hereditary Jacobites, his uncle the leader of the tory interest in the county of ——, his father a disobliged and discontented courtier, his tutor a non-juror, and the author of two treasonable volumes—this youth, I say, enters into G——'s dragoons, bringing with him a body of young fellows from his uncle's estate, and who have not sticked at avowing, in their way, the high-church principles they learned at Waverley-Honour, in their disputes with their comrades. To these men young Waverley is unusually attentive; they are supplied with money beyond a soldier's wants, and inconsistent with his discipline; and are under the management of a favourite serjeant, through whom they hold an unusually close communication with their captain, and affect to consider themselves as independent of the other officers, and superior to their comrades."

"All this, my dear Major, is the natural consequence of their attachment to their young landlord, and their finding themselves among a regiment levied chiefly in the north of Ireland and west of Scotland, and disposed to quarrel with them, both as Englishmen, and as of the Church of England."

"Well said, parson!—I would some of your synod heard you—But let me go on. This young man obtains leave of absence—goes to Tully-Veolan—the principles of the Baron of Bradwardine are pretty well known, not to mention that this lad's uncle bought him off in the year fifteen. He engages there in a brawl, in which he is said to have disgraced the commission he wore. Colonel G—— writes to him, first mildly, then more sharply—I think you will not doubt his having done so, since he says so; the mess invite him to explain the quarrel in which he is said to have been engaged; he neither replies to his commander nor his comrades. In the meanwhile his soldiers become mutinous and disorderly, and at length, while the rumour of this unhappy rebellion becomes general, his favourite Serjeant Houghton, and another fellow, are detected in correspondence with a French emissary, accredited, as he says, by Captain Waverley, who urges him, according to the men's confession, to desert with the troop and join their captain, who was with Prince Charles. In the meanwhile this trusty captain is, by his own admission, residing at Glennaquoich with the most active, subtle, and desperate Jacobite in Scotland; he goes with him at least as far as their famous hunting rendezvous, and I fear a little farther. Meanwhile two other summonses are sent him; one warning him of the disturbance in his troop, another peremptorily ordering him to repair to the regiment, which indeed common sense might have dictated, when he observed rebellion thickening all round him. He returns an absolute refusal, and throws up his commission."

"He had been already deprived of it."

"But he regrets that the measure had anticipated his resignation. His baggage is seized at his quarters, and at Tully-Veolan, and is found to contain a stock of pestilent jacobitical pamphlets, enough to poison a whole country, besides the unprinted lucubrations of his worthy friend and tutor Mr Pembroke."

"He says he never read them."

"In an ordinary case I should believe him, for they are as stupid and pedantic in composition as mischievous in their tenets. But can you suppose any thing but value for the principles they maintain, would induce a young man of his age to lug such trash about with him? Then, when news arrive of the approach of the rebels, he sets out in a sort of disguise, refusing to tell his name; and, if that old fanatic tell truth, attended by a very suspicious character, and mounted on a horse known to have belonged to Glennaquoich, and bearing on his person letters from his family expressing high rancour against the house of Brunswick, and a copy of verses in praise of one Wogan, who abjured the service of the parliament to join the Highland insurgents, when in arms to restore the house of Stuart, with a body of English cavalry— the very counterpart of his own plot—and summed up with a Go and do thou likewise, from that loyal subject, and most safe and peaceable character, Fergus Mac-Ivor of Glennaquoich, Vich Ian Vohr, and so forth. And, lastly," continued Major Mellville, warming in the detail of his arguments, "where do we find this second edition of Cavaliero Wogan? Why, truly, in the very tract most proper for execution of his design, and pistolling the first of the king's subjects who ventures to question his intentions."

Mr Morton prudently abstained from argument, which he perceived would only harden the magistrate in his opinion, and barely asked how he intended to dispose of the prisoner?

"It is a question of some difficulty, considering the state of the country."

"Could you not detain him (being such a gentleman-like young man) here in your own house, out of harm's way, till this storm blow over?"

"My good friend, neither your house nor mine will be long out of harm's way, even were it legal to confine him here. I have just learned that the commander-in-chief, who marched into the Highlands to seek out and disperse the insurgents, has declined giving them battle at Corryerick, and marched on northwards with all the disposable force of government to Inverness, John-o'-Groat's House, or the devil, for what I know, leaving the road to the low country open and undefended to the Highland army."

"Good God! Is the man a coward, a traitor, or an idiot?"

"None of the three, I believe. He has the common-place courage of a common soldier, is honest enough, does what he is commanded, and understands what is told him, but is as fit to act for himself, in circumstances of importance, as I, my dear parson, to occupy your pulpit."

This important public intelligence naturally diverted the discourse from Waverley for some time; at length, however, the subject was resumed.

"I believe," said Major Mellville, "that I must give this young man in charge to some of the detached parties of armed volunteers, who were lately sent out to overawe the disaffected districts. They are now recalled towards Stirling, and a small body comes this way to-morrow or next day, commanded by the westland-man—what's his name?— You saw him, and said he was the very model of one of Cromwell's military saints."

"Gilfillan, the Cameronian. I wish the young gentleman may be safe with him. Strange things are done in the heat and hurry of minds in so agitating a crisis, and I fear Gilfillan is of a sect which has suffered persecution without learning mercy."

"He has only to lodge Mr Waverley in Stirling Castle: I will give strict injunctions to treat him well. I really cannot devise any better mode for securing him, and I fancy you would hardly advise me to encounter the responsibility of setting him at liberty."

"But you will have no objection to my seeing him to-morrow in private?"

"None, certainly; your loyalty and character are my warrant. But with what view do you make the request?"

"Simply to make the experiment whether he may not be brought to communicate to me some circumstances which may hereafter be useful to alleviate, if not to exculpate, his conduct."

The friends now parted and retired to rest, each filled with the most anxious reflections on the state of the country.

Chapter Ten

A CONFIDANT

WAVERLEY awoke in the morning from troubled dreams and unrefreshing slumbers, to a full consciousness of the horrors of his situation. How it might terminate he knew not. He might be delivered up to military law, which, in the midst of civil war, was not likely to be scrupulous in the choice of its victims, or the quality of the evidence. Nor did he feel much more comfortable at the thoughts of a trial before a Scottish court of justice, where he knew the laws and forms differed in many respects from those of England, and had been taught to believe, however erroneously, that the liberty and rights of the subject were less carefully protected. A sentiment of bitterness rose in his mind against the government, which he considered as the author of his embarrassment and peril, and he cursed internally his scrupulous rejection of Mac-Ivor's invitation to accompany him to the field. "Why did not I," he said to himself, "like other men of honour, take the earliest opportunity to welcome to Britain the descendant of her ancient kings, and lineal heir of her throne? Why did not I

> Unthread the rude eye of rebellion,
> And welcome home again discarded faith,
> Seek out Prince Charles, and fall before his feet?

"All that has been recorded of excellence and worth in the house of Waverley has been founded upon their loyal faith to the house of Stuart. From the interpretation which this Scotch magistrate has put upon the letters of my uncle and father, it is plain I ought to have understood them as marshalling me to the course of my ancestors; and it has been my gross dulness, joined to the obscurity of expression which they adopted for the sake of security, that has confounded my judgment. Had I yielded to the first generous impulse of indignation, when I learned that my honour was practised upon, how different had been my present situation! I had then been free and in arms, fighting, like my forefathers, for love, for loyalty, and for fame. And now I am here, netted and in the toils, at the disposal of a suspicious, stern, and cold-hearted man, perhaps to be turned over to the solitude of a dungeon, or the infamy of a public execution. O Fergus! how true has your prophecy proved! and how soon, how very soon, has it been accomplished!"

While Edward was ruminating on these painful subjects of contemplation, and very naturally, though not quite so justly, bestowing upon the reigning dynasty that blame which was due to chance, or, in part at least, to his own unreflecting conduct, Mr Morton availed himself of Major Mellville's permission to pay him an early visit.

Waverley's first impulse was to intimate a desire that he might not be disturbed with questions or conversation, but he suppressed it upon observing the benevolent and reverend appearance of the clergyman who had rescued him from the immediate violence of the villagers.

"I believe, sir," said the unfortunate young man, "that in any other circumstances I should have had as much gratitude to express to you as the safety of my life may be worth; but such is the present tumult of my mind, and my anticipation of what I am yet likely to endure, that I can hardly offer you thanks for your interposition."

Mr Morton replied, that, far from making any claim upon his good opinion, his only wish and the sole purpose of his visit was to find out the means of deserving it. "My excellent friend, Major Mellville," he continued, "has feelings and duties as a soldier and public functionary, by which I am not fettered; nor can I always coincide in opinions which he forms, perhaps with too little allowance for the imperfections of human nature." He paused, and then proceeded; "I do not intrude myself on your confidence, Mr Waverley, for the purpose of learning any circumstance, the knowledge of which can be prejudicial either to yourself or to others; but I own my earnest wish is, that you would intrust me with any particulars which could lead to your exculpation. I can solemnly assure you they will be deposited with a faithful, and, to the extent of his limited powers, a zealous agent."

"You are, sir, I presume, a presbyterian clergyman?"—Mr Morton bowed.—"Were I to be guided by the prepossessions of education, I might distrust your friendly professions in my case; but I have observed that similar prejudices are nourished in this country against your professional brethren of the episcopal persuasion, and I am willing to believe them equally unfounded in both cases."

"Evil to him that thinks otherwise," said Mr Morton; "or who holds church government or ceremonies as the gage of Christian faith or moral virtue."

"But," continued Waverley, "I cannot perceive why I should trouble you with a detail of particulars, out of which, after revolving them as carefully as possible in my recollection, I find myself unable to explain much of what is charged against me. I know, indeed, that I am innocent, but I hardly see how I can hope to prove myself so."

"It is for that very reason, Mr Waverley, that I venture to solicit your confidence. My knowledge of individuals in this country is pretty general, and can upon occasion be extended. Your situation will, I fear, preclude your taking those active steps for recovering intelligence, or tracing imposture, which I would willingly undertake in your behalf; and if you are not benefitted by my exertions, at least they cannot be prejudicial to you."

Waverley, after a few minutes reflection, was convinced that his reposing confidence in Mr Morton, so far as he himself was concerned, could hurt neither Mr Bradwardine nor Fergus Mac-Ivor, both of whom had openly assumed arms against the government, and that it might possibly, if the professions of his new friend corresponded in sincerity with the earnestness of his expression, be of some service to himself. He therefore ran briefly over most of the events with which the reader is already acquainted, suppressing his attachment to Flora, and indeed neither mentioning her nor Rose Bradwardine in the course of his narrative.

Mr Morton seemed particularly struck with the account of Waverley's visit to Donald Bean Lean. "I am glad," he said, "you did not mention this circumstance to the Major. It is capable of great misconstruction on the part of those who do not consider the power of curiosity and the influence of romance as motives of youthful conduct. When I was a young man like you, Mr Waverley, any such hairbrained expedition (I beg your pardon for the expression) would have had inexpressible charms for me. But there are men in the world who will not believe that danger and fatigue are often incurred without any very adequate cause, and therefore who are sometimes led to assign motives of action entirely foreign to the truth. This man Bean Lean is renowned through the country as a sort of Robin Hood, and the stories which are told of his address and enterprise are the common tales of the winter fire-side. He certainly possesses talents beyond the rude sphere in which he moves; and, being neither destitute of ambition nor cumbered with scruples, he will probably attempt, by every means, to distinguish himself during the period of these unhappy commotions."—Mr Morton then made a careful memorandum of the various particulars of Waverley's interview with Donald Bean, and the other circumstances which Edward communicated.

The interest which this good man seemed to take in his misfortunes, above all, the full confidence he appeared to repose in his innocence, had the natural effect of softening Edward's heart, whom the coldness of Major Mellville had taught to believe that the world was leagued to oppress him. He shook Mr Morton warmly by the hand, and, assuring him that his kindness and sympathy had relieved his mind of a heavy load, told him, that whatever might be his own fate, he belonged to a family who had both gratitude and the power of displaying it. The earnestness of his thanks called drops to the eyes of the worthy clergyman, who was doubly interested in the cause for which he had volunteered his services, by observing the genuine and undissembled feelings of his young friend.

Edward now enquired if Mr Morton knew what was likely to be his destination.

"Stirling Castle," replied his friend; "and so far I am well pleased for your sake, for the governor is a man of honour and humanity. But I am more doubtful of your treatment upon the road; Major Mellville is involuntarily obliged to intrust the custody of your person to another."

"I am glad of it. I detest that cold-blooded calculating Scotch magistrate. I hope he and I shall never meet more: he had neither sympathy with my innocence nor with my wretchedness; and the petrifying accuracy with which he attended to every form of civility, while he tortured me by his questions, his suspicions, and his inferences, was as tormenting as the racks of the Inquisition. Do not vindicate him, my dear sir, for that I cannot hear with patience; tell me rather who is to have the charge of so important a state prisoner as I am?"

"I believe a person called Gilfillan, one of the sect who are termed Cameronians."

"I never heard of them."

"They claim to represent the more strict and severe presbyterians, who, in Charles II.'s and James II.'s days, refused to profit by the toleration, or indulgence, as it was called, which was extended to others of that religion. They held conventicles in the open fields, and, being treated with great violence and cruelty by the Scottish government, more than once took arms during these reigns. They take their name from their leader, Richard Cameron."

"I recollect;—but did not the triumph of presbytery at the Revolution extinguish that sect?"

"By no means; that great event fell yet far short of what they proposed, which was nothing less than the complete establishment of the church upon the grounds of the old Solemn League and Covenant. Indeed, I believe they scarce knew what they wanted; but being then a numerous body of men, and not unacquainted with the use of arms, they kept themselves together as a separate party in the state, and at the time of the Union had nearly formed a most unnatural league with their old enemies, the Jacobites, to oppose that important national measure. Since that time their numbers have gradually diminished; but a good many are still to be found in the western counties, and several, with a better temper than in 1707, have now taken arms for government. This person, whom they call Gifted Gilfillan, has been long a leader among them, and now heads a small party, which will pass here to-day or to-morrow on their march toward Stirling, under whose escort Major Mellville proposes you shall travel. I would willingly speak to Gilfillan in your behalf; but, having deeply imbibed all the prejudices of his sect, and being of the same fierce disposition, he would pay little regard to the remonstrance of an Erastian divine, as he would politely term me.—And now farewell, my young friend, for the present; I must not weary out the Major's indulgence, that I may obtain his permission to visit you again in the course of the day."

Chapter Eleven

THINGS MEND A LITTLE

ABOUT NOON Mr Morton returned and brought an invitation from Major Mellville that Mr Waverley would honour him with his company to dinner, notwithstanding the unpleasant circumstances which detained him at Cairnvreckan, from which he should heartily rejoice to see Mr Waverley completely extricated. The truth was, that Mr Morton's favourable report and opinion had somewhat staggered the preconceptions of the old soldier concerning Edward's supposed accession to the mutiny in the regiment; and in the unfortunate state of the country, the mere suspicion of disaffection, or an inclination to join the insurgent Jacobites, might infer criminality indeed, but certainly not dishonour. Besides, a person whom the Major trusted, had reported to him a contradiction of the agitating news of the preceding evening. According to this second edition of the intelligence, the Highlanders had withdrawn from the Lowland frontier with the purpose of following the government army in their march to Inverness. The Major was at a loss, indeed, to reconcile this information with the well-known abilities of some of the gentlemen in the Highland army, yet it was the course which was likely to be most agreeable to others. He remembered the same policy had detained them in the north in the year 1715, and he anticipated a similar termination to the insurrection, as upon that occasion. This news put him in such good humour, that he readily acquiesced in Mr Morton's proposal to pay some hospitable attention to his unfortunate guest, and voluntarily added, he hoped the whole affair would prove a youthful *escapade* which might be easily atoned by a short confinement.

The kind mediator had some trouble to prevail on his young friend to accept the invitation. He dared not urge to him the real motive, which was a good-natured wish to secure a favourable report of Waverley's case from Major Mellville to Governor Blakeney. He remarked, from the flashes of our hero's spirit, that touching upon this topic would be sure to defeat his purpose. He therefore pleaded that the invitation argued the Major's disbelief of any part of the accusation, which was inconsistent with Waverley's conduct as a soldier and man of honour, and that to decline his courtesy might be interpreted into a consciousness that it was unmerited. In short, he so far satisfied Edward that the manly and proper course was to meet the Major on easy terms, that, suppressing his strong dislike again to encounter his cold and punctilious civility, Waverley agreed to be guided by his new friend.

The meeting was stiff and formal enough. But Edward, having accepted the invitation, and his mind being really soothed and relieved by the kindness of Morton, held himself bound to behave with ease, though he could not affect cordiality. The Major was somewhat of a *bon-vivant*, and his wine was excellent. He told his old campaign stories, and displayed much knowledge of men and manners. Mr Morton had an internal fund of placid and quiet gaiety, which seldom failed to enliven any small party in which he found himself pleasantly seated. Waverley, whose life was a dream, gave ready way to the predominating impulse, and became the most lively of the party. He had at all times remarkable natural powers of conversation, though easily silenced by discouragement. On the present occasion, he piqued himself upon leaving on the minds of his companions a favourable impression of one who, under such disastrous circumstances, could sustain his misfortunes with ease and gaiety. His spirits, though not unyielding, were abundantly elastic, and soon seconded his efforts. The trio were engaged in very lively discourse, apparently delighted with each other, and the kind host was pressing a third bottle of Burgundy, when the sound of a drum was heard at some distance. The Major, who, in the glee of the old soldier, had forgot the duties of the magistrate, cursed, with a muttered military oath, the circumstance which recalled him to his official functions. He rose and went toward the window, which commanded a very near view of the highroad, and he was followed by his guests.

The drum advanced, beating no measured martial tune, but a kind of rub-a-dub-dub, like that with which the fire-drum startles the slumbering artizans of a Scottish burgh. It is the object of this history to do justice to all men. I must therefore record, in justice to the drummer, that he protested he could beat any known march or point of war used in the British army, and had accordingly commenced with "Dumbarton's Drums," when he was silenced by Gifted Gilfillan, the commander of the party, who refused to permit his followers to move to this profane, and even, as he said, persecutive tune, and commanded the drummer to beat the 119th Psalm. As this was beyond the capacity of the drubber of sheep-skin, he was fain to have recourse to the inoffensive row-dow-dow, as a harmless substitute for the sacred music which his instrument or skill were unable to perform. This may be held a trifling anecdote, but the drummer in question was no less than town-drummer of Anderton. I remember his successor in office a member of that enlightened body, the British Convention: Be his memory, therefore, treated with due respect.

Chapter Twelve

A VOLUNTEER SIXTY YEARS SINCE

UPON HEARING the unwelcome sound of the drum, Major Mellville hastily opened a sashed door, and stepped out upon a sort of terrace which divided his house from the high-road from which the martial music proceeded. Waverley and his new friend followed him, though probably he would have dispensed with their attendance. They soon recognized in solemn march, first, the performer upon the drum; secondly, a large flag of four compartments, in which were inscribed the words, COVENANT, KIRK, KING, KINGDOMS. The person who was honoured with this charge was followed by the commander of the party, a thin, dark, rigid-looking man, about sixty years old. The spiritual pride, which, in mine Host of the Candlestick, mantled in a sort of supercilious hypocrisy, was, in this man's face, elevated and yet darkened by genuine and undoubting fanaticism. It was impossible to behold him without the imagination placing him in some strange crisis, where religious zeal was the ruling principle. A martyr at the stake, a soldier in the field, a lonely and banished wanderer consoled by the intensity and supposed purity of his faith under every earthly privation; perhaps a persecuting inquisitor, as terrific in power as unyielding in adversity; any of these seemed congenial characters to this personage. With these high traits of energy, there was something in the affected precision and solemnity of his deportment and discourse, that bordered upon the ludicrous; so that, according to the mood of the spectator's mind, and the light under which Mr Gilfillan presented himself, one might have feared, or admired, or laughed at him. His dress was that of a west-country peasant, of better materials indeed than that of the lower rank, but in no respect affecting either the mode of the age, or of the Scottish gentry at any period. His arms were a broad-sword and pistols, which, from the antiquity of their appearance, might have seen the rout of Pentland, or Bothwell Brigg.

As he came up a few steps to meet Major Mellville, and touched solemnly, but slightly, his huge and overbrimmed blue bonnet, in answer to the Major, who had courteously raised his small triangular gold-laced hat, Waverley was irresistibly impressed with the idea that he beheld a leader of the Roundheads of yore, in conference with one of Marlborough's captains. The group of about thirty armed men who followed this gifted commander, was of a motley description. They were in ordinary Lowland dresses, of different colours, which, contrasted with the arms which they bore, gave them an irregular and mobbish appearance, so much is the eye accustomed to connect uniformity of dress with the military character. In front were a few who apparently partook of their leader's enthusiasm; men obviously to be feared in a combat where their natural courage was exalted by religious zeal. Others puffed and strutted, filled with the importance of carrying arms, and all the novelty of their situation, while the rest, apparently fatigued with their march, dragged their limbs listlessly along, or straggled from their companions to procure such refreshments as the neighbouring cottages and ale-house afforded. "Six grenadiers of Ligonier's," thought the Major to himself, as his mind reverted to his own military experience, "would have sent all these fellows to the right about."

Greeting, however, Mr Gilfillan civilly, he requested to know if he had received the letter he sent to him upon his march, and could undertake the charge of the state-prisoner whom he there mentioned, as far as Stirling Castle. "Yea," was the concise reply of the Cameronian leader, in a voice which seemed to issue from the very *penetralia* of his person.

"But your escort, Mr Gilfillan, is not so strong as I expected."

"Some of the people," replied Gilfillan, "hungered and were athirst by the way, and tarried until their poor souls were refreshed with the word."

"I am sorry, sir, you did not trust to your refreshing your men at Cairnvreckan; whatever my house contains is at the command of persons employed in the service."

"It was not of creature-comforts I spake," answered the Covenanter, regarding Major Mellville with something like a smile of contempt, "howbeit, I thank you; but the people remained waiting upon the precious Mr Jabesh Rentowel for the out-pouring of the afternoon exhortation."

"And have you, sir, when the rebels are about to spread themselves through this country, actually left a great part of your command at a field-preaching?"

Gilfillan again smiled scornfully as he made this indirect answer,— "Even thus are the children of this world wiser in their generation than the children of light."

"However, sir," said the Major, "as you are to take charge of this gentleman to Stirling, and deliver him, with these papers, into the hands of Governor Blakeney, I beseech you to observe some rules of military discipline upon your march. For example, I would advise you to keep your men more closely together, and that each, in his march, should cover his file-leader, instead of straggling like geese upon a common; and, for fear of surprise, I further recommend to you to form a small advanced party of your best men, with a single vidette in front of the whole march, so that when you approach a village or wood"—(Here the Major interrupted himself)—"But as I don't observe you listen to me, Mr Gilfillan, I suppose I need not give myself the trouble to say more upon the subject. You are a better judge, unquestionably, than I am of the measures to be pursued. But one thing I would have you well aware of, that you are to treat this gentle-man, your prisoner, with no rigour or incivility, and are to subject him to no other restraint than is necessary for his security."

"I have looked into my commission," said Mr Gilfillan, "subscribed by a worthy and professing nobleman, William Earl of Glencairn, nor do I find it therein set down that I am to receive any charges or commands anent my doings from Major William Mellville of Cairn-vreckan."

Major Mellville reddened even to the very ears, which appeared beneath his neat military side-curls, the more so as he observed Mr Morton smile at the same moment. "Mr Gilfillan," he answered, with some asperity, "I beg ten thousand pardons for interfering with a person of your importance. I thought, however, that you having been bred a grazier, if I mistake not, there might be occasion to remind you of the difference between Highlanders and Highland cattle; and if you should happen to meet with any gentleman who has seen service, and is disposed to speak upon the subject, I should imagine listening to him would do you no sort of harm. But I have done, and have only once more to recommend this gentleman to your civility as well as your custody.—Mr Waverley, I am truly sorry we should part in this way; but I trust, when you are again in this country, I may have an opportunity to render Cairnvreckan more agreeable than circumstances have permitted on this occasion."

So saying, he shook our hero by the hand. Morton also took an affectionate farewell; and Waverley having mounted his horse, with a musqueteer leading it by the bridle, and a file upon each side to prevent his escape, set forward upon the march with Gilfillan and his party. Through the little village they were accompanied with the shouts of the children, who cried out, "Eh! see to the Southland gentleman, that's gaun to be hanged for shooting lang Johnie Micklewrath the smith."

Chapter Thirteen

AN INCIDENT

THE DINNER-HOUR of Scotland Sixty Years since was two o'clock. It was therefore about four o'clock of a delightful autumn afternoon that Mr Gilfillan commenced his march, in hopes, although Stirling was eighteen miles distant, he might be able, by becoming a borrower on the night for an hour or two, to reach it that evening. He therefore put forth his strength, and marched stoutly along at the head of his followers, eyeing our hero from time to time as if he longed to enter into controversy with him. At length, unable to resist the temptation, he slackened his pace till he was alongside of his prisoner's horse, and after marching a few steps in silence abreast of him, he suddenly asked,—"Can ye say wha the carle was wi' the black coat and the mousted head wha was wi' the Laird of Cairnvreckan?"

"A presbyterian clergyman," answered Waverley.

"Presbyterian! a wretched Erastian, or rather an obscured prelatist, —a favourer of the black indulgence;—ane of these dumb dogs that cannot bark; they tell ower a clash of terror and a clatter of comfort in their sermons, without ony sense or savour or life—Ye've been fed in siccan a fauld, belike?"

"No; I am of the Church of England."

"And they're just neighbour-like, and nae wonder they gree sae weel. Wha wad hae thought the goodly structure of the Reformed Kirk of Scotland, built up by our fathers in 1642, wad hae been defaced by carnal ends and the corruptions of the time;—ay, wha would hae thought the carved work of the sanctuary would hae been sae soon cut down!"

To this lamentation, which one or two of the assistants chorussed with a deep groan, our hero judged it unnecessary to make any reply. Whereupon Mr Gilfillan, resolving that he should be a hearer at least, if not a disputant, proceeded in his Jeremiad.

"And now is it wonderful, when, for lack of exercise anent the call to the ministry and the duty of the day, ministers fall into sinful compliances with patronage and indemnities, and oaths and bonds, and other corruptions, is it wonderful, I say, that you, sir, and other sick-like unhappy persons, should labour to build up your auld Babel of iniquity, as in the bluidy persecuting saint-killing times? I trow, gin ye ware na blinded wi' the graces and favours, and services and enjoyments, and employments and inheritances, of this wicked world, I could prove to you, by the Scripture, in what a filthy rag ye put your trust; and that your surplices and your copes and vestments are but cast-off garments of the muckle harlot, that sitteth upon seven hills and drinketh of the cup of abomination. But I trow ye are deaf as adders upon that side of the head—Ay, ye are deceived with her enchantments, and ye traffic with her merchandize, and ye are drunk with the cup of her fornication!"

How much longer this military theologist might have continued his invective, in which he spared nobody but the scattered remnant of *hill-folk*, as he called them, is absolutely uncertain. His matter was copious, his voice powerful, and his memory strong; so there was little chance of his ending the exhortation till the party reached Stirling, had not his attention been attracted by a pedlar who had joined the march from a cross-road, and who sighed or groaned with great regularity at all fitting pauses of his homily.

"And what may ye be, friend?" said Gilfillan.

"A puir pedlar, that's bound for Stirling, and craves the protection of your honour's party in these kittle times. Ah! your honour has a notable faculty in searching and in explaining the secret,—ay, the secret and obscure and—incomprehensible—causes of the backslidings of the land; aye, your honour touches the root of the matter."

"Friend," said Gilfillan, with a more complacent voice than he had hitherto used, "honour not me. I do not go out to park-dikes, and to steadings, and to market-towns, to have herds and cottars and burghers pull aff their bonnets to me as they do to Major Mellville o' Cairnvreckan, and call me laird, or captain, or honour; —no, my sma' means, whilk are not worth aboon twenty thousand mark, have had the blessing of increase, but the pride of my heart has not increased with them—Nor do I delight to be called captain, though I have the subscribed commission of that gospel-searching nobleman, the Earl of Glencairn, in whilk I am so designated. While I live, I am and will be called Habakkuk Gilfillan, who will stand up for the standards of doctrine agreed to by the ance-famous Kirk of Scotland, before she trafficked with the accursed Achan, while he has a plack in his purse, or a drap o' bluid in his body."

"Ah," said the pedlar, "I have seen your land about Mauchlin—a fertile spot; your lines have fallen in pleasant places;—and siccan a breed o' cattle is not in ony lord's land in Scotland."

"Ye say right,—ye say right, friend," retorted Gilfillan eagerly, for he was not inaccessible to flattery upon this subject. "Ye say right; they are the real Lancashire, and there's no the like o' them even at the Mains of Kilmaurs;" and he then entered into a discussion of their excellencies, to which our readers would probably be as indifferent as our hero. After this excursion, the leader returned to his theological discussions, while the pedlar, less profound upon those mystic points, contented himself with groaning, and expressing his edification at suitable intervals.

"What a blessing it would be to the puir blinded popish nations among which I hae sojourned, to have siccan a light to their paths! I hae been as far as Muscovia in my sma' trading way, as a travelling merchant; and I hae been through France, and the Low Countries, and a' Poland, and maist feck o' Germany, and O! it would grieve your honour's soul to see the mumming, and the singing, and massing, that's in the kirk, and the piping that's in the quire, and the heathenish dancing and dicing upon the Sabbath."

This set Gilfillan off upon the Book of Sports and the Covenant, and the Engagers, and the Protesters, and the Whiggamores' Raid, and the Assembly of Divines at Westminster, and the Longer and Shorter Catechism, and the Excommunication at Torwood, and the slaughter of Archbishop Sharpe. This last topic again led him into the lawfulness of defensive arms, on which subject he uttered much more sense than could have been expected from some other parts of his harangue, and attracted even Waverley's attention, who had hitherto been lost in his own sad reflections. Mr Gilfillan then considered the lawfulness of a private man standing forth as the avenger of public oppression, and as he was labouring with great earnestness the cause of Mas James Mitchell, an incident occurred which interrupted his harangue.

The rays of the sun were lingering on the very verge of the horizon as the party ascended a hollow and somewhat steep path, which led to the summit of a rising ground. The country was uninclosed, being part of a very extensive heath or common; but it was far from level, exhibiting in many places hollows filled with furze and broom; in others, little dingles of stunted brushwood. A thicket of the latter description crowned the hill up which the party ascended. The foremost of the band, being the stoutest and most active, had pushed on, and, having surmounted the ascent, were out of ken for the present.

Gilfillan, with the pedlar, and the small party who were Waverley's more immediate guard, were near the top of the ascent, and the remainder straggled after them at a considerable interval.

Such was the situation of matters, when the pedlar missing, as he said, a little doggie which belonged to him, began to halt and whistle for it. This repeated more than once gave offence to the rigour of his companion, the rather because it appeared to indicate inattention to the treasures of theological and controversial knowledge which he was pouring out for his edification. He therefore signified gruffly, that he could not waste his time in waiting for an useless cur.

"But if your honour wad consider the case of Tobit"——

"Tobit!" exclaimed Gilfillan, with great heat; "Tobit and his dog both are altogether heathenish and apocryphal, and none but a prelatist or a papist would draw them into question. I doubt I ha'e been mista'en in you, friend."

"Very like," answered the pedlar, with great composure; "but ne'ertheless I shall take leave to whistle again upon poor Bawty."

His last signal was answered in an unexpected manner; for six or eight stout Highlanders, who lurked among the copse and brushwood, sprung into the hollow way, and began to lay about them with their claymores. Gilfillan, unappalled at this undesirable apparition, cried manfully, "The sword of the Lord and of Gideon!" and, drawing his broad-sword, would probably have done as much credit to the good old cause as any of its doughty champions at Drumclog, when behold! the pedlar, snatching a musket from the person who was next him, bestowed the butt of it with such emphasis on the head of his late instructor in the Cameronian creed, that he was forthwith levelled to the ground. In the confusion which ensued, the horse which bore our hero was shot by one of Gilfillan's party, as he discharged his firelock at random. Waverley fell with, and indeed under, his horse, and sustained some severe contusions. But he was almost instantly extricated from the fallen steed by two Highlanders, who, each seizing him by the arm, hurried him away from the scuffle and from the high-road. They ran with great speed, half supporting and half dragging our hero, who could however distinguish a few dropping shots fired about the spot which he had left. This, as he afterwards learned, proceeded from Gilfillan's party, who had now assembled, the stragglers in front and rear having joined the others. At their approach the Highlanders drew off, but not before they had rifled Gilfillan and two of his people, who remained on the spot grievously wounded. A few shots were exchanged betwixt them and the westlanders. But the latter, being now without a commander, and apprehensive of a second ambush, did not make any serious effort to recover their prisoner, judging it more

wise to proceed on their journey to Stirling, carrying with them their
wounded captain and comrades.

Chapter Fourteen

WAVERLEY IS STILL IN DURESSE

THE VELOCITY, and indeed violence, with which Waverley was
hurried along, nearly deprived him of sensation; for the injury he had
received from his fall prevented him from aiding himself so effectually
as he might otherwise have done. When this was observed by his
conductors, they called to their aid two or three others of the party,
and swathing our hero's body in one of their plaids, divided his weight
by that means among them, and transported him at the same rapid rate
as before, without any exertion of his own. They spoke little, and that
in Gaelic; and did not slacken their pace till they had run nearly two
miles, when they abated their extreme rapidity, but continued still to
walk very fast, relieving each other occasionally.

Our hero now endeavoured to address them, but was only answered
with "Niel Sassenagh," that is, "no English," being, as Waverley well
knew, the constant reply of a Highlander, when he either does not
understand, or does not chuse to reply to an Englishman or Lowlander. He then mentioned the name of Vich Ian Vohr, concluding
that he was indebted to his friendship for his rescue from the clutches
of Gifted Gilfillan. But neither did this produce any mark of recognition from his escort.

The twilight had given place to moonshine before the party halted
upon the brink of a precipitous glen, which, as partially enlightened by
the moon-beams, seemed full of trees and tangled brushwood. Two
of the Highlanders dived into it by a small foot-path, as if to explore its
recesses, and one of them returning in a few minutes, said something
to his companions, who instantly raised their burthen, and bore him,
with great attention and care, down the narrow and abrupt descent.
Notwithstanding their precautions, however, Waverley's person
came more than once into contact, rudely enough, with the projecting
stumps and branches which overhung the pathway.

At the bottom of the descent, and, as it seemed, by the side of a
brook, (for Waverley heard the rushing of a considerable body of
water, although its stream was invisible in the darkness,) the party
again stopped before a small and rudely-constructed hovel. The door
was open, and the inside of the premises appeared as uncomfortable
and rude as its situation and exterior foreboded. There was no

appearance of a floor of any kind; the roof seemed rent in several places; the walls were composed of loose stones and turf, and the thatch of branches of trees. The fire was in the centre, and filled the whole wigwam with smoke, which escaped as much through the door as by means of a circular aperture in the roof. An old, withered Highland sybil, the only inhabitant of this forlorn mansion, appeared busy in the preparation of some food. By the light which the fire afforded, Waverley could discover that his attendants were not of the clan of Ivor, for Fergus was particularly strict in requiring from his followers that they should wear the tartan striped in the mode peculiar to their race; a mark of distinction anciently general through the Highlands, and still maintained by those Chiefs who were proud of their lineage, or jealous of their separate and exclusive authority.

Edward had lived at Glennaquoich long enough to be aware of a distinction which he had repeatedly heard noticed, and now satisfied that he had no interest with his attendants, he glanced a disconsolate eye around the interior of the cabin. The only furniture, excepting a washing tub, and a wooden press, called in Scotland an *ambry*, sorely decayed, was a large wooden bed, planked, as is usual, all round, and opening by a sliding pannel. In this recess the Highlanders deposited Waverley, after he had by signs declined any refreshment. His slumbers were broken and unrefreshing; strange visions passed before his eyes, and it required constant and reiterated efforts of mind to dispel them. Shivering, violent headache, and shooting pains in his limbs, succeeded these symptoms; and in the morning it was evident to his Highland attendants, or guard, for he knew not in which light to consider them, that Waverley was quite unfit to travel.

After a long consultation among themselves, six of the party left the hut with their arms, leaving behind an old and a young man. The former undressed Waverley, and bathed the contusions, which swelling and livid colour now made conspicuous. His own portmanteau, which the Highlanders had not failed to bring off, supplied him with linen, and, to his great surprise, was, with all its contents, freely resigned to his use. The bedding of his couch seemed clean and comfortable, and his aged attendant closed the door of the bed, for it had no curtain, after a few words of Gaelic, from which Waverley gathered that he exhorted him to repose. So behold our hero for the second time the patient of a Highland Esculapius, but in a situation much more uncomfortable than when he was the guest of the worthy Tomanrait.

The symptomatic fever, which accompanied the injuries he had sustained, did not abate till the third day, when it gave way to the care of his attendants and the strength of his constitution, and he could now raise himself in his bed, though not without pain. He observed, however, that there was a great disinclination, on the part of the old woman who acted as his nurse, as well as on that of the elderly Highlander, to permit the door of the bed to be left open, so that he might amuse himself with observing their motions. And at length, after Waverley had repeatedly drawn open, and they had as frequently shut, the hatchway of his cage, the old gentleman put an end to the contest, by securing it on the outside with a nail so effectually that the door could not be drawn till this exterior impediment was removed.

While musing upon the cause of this contradictory spirit in persons whose conduct intimated no purpose of plunder, and who, in all other points, appeared to consult his welfare and his wishes, it occurred to our hero that, during the worst crisis of his illness, a feminine figure, younger than his old Highland nurse, had appeared to flit around his couch. Of this indeed he had but a very indistinct recollection, but his suspicions were confirmed when, attentively listening, he often heard, in the course of the day, the voice of another female conversing in whispers with his attendant. Who could it be? And why should she apparently desire concealment? Fancy immediately roused herself, and turned to Flora Mac-Ivor. But after a short conflict between his eager desire to believe she was in his neighbourhood, guarding, like an angel of mercy, the couch of his sickness, Waverley was compelled to conclude that his conjecture was altogether improbable; since, to suppose she had left her comparatively safe situation at Glennaquoich to descend into the low country, now the seat of civil war, and to inhabit such a lurking-place as this, was a thing hardly to be imagined. Yet his heart bounded as he sometimes could distinctly hear the trip of a light female step glide to or from the door of the hut, or the suppressed sounds of a female voice, of softness and delicacy, hold dialogue with the hoarse inward croak of old Janet, for so he understood his antiquated attendant was denominated.

Having nothing else to amuse his solitude, he employed himself in contriving some plan to gratify his curiosity, in despite of the sedulous caution of Janet and the old Highland Janizary, for he had never seen the young fellow since the first morning. At length, upon accurate examination, the infirm state of his wooden prison-house appeared to supply the means of gratifying his curiosity, for out of a spot which was somewhat decayed he was able to extract a nail. Through this minute aperture he could perceive a female form, wrapped in a plaid, in the act of conversing with Janet. But, since the days of our grandmother Eve, the gratification of inordinate curiosity has generally borne its penalty in disappointment. The form was not that of Flora, nor was the face visible; and to crown his disappointment, while he laboured with the nail to enlarge the hole, that he might obtain a more complete view, a slight noise betrayed his purpose, and the object of his curiosity instantly disappeared, nor, so far as he could observe, did she again revisit the cottage.

All precautions to blockade his view were from that time abandoned, and he was not only permitted, but assisted, to rise, and quit what had been, in a literal sense, his couch of confinement. But he was not allowed to leave the hut; for the young Highlander had now rejoined his senior, and one or other was constantly on the watch. Whenever Waverley approached the cottage door, the centinel upon duty civilly, but resolutely, placed himself against it and opposed his exit, accompanying his action with signs which seemed to imply there was danger in the attempt, and an enemy in the neighbourhood. Old Janet appeared anxious and upon the watch, and Waverley, who had not yet recovered strength enough to attempt to take his departure in spite of the opposition of his hosts, was under the necessity of remaining patient. His fare was, in every point of view, better than he could have conceived; for poultry, and even wine, were no strangers to his table. The Highlanders never presumed to eat with him, and, unless in the circumstance of watching him, treated him with great respect. His sole amusement was gazing from the window, or rather the shapeless aperture which was meant to answer the purpose of a window, upon a large and rough brook, which raged and foamed through a rocky channel, closely canopied with trees and bushes, about ten feet beneath the site of his house of captivity.

Upon the sixth day of his confinement, Waverley found himself so well that he began to meditate an escape from this dull and miserable prison-house, thinking any risk which he might incur in the attempt preferable to the stupifying and intolerable uniformity of Janet's retirement. The question indeed occurred, where he was to direct his course when again at his own disposal. Two schemes seemed practicable, yet both attended with danger and difficulty. One was to go back to Glennaquoich, and join Fergus Mac-Ivor, by whom he was sure to be kindly received; and in his present state of mind, the rigour with which he had been treated fully absolved him in his own eyes from his allegiance to the existing government. The other project was an endeavour to attain the nearest Scottish sea-port, and thence to take shipping for England. His mind wavered between these plans, and probably, if he had effected his escape in the manner he proposed, he would have been finally determined by the comparative facility by which either might have been executed. But his fortune had settled that he was not to be left to his option.

Upon the evening of the seventh day the door of the hut suddenly opened, and two Highlanders entered, whom Waverley recognized as having been a part of his original escort to this cottage. They conversed for a short time with the old man and his companion, and then made Waverley understand, by very significant signs, that he was to prepare to accompany them. This was a joyful annunciation. What had already passed during his confinement made it evident no personal injury was designed to him; and his romantic spirit, having recovered during his repose much of that elasticity which anxiety, resentment, disappoint- ment, and the mixture of unpleasant feelings excited by his late adven- tures had for a time subjugated, was now wearied with inaction. His passion for the wonderful, although it is the nature of such dispositions to be excited by that degree of danger which merely gives dignity to the feeling of the individual exposed to it, had sunk under the extraord- inary and apparently unsurmountable evils by which he appeared environed at Cairnvreckan. In fact, this compound of intense curiosity and exalted imagination forms a peculiar species of courage, which somewhat resembles the light usually carried by a miner, sufficiently competent indeed to afford him guidance and comfort during the ordinary perils of his labour, but certain to be extinguished should he encounter the more formidable hazard of earth-damps or pestiferous vapours. It was now, however, once more rekindled, and with a throb- bing mixture of hope, awe, and anxiety, Waverley watched the group before him, as those who were just arrived snatched a hasty meal, and the others assumed their arms, and made brief preparations for their departure.

As he sat in the smoky hut, at some distance from the fire, around which the others were crowded, he felt a gentle pressure upon his arm. He looked round—It was Alice, the daughter of Donald Bean Lean. She shewed him a packet of papers in such a manner that the motion was remarked by no one else, put her finger for a second to her lips, and passed on, as if to assist old Janet in packing Waverley's clothes in his portmanteau. It was obviously her wish he should not seem to recognize her; yet she repeatedly looked back at him, as an opportunity occurred of doing so unobserved, and when she saw that he remarked what she did, she folded the packet with great address and speed in one of his shirts as she deposited it in the portmanteau.

Here then was fresh food for conjecture. Was Alice his unknown warden, and was this maiden of the cavern the tutelar genius that watched his bed during his sickness? Was he in the hands of her father? and if so, what was his purpose? Spoil, his usual object, seemed in this case neglected; for not only Waverley's property was restored, but his purse, which might have tempted this professional plunderer, had been all along suffered to remain in his possession. All this perhaps the packet would explain; but it was plain from Alice's manner that she desired he should consult it in secret. Nor did she again seek his eye after she had satisfied herself that her manœuvre was observed and understood. On the contrary, she shortly afterwards left the hut, and it was only as she tript out from the door, that, favoured by the obscurity, she gave Waverley a parting smile and nod of significance, ere she vanished in the dark glen.

The young Highlander was repeatedly dispatched by his comrades as if to collect intelligence. At length, when he had returned for the third or fourth time, the whole party arose, and made signs to our hero to accompany them. Before his departure, however, he shook hands with old Janet, who had been so sedulous in his behalf, and added substantial marks of his gratitude for her attendance.

"God bless you! God prosper you, Captain Waverley!" said Janet, in good Lowland Scotch, though he had never hitherto heard her utter a syllable, save in Gaelic. But the impatience of his attendants prohibited his asking any explanation.

Chapter Fifteen

A NOCTURNAL ADVENTURE

THERE WAS a moment's pause when the whole party had got out of the hut, and the Highlander who assumed the command, and who, in Waverley's awakened recollection, seemed to be the same tall figure who had acted as Donald Bean Lean's lieutenant, by whispers and signs imposed the most strict silence. He delivered to Edward a sword and steel pistol, and, pointing up the track, laid his hand on the hilt of his own claymore, as if to make him sensible they might have occasion to use force to make good their passage. He then placed himself at the head of the party, who moved up the pathway in single or Indian file, Waverley being placed nearest to their leader. He moved with great precaution, as if to avoid giving any alarm, and halted as soon as he came to the verge of the ascent. Waverley was soon sensible of the reason, for he heard at no great distance an English centinel call out "All's well." The heavy sound sunk on the night-wind down the woody glen, and was answered by the echoes of its banks. A second, third, and fourth time the signal was repeated fainter and fainter, as if at a greater and greater distance. It was obvious a party of soldiers were near, and upon their guard, though not sufficiently so to detect men skilful in every art of predatory warfare, like those with whom he now watched their ineffectual precautions.

When these sounds had died upon the silence of the night, the Highlanders began their march swiftly, yet with the most cautious silence. Waverley had little time, or indeed disposition for observation, and could only discern that they passed at some distance from a large building, in the windows of which a light or two yet seemed to twinkle. A little farther on, the leading Highlander snuffed the wind like a setting spaniel, and then made a signal to his party again to halt. He stooped down upon all fours, wrapped up in his plaid, so as to be scarce distinguishable from the heathy ground on which he moved, and advanced in this posture to reconnoitre. In a short time he returned, and dismissed his attendants excepting one; and, intimating to Waverley that he must imitate his cautious mode of proceeding, all three crept forward on hands and knees.

After proceeding a greater way in this inconvenient manner than was at all comfortable to his shins, Waverley perceived the smell of smoke, which probably had been much sooner distinguished by the more acute nasal organs of his guide. It proceeded from the corner of a low and ruinous sheep-fold, the walls of which were made of loose stones, as is usual in Scotland. Close by this low wall the Highlander guided Waverley, and, in order probably to make him sensible of his danger, or perhaps to obtain the full credit of his own dexterity, he intimated to him, by sign and example, that he might raise his head so as to peep into the sheep-fold. Waverley did so, and beheld an outpost of four or five soldiers lying by their watch-fire. They were asleep, all except the centinel, who paced backwards and forwards with his fire-lock on his shoulder, which gleamed red in the light of the fire as he crossed and re-crossed before it in his short walk, casting his eye frequently to that part of the heavens from which the moon, hitherto obscured by mist, seemed now about to make her appearance.

In the course of a minute or two, by one of those sudden changes of atmosphere incident to a mountainous country, a breeze arose, and swept before it the clouds which had covered the horizon, and the night planet poured her full effulgence upon a wide and blighted heath, skirted indeed with copsewood and stunted trees in the quarter from which they had come, but open and bare to the observation of the centinel in that to which their course tended. The wall of the sheep-fold indeed concealed them as they lay, but any advance beyond its shelter seemed impossible without certain discovery.

The Highlander eyed the blue vault, but far from blessing the useful light with Homer's, or rather Pope's, benighted peasant, he muttered a Gaelic curse upon the unseasonable splendour of *Mac-Farlane's buat* (*i.e.* lanthorn). He looked anxiously around for a few minutes, and then apparently took his resolution. Leaving his attendant with Waverley, after motioning to Edward to remain quiet, and giving his comrade directions in a brief whisper, he retreated, favoured by the irregularity of the ground, in the same direction and in the same manner as they had advanced. Edward, turning his head after him, could perceive him crawling on all fours with the dexterity of an Indian, availing himself of every bush and inequality to escape observation, and never passing over the more exposed parts of his tract until the centinel's back was turned from him. At length he reached the thickets and underwood which partly covered the moor in that direction, and probably extended to the verge of the glen where Waverley had been so long an inhabitant. Behind these the Highlander disappeared, but it was only for a few minutes, for he suddenly issued forth from a different part of the thicket, and advancing boldly upon the open heath, as if to invite discovery, he levelled his piece and fired at the centinel. A wound in the arm proved a disagreeable interruption to the poor fellow's meteorological observations, as well as to the tune of Nancy Dawson, which he was whistling. He returned the fire ineffectually, and his comrades, starting up at the alarm, advanced alertly towards the spot from which the first shot had issued. The Highlander, after giving them a full view of his person, dived among the thickets, for his *ruse de guerre* had now perfectly succeeded.

While the soldiers pursued the cause of their disturbance in one direction, Waverley, adopting the hint of his remaining attendant, made the best of his speed in that which his guide originally intended to pursue, and which now (the attention of the soldiers being drawn to a different quarter) was unobserved and unguarded. When they had run about a quarter of a mile, the brow of a rising ground, which they had surmounted, concealed them from further risk of observation. They still heard, however, at a distance, the shouts of the soldiers as they hallooed to each other upon the heath, and they could also hear the distant roll of a drum beating to arms in the same direction. But these hostile sounds were now far in their rear, and died upon the breezes as they rapidly advanced.

When they had walked about half an hour along open and waste ground of the same description, they came to the stump of an ancient oak, which from its relics appeared to have been at one time a tree of very large size. In an adjacent hollow they found several Highlanders, with a horse or two. They had not joined them above a few minutes, which Waverley's attendant employed, in all probability, in communicating the cause of their delay, (for the words Duncan Douroch were often repeated,) when Duncan himself appeared, out of breath indeed, and with all the symptoms of having run for his life, but laughing, and in high spirits at the success of the stratagem by which

he had baffled his pursuers. This indeed Waverley could easily conceive might be a matter of no great difficulty to the active mountaineer,
who was perfectly acquainted with the ground, and traced his course
with a firmness and confidence to which his pursuers must have been
strangers. The alarm which he excited seemed still to continue, for a
dropping shot or two were heard at a great distance, which seemed to
serve as an addition to the mirth of Duncan and his comrades.

The mountaineer now resumed the arms with which he had
entrusted our hero, giving him to understand that the dangers of the
journey were happily surmounted. Waverley was then mounted upon
one of the horses, a change which the fatigue of the night and his
recent illness rendered exceedingly acceptable. His portmanteau was
placed on another poney, Duncan mounted a third, and they set
forward at a round pace, accompanied by their escort. No other incident marked the course of that night's journey, and at the dawn of
morning they attained the banks of a rapid river. The country around
was at once fertile and romantic. Steep banks of wood were broken by
corn fields, which this year promised an abundant harvest, already in a
great measure cut down.

On the opposite bank of the river, and partly surrounded by a
winding of its stream, stood a large and massive castle, the half-ruined
turrets of which were already glittering in the first rays of the sun. It
was in form an oblong square, of size sufficient to contain a large court
in the centre. The towers at each angle of the square rose higher than
the walls of the building, and were in their turn surmounted by turrets,
differing in height and irregular in shape. Upon one of these a centinel
watched, whose bonnet and plaid, streaming in the wind, declared
him to be a Highlander, as a broad white ensign, which floated over
another tower, announced that the garrison was held by the insurgent
adherents of the house of Stuart.

Passing hastily through a small and mean village, where their
appearance excited neither surprise nor curiosity in the few peasants
whom the labours of the harvest began to summon from their repose,
the party crossed an ancient and narrow bridge of several arches, and
turning to the left, up an avenue of huge old sycamores, Waverley
found himself in front of the gloomy yet picturesque structure which
he had admired at a distance. An huge iron-grated door, which formed
the exterior defence of the gateway, was already thrown back to receive
them; and a second, heavily constructed of oak, and studded thickly
with iron nails, being next opened, admitted them into the interior
court-yard. A gentleman, dressed in the Highland garb, and having a
white cockade in his bonnet, assisted Waverley to dismount from his
horse, and with much courtesy bid him welcome to the castle.

The governor, for so we must term him, having conducted Waverley to a half-ruinous apartment, where, however, there was a small camp-bed, and having offered him any refreshment which he desired, was then about to leave him.

"Will you not add to your civilities," said Waverley, after having made the usual acknowledgment, "by having the kindness to inform me where I am, and whether or not I am to consider myself as a prisoner?"

"I am not at liberty to be so explicit upon this subject as I could wish. Briefly, however, you are in the Castle of Doune, in the district of Menteith, and in no danger whatever."

"And how am I assured of that?"

"By the honour of Donald Stuart, governor of the garrison, and lieutenant-colonel in the service of his Royal Highness Prince Charles Edward." So saying he hastily left the apartment, as if to avoid further discussion.

Our hero, exhausted by the fatigues of the night, now threw himself upon the bed, and was in a few minutes fast asleep.

Chapter Sixteen

THE JOURNEY IS CONTINUED

BEFORE WAVERLEY awakened from his repose, the day was far advanced, and he began to feel that he had past many hours without food. This was soon furnished in form of a copious breakfast, but Colonel Stuart, as if wishing to avoid the queries of his guest, did not again present himself. His compliments were, however, delivered by a servant, with an offer to provide any thing in his power that could be useful to Captain Waverley on his journey, which he intimated would be continued that evening. To Waverley's farther enquiries, the servant opposed the impenetrable barrier of real or affected ignorance and stupidity. He removed the table and provisions, and Waverley was again consigned to his own meditations.

As he contemplated the strangeness of his fortune, which seemed to delight in placing him at the disposal of others, without the power of directing his own motions, Edward's eye suddenly rested upon his portmanteau, which had been deposited in his apartment during his sleep. The mysterious appearance of Alice, in the cottage of the glen, immediately rushed upon his mind, and he was about to secure and examine the packet which she had deposited among his clothes, when the servant of Colonel Stuart again made his appearance, and took up the portmanteau upon his shoulders.

"May I not take out a change of linen, my friend?"

"Your honour sall get ane o' the colonel's ain ruffled sarks, but this maun gang in the baggage-cart."

And so saying, he very coolly carried off the portmanteau, without awaiting farther remonstrance, leaving our hero in a state where disappointment and indignation struggled for the mastery. In a few minutes he heard a cart rumble out of the rugged court-yard, and made no doubt that he was now dispossessed, for a space at least, if not for ever, of the only documents which seemed to promise some light upon the dubious events which had of late influenced his destiny. With such melancholy thoughts he had to beguile about four or five hours of solitude.

When this space was elapsed, the trampling of horse was heard in the court-yard, and Colonel Stuart soon after made his appearance to request his guest to take some farther refreshment before his departure. The offer was accepted, for a late breakfast had by no means left our hero incapable of doing honour to dinner, which was now presented. The conversation of his host was that of a plain country gentleman, mixed with some soldier-like sentiments and expressions. He cautiously avoided any reference to the military operations or civil politics of the time, and to Waverley's direct enquiries concerning some of these points, replied equally directly, that he was not at liberty to converse upon such topics.

When dinner was finished, the governor arose, and wishing Edward a good journey, told him that his servant having informed him that his baggage had been sent forward, he had taken the freedom to supply him with such changes of linen as he might find necessary till he was again possessed of his own. With this compliment he disappeared. A servant acquainted Waverley an instant afterwards, that his horse was ready.

Upon this hint he descended into the court-yard, and found a trooper holding a saddled horse, on which he mounted, and sallied from the portal of Doune Castle, attended by about a score of armed men on horseback. These had less the appearance of regular soldiers than of individuals who had suddenly assumed arms from some pressing motive of unexpected emergence. Their uniform, which was an affected imitation of that of French chasseurs, was in many respects incomplete, and sate awkwardly upon those who wore it. Waverley's eye, accustomed to look at a well-disciplined regiment, could easily discover that the motions and habits of his escort were not those of trained soldiers, and that although expert enough in the management of their horses, their skill was that of huntsmen or grooms, rather than of troopers. Their horses were not trained to the regular pace so necessary to execute simultaneous and combined movements and formations; nor did they seem *bitted* (as it is technically expressed) for the use of the sword. The men, however, were stout hardy-looking fellows, and might be individually formidable as irregular cavalry. The commander of this small party was mounted upon an excellent hunter, and although dressed in uniform, his change of apparel did not prevent Waverley from recognizing his old acquaintance, Mr Falconer of Balmawhapple.

Now, although the terms upon which Edward had met with this gentleman were none of the most friendly, he would have sacrificed every recollection of their foolish quarrel, for the pleasure of enjoying once more the social intercourse of question and answer, from which he had been so long excluded. But apparently the remembrance of his defeat by the Baron of Bradwardine, of which Edward had been the unwilling cause, still rankled in the mind of the low-bred, and yet proud, laird. He carefully avoided giving the least sign of recognition, riding doggedly at the head of his men, who, though scarce equal in numbers to a serjeant's party, were denominated Captain Falconer's troop, and preceded by a trumpet, which sounded from time to time, and a standard, borne by Cornet Falconer, the laird's younger brother. The lieutenant, an elderly man, had much the air of a low sportsman and boon companion; an expression of dry humour predominated in his countenance over features of a vulgar cast, which indicated habitual intemperance. His cocked hat was set knowingly upon one side of his head, and while he whistled the "Bob of Dumblane" under the influence of half a mutchkin of brandy, he seemed to trot merrily forwards, with a happy indifference to the state of the country, the conduct of the party, the end of the journey, and all other sublunary matters whatever.

From this wight, who now and then dropped alongside of his horse, Waverley hoped to acquire some information, or at least to beguile the way with talk. "A fine evening, sir," was Edward's salutation.

"Ow, ay! a bra' night," replied the lieutenant, in broad Scotch of the more vulgar description.

"And a fine harvest, apparently," continued Waverley, following up his first attack.

"Ay, the aits will be got bravely in; but the farmers, deil burst them, and the corn-mongers, will mak the auld price gude against them as has horses till keep."

"You perhaps act as quarter-master, sir?"

"Ay, quarter-master, riding-master, and lieutenant. And, to be sure, whae's fitter to look after the breaking and the keeping of the poor beasts than mysell, that bought and sold every one of them?"

"And, pray, sir, if it be not too great freedom, may I beg to know where we are going just now?"

"A fule's errand, I fear," answered this communicative personage.

"In that case, I should have thought a person of your appearance would not have been found upon the road."

"Vera true, vera true, sir—But every why has its wherefore—Ye maun ken the laird there bought a' thir beasts frae me to munt his troop, and agreed to pay for them according to the necessities and prices of the time—But then he had na the ready penny, and I hae been advised his bond will no be worth a boddle against the estate, and then I had a' my dealers to settle with at Martinmas—and so as he vera kindly offered me this commission, and as the auld *Fifteen* wad never help me to my siller for sending out naigs against the government, why, conscience! sir, I thought my best chance for payment was e'en to *gae out* mysell—and ye may judge, sir, that as I hae dealt a' my life in halters, I think nae mickle o' putting my craig in peril of a St John-stone's tippet."

"You are not, then, by profession a soldier?"

"Na, na, thank God," answered this doughty partizan, "I was nae bred at sae short a tether—I was brought up to hack and manger—I was bred a horse-couper, sir—and if I might live to see you at Whit-son-tryst, or at Staneshaw-bank, or the winter fair at Hawick, and ye wanted a spanker that would lead the field, I'se be caution I would serve ye easy, for Jamie Jinker was ne'er the lad to impose upon a gentleman—Ye're a gentleman, sir, and should ken a horse's points—ye see that through-ganging thing that Balmawhapple's on—I selled her till him—She was bred out of Lick-the-Ladle, which wan the king's plate at Caverton-Edge, by Duk Hamilton's Dusty-Foot," &c. &c. &c.

But as Jinker was entered full sail upon the pedigree of Balma-whapple's mare, having already got as far as great grandsire and grand-dam, and while Waverley was watching for an opportunity to obtain from him intelligence of more interest, the noble captain checked his horse until they came up, and then, without appearing to notice Edward directly, said sternly to the genealogist, "I thought, lieutenant, my orders were precise, that no one should speak to the prisoner."

The metamorphosed horse-dealer was silenced, of course, and slunk to the rear, where he consoled himself by entering into a vehement dispute upon the price of hay with a farmer, who had reluctantly followed his laird to the field, rather than give up his farm, whereof the lease had just expired.

Waverley was therefore once more consigned to silence, foreseeing that farther attempt at conversation with any of the party would only give Balmawhapple a wished-for opportunity to display the insolence of authority, and the sulky spite of a temper naturally dogged, and rendered worse by habits of low indulgence and the incense of servile adulation.

In about two hours time, the party were near the Castle of Stirling, over whose battlements the union flag was brightening as it waved in the evening sun. To shorten his journey, or perhaps to display his importance and insult the English garrison, Balmawhapple, inclining to the left, took his route through the royal park, which reaches to and surrounds the rock upon which the fortress is situated.

With a mind more at ease, Waverley could not have failed to admire the mixture of romance and beauty which renders interesting the scene through which he was now passing—the field which had been the scene of the tournaments of old—the rock from which the ladies beheld the contest, while each made vows for the success of some favourite knight—the towers of the Gothic church where these vows might be paid—and, surmounting all, the fortress itself, at once a castle and a palace, where valour received the prize from royalty, and knights and dames closed the evening amid the revelry of the dance, the song, and the feast. All these were objects fitted to arouse and interest a romantic imagination.

But Waverley had other subjects of meditation, and an incident soon occurred of a nature to disturb meditation of any kind. Balmawhapple, in the pride of his heart, as he wheeled his little body of cavalry around the base of the castle, commanded his trumpet to sound a flourish, and his standard to be displayed. This insult produced apparently some sensation; for when the cavalcade was at such distance from the southern battery as to admit a gun being so much depressed as to bear upon them, a flash of fire issued from one of the embrazures upon the rock; and ere the report, with which it was attended, could be heard, the rushing sound of a cannon-ball passed over Balmawhapple's head, and the bullet burying itself in the ground at a few yards distance, covered him with the earth which it drove up. There was no need to bid the party trudge. In fact, every man acting upon the impulse of the moment, Mr Jinker's steeds were soon brought to shew their mettle, and the cavaliers retreating with more speed than regularity, never *struck a trot*, as the lieutenant afterwards observed, until an intervening eminence had secured them from any repetition of so undesirable a compliment on the part of Stirling Castle. I must do Balmawhapple, however, the justice to say, that he not only kept the rear of his troop, and laboured to maintain some order among them, but in the height of his gallantry answered the fire of the castle by discharging one of his horse-pistols at the battlements; although, the distance being nearly half a mile, I could never learn that this measure of retaliation was attended with any particular effect.

The travellers now passed the memorable field of Bannockburn, and reached the Torwood, a place glorious or terrible to the recollections of the Scottish peasant, as the feats of Wallace, or the cruelties of Wude Willie Grime, predominate in his recollection. At Falkirk, a town formerly famous in Scottish history, and soon to be again distinguished as the scene of military events of importance, Balmawhapple proposed to halt and repose his troop for the evening. This was performed with very little regard to military discipline, as his worthy quarter-master was only solicitous to discover where the best brandy might be come at. Centinels were deemed unnecessary, and the only vigils performed were those of such of the party as could procure liquor. A few resolute men might easily have cut off the detachment; but of the inhabitants some were favourable, many indifferent, and the rest overawed. So nothing memorable occurred in the course of the evening, excepting that Waverley's rest was sorely interrupted by the revellers hallooing forth their Jacobite songs, without remorse or mitigation of voice.

Early in the morning they were again mounted, and on the road to Edinburgh, though the pallid visages of some of the troop betrayed that they had spent a night of sleepless debauchery. They halted at Linlithgow, distinguished by its ancient palace, which, Sixty Years since, was entire and habitable, but the venerable ruins of which, *not quite Sixty Years since*, very narrowly escaped the unworthy fate of being converted into a barrack for French prisoners! May repose and blessings attend the ashes of the patriotic statesman, who, amongst his last services to Scotland, interposed to prevent this profanation.

As they approached the metropolis of Scotland, through a champaign and cultivated country, the sounds of war began to be heard. The distant, yet distinct report of heavy cannon, fired at intervals, apprized Waverley that the work of destruction was going forward. Even Balmawhapple seemed moved to take some precautions, by sending an advanced party in front of his troop, keeping the main body in tolerable order, and moving steadily forward.

Marching in this manner they speedily reached an eminence, from which they could view Edinburgh stretching along the ridgy hill which slopes eastward from the Castle. The latter, being in a state of siege, or rather of blockade, by the northern insurgents, who had already occupied the town for two or three days, fired at intervals upon such parties of Highlanders as exposed themselves, either on the main street, or elsewhere in the vicinity of the fortress. The morning being calm and fair, the effect of this dropping fire was to invest the Castle in wreaths of smoke, the edges of which dissipated slowly in the air, while the central veil was darkened ever and anon by fresh clouds poured forth from the battlements; the whole giving, by the partial concealment, an appearance of grandeur and gloom, rendered more terrific when Waverley reflected on the cause by which it was produced, and that each explosion might ring the brave man's knell.

Ere they approached the city, the partial cannonade had wholly ceased. Balmawhapple, however, having in his recollection the unfriendly greeting which his troop had received from the battery at Stirling, had apparently no wish to tempt the forbearance of the artillery of the Castle. He therefore left the direct road, and sweeping considerably to the southward, so as to keep out of range of the cannon, approached the ancient palace of Holy-Rood, without having entered the walls of the city. He then drew up his men in front of this venerable pile, and delivered Waverley to the custody of a guard of Highlanders, whose officer conducted him into the interior of the building.

A long, low, and ill-proportioned gallery, hung with pictures, affirmed to be the portraits of kings, who, if they ever flourished at all, lived several hundred years before the invention of painting in oil colours, served as a sort of guard-chamber, or vestibule, to the apartments which the adventurous Charles Edward now occupied in the palace of his ancestors. Officers, both in Highland and Lowland garb, passed and re-passed in haste, or loitered in the hall, as if waiting for orders. Secretaries were engaged in making out passes, musters, and returns. All seemed busy, and earnestly intent upon something of importance; but Waverley was suffered to remain seated in the recess of a window unnoticed by any one, in anxious reflection upon the crisis of his fate, which seemed now rapidly approaching.

Chapter Seventeen

AN OLD AND A NEW ACQUAINTANCE

WHILE HE was deep sunk in his reverie, the rustle of tartans was heard behind him, a friendly arm clasped his shoulders, and a friendly voice exclaimed,

"Said the Highland prophet sooth? Or must second-sight go for nothing?"

Waverley turned and was warmly embraced by Fergus Mac-Ivor.

"A thousand welcomes to Holy-Rood, once more possessed by her legitimate sovereign! did I not say we should prosper, and that you would fall into the hands of the Philistines if you parted from us?"

"Dear Fergus, it is long since I have heard a friend's voice. Where is Flora?"

"Safe, and a triumphant spectator of our success."

"In this place?"

"Ay, in this city at least, and you shall see her; but first you must meet a friend whom you little think of, who has been frequent in his enquiries after you."

Thus saying, he dragged Waverley by the arm out of the guard-chamber, and ere he knew where he was conducted, Edward found himself in a presence-room fitted up with some attempt at royal state.

A young man, wearing his own fair hair, distinguished by the dignity of his mien and the noble expression of his well-formed and regular features, advanced out of a circle of military gentlemen and Highland chiefs, by whom he was surrounded. In his easy and graceful manners, Waverley afterwards thought he could have discovered his high birth and rank, although the star on his breast, and the embroidered garter at his knee, had not appeared as its indications.

"Let me present to your Royal Highness," said Fergus, bowing profoundly—

"The descendant of one of the most ancient and loyal families in England," said the young Chevalier, interrupting him. "I beg pardon for interrupting you, my dear Mac-Ivor, but no master of ceremonies is necessary to present a Waverley to a Stuart."

Thus saying, he extended his hand to Edward with the utmost courtesy, who could not, had he desired it, have avoided rendering him the homage which seemed due to his rank, and was certainly the right of his birth. "I am sorry to understand, Mr Waverley, that owing to circumstances which have been as yet but ill explained, you have suffered some restraint among my followers in Perthshire, and on your march here; but we are in such a situation that we hardly know our friends, and I am even at this moment uncertain whether I can have the pleasure of considering Mr Waverley among mine."

He then paused for an instant, but before Edward could adjust a suitable reply, or even arrange his thoughts as to its purport, he took out a paper, and proceeded:—"I should indeed have no doubts upon this subject, if I could trust to this proclamation sent forth by the friends of the Elector of Hanover, in which they rank Mr Waverley among the nobility and gentry who are menaced with the pains of high treason for loyalty to their legitimate sovereign. But I desire to gain no adherents save from affection and conviction; and if Mr Waverley inclines to prosecute his journey to the south, or to join the forces of the Elector, he shall have my passport and free permission to do so; and I can only regret that my power cannot extend to protect him against the probable consequences of such a measure.—But," continued Charles Edward, after another short pause, "if Mr Waverley should, like his ancestor, Sir Nigel, determine to embrace a cause which has little to recommend it but its justice, and follow a prince who throws himself upon the affections of his people to recover the throne of his ancestors, or perish in the attempt, I can only say, that among these nobles and gentlemen he will find worthy associates in a gallant enterprize, and will follow a master who may be unfortunate, but I trust will never be ungrateful."

The politic Chieftain of the race of Ivor knew his advantage in introducing Waverley to this personal interview with the royal Adventurer. Unaccustomed to the address and manner of a polished court, in which Charles was eminently skilful, his words and his kindness penetrated the heart of our hero, and easily outweighed all prudential motives. To be thus personally solicited for assistance by a prince, whose form and manners, as well as the spirit which he displayed in this singular enterprize, answered his ideas of a hero of romance—to be courted by him in the ancient halls of his paternal palace, recovered by the sword which he was already bending towards other conquests, gave Edward, in his own eyes, the dignity and importance which he had ceased to consider as his attributes. Rejected, slandered, and threatened upon the one side, he was irresistibly attracted to the cause which the prejudices of education, and the political principles of his family, had already recommended as the most just. These thoughts rushed through his mind like a torrent, sweeping before them every consideration of an opposite tendency,—the time, besides, admitted of no deliberation,—and Waverley, kneeling to Charles Edward, devoted his heart and sword to the vindication of his rights.

The Prince (for although unfortunate in the faults and follies of his forefathers, we shall here, and elsewhere, give him the title due to his birth) raised Waverley from the ground, and embraced him with an expression of thanks too warm not to be genuine. He also thanked Fergus Mac-Ivor repeatedly for having brought him such an adherent, and presented Waverley to the various noblemen, chieftains, and officers who were about his person, as a young gentleman of the highest hopes and prospects, in whose bold and enthusiastic avowal of his cause they might see an evidence of the sentiments of the English families of rank at this important crisis. Indeed, this was a point much doubted among the adherents of the house of Stuart; and as a well-founded disbelief in the co-operation of the English Jacobites kept many Scottish men of rank from his standard, and diminished the courage of those who had joined it, nothing could be more seasonable for the Chevalier than the open declaration in his favour of the representative of the house of Waverley-Honour, so long known as cavaliers and royalists. This Fergus had foreseen from the beginning. He really loved Waverley, because their feelings and projects never thwarted each other; he hoped to see him united with Flora, and he rejoiced that they were effectually engaged in the same cause. But, as we before hinted, he also exulted as a politician in beholding secured to his party a partizan of such consequence; and he was far from insensible to the personal importance which he himself gained with the Prince, from having so materially assisted in making the acquisition.

Charles Edward, on his part, seemed eager to shew his attendants the value which he attached to his new adherent, by entering immediately, as in confidence, upon the circumstances of his situation. "You have been secluded so much from intelligence, Mr Waverley, from causes with which I am but indistinctly acquainted, that I presume you are even yet unacquainted with the important particulars of my present situation. You have, however, heard of my landing in the remote district of Moidart, with only seven attendants, and of the numerous chiefs and clans whose loyal enthusiasm at once placed a solitary adventurer at the head of a gallant army. You must also, I think, have learned, that the commander-in-chief of the Hanoverian Elector marched into the Highlands at the head of a numerous and well-appointed military force, with the intention of giving us battle, but that his courage failed him when we were within three hours' march of each other, so that he fairly gave us the slip, and marched northward to Aberdeen, leaving the low country open and undefended. Not to lose so favourable an opportunity, I marched on to this metropolis, driving before me two regiments of horse, who had threatened to cut to pieces every Highlander who should venture to pass Stirling; and while discussions were carrying forward among the magistracy and citizens whether they should defend themselves or surrender, my good friend Lochiel, (laying his hand on the shoulder of that gallant and accomplished chieftain) saved them the trouble of farther deliberation, by entering the gates with five hundred Camerons. Thus far, therefore, we have done well; but, in the meanwhile, this doughty general's nerves being braced by the keen air of Aberdeen, he has taken shipping for Dunbar, and I have just received certain information that he landed there yesterday. His purpose must unquestionably be to march towards us to recover possession of the capital. Now there are two opinions in my council of war. One, that being inferior probably in numbers, and certainly in discipline and military appointments, not to mention our total want of artillery, and the weakness of our handful of cavalry, it will be safest to fall back towards the mountains, and there protract the war until fresh succours arrive from France, and the whole body of the Highland clans shall have taken arms in our favour. The opposite opinion maintains, that a retrograde movement, in our circumstances, is certain to throw utter discredit on our arms and undertaking; and, far from gaining us new partizans, will be the means of disheartening those who have joined our standard. The officers who use these last arguments, among whom is your friend Fergus Mac-Ivor, maintain, that if the Highlanders are strangers to the usual military discipline of Europe, the soldiers whom they are to encounter are no less strangers to their peculiar and formidable mode of attack; that the attachment and courage of the chiefs and gentlemen is not to be doubted; and that as they will be in the midst of the enemy, their clans-men will as surely follow them; in fine, that having drawn the sword, we should throw away the scabbard, and trust our cause to battle and to the God of Battles. Will Mr Waverley favour us with his opinion in these arduous circumstances?"

Waverley coloured high betwixt pleasure and modesty at the distinction implied in this question, and answered, with equal spirit and readiness, that he could not venture to offer an opinion as derived from military skill, but that the counsel would be far the most acceptable to him which should first afford him an opportunity to evince his zeal in his Royal Highness's service.

"Spoken like a Waverley," answered Charles Edward, "and that you may hold a rank in some degree corresponding to your name, allow me, instead of the captain's commission which you have lost, to offer you the brevet rank of major in my service, with the advantage of acting as one of my aids-de-camp until you can be attached to a regiment, of which I hope several will be speedily embodied."

"Your Royal Highness will forgive me," answered Waverley, for his recollection turned to Balmawhapple and his scanty troop, "if I decline accepting any rank until the time and place where I may have interest enough to raise a sufficient body of men to make my command useful to your Royal Highness's service. In the meanwhile, I hope for your permission to serve as a volunteer under my friend Fergus Mac-Ivor."

"At least," said the Prince, who was obviously pleased with this proposal, "allow me the pleasure of arming you after the Highland fashion." With these words, he unbuckled the broadsword which he wore, the belt of which was plated with silver, and the steel basket-hilt richly and curiously inlaid. "The blade," said the Prince, "is a genuine Andrea Ferrara, it has been a sort of heir-loom in our family; but I am convinced I put it into better hands than my own, and will add to it pistols of the same workmanship.—Colonel Mac-Ivor, you must have much to say to your friend; I will detain you no longer from your private conversation, but remember we expect you both to attend us in the evening. It may be perhaps the last night we may enjoy in these halls, and as we go to the field with a clear conscience, we will spend the eve of battle merrily."

Thus licensed, the Chief and Waverley left the presence-chamber.

Chapter Eighteen

THE MYSTERY BEGINS TO BE CLEARED UP

"How do you like him?" was Fergus's first question, as they descended the large stone staircase.

"A prince to live and die under," was Waverley's enthusiastic answer.

"I knew you would think so when you saw him, and I intended you should have met earlier, but was prevented by your sprain. And yet he has his foibles, or rather he has difficult cards to play, and his Irish officers, who are much about him, are but sorry advisers,—they cannot discriminate among the numerous pretensions that are set up. Would you think it—I have been obliged for the present to suppress an earl's patent, granted for services rendered ten years ago, for fear of exciting the jealousy, forsooth, of C—— and M——. But you were very right, Edward, to refuse the situation of aid-de-camp. There are two vacant indeed, but Clanronald and Lochiel, and almost all of us, have requested one for young Aberchallader, and the Lowlanders and the Irish party are equally desirous to have the other for the Master of F——. Now, if either of these candidates were to be superseded in your favour, you would make enemies. And then I am surprised that the Prince should have offered you a majority, when he knows very well that nothing short of lieutenant-colonel will satisfy others, who cannot bring one hundred and fifty men to the field. But patience, cousin, and shuffle the cards! It is all very well for the present, and we must have you properly equipped for the evening in your new costume; for, to say truth, your outward man is scarce fit for a court."

"Why, my shooting jacket has seen service since we parted; but that, probably, you know as well or better than I."

"You do my second-sight too much honour. We were so busy, first with the scheme of giving battle to Cope, and afterwards with our operations in the Lowlands, that I could only give general directions to such of our people as were left in Perthshire to respect and protect you should you come in their way. But let me hear the full story of your adventures, for they have reached us in a very partial and mutilated manner."

Waverley then detailed at length the circumstances with which the reader is already acquainted, to which Fergus listened with great attention. By this time they had reached the door of his quarters, which he had taken up in a small paved court, retiring from the street, at the house of a buxom widow of forty, who seemed to smile very graciously upon the handsome young Chief, being a person with whom good looks and good humour were sure to secure an interest, whatever might be the party's political opinions. Here Callum Beg received them with a smile of recognition. "Callum," said the Chief, "call Shemus an Snaht," (James of the Needle.) This was the hereditary tailor of Vich Ian Vohr. "Shemus, Mr Waverley is to wear the *cath d'ath*, (battle colour or tartan;) his trews must be ready in four hours. You know the measure of a well-made man: two double nails to the small of the leg"——

"Eleven from haunch to heel, seven round the waist—I give your honour leave to hang Shemus, if there's a pair of sheers in the Highlands that has a baulder sneck than hers ain at the *cumadh an truais*," (shape of the trews.)

"Get a plaid of Mac-Ivor tartan, and sash," continued the Chieftain, "and a blue bonnet of the Prince's pattern, at Mr Mouat's the haberdasher. My short green coat, with silver lace, will fit him exactly, and I have never worn it. Tell Ensign Maccombich to pick out a handsome target from among mine. The Prince has given Mr Waverley broadsword and pistols, I will furnish him with a dirk and purse; add but a pair of low-heeled shoes, and then, my dear Edward, (turning to him) you will be a complete son of Ivor."

These necessary directions given, the Chieftain resumed the subject of Waverley's adventures. "It is plain," he said, "that you have been in the custody of Donald Bean Lean. You must know that when I marched away my clan to join the Prince, I laid my injunctions on that worthy member of society to perform a certain piece of service, which done, he was to join me with all the force he could muster. But instead of doing so, the gentleman, finding the coast clear, thought it better to make war on his own account, and has scoured the country, plundering, I believe, both friend and foe, under pretence of levying *blackmail*, sometimes as if by my authority, and sometimes (and be cursed to his consummate impudence) in his own great name. Upon my honour, if I live to see the cairn of Benmore again, I will be tempted to hang that fellow. Now I recognise his hand particularly in the mode of your rescue from that canting rascal Gilfillan, and I have little doubt that Donald himself played the part of the pedlar on that occasion; but how he should not have plundered you, or put you to ransom, or availed himself in some way or other of your captivity for his own advantage, passes my judgment."

"When and how did you hear of my confinement?" said Waverley.

"The Prince himself told me," said Fergus, "and enquired very minutely into your history. He then mentioned your being at that moment in the power of one of our northern parties—you know I could not ask him to explain particulars—and requested my opinion about disposing of you. I recommended that you should be brought here as a prisoner, because I did not wish to prejudice you farther with the English government, in case you pursued your purpose of going southward. I knew nothing, you must recollect, of the charge brought against you of aiding and abetting high treason, which I presume has some share in changing your original plan. That sullen, good-for-nothing brute Balmawhapple was sent to escort you from Doune, with what he calls his troop of horse. As to his behaviour, in addition to his natural antipathy to every thing that resembles a gentleman, I presume his adventure with Bradwardine rankles in his recollection, the rather that I dare say his mode of telling that story contributed to the evil reports which reached your quondam regiment."

"Very likely," said Waverley; "but now surely, my dear Fergus, you may find time to tell me something of Flora."

"Why, I can only tell you that she is well, and residing for the present with a relation in this city. I thought it better she should come here, as since our success a good many ladies of rank attend our military court; and I assure you, that there is a sort of consequence annexed to the relatives of such a person as Flora Mac-Ivor, and where there is such a justling of claims and requests a man must use every fair means to enhance his importance."

There was something in this last sentence which grated on Waverley's feelings. He could not bear that Flora should be considered as conducing to her brother's preferment, by the admiration which she must unquestionably attract; and although it was in strict correspondence with many points of Fergus's character, it shocked him as selfish, and unworthy of his sister's high mind and his own independent pride. Fergus, to whom such manœuvres were familiar, as to one brought up at the French court, did not observe the unfavourable impression which he had unwarily made upon his friend's mind, and concluded by saying, "that they would hardly see Flora before the evening, when she would be at the concert and ball, with which the Prince's party were to be entertained. She and I had a quarrel about her not appearing to take leave of you. I am unwilling to renew it, by

soliciting her to receive you this morning; and perhaps my doing so
might not only be ineffectual, but prevent your meeting this evening."

While thus conversing, Waverley heard in the court, before the
windows of the parlour, a well-known voice. "I aver to you, my worthy
friend," said the speaker, "that it is a total dereliction of military
discipline; and were you not as it were a *tyro*, your purpose would
deserve strong reprobation. For a prisoner of war is on no account to
be coerced with fetters, or debinded in *ergastulo*, as would have been
the case had you put this gentleman into the pit of the peel-house at
Balmawhapple. I grant, indeed, that such a prisoner may for security
be coerced in *carcere*, that is, in a public prison."

The growling voice of Balmawhapple was heard as taking leave in
displeasure, but the word "land-louper" alone was distinctly audible.
He had disappeared before Waverley had reached the court, in order
to greet the worthy Baron. The uniform in which he was now attired
seemed to have added fresh stiffness and rigidity to his tall perpendicular figure; and the consciousness of military command and authority
had increased, in the same proportion, the self-importance of his
demeanour, and dogmatism of his conversation.

He received Waverley with his usual kindness, and expressed
immediate anxiety to hear an explanation of the circumstances attending the loss of his commission in G——'s dragoons; "not," he said,
"that he had the least apprehension of his young friend having
done aught which could merit such ungenerous treatment as he had
received from government, but because it was right and seemly that
the Baron of Bradwardine should be, in point of trust and in point of
power, fully able to refute all calumnies against the heir of Waverley-
Honour, whom he had so much right to regard as his own son."

Fergus Mac-Ivor, who had now joined them, went hastily over the
circumstances of Waverley's story, and concluded with the flattering
reception he had met from the young Chevalier. The Baron listened
in silence, and at the conclusion shook Waverley heartily by the hand,
and congratulated him upon entering the service of his lawful Prince.
"For," continued he, "although it has been justly held in all nations a
matter of scandal and dishonour to infringe the *sacramentum militare*,
and that whether it was taken by each soldier singly, whilk the Romans
denominated *per conjurationem*, or by one soldier in name of the rest;
yet no one ever doubted that the allegiance so sworn was discharged
by the *dimissio*, or discharging of a soldier, whose case would be as
hard as that of colliers, salters, and other slaves of the soil, were it to be
accounted otherwise. This is something like the brocard expressed by
the learned Sanchez in his work *De Jure-jurando*, which you have
questionless consulted upon this occasion. As for those who have

calumniated you by leasing-making, I protest to Heaven I think they have justly incurred the penalty of the *Memmia lex*, also called *lex Remmia*, which is prelected upon by Tullius in his oration *In Verrem*. I should have deemed, however, Mr Waverley, that before destining yourself to any special service in the army of the Prince, ye might have enquired what rank the Baron of Bradwardine held there, and whether he would not have been peculiarly happy to have had your services in the regiment of horse which he is now about to levy."

Edward eluded this reproach by pleading the necessity of giving an immediate answer to the Prince's proposal, and his uncertainty at the moment whether his friend the Baron was with the army, or engaged upon service elsewhere.

This punctilio being settled, Waverley made enquiry after Miss Bradwardine, and was informed she had come to Edinburgh with Flora Mac-Ivor, under guard of a party of the Chieftain's men. This step was indeed necessary, Tully-Veolan having become a very unpleasant, and even dangerous place of residence for an unprotected young lady, on account of its vicinity both to the Highlands and to one or two large villages, which, from aversion as much to the caterans as zeal for presbytery, had declared themselves on the side of government, and formed irregular bodies of partizans, who had frequent skirmishes with the mountaineers, and sometimes attacked the houses of the Jacobite gentry.

"I would propose to you," continued the Baron, "to walk as far as my quarters in the Luckenbooths, and to admire in your passage the High Street, whilk is, beyond a shadow of dubitation, finer than any street, whether in London or Paris. But Rose, poor thing, is sorely discomposed with the firing of the Castle, though I have proved to her from Blondel and Coehorn, that it is impossible a bullet can reach these buildings; and, besides, I have it in charge from his Royal Highness to go to the camp, or leaguer of our army, to see that the men do *conclamare vasa*, that is, truss up their bag and baggage for to-morrow's march."

"That will be easily done by most of us," said Mac-Ivor, laughing.

"Craving your pardon, Colonel Mac-Ivor, not quite so speedily as ye seem to opine. I grant most of your folks left the Highlands, expedited as it were, and free from the incumbrance of baggage, but it is unspeakable the quantity of useless sprechery which they have collected on their march. I saw one fellow of yours (craving your pardon once more) with a pier-glass upon his back."

"Ay," said Fergus, still in good humour, "he would have told you, if you had questioned him, *a ganging foot is aye getting.*—But come, my dear Baron, you know as well as I, that a hundred Uhlans, or a single troop of Schmirschitz's Pandours, would make more havoc in a country than the knight of the mirror and all the rest of our clans put together."

"And that is very true likewise," said the Baron; "they are, as the heathen author says, *ferociores in aspectu, mitiores in actu*, of a torrid and grim visage, but more benign in demeanour than their physiognomia or aspect might infer.—But I stand here speaking with you two youngsters, when I should be in the King's Park."

"But you will dine with Waverley and me on your return? I assure you, Baron, though I can live like a Highlander when needs must, I remember my Paris education, and understand perfectly *faire la meilleure chère*."

"And wha the deil doubts it," quoth the Baron, laughing, "when you bring only the cookery, and the Good Town must furnish the materials?—Well, I have some business in the town too: But I'll join you at three, if the vivers can tarry so long." So saying, he took leave of his friends, and went to look after the charge which had been assigned him.

Chapter Nineteen

A SOLDIER'S DINNER

JAMES OF THE NEEDLE was a man of his word, when whiskey was no party to the contract; and upon this occasion Callum Beg, who still thought himself in Waverley's debt, since he had declined accepting compensation at the expence of mine Host of the Candlestick's person, took this opportunity of discharging the obligation, by mounting guard over the hereditary tailor of Sliochd nan Ivor; and, as he expressed himself, targed him tightly till the finishing of the job. To rid himself of this restraint, Shemus's needle flew through the tartan like lightning; and as the artist kept chaunting some dreadful skirmish of Fin Macoul, he accomplished at least three stitches to the death of every hero. The dress was, therefore, soon ready, for the short coat fitted the wearer, and the rest of the apparel required little adjustment.

When our hero fairly assumed the "garb of old Gaul," which was well calculated to give an appearance of strength to a figure, which, though tall and well-made, was rather elegant than robust, I hope my fair readers will excuse him if he looked at himself in the mirror more than once, and could not help acknowledging that the reflection seemed that of a very handsome young fellow. In fact, there was no disguising it. His light-brown hair, for he wore no periwig, notwithstanding the universal fashion of the time, became the bonnet which surmounted it. His person promised firmness and agility, to which the ample folds of the tartan added an air of dignity. His blue eye seemed of that kind,

> Which melted in love, and which kindled in war.

And an air of bashfulness, which was in reality the effect of want of habitual intercourse with the world, gave interest to his features, without injuring their grace or intelligence.

"He's a pratty man; a very pratty man," said Evan Dhu (now Ensign Maccombich) to Fergus's buxom landlady.

"He's vera weel," said the Widow Flockhart, "but no naithing so well-far'd as your colonel, ensign."

"I was na comparing them," quoth Evan, "nor was I speaking about his being well-favoured; but only that Mr Waverley looks clean-made and *deliver*, and like a proper lad o' his quarters, that will not cry barley in a brulzie. And, indeed, he's gleg aneuch at the broadsword and target. I hae played wi' him mysel at Glennaquoich, and sae has Vich Ian Vohr, often of a Sunday afternoon."

"Lord forgive ye, Ensign Maccombich, I'm sure the colonel wad never do the like o' that."

"Hout! hout! Mrs Flockhart, we're young blude, ye ken; and young saints, auld deils."

"But will ye fight wi' Sir John Cope, the morn, Ensign Maccombich?"

"Troth I'se ensure him, an he'll bide us, Mrs Flockhart."

"And will ye face these tearing chields, the dragoons, Ensign Maccombich?"

"Claw for claw, as Conan said to Satan, Mrs Flockhart, and the deevil tak the shortest nails."

"And will the Colonel venture on the bagganets himsel?"

"Ye may swear it, Mrs Flockhart; the very first man will he be, by Saint Phedar."

"Merciful goodness! and if he's killed amang the red coats!"

"Troth, if it should sae befall, Mrs Flockhart, I ken ane that will na be living to weep for him. But we maun a' live the day, and have our dinner; and there's Vich Ian Vohr has packed his *dorlach*, and Mr Waverley's wearied wi' majoring yonder afore the muckle pier-glass, and that grey auld stoor carle, the Baron o' Bradwardine, that shot young Ronald of Ballenkeiroch, he's coming down the close wi' that droghling, coghling baillie body they ca' Macwhupple, just like the Laird o' Kittlegab's French cook, wi' his turnspit doggie trindling ahint him, and I am as hungry as a gled, my bonny dow; sae bid Kate set on the broo', and do ye put on your pinners, for ye ken Vich Ian

Vohr winna sit down till ye be at the head o' the table;—and dinna forget the pint bottle o' brandy, my woman."

This hint produced dinner. Mrs Flockhart, smiling in her weeds like the sun through a mist, took the head of the table, thinking within herself perhaps, that she cared not how long the rebellion lasted that brought her into company so much above her usual associates. She was supported by Waverley and the Baron, with the advantage of the Chieftain *vis-à-vis*. The men of peace and of war, that is, Baillie Macwheeble and Ensign Maccombich, after many profound congés to their superiors and each other, took their places on each side of the Chieftain. Their fare was excellent, time, place, and circumstances considered, and Fergus's spirits were extravagantly high. Regardless of danger, and sanguine from temper, youth, and ambition, he saw in imagination all his prospects crowned with success, and was totally indifferent to the probable alternative of a soldier's grave. The Baron apologized slightly for bringing Macwheeble. They had been providing, he said, for the expences of the campaign. "And, by my faith," said the old man, "as I think this will be my last, so I just end where I began —I hae evermore found the sinews of war, as a learned author calls the *caisse militaire*, more difficult to come by than either its flesh, blood, or bones."

"What, have you raised our only efficient body of cavalry, and got ye none of the louis d'ors out of the Doutelle to help you?"

"No, Glennaquoich; cleverer fellows have been before me."

"That's a scandal," said the young Highlander; "but you will share what is left of my subsidy: It will save you an anxious thought to-night, and be all one to-morrow, for we shall all be provided for one way or other before the sun sets." Waverley, blushing deeply, but with great earnestness, pressed the same request. "I thank ye baith, my good lads," said the Baron, "but I will not infringe upon your peculium. Baillie Macwheeble has provided the sum which is necessary."

Here the Baillie shifted, and fidgetted about in his seat, and appeared extremely uneasy. At length, after several preliminary hems, and much tautological expression of his devotion to his honour's service, by night or day, living or dead, he began to insinuate, "that the banks had removed all their ready cash into the Castle;—that, nae doubt, Sandie Goldie, the silversmith, would do mickle for his honour; but there was little time to get the wadset made out; and, doubtless, if his honour, Glennaquoich, or Mr Waaverley, could accommodate"——

"Let me hear of no such nonsense, sir," said the Baron in a tone which rendered Macwheeble mute, "but proceed as we accorded before dinner, if it be your wish to remain in my service."

To this peremptory order the Baillie, though he felt as if condemned to suffer a transfusion of blood from his own veins into those of the Baron, did not presume to make any reply. After fidgetting a little while longer, however, he addressed himself to Glennaquoich, and told him, if his honour had mair ready siller than was sufficient for his occasions in the field, he could put it out at use for his honour in safe hands, and at great profit at this time. At this proposal Fergus laughed heartily, and answered, when he had recovered his breath,—"Many thanks, Baillie; but you must know it is a general custom among us soldiers to make our landlady our banker. Here, Mrs Flockhart," said he, taking four or five broad pieces out of a well-filled purse, and tossing the purse itself, with its remaining contents, into her apron, "these will serve my occasions; do you take the rest: Be my banker if I live, and my executor if I die; but take care to give something to the Highland cailliachs that shall cry the coronach loudest for the last Vich Ian Vohr."

"It is the *testamentum militare*," quoth the Baron, "whilk, amang the Romans was privilegiate to be nuncupative;" but the soft heart of Mrs Flockhart was melted within her at the Chieftain's speech; she set up a lamentable blubbering, and positively refused to touch the bequest, which Fergus was therefore obliged to resume. "Well, then," said the Chief, "if I fall, it will go to the grenadier that knocks my brains out, and I shall take care he works hard for it."

Baillie Macwheeble was again tempted to put in his oar, for where cash was concerned, he did not willingly remain silent. "Perhaps he had better carry the goud to Miss Mac-Ivor, in case of mortality, or accidents of war. It might take the form of a *mortis causa* donation in the young leddie's favour, and wad cost but the scrape of a pen to make it out."

"The young lady," said Fergus, "should such an event happen, will have other matters to think of than these wretched louis d'ors."

"True—undeniable—there's nae doubt o' that; but your honour kens that a full sorrow"——

"Is endurable by most folks more easily than a hungry one. True, Baillie, very true; and I believe there may even be some who would be consoled by such a reflection for the loss of the whole existing generation; but there is a sorrow which knows neither hunger nor thirst; and poor Flora"——He paused, and the whole company sympathized in his emotion. The Baron's thoughts naturally reverted to the unprotected state of his daughter, and the big tear came to the veteran's eye. "If I fall, Macwheeble, you have all my papers, and know all my affairs; be just to Rose."

The Baillie was a man of earthly mould after all, a good deal of dirt and dross about him undoubtedly, but some kindly and just feelings he had, especially where the Baron or his young mistress were concerned. He set up a lamentable howl. "If this doleful day should come, while Duncan Macwheeble had a boddle, it should be Miss Rose's. He wad scroll for a plack the sheet, or she kend what it was to want; if indeed a' the bonnie barony o' Bradwardine and Tully-Veolan, with the fortalice and manor-place thereof (he kept sobbing and whining at every pause) tofts—crofts—mosses—muirs—outfield—infield—buildings—orchards—dove-cotes—with the rights of net and coble in the water and loch of Veolan—tiends, parsonage and vicarage—annexis—connexis—rights of pasturage—fuel—feal and divot—parts, pendicles, and pertinents whatsoever—(here he had recourse to the end of his long cravat to wipe his eyes, which overflowed, in spite of him, at the ideas this technical jargon conjured up)—all as more fully described in the proper evidents and titles thereof—and lying within the parish of Bradwardine and the shire of Perth—if, as aforesaid, they must all pass from my master's child to Inch-Grubbit, wha's a whig and a Hanoverian, and be managed by his doer, Jamie Howie, wha's no fit to be a birlieman, let be a baillie"——

The beginning of this lamentation really had something affecting, but the conclusion rendered laughter irresistible. "Never mind, Baillie," said Ensign Maccombich, "for the gude auld times of rugging and riving (pulling and tearing) are come back again, an' Sneckus Mac-Snackus, and all the rest of your friends, maun give place to the longest claymore."

"And that claymore shall be ours, Baillie," said the Chieftain, who saw that Macwheeble looked very blank at this intimation.

> "We'll give them the metal our mountain affords,
> Lillibulero, bullen a la,
> And in place of broad-pieces, we'll pay with broad-swords,
> Lero, lero, &c.
> With duns and with debts we will soon clear our score,
> Lillibulero, &c.
> For the man that's thus paid will crave payment no more,
> Lero, lero, &c.

"But come, Baillie, be not cast down; drink your wine with a joyous heart; the Baron shall return safe and victorious to Tully-Veolan, and unite Killancureit's lairdship with his own, since the cowardly half-bred swine will not turn out for the Prince like a gentleman."

"To be sure, they lie maist ewest," said the Baillie, wiping his eyes, "and should naturally fall under the same factory."

"And I," proceeded the Chieftain, "shall take care of myself, too; for you must know I have to complete a good work here, by bringing Mrs Flockhart into the bosom of the Catholic church, or at least half

way, and that is to your episcopal meeting-house. O, Baron! if you
heard her fine counter-tenor admonishing Kate and Matty in the
morning, you, who understand music, would tremble at the idea of
hearing her shrieking in the psalmody of Haddo's-hole."

"Lord forgive you, Colonel, how ye rin on! but I hope your honours
will tak tea before you gang to the palace, and I maun go and mask it
for you."

So saying, Mrs Flockhart left the gentlemen to their own conversation, which, as might be supposed, turned chiefly upon the approaching events of the campaign.

Chapter Twenty

THE BALL

ENSIGN MACCOMBICH having gone to the Highland camp upon
duty, and Baillie Macwheeble having retired to digest his dinner, and
Evan Dhu's intimation of martial law, in some blind change-house,
Waverley, with the Baron and the Chieftain, proceeded to Holyrood-
House. The two last were in full tide of spirits, and the Baron rallied in
his way our hero upon the handsome figure which his new dress
displayed to advantage. "If you have any design upon the heart of a
bonny Scottish lassie, I would premonish you when you address her to
remember the words of Virgilius:

> Nunc insanus amor duri me Martis in armis,
> Tela inter media atque adversos detinet hostes.

Whilk verses Robertson of Struan, Chief of the clan Donnochy, unless
the claims of Lude ought to be preferred *primo loco*, has thus elegantly
rendered:

> For cruel love has gartan'd low my leg,
> And clad my hurdies in a philabeg.

Although indeed ye wear the trews, a garment whilk I approve most of
the two, as more ancient and seemly."

"Or rather," said Fergus, "hear my song:

> She wadna hae a Lowland laird,
>   Nor be an English lady;
> But she's away with Duncan Græme,
>   And he's rowed her in his plaidy."

By this time they reached the palace of Holy-Rood, and were
announced respectively as they entered the apartments.

It is but too well known how many gentlemen of rank, education,
and fortune took a concern in the ill-fated and desperate undertaking
of 1745. The ladies also of Scotland very generally espoused the cause

of the gallant and handsome young Prince, who threw himself upon the mercy of his countrymen, rather like a hero of romance than a calculating politician. It is not therefore to be wondered that Edward, who had spent the greater part of his life in the solemn seclusion of Waverley-Honour, should have been dazzled at the liveliness and elegance of the scene now exhibited in the long-deserted halls of the Scottish palace. The accompaniments, indeed, fell far short of splendour, being but such as the confusion and hurry of the time admitted. Still, however, the general effect was striking, and, the rank of the company considered, might well be called brilliant.

It was not long before the lover's eye discovered the object of his attachment. Flora Mac-Ivor was in the act of returning to her seat, near the top of the room, with Rose Bradwardine by her side. Among much elegance and beauty, they had attracted a general degree of the public attention, being certainly two of the handsomest women present. The Prince took much notice of both, particularly of Flora, with whom he danced, a preference which she probably owed to her foreign education, and command of the French and Italian languages.

When the bustle attending the conclusion of the dance permitted, Edward, almost intuitively, followed Fergus to the place where Miss Mac-Ivor was seated. The sensation of hope, with which he had nursed his affection in absence of the beloved object, seemed to vanish in her presence, and, like one striving to recover the particulars of a forgotten dream, he would have given the world at that moment to have recollected the grounds on which he had founded expectations which now seemed so delusive. He accompanied Fergus with downcast eyes, tingling ears, and the sensation of a criminal, who, while he moves slowly through the crowds who have assembled to behold his execution, receives no clear sensation either from the noise which fills his ears, or the tumult on which he casts his wandering look.

Flora seemed a little—a very little—affected and discomposed at his approach. "I bring you an adopted son of Ivor," said Fergus.

"And I receive him as a second brother," replied Flora.

There was a slight emphasis on the word which would have escaped every ear but one that was feverish with apprehension. It was however distinctly marked, and, combined with her whole tone and manner, plainly intimated, "I will never think of Mr Waverley as a more intimate connection." Edward stopped, bowed, and looked at Fergus, who bit his lip, a movement of anger which proved that he also put a sinister interpretation on the reception which his sister had extended his friend. "This then is an end of my day-dream!" Such was Waverley's first thought, and it was so exquisitely painful as to banish from his cheek every drop of blood.

"Good God!" said Rose Bradwardine, "he is not yet recovered!"

These words, which she uttered with great emotion, were over-heard by the Chevalier himself, who stepped hastily forward, and, taking Waverley by the hand, enquired kindly after his health, and added, that he wished to speak with him. By a strong and sudden effort, which the circumstances rendered indispensable, Waverley recovered himself so far as to follow the Chevalier in silence to a sort of recess in the apartment.

Here the Prince detained him for some time, asking various questions about the great tory and catholic families of England, their connections, their influence, and the state of their affections towards the house of Brunswick. To these queries Edward could not at any time have given more than general answers, and it may be supposed that, in the present state of his feelings, his responses were indistinct even to confusion. The Chevalier smiled once or twice at the incongruity of his replies, but continued the same style of conversation, although he found himself obliged to occupy the principal share of it, until he perceived that Waverley had recovered his presence of mind. It is probable that this long audience was partly meant to further the idea which the Prince desired should be entertained among his followers, that Waverley was a character of political influence. But it appeared from his concluding expressions that he had a different and good-natured motive, personal to our hero, for prolonging the conference. "I cannot resist the temptation," he said, "of boasting of my own discretion as a lady's confidant. You see, Mr Waverley, that I know all, and I assure you I am deeply interested in the affair. But, my good young friend, you must put a more severe restraint upon your feelings. There are many here whose eyes can see as clearly as mine, but the prudence of whose tongues may not be equally trusted."

So saying, he turned easily away, and joined a circle of officers at a few paces distance, leaving Waverley to meditate upon his parting expression, which, though not intelligible to him in its whole purport, was sufficiently so in the caution which the last words recommended. Making therefore an effort to shew himself worthy of the interest which his new master had expressed, by instant obedience to his recommendation, he walked up to the spot where Flora and Miss Bradwardine were still seated, and having made his compliments to the latter, he succeeded, even beyond his own expectation, in entering into conversation upon general topics.

If, my dear reader, thou hast ever happened to take post-horses at ——, or at ——, (one at least of which blanks, or more probably both, you will be able to fill up from an inn near your own residence,) you must have observed, and doubtless with sympathetic pain, the reluctant agony with which the poor jades at first apply their galled necks to the collars of the harness. But when the irresistible arguments of the post-boy have prevailed upon them to proceed a mile or two, they will become callous to the first sensation; and being *warm in the harness*, as the said post-boy may term it, proceed as if their withers were altogether unwrung. This simile so much corresponds with the state of Waverley's feelings in the course of this memorable evening, that I prefer it (especially as being, I trust, wholly original) to any more splendid illustration, with which Byshe's Art of Poetry might supply me.

Exertion, like virtue, is its own reward; and our hero had, moreover, other stimulating motives for persevering in a display of affected composure and indifference to Flora's obvious unkindness. Pride, which applies its caustic as an useful, though severe, remedy for the wounds of affection, came rapidly to his aid. Distinguished by the favour of a Prince, destined, he had room to hope, to play a conspicuous part in the revolution which awaited a mighty kingdom, excelling probably in mental acquirements, and equalling at least, in personal accomplishments, most of the noble and distinguished persons with whom he was now ranked, young, wealthy, and high born, could he, or ought he to droop beneath the frown of a capricious beauty?

> O nymph, unrelenting and cold as thou art,
> My bosom is proud as thine own.

With the feeling expressed in these beautiful lines (which however were not then written,) Waverley determined upon convincing Flora that he was not to be depressed by a rejection, in which his vanity whispered that perhaps she did her own prospects as much injustice as his. And, to aid this change of feeling, there lurked the secret and unacknowledged hope, that she might learn to prize his affection more highly when she did not conceive it to be altogether within her own choice to attract or repulse it. There was a mystic tone of encouragement also in the Chevalier's words, though he feared they only referred to the wishes of Fergus in favour of an union between him and his sister. But the whole circumstances of time, place, and incident, combined at once to awaken his imagination, and to call upon him for a manly and decisive tone of conduct, leaving to fate to dispose of the issue. Should he appear to be the only one sad and disheartened on the eve of battle, how greedily would the tale be commented upon by the slander which had been already but too busy with his fame? Never, never, he internally resolved, shall my unprovoked enemies possess such an advantage over my reputation.

Under the influence of these mixed sensations, and cheered at times by a smile of intelligence and approbation from the Prince as he passed the group, Waverley exerted his powers of fancy, intelligence, and eloquence, and attracted the general admiration of the company. The conversation gradually assumed the tone best qualified for the display of his talents and acquisitions. The gaiety of the evening was exalted in character, rather than checked, by the approaching dangers of to-morrow. All nerves were strung for the future, and prepared to enjoy the present. This mood of mind is highly favourable for the exercise of the powers of imagination, for poetry, and for that elo-quence which is allied to poetry. Waverley, as we have elsewhere observed, possessed at times a wonderful flow of rhetoric; and on the present occasion, he touched more than once the higher notes of feeling, and then again ran off in a wild voluntary of fanciful mirth. He was supported and excited by kindred spirits, who felt the same impulse of mood and time; and even those of more cold and calculat-ing habits were hurried along by the torrent. Many ladies declined the dance, which still went forward, and, under various pretences, joined the party to which the "handsome young Englishman" seemed to have attached himself. He was presented to several of the first rank, and his manners, which for the present were altogether free from the bashful restraint by which, in a moment of less excitation, they were usually clouded, gave universal delight.

Flora Mac-Ivor appeared to be the only female present who regarded him with a degree of coldness and reserve; yet even she could not suppress a sort of wonder at talents, which, in the course of their acquaintance, she had never seen displayed with equal brilliancy and impressive effect. I do not know whether she might not feel a momentary regret at having taken so decisive a resolution upon the addresses of a lover, who seemed fitted so well to fill a high place in the highest stations of society. Certainly she had hitherto accounted among the incurable deficiencies of Edward's disposition, the *mauv-aise honte*, which, as she had been educated in the first foreign circles, and was little acquainted with the shyness of English manners, was, in her opinion, too nearly related to timidity and imbecillity of disposi-tion. But if a passing wish occurred that Waverley could have rendered himself uniformly thus amiable and attractive, its influence was momentary; for circumstances had arisen since they met which rendered, in her eyes, the resolution she had formed respecting his addresses final and irrevocable.

With opposite feelings Rose Bradwardine bent her whole soul to listen. She felt a secret triumph at the public tribute paid to one, whose merit she had learned to prize too early and too fondly. Without a thought of jealousy, without a feeling of fear, pain, or doubt, and undisturbed by a single selfish consideration, she resigned herself to the pleasure of observing the general murmur of applause. When Waverley spoke, her ear was exclusively filled with his voice; when others answered, her eye took its turn of observation, and seemed to watch his reply. Perhaps the delight which she experienced in the course of that evening, though transient, and followed by much sorrow, is in its nature the most pure and disinterested which the human mind is capable of enjoying.

"Baron," said the Chevalier, "I would not trust my mistress in the company of your young friend. He is really, though somewhat romantic, one of the most fascinating young men whom I have ever seen."

"And by my honour, sir," said the Baron, "the lad can sometimes be as dowff as a sexagenary like myself. If your Royal Highness had seen him dreaming and dozing about the banks of Tully-Veolan like an hypochondriac person, or, as Burton's Anatomia hath it, a phrenesiac or lethargic patient, you would wonder where he hath sae suddenly acquired all this fine sprack festivity and jocularity."

"Truly," said Fergus Mac-Ivor, "I think it can only be the inspiration of the tartans; for though Waverley be always a man of sense and honour, I have hitherto often found him a very absent and inattentive companion."

"We are the more obliged to him," said the Chevalier, "for having reserved for this evening qualities which even such intimate friends had not discovered.—But come, gentlemen, the night advances, and the business of to-morrow must be early thought upon. Each take charge of his fair partner, and honour a small refreshment with your company."

He led the way to another suite of apartments, and assumed the seat and canopy at the head of a long range of tables, with an air of dignity mingled with courtesy which well became his high birth and lofty pretensions. An hour had hardly flown away when the musicians played the signal for parting, so well known in Scotland.

"Good night then," said the Chevalier, rising; "Good night, and joy be with you!—Good night, fair ladies, who have so highly honoured a proscribed and banished Prince.—Good night, my brave friends; may the happiness we have this evening experienced be an omen of our return to these our paternal halls, speedily and in triumph, and of many and many future meetings of mirth and pleasure in the palace of Holy-Rood!"

When the Baron of Bradwardine afterwards mentioned this adieu of the Chevalier, he never failed to repeat, in a melancholy tone,

"Audiit, et voti Phœbus succedere partem
Mente dedit; partem volucres dispersit in auras;

which," as he added, "is weel rendered into English metre by my friend Bangour;

> Ae half the prayer wi' Phœbus grace did find,
> The t'other half he whistled down the wind."

Chapter Twenty-One

THE MARCH

THE CONFLICTING passions and exhausted feelings of Waverley had resigned him to late but sound repose. He was dreaming of Glennaquoich, and had transferred to the halls of Ian nan Chaistel the festal train which so lately graced those of Holy-Rood. The pibroch too was distinctly heard; and this at least was no delusion, for the "proud step of the chief piper" of the "chlain Mac-Ivor" was perambulating the court before the door of his Chieftain's quarters, and as Mrs Flockhart, apparently no friend to his minstrelsy, was pleased to observe, "garring the very stane and lime wa's dinnle wi' his screeching." Of course it soon became too powerful for Waverley's dream, with which it had at first rather harmonized.

The sound of Callum's brogues in his apartment, (for Mac-Ivor had again assigned Waverley to his care) was the next note of parting. "Winna yere honour bang up? Vich Ian Vohr and ta Prince are awa' to the lang green glen ahint the clachan at they ca' King's Park, and mony ane's on his ain shanks the day that will be carried on ither folks' ere night."

Waverley sprung up, and, with Callum's assistance and instructions, adjusted his tartans in proper costume. Callum told him also, "tat his leather dorlach wi' the lock on her was come frae Doune, and she was awa' again in the wain wi' Vich Ian Vohr's walise."

By this periphrasis Waverley readily apprehended his portmanteau was intended. He thought upon the mysterious packet of the maid of the cavern, which seemed always to escape him when within his very grasp. But this was no time for indulgence of curiosity; and having declined Mrs Flockhart's compliment of a *morning, i. e.* a matutinal dram, being probably the only man in the Chevalier's army by whom such a courtesy would have been rejected, he made his adieus, and departed with Callum.

"Callum," said he, as they proceeded down a dirty close to gain the southern skirts of the Canongate, "what shall I do for a horse?"

"Ta deil ane ye maun think of," said Callum. "Vich Ian Vohr's marching on foot at the head o' his kin, (no to say the Prince, wha does the like,) wi' his target on his shoulder, and ye maun e'en be neighbour like."

"And so I will, Callum,—give me my target;—so, there we are fixed. How does it look?"

"Like the bra' Highlander at's painted on the board afore the mickle change-house they ca' Luckie Middlemass's," answered Callum; meaning, I must observe, a high compliment, for, in his opinion, Luckie Middlemass's sign was an exquisite specimen of art. Waverley, however, not feeling the full force of this polite simile, asked him no farther questions.

Upon extricating themselves from the mean and dirty suburbs of the metropolis, and emerging into the open air, Waverley felt a renewal both of health and spirits, and turned his recollection with firmness upon the events of the preceding evening, and with hope and resolution towards those of the approaching day.

When he had surmounted a small craggy eminence, called St Leonard's Hill, the King's Park, or the hollow between the mountain of Arthur's Seat, and the rising grounds on which the southern part of Edinburgh is now built, lay beneath him, and displayed a singular and animating prospect. It was occupied by the army of the Highlanders, now in the act of preparing for their march. Waverley had already seen something of the kind at the hunting-match which he attended with Fergus Mac-Ivor, but this was upon a scale of much greater magnitude, and incomparably deeper interest. The rocks, which formed the back-ground of the scene, and the very sky itself, rung with the clang of the bagpipers, summoning forth, each with his appropriate pibroch, his chieftain and clan. The mountaineers, rousing themselves from their couch under the canopy of heaven, with the hum and bustle of a confused and irregular multitude, like bees alarmed and arming in their hives, seemed to possess all the pliability of movement fitted to execute military manœuvres. Their motions appeared spontaneous and confused, but the result was order and regularity; so that a general must have praised the conclusion, though a martinet might have ridiculed the method by which it was attained.

The sort of complicated medley created by the hasty arrangement of the various clans under their respective banners, for the purpose of getting into the order of march, was in itself a gay and lively spectacle. They had no tents to strike, having generally, and by choice, slept upon the open field, although the autumn was now waning, and the nights beginning to be frosty. After forming for a little while, there was exhibited a changing, fluctuating, and confused appearance of waving tartans and floating plumes, and of banners displaying the proud gathering word of Clanronald, *Ganion Coheriga*—(gainsay who dares;) *Loch-Sloy*, the watchword of the Mac-Farlanes; *Forth, fortune, and fill the fetters*, the motto of the Marquis of Tullibardine; *Bydand*, that of Lord Lewis Gordon; and the appropriate signal words and emblems of many other chieftains and clans.

At length the mixed and wavering multitude arranged themselves into a narrow and dusky column of great length, stretching through the whole extent of the valley. In the front of the column the standard of the Chevalier was displayed, bearing a red cross upon a white ground, with the motto *Tandem Triumphans*. The few cavalry, being chiefly Lowland gentry, with their domestic servants and retainers, formed the advanced-guard of the army, and their standards, of which they had rather too many in respect of their numbers, were seen waving upon the extreme verge of the horizon. Many members of this body, among whom Waverley accidentally remarked Balmawhapple and his lieutenant, Jinker, (which last, however, had been reduced, with several others, by the advice of the Baron of Bradwardine, to the situation of what he called reformed officers, or reformadoes,) added to the liveliness, though by no means to the regularity, of the scene, by galloping their horses as fast forward as the press would permit, to join their proper station in the van. The fascinations of the Circes of the High Street, and the potions of strength with which they had been drenched over night, had probably detained these heroes within the walls of Edinburgh somewhat later than was consistent with their morning duty. Of such loiterers, the more prudent took the longer and circuitous, but more open route, to attain their place in the march, by keeping at some distance from the infantry, and making their way through the inclosures to the right, at the expence of leaping over or pulling down the dry stone fences. The irregular appearance and vanishing of these small parties, as well as the confusion occasioned by those who endeavoured, though generally without effect, to press to the front through the crowd of Highlanders, maugre their curses, oaths, and opposition, added to the picturesque wildness, what it took from the military regularity, of the scene.

While Waverley gazed upon this remarkable spectacle, rendered yet more impressive by the occasional discharge of cannon-shot from the Castle at the Highland guards as they were withdrawn from its vicinity to join their main body, Callum, with his usual freedom of interference, reminded him that Vich Ian Vohr's folk were nearly at the head of the column of march which was still distant, and that "they would gang very fast after the cannon fired." Thus admonished, Waverley walked briskly forward, yet often casting a glance upon the darksome clouds of warriors who were collected before and beneath him. A nearer view, indeed, rather diminished the effect impressed on the mind by the more distant appearance of the army. The leading men of each clan were well armed with broadsword, target, and fusee, to which all added the dirk, and most the steel pistol. But these consisted of gentlemen, that is, relations of the chief, however distant, and who had an immediate title to his countenance and protection. Finer and hardier men than these could not have been selected out of any army in Christendom; and the free and independent habits which each possessed, and which each was yet so well taught to subject to the command of his chief, and the peculiar mode of discipline adopted in Highland warfare, rendered them equally formidable by their individual courage and high spirit, and from their rational conviction of the necessity of acting in unison, and of giving their national mode of attack the fullest opportunity of success.

But, in a lower rank to these, there were found individuals of an inferior description, the peasantry of the country, who, although they did not allow themselves to be so called, and claimed often, with apparent truth, to be of more ancient descent than the masters whom they served, bore, nevertheless, the livery of extreme penury, being indifferently accoutred, and worse armed, half naked, stinted in growth, and miserable in aspect. Each important clan had some of these Helots attached to them;—thus the M'Couls, though tracing their descent from Comhal, the father of Finn, or Fingal, were a sort of Gibeonites, or hereditary servants to the Stuarts of Appine. The Macbeaths, descended from the unhappy monarch of that name, were subjects to the Morays, and clan Donnochy, or Robertsons of Athole; and many other examples might be given, but for hurting any pride of clanship which may yet be left, and thereby drawing a Highland tempest into the shop of my publisher. Now these same Helots, though forced into the field by the arbitrary authority of the chieftains under whom they hewed wood and drew water, were, in general, very sparingly fed, ill dressed, and worse armed. The latter circumstance was indeed owing chiefly to the general disarming act, which had been carried into effect ostensibly through the whole Highlands, although most of the chieftains contrived to elude its influence by retaining the weapons of their own immediate clansmen, and delivering up those of less value which they collected from these inferior satellites. It followed, as a matter of course, that, as we have already hinted, many of these poor fellows were brought to the field in a very wretched condition.

From this it happened, that, in bodies, the van of which were admirably well armed in their own fashion, the rear resembled actual banditti. Here was a pole-axe, there a sword without a scabbard; here a gun without a lock, there a scythe set straight upon a pole; and some had only their dirks, and bludgeons or stakes pulled out of hedges. The grim, uncombed, and wild appearance of these men, most of whom gazed with all the admiration of ignorance upon the most ordinary productions of domestic art, created surprise in the Lowlands, but it also created terror. So little was the condition of the Highlands known at that late period, that the character and appearance of their population, while thus sallying forth as military adventurers, conveyed to the south country Lowlanders as much surprise as if an invasion of African negroes, or Esquimaux Indians, had issued forth from the northern mountains of their own native country. It cannot therefore be wondered if Waverley, who had hitherto judged of the Highlanders generally, from the samples which the policy of Fergus had from time to time exhibited, should have felt damped and astonished at the daring attempt of a body not then exceeding four thousand men, and of those not above half the number, at the utmost, well armed, to change the fate, and alter the dynasty, of the British kingdoms.

As he moved along the column, which still remained stationary, an iron gun, the only piece of artillery possessed by the army which meditated so important a revolution, was fired as the signal of march. The Chevalier had expressed a wish to leave this useless piece of ordnance behind him; but, to his surprise, the Highland chiefs interposed to solicit that it might accompany their march, pleading the prejudices of their followers, who, little accustomed to artillery, attached a degree of absurd importance to this field-piece, and expected it would contribute essentially to a victory which they could only owe to their own muskets and broad-swords. Two or three French artillerymen were therefore appointed to the management of this military engine, which was drawn along by a string of Highland ponies, and was, after all, only used for the purpose of firing signals.

No sooner was its voice heard upon the present occasion, than the whole line was in motion. A wild cry of joy from the advancing battalions rent the air, and was then lost in the shrill clangour of the bagpipes, as the sound of these, in their turn, was partially drowned by the heavy tread of so many men put at once into motion. The banners glittered and shook as they moved forward, and the horse hastened to occupy their station as the advanced guard, and to push on reconnoitering parties to ascertain and report the motions of the enemy. They vanished from Waverley's eye as they wheeled round the basis of Arthur's Seat, under the remarkable ridge of basaltic rocks which front the little lake of Duddingston.

The infantry followed in the same direction, regulating their pace by another body which occupied a road more to the southward. It cost

Edward some exertion of activity to attain the place which Fergus's
followers occupied in the line of march.

Chapter Twenty-Two

AN INCIDENT GIVES RISE TO UNAVAILING REFLECTIONS

WHEN WAVERLEY reached that part of the column which was filled
by the clan of Mac-Ivor, they halted, formed, and received him with a
triumphant flourish upon the bagpipes, and a loud shout of the men,
most of whom knew him personally, and were delighted to see him in
the dress of their country and of their sept. "You shout," said a
Highlander of a neighbouring clan to Evan Dhu, "as if the Chieftain
were just come to your head."

"*Mar e Bran is e brathair*, If it be not Bran, it is Bran's brother," was
the proverbial reply of Maccombich.

"O, then, it is the handsome Sassenach Duihne Wassal, that is to be
married to Lady Flora?"

"That may be, or it may not be; and it is neither your matter nor
mine, Gregor."

Fergus advanced to embrace the volunteer, and afford him a warm
and hearty welcome; but he thought it necessary to apologize for the
diminished numbers of his battalion, (which did not exceed three
hundred men) by observing, he had sent a good many out upon
parties. The fact was, that the defection of Donald Bean Lean had
deprived him of at least thirty hardy fellows, whose services he had
fully reckoned upon, and many of his occasional adherents had been
recalled by their several chiefs to the standards to which they most
properly owed their allegiance. The rival chief of the great northern
branch also of his own clan, had mustered his people, although he had
not yet declared either for the government or for the Chevalier, and by
his intrigues had in some degree diminished the force with which
Fergus took the field. To make amends for these disappointments, it
was universally admitted that the followers of Vich Ian Vohr, in point
of appearance, equipment, arms, and dexterity in using them, equalled
the most choice troops that followed the standard of Charles Edward.
Old Ballenkeiroch acted as his major; and, with the other officers who
had known Waverley when at Glennaquoich, gave our hero a cordial
reception, as the sharer of their future dangers and expected honours.

The route pursued by the Highland army after leaving the village of
Duddingston, was, for some time, the common post-road betwixt
Edinburgh and Haddington, until they crossed the Esk, at Mussel-

burgh, when, instead of keeping the low grounds towards the sea, they turned more inland, and occupied the brow of the eminence called Carberry-Hill, a place already distinguished in Scottish history as the spot where the lovely Mary surrendered herself to her insurgent subjects. This direction was chosen because the Chevalier had received notice that the army of the government had quartered the night before to the west of Haddington, with the intention of falling down towards the sea-side, and approaching Edinburgh by the lower coast-road. By keeping the height which overhung that road in many places, it was hoped the Highlanders might find an opportunity of attacking them to advantage. The army therefore halted upon the ridge of Carberry-Hill, both to refresh the soldiers, and as a central situation from which their march could be directed to any point that the motions of the enemy might render most advisable. While they remained in this position, a messenger came in haste to desire Mac-Ivor to come to the Prince, and added, that their advanced post had had a skirmish with some of the enemy's cavalry, and that the Baron of Bradwardine had sent in a few prisoners.

Waverley walked forward out of the line to satisfy his curiosity, and soon observed five or six of the troopers, who, covered with dust, had galloped in to announce that the enemy were in full march westward along the coast. Passing still a little farther on, he was struck with a groan which issued from a hovel,—he approached the spot, and heard a voice, in the provincial English of his native county, which endeavoured, though frequently interrupted by pain, to repeat the Lord's Prayer. The voice of distress always found a ready answer in our hero's bosom. He entered the hovel, which seemed to be intended for what is called, in the pastoral counties of Scotland, a *smearing-house;* and in its obscurity Edward could only at first discern a sort of red bundle; for those who had stripped the wounded man of his arms, and part of his clothes, had left him the dragoon-cloak in which he was enveloped.

"For the sake of God," said the wounded man, as he heard Waverley's step, "give me a single drop of water!"

"You shall have it," answered Waverley, at the same time raising him in his arms, bearing him to the door of the hut, and giving him some drink from his flask.

"I should know that voice," answered the man; but looking on Edward's dress with a bewildered look,—"no, this is not the young squire."

This was the common phrase by which Edward was distinguished on the estate of Waverley-Honour, and the sound now thrilled to his heart with the thousand recollections which the well-known accents of his native country had already contributed to awaken. "Houghton!" he said, gazing on the ghastly features which death was fast disfiguring, "can this be you?"

"I never thought to hear an English voice again," said the wounded man; "they left me to live or die here as I could, when they found I would say nothing about the strength of the regiment. But, O! squire, how could you stay from us so long, and let us be tempted by that fiend of the pit, Ruffen;—we would have followed you through flood and fire, to be sure."

"Ruffen! I assure you, Houghton, you have been vilely imposed upon."

"I often thought so," said Houghton, "though they shewed us your very seal; and so Tims was shot, and I was reduced to the ranks."

"Do not exhaust your strength in speaking," said Edward, "I will get you a surgeon presently."

He saw Mac-Ivor approaching, who was now returning from head-quarters, where he had attended a council of war, and hastened to meet him. "Brave news!" shouted the Chief; "we shall be at it in less than two hours. The Prince has put himself at the head of the advance; and, as he drew his sword, called out, 'My friends, I have thrown away the scabbard.' Come, Waverley, we move instantly."

"A moment,—a moment; this poor prisoner is dying;—where shall I find a surgeon?"

"Why, where should you? we have none, you know, but two or three French fellows, who, I believe, are little better than *garçons apothicaires*."

"But the man will bleed to death."

"Poor fellow! But it will be a thousand men's fate before night; so come along."

"I cannot; I tell you he is a son of a tenant of my uncle's."

"O, if he's a follower of yours, he must be looked to; I'll send Callum to you; but diaoul!—ceade millia molligheart," continued the impatient Chieftain,—"what made an old soldier, like Bradwardine, send dying men here to cumber us?"

Callum came with his usual alertness, and, indeed, Waverley rather gained than lost in the opinion of the Highlanders, by his anxiety about the wounded man. They would not have understood the general philanthropy, which rendered it almost impossible for Waverley to have past any person in such distress; but, as apprehending that the sufferer was one of his *following*, they unanimously allowed that Waverley's conduct was that of a kind and considerate chieftain, who merited the attachment of his people. In about a quarter of an hour poor Humphrey breathed his last, praying his young master, when he returned to Waverley-Honour, to be kind to old Job Houghton and his dame, and conjuring him not to fight with these wild petticoat-men against old England.

When his last breath was drawn, Waverley, who had beheld with sincere sorrow, and no slight tinge of remorse, the final agonies of mortality, now witnessed for the first time, commanded Callum to remove the body into the hut. This the young Highlander performed, not without examining the pockets of the defunct, which, however, he remarked, had been pretty well spung'd. He took the cloak, however, and proceeding with the provident caution of a spaniel hiding a bone, concealed it among some furze, and carefully marked the spot, observing, that if he chanced to return that way, it would be an excellent rokelay for his auld mother, Elspat.

It was by a considerable exertion that they regained their place in the marching column, which was now moving rapidly forward to occupy the high grounds above the village of Tranent, between which and the sea lay the purposed march of the opposite army.

This melancholy interview with his late serjeant forced many unavailing and painful reflections upon Waverley's mind. It was clear, from the confession of the man, that Colonel G——'s proceedings had been strictly warranted, and even rendered indispensable, by the steps taken in Edward's name to induce the soldiers of his troop to mutiny. The circumstance of the seal, he now, for the first time, recollected, and that he had lost it in the cavern of the robber, Bean Lean. That the artful villain had secured it, and used it as the means of carrying on an intrigue in the regiment for his own purposes, was sufficiently evident; and Edward had now little doubt that in the packet placed in his portmanteau by his daughter, he should find farther light upon his proceedings. In the meanwhile, the repeated expostulation of Houghton,—"Ah, squire, why did you leave us?" rung like a knell in his ears.

"Yes," said he, "I have indeed acted towards you with thoughtless cruelty. I brought you from your paternal fields, and the protection of a generous and kind landlord, and when I had subjected you to all the rigour of military discipline, I shunned to bear my own share of the burthen, and wandered from the duties I had undertaken, leaving alike those whom it was my business to protect, and my own reputation, to suffer under the artifices of villainy. O, indolence and indecision of mind! if not in yourselves vices, to how much exquisite misery do you frequently prepare the way!"

Chapter Twenty-Three

THE EVE OF BATTLE

ALTHOUGH the Highlanders marched on very fast, the sun was declining when they arrived upon the brow of those high grounds which command an open and extensive plain stretching northwards to the sea, on which are situated, but at a considerable distance from each other, the small villages of Seaton and Cockenzie, and the larger one of Preston. The low coast-road to Edinburgh passed through this plain, issuing upon it from the inclosures of Seaton-house, and at the town or village of Preston again entering the defiles of an inclosed country. By this way the English general had chosen to approach the metropolis, both as most commodious for his cavalry, and as being probably of opinion that by doing so, he would meet in front with the Highlanders advancing from Edinburgh in the opposite direction. In this he was mistaken, for the sound judgment of the Chevalier, or of those to whose advice he listened, left the direct passage free, but occupied the strong ground by which it was overlooked and commanded.

When the Highlanders reached the heights commanding the plain described, they were immediately formed in array of battle along the brow of the hill. Almost at the same instant, the van of the English appeared issuing from among the trees and inclosures of Seaton, with the purpose of occupying the plain between the high ground and the sea. The space which divided the armies being only about half a mile in breadth, Waverley could plainly see the squadrons of dragoons issue, one after another, from the defiles, with their videttes in front, and form upon the plain, with their front opposed to the line of the Prince's army. They were followed by a train of field-pieces, which, when they reached the flank of the dragoons, were also brought into line, and pointed against the heights. The march was continued by three or four regiments of infantry marching in open column, their fixed bayonets shewing like successive hedges of steel, and their arms glancing like lightning, as, at a signal given, they at once wheeled into line, and were placed in direct opposition to the Highlanders. A second train of artillery, with another regiment of horse, closed the long march, and formed on the left flank of the infantry, the whole line facing southwards.

While the English army went through these evolutions, the Highlanders shewed equal promptitude and zeal for battle. As fast as the clans came upon the ridge which fronted their enemy, they were formed into line, so that both armies got into complete order of battle at the same moment. When this was accomplished, the Highlanders set up a tremendous yell, which was re-echoed by the heights behind them. The regulars, who were in high spirits, returned a loud shout of defiance, and fired one or two of their cannon, upon an advanced post of the Highlanders. The latter displayed great earnestness to proceed instantly to the attack, Evan Dhu urging to Fergus, by way of argument, that "the *sidier roy* was tottering like an egg upon a staff, and that they had a' the vantage of the onset, for even a haggis (God bless her!) could charge down hill."

But the ground through which the mountaineers must have descended, although not of great extent, was impracticable in its character, being not only marshy, but intersected with walls of dry stone, and traversed in its whole length by a very broad and deep ditch, circumstances which must have given the musketry of the regulars dreadful advantages. The authority of the commanders was therefore interposed to curb the impetuosity of the Highlanders, and only a few marksmen were sent down the descent to skirmish with the enemy's advanced posts, and to reconnoitre the ground.

Here then was a military spectacle of no ordinary interest, or usual occurrence. The two armies, so different in aspect and discipline, yet each admirably trained to their peculiar mode of war, upon whose conflict the temporary fate at least of Scotland appeared to depend, now faced each other like two gladiators in the arena, each meditating upon the mode of attacking their enemy. The leading officers and the general's staff of each army could be distinguished in front of their lines, busied with their spy-glasses to watch each other's motions, and occupied in dispatching the orders and receiving the intelligence conveyed by the aids-de-camp and orderly-men, who gave life to the scene by galloping along in different directions, as if the fate of the day depended upon the speed of their horses. The space between the armies was at times occupied by the partial and irregular contest of individual sharp-shooters, and a hat or bonnet was occasionally seen to fall, or a wounded man was borne off by his comrades. These, however, were but trifling skirmishes, for it suited the view of neither party to advance in that direction. From the neighbouring hamlets, the peasantry cautiously shewed themselves as if watching the issue of the expected engagement; and at no great distance in the bay were two square-rigged vessels bearing the English flag, whose tops and yards were crowded with less timid spectators.

When this awful pause had lasted for a short time, Fergus, with another Chieftain, received orders to detach their clans towards the village of Preston, in order to threaten the right flank of Cope's army, and compel him to a change of disposition. In order to execute these orders, the Chief of Glennaquoich occupied the church-yard of Tranent, a commanding situation, and a convenient place, as Evan Dhu remarked, for any gentleman who might have the misfortune to be killed, and chanced to be curious about Christian burial. To check or dislodge this party, the English general detached two guns, escorted by a strong party of cavalry. They approached so near that Waverley could plainly recognize the standard of the troop he had formerly commanded, and hear the trumpets and kettle-drums sound the advance, which he had so often obeyed. He could hear, too, the well-known word given in the English dialect, by the equally well-distinguished voice of the commanding officer for whom he had once felt so much respect. It was at that instant, that looking around him, he saw the wild dress and appearance of his Highland associates, heard their whispers in an uncouth and unknown language, looked upon his own dress, so unlike that which he had worn from his infancy, and wished to awake from what seemed at the moment a dream, strange, horrible, and unnatural. "Good God," he thought, "am I then a traitor to my country, a renegade to my standard, and a foe, as that poor dying wretch expressed himself, to my native England!"

Ere he could digest or smother the recollection, the tall military form of his late commander came full in view, for the purpose of reconnoitering. "I can hit him now," said Callum, cautiously raising his fusee over the wall under which he lay couched, scarce sixty yards distance.

Edward felt as if he were about to see a parricide committed in his presence; for the venerable grey hair and striking countenance of the veteran, recalled the almost paternal respect with which his officers universally regarded him. But ere he could say "Hold," an aged Highlander, who lay beside Callum Beg, stopped his arm. "Spare your shot," said the seer, "his hour is not yet come. But let him beware of to-morrow—I see his winding-sheet high upon his breast."

Callum, flint to other considerations, was penetrable to superstition. He turned pale at the words of the *Taishatr*, and recovered his piece. Colonel G——, unconscious of the danger he had escaped, turned his horse round, and rode slowly back to the front of his regiment.

By this time the regular army had assumed a new line, with one flank inclined towards the sea, and the other resting upon the village of Preston; and, as similar difficulties occurred in attacking their new position, Fergus and the rest of the detachment were recalled to their former post. This alteration created the necessity of a corresponding change in General Cope's army, which was again brought into a line parallel with that of the Highlanders. In these manœuvres on both sides the day-light was nearly consumed, and both armies prepared to rest upon their arms for the night in the lines which they respectively occupied.

"There will be nothing done to-night," said Fergus to his friend Waverley; "ere we wrap ourselves in our plaids, let us go see what the Baron is about in rear of the line."

When they approached his post, they found the good old careful officer, after having sent out his night patroles and posted his centinels, engaged in reading the Evening Service of the Episcopal Church to the remainder of his troop. His voice was loud and sonorous, and though his spectacles upon his nose, and the appearance of Saunders Saunderson, in military array, performing the functions of clerk, had something ludicrous, yet the circumstances of danger in which they stood, the military costume of the audience, and the appearance of their horses, saddled and picquetted behind them, gave an impressive and solemn effect to the office of devotion.

"I have confessed to-day, ere you were awake," whispered Fergus to Waverley, "yet I am not so strict a catholic as to refuse to join in this good man's prayers." Edward assented, and they remained till the Baron had concluded the service.

As he shut the book, "Now, lads," said he, "have at them in the morning with heavy hands and light consciences." He then kindly greeted Mac-Ivor and Waverley, who requested to know his opinion of their situation. "Why, you know Tacitus saith, '*In rebus bellicis maxime dominatur Fortuna*,' which is equiponderate with our vernacular adage, 'Luck can maist in the mellee.' But credit me, gentlemen, yon man is not a deacon of his craft. He damps the spirits of the poor lads he commands, by keeping them on the defensive, whilk of itself implies inferiority or fear. Now will they lie on their arms yonder, as anxious and as ill at ease as a toad under a harrow, while our men will be quite fresh and blithe for action in the morning.—Well, good night —One thing troubles me, but if to-morrow goes well off, I will consult you about it, Glennaquoich."——

"I could almost apply to Mr Bradwardine the character which Henry gives of Fluellen," said Waverley, as his friend and he walked towards their *bivouac*:

> "Though it appears a little out of fashion,
> There is much care and valour in this 'Scotchman.'"

"He has seen much service," answered Fergus, "and one is sometimes astonished to find how much nonsense and reason are mingled in his composition. I wonder what can be troubling his mind—probably something about Rose.—Hark! the English are setting their watch."

The roll of the drums and shrill accompaniment of the fifes swelled up the hill—died away—resumed its thunder—and was at length hushed. The trumpets and kettle-drums of the cavalry were next heard to perform the beautiful and wild point of war appropriated as signal for that piece of nocturnal duty, and then finally sunk upon the wind with a shrill and mournful cadence.

The friends, who had now reached their post, stood and looked round them ere they lay down to rest. The western sky twinkled with stars, but a frost-mist rising from the ocean, covered the eastern horizon, and rolled in white wreaths along the plain where the adverse army lay couched upon their arms. Their advanced posts were pushed as far as the side of the great ditch at the bottom of the descent, and had kindled large fires at different intervals, gleaming with obscure and hazy lustre through the heavy fog which appeared to encircle them with a doubtful halo.

The Highlanders, "thick as leaves in Valambrosa," lay stretched upon the ridge of the hill, buried (excepting their centinels) in the most profound repose. "How many of these brave fellows will sleep more soundly before to-morrow night, Fergus!"

"You must not think of that. You must only think of your sword, and by whom it was given. All other reflections are now TOO LATE."

With the opiate contained in this undeniable remark, Edward endeavoured to lull the tumult of his conflicting feelings. The Chieftain and he combining their plaids, made a comfortable and warm couch. Callum, sitting down at their head, (for it was his duty to watch upon the immediate person of the Chief,) began a long mournful song in Gaelic, to a low and uniform tune, which, like the sound of the wind at a distance, soon lulled them both to sleep.

Chapter Twenty-Four

THE CONFLICT

WHEN THEY had slept for a few hours, they were awakened, and summoned to attend the Prince. The distant village clock was heard to toll three as they hastened to the place where he lay. He was already surrounded by his principal officers and the chiefs of clans. A bundle of pease-straw, which had been lately his couch, now served for his seat. Just as Fergus reached the circle, the consultation had broken up. "Courage, my brave friends!" said the Chevalier, "and each one put himself instantly at the head of his command. A faithful friend has offered to guide us by a practicable, though narrow and circuitous route, which, sweeping to our right, traverses the broken ground and morass, and enables us to gain the firm and open plain, upon which the enemy are lying. This difficulty surmounted, Heaven and your good swords must do the rest."

The proposal spread unanimous joy, and each leader hastened to get his men into order with as little noise as possible. And the army, moving by its right from off the ground on which they had rested, soon entered the path through the morass, conducting their march with astonishing silence and great rapidity. The mist had not risen to the higher grounds, so that for some time they had the advantage of star-light. But this was lost as the stars faded before approaching day, and as the head of the marching column, continuing its descent, plunged as it were into the heavy ocean of fog, which rolled its white waves over the whole plain, and over the sea, by which it was bounded. Some difficulties were now to be encountered, inseparable from darkness, a narrow, broken, and marshy path, and the necessity of preserving union in the march. These, however, were less inconvenient to High-landers, from their habits of life, than they would have been to any other troops, and they continued a steady and swift movement.

As the clan of Ivor approached the firm ground, following the tract of those who preceded them, the challenge of a patrole was heard through the mist, though they could not see the dragoon by whom it was made—"Who goes there?"

"Hush!" cried Fergus, "hush! let none answer, as he values his life —press forward;" and they continued their march with silence and rapidity.

The patrole fired his carabine upon the body, and the report was instantly followed by the clang of his horse's feet as he galloped off. "*Hylax in limine latrat*," said the Baron of Bradwardine, who heard the shot; "that loon will give the alarm."

The clan of Fergus had now gained the firm plain, which had lately borne a large crop of corn. But the harvest was gathered in, and the expanse was unbroken by tree, bush, or interruption of any kind. The rest of the army were following fast, when they heard the drums of the enemy beat the general. Surprise, however, had made no part of their plan, so they were not disconcerted by this intimation that the foe was upon his guard, and prepared to receive them. It only hastened their dispositions for the combat, which were very simple.

The Highland army, which now occupied the eastern end of the wide plain, or corn field, so often referred to, was drawn up in two lines, extending from the morass towards the sea. The first was des-tined to charge the enemy, the second to act as a reserve. The few horse, whom the Prince headed in person, remained between the two lines. The Adventurer had intimated a resolution to charge in person at the head of his first line; but his purpose was deprecated by all around him, and he was though with difficulty induced to abandon it.

Both lines now moving forwards, the first prepared for instant combat. The clans, of which it was composed, formed each a sort of separate phalanx, narrow in front, and in depth ten, twelve, or fifteen files, according to the strength of the following. The best armed and best born, for the words were synonymous, were placed in front of each of these irregular subdivisions. The others in the rear shouldered forwards the front, and by their pressure added both physical impulse, and additional ardour and confidence, to those who were first to encounter the danger.

"Down with your plaid, Waverley," cried Fergus, throwing off his own; "we'll win silks for our tartans before the sun is above the sea."

The clansmen on every side stript their plaids, prepared their arms, and there was an awful pause of about three minutes, during which the men, pulling off their bonnets, raised their faces to heaven, and uttered a short prayer. Waverley felt his heart at that moment throb as it would have burst from his bosom. It was not fear, it was not ardour,—it was a compound of both, a new and deeply energetic impulse, that with its first emotion chilled and astounded, then fevered and maddened his mind. The sounds around him combined to exalt his enthusiasm; the pipes played, and the clans rushed forwards, each in its own dark column. As they advanced they mended their pace, and the muttering sounds of the men to each other began to swell into a wild cry.

At this moment the sun, which was now above the horizon, dispelled the mists. The vapours rose like a curtain, and shewed the two armies in the act of closing. The line of the regulars was formed directly fronting the attack of the Highlanders;—it glittered with the appointments of a complete army, and was flanked by cavalry and artillery. But the sight impressed no terror on the assailants. "Forward, sons of Ivor," cried their Chief, "or the Camerons will draw the first blood." They rushed on with a tremendous yell.

The rest is well known. The horse, who were commanded to charge the advancing Highlanders in the flank, received a fire from their fusees as they ran on, and, seized with a disgraceful panic, wavered, halted, disbanded, and galloped from the field. The artillery-men, deserted by the cavalry, fled after discharging their pieces, and the Highlanders, who dropped their guns when fired, and drew their broad-swords, rushed with headlong fury against the infantry.

It was at this moment of confusion and terror that Waverley re-marked an English officer, apparently of high rank, standing alone and unsupported by a field-piece, which, after the flight of the men by whom it was wrought, he had himself levelled and discharged against the clan of Mac-Ivor, the nearest group of Highlanders within his aim. Struck with his tall martial figure, and eager to save him from inevitable destruction, Waverley outstripped for an instant even the speediest of the warriors, and reaching the spot first, called to him to surrender. The officer replied by a thrust with his sword, which Waverley received in his target, and in turning it aside the weapon broke. At the same time the battle-axe of Dugald Mahony was in the act of descending upon the Englishman's head. Waverley intercepted and prevented the blow, and the officer, perceiving farther resistance unavailing, and struck with Edward's generous anxiety for his safety, resigned the fragment of his sword, and was committed by Waverley to Dugald, with a strict charge to use him well, and not to pillage his person, promising him, at the same time, full indemnification for the spoil.

On Edward's right the battle still raged fierce and thick. The English infantry, trained in the wars of Flanders, stood their ground with great courage. But their extended files were pierced and broken in many places by the close masses of the clans; and in the personal struggle which ensued, the nature of the Highlanders' arms, and their extraordinary fierceness and activity, gave them a decided superiority over those who had been accustomed to trust much to their array and discipline, and now felt that the one was broken and the other useless. Waverley, as he cast his eyes towards this scene of smoke and slaughter, observed Colonel G——, deserted by his own soldiers in spite of all his attempts to rally them, yet spurring his horse through the field to take the command of a small body of infantry, who, with their backs arranged against the wall of his own park, (for his house was close by the field of battle,) continued a desperate and unavailing resistance. Waverley could perceive that he had already received several wounds, his clothes and saddle being marked with blood. To save this good and brave man, became the instant object of Edward's anxious exertions. But he only could witness his fall. Ere Edward could make his way among the Highlanders, who, furious and eager for spoil, now thronged upon each other, he saw his former commander brought from his horse by the blow of a scythe, and beheld him receive, while on the ground, more wounds than would have let out twenty lives. When Waverley came up, however, perception had not entirely fled. The dying warrior seemed to recognize Edward, for he fixed his eye upon him with an upbraiding yet sorrowful look, and appeared to struggle for utterance. But he felt that death was dealing closely with him, and resigning his purpose, and folding his hands as if in devotion, he gave up his soul to his Creator. The look with which he regarded Waverley in his dying moments did not strike him so deeply at that crisis of hurry and confusion, as when it recurred to his imagination at the distance of some time.

Loud shouts of triumph now echoed over the whole field. The battle was fought and won, and the whole baggage, artillery, and military stores of the regular army remained in possession of the victors. Never was a victory more complete. Scarce any escaped from the battle, excepting the cavalry who had left it at the very onset, and even these were broken into different parties and scattered all over the country. The loss of the victors was very trifling. So far as our tale is concerned, we have only to relate the fate of Balmawhapple, who, mounted on a horse as headstrong and stiff-necked as the rider, pursued the flight of the dragoons until about four miles from the field of battle, when some dozen of the fugitives took heart of grace, turned round, and cleaving his skull with their broad-swords, satisfied the world that the unfortunate gentleman had actually brains, the end of his life thus giving proof of a fact greatly doubted during its progress. His death was lamented by few. Most who knew him agreed in the pithy observation of Ensign Maccombich, that there "was mair *tint* (lost) at Sherriff-Muir." His friend, Lieutenant Jinker, bent his eloquence only to exculpate his favourite mare from any share in contributing to the catastrophe. "He had tauld the laird a thousand times," he said, "that it was a burning shame to pit a martingale upon the puir thing, when he would needs ride her wi' a curb of half a yard lang; and that he could na but bring himsel (no to say her) to some mischief, by flinging her down, or otherwise; whereas if he had had a wee bit rinning ring on the snafle, she wad hae rein'd as cannily as a cadger's pownie."

Such was the elegy of the Laird of Balmawhapple.

END OF VOLUME SECOND

WAVERLEY

OR,

'TIS SIXTY YEARS SINCE

VOLUME III

<hr />

Chapter One

AN UNEXPECTED EMBARRASSMENT

WHEN THE battle was over, and all things coming again into order, the Baron of Bradwardine, returning from the duty of the day, and having disposed those under his command in their proper stations, sought the Chieftain of Glennaquoich and his friend Edward Waverley. He found the former busied in determining disputes among his clansmen about points of precedence and deeds of valour, besides sundry high and doubtful questions concerning plunder. The most important of the last respected the property of a gold watch, which had once belonged to some unfortunate English officer. The party against whom judgment was awarded consoled himself by observing, "She (*i. e.* the watch, which he took for a living animal,) died the very night that Vich Ian Vohr gave her to Murdoch;" the machine having, in fact, stopped for want of winding up.

It was just when this important question was decided, that the Baron of Bradwardine, with a careful and yet important expression of countenance, joined the two young men. He descended from his reeking charger, the care of which he recommended to one of his grooms. "I seldom ban, sir," said he to the man; "but if ye play ony of your houndsfot tricks, and leave puir Berwick before he's sorted, to run after spuilzie, deil be wi' me if I do not give your craig a thraw." He then stroked with great complacence the animal which had borne him through the fatigues of the day, and having taken a tender leave of him,

—"Weel, my good young friends, a glorious and decisive victory," said he; "but these loons of troopers fled over soon. I would have liked to have shewn you the true points of the *prælium equestre*, or equestrian combat, whilk their cowardice has postponed, and which I hold to be the pride and terrour of warfare. Well, I have fought once more in this old quarrel, though I admit I could not be so far *ben* as you lads, being that it was my point of duty to keep together our handful of horse. And no cavalier ought in ony wise to begrudge honour that befalls his companions, even though they are ordered upon thrice his danger, whilk another time, by the blessing of God, may be his own case.— But, Glennaquoich, and you, Mr Waverley, I pray ye to give me your best advice on a matter of mickle weight, and which deeply affects the honour of the house of Bradwardine.—I crave your pardon, Ensign Maccombich, and yours, Inveraughlin, and yours, Edderalshendrach, and yours, sir."

The last person he addressed was Ballenkeiroch, who, remembering the death of his son, loured on him with a look of savage defiance. The Baron, quick as lightning at taking umbrage, had already bent his brow, when Glennaquoich dragged his major off the spot, and remonstrated with him, in the authoritative tone of a chieftain, on the madness of reviving a quarrel in such a moment.

"The ground is cumbered with carcases," said the old mountaineer, turning sullenly away; "*one more* would hardly have been ken'd upon it, and if it was na for yoursell, Vich Ian Vohr, that one should be Bradwardine's or mine."

The Chief soothed while he hurried him away, and then returned to the Baron. "It is Ballenkeiroch," said he, in an under and confidential voice, "father of the young man who fell in the unlucky affair eight years since at the Mains."

"Ah!" said the Baron, instantly relaxing the doubtful sternness of his features, "I can take mickle frae a man to whom I have unhappily rendered sic a displeasure as that. Ye were right to apprize me, Glennaquoich; he may look as black as midnight at Martinmas ere Cosmo Comyne Bradwardine shall say he does him wrang.—Ah! I hae nae male lineage, and I should bear with one I have made childless, though ye are aware the blood-wit was made up to your ain satisfaction by assythment, and that I have since expedited letters of slains.—Well, as I said, I have no male issue, and yet it is needful that I maintain the honour of my house; and it is on that score I prayed ye for your peculiar and private attention."

The two young men awaited in anxious curiosity. "I doubt na, lads, but your education has been sae seen to, that ye understand the true nature of the feudal tenures?"

Fergus, afraid of an endless dissertation, answered, "Intimately, Baron," and touched Waverley, as a signal to express no ignorance.

"And ye are aware, I doubt not, that the holding of the Barony of Bradwardine is of a nature alike honourable and peculiar, being blanch, (which Craig opines ought to be Latinated *blancum*, or rather *francum*, a free holding,) *pro servitio detrahendi, seu exuendi, caligas regis post battalliam.*" Here Fergus turned his falcon eye upon Edward, with an almost imperceptible rise of his eyebrow, to which his shoulders corresponded in the same degree of elevation. "Now, two points of dubitation occur to me upon this topic. First, whether this service, or feodal homage, be at any any event due to the person of the Prince, the words being, *per expressum, caligas regis*, the boots of the king himself; and I pray your opinion anent that particular before we proceed farther."

"Why, he is Prince Regent," answered Mac-Ivor, with laudable composure of countenance; "and in the court of France all the honours are rendered to the person of the Regent which are due to that of the King. Besides, were I to pull off either of their boots, I would render that service to the young Chevalier ten times more willingly than to his father."

"Ay, but I talk not of personal predilections. However, your authority is of great weight as to the usages of the court of France: And doubtless the Prince, as *alter ego*, may have a right to claim the *homagium* of the great tenants of the crown, since all faithful subjects are commanded, in the commission of regency, to respect him as the King's own person. Far, therefore, be it from me to diminish the lustre of his authority, by withholding this act of homage, so peculiarly calculated to give it splendour; for I question if the Emperor of Germany himself hath his boots taken off by a free baron of the empire. But here lieth the second difficulty—The Prince wears no boots, but simply brogues and trews."

This last dilemma had almost disturbed Fergus's gravity.

"Why," said he, "you know, Baron, the proverb tells us, 'It's ill taking the breeks off a Highlandman,'—and the boots are here in the same predicament."

"The word *caligæ*, however," continued the Baron, "though I admit, that, by family tradition, and even in our ancient evidents, it is explained *lie* BOOTS, means, in its primitive sense, rather sandals; and Caius Cæsar, the nephew and successor of Caius Tiberius, received the agnomen of Caligula, *a caligulis, sive caligis levioribus, quibus adolescentior usus fuerat in exercitu Germanici patris sui*. And the *caligæ* were also proper to the monastic bodies; for I read in an ancient Glossarium, upon the Rule of St Benedict, in the Abbey of St Amand, that *caligæ* were tied with latchets."

"That will apply to the brogues," said Fergus.

"It will so, my dear Glennaquoich, and the words are express; *Caligæ dictæ sunt quia ligantur; nam socci non ligantur, sed tantum intromittuntur;* that is, *caligæ* are denominated from the ligatures, wherewith they are bound; whereas *socci*, which may be analogous to our slippers, are only slipped upon the feet. The words of the charter are also alternative, *exuere seu detrahere;* that is, to *undo*, as in the case of sandals or brogues; and to *pluck off*, as we say vernacularly, concerning boots. Yet I would we had more light; but I fear there is little chance of finding hereabout any erudite author, *de re vestiaria.*"

"I should doubt it very much," said the Chieftain, looking around on the straggling Highlanders, who were returning loaded with spoils of the slain, "though the *res vestiaria* itself seems to be in some request at present."

This remark coming within the Baron's idea of jocularity, he honoured it with a smile, but immediately resumed what to him appeared very serious business.

"Baillie Macwheeble indeed holds an opinion, that this honorary service is due from its very nature, *si petatur tantum*, only if his Royal Highness shall require of the great tenant of the crown to perform that personal duty: and indeed he pointed out the case in Dirleton's Doubts and Queries, Grippit *versus* Spicer, anent the eviction of an estate *ob non solutum canonem*, that is, for non-payment of feu-duty of three pepper-corns yearly, whilk were taxt to be worth seven-eighths of a penny Scots, in whilk the defender was assoilzied. But I deem it safest, wi' your good favour, to place myself in the way of rendering the Prince this service, and to proffer performance thereof; and I shall cause the Baillie to attend with a schedule of a protest, whilk he has here prepared, (taking out a paper,) intimating, that if his Royal Highness shall accept of other assistance at pulling off his *caligæ*, (whether the same shall be rendered boots or brogues,) save that of the said Baron of Bradwardine, who is in presence ready and willing to perform the same, it shall in no-wise impinge or prejudice the right of the said Cosmo Comyne Bradwardine to perform the said service in future; nor shall it give any esquire, valet of the chamber, squire, or page, whose assistance it may please his Royal Highness to employ, any right, title, or ground, for evicting from the said Cosmo Comyne Bradwardine the estate and barony of Bradwardine, and others held as aforesaid, by the due and faithful performance thereof."

Fergus highly applauded this arrangement; and the Baron took a friendly leave of them, with a smile of contented importance upon his visage.

"Long live our dear friend, the Baron!" exclaimed the Chief, so soon as he was out of hearing, "for the most absurd original that exists north of Tweed. I wish to heaven I had recommended him to attend the circle this evening with a boot-ketch under his arm. I think he might have adopted the suggestion, if it had been made with suitable gravity."

"And how can you take pleasure in making a man of his worth so ridiculous?"

"Begging pardon, my dear Waverley, you are as ridiculous as he. Why, do you not see the man's whole mind was wrapped up in this ceremony? He has heard and thought of it since infancy, as the most august privilege and ceremony in the world; and I doubt not but the expected pleasure of performing it was a principal motive with him for taking up arms. Depend upon it, had I endeavoured to divert him from exposing himself, he would have treated me as an ignorant, conceited coxcomb, or perhaps might have taken a fancy to cut my throat; a pleasure which he once proposed to himself upon some point of etiquette, not half so important, in his eyes, as this matter of boots or brogues, or whatever the *caligæ* shall finally be pronounced by the learned. But I must go to head-quarters, to prepare the Prince for this extraordinary scene. My information will be well taken, for it will give him a hearty laugh at present, and put him on his guard against laughing, when it might be very *mal-a-propos*. So, *au revoir*, my dear Waverley."

Chapter Two

THE ENGLISH PRISONER

THE FIRST occupation of Waverley, after he parted from the Chieftain, was to go in quest of the officer whose life he had saved. He was guarded along with his companions in misfortune, who were very numerous, in a gentleman's house near the field of battle.

Upon entering the room, where they stood crowded together, Waverley easily recognized the object of his visit, not only by the peculiar dignity of his appearance, but by the appendage of Dugald Mahony, with his battle-axe, who had stuck to him from the moment of his capture, as if he had been skewered to his side. This close attendance was, perhaps, for the purpose of securing his promised reward from Edward, but it also operated to save the English gentleman from being plundered in the scene of general confusion; for Dugald sagaciously argued, that the amount of the salvage which he might be allowed, would be regulated by the state of the prisoner, when he should deliver him over to Waverley. He hastened to assure Waverley, that he had "keepit ta *sidier roy* haill, and that he was na a plack the waur since the fery moment whan his honour forbad her to gie him a bit clamhewit wi' her Lochaber axe."

Waverley assured Dugald of a liberal recompence, and, approaching the English officer, expressed his anxiety to do any thing which might contribute to his convenience under his present unpleasant circumstances.

"I am not so unexperienced a soldier, sir," answered the Englishman, "as to complain of the fortune of war. I am only grieved to see those scenes acted in our own island, which I have often witnessed elsewhere with comparative indifference."

"Another such day as this," said Waverley, "and I trust the cause of your regrets will be removed, and all will again return to peace and order."

The officer smiled and shook his head. "I must not forget my situation so far as to attempt a formal confutation of that opinion; but, notwithstanding your success, and the valour which won it, you have undertaken a task to which your strength appears wholly inadequate."

At this moment Fergus pushed into the press.

"Come, Edward, come along. The Prince has gone to Pinkie-house for the night; and we must follow or lose the whole ceremony of the *caligæ*. Your friend, the Baron, has been guilty of a great piece of cruelty; he has insisted upon dragging Baillie Macwheeble out to the field of battle. Now, you must know, the Baillie's greatest horror is an armed Highlander, or a loaded gun. And there he stands listening to the Baron's instructions, concerning the protest; and ducking his head, like a sea-gull, at the report of every gun and pistol that our idle boys are firing upon the field; and undergoes, by way of penance, at every symptom of flinching, a severe rebuke from his patron, who would not admit the discharge of a whole battery of cannon within point-blank distance, as an apology for neglecting a discourse, in which the honour of his family is interested."

"But how has Mr Bradwardine got him to venture so far?"

"Why, he had come as far as Musselburgh, I fancy, in hopes of making some of our wills; and the peremptory commands of the Baron dragged him forwards to Preston after the battle was over. He complains of one or two of our ragamuffians having put him in peril of his life, by presenting their pieces at him; but as they limited his ransom to an English penny, I don't think we need trouble the provost-martial upon that subject.—So, come along, Waverley."

"Waverley!" said the English officer, with great emotion, "the nephew of Sir Everard Waverley, of——shire."

"The same, sir," replied our hero, somewhat surprised at the tone in which he addressed him.

"I am at once happy and grieved," said the prisoner, "to have met with you."

"I am ignorant, sir," answered Waverley, "how I have deserved so much interest."

"Did your uncle never mention a friend called Talbot?"

"I have heard him talk with great regard of such a gentleman——a colonel, I believe, in the army, and the husband of Lady Emily Blande-ville; but I thought Colonel Talbot had been abroad."

"I am just returned; and being in Scotland, thought it my duty to act where my services promised to be useful. Yes, Mr Waverley, I am that Colonel Talbot, the husband of the lady you have named; and I am proud to acknowledge, that I owe alike my professional rank and my domestic happiness to your generous and noble-minded relative. Good God! that I should find his nephew and heir in such a dress, and engaged in such a cause!"

"Sir," said Fergus, haughtily, "the dress and cause are those of men of birth and honour."

"My situation forbids me to dispute your assertion; otherwise it were no difficult matter to shew, that neither courage nor pride of lineage can gild a bad cause. But, with Mr Waverley's permission, and yours, sir, if yours also must be asked, I would willingly speak a few words with him on affairs connected with his family."

"Mr Waverley, sir, regulates his own motions; you will follow me, I suppose, to Pinkie," said Fergus, turning to Edward, "when you have finished your discourse with this new acquaintance?" So saying, the Chief of Glennaquoich adjusted his plaid with rather more than his usual air of haughty assumption, and left the apartment.

The interest of Waverley readily procured for Colonel Talbot the freedom of adjourning to a large garden, belonging to his place of confinement. They walked a few paces in silence, Colonel Talbot apparently studying how to open what he had to say; at length he addressed Edward.

"Mr Waverley, you have this day saved my life; and yet I would to God that I had lost it, ere I had found you wearing the uniform and cockade of these men."

"I forgive your reproach, Colonel Talbot—it is well meant, and your education and prejudices render it natural. But there is nothing extraordinary in finding a man, whose honour has been publicly and unjustly assailed, in the situation which promised most fair to afford him satisfaction on his calumniators."

"I should rather say, in the situation most likely to confirm the reports which they have circulated," said Colonel Talbot, "by following the very line of conduct ascribed to you. Are you aware, Mr Waverley, of the infinite distress, and even danger, which your present conduct has occasioned to your nearest relatives?"

"Danger?"

"Yes, sir, danger. When I left England, your uncle and father had been obliged to find heavy bail, to answer a charge of treason, to which they were only admitted by exertion of the most pressing interest. I came down to Scotland, with almost the sole purpose of rescuing you from the gulf into which you have precipitated yourself; nor can I estimate the consequences to your family, of your having openly joined the rebellion, since the very suspicion of your intentions was so perilous to them. Most deeply do I regret, that I did not meet you before this last and fatal error."

"I am really ignorant why Colonel Talbot should have taken so much trouble on my account."

"Mr Waverley, I am dull at apprehending irony; and therefore I shall answer your words according to their plain meaning. I am indebted to your uncle for benefits greater than those which a son owes to a father. I acknowledge to him the duty of a son; and as I know there is no manner in which I can requite his kindness so well as by serving you, I will serve you, if possible, whether you will permit me or no; the personal obligation which you have this day laid me under, (although, in common estimation, as great as one human being can bestow on another,) adds nothing to my zeal in your behalf; nor can it be abated by any coldness with which you may please to receive it."

"Your intentions may be kind, sir, but your language is harsh, or at least peremptory."

"On my return to England, after long absence, I found your uncle, Mr Waverley, in the custody of a king's messenger, in consequence of the suspicion brought upon him by your conduct. He is my oldest friend—how often shall I repeat it—my best benefactor! he sacrificed his own views of happiness to mine—he never uttered a word, he never harboured a thought, that benevolence itself might not have thought or spoken. I found this man in confinement, rendered harsher to him by his habits of life, his natural dignity of feeling, and—forgive me, Mr Waverley,—by the cause through which this calamity had come upon him. I cannot disguise from you my feelings upon this occasion; they were most painfully unfavourable to you. Having, by my family interest, which you probably know is not inconsiderable, succeeded in obtaining Sir Everard's release, I set out for Scotland. I saw Colonel G——, a man whose fate alone is sufficient to render this insurrection for ever execrable. In the course of conversation with him, I found, that, from late circumstances, from a re-examination of the persons engaged in the mutiny, and from his original good opinion of your character, he was much softened towards you; and I doubted not, that if I could be so fortunate as to discover you, all might yet have been well. But this unnatural rebellion has ruined all.—I have, for the first time, in a long and active military life, seen Britons disgrace themselves by a panic flight, and that before a foe without either arms or discipline: And now I find the heir of my dearest friend—the son, I may say, of his affections—sharing a triumph, for which he ought the first to have blushed. Why should I lament G——! his lot was happy, compared to mine."

There was so much dignity in Colonel Talbot's manner, such a mixture of military pride and manly sorrow, and the news of Sir Everard's imprisonment was told in so deep a tone of feeling, that Edward stood mortified, abashed, and distressed, in presence of the prisoner, who owed to him his life not many hours before. He was not sorry when Fergus interrupted their conference a second time.

"His Royal Highness commanded Mr Waverley's attendance." Colonel Talbot threw upon Edward a reproachful glance, which did not escape the quick eye of the Highland Chief. "His *immediate* attendance," he repeated with considerable emphasis. Waverley turned again towards the Colonel.

"We shall meet again," he said; "in the meanwhile, every possible accommodation"——

"I desire none," said the Colonel; "let me fare like the meanest of those brave men, who, on this day of calamity, have preferred wounds and captivity to flight; I would almost exchange places with one of those who has fallen, to know that my words have made a suitable impression on your mind."

"Let Colonel Talbot be carefully secured," said Fergus to the Highland officer, who commanded the guard over the prisoners; "it is the Prince's particular command; he is a prisoner of the utmost importance."

"But let him want no accommodation suitable to his rank," said Waverley.

"Consistent always with secure custody," reiterated Fergus. The officer signified his acquiescence in both commands, and Edward followed Fergus to the garden gate, where Callum Beg, with three saddle-horses, awaited them. Turning his head, he saw Colonel Talbot re-conducted to his place of confinement by a file of Highlanders; he lingered on the threshold of the door, and made a signal with his hand towards Waverley, as if enforcing the language he had held towards him.

"Horses," said Fergus, as he mounted, "are now as plenty as black-berries; every man may have them for catching. Come, let Callum adjust your stirrups, and let us to Pinkie-house as fast as these *ci-devant* dragoon-horses chuse to carry us."

Chapter Three

RATHER UNIMPORTANT

"I WAS turned back," said Fergus to Edward, "by a message from the Prince. But I suppose you know the value of this most noble Colonel Talbot as a prisoner. He is held one of the best officers among the red-coats; a special friend and favourite of the Elector himself, and of that dreadful hero, the Duke of Cumberland, who has been sum-moned from his triumphs at Fontenoy, to come over and devour us poor Highlanders alive—But what the devil makes you look so dejected? Has he been telling you how the bells of St James's ring? Not 'turn again Whittington,' like those of Bow, in the days of yore?"

"Fergus?"

"Nay, I cannot tell what to make of you:—you are blown about with every wind of doctrine. Here have we gained a victory, unparalleled in history—and your behaviour is praised by every living mortal to the skies—and the Prince is eager to thank you in person—and all our beauties of the white rose are pulling caps for you,—and you, the *preux chevalier* of the day, are stooping on your horse's neck like a butter-woman riding to market, and looking as black as a funeral!"

"I am sorry for poor Colonel G——'s death: he was once very kind to me."

"Why, then, be sorry for five minutes, and then be glad again; his chance to-day may be ours to-morrow; and what does it signify? The next best thing to victory is honourable death, but it is a *pis-aller*, and one would rather a foe had it than one's self."

"But Colonel Talbot has informed me that my father and uncle are both imprisoned by government on my account."

"We'll put in bail, my boy; old Andrew Ferrara shall lodge his security; and I should like to see him put to justify it in Westminster-hall!"

"Nay, they are already at liberty upon bail of a more civic descrip-tion."

"Then why is thy noble spirit cast down, Edward? Dost think that the Elector's ministers are such doves as to set their enemies at liberty at this critical moment, if they could or durst confine and punish them? Assure thyself that either they have no charge against your relations on which they can continue their imprisonment, or else they are afraid of our friends, the jolly cavaliers of Old England. At any rate, you need not be apprehensive upon their account; and we will find some means of conveying to them assurances of your safety."

Edward was silenced, but not satisfied, with these reasons. He had now been more than once shocked at the small degree of sympathy which Fergus exhibited for the feelings even of those whom he loved, if they did not correspond with his own mood at the time, and more especially if they thwarted him while earnest in a favourite pursuit. Fergus sometimes indeed remarked that he had offended Waverley, but, always intent upon some favourite plan or project of his own, he was never sufficiently aware of the extent or duration of his displeasure, so that the reiteration of these petty offences somewhat cooled the volunteer's extreme attachment to his officer.

The Chevalier received Waverley with his usual favour, and paid him many compliments on his distinguished bravery. He then took him apart, made many enquiries concerning Colonel Talbot, and when he had received all the information which Edward was able to give concerning him and his connections, he proceeded,—"I cannot but think, Mr Waverley, that since this gentleman is so particularly connected with our worthy and excellent friend, Sir Everard Waverley, and since his lady is of the house of Blandeville, whose devotion to the true and loyal principles of the Church of England is so generally known, the colonel's own private sentiments cannot be unfavourable to us, whatever mask he may have assumed to accommodate himself to the times."

"If I am to judge from the language he this day held to me, I am under the necessity of differing widely from your Royal Highness."

"Well, it is worth making a trial at least. I therefore entrust you with the charge of Colonel Talbot, with power to act concerning him as you think most advisable; and I trust you will find means of ascertaining what are his real dispositions towards our Royal Father's restoration."

"I am convinced," said Waverley, bowing, "that if Colonel Talbot chuses to grant his parole, it may be securely depended upon; but if he refuses it, I trust your Royal Highness will devolve on some other person than the nephew of his friend, the task of laying him under the necessary restraint."

"I will trust him with no person but you," said the Prince, smiling, but peremptorily repeating his mandate; "it is of importance to my service that there should appear to be a good intelligence between you, even if you are unable to gain his confidence in earnest. You will therefore receive him into your quarters, and in case he declines giving his parole, you must apply for a proper guard. I beg you will go about this directly. We return to Edinburgh to-morrow."

Being thus remanded to the vicinity of Preston, Waverley lost the Baron of Bradwardine's solemn act of homage. So little, however, was he at this time "in love with vanity," that he had quite forgot the ceremony in which Fergus had laboured to engage his curiosity. But next day a formal gazette was circulated, containing a detailed account of the battle of Gladsmuir, as the Highlanders chose to denominate their victory. It concluded with an account of the court held by the Chevalier at Pinkie-house in the evening, which contained this among other high-flown descriptive paragraphs:

"Since that fatal treaty which annihilated Scotland as an independent Nation, it has not been our happiness to see her Princes receive, and her nobles discharge, those acts of feudal homage, which, founded upon the splendid actions of Scottish valour, recall the memory of her early history, with the manly and chivalrous simplicity of the ties which united to the crown the lineage of the warriors by whom it was repeatedly upheld and defended. But upon the evening of the 20th, our memories were refreshed with one of those ceremonies which belong to the ancient days of Scotland's glory. After the circle was formed, Cosmo Comyne Bradwardine, of that Ilk, Colonel in the service, &c. &c. &c. came before the Prince, attended by Mr D. Macwheeble, the Baillie of his ancient Barony of Bradwardine, (who, we understand, has been lately named a commissary,) and, under form of instrument, claimed permission to perform, to the person of His Royal Highness, as representing his father, the service used and wont for which under a Charter of Robert Bruce (of which the original was produced and inspected by the Master of His Royal Highness's Chancery for the time being) the claimant held the Barony of Bradwardine, and lands of Tully-Veolan. The claim being admitted and registered, His Royal Highness having placed his foot upon a cushion, the Baron of Bradwardine, kneeling upon his right knee, proceeded to undo the latchet of the brogue, or low-heeled Highland shoe, which our gallant young Hero wears in compliment to his brave followers. When this was performed, His Royal Highness declared the ceremony completed; and, embracing the gallant veteran, protested that nothing but compliance with an ordinance of Robert Bruce, could have induced him to receive even the symbolical performance of a menial office from hands which had fought so bravely to put the crown upon the head of his father. The Baron of Bradwardine then took instruments in the hands of Mr Commissary Macwheeble, bearing, that all points and circumstances of the act of homage had been *rite et solenniter acta et peracta*, and a corresponding entry was made in the protocol of the Lord High Chamberlain, and in the record of Chancery. We understand that it is in contemplation of His Royal Highness, when His Majesty's pleasure can be known, to raise Colonel Bradwardine to the peerage, by the title of Viscount Bradwardine of Bradwardine and Tully-Veolan, and that, in the meanwhile, His Royal Highness, in his father's name and authority, has been pleased to grant him an honourable augmentation to his paternal coat-of-arms, being a budget or boot-jack, disposed saltier-wise with a naked broad-sword, to be borne in the dexter cantle of the shield; and, as an additional motto on a scroll beneath, the words, 'Draw and draw off.'"

"Were it not for the recollection of Fergus's raillery," thought Waverley to himself when he had perused this long and grave document, "how very tolerably would all this sound, and how little should I have thought of connecting it with the ridiculous! Well, after all, every thing has its fair as well as its seamy side; and truly I do not see why the Baron's boot-jack may not stand as fair in heraldry as the water-buckets, waggons, cart-wheels, plough-socks, shuttles, candlesticks, and other ordinaries, conveying ideas of any thing save chivalry, which appear in the arms of some of our most ancient gentry."— This, however, is an episode in respect to the principal story.

When Waverley returned to Preston, and rejoined Colonel Talbot, he found him recovered from the strong and obvious emotion with which a concurrence of unpleasing events had affected him. He had recovered his natural manner, which was that of the English gentleman and soldier, manly, open, and generous, but not unsusceptible of prejudice against those of a different country, or who were opposed in political tenets. When Waverley acquainted Colonel Talbot with the Chevalier's purpose to commit him to his charge, "I did not think to have owed so much obligation to that young gentleman," he said, "as is implied in this destination. I can at least willingly join in the prayer of the honest presbyterian clergyman, that as he has come among us seeking an earthly crown, his labour may be speedily rewarded with a heavenly one. I will willingly give my parole not to attempt an escape without your knowledge, since, in fact, it was to meet you I came to Scotland; and I am glad it has happened even under this predicament. But I suppose we shall be but a short time together. Your Chevalier, (that is a name we may both give to him) with his plaids and blue caps, will, I presume, be continuing his crusade southwards?"

"Not as I hear; I believe the army makes some stay in Edinburgh, to collect reinforcements."

"And besiege the Castle?" said Talbot, smiling sarcastically; "well,

256 WAVERLEY Vol. 3, ch. 4

unless my old commander, Guest, turn false metal, or the castle-rock sink into the North Loch, events which I deem equally probable, I think we shall have some time to make up our acquaintance. I have a guess that this gallant Chevalier has a design that I should be your proselyte, and as I wish you to be mine, there cannot be a more fair proposal. But, as I spoke to-day under the influence of feelings I rarely give way to, I hope you will excuse my entering again upon controversy, till we are somewhat better acquainted."

Chapter Four

INTRIGUES OF LOVE AND POLITICS

IT IS NOT necessary to record in these pages the triumphant entrance of the Chevalier into Edinburgh after the decisive affair of Preston. One circumstance, however, may be noticed, because it illustrated the high spirit of Flora Mac-Ivor. The Highlanders, by whom the Prince was surrounded, in the license and extravagance of this joyful moment, fired their pieces repeatedly, and one of these having been accidentally loaded with ball, the bullet grazed the young lady's temple as she waved her handkerchief from a balcony. Fergus, who beheld the accident, was at her side in an instant; and, on seeing that the wound was trifling, he drew his broad-sword, with the purpose of rushing down upon the man by whose carelessness she had incurred so much danger, when, holding him firm by the plaid, "Do not harm the poor fellow," she cried, "for Heaven's sake do not harm him! but thank God with me that the accident happened to Flora Mac-Ivor; for had it befallen a whig they would have pretended that the shot was fired on purpose."

Waverley escaped the alarm which this accident would have occasioned to him, as he was unavoidably delayed by the necessity of accompanying Colonel Talbot to Edinburgh.

They performed the journey together on horseback, and for some time, as if to sound each other's feelings and sentiments, they conversed upon general and ordinary topics.

When Waverley again entered upon the subject which he had most at heart, the situation namely of his father and his uncle, Colonel Talbot seemed now rather desirous to alleviate than to aggravate his anxiety. This appeared particularly to be the case when he had heard Waverley's history, which he did not scruple to confide to him. "And so," said the Colonel, "there has been no malice prepense, as lawyers, I think, term it, in this rash step of yours; and you have been trepanned into the service of this Italian knight-errant by a few civil speeches from him and one or two of his Highland recruiting serjeants. It is sadly foolish to be sure, but not nearly so bad as I was led to expect. However, you cannot desert at the present moment, that seems impossible. But I have little doubt that in the dissensions incident to this heterogeneous mass of wild and desperate men, some opportunity may arise, by availing yourself of which, you may extricate yourself honourably from your rash engagement before the bubble burst. If this can be managed, I would have you go to a place of safety in Flanders, which I shall point out. And I think I can secure your pardon from government after a few months' residence abroad."

"I cannot permit you, Colonel Talbot, to speak of any plan which turns on my deserting an enterprise, in which I may have engaged hastily, but certainly voluntarily, and with the purpose of abiding the issue."

"Well," said Colonel Talbot, smiling, "leave me my thoughts and hopes at least at liberty, if not my speech. But have you never examined your mysterious packet?"

"It is in my baggage; we shall find it in Edinburgh."

In Edinburgh they soon arrived. Waverley's quarters had been assigned to him, by the Prince's express orders, in a handsome lodging, where there was accommodation for Colonel Talbot. His first business was to examine his portmanteau, and, after a very short search, out tumbled the expected packet. Waverley opened it eagerly. Under a blank cover, simply addressed to E. Waverley, Esq. he found a number of open letters. The uppermost were two from Colonel G——, addressed to himself. The earliest in date was a kind and gentle remonstrance for neglect of the writer's advice, respecting the disposal of his time during his leave of absence, the renewal of which he reminded Captain Waverley would speedily expire. "Indeed," the letter proceeded, "had it been otherwise, the news from abroad, and my instructions from the War Office, must have compelled me to recall it, as there is great danger, since the disaster in Flanders, both of foreign invasion and insurrection among the disaffected at home. I therefore entreat you will repair, as soon as possible, to the head-quarters of the regiment; and I am concerned to add, that this is still the more necessary, as there is some discontent in your troop, and I postpone enquiring into particulars until I can have the advantage of your assistance."

The second letter, dated eight days later, was in such a style as might have been expected from the Colonel's receiving no answer to the first. It reminded Waverley of his duty, as a man of honour, an officer, and a Briton; took notice of the increasing dissatisfaction of his men, and that some of them had been heard to hint, that their Captain encouraged and approved their mutinous behaviour; and, finally, the writer expressed the utmost regret and surprise that he had not obeyed his commands by repairing to head-quarters, reminded him that his leave of absence had been recalled, and conjured him, in a style in which paternal remonstrance was mingled with military authority, to redeem his error by immediately joining his regiment. "That I may be certain," concluded the letter, "that this actually reaches you, I dispatch it by Corporal Tims, with orders to deliver it into your own hand."

Upon reading these letters, Waverley, with great bitterness of feeling, was compelled to make the *amende honorable* to the memory of the brave and excellent writer. For surely, as Colonel G—— must have had every reason to conclude they had come safely to hand, less could not follow, in their being neglected, than that third and final summons, which Waverley actually received at Glennaquoich, though too late to obey it. And his being superseded, in consequence of his apparent neglect of this last command, was so far from being a harsh or severe proceeding, that it was plainly inevitable. The next letter he unfolded was from the major of the regiment, acquainting him that a report to the disadvantage of his reputation, was public in the country, stating, that one Mr Falconer of Ballihopple, or some such name, had proposed, in his presence, a treasonable toast, which he permitted to pass in silence, although it was so gross an affront to the royal family, that a gentleman in company, not remarkable for his zeal for government, had nevertheless taken the matter up, and that Captain Waverley had thus suffered another, comparatively unconcerned, to resent an affront directed against him personally as an officer, and to go out with the person by whom it was offered. The Major concluded, that no one of Captain Waverley's brother officers could believe this scandalous story, but that his own honour, equally with that of the regiment, depended upon its being instantly contradicted by his authority, &c. &c. &c.

"What do you think of all this?" said Colonel Talbot, to whom Waverley silently handed the letters after he had perused them.

"Think?—it renders thought impossible. It is enough to drive me mad."

"Be calm, my young friend, let us see what are these dirty scrawls which follow."

The first was addressed, "For Master W. Ruffen These."—

"D^r. Sur Sum of our yong Gulpins wul not bite thof I tuold them you shoed me the Squoire's own seel. But Tims will deliver you the

lettrs as desired and tell ould Addem he gave them to Squoir's hond, as to be sure yours is the same and shall be reddy for signol and hoy for Hoy Church and Sachefrel as fadur sings at harvest whome.
"Yrs deer Sur

"H. H.

"Poscriff. Do'e tell Squoir we longs to heer from him and has dootings about his not writing himsell and liftenant Bottler is smoky."

"This Ruffen, I suppose, then, is your Donald of the Cavern, who has intercepted your letters, and carried on a correspondence with the poor devil Houghton, as if under your authority?"

"It seems too true. But who can Addem be?"

"Possibly Adam, for poor Gardiner, a sort of pun on his name."

The other letters were to the same purpose, and they soon received complete light upon Donald Bean's machinations.

John Hodges, one of Waverley's servants, who had remained with the regiment, and had been taken at Preston, now made his appearance. He had sought out his master with the purpose of again entering his service. From this fellow they learned, that some time after Waverley had gone from the head-quarters of the regiment, a pedlar, called Ruthven, Ruffen, or Rivane, known among the soldiers by the name of Wily Will, had made frequent visits to the town of ——. He appeared to possess plenty of money, sold his commodities very cheap, seemed always willing to treat his friends at the ale-house, and easily ingratiated himself with many of Waverley's troop, particularly Serjeant Houghton, and one Tims, also a non-commissioned officer. To these he unfolded, in Waverley's name, a plan for leaving the regiment and joining him in the Highlands, where report said the clans had already taken arms in great numbers. The men, who had been educated as Jacobites, so far as they had any opinions at all, and who knew their landlord, Sir Everard, had always been supposed to hold such tenets, easily fell into the snare. That Waverley was at a distance in the Highlands, was received as a sufficient excuse for transmitting his letters through the medium of the pedlar; and the sight of his well-known seal seemed to authenticate the negociations in his name, where writing might have been dangerous. The cabal, however, began to take air, from the premature mutinous language of those concerned. Wily Will justified his appellative; for, after suspicion arose, he was seen no more. When the Gazette appeared, in which Waverley was superseded, great part of his troop broke out into actual mutiny, but were surrounded and disarmed by the rest of the regiment. In consequence of the sentence of a court-martial, Houghton and Tims were condemned to be shot, but afterwards permitted to cast lots for life. Houghton, the survivor, shewed much penitence, being convinced, from the rebukes and explanations of Colonel G——, that he had really engaged in a very heinous crime. It is remarkable, that as soon as the poor fellow was satisfied of this, he became also convinced that the instigator had acted without authority from Edward, saying, "if it was dishonourable and against Old England, the squire could know nought about it: he never did, or thought to do, any thing dishonourable, no more didn't Sir Everard, nor none of them afore him, and in that belief he would live and die that Ruffen had done it all of his own head."

The strength of conviction with which he expressed himself upon this subject, as well as his assurances that the letters intended for Waverley had been delivered to Ruthven, had made that revolution in Colonel G——'s opinion which he expressed to Talbot.

The reader has long since understood that Donald Bean Lean played the part of tempter on this occasion. His motives were shortly these. Of an active and intriguing spirit, he had been long employed as a subaltern agent and spy by those in the confidence of the Chevalier, to an extent beyond what was suspected even by Fergus Mac-Ivor, whom, though obliged to him for protection, he regarded with fear and dislike. To success in this political department, he naturally looked for raising himself by some bold stroke above his present hazardous and precarious trade of rapine. He was particularly employed in learning the strength of the regiments in Scotland, the character of the officers, &c. and had long had his eye upon Waverley's troop, as open to temptation. Donald even believed that Waverley himself was at bottom in the Stuart interest, which seemed confirmed by his long visit to the jacobite Baron of Bradwardine. When, therefore, he came to his cave with one of Glennaquoich's attendants, the robber, who could never appreciate his real motive was mere curiosity, was so sanguine as to hope that his own talents were to be employed in some intrigue of consequence, under the auspices of this wealthy young Englishman. Nor was he undeceived by Waverley's neglecting all his hints and the openings afforded for explanation. His conduct passed for prudent reserve, and somewhat piqued Donald Bean, who, supposing himself left out of a secret where confidence promised to be so advantageous, determined to have his share in the drama, whether a regular part were assigned him or no. For this purpose, during Waverley's sleep, he possessed himself of his seal, as a token to be used to any of the troopers whom he might discover to be possessed of the captain's confidence. His first journey to ——, the town where the regiment was quartered, undeceived him in his original supposi-

tion, but opened to him a new field of action. He knew there would be
no service so well rewarded by the friends of the Chevalier, as seducing
a part of the regular army to his standard. For this purpose he opened
the machinations with which the reader is already acquainted, and
which form a clew to all the intricacies and obscurities of the narrative
previous to Waverley's leaving Glennaquoich.

By Colonel Talbot's advice, Waverley declined retaining in his
service the lad whose evidence had thrown additional light on these
intrigues. He represented to him it would be doing the man an injury
to engage him in a desperate undertaking, and that, whatever should
happen, his evidence would go some length, at least, in explaining the
circumstances under which Waverley himself had embarked in it.
Waverley therefore wrote a short state of what had happened to his
uncle and his father, cautioning them, however, in the present circumstances, not to attempt to answer his letter. The Colonel added long
dispatches as well as letters to his own family. Talbot then gave the
man a letter to the commander of one of the English vessels of war
cruizing in the firth, requesting him to put the bearer ashore at Berwick, with a pass to proceed to ——shire. The man was then furnished with money to make an expeditious journey, and directed to get
on board the ship by means of bribing a fishing-boat, which, as they
afterwards learned, he easily effected.

Tired of the attendance of Callum Beg, who, he thought, had some
disposition to act as a spy on his motives, Waverley hired as his servant
a simple Edinburgh swain, who had mounted the white cockade in a fit
of spleen and jealousy, because Jenny Jop had danced a whole night
with Corporal Bullock of the Fusileers.

Chapter Five

INTRIGUES OF SOCIETY AND LOVE

COLONEL Talbot became more kindly in his demeanour towards
Waverley after the confidence he had reposed in him, and as they were
necessarily much together, the character of the Colonel rose in Waverley's estimation. There seemed at first something harsh in his strong
expressions of dislike and censure, although no one was in the general
case more open to conviction. The habit of authority also had
given his manners some peremptory hardness, notwithstanding the
polish which they had received from his intimate acquaintance with
the higher circles. As a specimen of the military character, he differed
from all whom Waverley had as yet seen. The soldiership of the Baron

of Bradwardine was marked by pedantry; that of Major Mellville by a sort of martinet attention to the minutiæ and technicalities of discipline, rather suitable to one who was to manœuvre a battalion, than to him who was to command an army; the military spirit of Fergus was so much warped and blinded with his plans and political views, that it was that of a petty sovereign, rather than of a soldier. But Colonel Talbot was in every point the English soldier. His whole soul was devoted to the service of his king and country, without feeling any pride in knowing the theory of his art with the Baron, or its practical minutiæ with the Major, or in applying his science to secure his own particular plans, like the Chieftain of Glennaquoich. Added to this, he was a man of extended knowledge and cultivated taste, although strongly tinged, as we have already observed, with those prejudices which are peculiarly English.

The character of Colonel Talbot dawned upon Edward by degrees; for the delay of the Highlanders in the fruitless siege of Edinburgh Castle occupied several weeks, during which Waverley had little to do, excepting to seek such amusement as society afforded. He would willingly have persuaded his new friend to become acquainted with some of his former intimates. But the Colonel, after one or two visits, shook his head, and declined farther experiment. Indeed he went farther, and characterized the Baron as the most intolerable formal pedant he had ever had the misfortune to meet with, and the Chief of Glennaquoich as a Frenchified Scotchman, possessing all the cunning and plausibility of the nation where he was educated, with the proud, vindictive, and turbulent humour of that of his birth. "If the devil," he said, "had sought out an agent expressly for the purpose of embroiling this miserable country, I do not think he could find a better than such a fellow as this, whose temper seems equally active, supple, and mischievous, and who is followed, and implicitly obeyed, by a gang of such cut-throats as those whom you are pleased to admire so much."

The ladies of the party did not escape his censure. He allowed that Flora Mac-Ivor was a fine woman, and Rose Bradwardine a pretty enough girl. But he alleged that the former destroyed the effect of her beauty by an affectation of the grand airs which she had probably seen practised in the mock court of St Germains. As for Rose Bradwardine, he said it was impossible for any mortal to admire such an uninformed little thing, whose small portion of education was as ill adapted to her sex or youth, as if she had appeared with one of her father's old campaign coats upon her person for her sole garment. Now all this was mere spleen and prejudice in the excellent Colonel, with whom the white cockade on the breast, the white rose in the hair, and the *Mac* at the beginning of a name, would have made a devil out of an angel; and indeed he himself jocularly allowed, that he could not have endured Venus herself, if she had been announced in a drawing-room by the name of Miss Mac-Jupiter.

Waverley, it may easily be believed, looked upon these young ladies with very different eyes. During the period of the siege, he paid them almost daily visits, although he observed with deep regret that his suit made as little progress in the affections of the former, as the arms of the Chevalier in subduing the fortress. She maintained with rigour the rule she had laid down of treating him with indifference, without either affecting to avoid him or to shun intercourse with him. Every word, every look, was strictly regulated to accord with her system, and neither the dejection of Waverley, nor the anger which Fergus scarcely suppressed, could extend Flora's attention to Edward beyond that which the most ordinary politeness demanded. On the other hand, Rose Bradwardine gradually rose in his opinion. He had several opportunities of remarking, that as her extreme timidity wore off, her manners assumed a higher character; that the agitating circumstances of the stormy time seemed to call forth a certain dignity of feeling and expression, which he had not formerly observed; and that she omitted no opportunity within her reach to extend her knowledge and refine her taste.

Flora Mac-Ivor called Rose her pupil, and was attentive to assist her in her studies, and to fashion both her taste and understanding. It might have been remarked by a very close observer, that in the presence of Waverley she was much more desirous to exhibit her friend's excellencies than her own. But I must request of the reader to suppose, that this kind and disinterested purpose was concealed by the most cautious delicacy and by her studiously shunning the most distant approach to affectation. So that it was as unlike the usual exhibition of one pretty woman affecting to *proner* another, as the friendship of David and Jonathan might be to the intimacy of two Bond-street loungers. The fact is, that though the effect was felt, the cause could hardly be observed. Each of the ladies, like two excellent actresses, were perfect in their parts, and performed them to the delight of the audience; and such being the case, it was almost impossible to discover that the elder had constantly ceded to her friend that which was most suitable to her talents.

But to Waverley, Rose Bradwardine possessed an attraction which few men can resist, from the marked interest which she took in every thing which affected him. She was too young and too inexperienced to estimate the full force of the constant attention which she paid to him. Her father was too abstracted in learned and military discussions to observe her partiality, and Flora Mac-Ivor did not alarm her by remonstrance, because she saw in this line of conduct the most probable chance of her securing at length a return of affection. The truth is, that in her first conversation after their meeting, Rose had discovered the state of her mind to that acute and intelligent friend, although she was not herself aware of it. From that time, Flora was not only determined upon the final rejection of Waverley's addresses, but became anxious that they should, if possible, be transferred to her friend. Nor was she less interested in this plan that she knew her brother had from time to time talked, as between jest and earnest, of paying his suit to Miss Bradwardine. She knew that Fergus had the true continental latitude of opinion respecting the institution of marriage, and would not have given his hand to an angel, unless for the purpose of strengthening his alliances, and increasing his influence and wealth. The Baron's whim of transferring his estate to the distant heir male, instead of his own daughter, was therefore likely to be an insurmountable obstacle to his entertaining any serious thoughts of Rose Bradwardine. Indeed, Fergus's brain was a perpetual work-shop of scheme and intrigue, of every possible kind and description; while, like many a mechanic of more ingenuity than steadiness, he would often unexpectedly, and without any apparent motive, abandon one plan, and go earnestly to work upon another, which was either fresh from the forge of his imagination, or had at some former period been flung aside half finished. It was therefore often difficult to guess what line of conduct he might finally adopt upon any given occasion.

Although Flora was sincerely attached to her brother, whose high energies might indeed have commanded her admiration even without the ties which bound them together, she was by no means blind to his faults, which she considered as most dangerous to the hopes of any woman, who should found her ideas of a happy marriage in the peaceful enjoyment of domestic society, and the exchange of mutual and engrossing affection. The real disposition of Waverley, on the other hand, notwithstanding his dreams of tented fields and military honour, seemed exclusively domestic. He asked and received no share in the busy scenes which were constantly passing around him, and was rather annoyed than interested by the discussion of contending claims, rights, and interests, which often passed in his presence. All this pointed him out as the person formed to make happy a spirit like that of Rose, which corresponded with his own.

She remarked this point in Waverley's character one day while she sat with Miss Bradwardine. "His genius and elegant taste," answered Rose, "cannot be interested in such trifling discussions. What is it to him, for example, whether the Chief of the Mac——, who has brought out only fifty men, should be a colonel or a captain? and how could Mr

Waverley be supposed to interest himself in the violent altercation between your brother and young Corrinaschian, whether the post of honour be due to the eldest cadet of a clan or the youngest?"

"My dear Rose, if he were the hero you suppose him, he would interest himself in these matters, not indeed as important in themselves, but for the purpose of mediating between the ardent spirits who actually do make them the subject of discord. You saw when Corrinaschian raised his voice in great passion, and laid his hand upon his sword, Waverley lifted his head as if he had just awaked from a dream, and asked, with great composure, what the matter was."

"Well, and did not the laughter they fell into at his absence of mind serve better to break off the dispute, than any thing he could have said to them?"

"True, but not quite so creditably for Waverley, as if he had brought them to their senses by force of reason."

"Would you have him peace-maker general between all the gun-powder Highlanders in the army? I beg your pardon, Flora, your brother, you know, is out of the question; he has more sense than half of them. But can you think the fierce, hot, furious spirits, of whose brawls we see much and hear more, and who terrify me out of my life every day in the world, are at all to be compared to Waverley?"

"I do not compare him with these uneducated men, my dear Rose. I only lament that, with his talents and genius, he does not assume that place in society for which they eminently fit him, and that he does not lend their full impulse to the noble cause in which he has enlisted. Are there not Lochiel, and P——, and M——, and G——, all men of the highest education, as well as the first talents: why will he not stoop like them to be alive and useful?—I often believe his zeal is frozen by that proud cold-blooded Englishman, whom he now lives with so much."

"Colonel Talbot—he is a very disagreeable person, to be sure. He looks as if he thought no Scottish-woman worth the trouble of handing her a cup of tea. But Waverley is so gentle, so well informed."

"Yes, he can admire the moon, and quote a stanza from Tasso."

"Besides, you know how he fought."

"For mere fighting," answered Flora, "I believe all men (that is, who deserve the name) are pretty much alike: there is generally more courage required to run away. They have besides, when confronted with each other, a certain instinct for strife, as we see in other male animals, such as dogs, bulls, and so forth. But high and perilous enterprize is not Waverley's forte. He would never have been his celebrated ancestor Sir Nigel, but only Sir Nigel's eulogist and poet. I will tell you where he will be at home, my dear, and in his place,—in the quiet circle of domestic happiness, lettered indolence, and elegant enjoyment of Waverley-Honour. And he will refit the old library in the most exquisite Gothic taste, and garnish its shelves with the rarest and most valuable volumes;—and he will draw plans and landscapes, and write verses, and rear temples, and dig grottoes;—and he will stand in a clear summer night in the colonnade before his Hall, and gaze on the deer as they stray in the moonlight, or lie shadowed by the boughs of the huge old fantastic oaks, and he will repeat verses to his beautiful wife, who shall hang upon his arm;—and he will be a happy man."

"And she will be a happy woman," thought poor Rose. But she only sighed, and dropped the conversation.

Chapter Six

FERGUS, A SUITOR

WAVERLEY had, indeed, as he looked closer upon the state of the Chevalier's court, less reason to be satisfied with it. It contained, as they say an acorn includes all the ramifications of the future oak, as many seeds of *tracasserie* and intrigue as might have done honour to the court of a large empire. Each person of importance had some separate object, which he pursued with a fury that Waverley considered as altogether disproportioned to its importance. Almost all had their causes of discontent, although the most legitimate was that of the worthy old Baron, who was only distressed on account of the common cause.

"We will hardly," said he one morning to Waverley when they had been viewing the castle, "gain the obsidional crown, which you wot well was made of the roots or grain which takes root within the place besieged, or it may be of the herb woodbind, *paretaria*, or pellitory; we will not, I say, gain it by this same blockade or leaguer of Edinburgh Castle." For this opinion he gave more learned and satisfactory reasons than the reader may care to hear repeated.

Having escaped from the old gentleman, Waverley went to Fergus's lodgings by appointment, to await his return from Holyrood-House. "I am to have a particular audience to-morrow," said Fergus to Waverley overnight, "and you must meet me to wish me joy of the success which I securely anticipate."

The morrow came, and in the Chief's apartment he found Ensign Maccombich waiting to make report of his turn of duty in a sort of ditch which they had dug across the Castle-hill, and called a trench. In a short time the Chief's voice was heard on the stair in a tone of impatient fury,—"Callum,—why, Callum Beg,—Diaoul!—" He entered the room with all the marks of a man agitated by a towering passion; and there were few upon whose features rage produced a more violent effect. The veins of his forehead swelled when he was in such agitation; his nostril became dilated; his cheek and eye inflamed; and his look that of a demoniac. These appearances of half-suppressed rage were the more frightful, because they were obviously caused by a strong effort to temper with discretion an almost ungovernable paroxysm of passion, and resulted from an internal conflict of the most dreadful kind, which agitated his whole frame of mortality.

As he entered the apartment, he unbuckled his broad-sword, and throwing it down with such violence that the weapon rolled to the other end of the room, "I know not what," he exclaimed, "withholds me from taking a solemn oath that I will never more draw it in his cause—Load my pistols, Callum, and bring them hither—instantly, instantly!"

Callum, whom nothing ever startled, dismayed, or disconcerted, obeyed very coolly. Evan Dhu, upon whose brow the suspicion that his Chief had been insulted, called up a corresponding storm, swelled in sullen silence, awaiting to learn where or upon whom vengeance was to descend.

"So, Waverley, you are there," said the Chief, after a moment's recollection; "Yes, I remember I asked you to share my triumph, and you have come to witness my—disappointment, we shall call it." Evan now presented the written report he had in his hand, which Fergus threw from him with great passion. "I wish to God," he said, "the old den would tumble down above the heads of the fools who attack it, and the knaves who defend it. I see, Waverley, you think I am mad—Leave us, Evan, but be within call."

"The Colonel's in an unco kippage," said Mrs Flockhart to Evan as he descended; "I wish he may be weel,—the very veins on his brent brow are swelled like whip-cord; wad he no tak something?"

"He usually lets blood for these fits," answered the Highland Ancient with great composure.

When his officer left the room, the Chieftain gradually reassumed some degree of composure. "I know, Waverley," he said, "that Colonel Talbot has persuaded you to curse ten times a-day your engagement with us;—nay, never deny it, for I am at this moment tempted to curse my own. Would you believe it, I made this very morning two suits to the Prince, and he has rejected them both; what do you think of it?"

"What can I think till I know what your requests were?"

"Why, what signifies what they were, man? I tell you it was I that made them; I, to whom he owes more than to any three that have joined the standard, for I negociated the whole business, and brought in all the Perthshire men when not one would have stirred. I am not likely, I think, to ask any thing very unreasonable, and if I did, they might have stretched a point.—Well, but you shall know all, now that I can draw my breath again with some freedom.—You remember my earl's patent; it is dated some years back, for services then rendered, and certainly my merit has not been diminished, to say the least, by my subsequent behaviour. Now, sir, I value this bauble of a coronet as little as you, or any philosopher on earth; for I hold that the chief of such a clan as the Sliochd nan Ivor is superior in rank to any earl in Scotland. But I had a particular reason for assuming this cursed title at this time. You must know I learned accidentally that the Prince has been pressing that old foolish Baron of Bradwardine to disinherit his male heir, a nineteenth or twentieth cousin, who has taken a command in the Elector of Hanover's militia, and to settle his estate upon your pretty little friend, Rose; and this, as being the command of his king and overlord, who may alter the destination of a fief at pleasure, the old gentleman seems well reconciled to."

"And what becomes of the homage?"

"Curse the homage!—I believe Rose is to pull off the queen's slipper on her coronation-day, or some such trash. Well, sir, as Rose Bradwardine would always have made a suitable match for me, but for this idiotical predilection of her father for the heir-male, it occurred to me there now remained no obstacle unless that the Baron might expect his daughter's husband to take the name of Bradwardine, (which you know would be impossible in my case) and that this might be evaded by my assuming the title to which I had so good a right, and which, of course, would supersede that difficulty. If she was to be also Viscountess Bradwardine, in her own right, after her father's demise, so much the better; I could have no objection."

"But, Fergus," said Waverley, "I had no idea that you had any affection for Miss Bradwardine, and you are always sneering at her father."

"I have as much affection for Miss Bradwardine, my good friend, as I think it necessary to have for the future mistress of my family, and the mother of my children. She is a very pretty intelligent girl, is certainly of one of the very first Lowland families, and, with a little of Flora's instructions and forming, will make a very good figure. As to her father, he is an original, it is true, and an absurd enough one; but he has given such severe lessons to Sir Hew Halbert, that dear defunct the Laird of Balmawhapple, and others, that nobody dare laugh at him, so his absurdity goes for nothing. I tell you there could have been no earthly objection—none. I had settled the thing entirely in my own mind."

"But had you asked the Baron's consent, or Rose's?"

"To what purpose? To have spoke to the Baron before I had assumed my title, would have only provoked a premature and irritating discussion on the subject of the change of name. Whereas as Earl of Glennaquoich I had only to propose to him to carry his d—d bear and boot-jack *party per pale*, or in a scutcheon of pretence, or in a separate shield perhaps—any way that would not blemish my own coat-of-arms. And as to Rose, I don't see what objection she could have made, if her father was satisfied."

"Perhaps the same that your sister makes to me, you being satisfied."

Fergus gave a broad stare at the comparison which this supposition implied, but cautiously suppressed the answer which rose to his tongue. "O, we should easily have arranged all that—So, sir, I craved a private interview, and this morning was assigned, and I asked you to meet me here, thinking, like a fool, that I should want your countenance as bride's-man. Well—I state my pretensions—they are not denied—the promises so repeatedly made, and the patent granted—they are acknowledged. But when I propose, as a natural consequence, to assume the rank which the patent bestowed, I have the old story of the jealousy of C—— and M—— trumpt up against me. I resist this pretext, and offer to procure their written acquiescence, in virtue of the date of my patent as prior to their silly claims—I assure you I would have had such a consent from them, if it had been at point of the sword—And then out comes the real truth; and he dares to tell me, to my face, that my patent must be suppressed for the present, for fear of disgusting that rascally coward and *faineant*—(naming the rival chief of the northern branch of his own clan) who has no better title to be a chieftain than I to be Emperor of China; and who is pleased to shelter his dastardly reluctance to come out agreeable to his promise twenty times pledged, under a pretended jealousy of the Prince's partiality to me. And, to leave this miserable driveller without a pretence for his cowardice, the Prince asks it as a personal favour of me, forsooth, not to press my just and reasonable request at this moment. After this put your faith in princes!"

"And did your audience end here?"

"End? O no: I was determined to leave him no pretence for his ingratitude, and therefore I stated, with all the composure I could muster, for I promise you I trembled with passion, the particular reasons I had for wishing that his Royal Highness would impose upon me any other mode of exhibiting my duty and devotion, as my views in life made, what would at any other time have been a mere trifle, at this crisis, a severe sacrifice; and then I explained to him my full plan."

"And what did the Prince answer?"

"Answer? why—it is well it is written, curse not the king, no, not in thy thought!—why, he answered, that truly he was glad I had made him my confidant to prevent more grievous disappointment, for he could assure me, upon the word of a Prince, that Miss Bradwardine's affections were engaged, and he was under a particular promise to favour them. 'So, my dear Fergus,' said he, with his most gracious cast of smile, 'as the marriage is utterly out of question, there need be no hurry you know about the earldom.' And so he glided off, and left me *planté la*."

"And what did you do?"

"I'll tell you what I *could* have done at that moment—sold myself to the devil or the Elector, which ever offered the dearest revenge.— However, I am now cool. I know he intends to marry her to some of his rascally Frenchmen, or his Irish officers, but I will watch them close; and let the man that would supplant me look well to himself.—*Bisogna coprirsi, Signor*."

After some farther conversation, unnecessary to be detailed, Waverley took leave of the Chieftain, whose fury had now subsided into a deep and strong desire of vengeance, and returned home, scarce able to analyze the mixture of feelings which the narrative had awakened in his own bosom.

Chapter Seven

"TO ONE THING CONSTANT NEVER."

"I AM THE very child of caprice and folly," said Waverley to himself, as he bolted the door of his apartment, and paced it with hasty steps— "What is it to me that Fergus Mac-Ivor should wish to marry Rose Bradwardine?—I love her not—I might have been loved by her perhaps—but I rejected her simple, natural, and affecting attachment, instead of cherishing it into tenderness, and dedicated myself to one who will never love mortal man, unless old Warwick, the King-maker, should arise from the dead. The Baron too—I would not have cared about his estate, and so the name would have been no stumbling-block. The devil might have taken the barren moors, and drawn off the royal *caligæ*, for what I would have cared. But framed as she is for domestic affection and tenderness, for giving and receiving all those kind and quiet attentions which sweeten life to those who pass it together, she is sought by Fergus Mac-Ivor. He will not use her ill to be sure—of that he is incapable—but he will neglect her after the first month; he will be too intent on subduing some rival chieftain, on circumventing some favourite at court, on gaining some heathy hill and lake, or adding to his bands some new troop of caterans, to enquire what she does, or how she amuses herself.

> And then will canker sorrow eat her bud,
> And chase the native beauty from her cheek;
> And she will look as hollow as a ghost,
> As dim and meagre as an ague fit,
> And so she'll die.

And such a catastrophe of the most gentle creature on earth might have been prevented, if Mr Edward Waverley had had his eyes!— Upon my word I cannot understand how I thought Flora so much, that is, so *very* much handsomer than Rose. She is taller indeed, and her manner more formed; but many people think Miss Bradwardine's more natural; and she is certainly much younger. I should think Flora is two years older than I am—I will look at them particularly this evening."

And with this resolution Waverley went to drink tea (as the fashion was Sixty Years since) at the house of a lady of quality, attached to the cause of the Chevalier, where he found, as he expected, both the ladies. All rose as he entered, but Flora immediately resumed her place, and the conversation in which she was engaged. Rose, on the contrary, almost imperceptibly made a little way in the crowded circle for his advancing the corner of a chair.—"Her manner, upon the whole, is most engaging," thought Waverley.

A dispute occurred whether the Gaelic or Italian language was most liquid and best adapted for poetry: the opinion for the Gaelic, which probably might not have found supporters elsewhere, was here fiercely defended by seven Highland ladies, who talked at the top of their lungs, and screamed the company deaf, with examples of Celtic *euphonia*. Flora, observing the Lowland ladies sneer at the comparison, produced some reasons to shew that it was not altogether so absurd; but Rose, when asked for her opinion, gave it with animation in praise of Italian, which she had studied with Waverley's assistance. "She has a more correct ear than Flora, though a less accomplished musician," said Waverley to himself. "I suppose Miss Mac-Ivor will next compare Mac-Murrough nan Fonn to Ariosto."

Lastly, it so befell that the ladies differed whether Fergus who was present should be asked to perform on the flute, at which he was an adept, or Waverley invited to read a play of Shakspeare; and the lady of the tea-table good humouredly undertook to collect the votes of the company for poetry or music, under the condition, that the gentleman whose talents were not laid under contribution that evening, should contribute them to enliven the next. It chanced that Rose had the casting vote. Now Flora, who seemed to impose it as a rule upon herself never to countenance any proposal which might seem to encourage Waverley, had voted for music, providing the Baron would take his violin to accompany Fergus. "I wish you joy of your taste, Miss Mac-Ivor," thought Edward as they sought for his book. "I thought it better when we were at Glennaquoich; but certainly the Baron is no great performer, and Shakspeare is worth listening to."

Romeo and Juliet was selected, and Edward read with great taste, feeling, and spirit, several scenes from that play. All the company applauded with their hands, and many with their tears. Flora, to whom the drama was well known, was among the former. Rose, to whom it was altogether new, belonged to the latter class of admirers. "She has more feeling too," said Waverley internally.

The conversation turning upon the incidents of the play, and upon the characters, Fergus declared that the only one worth naming, as a man of fashion and spirit, was Mercutio. "I could not," he said, "quite follow all his old-fashioned wit, but he must have been a very pretty fellow according to the ideas of his time."

"And it was a shame," said Ensign Maccombich, who usually followed his colonel every where, "for that Tibbert, or Taggart, or what was his name, to stick him under the other gentleman's arm while he was redding the fray."

The ladies, of course, declared loudly in favour of Romeo, but this opinion did not go undisputed. The mistress of the house, and several other ladies in company severely reprobated the levity with which the hero transfers his affection from Rosaline to Juliet. Flora remained silent until her opinion was repeatedly requested, and then answered, she thought the circumstance objected to, not only reconcileable to nature, but such as in the highest degree evinced the art of the poet. "Romeo is described as a young man, peculiarly susceptible of the softer passions; his love is at first fixed upon a woman who could afford it no return; this he repeatedly tells you,—

From love's weak childish bow she lives unharmed;

and again,—

She hath forsworn to love.

"Now, as it was impossible that Romeo's love, supposing him a reasonable being, could continue without hope, the poet has, with great art, seized the moment when he was reduced actually to despair, to throw in his way an object more accomplished than her by whom he had been rejected, and who is disposed to repay his attachment. I can scarce conceive a situation more calculated to enhance the ardour of

Romeo's affection for Juliet, than his being at once raised by her from the state of drooping melancholy, in which he appears first upon the scene, to the ecstatic state in which he exclaims—

> ——come what sorrow can,
>> It cannot countervail the exchange of joy
>> That one short minute gives me in her sight."

"Good now, Miss Mac-Ivor," said a young lady of quality, "do you mean to cheat us out of our prerogative? will you persuade us love cannot subsist without hope, or that the lover must become fickle if the lady is cruel? O fie! I did not expect such an unsentimental conclusion."

"A lover, my dear Lady Betty, may, I conceive, persevere in his suit under very discouraging circumstances. Affection can (now and then) withstand very severe storms of rigour, but not a long polar frost of downright indifference. Don't, even with *your* attractions, try the experiment upon any lover whose faith you value. Love will subsist on wonderfully little hope, but not altogether without it."

"It will be just like Duncan Mac-Girdie's mare," said Evan, "if your ladyships please; he wanted to use her by degrees to live without meat, and just as he had put her on a straw a-day the poor thing died!"

Evan's illustration set the company a-laughing, and the discourse took a different turn. Shortly afterwards the party broke up, and Edward returned home, musing on what Flora had said. "I will love my Rosaline no more," said he; "she has given me a broad enough hint for that; and I will speak to her brother, and resign my suit. But for a Juliet—would it be handsome to interfere with Fergus's pretensions?—But it is impossible they can ever succeed: and should they miscarry, what then?—why then—*alors comme alors*."

And with this resolution, of being guided by circumstances, did our hero commit himself to repose.

Chapter Eight

A BRAVE MAN IN SORROW

IF MY FAIR READERS should be of opinion that my hero's levity in love is altogether unpardonable, I must remind them, that all his griefs and difficulties did not arise from that sentimental source. Even the lyrical poet, who complains so feelingly of the pains of love, could not forget, that, at the same time, he was "in debt and in drink," which, doubtless, were great aggravations of his distress. There were, indeed, whole days in which Waverley thought neither of Flora nor of Rose Bradwardine, but which were spent in melancholy conjectures upon the probable state of matters at Waverley-Honour, and the dubious issue of the civil contest in which he was engaged. Colonel Talbot often engaged him in discussions upon the justice of the cause he had espoused. "Not," he said, "that it is possible for you to quit it at this present moment, for, come what come will, you must stand by your rash engagement. But I wish you to be aware that the right is not with you; that you are fighting against the real interests of your country; and that you ought, as an Englishman and a patriot, to take the first opportunity to leave this unhappy expedition before the snow-ball melt."

In such political disputes, Waverley usually opposed the common arguments of his party, with which it is unnecessary to trouble the reader. But he had little to say when the Colonel urged him to compare the strength by which they had undertaken to overthrow the government, with that which was now assembling very rapidly for its support. To this statement Waverley had but one answer: "If the cause I have undertaken be perilous, there would be the greater disgrace in abandoning it." And in his turn he generally silenced Colonel Talbot, and succeeded in changing the subject.

One night, when, after a long dispute of this nature, the friends had separated, and our hero had retired to bed, he was awaked about midnight by a suppressed groan. He started up and listened; it came from the apartment of Colonel Talbot, which was divided from his own by a wainscotted partition, with a door of communication. Waverley approached this door, and distinctly heard one or two deep-drawn sighs. What could be the matter? The Colonel had parted from him, apparently, in his usual state of spirits—he must have been taken suddenly ill. Under this impression, he opened the door of communication very gently, and perceived the Colonel, in his night-gown, seated by a table, on which lay a letter and picture. He raised his head hastily, as Edward stood uncertain whether to advance or retire, and Waverley perceived that his cheeks were stained with tears.

As if ashamed at being found giving way to such emotion, Colonel Talbot rose with apparent displeasure. "I think, Mr Waverley, my own apartment, and the hour, might have secured even a prisoner against"——

"Do not say *intrusion*, Colonel Talbot; I heard you——breathe hard—and feared you were ill; that alone could have induced me to break in upon you."

"I am well," said the Colonel, "perfectly well."

"But you are distressed: is there any thing can be done?"

"Nothing, Mr Waverley; I was only thinking of home—and some unpleasant occurrences there."

"Good God, my uncle?"

"No, it is a grief entirely my own; I am ashamed you should have seen it disarm me so much; but it must have its course at times, that it may be at others more decently supported. I would have kept it secret from you; for I think it will grieve you, and yet you can administer no consolation. But you have surprised me.—I see you are surprised yourself,—and I hate mystery. Read that letter."

The letter was from Colonel Talbot's sister, and in these words:

"I received yours, my dearest brother, by Hodges. Sir E. W. and Mr R. W. are still at large, but are not permitted to leave London. I wish to heaven I could give you as good an account of matters in the square. But the news of the unhappy affair at Preston came upon us, with the dreadful addition that you were among the fallen. You know Lady Emily's state of health, when your friendship for Sir E. induced you to leave her. She was much harassed with the sad accounts from Scotland of the rebellion having broken out; but kept up her spirits, as, she said, it became your wife, and for the sake of the future heir, so long hoped for in vain. Alas, my dear brother, these hopes are now ended! notwithstanding all my watchful care, this unhappy rumour reached her without preparation. She was taken ill immediately; and the poor infant scarce survived its birth. Would to God this were all! But although the contradiction of the horrible report by your own letter has greatly revived her spirits, yet Dr —— apprehends, I grieve to say, serious, and even dangerous, consequences to her health, especially from the uncertainty in which she must necessarily remain for some time, aggravated by the ideas she has formed, of the ferocity of those with whom you are a prisoner.

"Do therefore, my dear brother, as soon as this reaches you, endeavour to gain your release by parole, by ransom, or any way that is practicable. I do not exaggerate Lady Emily's state of health; but I must not—dare not suppress the truth. Ever, my dear Philip, your most affectionate sister,

"LUCY TALBOT."

Edward stood motionless when he had perused this letter, for the conclusion was inevitable, that, by the Colonel's journey in quest of him, he had incurred this heavy calamity. It was severe enough, even in its irremediable part; for Colonel Talbot and Lady Emily, long without a family, had fondly exulted in the hopes which were now blasted. But this disappointment was nothing to the extent of the threatened evil; and Edward, with horror, regarded himself as the original cause of both.

Ere he could collect himself sufficiently to speak, Colonel Talbot had recovered his usual composure of manner, though his troubled eye denoted his mental agony.

"She is a woman, my young friend, who may justify even a soldier's tears." He reached him the miniature, exhibiting features which fully vindicated the eulogium; "and yet, God knows, what you see of her there is the least of the charms she possesses—possessed, I should perhaps say—but God's will be done."

"You must fly—you must fly instantly to her relief. It is not—it shall not be too late."

"Fly? how is it possible? I am a prisoner—upon parole."

"I am your keeper—I restore your parole—I am to answer for you."

"You cannot do so consistently with your duty; nor can I accept a discharge from you, with due regard to my own honour—you would be made responsible."

"I will answer it with my head, if necessary. I have been the unhappy cause of the loss of your child, make me not the murderer of your wife."

"No, my dear Edward," said Talbot, taking him kindly by the hand, "you are in no respect to blame; and if I concealed this domestic distress for two days, it was lest your sensibility should view it in that light. You could not think of me, hardly knew of my existence, when I left England in quest of you. It is a responsibility, heaven knows, sufficiently heavy for mortality, that we must answer for the foreseen and direct result of our actions,—for their indirect and consequential operation, the great and good Being, who alone can foresee the dependence of human events on each other, hath not pronounced his frail creatures liable."

"But that you should have left Lady Emily in the situation the most interesting to a husband, to seek a"——

"I only did my duty, and I do not, and ought not to regret it. If the path of gratitude and honour were always smooth and easy, there would be little merit in following it—but it moves often in contradiction to our interest and passions, and sometimes to our better affections. These are the trials of life, and this, though not the least bitter," (the tears came unbidden to his eyes,) "is not the first which it has been my fate to encounter—but we will talk of this to-morrow," wringing Waverley's hand. "Good night; strive to forget it for a few hours. It will dawn, I think, by six, and it is now past two. Good night."

Edward retired, without trusting his voice with a reply.

Chapter Nine

EXERTION

WHEN COLONEL TALBOT entered the breakfast-parlour next morning, he learned from Waverley's servant that our hero had been abroad at an early hour, and was not yet returned. The morning was well advanced before he again appeared. He arrived out of breath, but with an air of joy that astonished Colonel Talbot.

"There," said he, throwing a paper on the table, "there is my morning's work. Alick, pack up the Colonel's clothes. Make haste, make haste."

The Colonel examined the paper with astonishment. It was a pass from the Chevalier to Colonel Talbot, to repair to Leith, or any other port in possession of his Royal Highness's troops, and there to embark for England, or elsewhere, at his free pleasure; he only giving his parole of honour not to bear arms against the house of Stuart for the space of a twelvemonth.

"In the name of God," said the Colonel, his eyes sparkling with eagerness, "how did you obtain this?"

"I was at the Chevalier's levee as soon as he usually arises. He was gone to the camp at Duddingston. I pursued him thither; asked and obtained an audience—but I will tell you not a word more, unless I see you begin to pack."

"Before I know whether I can avail myself of this passport, or how it was obtained?"

"O, you can take out the things again, you know;—now I see you busy, I will go on. When I first mentioned your name, his eyes sparkled almost as bright as yours did two minutes since. 'Had you,' he earnestly asked, 'shewn any sentiments favourable to his cause?' 'Not in the least, nor was there any hope you would do so.' His countenance fell. I requested your freedom. 'Impossible,' he said; 'your importance as a friend and confidant of such and such personages made my request altogether extravagant.' I told him my own story and yours; and asked him to judge what my feelings must be by his own. He has a heart, and a kind one, Colonel Talbot, you may say what you please. He took a sheet of paper, and wrote the pass with his own hand. 'I will not trust myself with my council,' he said, 'they will argue me out of what is right. I will not endure that a friend, valued as I value you, should be loaded with the painful reflections which must afflict you in case of farther misfortune in Colonel Talbot's family; nor will I keep a brave enemy a prisoner under such circumstances. Besides,' said he, 'I think I can justify myself to my prudent advisers by pleading the good effect such lenity will produce on the minds of the great English families with whom Colonel Talbot is connected.' "

"There the politician peeped out," said the Colonel.

"Well, at least he concluded like a king's son;—'Take the passport; I have added a condition for form's sake; but if the Colonel objects to it, let him depart without giving any parole whatever. I come here to war with men, but not to distress or endanger women.' "

"I never thought to have been so much indebted to the Pretend——"

"To the Prince," said Waverley, smiling.

"To the Chevalier," said the Colonel; "it is a good travelling name, and which we may both freely use. Did he say any thing more?"

"Only asked if there was any thing else he could oblige me in; and when I replied in the negative, he shook me by the hand, and wished all his followers were as considerate, since some friends of mine not only asked all he had to bestow, but many things which were entirely out of his power, or that of the greatest sovereign upon earth. Indeed, he said, no prince seemed, in the eyes of his followers, so like the deity as himself, if you were to judge from the extravagant requests which were daily preferred to him."

"Poor young gentleman," said the Colonel, "I suppose he begins to feel the difficulties of his situation. Well, dear Waverley, this is more than kind, and shall not be forgotten while Philip Talbot can remember any thing. My life—pshaw—let Emily thank you for that—this is a favour worth fifty lives. I cannot hesitate upon giving my parole in the circumstances: there it is—(he wrote it out in form)—And now, how am I to get off?"

"All that is settled: your knapsack is packed, my horses wait, and a boat has been engaged, by the Prince's permission, to put you on board the Fox frigate. I sent a messenger down to Leith on purpose."

"That will do excellently. Captain Beaver is my particular friend: he will put me ashore at Berwick or Shields, from which I can ride post to London;—and you must entrust me with the packet of papers which you recovered by means of your Miss Bean Lean. I may have an opportunity of using them to your advantage.—But I see your Highland friend Glen—— what do you call his barbarous name? and his orderly with him. I must not call him his orderly cut-throat any more, I suppose. See how he walks as if the world were his own, with the bonnet on one side of his head, and his plaid puffed out across his breast. I should like now to meet that youth where my hands were not tied: I would tame his pride, or he should tame mine."

"For shame, Colonel Talbot; you swell at sight of the tartan, as the bull is said to do at scarlet. You and Mac-Ivor have some points not much unlike, so far as national prejudice is concerned."

The latter part of this discourse passed in the street. They passed the Chief, the Colonel punctiliously and he sternly greeting each other, like two duellists before they take their ground. It was evident the dislike was mutual. "I never see that surly fellow that dogs his heels," said the Colonel, after he had mounted his horse, "but he reminds me of lines I have somewhere heard—upon the stage, I think;

—Close behind him
Stalks sullen Bertram, like a sorcerer's fiend,
Pressing to be employed."

"I assure you," said Waverley, "you judge harshly and injuriously of the Highlanders."

"Not a whit, not a whit; I cannot spare them a jot; I cannot bate them an ace. Let them stay in their own barren mountains, and puff and swell, and hang their bonnets on the horns of the moon if they have a mind; but what business have they to come where people wear breeches and speak an intelligible language?—I mean intelligible in comparison to their gibberish, for even the Lowlanders talk a kind of English little better than the Negroes in Jamaica. I could pity the Pre——, I mean the Chevalier himself, for having so many desperadoes about him. And they learn their trade so early. There is a kind of subaltern imp, for example, a sort of sucking devil, whom your friend Glena—Glenamuck there, has sometimes in his train. To look at him, he is about fourteen in years; but he is a century old in mischief and villainy. He was playing at quoits the other day in the court; a gentleman, a decent-looking person enough, came past, and as a quoit hit his shin, he lifted his cane: But my young bravo whips out his pistol, like Beau Clincher in the Trip to the Jubilee, and had not a shrill scream of *Gardez l'eau*, from an upper window, set all parties a-scampering for fear of the inevitable consequences, the poor gentleman would have lost his life by the hands of that little cockatrice."

"A fine character you'll give of Scotland upon your return, Colonel Talbot."

"O, Justice Shallow shall save me the trouble—Barren, barren, beggars all, beggars all—marry, good air,—and that only when you are out of Edinburgh, and not yet come to Leith, as is our case at present."

In a short time they arrived at the sea-port:—

The boat rock'd at the pier of Leith,
Full loud the wind blew down the ferry;
The ship rode at the Berwick Law——

"Farewell, Colonel; may you find all as you would wish it. Perhaps we may meet sooner than you expect: they talk of an immediate route for England."

"Tell me nothing of that," said Talbot; "I wish to carry no news of your motions."

"Simply then, adieu. Say, with a thousand kind greetings, all that is dutiful and affectionate to Sir Everard and Aunt Rachael—Speak of me as kindly as you can—think of me as indulgently as your conscience will permit, and once more adieu."

"And adieu, my dear Waverley; many, many thanks for your kindness. Unplaid yourself on the first opportunity. I shall ever think of you with gratitude, and the worst of my censure shall be, *Que diable alloit il faire dans cette galere?*"

And thus they parted, Colonel Talbot going on board of the boat, and Waverley returning to Edinburgh.

Chapter Ten

THE MARCH

IT IS NOT our purpose to intrude upon the province of history. We shall therefore only remind our reader, that about the beginning of November the young Chevalier, at the head of about six thousand men at the utmost, resolved to peril his cause upon attempting to penetrate into the centre of England, although aware of the mighty preparations which were made for their reception. They set forwards on this crusade in weather which would have rendered any other troops incapable of marching, but which in reality gave these active mountaineers advantages over a less hardy enemy. In defiance of a superior army lying upon the Borders, under Field-Marshal Wade, they besieged and took Carlisle, and soon afterwards prosecuted their daring march to the southward.

As Colonel Mac-Ivor's regiment marched in the van of the clans, he and Waverley, who now equalled any Highlander in endurance of fatigue, and was become somewhat acquainted with their language, were perpetually at its head. They marked the progress of the army, however, with very different eyes. Fergus, all air and fire, and confident against the world in arms, measured nothing but that every step was a yard nearer London. He neither asked, expected, nor desired any aid, except that of the clans, to place the Stuarts once more on the throne; and when by chance a few adherents joined the standard, he always considered them in the light of new claimants upon the favour of the future monarch, who must therefore subtract for their gratification so much of the bounty which should be shared among his Highland followers.

Edward's views were very different. He could not but observe, that in those towns in which they proclaimed James the Third, "no man cried, God bless him." The mob stared and listened, heartless, stupified, and dull, but gave few signs even of that boisterous spirit, which induces them to shout upon all occasions for the mere exercise of their most sweet voices. The Jacobites had been taught to believe that the north-western counties abounded with wealthy squires and hardy yeomen, devoted to the cause of the White Rose. But of the wealthier tories they saw little. Some fled from their houses, some feigned themselves sick, some surrendered themselves to the government as suspected persons. Of such as remained, the ignorant gazed with astonishment, mixed with horror and aversion, at the wild appearance, unknown language, and singular garb of the Scottish clans. And to the more prudent, their scanty numbers, apparent deficiency in discipline, and poverty of equipment, seemed certain tokens of the calamitous termination of their rash undertaking. Thus the few who joined them were such as bigotry of political principle blinded to consequences, or broken fortunes induced to hazard all upon a risk so desperate.

The Baron of Bradwardine being asked what he thought of these recruits, took a long pinch of snuff, and answered drily, "that he could not but have an excellent opinion of them, since they resembled precisely the followers who attached themselves to the good King David at the cave of Adullam; *videlicet*, every one that was in distress, and every one that was in debt, and every one that was discontented, which the Vulgate renders bitter of soul; and doubtless," he said, "they will prove mighty men of their hands, and there is much need that they should, for I have seen many a sour look cast upon us."

But none of these considerations grieved Fergus. He admired the luxuriant beauty of the country, and the situation of many of the seats which they passed. "Is Waverley Hall like that house, Edward?"

"It is one half larger."

"Is your uncle's park as fine a one as that?"

"It is three times as extensive, and rather resembles a forest than a mere park."

"Flora will be a happy woman."

"I hope Miss Mac-Ivor will have much reason for happiness, unconnected with Waverley-Honour."

"I hope so too; but, to be mistress of such a place will be a pretty addition to the sum total."

"An addition the want of which, I trust, will be amply supplied by some other means."

"How," said Fergus, stopping short, and turning upon Waverley—"How am I to understand that, Mr Waverley? Had I the pleasure to hear you aright?"

"Perfectly right, Fergus."

"And I am to understand then that you no longer desire my alliance and my sister's hand?"

"Your sister has refused mine, both directly, and by all the usual means by which ladies repress undesired attentions."

"I have no idea of a lady dismissing or a gentleman withdrawing his suit, after it has been approved of by her legal guardian, without giving him an opportunity of talking the matter over with the lady. You did not, I suppose, expect my sister to drop into your mouth like a ripe plum, the first moment you chose to open it?"

"As to the lady's title to dismiss her lover, Colonel, it is a point which you must argue with her, as I am ignorant of the customs of the Highlands in that particular. But as to my title to acquiesce in a rejection from her without any appeal to your interest, I will tell you plainly, without meaning to undervalue Miss Mac-Ivor's admitted beauty and accomplishments, that I would not take the hand of an angel, with an empire for her dowry, if her consent were extorted by the importunity of friends and guardians, and did not flow from her own free inclination."

"An angel, with the dowry of an empire," repeated Fergus, in a tone of bitter irony, "is not very likely to be pressed upon a ——shire squire. But, sir," changing his tone, "if Flora Mac-Ivor have not the dowry of an empire, she is *my* sister, and that is sufficient at least to secure her against being treated with any thing approaching to levity."

"She is Flora Mac-Ivor, sir, which to me, were I capable of treating any woman with levity, would be a more effectual protection."

The brow of the Chieftain was now fully clouded, but Edward felt too indignant at the unreasonable tone which he had adopted to avert the storm by the least concession. They had both stood still while this short dialogue passed; and Fergus seemed half disposed to say something more violent; but, by a strong effort, suppressed his passion, and, turning his face forward, walked sullenly on. As they had always hitherto walked together, and almost constantly side by side, Waverley pursued his course silently in the same direction, determined to let the Chief take his own time in recovering the good humour which he had so unreasonably discarded, and firm in his resolution not to bate him an inch of dignity.

After they had marched on in this sullen manner about a mile,

Fergus resumed the discourse in a different tone. "I believe I was warm, my dear Edward, but you provoke me with your want of knowledge of the world. You have taken pet at some of Flora's prudery, or high-flying notions of loyalty, and now, like a child, you quarrel with the play-thing you have been crying for, and beat me, your faithful keeper, because my arms cannot reach to Edinburgh to hand it to you. I am sure, if I was passionate, the mortification at losing the alliance of such a friend, after your arrangement had been the talk of both Highlands and Lowlands, and that without so much as knowing why or wherefore, might well provoke calmer blood than mine. I shall write to Edinburgh, and put all to rights; that is, if you desire I should do so; as indeed I cannot suppose that your good opinion of Flora, it being such as you have often expressed to me, can be at once laid aside."

"Colonel Mac-Ivor," said Edward, who had no mind to be hurried farther or faster than he chose in a matter which he already considered as broken off, "I am fully sensible of the value of your good offices; and certainly, by your zeal on my behalf in such an affair, you do me no small honour. But as Miss Mac-Ivor has made her election freely and voluntarily, and as all my attentions in Edinburgh were received with more than coldness, I cannot, in justice either to her or to myself, consent that she should again be harassed upon this topic. I would have mentioned this to you some time since; but you saw the footing upon which we stood together and must have understood it. Had I thought otherwise, I would have earlier spoken—but I had a natural reluctance to enter upon a subject so painful to us both."

"O, very well, Mr Waverley, the thing is at an end. I have no occasion to press my sister upon any man."

"Nor have I any occasion to court repeated rejection from the same young lady."

"I shall make due enquiry, however," said the Chieftain, without noticing the interruption, "and learn what my sister thinks of all this; we will then see whether it is to end here."

"Respecting such enquiries, you will of course be guided by your own judgement. It is, I am aware, impossible Miss Mac-Ivor can change her mind; and were such an unsupposable case to happen, it is certain I will not change mine. I only mention this to prevent any possibility of future misconstruction."

Gladly at that moment would Mac-Ivor have put their quarrel to a personal arbitrement; his eye flashed fire, and he measured Edward as if to chuse where he might best implant a mortal wound. But although we do not now quarrel according to the modes and figures of Caranza or Vincent Saviola, no one knew better than Fergus that there must be some decent pretext for a mortal duel. For instance, you may challenge a man for treading on your corn in a crowd, or for pushing you up to the wall, or for taking your seat in the theatre. But the modern code of honour will not permit you to found a quarrel upon your right of compelling a man to continue addresses to a female relative, which the fair lady has already refused. So that Fergus was compelled to stomach this supposed affront, until the whirligig of time, whose motion he promised himself he would watch most sedulously, should bring about an opportunity of revenge.

Waverley's servant always led a saddle-horse for him in the rear of the battalion to which he was attached, though his master seldom rode him. But now, incensed at the domineering and unreasonable conduct of his late friend, he fell behind the column, and mounted his horse, resolving to seek the Baron of Bradwardine, and request permission to volunteer in his troop, instead of the Mac-Ivor regiment.

"A happy time of it I should have had," thought he, after he was mounted, "to have been so closely allied to this superb specimen of pride and self-opinion and passion. A colonel! why, he should have been a generalissimo—a petty chief of three or four hundred men! his pride might suffice for the Cham of Tartary—the Grand Seignior— the Great Mogul! I am well free of him. Were Flora an angel, she would bring with her a second Lucifer of ambition and wrath for a brother-in-law."

The Baron, whose learning (like Sancho's jests, while in the Sierra Morena,) seemed to grow mouldy for want of exercise, joyfully embraced the opportunity of Waverley's offering his service in his regiment, to bring it into some exertion. The good-natured old gentleman, however, laboured to effect a reconciliation between the two quondam friends. Fergus turned a cold ear to his remonstrances, though he gave them a respectful hearing; and as for Waverley, he saw no reason why he should be the first in courting a renewal of the intimacy which the Chieftain had so unreasonably disturbed. The Baron then mentioned the matter to the Prince, who, anxious to prevent quarrels in his little army, declared, he would himself remonstrate with Colonel Mac-Ivor on the unreasonableness of his conduct. But, in the hurry of their march, it was a day or two before he had an opportunity to exert his influence in the manner he proposed.

In the meanwhile, Waverley turned the instructions he had received while in G——'s dragoons to some account, and assisted the Baron in his command as a sort of adjutant. "*Parmi les aveugles un borgne est roi*," says the French proverb; and the cavalry, which consisted chiefly of Lowland gentlemen, their tenants and servants, formed a high opinion of Waverley's skill, and a great attachment to his person. This was indeed partly owing to the satisfaction which they felt at the distinguished English volunteer's leaving the Highlanders to rank among them; for there was a latent grudge between the horse and foot, not only owing to the difference of the services, but because most of the gentlemen, living near the Highlands, had at one time or other had quarrels with the tribes in their vicinity, and all of them looked with a jealous eye on the Highlanders' avowed pretensions to superior valour and utility in the Prince's service.

Chapter Eleven

THE CONFUSION OF KING AGRAMANT'S CAMP

IT WAS Waverley's custom sometimes to ride a little off from the main body to look at any object of curiosity which occurred upon the march. They were now in Lancashire, when, attracted by a castellated old hall, he left the squadron for half an hour, to take a survey and slight sketch of it. As he returned down the avenue, he was met by Ensign Maccombich. This man had contracted a sort of regard for Edward since the day of his first seeing him at Tully-Veolan, and introducing him to the Highlands. He seemed to loiter, as if on purpose to meet with our hero. Yet, as he passed him, he only approached his stirrup, and said in Gaelic, *'N aire!*, that is, Beware! and then walked swiftly on, shunning all further communication.

Edward, somewhat surprised at this hint, followed with his eyes the course of Evan, who speedily disappeared among the trees. His servant, Alick Polwarth, who was in attendance, also looked after the Highlander, and then rode up close to his master.

"The ne'er be in me, sir, if I think you're safe amang these Highland runthereouts."

"What do you mean, Alick?"

"The Mac-Ivors, sir, hae gotten it into their heads, that ye hae affronted their young leddy, Miss Flora, and I hae heard mae nor ane say they wadna tak muckle to mak a black-cock o' ye—And ye ken yeresell there's mony o' them wadna mind a bawbee the weising a ball through the Prince himsell, an the Chief gae them the wink; or whether he did or no, if they thought it wad please him when it was done."

Waverley, though confident that Fergus Mac-Ivor was incapable of such treachery, was by no means equally sure of the forbearance of his followers. He knew, that where the honour of the Chief or his family was supposed to be touched, the happiest man would be the first that could avenge the stigma; and he had often heard them quote a proverb that the best revenge was the most speedy and most safe. Coupling this with the hint of Evan, he judged it most prudent to set spurs to his horse, and ride briskly back to the squadron. Ere he reached the end of the long avenue, however, a ball whistled past him, and the report of a pistol was heard.

"It was that deevil's buckie, Callum Beg," said Alick; "I saw him whisk away through amang the reises."

Edward, justly incensed at this act of treachery, galloped out of the avenue, and observed the battalion of Mac-Ivors at some distance moving along the common, in which it terminated. He also saw an individual running very fast to join the party; this he concluded was the intended assassin, who, by leaping an inclosure, might easily make a much shorter path to the main body than he could find on horseback. Unable to contain himself, he commanded Alick to go to the Baron of Bradwardine, who was at the head of his regiment about half a mile in front, and acquaint him with what had happened. He himself immediately rode up to Fergus's regiment. The Chief himself was in the act of joining them. He was on horseback, having been waiting upon the Prince. On perceiving Edward approaching, he put his horse in motion towards him.

"Colonel Mac-Ivor," said Waverley, without any farther salutation, "I have to inform you that one of your people has this instant fired at me from a lurking-place."

"As that (excepting the circumstance of the lurking-place) is a pleasure which I presently propose to myself, I should be glad to know which of my clansmen dared to anticipate me."

"I shall certainly be at your command whenever you please; the gentleman who took your office upon himself is your page there, Callum Beg."

"Stand forth from the ranks, Callum! Did you fire at Mr Waverley?"

"No," answered the unblushing Callum.

"You did," said Alick Polwarth, who was already returned, having met a trooper by whom he dispatched an account of what was going forward to the Baron of Bradwardine, while he himself returned to his master at full gallop, neither sparing the rowels of his spurs, nor the sides of his horse. "You did; I saw you as plainly as I ever saw the auld kirk at Coudingham."

"You lie," replied Callum, with his usual impenetrable obstinacy. The combat between the knights would certainly, as in the days of chivalry, have been preceded by an encounter between the squires, for Alick was a stout-hearted Merse-man, and feared the bow of Cupid far more than a Highlander's dirk or claymore. But Fergus, with his usual tone of decision, demanded Callum's pistol. The cock was down, the pan and muzzle were black with the smoke; it had been that instant fired.

"Take that," said Fergus, striking the boy upon the head with the heavy pistol butt with his whole force,—"take that for acting without orders, and lying to disguise it." Callum received the blow without appearing to flinch from it, and fell without sign of life. "Stand still, upon your lives," said Fergus to the rest of the clan; "I blow out the brains of the first man who interferes between Mr Waverley and me." They stood motionless; Evan Dhu alone shewed symptoms of vexation and anxiety. Callum lay on the ground bleeding copiously, but no one ventured to give him any assistance. It seemed as if he had gotten his death-blow.

"And now for you, Mr Waverley; please to turn your horse twenty yards with me upon the common." Waverley complied; and Fergus, confronting him when they were a little way from the line of march, said, with great affected coolness, "I could not but wonder, sir, at the fickleness of taste which you were pleased to express the other day. But it was not an angel, as you justly observed, who had charms for you, unless she brought an empire for her fortune. I have now an excellent commentary upon that obscure text."

"I am at a loss even to guess at your meaning, Colonel Mac-Ivor, unless that it seems plain you intend to fasten a quarrel upon me."

"Your affected ignorance shall not save you, sir. The Prince,—the Prince himself has acquainted me with your manœuvres. I little thought that your engagements with Miss Bradwardine were the reason of your breaking off your intended match with my sister. I suppose the information that the Baron had altered the destination of his estate, was quite a sufficient reason for slighting your friend's sister, and carrying off your friend's mistress."

"Did the Prince tell you I was engaged to Miss Bradwardine?— Impossible."

"He did, sir; so, either draw and defend yourself, or resign your pretensions to the lady."

"This is absolute madness," exclaimed Waverley, "or some strange mistake!"

"O! no evasion! draw your sword," said the infuriated Chieftain,— his own was already unsheathed.

"Must I fight in a madman's quarrel?"

"Then give up now, and for ever, all pretensions to Miss Bradwardine's hand."

"What title have you," cried Waverley, utterly losing command of himself, "what title have you, or any man living, to dictate such terms to me?" And he also drew his sword.

At this moment, the Baron of Bradwardine, followed by several of his troop, came up upon the spur, some from curiosity, others to take part in the quarrel, which they indistinctly understood had broken out between the Mac-Ivors and their corps. The clan, seeing them approach, put themselves in motion to support their Chieftain, and a scene of confusion commenced which seemed likely to terminate in bloodshed. A hundred tongues were in motion at once. The Baron lectured, the Chieftain stormed, the Highlanders screamed in Gaelic, the horsemen cursed and swore in Lowland Scotch. At length matters came to such a pass, that the Baron threatened to charge the Mac-Ivors unless they resumed their ranks, and many of them, in return, presented their fire-arms at him and the other troopers. The confusion was privately fostered by old Ballenkeiroch, who made no doubt that his own day of vengeance was arrived. When, behold! a cry arose of "Room! Make way! *gare! gare! place à Monseigneur! place à Monseigneur!*" This announced the approach of the Prince, who came up with a party of Fitz-James's foreign dragoons that acted as his body guard. His arrival produced some degree of order. The Highlanders reassumed their ranks, the cavalry fell in and formed squadron, and the Baron and Chieftain were silent.

The Prince called them and Waverley before him. Having heard the original cause of the quarrel through the villainy of Callum Beg, he ordered him into custody of the provost-marshal for immediate execution, in the event of his surviving the chastisement inflicted by his Chieftain. Fergus, however, in a tone betwixt claiming a right and asking a favour, requested he might be left at his disposal, and promised his punishment should be exemplary. To deny this might have seemed to encroach on the patriarchal authority of the Chieftains, of which they were very jealous, and they were not persons to be disobliged. Callum was therefore left to the justice of his own tribe.

The Prince next demanded to know the new cause of quarrel between Colonel Mac-Ivor and Waverley. There was a pause. Both gentlemen found the presence of the Baron of Bradwardine (for by this time all three had approached the Chevalier by his command) an insurmountable barrier against entering upon a subject where the name of his daughter must unavoidably be mentioned. They turned their eyes on the ground, with looks in which shame and embarrassment were mingled with displeasure. The Prince, who had been educated among the discontented and mutinous spirits of the court of St Germains, where feuds of every kind were the daily subject of solicitude to the dethroned sovereign, had served his apprenticeship, as old Frederick of Prussia would have said, to the trade of royalty. To promote or restore concord amongst his followers was indispensable. Accordingly he took his measures.

"Monsieur de Beaujeu!"

"Monseigneur!" said a young handsome French cavalry officer, who was in attendance.

"Ayez la bonté d'alligner ces montagnards là, ainsi que la cavalerie, s'il vous plait, et de les remettre à la marche. Vous parlez si bien l'Anglois, cela ne vous donneroit pas beaucoup de peine."

"Ah! pas de tout, Monseigneur," replied Mons. le Compte de Beaujeu, his head bending down to the neck of his little dancing, prancing, highly-managed charger. Accordingly he *piaffed* away in high spirits and confidence to the head of Fergus's regiment, although understanding not a word of Gaelic, and very little English.

"Messieurs les sauvages Ecossois—dat is—gentilmans savages— have de goodness d'arranger vous."

The clan comprehending the order more from the gesture than the words, and seeing the Prince himself present, hastened to dress their ranks.

"Ah! ver well! dat is fort bien!" said the Count de Beaujeu. "Gentil- mans sauvages—mais, très bien—Eh bien!—Qu'est ce que vous appellez visage, Monsieur?" (to a lounging trooper who stood by him) "Ah, oui! *face*—Je vous remercie, Monsieur.—Gentilshommes, have de goodness to make de face to de right par files, dat is, by file. Marsh! —Mais, très bien—encore, Messieurs; il faut vous mettre à la marche —Marchez donc, au nom de Dieu, parceque j'ai oublié le mot Anglois—mais vous êtes des braves gens, et me comprenez très bien."

The Count then hastened to put the cavalry in motion. "Gentilmens cavalrie, you must fall in—Ah! par ma foi, I did not say fall off! I am a fear de littel gros fat gentilmans is mush hurt. Ah, mon dieu! c'est le commissaire qui nous a apporté les premières nouvelles de ce maudit fracas. Je suis trop faché, Monsieur!"

But poor Macwheeble, who, with a sword stuck across him, and a white cockade as large as a pan-cake, now figured in the character of commissary, being overturned in the bustle occasioned by the troopers hastening to get themselves in order in the Prince's presence, before he could rally his galloway, slunk to the rear amid the unrestrained laughter of the spectators.

"Eh bien, Messieurs, wheel to de right by trees—dat is it! Et Mon- sieur de Bradwardine, ayez la bonté de vous mettre à la tête de votre régiment, car, par dieu, je n'en puis plus."

The Baron of Bradwardine was obliged to go to the assistance of Monsieur de Beaujeu, after he had fairly expended his few English military phrases. One purpose of the Chevalier was thus answered.

The other he proposed was, that in the eagerness to hear and comprehend commands issued through such an indistinct medium in his own presence, the thoughts of the soldiers in both corps might get a current different from the angry channel in which they were flowing at the time.

Charles Edward was no sooner left with the Chieftain and Waverley, the rest of his attendants being at some distance, than he said, "If I owed less to your disinterested friendship, I could be most seriously angry with both of you for this very extraordinary and causeless broil, at a moment when my father's service so decidedly demands the most perfect unanimity. But the worst of my situation is, that my very best friends think themselves at liberty to ruin themselves, as well as the cause they are engaged in, upon the slightest caprice."

Both the young men protested their resolution to submit every difference to his arbitration. "Indeed," said Edward, "I hardly know of what I am accused. I sought Colonel Mac-Ivor merely to mention to him that I had nearly escaped assassination at the hand of his immediate dependant, a dastardly revenge of which I knew him to be incapable. As to the cause for which he was disposed to fasten a quarrel upon me, I am so ignorant of it that I only know he accuses me most unjustly of having engaged the affections of a young lady in prejudice of his pretensions."

"If there is an error," said the Chieftain, "it arises from a conversation which I held this morning with his Royal Highness himself."

"With me?" said the Chevalier; "is it possible Colonel Mac-Ivor can have so far misunderstood me?"

He then led Fergus aside, and after five minutes earnest conversation, spurred his horse towards Edward. "Is it possible—nay, ride up, Colonel, for I desire no secrets—Is it possible, Mr Waverley, that I am mistaken in supposing that you are an accepted lover of Miss Bradwardine? a fact of which I was by circumstances, though not by communication from you, so absolutely convinced, that I alleged it to Vich Ian Vohr this morning as a reason why, without offence to him, you might not continue to be ambitious of an alliance, which to an unengaged person, even though once repulsed, holds out too many charms to be lightly laid aside."

"Your Royal Highness," said Waverley, "must have founded on circumstances altogether unknown to me, when you did me the distinguished honour of supposing me an accepted lover of Miss Bradwardine. I feel the distinction implied in the supposition, but I have no title to it. For the rest, my confidence in my own merit is too justly slight to admit of my hoping for better success in any quarter after positive rejection."

The Chevalier was silent for a moment, looking steadily at them both, and then said, "Upon my word, Mr Waverley, you are a less happy man than I conceived I had very good reason to think you. But now, gentlemen, allow me to be umpire in this matter, not as Prince Regent, but as Charles Stuart, a brother adventurer with you in the same gallant cause. Lay my pretensions entirely out of view, and consider your own honour, and how far it is well, or becoming, to give our enemies the advantage, and our friends the scandal, of shewing that, few as we are, we are not united. And forgive me if I add, that the names of the ladies who have been mentioned, crave more respect from us all than to be made themes of discord."

He took Fergus a little apart, and spoke to him very earnestly for two or three minutes, and then returning to Waverley, said, "I believe I have satisfied Colonel Mac-Ivor, that his resentment was founded upon a misconception, to which, indeed, I myself gave rise, and I trust Mr Waverley is too generous to harbour any recollection of what is passed, when I assure him such is the case.—You must state this matter properly to your clan, Vich Ian Vohr, to prevent a recurrence of their precipitate violence." Fergus bowed. "And now, gentlemen, let me have the pleasure to see you shake hands."

They advanced coldly, and with measured steps, each apparently reluctant to appear most forward in concession. They did, however, shake hands, and parted, taking a respectful leave of the Chevalier.

Charles Edward then rode to the head of the Mac-Ivors, threw himself from his horse, begged a drink out of old Ballenkeiroch's cantine, and marched about half a mile along with them, enquiring into the history and connections of Sliochd nan Ivor, adroitly using the few words of Gaelic he possessed, and affecting a great desire to learn it more thoroughly. He then mounted his horse once more, and galloped to the Baron's cavalry, which was in front, halted them, and examined their accoutrements and state of discipline; took notice of the principal gentlemen, and even of the cadets; enquired after their ladies, and commended their horses; rode about an hour with the Baron of Bradwardine; and endured three long stories about Field-Marshal the Duke of Berwick.

"Beaujeu, mon cher ami," said he as he returned to his usual place in the line of march, "que mon métier de prince-errant est ennuyant, par fois. Mais, courage! c'est le grand jeu après tout."

Chapter Twelve

A SKIRMISH

THE READER need hardly be reminded, that, after a council of war held at Derby upon the 5th of December, the Highlanders relinquished their desperate attempt to penetrate farther into England, and, greatly to the distress of their young and daring leader, positively determined to return northward. They commenced their retreat accordingly, and, by their extreme celerity of movement, outstripped the motions of the Duke of Cumberland, who now pursued them with a very large body of cavalry.

This retreat was a virtual resignation of their towering hopes. None had been so sanguine as Fergus Mac-Ivor, none, consequently, was so cruelly mortified at this change of measures. He argued, or rather remonstrated, with the utmost vehemence at the council of war; and, when his opinion was rejected, shed tears of grief and indignation. From that moment his whole manner was so much altered, that he could scarcely have been recognised for the same soaring and ardent spirit, for whom the earth seemed too narrow but a week before. The retreat had continued for several days, when Edward, to his surprise, early upon the 18th of December, received a visit from the Chieftain in his quarters in a hamlet, about half way between Shap and Penrith.

Having had no intercourse with the Chieftain since their rupture, Edward waited with some anxiety an explanation of this unexpected visit; nor could he help being surprised, and somewhat shocked, with the change in his appearance. His eye had lost much of its fire; his cheek was hollow, his voice was languid, even his gait seemed less firm and elastic than it was wont; and his dress, to which he used to be particularly attentive, was now carelessly flung about him. He invited Edward to walk out with him by a little river in the vicinity; and smiled in a melancholy manner when he observed him take down and buckle on his sword. As soon as they were in a wild sequestered path by the side of the stream, "Our fine adventure is now totally ruined, Waverley, and I wish to know what you intend to do:—nay, never stare at me, man. I tell you I received a packet from my sister yesterday, and, had I got the information it contains sooner, it would have prevented a quarrel, which I am always vexed when I think of. In a letter written after our dispute, I acquainted her with the cause of it, and she now replies to me, that she never had, nor could have, any purpose of giving you encouragement; so that it seems I have acted like a madman—poor Flora—she writes in high spirits; what a change will the news of this unhappy retreat make in her state of mind!"

Waverley, who was really much affected by the deep tone of melancholy with which Fergus spoke, affectionately entreated him to banish from his remembrance any unkindness which had arisen between them, and they once more shook hands, but now with sincere cordiality. Fergus again enquired of Waverley what he intended to do. "Had you not better leave this luckless army, and get down before us to Scotland, and embark for the continent from some of the eastern ports that are still in our possession? When you are out of the kingdom, your friends will easily negociate your pardon; and, to tell you the truth, I wish you would carry Rose Bradwardine with you as your wife, and take Flora also under your joint protection."—Edward stared—"She loves you, and I believe you love her, though, perhaps, you have not found it out, for you are not celebrated you know for knowing your own mind very pointedly." He said this with a sort of smile.

"How," answered Edward, "can you advise me to desert the expedition in which we are all embarked?"

"Embarked? the vessel is going to pieces, and it is full time for all who can to get into the long-boat and leave her."

"Why, what will other gentlemen do, and why did the Highland Chiefs consent to this retreat, if it is so ruinous?"

"O, they think that, as on former occasions, the heading, hanging, and forfeiting, will chiefly fall to the lot of the Lowland gentry; that they will be left secure in their poverty and in their fastnesses, there, according to their proverb, 'to listen to the wind upon the hill till the waters abate.' But they will be disappointed; they have been too often troublesome to be repeatedly passed over, and this time John Bull has been too heartily frightened to recover his good humour for some time. The Hanoverian ministers always deserved to be hanged for rascals, but now, if they get the power in their hands,—as soon or late they must, since there is neither rising in England nor assistance from France,—they will deserve the gallows as fools if they leave a single clan in the Highlands in a situation to be again troublesome to government. Ay, they will make root and branch work, I warrant them."

"And while you recommend flight to me, a counsel which I will rather die than embrace, what are your own views?"

"O, my fate is settled. Dead or captive I must be before to-morrow."

"What do you mean by that? The enemy is still a day's march in our rear, and if he comes up, we are still strong enough to keep him in check. Remember Gladsmuir."

"What I tell you is true notwithstanding, so far as I am individually concerned."

"Upon what authority can you found so melancholy a prediction?"

"On one which never failed a person of my house—I have seen," he said, lowering his voice, "the Bodach glas."

"Bodach glas?"

"Yes: Have you been so long at Glennaquoich, and never heard of the grey spectre? though indeed there is a certain reluctance among us to mention him."

"No, never."

"Ah! it would have been a tale for poor Flora to have told you. Or if that hill were Benmore, and that long blue lake, which you see just winding towards yon mountainous country, were Loch Tay, or my own Loch an Ri, the tale would be better suited with scenery. However, let us sit down on this knoll; even Saddleback and Ulswater will suit what I have to say better than the English hedgerows, inclosures, and farm-houses. You must know, then, that when my ancestor, Ian nan Chaistel, wasted Northumberland, there was associated with him in the expedition a sort of southland chief, or captain of a band of Lowlanders, called Halbert Hall. In their return through the Cheviots, they quarrelled about the division of the great booty they had acquired, and came from words to blows. The Lowlanders were cut off to a man, and their chief fell the last, covered with wounds, by the sword of my ancestor. Since that time, his spirit has crossed the path of the Vich Ian Vohr of the day when any great disaster was impending, but especially before approaching death. My father saw him twice; once before he was made prisoner at Sherriff-Muir; another time on the morning of the day on which he died."

"How can you, my dear Fergus, tell such nonsense with a grave face?"

"I do not ask you to believe it; but I tell you the truth, ascertained by three hundred years' experience at least, and last night by my own eyes."

"The particulars, for heaven's sake."

"I will, on condition you will not attempt a jest upon the subject.— Since this unhappy retreat commenced, I have scarce ever been able to sleep for thinking of my clan, and Flora, and this poor Prince, whom they are leading back like a dog in a string, whether he will or no, and the downfall of my family. Last night I felt so feverish that I left my quarters, and walked out, in hopes the keen frost air would brace my nerves—I cannot tell how much I dislike going on, for I know you will hardly believe me. However—I crossed a small foot-bridge, and kept walking back and forwards, when I observed with surprise, by the clear moonlight, a tall figure in a grey plaid, such as shepherds wear in the south of Scotland, which, move at what pace I would, kept regularly about four yards before me."

"You saw a Cumberland peasant in his ordinary dress, probably."

"No: I thought so at first, and was astonished at the man's audacity in daring to dog me. I called to him, but received no answer. I felt an anxious throbbing at my heart, and to ascertain what I dreaded, I stood still and turned myself on the same spot successively to the four points of the compass—By Heaven, Edward, turn where I would, the figure was instantly before my eyes, at precisely the same distance! I was then convinced it was the Bodach glas. My hair bristled, and my knees shook—I manned myself, however, and determined to return to my quarters—My ghastly visitant glided before me, (for I could not say he walked,) until he reached the foot-bridge: there he stopped, and turned full round. I must either wade the river, or pass him as close as I am to you. A desperate courage, founded on the belief that my death was near, made me resolve to make my way in despite of him. I made the sign of the cross, drew my sword, and uttered, 'In the name of God, Evil Spirit, give place!' 'Vich Ian Vohr,' it said, in a voice that made my very blood curdle, 'beware of to-morrow!' It seemed at that moment not half a yard from my sword's point; but the words were no sooner spoken than it was gone, and nothing appeared further to obstruct my passage. I got home, and threw myself on my bed, where I spent a few hours heavily enough; and this morning, as no enemy was reported to be near us, I took my horse, and rode forward to make up matters with you. I would not willingly fall, until I am in charity with a wronged friend."

Edward had little doubt that this phantom was the operation of an exhausted frame, and depressed spirits, working upon the belief common to all Highlanders in such superstitions. He did not the less pity Fergus, for whom, in his present distress, he felt all his former regard revive. With the view of diverting his mind from these gloomy images, he offered, with the Baron's permission, which he knew he could readily obtain, to remain in his quarters till Fergus's corps should come up, and march with them as usual. The Chief seemed much pleased, yet hesitated to accept the offer. "We are, you know, in the rear—the post of danger in a retreat."

"And therefore the post of honour."

"Well—let Alick have your horse in readiness, in case we should be over-matched, and I shall be delighted to have your company once more."

The rear-guard were late in making their appearance, having been delayed by various accidents, and by the badness of the roads. At length they entered the hamlet. When Waverley joined the clan Mac-Ivor, arm-in-arm with their Chieftain, all the resentment they had entertained against him seemed blown off at once. Evan Dhu received him with a grin of congratulation; and even Callum, who was running about as active as ever, pale indeed, and with a great patch upon his head, appeared delighted to see him.

"That gallows-bird's skull," said Fergus, "must be harder than marble: the lock of the pistol was actually broken."

"How could you strike so young a lad so hard?"

"Why, if I did not strike hard sometimes, the rascals would forget themselves."

They were now in full march, every caution being taken to prevent surprise. Fergus's people, and a fine clan-regiment from Badenoch, commanded by Cluny Mac-Pherson, had the rear. They had passed a large open moor, and were entering into the inclosures which surround a small village called Clifton. The winter sun had set, and Edward began to rally Fergus upon the false predictions of the Grey Spirit. "The ides of March are not past," said Mac-Ivor, with a smile; when, suddenly casting his eyes back on the moor, a large body of cavalry was indistinctly seen to hover upon its brown and dark surface. To line the inclosures facing the open ground, and the road by which the enemy must move from it upon the village, was the work of a short time. While these manœuvres were accomplishing, night sunk down, dark and gloomy, though the moon was at full. Sometimes, however, she gleamed forth a dubious light upon the scene of action.

The Highlanders did not long remain undisturbed in the defensive position they had adopted. Favoured by the night, one large body of dismounted dragoons attempted to force the inclosures, while another, equally strong, strove to penetrate by the high-road. Both were received by such a heavy fire as disconcerted their ranks, and effectually checked their progress. Unsatisfied with the advantage thus gained, Fergus, to whose ardent spirit the approach of danger seemed to restore all its elasticity, drawing his sword, and calling out "Claymore!" encouraged his clan, by voice and example, to rush down upon the enemy. Mingling with the dismounted dragoons, they forced them at the sword-point to fly to the open moor, where a considerable number were cut to pieces. But the moon, which suddenly shone out, shewed to the English the small number of assailants, disordered by their own success. Two squadrons of horse moving to the support of their companions, the Highlanders endeavoured to recover the inclosures. But several of them, amongst others their brave Chieftain, were cut off and surrounded before they could effect their purpose. Waverley, looking eagerly for Fergus, from whom, as well as from the retreating body of his followers, he had been separated in the darkness and tumult, saw him with Evan Dhu and Callum defending themselves desperately against a dozen of horsemen, who were hewing at them with their long broad-swords. The moon was at that moment again totally overclouded, and Edward, in the obscurity, could neither bring aid to his friends, nor discover which way lay his own road to rejoin the rear-guard. After once or twice narrowly escaping being slain or made prisoner by parties of the cavalry whom he encountered in the darkness, he at length reached an inclosure, and, clambering over it, concluded himself in safety, and on the way to the Highland forces, whose pipes he heard at some distance. For Fergus hardly a hope remained, unless that he might be made prisoner. Revolving his fate with sorrow and anxiety, the superstition of the Bodach glas recurred to Edward's recollection, and he said to himself, with internal surprise, "What, can the devil speak truth?"

Chapter Thirteen

A CHAPTER OF ACCIDENTS

EDWARD was in a most unpleasant and dangerous situation. He soon lost the sound of the bagpipes; and what was yet more unpleasant, when, after searching long in vain, and scrambling through many enclosures, he at length approached the high road, he learned, from the unwelcome noise of kettle-drums and trumpets, that the English cavalry now occupied it, and consequently were between him and the Highlanders. Precluded, therefore, from advancing in a straight direction, he resolved to avoid the English military, and endeavour to join his friends, by making a circuit to the left, for which a beaten path, deviating from the main road in that direction, seemed to afford facilities. The path was muddy, and the night dark and cold; but even these inconveniences were hardly felt among the apprehensions which falling into the hands of the King's forces reasonably excited in his bosom.

After walking about three miles, he at length reached a hamlet. Conscious that the common people were in general unfavourable to the cause he had espoused, yet anxious, if possible, to procure a horse and guide to Penrith, where he hoped to find the rear, if not the main body of the Chevalier's army, he approached the ale-house of the place. There was a great noise within: he paused to listen. A round English oath or two, and the burden of a campaign song, convinced him the hamlet also was occupied by the Duke of Cumberland's soldiers. Endeavouring to retire from it as softly as possible, and blessing the obscurity which he had hitherto murmured against, Waverley groped his way the best he could along a small paling, which seemed the boundary of some cottage garden. As he reached the gate of this little enclosure, his outstretched hand was grasped by that of a female, whose voice at the same time uttered, "Edward, is't thou, man?"

"Here is some cursed mistake," thought Edward, struggling, but gently, to disengage himself.

"Nean o' thy foun, noo, man, or the redcoats will hear thee; they hae been houlerying and poulerying every ane that past eal-house-door this neight to make them drive their waggons and sick loike. Come into feyther's, or they'll do ho a mischief."

"A good hint," thought Edward, following the girl through the little garden into a brick-paved kitchen, where she set herself to kindle a match at an expiring fire, and with the match to light a candle. She had no sooner looked on Edward, than she dropped the light, with a shrill scream of, "O feyther, feyther!"

The father, thus invoked, speedily appeared—a sturdy old farmer, in a pair of leathern breeches, and boots pulled on without stockings, having just started from his bed; the rest of his dress was only a Westmoreland statesman's robe-de-chambre, that is, his shirt. His figure was displayed to advantage, by a candle which he bore in his left hand; in his right he brandished a poker.

"What hast got here, wench?"

"Oh!" cried the poor girl, almost going off in hysterics, "I thought it was Ned Williams, and it's one of the plaid-men."

"And what was thee ganging to do wi' Ned Williams at this toime o' neet?" To this, which was, perhaps, one of the numerous class of questions more easily asked than answered, the rosy-cheeked damsel made no reply, but continued sobbing and wringing her hands.

"And thee, lad, doest ho know that the dragoons be a town? doest know that, mon? ad they'll sliver thee loike a turnip, mon."

"I know my life is in great danger," said Waverley, "but if you can assist me, I will reward you handsomely. I am no Scotchman, but an unfortunate English gentleman."

"Be ho Scot or no," said the honest farmer, "I wish thou hadst kept the other side of the hallan; but, since thou art here, Jacob Jopson will betray no man's bluid—and the plaids were gay canny, and did not do so much mischief when they were here yesterday."

Accordingly, he set seriously about sheltering and refreshing our hero for the night. The fire was speedily rekindled, but with precaution against its light being seen from without. The jolly yeoman cut a rasher of bacon, which Cicely soon broiled, and her father added a swingeing tankard of his best ale. It was settled that Edward should remain till the troops marched in the morning, then buy a horse from the farmer, and, with the best directions that could be obtained, endeavour to overtake his friends. A clean, though coarse bed, received him after the fatigues of this unhappy day.

With the morning arrived the news that the Highlanders had evacuated Penrith, and marched off towards Carlisle; that the Duke of Cumberland was in possession of Penrith, and that detachments of his army covered the roads in every direction. To attempt to get through undiscovered would be an act of the most frantic temerity. Ned Williams (the right Edward) was now called to council by Cicely and her father. Ned, who perhaps did not care that his handsome namesake should remain too long in the same house with his sweetheart for fear of fresh mistakes, proposed that Edward, exchanging his uniform and plaid for the dress of the country, should go with him to his father's farm near Ulswater, and remain in that undisturbed retirement until the military movements in the country should have ceased to render his departure hazardous. A price was also agreed upon, at which the stranger might board with Farmer Williams, if he thought proper, till he could depart with safety. It was of moderate amount, the distress of his situation, among this honest and simple-hearted race, being considered as no reason for increasing their demand on this account.

The necessary articles of dress were accordingly procured, and, by following bye-paths, known to the young farmer, they hoped to escape any unpleasant rencontre. A recompence of their hospitality was refused peremptorily by old Jopson and his cherry-cheeked daughter; a kiss paid the one, and a hearty shake of the hand the other. Both seemed anxious for their guest's safety, and took leave of him with kind wishes.

In the course of their route, Edward, with his guide, traversed those fields which the night before had been the scene of action. A brief gleam of December's sun shone sadly on the broad heath, which, towards the spot where the great north-west road entered the inclosures of Lord Lonsdale's property, exhibited dead bodies of men and horses, and the usual companions of war, a number of carrion crows, hawks, and ravens.

"And this, then, was thy last field," thought Waverley, his eyes filling at the recollection of the many splendid points of Fergus's character, and of their former intimacy, all his passions and imperfections forgotten—"here fell the last Vich Ian Vohr, on a nameless heath; and in an obscure night-skirmish was quenched that ardent spirit, who thought it little to cut a way for his master to the British throne! Ambition, policy, bravery, all far beyond their sphere, here learned the fate of mortals. The sole support, too, of a sister, whose spirit, as proud and unbending, was even more exalted than thine own; here ended all thy hopes for Flora, and the long and valued line which it was thy boast to raise yet more highly by thy adventurous valour."

As these ideas pressed on Waverley's mind, he resolved to go upon the open heath, and search if, among the slain, he could discover the body of his friend, with the pious intention of securing the last rites of sepulture. The timorous young man who accompanied him remonstrated upon the danger of the attempt, but Edward was determined. The followers of the camp had already stripped the dead of all they could carry away; but the country-people, unused to scenes of blood, had not yet approached the field of action, though some stood fearfully gazing at a distance. About sixty or seventy dragoons lay slain within the first inclosure, upon the high-road, and upon the open moor. Of the Highlanders, not above a dozen had fallen, chiefly those who, venturing too far on the moor, could not regain the strong ground. He could not find the body of Fergus among the slain. In a little knot, separated from the others, lay the carcases of three English dragoons, two horses, and the page Callum Beg, whose hard skull a trooper's broadsword had at length effectually cloven. It was possible his clan had carried off the body, but it was also possible Fergus had escaped, especially as Evan Dhu, who would never leave his Chief, was not found among the dead. Or Fergus might be prisoner, and the less formidable denunciation inferred from the appearance of the Bodach glas might have proved the true one. The approach of a party, sent for the purpose of compelling the country-people to bury the dead, and who had already assembled several peasants for that purpose, now compelled Edward to rejoin his guide, who awaited him in great anxiety and fear under shade of the plantations.

After leaving this field of death, the rest of their journey was happily accomplished. At the house of Farmer Williams, Edward passed for a young kinsman, bred to be a clergyman, who was come to reside there till the civil tumults permitted him to pass through the country. This silenced suspicion among the kind and simple yeomanry of Cumberland, and accounted sufficiently for the grave manners and retired habits of their new guest. The precaution became more necessary than Waverley had anticipated, as a variety of incidents prolonged his stay at Fasthwaite, as the farm was called.

A tremendous fall of snow rendered his departure impossible for more than ten days. When the roads began to become a little practicable, they successively received news of the retreat of the Chevalier into Scotland; then, that he had abandoned the frontiers, retiring upon Glasgow; and that the Duke of Cumberland had formed the siege of Carlisle. His army, therefore, barred all possibility of Waverley's escaping into Scotland in that direction. On the eastern border, Marshal Wade, with a large force, was advancing upon Edinburgh, and all along the frontier, parties of militia, volunteers, and partizans, were in arms to suppress insurrection, and apprehend such stragglers from the Highland army as had been left in England. The surrender of Carlisle, and the severity with which the rebel garrison were threatened, soon formed an additional reason against venturing upon a solitary and hopeless journey through a hostile country and a large army, to carry the assistance of a single sword to a cause which seemed altogether desperate.

In this solitary and secluded situation, without the advantage of company or conversation with men of cultivated minds, the arguments of Colonel Talbot often recurred to the mind of our hero. A still more anxious recollection haunted his slumbers—it was the dying look and gesture of Colonel G——. Most devoutly did he hope, as the rarely-occurring post brought news of skirmishes with various success, that it might never again be his lot to draw his sword in civil conflict. Then his mind turned to the supposed death of Fergus, to the desolate situation of Flora, and, with yet more tender recollection, to that of Rose Bradwardine, who was destitute of the devoted enthusiasm of loyalty, which, to her friend, hallowed and exalted misfortune. These reveries he was permitted to enjoy, undisturbed by queries or interruption; and it was in many a winter walk by the shores of Ulswater, that he acquired a more complete mastery of a spirit tamed by adversity, than his former experience had given him; and that he felt himself entitled to say firmly, though perhaps with a sigh, that the romance of his life was ended, and that its real history had now commenced. He was soon called upon to justify his pretensions to reason and philosophy.

Chapter Fourteen

A JOURNEY TO LONDON

THE FAMILY at Fasthwaite were soon attached to Edward. He had, indeed, that gentleness and urbanity which almost universally attracts corresponding kindness, and to their simple ideas his learning gave him consequence, and his sorrows interest. The last he ascribed, evasively, to the loss of a brother in the skirmish near Clifton; and in that primitive state of society, where the ties of affection were highly prized, his continued depression excited sympathy, but not surprise.

In the end of January, his more lively powers were called out by the happy union of Edward Williams, the son of his host, with Miss Cicely Jopson. Our hero could not cloud with sorrow the festivity attending the wedding of two persons to whom he was so highly obliged. He therefore exerted himself, danced, sung, played at the various rural games of the day, and was the blithest of the company. The next morning, however, he had more serious matters to think of.

The clergyman who had married the young couple was so much pleased with the supposed student of divinity, that he came next day from Penrith on purpose to pay him a visit. This might have been a puzzling chapter had he entered into any examination of our hero's supposed theological studies; but fortunately he loved better to hear and communicate the news of the day. He brought with him two or three old newspapers, in one of which Edward found a piece of intelligence that soon rendered him deaf to every word which the Reverend Mr Twigtythe was saying upon the news from the north, and the prospect of the Duke's speedily overtaking and crushing the rebels. This was an article in these, or nearly these words:

"Died at his house, in Hill-Street, Berkeley-Square, upon the 10th inst., Richard Waverley, Esq., second son to Sir Giles Waverley of Waverley-Honour, &c. &c. He died of a lingering disorder, augmented by the unpleasant predicament of suspicion in which he stood, having been obliged to find bail, to a high amount, to meet an impending accusation of high treason. An accusation of the same grave crime hangs over his elder brother, Sir Everard Waverley, the representative of that ancient family; and we understand the day of his trial will be fixed early in the next month, unless Edward Waverley, son of the deceased Richard, and heir to the Baronet, shall surrender himself to justice. In that case, we are assured it is his Majesty's gracious purpose to drop further proceedings upon the charge against Sir Everard. This unfortunate young gentleman is ascertained to have been in arms in the Pretender's service, and to have marched along with the Highland troops into England. But he has not been heard of since the skirmish at Clifton upon 18th December last."

Such was this distracting paragraph.—"Good God! am I then a parricide?—Impossible! my father, who never shewed me the affection of a father while he lived, cannot have been so much affected by my supposed death as to hasten his own—no, I will not believe it,—it were distraction to entertain for a moment such a horrible idea. But it were, if possible, worse than parricide to suffer any danger to hang over my noble and generous uncle, who has ever been more to me than a father, if such evil can be averted by any sacrifice on my part!"

While these reflections passed like the sting of scorpions through Waverley's sensorium, the worthy divine was startled in a long disquisition on the battle of Falkirk by the ghastliness which they communicated to his looks, and asked him if he was ill. Fortunately the bride, all smirk and blush, had just entered the room. Mrs Williams was none of the brightest of women, but she was good-natured, and readily concluding that Edward had been shocked by disagreeable news in the papers, interfered so judiciously, that, without exciting suspicion, she drew off Mr Twigtythe's attention, and engaged it until he soon after took his leave. Waverley immediately explained to his friends that he was under the necessity of going to London with as little delay as possible.

One cause of delay, however, did occur, to which Waverley had been very little accustomed. His purse, though well stocked when he first went to Tully-Veolan, had not been reinforced since that period; and although his life since had not been of a nature to exhaust it hastily, for he had lived chiefly with his friends or with the army, yet he found, that after settling with his kind landlord, he would be too poor to encounter the expence of travelling post. The best course, therefore, seemed to be to get into the great north road about Boroughbridge, and there take a place in the Northern Diligence, a huge old-fashioned tub, drawn by three horses, which completed the journey from Edinburgh to London (God willing, as the advertisements expressed it) in three weeks. Our hero, therefore, took an affectionate farewell of his Cumberland friends, whose kindness he promised never to forget, and tacitly hoped one day to acknowledge, by substantial proofs of gratitude. After some petty difficulties and vexatious delays, and after putting his dress into a shape better befitting his rank, though perfectly plain and simple, he accomplished crossing the country, and found himself in the desired vehicle *vis-à-vis* to Mrs Nosebag, the lady of Lieutenant Nosebag, adjutant and riding-master of the —— dragoons, a jolly woman of about fifty, wearing a blue habit, faced with scarlet, and grasping a silver-mounted horse-whip.

This lady was one of those active members of society who take upon them *faire les frais de la conversation*. She was just returned from the north, and informed Edward how nearly her regiment had cut the petticoat people into ribbands at Falkirk, "only somehow there was one of those nasty awkward marshes that they are never without in Scotland, I think, and so our poor dear little regiment suffered something, as my Nosebag says, in that unsatisfactory affair. You, sir, have served in the dragoons?" Waverley was taken so much at unawares, that he acquiesced.

"O, I knew it at once; I saw you were military from your air, and I was sure you could be none of the foot-wobblers, as my Nosebag calls them. What regiment, pray?" Here was a delightful question. Waverley, however, justly concluded this good lady had the whole army-list by heart; and, to avoid detection by adhering to truth, answered, "G——'s dragoons, ma'am; but I have retired some time."

"O, those as won the race at the battle of Preston, as my Nosebag says. Pray, sir, were you there?"

"I was so unfortunate, madam, as to witness that engagement."

"And that was a misfortune that few of G——'s staid to witness, I believe, sir—ha! ha! ha! I beg your pardon; but a soldier's wife loves a joke."

"Devil confound you," thought Waverley; "what infernal luck has penned me up with this inquisitive hag!"

Fortunately the good lady did not stick long to one subject. "We are coming to Ferrybridge, now," she said, "where there was a party of *ours* left to support the beadles, and constables, and justices, and these sort of creatures that are examining passes and stopping rebels, and all that." They were hardly in the inn before she dragged Waverley to the window, exclaiming, "Yonder comes Corporal Bridoon, of our poor dear troop; he's coming with the constable man; he's one of my lambs, as Nosebag calls 'em. Come, Mr a—a—a,—pray what's your name, sir?"

"Butler, madam," said Waverley, resolved rather to make free with the name of a former fellow-officer, than run the risk of detection by inventing one not to be found in the regiment.

"O, you got a troop lately, when that shabby fellow, Waverley, went over to the rebels—Lord, I wish our old cross Captain Crump would go over to the rebels, that Nosebag might get the troop.—Lord, what can Bridoon be standing swinging upon the bridge for? I'll be hanged if he a'nt hazy, as Nosebag says—Come, sir, as you and I belong to the service, we'll go put the rascal in mind of his duty."

Waverley, with feelings more easily conceived than described, saw himself obliged to follow this doughty female commander. The gallant corporal was as like a lamb as a drunk corporal of dragoons, about six feet high, with very broad shoulders, and very thin legs, not to mention a great scar across his nose, could well be. Mrs Nosebag addressed him with something which, if not an oath, sounded very like one, and commanded him to attend to his duty. "You be d—d for a ——," commenced the gallant cavalier; but looking up in order to suit the action to the words, and also to enforce the epithet which he meditated, with an adjective applicable to the party, he recognised the speaker, made his military salam, and altered his tone.—"Lord love

your handsome face, Madam Nosebag, is it you? Why, if a poor fellow
does happen to fire a slug of a morning, I am sure you were never the
lady to bring him to harm."

"Well, you rapscallion, go mind your duty; this gentleman and I
belong to the service; but be sure you look after that shy cock in the
slouched hat that sits in the corner of the coach. I believe he's one of
the rebels in disguise."

"D—n her gooseberry wig," said the corporal, when she was out of
hearing, "that gimlet-eyed jade, mother-adjutant, as we call her, is a
greater plague to the regiment than provost-marshal, serjeant-major,
and old Hubble-de-Shuff, the colonel, into the bargain. Come, Master Constable, let's see if this shy cock, as she calls him, (who, by the
way, was a Quaker, from Leeds, with whom Mrs Nosebag had had
some tart argument on the legality of bearing arms,) will stand godfather to a nip of brandy, for your Yorkshire ale is cold on my stomach."

The vivacity of this good lady, as it helped Edward out of this
scrape, was like to have drawn him into one or two others. In every
town where they stopped, she wished to examine the corps de garde, if
there was one, and once very narrowly missed introducing Waverley
to a recruiting-serjeant of his own regiment. Then she Captain'd and
Butler'd him till he was almost mad with vexation and anxiety; and
never was he more rejoiced in his life at the termination of a journey,
than when the arrival of the coach in London freed him from the
attentions of Madam Nosebag.

Chapter Fifteen

WHAT'S TO BE DONE NEXT?

IT WAS twilight when they arrived in town, and having shaken off his
companions, and walked through a good many streets to avoid the
possibility of being traced by them, Edward took a hackney-coach and
drove to Colonel Talbot's house, in one of the principal squares at the
west end of the town. That gentleman, by the death of relations, had
succeeded since his marriage to a large fortune, possessed considerable political interest, and lived in what is called great style.

When Waverley knocked at his door, he found it at first difficult to
procure admittance, but at length was shewn into an apartment where
the Colonel was at table. Lady Emily, whose very beautiful features
were still pallid from indisposition, sate opposite to him. The instant
he heard Waverley's voice, he started up and embraced him. "Frank

Stanley, my dear boy, how do ye do?—Emily, my love, this is young Stanley."

The blood rushed to the lady's cheek as she gave Waverley a reception, in which courtesy was mingled with kindness, while her trembling hand and faultering voice shewed how much she was startled and discomposed. Dinner was hastily replaced, and while Waverley was engaged in refreshing himself, the Colonel proceeded—"I wonder you have come here, Frank; the doctors tell me the air of London is very bad for your complaints. You should not have risked it. But I am delighted to see you, and so is Emily, though I fear we must not count upon your staying long."

"Some particular business brought me up," muttered Waverley.

"I supposed so, but I sha'n't allow you to stay long.—Spontoon, (to an elderly military looking servant out of livery) take away these things, and answer the bell yourself if I ring. Don't let any of the other fellows disturb us—My nephew and I have business to talk of."

When the servants had retired, "In the name of God, Waverley, what has brought you here? It may be as much as your life is worth."

"Dear Mr Waverley," said Lady Emily, "to whom I owe so much more than acknowledgements can ever pay, how could you be so rash?"

"My father—my uncle—this paragraph," he handed the paper to Colonel Talbot.

"I wish to Heaven these scoundrels were condemned to be squeezed to death in their own presses," said Talbot. "I am told there are not less than a dozen of their papers now published in town, and no wonder that they are obliged to invent lies to find sale for their journals. It is true, however, my dear Edward, that you have lost your father; but as to this flourish of his unpleasant situation having grated upon his spirits, and hurt his health—the truth is—for though it is harsh to say so now, yet it will relieve your mind from the idea of weighty responsibility—the truth then is, that Mr Richard Waverley, through this whole business, showed great want of sensibility, both to your situation and that of your uncle; and the last time I saw him, he told me, with great glee, that as I was so good as take charge of your interests, he had thought it best to patch up a separate negociation for himself, and make his peace with government through some channels which former connections left still open to him."

"And my uncle, my dear uncle?"

"Is in no danger whatsoever. It is true (looking at the date of the paper) there was a foolish report some time ago to the purport here quoted, but it is entirely false. Sir Everard is gone down to Waverley-Honour, freed from all uneasiness, unless upon your account. But you are in peril yourself—your name is in every proclamation—warrants are out to apprehend you. How and when did you come here?"

Edward told his story at length, suppressing his quarrel with Fergus; for, being himself partial to the Highlanders, he did not wish to give any advantage to the Colonel's national prejudice against them.

"Are you sure it was your friend Glen's foot-boy you saw dead on Clifton-Moor?"

"Quite positive."

"Then that little limb of the devil has cheated the gallows, for cut-throat was written in his face, though (turning to Lady Emily) it was a very handsome face too. But for you, Edward, I wish you would go down again to Cumberland, or rather I wish you had never stirred from thence, for there is an embargo in all the sea-ports, and a strict search for adherents of the Pretender, and the tongue of that confounded woman will wag in her head like the clack of a mill, till some how or other she will detect Lieutenant Butler to be a feigned personage."

"Do you know any thing," asked Waverley, "of my fellow-traveller?"

"Her husband was my serjeant-major for six years: she was a buxom widow with a little money—he married her—was steady, and got on by being a good drill. I must send Spontoon to see what she is about: he will find her out among the old regimental connections. To-morrow you must be indisposed, and keep your room from fatigue. Lady Emily is to be your nurse, and Spontoon and I your attendants. You bear the name of a near relation of mine, whom none of my present people ever saw except Spontoon, so there will be no immediate danger. So pray feel your head ache and your eyes grow heavy as soon as possible, that you may be put upon the sick list; and, Emily, do you order an apartment for Frank Stanley, with all the attentions which an invalid may require."

In the morning the Colonel visited his guest. "Now," said he, "I have some good news for you. Your reputation as a gentleman and officer is effectually cleared of neglect of duty, and accession to the mutiny in G——'s regiment. I have had a correspondence on this subject with a very zealous friend of yours, your Scotch parson, Morton; his first letter was addressed to Sir Everard, but I relieved the good Baronet of the trouble of answering it. You must know, that your free-booting acquaintance, Donald of the Cave, has at length fallen into the hands of the Philistines. He was driving off the cattle of a certain proprietor called Killam—something or other."

"Killancureit?"

"The same—now this gentleman being, it seems, a great farmer, and having a special value for his breed of cattle, being, moreover, rather of a timid disposition, had got a party of soldiers to protect his property. So Donald run his head unawares into the lion's mouth, and was defeated and made prisoner. Being ordered for execution, his conscience was assailed on the one hand by a catholic priest, on the other by your friend Morton. He repulsed the catholic chiefly on account of the doctrine of extreme unction, which this economical gentleman censured as an excessive waste of oil. So his conversion from a state of impenitence fell to Mr Morton's share, who, I dare say, acquitted himself excellently, though, I suppose, Donald made but a queer kind of Christian after all. He confessed, however, before a magistrate, one Major Mellville, who seems to have been a correct friendly sort of person, his full intrigue with Houghton, explaining particularly how it was carried on, and fully acquitting you of the least accession to it. He also mentioned his rescuing you from the hands of the volunteer officer, and sending you, by orders of the Pret—Chevalier I mean—as a prisoner to Doune, from whence he understood you were carried prisoner to Edinburgh. These are particulars which cannot but tell in your favour. He hinted that he had been employed to deliver and to protect you, and rewarded for doing so; but he would not confess by whom, alleging, that though he would not have minded breaking any ordinary oath to satisfy the curiosity of Mr Morton, to whose pious admonitions he owed so much, yet, in the present case, he had been sworn to silence upon the edge of his dirk, which, it seems, constituted, in his opinion, an inviolable obligation."

"And what is become of him?"

"O, he was hanged at Stirling after the rebels raised the siege, with his lieutenant, and four plaids besides; he having the advantage of a gallows more lofty than his friends."

"Well, I have little cause either to regret or rejoice at his death—he has done me both good and harm to a very considerable extent."

"His confession, at least, will serve you materially, since it wipes from your character all those suspicions which gave the accusation against you a complexion of a nature different from that with which so many unfortunate gentlemen, now, or lately, in arms against the government, may be justly charged. Their treason—I must give it its name, though you participate in its guilt—is an action arising from mistaken virtue, and therefore cannot be classed as disgraceful, though it be doubtless highly criminal. Where the guilty are so numerous, clemency must be extended to far the greater number; and I have little doubt to procure a remission for you, providing we can keep you out of the claws of Justice till she has selected and gorged upon her victims. For in this, as in other cases, it will be according to the vulgar proverb, First come first served. Besides, government are desirous at present to intimidate the English Jacobites, among whom they can find few examples for punishment; this is a vindictive and timid feeling which will soon wear off, for, of all nations, the English are least blood-thirsty by nature. But it exists at present, and you must, therefore, be kept out of the way in the meanwhile."

Now entered Spontoon with an anxious countenance. By his regimental acquaintances he had traced out Madam Nosebag, and found her full of ire, fuss, and fidget, at discovery of an impostor, who had travelled from the north with her under the assumed name of Captain Butler of G——'s dragoons. She was going to lodge an information on the subject, to have him sought for as an emissary of the Pretender; but Spontoon, (an old soldier,) while he pretended to approve, contrived to make her delay her intention. No time, however, was to be lost; the accuracy of this good dame's description might probably lead to the discovery that Waverley was the pretended Captain Butler; an identification fraught with danger to Edward, perhaps to his uncle, and even to Colonel Talbot. Which way to direct his course was now the question.

"To Scotland," said Waverley.

"To Scotland?" said the Colonel; "with what purpose?——not to engage again with the rebels, I hope."

"No—I consider my engagement ended, when, after all my efforts, I could not rejoin them, and now by all accounts they are gone to make a winter campaign in the Highlands, where such adherents as I am would rather be burdensome than useful. Indeed, it seems likely that they only prolong the war to place the Chevalier's person out of danger, and to make some terms for themselves. To burden them with my presence would just add another party, whom they would not give up, and could not defend. I understand they left almost all their English adherents in garrison at Carlisle, for that very reason—And on a more general view, Colonel, to confess the truth, though it may lower me in your opinion, I am heartily tired of the trade of war, and am, as Fletcher's Humorous Lieutenant says, 'even as weary of this fighting' "——

"Fighting? pooh! what have you seen but a skirmish or two?——Ah! if you saw war on the grand scale—sixty or a hundred thousand men in the field on each side."

"I am not at all curious, Colonel,—Enough, says our homely proverb, is as good as a feast. The plumed troops and the big war used to enchant me in poetry, but the night marches, vigils, couches under the winter sky, and such accompaniments of the glorious trade, are not at all to my taste in practice;—then for dry blows, I had my fill of fighting at Clifton, where I escaped by a hair's-breadth half a dozen times, and you, I should think"——He stopped.

"Had enough at Preston, you mean to say," said the Colonel, laughing; "but 'tis my vocation, Hal."

"It is not mine though," said Waverley; "and having honourably got rid of the sword which I drew only as a volunteer, I am quite satisfied with my military experience, and shall be in no hurry to take it up again."

"I am very glad you are of that mind,—but then what would you do in the north?"

"In the first place, there are some sea-ports on the eastern coast of Scotland still in the hands of the Chevalier's friends; should I gain any of them, I can easily embark for the continent."

"Good—your second reason?"

"Why, to speak the very truth, there is a person in Scotland upon whom I now find that my happiness depends more than I was always aware, and about whose situation I am very anxious."

"Then Emily was right, and there is a love affair in the case after all; and which of these two pretty Scotchwomen, whom you insisted upon my admiring, is the distinguished fair? not Miss Glen—— I hope."

"No."

"Ah, pass for the other; simplicity may be improved, but pride and conceit never. Well, I don't discourage you; I think it will please Sir Everard, from what he said when I jested with him about it; only I hope that intolerable papa, with his brogue, and his snuff, and his Latin, and his intolerable long stories about the Duke of Berwick, will find it necessary hereafter to be an inhabitant of foreign parts. But as to the daughter, though I think you might find as fitting a match in England, yet, if your heart be really set upon this Scotch rose-bud, why the Baronet has a great opinion of her father and of his family, and he wishes much to see you married and settled, both for your own sake and for that of the three ermines passant, which may otherwise pass away altogether. But I will bring you his mind fully upon the subject, since you are debarred correspondence for the present, for I think you will not be long in Scotland before me."

"Indeed! and what can induce you to think of returning to Scotland? No relenting longing towards the land of mountains and floods, I am afraid."

"None, on my word; but Emily's health is now, thank God, re-established, and, to tell you the truth, I have little hopes of concluding the business which I have at present most at heart, until I can have a personal interview with his Royal Highness the Commander in Chief; for, as Fluellen says, 'the Duke doth love me well, and I thank heaven I have deserved some love at his hands.' I am now going out for an hour or two to arrange matters for your departure; your liberty extends to the next room, Lady Emily's parlour, where you will find her when you are disposed for music, reading, or conversation. We have taken measures to exclude all servants but Spontoon, who is as true as steel."

In about two hours Colonel Talbot returned, and found his young friend conversing with his lady, she pleased with his manners and information, and he delighted at being restored, though but for a moment, to society of his own rank, from which he had been for some time secluded.

"And now," said the Colonel, "hear my arrangements, for there is little time to lose. This youngster, Edward Waverley, alias Williams, alias Captain Butler, must continue to pass by his fourth *alias* of Francis Stanley, my nephew; he shall set out to-morrow for the north, and the chariot shall take him the first two stages. Spontoon shall then attend him; and they shall ride post as far as Huntingdon; and the presence of Spontoon, well known on the road as my servant, will check all disposition to enquiry. At Huntingdon you will meet the real Frank Stanley. He is studying at Cambridge; but, a little while ago, doubtful if Emily's health would permit me to go down to the north myself, I procured him a passport from the Secretary of State's office to go in my stead. As he went chiefly to look after you, his journey is now unnecessary. He knows your story; you will dine together at Huntingdon; and perhaps your wise heads may hit upon some plan for removing or diminishing the danger of your farther progress northward. And now, (taking out a morocco case,) let me put you in funds for the campaign."

"I am ashamed, my dear Colonel"——

"Nay, you should command my purse in any event; but this money is your own. Your father, considering the chance of your being attainted, left me his trustee for your advantage. So that you are worth above L.15,000, besides Brere-wood Lodge—a very independent person, I promise you. There are bills here for L.200; any larger sum you may have, or credits abroad as soon as your motions require it."

The first use which occurred to Waverley of his newly-acquired wealth, was to write to honest Farmer Jopson, requesting his acceptance of a silver tankard on the part of his friend Williams, who had not forgotten the night of the eighteenth December last. He begged him at the same time carefully to preserve for him his Highland garb and accoutrements, particularly the arms, curious in themselves, and to which the friendship of the donors gave additional value. Lady Emily undertook to find some suitable token of remembrance, likely to flatter the vanity and please the taste of Mrs Williams; and the Colonel, who was a kind of farmer, promised to send the Ulswater patriarch an excellent team of horses for cart and plough.

One happy day Waverley spent in London; and, travelling in the manner projected, he met with Frank Stanley at Huntingdon. The two young men were acquainted in a minute.

"I can read my uncle's riddle," said Stanley; "the cautious old soldier did not care to hint to me that I might hand over to you this passport, which I have no occasion for; but if it should afterwards come out as the rattle-pated trick of a young Cantab, *cela ne tire à rien*. You are therefore to be Francis Stanley, with his passport." This proposal appeared in effect to alleviate a great part of the difficulties which Edward must otherwise have encountered at every turn; and accordingly he scrupled not to avail himself of it, the more especially as he had discarded all political purposes from his present journey, and could not be accused of furthering machinations against the government while travelling under protection of a Secretary's passport.

The day passed merrily away. The young student was inquisitive about Waverley's campaigns, and the manners of the Highlands. Edward was obliged to satisfy his curiosity by whistling a pibroch, dancing a strathspey, and singing a Highland song. The next morning Stanley rode a stage northwards with his new friend, and parted from him with great reluctance, upon the remonstrances of Spontoon, who, accustomed to submit to discipline, was rigid in enforcing it.

Chapter Sixteen

DESOLATION

WAVERLEY riding post, as was the usual fashion of the period, without any adventure, save one or two queries, which the talisman of his passport sufficiently answered, reached the borders of Scotland. Here he heard the tidings of the decisive battle of Culloden. It was no more than he had long expected, though the success at Falkirk had thrown a faint and setting gleam over the arms of the Chevalier. Yet it came upon him like a shock, by which he was for a time altogether unmanned. The generous, the courteous, the noble-minded Adventurer, was then a fugitive, with a price upon his head; his adherents, so brave, so enthusiastic, so faithful, were dead, imprisoned, or exiled. Where, now, was the exalted and high-souled Fergus, if, indeed, he had survived the night of Clifton? Where the pure-hearted and primitive Baron of Bradwardine, whose foibles seemed foils to set off the disinterestedness of his disposition, his genuine goodness of heart, and unshaken courage? Those two who clung for support to these fallen columns, Rose and Flora, where were they to be sought, and in what distress must not the loss of their natural protectors have involved them? Of Flora, he thought with the regard of a brother for a sister; but of Rose, with a sensation far more deep and tender. It might be yet his fate to supply the want of those guardians they had lost. Agitated by these thoughts he precipitated his journey.

When he arrived at Edinburgh, where his enquiries must necessarily commence, he felt the full difficulty of his situation. Many inhabitants of that city had seen and known him as Edward Waverley; how, then, could he avail himself of a passport as Francis Stanley? He resolved, therefore, to avoid all company, and to move northward as soon as possible. He was, however, to await a day or two here in expectation of a letter from Colonel Talbot, and he was also to leave his own address, under his feigned character, at a place agreed upon. With this purpose he sallied out in the dusk through the well-known streets, carefully shunning observation, but in vain—one of the first persons whom he met at once recognized him. It was Mrs Flockhart, Fergus Mac-Ivor's good-humoured landlady.

"Gude guide us, Mr Waverley, is this you? na, ye need na be feared for me. I wad betray nae gentleman in your circumstances—eh, lack-a-day! lack-a-day! here's a change o' markets; how merry Colonel Mac-Ivor and you used to be in our house!" And the good-natured widow shed a few natural tears. As there was no resisting her claim of acquaintance, Waverley acknowledged it with a good grace, as well as the danger of his own situation. "As it is in the darkening, sir, wad ye just step in bye to our house, and tak a dish of tea? and I am sure if ye like to sleep in the little room, I wad tak care ye are na disturbed, and nae body wad ken ye; for Kate and Matty, the limmers, gaed aff wi' twa o' Hawley's dragoons, and I hae twa new queans instead o' them."

Waverley accepted her invitation, and engaged the lodging for a night or two, satisfied he would be safer in the house of this simple creature than any where else. When he entered the parlour, his heart swelled to see Fergus's bonnet, with the white cockade, hanging beside the little mirror.

"Ay," said Mrs Flockhart, sighing, as she observed the direction of his eyes, "the poor Colonel bought a new ane just the day before the march, and I winna let them tak that ane doon, but just to brush it ilka day mysell, and whiles I look at it till I just think I hear him cry to Callum to bring him his bonnet, as he used to do when he was ganging out.—It's unco silly—the neighbours ca' me a Jacobite—but they may say their say—I am sure it's no for that—but he was as kind-hearted a gentleman as ever lived, and as weel-fa'rd too—Oh, d'ye ken, sir, whan he is to suffer?"

"Suffer! why, where is he?"

"Eh, Lord's sake! d'ye no ken? The poor Hieland body, Dugald Mahony, came here a while since wi' ane o' his arms cut off, and a sair clour in the head—Ye'll mind Dugald, he carried aye an axe on his shouther—and he came here just begging, as I may say, for something to eat—And he tauld us the Chief, as they ca'd him, (but I aye ca' him the Colonel,) and Ensign Maccombich, that ye mind weel, were ta'en somewhere beside the English border, when it was sae dark that his folk never missed him till it was ower late, and they were like to gang clean daft. And he said that little Callum Beg, (he was a bauld mischievous callant that,) and your honour, were killed that same night in the tuilzie, and mony mae bra' men. But he grat when he spak o' the Colonel, ye never saw the like. And now the word gangs the Colonel is to be tried, and to suffer wi' them that were ta'en at Carlisle."

"And his sister?"

"Ay, that they ca'd the Lady Flora—weel, she's away up to Carlisle to him, and lives wi' some grand papist lady thereabouts to be near him."

"And," said Edward, "the other young lady?"

"Whilk other? I ken only of ae sister the Colonel had."

"I mean Miss Bradwardine," said Edward.

"Ou, ay—the laird's daughter, she was a very bonny lassie, poor thing, but far shyer than Lady Flora."

"Where is she, for God's sake?"

"Ou, wha kens where ony o' them is now? puir things, they're sair ta'en down for their white cockades and their white roses; but she gaed north to her father's in Perthshire, when the government troops came back to Edinbro'. There were some pretty men amang them, and ane Major Whacker was quartered on me, a very civil gentleman, but O Mr Waaverley, he was naething sae weel fa'rd as the poor Colonel."

"Do you know what is become of Miss Bradwardine's father?"

"The auld laird? na, naebody kens that; but they say he fought very sair in this last bluidy battle at Inverness; and Deacon Clank, the white-iron smith, says that the government folk are sair agane him for having been *out* twice; and troth he might hae ta'en warning, but there's nae fule like an auld fule—the puir Colonel was only out anes."

Such lamentations contained almost all the simple-hearted widow knew of the fate of her late lodgers and acquaintances, but it was enough to determine Edward, at all hazards, to proceed instantly to Tully-Veolan, where he concluded he should see, or at least hear something of Rose. He therefore left a letter for Colonel Talbot at the place agreed upon, signed by his assumed name, and giving for his address the post town next to the Baron's residence.

From Edinburgh to Perth he took post-horses, resolving to make the rest of his journey on foot; a mode of travelling to which he was partial, and which had the advantage of permitting a deviation from the road when he saw parties of military at a distance. His campaign had considerably strengthened his constitution, and improved his habits of enduring fatigue. His baggage he sent before him as opportunity occurred.

As he advanced northward, the traces of war became visible. Broken carriages, dead horses, unroofed cottages, woods felled for palisades, and bridges destroyed, or only partially repaired—all indicated the movements of hostile armies. In those places where the gentry were attached to the Stuart cause, their houses seemed dismantled or deserted, the usual course of what may be called ornamental labour totally interrupted, and the remaining inhabitants gliding about with fear, sorrow, and dejection in their faces.

It was near evening when he approached the village of Tully-Veolan, with feelings and sentiments how different from those which attended his first entrance. Then life was so new to him that a dull or disagreeable day was one of the greatest misfortunes which his imagination anticipated, and it seemed to him that his time ought only to be consecrated to elegant or amusing study, and relieved by lively society or youthful frolic. Now, how changed, how saddened, yet how elevated was his character, within the course of a very few months! Danger and misfortune are rapid, though severe teachers. "A sadder and a wiser man," he felt, in internal confidence and mental dignity, a compensation for the gay dreams which in his case experience had so rapidly dissolved.

As he approached the village, he saw, with surprise and anxiety, that a party of soldiers were quartered near it, and what was worse, that they seemed stationary there. This he conjectured from a few tents which he beheld glimmering upon what was called the common-moor. To avoid the risk of being stopped and questioned in a place where he was so likely to be recognized by some of the villagers, he fetched a large circuit, altogether avoiding the hamlet, and approaching the upper gate of the avenue by a bye-path well known to him. A single glance announced that great changes had taken place. One leaf of the gate, entirely broken down, and split up for fire wood, lay in piles ready to be taken away; the other swung uselessly about upon its loosened hinges. The battlements above the gate were broken and thrown down, and the two carved Bears, which were said to have done centinels' duty upon the top for centuries, now hurled from their posts, lay among the rubbish. The avenue was sorely wasted. Several large trees were felled and left lying across the path; and the cattle of the villagers, and the more rude hoofs of dragoon horses, had poached into black mud the verdant turf which Waverley had so much admired.

Upon entering the court-yard, Edward saw the fears realized which these circumstances had excited. The place had been sacked by the King's troops, who, in wanton mischief, had even attempted to burn it; and though the thickness of the walls had resisted the fire, unless to a partial extent, the stables and out-houses were totally consumed. The towers and pinnacles of the main building were scorched and blackened; the pavement broken and shattered; the doors torn down entirely, or hanging by a single hinge; the windows dashed in and demolished, and the court strewed with articles of furniture broken into fragments. These accessaries of ancient distinction, to which the Baron, in the pride of his heart, had attached so much importance and veneration, were treated with peculiar contumely. The fountain was demolished, and the spring, which had supplied it, now flooded the court-yard. The stone bason seemed to be destined for a drinking-trough for cattle, from the manner in which it was arranged upon the ground. The whole tribe of Bears, large and small, had experienced as little favour as those at the head of the avenue, and one or two of the family pictures, which had served for targets to the soldiers, lay on the ground in tatters. With an aching heart, as may well be imagined, Edward viewed these wrecks of a mansion so respected. But his anxiety to learn the fate of the proprietors, and his fears as to what that fate might be, increased with every step. When he entered upon the terrace, new scenes of desolation were visible. The ballustrade was broken down, the walks destroyed, the borders overgrown with weeds, and the fruit-trees cut down or grubbed up. In one copartment of this old-fashioned garden were two immense horse-chesnut trees, of whose size the Baron was particularly vain: too lazy, perhaps, to cut them down, the spoilers, with malevolent ingenuity, had mined them, and placed a quantity of gunpowder in the cavity. One had been shivered to pieces by the explosion, and the wreck lay scattered around, encumbering the ground it had so long shadowed. The other mine had been more partial in its effect. About one-fourth of the trunk of the tree was torn from the mass, which, mutilated and defaced on the one side, still spread on the other its ample and undiminished boughs.

Amid these general marks of ravage, there were some which more particularly addressed the feelings of Waverley. Viewing the front of the building, thus wasted and defaced, his eyes naturally sought the little balcony which more properly belonged to Rose's apartment— her *troisième*, or rather *cinquième étage*. It was easily discovered, for beneath it lay the stage-flowers and shrubs, with which it was her pride to decorate it, and which had been hurled from the bartizan—several of her books lay mingled with broken flower-pots and other remnants. Amongst these Waverley distinguished one of his own, a small copy of Ariosto, and gathered it as a treasure, though wasted by the wind and rain.

While yet plunged in the sad reflections which the scene excited, he was looking around for some one who might explain the fate of the inhabitants, he heard a voice from the interior of the building, singing, in well-remembered accents, an old Scottish song:

> "They came upon us in the night,
> And brake my bower and slew my knight;
> My servants a' for life did flee,
> And left us in extremitie.
>
> They slew my knight, to me sae dear;
> They slew my knight and drave his gear;
> The moon may set, the sun may rise,
> But a deadly sleep has closed his eyes."

"Alas," thought Edward, "is it thou?—poor helpless being–art thou alone left, to gibber and moan, and fill with thy wild and unconnected scraps of minstrelsy the halls that protected thee?" He then called first low, and then louder, "Davie—Davie Gellatley."

The poor simpleton shewed himself from among the ruins of a sort of green-house, that once terminated what was called the terrace walk, but at first sight of a stranger retreated, as if in terror. Waverley, remembering his habits, began to whistle a tune to which he was partial, which Davie had expressed great pleasure in listening to, and had picked up from him by the ear. Our hero's minstrelsy no more equalled that of Blondel, than poor Davie resembled Cœur de Lion; but the melody had the same effect of producing recognition. Davie again stole from his lurking place, but timidly, while Waverley, afraid of frightening him, stood motionless making the most encouraging signals he could devise.—"It's his ghaist," muttered Davie; yet, coming nearer, he seemed to acknowledge his living acquaintance. The poor fool himself seemed the ghost of what he was. The sort of peculiar dress in which he had been attired in better days, shewed only miserable rags of its whimsical finery, the lack of which was oddly supplied by the remnants of tapestried hangings, window curtains, and shreds of pictures, with which he had bedizened his tatters. His face, too, had lost its vacant and careless air, and the poor creature looked hollow-eyed, meagre, half-starved, and nervous, to a pitiable degree. After long reconnoitring, he approached Waverley with some confidence, looked him sadly in the face, and said, "A' dead and gane—a' dead and gane."

"Who are dead?" said Waverley, forgetting the incapacity of Davie to hold any connected discourse.

"Baron—and Baillie—and Saunders Saunderson—and Leddy Rose—(here he burst out a-weeping) bonnie Leddy Rose that sang sae sweet—A' dead and gane—dead and gane.

> But follow, follow me,
> While glow-worms light the lea,
> I'll shew ye where the dead should be—
>> Each in his shroud,
>> While winds pipe loud,
> And the red moon peeps dim through the cloud.
> Follow, follow me;
> Brave should he be
> That treads by the night the dead men's lea."

With these words, chaunted in a wild and earnest tone, he made a sign to Waverley to follow him, and walked rapidly towards the bottom of the garden, tracing the bank of the stream, which, it may be remembered, was its eastern boundary. Edward, over whom an involuntary shuddering stole at the import of his words, followed him in some hope of an explanation. As the house was evidently deserted, he could hope to find among the ruins no more rational informer.

Davie walking very fast, soon reached the extremity of the garden, and scrambled over the ruins of the wall which once had divided it from the wooded glen in which the old tower of Tully-Veolan was situated. He then jumped down into the bed of the stream, and, followed by Waverley, proceeded at a great pace, climbing over some fragments of rock, and turning with difficulty round others. They passed beneath the ruins of the castle, Waverley keeping up with his guide with difficulty, for the twilight began to fail. Following the descent of the stream a little lower, he totally lost him, but a twinkling light, which he now discovered among the tangled copse-wood and bushes, seemed a surer guide. He pursued a very uncouth path by its occasional guidance, and at length reached the door of a wretched hut. A fierce barking of dogs was at first heard, but it stilled at his approach. A voice sounded from within, and he held it most prudent to listen before he advanced.

"Wha hast thou brought here, thou unsonsy villain, thou?" said an old woman, apparently in great indignation. He heard Davie Gellatley, in answer, whistle a part of the tune by which he had recalled himself to the simpleton's memory, and had now no hesitation to knock at the door. There was a dead silence instantly within, except the deep growling of the dogs; and he next heard the mistress of the hut approach the door, not probably for the sake of undoing a latch, but of fastening a bolt. To prevent this, Waverley lifted the latch himself.

In front was an old wretched-looking woman, exclaiming, "Wha comes into folks' houses in this gait, at this time o' the night?" On one side, two grim and half-starved deer greyhounds laid aside their ferocity at his appearance, and seemed to recognise him. On the other side, half-concealed by the opened door, yet apparently seeking that concealment reluctantly, with a cocked pistol in his right hand, and his left in the act of drawing another from his belt, stood a tall boney gaunt figure in the remnants of a faded uniform, and a beard of three weeks' growth.

It was the Baron of Bradwardine.—It is unnecessary to add, that he threw aside his weapon, and greeted Waverley with a hearty embrace.

Chapter Seventeen

COMPARING OF NOTES

THE BARON'S story was short, when divested of the adages and common-places, Latin, English, and Scotch, with which his erudition garnished it. He insisted much upon his grief at the loss of Edward and of Glennaquoich, fought the fields of Falkirk and Culloden, and related how, after all was lost in the last battle, he had returned home with the idea he could more easily find shelter among his own tenants, and on his own estate, than elsewhere. A party of soldiers had been sent to lay waste his property, for clemency was not the order of the day. Their proceedings, however, were checked by an order from the civil court. The estate, it was found, could not be forfeited to the crown, to the prejudice of Malcolm Bradwardine of Inch-Grubbit, the heir-male, whose claim could not be prejudiced by the Baron's attainder, as deriving no right through him, and who, therefore, like other heirs of entail in the same situation, entered upon possession. But unlike many in similar circumstances, the new laird speedily shewed that he intended utterly to exclude his predecessor from all benefit or advantage in the estate, and to avail himself of the old Baron's evil fortune, to the full extent. This was the more ungenerous, as all the country knew that, from a romantic idea of not prejudicing this young man's right as heir-male, the Baron had refrained from settling his estate on his daughter. In the Baron's own words, "The matter did not coincide with the feelings of the commons of Bradwardine, Mr Waverley; and the tenants were slack and repugnant in payment of their mails and duties; and when my kinsman came to the village wi' the new factor, Mr James Howie, to lift the rents, some wanchancy person—I suspect

John Heatherblutter, the old game-keeper, that was out wi' me in the year fifteen—fired a shot at him in the gloaming. Whereby he was so affrighted, that I may say with Tullius in Catilinam, *Abiit, evasit, erupit, effugit*. He fled, sir, as one may say, incontinent to Stirling. And now he hath advertised the estate for sale, being himself the last substitute in this entail.—And if I were to grieve about sic matters, this would grieve me mair than its passing from my immediate possession, whilk, by the course of nature, must have happened in a few years. Whereas now it passes from the lineage that should have possessed it in *sæcula sæculorum*. But God's will be done, *humana perpessi sumus*. Sir John of Bradwardine—Black Sir John, as he is called—who was the common ancestor of our house and the Inch-Grubbits, little thought such a person would have sprung from his loins. Meantime, he has accused me to some of the *primates*, the rulers for the time, as if I were a cut-throat, and an abettor of bravoes and assassinates, and *coupe-jarrets*. And they have sent soldiers here to abide on the estate, and hunt me like a partridge upon the mountains, as Scripture says of good King David, or like our ain valiant Sir William Wallace,—not that I bring mysell into comparison with either.—I thought, when I heard you at the door of the hut, that they had driven the auld deer to his den at last; and so I e'en prepared to die at bay, like a buck of the first head.—But now, Janet, canna ye gie us something for supper?"

"Ow, ay, sir, I'll brander the moor-fowl that John Heatherblutter brought in this morning; and ye see puir Davie's roasting the black hen's eggs—I dare say, Mr Waaverley, ye never kend that the eggs that were sae weel roasted at supper in the Ha-house were aye turned by our Davie;—there's no the like o' him ony gate for powtering wi' his fingers amang the het peat-ashes, and roasting eggs." Davie all this while lay with his nose almost in the fire, nuzzling among the ashes, kicking his heels, mumbling to himself, and turning the eggs as they lay in the hot embers, as if to confute the proverb, that "there goes reason to roasting of eggs," and justify the eulogium which poor Janet poured out upon

Him whom she loved, her idiot boy.

"Davie's no sae silly as folks tak him for, Mr Waaverley; he wadna hae brought you here unless he had kend ye was a friend to his honour —indeed the very dogs kend ye, Mr Waaverley, for ye was aye kind to beast and body.—I can tell you a story o' Davie, wi' his Honour's leave: His Honour, ye see, being under hiding in thae sair times—the mair's the pity—he lies a' day, and whiles a' night, in the cove in the dern hag; but though it's a bieldy enough bit, and the auld gudeman o' Corse-cleugh has pang'd it wi' a kemple o' strae amaist, yet when the country's quiet, and the night very cauld, his Honour whiles creeps down here to get a warm at the ingle, and a sleep amang the blankets, and gangs awa' in the morning. And so ae morning siccan a fright as I got! twa unlucky red-coats were up for black-fishing, or some siccan ploy, for the neb o' them's never out of mischief; and they just got a glisk o' his honour as he gaed into the wood, and banged off a gun at him. I out like a jer-falcon, and cried,—'Wad they shute an honest woman's poor innocent bairn?' and I fleyt at them, and threepit it was my son; and they damned and swuir at me that it was the auld rebel, as the villains ca'd his Honour; and Davie was in the wood, and heard the tuilzie, and he, just out of his ain head, got up the auld grey maud that his Honour had flung off him to gang the faster, and he came out o' the very same bit o' the wood, majoring and looking about sae like his Honour, that they were clean beguiled, and thought they had letten aff their gun at crack-brained Sawney, as they ca' him; and they gae me sixpence, and twa saumon fish, to say naething about it to their officer.—Na, na, Davie's no just like other folk, puir fallow; but he's no sae silly as folk tak him for.—But, to be sure, how can we do aneugh for his Honour, when we and ours hae lived on his ground this twa hunder years; and when he keepit my puir Jamie at school and college, and even at the Ha'-house, till he gaed to a better place; and when he saved me frae being ta'en to Perth as a witch—Lord forgie them that would touch sic a puir silly auld body—and has maintained puir Davie at heck and manger maist feck o' his life?"

Waverley at length found an opportunity to interrupt Janet's narrative, by an enquiry after Miss Bradwardine.

"She's weel and safe, thank God! at the Duchran," answered the Baron; "the laird's distantly related to us, and more nearly to my chaplain, Mr Rubrick; and, though he be of Whig principles, yet he's not forgetful of auld friendships at this time. The Baillie's doing what he can to save something out of the wreck for puir Rose—but I doubt, I doubt, I shall never see her again, for I maun lay my banes in some far country."

"Hout na, your honour; ye were just as ill aff in the feifteen, and gat the bonnie barony back, an' a'; and now the eggs is ready, and the muir-cock's brandered, and there's ilk ane a trencher and some saut, and the heel o' the white loaf that came frae the Baillie's; and there's plenty o' brandy in the greybeard that Luckie Macleary sent down, and winna ye be supped like princes?"

"I wish one Prince, at least, of our acquaintance may be no worse off," said the Baron to Waverley, who joined him in cordial hopes for the safety of the unfortunate Chevalier.

They then began to talk of their future prospects. The Baron's plan was very simple. It was to escape to France, where, by the interest of his old friends, he hoped to get some military employment, for which he still conceived himself capable. He invited Waverley to go with him, a proposal in which Edward acquiesced, in case the interest of Colonel Talbot should fail in procuring his pardon. Tacitly he hoped the Baron would sanction his addresses to Rose, and give him a right to assist him in his exile, but he forebore to speak on this subject until his own fate should be decided. They then talked of Glennaquoich, for whom the Baron expressed great anxiety, although, he observed, he was "the very Achilles of Horatius Flaccus,

> Impiger, iracundus, inexorabilis, acer.

Which has been thus rendered vernacularly by Struan Robertson:

> A fiery etter-cap, a fractious chiel,
> As hot as ginger, and as stieve as steel."

Flora had a large and unqualified share of the good old man's sympathy.

It was now wearing late. Old Janet got into some kind of kennel behind the hallan; Davie had been long asleep and snoring between Ban and Buscar. These dogs had followed him to the hut after the mansion-house was deserted, and there constantly resided; and their ferocity, with the old woman's reputation of being a witch, contributed a good deal to keep people from the glen. With this view, Baillie Macwheeble supplied Janet underhand with meal for their maintenance, and also little articles of luxury for his patron's use, in which, however, much precaution was necessarily used. After some compliments, the Baron occupied his usual couch, and Waverley reclined in an easy chair of tattered velvet, which had once garnished the state bed-room of Tully-Veolan, (for the furniture of the mansion was now scattered through all the cottages in the vicinity,) and went to sleep as comfortably as in a bed of down.

Chapter Eighteen

MORE EXPLANATION

WITH THE first dawn of day, old Janet was scuttling about her house to wake the Baron, who usually slept sound and heavily.

"I must go back," he said to Waverley, "to my cove; will you walk down the glen wi' me?"

They went out together, and followed a narrow and entangled footpath, which the occasional passage of anglers, or wood-cutters, had traced by the side of the stream. On their way, the Baron explained to Waverley, that he would be under no danger in remaining a day or two at Tully-Veolan, and even in being seen walking about, if he used the precaution of pretending that he was looking at the estate as agent, or surveyor, for an English gentleman, who designed to be purchaser. With this view, he recommended to him to visit the Baillie, who still lived at the factor's house, called Little Veolan, about a mile from the village, though he was to remove next term. Stanley's passport would be an answer to the officer who commanded the military; and as to any of the country people who might recognise Waverley, the Baron assured him he was in no danger of being betrayed by them.

"I believe," said the old man, "half the people of the barony know that the auld laird is somewhere hereabout; for I see they do not suffer a single bairn to come here a bird-nesting; a practice, whilk, when I was in full possession of my power as baron, I was unable totally to interdict. Nay, I often find bits of things in my way, that the poor bodies, God help them! leave there, because they think they may be useful to me. I hope they will get a wiser master, and as kind a one as I was."

A natural sigh closed the sentence; but the quiet equanimity with which the Baron endured his misfortunes, had something in it venerable and even sublime. There was no fruitless repining, no turbid melancholy; he bore his lot, and the hardships which it involved, with a good-humoured, though serious composure, and used no irritating language against the prevailing party.

"I did what I thought my duty," said the good old man, "and questionless they are doing what they think theirs. It grieves me sometimes to look upon these blackened walls of the home of my ancestors; but doubtless officers cannot always keep the soldier's hand from depredation and spuilzie; and Gustavus Adolphus himself, as ye may read in Colonel Munro His Expedition with the worthy Scots regiment called Mac-Keyes regiment, did often permit it.—Indeed I have myself seen as sad sights as Tully-Veolan now is, when I served with the Marechal Duke of Berwick. To be sure we may say with Virgilius Maro, *Fuimus Troes*—and there's the end of an auld sang. But houses and families and men have a' stood lang enough when they have stood lang enough to fall wi' honour— And now I hae gotten a house that is not unlike a *domus ultima*"— they were now standing below a steep rock.—"We poor Jacobites," continued the Baron, looking up, "are now like the conies in Holy Scripture, (which the great traveller Pococke calleth Jerboa,) a feeble people, that make our abode in the rocks. So, fare ye well, my good lad, till we meet at Janet's in the even, for I must get into my

Patmos, which is no easy matter for my auld stiff limbs."

With that he began to ascend the rock, stepping, with the help of his hands, from one precarious footstep to another, till he got about half way up, where two or three bushes concealed the mouth of a hole, resembling an oven, into which the Baron insinuated, first his head and shoulders, and then, by slow gradation, the rest of his long body, his legs and feet finally disappearing, coiled up like a huge snake entering his retreat, or a long pedigree introduced with care and difficulty into the narrow pigeon-hole of an old cabinet. Waverley had the curiosity to clamber up and look in upon him in his den, as the lurking-place might well be termed. Upon the whole, he looked not unlike that ingenious puzzle, called *a reel in a bottle*, the marvel of children, (and some grown people too, myself for one,) who can neither comprehend the mystery how it has got in, or how it is to be taken out. The cave was very narrow, too low in the roof to admit of his standing, or almost of his sitting up, though he made some awkward attempts at the latter posture. His sole amusement was the perusal of his old friend Titus Livius, varied by occasionally scratching Latin proverbs and texts of Scripture with his knife on the roof and walls of his fortalice, which were of sand stone. And as the cave was dry and filled with clean straw and withered fern, "it made," as he said, coiling himself up with an air of snugness and comfort which contrasted strangely with his situation, "unless when the wind was due north, a very passable *gite* for an old soldier." Neither, as he observed, was he without sentries for the purpose of recognoscing. Davie and his mother were perpetually on the watch, to discover and avert danger; and it was singular what instances of address seemed dictated by the instinctive attachment of the poor simpleton, when his patron's safety was concerned.

With Janet, Edward now sought an interview. He had recognised her at first sight as the old woman who had nursed him during his sickness after his delivery from Gifted Gilfillan. The hut also, though a little repaired, and somewhat better furnished, was certainly the place of his confinement; and he now recollected on the common moor of Tully-Veolan the trunk of a large decayed oak, called the *trysting-tree*, which he had no doubt was the same at which the High-landers rendezvoused on that memorable night. All this he had com-bined in his imagination the night before; but reasons, which may probably occur to the reader, prevented him from catechising Janet in presence of the Baron.

He now commenced the task in good earnest; and the first question was, Who was the young lady who visited the hut during his illness? Janet paused for a moment; and then observed, that, to keep the secret now, would neither do good or ill to any body.

"It was just a leddy, that has na her equal in the world—Miss Rose Bradwardine!"

"Then Miss Rose was probably also the author of my deliverance," inferred Waverley, delighted at the confirmation of an idea which local circumstances had already induced him to entertain.

"I wot weel, Mr Waaverley, and that was she e'en; but sair, sair angry and affronted wad she hae been, puir thing, if she had thought ye had been ever to ken a word about the matter; for she gar'd me speak aye Gaelic when ye was in hearing, to mak ye trow ye were in the Hielands. I can speak it weel eneugh—my mother was a Hieland woman."

A few more questions now brought out the whole mystery respecting Waverley's deliverance from the bondage in which he left Cairn-vreckan. Never did music sound sweeter to an amateur than the drowsy tautology with which old Janet detailed every circumstance thrill upon the ears of Waverley. But my reader is not a lover, and I must spare his patience, by attempting to condense, within reasonable compass, the narrative which old Janet spread through a harangue of nearly two hours.

When Waverley communicated to Fergus the letter he had received from Rose Bradwardine, by Davie Gellatley, giving an account of Tully-Veolan being occupied by a small party of soldiers, that circumstance had struck upon the busy and active mind of the Chieftain. Eager to distress and narrow the posts of the enemy, desirous to prevent their establishing a garrison so near him, and willing also to oblige the Baron,—for he often had the idea of a marriage with Rose floating through his brain,—he resolved to send some of his people to drive out the red-coats, and to bring Rose to Glennaquoich. But just as he had ordered Evan with a small party on this duty, the news of Cope's having marched into the Highlands to meet and disperse the forces of the Chevalier, ere they came to a head, obliged him to join the standard with his whole forces.

He sent to Donald Bean to attend him; but that cautious freebooter, who well understood the value of a separate command, instead of joining, sent such apologies as the pressure of the time compelled Fergus to admit as current, though not without the internal resolution of being revenged on him for his procrastination, time and place convenient. However, as he could not amend the matter, he issued orders to Donald to descend into the low country, drive the soldiers from Tully-Veolan, and paying all respect to the mansion of the Baron, to take his abode somewhere near it, for protection of his daughter and family, and to harass and chase away any of the armed volunteers, or small parties of military, which he might find moving about in the vicinity.

As this charge formed a sort of "roving commission," which Donald proposed to interpret in the way most advantageous to himself, as he was relieved from the immediate terror of Fergus, and as he had from his secret services some interest in the councils of the Chevalier, he resolved to make hay while the sun shone. He achieved, without difficulty, the task of driving the soldiers from Tully-Veolan; but, although he did not venture to encroach upon the interior of the family, or to disturb Miss Rose, being unwilling to make himself a powerful enemy in the Chevalier's army,

> For well he knew the Baron's wrath was deadly,

yet he set about to raise contributions and exactions upon the tenantry, and otherwise to turn the war to his own advantage. Meanwhile he mounted the white cockade, and waited upon Rose with a pretext of great devotion for the service in which her father was engaged, and many apologies for the freedom he must necessarily use for the support of his people. It was at this moment that Rose learned, by open-mouthed fame, with all sort of exaggeration, that Waverley had killed the smith at Cairnvreckan, in an attempt to arrest him, had been cast into a dungeon by Major Mellville of Cairnvreckan, and was to be executed by martial law within three days. In the agony which these tidings excited, she proposed to Donald Bean the rescue of the prisoner. It was the very sort of service which he was desirous to undertake, judging it might constitute a merit of such a nature as would make amends for any peccadilloes which he might be guilty of in the country. He had the art, however, pleading all the while duty and discipline, to hold off until poor Rose, in the extremity of her distress, offered to bribe him to the enterprize, with some valuable jewels which had been her mother's.

Donald Bean, who had served in France, knew, and perhaps even over-estimated, the value of these trinkets. But he also perceived Rose's apprehensions of its being discovered that she had parted with her jewels for Waverley's liberation. Resolved this scruple should not part him and the treasure, he voluntarily offered to take an oath that he would never mention Miss Rose's share in the transaction, and fore-seeing convenience in keeping the oath, and no probable advantage from breaking it, he took the engagement—in order, as he told his lieutenant, to deal handsomely by the young lady,—in the only mode and form which, by a mental paction with himself, he considered as binding—he swore secrecy upon his drawn dirk. He was the more especially moved to this act of good faith by some attentions that Miss

Bradwardine shewed to his daughter Alice, which, while they gained the heart of that mountain damsel, highly gratified the pride of her father. Alice, who could now speak a little English, was very communicative in return for Rose's kindness, readily confided to her the whole papers respecting the intrigue with G——'s regiment, of which she was the depositary, and as readily undertook, at her instance, to restore them to Waverley without her father's knowledge. "For they may oblige the bonnie young lady and the handsome young gentleman," thought Alice, "and what use has my father for a whin bits o' scarted paper." The reader is aware that she took an opportunity of executing this purpose on the eve of Waverley's leaving the glen.

How Donald Bean executed his enterprise, the reader is aware. But the expulsion of the military from Tully-Veolan had given alarm, and, while he was lying in wait for Gilfillan, a strong party, such as he did not care to face, was sent to drive back the insurgents in their turn, to encamp there, and to protect the country. The officer, a gentleman and a disciplinarian, neither intruded himself on Miss Bradwardine, whose unprotected situation he respected, nor permitted his soldiers to commit any breach of discipline. He formed a little camp, upon an eminence, near the house of Tully-Veolan, and placed proper guards at the passes in the vicinity.

This unwelcome news reached Donald Bean Lean as he was returning to Tully-Veolan after the discomfiture of Gifted Gilfillan. Determined, however, to obtain the guerdon of his labour, he resolved, since approach to Tully-Veolan was impossible, to deposit his prisoner in Janet's cottage, a place, the very existence of which could hardly have been suspected even by those who had long lived in the vicinity, unless they had been guided thither, and which was utterly unknown to Waverley himself. This effected, he claimed and received his reward. The illness of Waverley was an event which deranged all their calculations. Donald was obliged to leave the neighbourhood with his people and seek more free course for his adventures elsewhere. At Rose's earnest entreaty, he left one old man, a herbalist, who was supposed to understand a little of medicine, to superintend Waverley during his illness.

In the meanwhile, new and fearful doubts started in Rose's mind. They were suggested by old Janet, who insisted, that a reward having been offered for the apprehension of Waverley, and his own personal effects being so valuable, there was no saying to what breach of faith Donald might be tempted. In an agony of grief and terror, Rose took the daring resolution of explaining to the Prince himself the danger in which Mr Waverley stood, judging that, both as a politician, and a man of honour and humanity, Charles Edward would interest himself to prevent his falling into the hands of the opposite party. This letter she at first thought of sending anonymously, but naturally feared it would not, in that case, be credited. She therefore subscribed her name, though with reluctance and terror, and consigned it in charge to a young man who, at leaving his farm to join the Chevalier's army, had made it his petition to her to have some sort of credentials to the Adventurer, from whom he hoped to obtain a commission.

The letter reached Charles Edward on his descent to the low country, and aware of the political importance of having it supposed that he was in correspondence with the English Jacobites, which might be inferred if he could attach this young gentleman to his person, he caused the most positive orders to be transmitted to Donald Bean Lean, to transmit Waverley, safe and uninjured, in person or effects, to the governor of Doune Castle. The freebooter dared not disobey, for the army of the Prince was now so near him that punishment might have followed; besides, he was a politician as well as a robber, and was unwilling to cancel the interest created through former secret services, by being refractory on this occasion. He therefore made a virtue of necessity, and transmitted orders to his lieutenant to convey Edward to Doune, which was safely accomplished in the mode mentioned in a former chapter. The governor of Doune was directed to send him to Edinburgh as a prisoner, because the Prince was apprehensive that Waverley, if set at liberty, might have reassumed his purpose of going into England, without affording him an opportunity of a personal interview. In this, indeed, he acted by advice of the Chieftain of Glennaquoich, with whom it may be remembered the Chevalier communicated upon the mode of disposing of Edward, though without telling him how he came to learn the place of his confinement.

This, indeed, Charles Edward considered as a lady's secret; for although Rose's letter was couched in the most cautious and general terms, and professed to be written merely from motives of humanity, and zeal for the Prince's service, yet she expressed so anxious a wish that she should not be known to have interfered, that the Chevalier was induced to suspect the deep interest which she took in Waverley's safety. This conjecture, which was well-founded, led, however, to false inferences, for the emotion which Edward displayed on approaching Flora and Rose at the ball at Holy-Rood was placed by the Chevalier to the account of the latter; and he concluded that the Baron's views about the settlement of his property, or some such obstacle, thwarted their mutual inclinations. Common Fame, it is true, frequently gave Waverley to Miss Mac-Ivor; but the Prince knew that common Fame is very prodigal in such gifts; and, examining strictly the behaviour of the ladies toward Waverley, he had no doubt that the young Englishman had no interest with Flora, and was beloved by Rose Bradwardine. Desirous to bind Waverley to his service, and wishing also to do a kind and friendly action, the Prince next assailed the Baron on the subject of settling his estate upon his daughter. Mr Bradwardine acquiesced; but the consequence was that Fergus was immediately induced to prefer his double suit for a wife and an earldom, which the Prince rejected, in the manner we have seen. The Chevalier, constantly engaged in his own multiplied affairs, had not hitherto sought any explanation with Waverley, though often meaning to do so. But after Fergus's declaration, he saw the necessity of appearing neutral between the rivals, devoutly hoping that the matter, which now seemed fraught with the seeds of strife, might be permitted to lie over till the termination of his expedition. But when on the march to Derby, Fergus, being questioned concerning his quarrel with Waverley, alleged as the cause, that Edward was desirous of retracting the suit he had made to his sister, the Chevalier plainly told him that he had himself observed Miss Mac-Ivor's behaviour to Waverley, and that he was convinced Fergus was under the influence of a great mistake in judging of Waverley's conduct, who, he had every reason to believe, was engaged to Miss Bradwardine. The quarrel which ensued between Edward and the Chieftain, is, I hope, still in the remembrance of the reader. These circumstances will serve to explain such points of our narration as, according to the custom of story-tellers, we deemed it fit to leave unexplained, for the purpose of exciting the reader's curiosity.

When Janet had once furnished the leading facts of this narrative, Waverley was easily enabled to apply the clue which they afforded to other mazes of the labyrinth, in which he had been engaged. To Rose Bradwardine, then, he owed the life which he now thought he could willingly have laid down to serve her. A little reflection convinced him, however, that to live for her sake was more convenient and agreeable, and that being possessed of independence, she might share it with him either in foreign countries or in his own. The pleasure of being allied to a man of the Baron's high worth, and who was so much valued by his uncle Sir Everard, was also an agreeable consideration, had any thing been wanting to recommend the match. His absurdities, which had appeared grotesquely ludicrous during his prosperity, seemed, in the sun-set of his fortune, to be harmonized and assimilated with the nobler features of his character, so as to add peculiarity without exciting ridicule. His mind occupied with such projects of future happiness, Edward sought Little Veolan, the habitation of Mr Duncan Macwheeble.

Chapter Nineteen

Now is Cupid a child of conscience—he makes restitution.

SHAKSPEARE

MR DUNCAN MACWHEEBLE, no longer Commissary or Baillie, though still enjoying the empty name of the latter dignity, had escaped proscription by an early secession from the insurgents' party, and by his insignificance.

Edward found him in his little office immersed among accounts papers. Before him was a huge bicker of oatmeal-porridge, and at the side thereof, a horn-spoon and a bottle of two-penny. Eagerly running his eye over a voluminous law-paper, he from time to time shovelled an immense spoonful of these nutritive viands into his capacious mouth. A pot-bellied Dutch bottle of brandy, which stood by, intimated either that this honest limb of the law had taken his *morning* already, or that he meant to season his porridge with such a digestive, or perhaps both circumstances might reasonably be inferred. His night-cap and morning gown had whilome been of tartan, but, equally cautious and frugal, the honest Baillie had got them dyed black, lest their original ill-omened colour might remind his visitors of his unlucky excursion to Derby. To sum up his picture, his face was daubed with snuff up to the eyes, and his fingers with ink up to the knuckles. He looked dubiously at Waverley as he approached the little green rail which fenced his desk and stool from the approach of the vulgar. Nothing could give the Baillie more annoyance than the idea of acquaintance being claimed by any of the unfortunate gentlemen, who were now so much more likely to want assistance than to afford profit. But this was the rich young Englishman—who knew what might be his situation?—he was the Baron's friend too—what was to be done?

While these reflections gave an air of absurd perplexity to the poor man's visage, Waverley, reflecting on the communication he was about to make to him, of a nature so ridiculously contrasted with the appearance of the individual, could not help bursting out a-laughing, as he checked the propensity to exclaim, with Syphax,—

—Cato's a proper person to entrust
A love-tale with.

As Mr Macwheeble had no idea of any person laughing heartily, who was either encircled by peril or oppressed by poverty, the hilarity of Edward's countenance greatly relieved the embarrassment of his own, and, giving him a tolerably hearty welcome to Little Veolan, he asked what he would chuse for breakfast. His visitor had, in the first place, something for his private ear, and begged leave to bolt the door. Duncan by no means liked this precaution, which savoured of danger to be apprehended; but he could not now draw back.

Convinced he might trust this man, as he could make it his interest to be faithful, Edward communicated his present situation and future schemes to Macwheeble. The wily agent listened with apprehension when he found Waverley was still in a state of proscription—was somewhat comforted by learning that he had a passport—rubbed his hands with glee when he mentioned the amount of his present fortune—opened huge eyes when he heard the brilliancy of his future expectations—but when he expressed his intention to share them with Miss Rose Bradwardine, extacy had almost deprived the honest man of his senses. The Baillie started from his three-footed stool like the Pythoness from her tripod; flung his best wig out of window, because the block on which it was placed stood in the way of his career; chucked his cap to the cieling, caught it as it fell; whistled Tulloch-gorum; danced a Highland fling with inimitable grace and agility, and then threw himself exhausted into a chair, exclaiming, "Lady Waaver-ley!—ten thousand a-year, the least penny!—Lord preserve my poor understanding!"—

"Amen, with all my heart," said Waverley; "but now, Mr Mac-wheeble, let us proceed to business." This word had somewhat a sedative effect, but the Baillie's head, as he expressed himself, was still "in the bees." He mended his pen, however, marked half a dozen sheets of paper with an ample marginal fold, whipped down Dallas of Saint Martins' Stiles from a shelf, where that venerable work roosted with Stair's Institutions, Dirleton's Doubts, Balfour's Practiques, and a parcel of old account-books—opened the volume at the article Con-tract of Marriage, and prepared to make what he called a "sma' min-ute, to prevent parties from resiling."

With some difficulty, Waverley made him comprehend that he was going a little too fast. He explained to him that he should want his assistance, in the first place, to make his residence safe for the time, by writing to the officer at Tully-Veolan, that Mr Stanley, an English gentleman, nearly related to Colonel Talbot, was upon a visit of busi-ness at Mr Macwheeble's, and, knowing the state of the country, had sent his passport for Captain Foster's inspection. This produced a polite answer from the officer, with an invitation to Mr Stanley to dine with him, which was declined, (as may readily be supposed,) under pretence of business.

Waverley's next request was, that Mr Macwheeble would dispatch a man and horse to ——, the post-town at which Colonel Talbot was to address him, with directions to wait there until the post should bring a letter for Mr Stanley, and then to forward it to Little Veolan with all speed. In a moment, the Baillie was in search of his apprentice (or servitor, as he was called Sixty Years since,) Jock Scriever, and in not much greater space of time, Jock was on the back of the white poney.

"Tak care ye guide him weel, sir, for he's aye been short in the wind since—a hem—Lord be gude to me! (in a low voice), I was going to come out wi'—since I rode whip and spur to fetch the Chevalier to redd Mr Waaverley and Vich Ian Vohr; and an uncanny coup I gat for my pains.—Lord forgie your honour! I might hae broken my neck—but troth it was in a venture, mae ways nor ane; but this maks amends for a'. Lady Waaverley!—ten thousand a-year!—Lord be gude to hus!"

"But you forget, Mr Macwheeble, we want the Baron's consent—the lady's—"

"Never fear, never fear—I'se be caution for them—I'se gie you my personal warrandice—ten thousand a-year! it dings Balmawhapple out and out—a year's rent's worth a' Balmawhapple, fee and life-rent! Lord make us thankful!"

To turn the current of his feelings, Edward enquired if he had heard any thing lately of the Chieftain of Glennaquoich?

"Not one word," answered Macwheeble, "but that he was still in Carlisle Castle, and was soon to be pannelled for his life. I dinna wish the young gentleman ill," he said, "but I hope that they that hae got him will keep him, and no let him back to this Hieland border again to plague us wi' black-mail, and a' manner o' violent, wrongous, and masterfu' oppression and spoliation, both by himself and others of his causing, sending, and hounding out. And he couldna tak care o' the siller when he had gotten it neither, but flang it a' into yon idle quean's lap at Edinburgh—but light come light gane. For my part, I never wish to see a kilt in the country again, nor a red-coat—nor a gun, for that matter, unless it were to shoot a patrick—they're a' tarr'd wi' ae stick; and when they've done ye wrang, even when ye hae gotten decreet of spuilzie, oppression, and violent profits against them, what better are ye?—they have na a plack to pay you—ye need never extract it."

With such discourse, and the intervening topics of business, the time passed until dinner, Macwheeble in the meanwhile promising to devise some mode of introducing Edward at the Duchran, where Rose at present resided, without risk of danger or suspicion, which seemed no very easy task, since the laird was a zealous friend to government. The poultry-yard had been laid under requisition, and cocky-leeky and Scotch collops soon reeked in the Baillie's little parlour. The landlord's corkscrew was just introduced into the muzzle of a pint-bottle of claret, (cribbed possibly from the cellars of Tully-Veolan,) when the sight of the grey poney passing the window at full trot, induced the Baillie, but with due precaution, to place it aside for the moment. Enter Jock Scriever with a packet for Mr Stanley; it is Colonel Talbot's seal; and Edward's fingers tremble as he undoes it. Two official papers, folded, signed, and sealed in all formality, drop out. They are hastily picked up by the Baillie, who had a natural respect for every thing resembling a deed, and glancing slily on their titles, his eyes, or rather spectacles, are greeted with "Protection by His Royal Highness to the person of Cosmo Comyne Bradwardine, Esq. of that ilk, commonly called Baron of Bradwardine, forfeited for his accession to the late rebellion"—the other a protection of the same tenor in favour of Edward Waverley, Esq. Colonel Talbot's letter was in these words:

"MY DEAR EDWARD,

"I am just arrived here, and yet I have finished my business. It has cost me some trouble though, as you shall hear. I waited upon his Royal Highness immediately upon my arrival, and found him in no very good humour for my purpose. Three or four Scotch gentlemen were just leaving his levee. After he had expressed himself to me very courteously: 'Would you think it,' he said, 'Talbot, here have been half a dozen of the most respectable gentlemen, and best friends to government north of the Forth, Major Mellville of Cairnvreckan, Rubrick of Duchran, and others, who have fairly wrung from me, by their downright importunity, a present protection, and the promise of a future pardon, for that stubborn old rebel whom they call Baron of Bradwardine. They allege his high personal character, and the clemency which he shewed to such of our people as fell into the rebels' hands, should weigh in his favour; especially as the loss of his estate is like to be a severe enough punishment. Rubrick has undertaken to keep him at his own house till things are settled in the country, but it's a little hard to be forced in a manner to pardon such a mortal enemy to the House of Brunswick.' This was no favourable moment for opening my business; however, I said I was rejoiced to learn that his Royal Highness was in the course of granting such requests, as it emboldened me to present one of the like nature in my own name. He was very angry, but I persisted; I mentioned the uniform support of our three votes, my brothers' and my own, in the House, touched modestly on services abroad, though valuable only in his Royal Highness having been pleased kindly to accept them, and founded pretty strongly on his own expressions of friendship and good-will. He was embarrassed, but obstinate. I hinted the policy of detaching, on all future occasions, the heir of such a fortune as your uncle's, from the machinations of the disaffected. But I made no impression. I mentioned the obligations which I lay under to Sir Everard, and to you personally, and claimed as the sole reward of my services, that he would be pleased to afford me the means of evincing my gratitude. I perceived that he still meditated a refusal, and taking my commission from my pocket, I said, as a last resource, that as his Royal Highness did not, under these pressing circumstances, think me worthy of a favour which he had not scrupled to grant to other gentlemen, whose services I could hardly judge more important than my own, I must beg leave to deposit, with all humility, my commission in his Royal Highness's hands, and to retire from the service. He was not prepared for this; he told me to take up my commission; said some very handsome things of my services, and granted my request. You are therefore once more a free man, and I have promised for you that you will be a good boy in future, and remember what you owe to the lenity of government. Thus you see *my* prince can be as generous as *yours*. I do not pretend, indeed, that he confers a favour with all the foreign graces and compliments of your Chevalier Errant. But he has a plain English manner, and the evident reluctance with which he grants your request, indicates the sacrifice which he makes of his own inclination to your wishes. —My friend, the adjutant-general, has procured me a duplicate of the Baron's protection, the original being in Major Mellville's possession, which I send to you, as I know that if you can find him you will have pleasure in being the first to communicate the joyful intelligence. He will of course repair to Duchran without loss of time, there to ride quarantine for a few weeks. As for you, I give you leave to escort him thither, and to stay a week there, as I understand a certain fair lady is in that quarter. And I have the pleasure to tell you, that whatever progress you can make in her good graces will be highly agreeable to Sir Everard and Mrs Rachael, who will never believe you settled in views and prospects, and the three ermines passant in actual safety, until you present them with a Mrs Edward Waverley. Now, certain love-affairs of my own—a good many years since—interrupted some measures which were then proposed in favour of the three ermines passant; so I am bound in honour to make them amends. Therefore make good use of your time, for when your week is expired, it will be necessary that you go to London to plead your pardon or something or other in the law court. Ever, dear Waverley, Yours most truly,

"PHILIP TALBOT."

Chapter Twenty

Happy the wooing
That's not long a-doing.

WHEN THE FIRST rapturous sensation occasioned by these excellent tidings had somewhat subsided, Edward proposed instantly to go down to the glen to acquaint the Baron with their import. But the cautious Baillie justly observed, that if the Baron were to appear instantly in public, the tenantry and villagers might become riotous in expressing their joy, and give offence to the "powers that be," a sort of persons for whom the Baillie always had unlimited respect. He therefore proposed that Mr Waverley should go to Janet Gellatley's, and bring the Baron up under cloud of night to Little Veolan, where he might once more enjoy the luxury of a good bed. In the mean while, he said, he himself would go to Captain Foster and shew him the Baron's protection, and obtain his countenance for harbouring him that night, and he would have horses ready on the morrow to set him on his way to the Duchran along with Mr Stanley, "whilk denomination, I apprehend, your honour will for the present retain," said the Baillie.

"Certainly, Mr Macwheeble; but will you not go down to the glen yourself in the evening to meet your patron?"

"That I wad wi' a' my heart; and mickle obliged to your honour for putting me in mind o' my bounden duty. But it will be past sun-set after I get back frae the Captain's, and at these unsonsy hours the glen has a bad name—there's something no that canny about auld Janet Gellatley. The laird he'll no believe thae things, but he was aye ower rash and venturesome—and feared neither man nor devil—and sae's seen o't. But right sure am I Sir George Mackenyie says that no divine can doubt there are witches, since the Bible says thou shalt not suffer them to live; and that no lawyer in Scotland can doubt it, since it's punishable by death by our law—there's baith law and gospel for it. An his honour winna believe Leviticus, he might aye believe the Statute-book—But he may tak his ain way o't—it's a' ane to Duncan Macwheeble. However, I shall send to ask up auld Janet this e'en; it's best no to lightly them that have that character—and we'll want Davie to turn the spit, for I'll gar Eppie put down a fat goose to the fire for your honours to your supper."

When it was near sun-set, Waverley hastened to the hut, and he could not but allow that superstition had chosen no improper locality, nor unfit object, for the foundation of her fantastic terrors. It resembled exactly the description of Spenser:

> There, in a gloomy hollow glen, she found
>   A little cottage built of sticks and reeds,
> In homely wise, and wall'd with sods around,
>   In which a witch did dwell in loathly weeds,
> And wilfull want, all careless of her needs;
>   So chusing solitary to abide
> Far from all neighbours, that her devilish deeds,
>   And hellish arts, from people she might hide,
> And hurt far off, unknown, whomever she espied.

He entered the cottage with these verses in his memory. Poor old Janet, bent double with age, and bleared with peat-smoke, was tottering about the hut with a birch broom, muttering to herself as she endeavoured to make her hearth and floor a little clean for the reception of her expected guests. Waverley's step made her start, look up, and fall a trembling, so much had her nerves been on the rack for her patron's safety. With difficulty Waverley made her comprehend that the Baron was now safe from personal danger; and when her mind had admitted that joyful news, it was equally hard to make her conceive how he was not to enter again upon possession of his estate. "It behoved to be," she said, "he wad get it back again; nae body wad be sae grippal as to tak his gear after they had gi'en him a pardon: and for that Inch-Grubbit, I could whiles wish mysell a witch for his sake, if I were nae feared the Enemy wad tak me at my word." Waverley then gave her some money, and promised that her fidelity should be rewarded. "How can I be rewarded, sir, sae weel, as just to see my auld master and Miss Rose come back and bruick their ain?"

Waverley now took leave of Janet, and soon stood beneath the Baron's Patmos. At a low whistle, he observed the veteran peeping out to reconnoitre, like an old badger with his head out of his hole. "Ye hae come rather early, my good lad," said he, descending; "I question if the red-coats hae beat the tattoo yet, and we're no that safe till then."

"Good news cannot be told too soon," said Waverley, and with infinite joy communicated to him the happy tidings. The old man stood for a moment in an attitude of silent devotion, then exclaimed, "Praise be to God!—I shall see my bairn again."

"And never, I hope, to part with her more," said Waverley.

"I trust in God, not—unless it be to win the means of supporting her—for my things are but in a bruckle state—but what signifies warld's gear?"

"And if," said Waverley, timidly, "there were a situation in life which would put Miss Bradwardine beyond the uncertainty of fortune, and in the rank to which she was born, would you object to it, my dear

Baron, because it would make one of your friends the happiest man in the world?"

The Baron turned, and looked at him with great earnestness.

"Yes," continued Edward, "I shall not consider my sentence of banishment as repealed, unless you will give me permission to accompany you to the Duchran, and"——

The Baron seemed collecting all his dignity to make a suitable reply upon what, at another time, he would have treated as the propounding a treaty of alliance between the houses of Bradwardine and Waverley. But his efforts were in vain; the father was too mighty for the baron; the pride of birth and rank were swept away in the joyful surprise; a slight convulsion passed rapidly over his features as he gave way to the feelings of nature, threw his arms round Waverley's neck, and sobbed out,—"My son, my son! if I had been to search the world, I would have made my choice here."

Edward returned the embrace with great sympathy of feeling, and for a little while they both kept silence. At length it was broken by Edward. "But, Miss Bradwardine?"

"She had never a will but her old father's; besides, you are a likely youth, of honest principles, and high birth;—no, she never had any other will than mine, and in my proudest days I could not have wished a mair eligible espousal for her than the nephew of my excellent old friend, Sir Everard. But I hope, young man, ye deal na rashly in this matter? I hope ye hae secured the approbation of your ain friends and allies, particularly of your uncle, who is *in loco parentis*. A! we maun tak heed o' that." Edward assured him that Sir Everard would think himself highly honoured in the flattering reception his proposal had met with, and that it had his entire approbation; in evidence of which, he put Colonel Talbot's letter into the Baron's hand. The Baron read it with great attention. "Sir Everard," he said, "always despised wealth in comparison of honour and birth; and indeed he hath no occasion to court the *Diva Pecunia*. Yet I now wish, since this Malcolm turns out such a parricide, for I can call him no better, as to think of alienating the family inheritance—I now wish (his eyes fixed on a part of the roof which was visible above the trees,) that I could have left Rose the auld hurley-house, and the riggs belanging to it.—And yet," said he, resuming more cheerfully, "it's may be as weel as it is; for, as Baron of Bradwardine, I might have thought it my duty to insist upon certain compliances respecting name and bearings, whilk now, as a landless laird wi' a tocherless daughter, no one can blame me for departing from."

"Heaven be praised (thought Edward to himself) that Sir Everard does not hear these scruples! the three ermines passant and the rampant bear would certainly have gone together by the ears." He then, with all the ardour of a young lover, assured the Baron, that he sought for his happiness only in Rose's hand, and thought himself as happy in her father's simple approbation, as if he had settled an earldom upon his daughter.

They now reached Little Veolan. The goose was smoking on the table, and the Baillie brandished his knife and fork. A joyous greeting took place between him and his patron. The kitchen, too, had its company. Auld Janet was established at the ingle-nook; Davie had turned the spit, to his immortal honour; and even Ban and Buscar, in the liberality of Macwheeble's joy, had been stuffed to the throat with food, and now lay snoring on the floor.

The next day conducted the Baron and his young friend to the Duchran, where the former was expected, in consequence of the success of the almost unanimous application of the Scottish friends of government in his favour. This had been so general and so powerful, that it was almost thought his estate might have been saved, had it not passed into the rapacious hands of his unworthy kinsman, whose right, arising out of the Baron's attainder, could not be affected by a pardon from the crown. The old gentleman, however, said, with his usual spirit, he was more gratified by the hold he possessed in the good opinion of his neighbours, than he would have been in being rehabilitated and restored *in integrum*, had it been found practicable.

We will not attempt to describe the meeting of the father and daughter—loving each other so affectionately, and separated under such perilous circumstances. Still less will we attempt to analyse the deep blush of Rose, at receiving the compliments of Waverley, or enquire whether she had any curiosity respecting the particular cause of his journey to Scotland at that period. We will not even trouble the reader with the hum-drum details of a courtship Sixty Years since. It is enough to say, that, under so strict a martinet as the Baron, all things were conducted in due form. He took upon himself, the morning after their arrival, the task of announcing the proposal of Waverley to Rose, which she heard with a proper degree of maidenly timidity. Fame does, however, say, that Waverley had, the evening before, found five minutes to apprize her of what was coming, while the rest of the company were looking at three twisted serpents, which formed a *jet d'eau* in the garden.

My fair readers will judge for themselves; but, for my part, I cannot conceive how so important an affair could be communicated in so short a space of time; at least, it certainly took a full hour in the Baron's mode of conveying it.

Waverley was now considered as a received lover in all the forms.

He was made, by dint of smirking and nodding, on the part of the lady of the house, to sit next Miss Bradwardine at dinner, to be Miss Bradwardine's partner at cards. If he came into the room, she of the four Miss Rubricks who chanced to be next Rose, was sure to recollect that her thimble, or her scissars, were at the other end of the room, in order to leave the seat nearest to Miss Bradwardine vacant for his occupation. And sometimes, if papa and mamma were not in the way to keep them on their good behaviour, the misses would titter a little. The old Laird of Duchran would also have his occasional jest, and the old lady her remark. Even the Baron could not refrain; but here Rose escaped every embarrassment but that of conjecture, for his wit was usually couched in a Latin quotation. The very footmen sometimes grinned too broadly, the maid-servants giggled mayhap too loud, and a provoking air of intelligence seemed to pervade the whole family. Alice Bean, the pretty maid of the cavern, who, after her father's *misfortune*, as she called it, had attended Rose as fille-de-chambre, smiled and smirked with the best of them. But Rose and Edward endured all these little vexatious circumstances as other folks have done before and since, and probably contrived some indemnification, since they are not supposed, on the whole, to have been particularly unhappy during Waverley's six days' stay at the Duchran.

It was finally arranged that he should go to Waverley-Honour to make the necessary arrangements for his marriage, thence to London to take the proper measures for pleading his pardon, and return as soon as possible to claim the hand of his plighted bride. Edward also intended in his journey to visit Colonel Talbot; but, above all, it was his most important object to learn the fate of the unfortunate Chief of Glennaquoich; to visit him at Carlisle, and to try whether any thing could yet be done for procuring, if not a pardon, a commutation at least, or alleviation of the punishment to which he was almost certain of being condemned; and, in case of the worst, to offer Flora an asylum with Rose, or otherwise assist her views in any mode which might seem possible. The fate of Fergus seemed hard to be averted. Edward had already striven to interest his friend, Colonel Talbot, in his behalf; but had been given distinctly to understand by his reply, that his credit in matters of that nature was totally exhausted.

The Colonel was still at Edinburgh, and proposed to wait there for some months upon business confided to him by the Duke of Cumberland. He was to be joined by Lady Emily, to whom easy travelling and goat's whey were recommended, and who was to journey northward, under the escort of Francis Stanley. Edward, therefore, met the Colonel at Edinburgh, who wished him joy in the kindest manner on his approaching happiness, and cheerfully undertook many commissions which our hero was necessarily obliged to delegate to his charge. But on the subject of Fergus he was inexorable. He satisfied Edward, indeed, that his interference would be unavailing. But, besides, Colonel Talbot owned that he could not conscientiously use any influence in favour of this unfortunate gentleman. "Justice, which demanded some penalty of those who had wrapped the whole nation in fear and in mourning, could not perhaps have selected a fitter victim. He came to the field with the fullest light upon the nature of his attempt. He had studied and understood the game. His father's fate could not intimidate him. The lenity of the laws, which had restored to him his father's property and rights, could not melt him. That he was brave, generous, and possessed many good qualities, only rendered him more dangerous. That he was enlightened and accomplished, made his crime less excusable. That he was an enthusiast in a wrong cause, only made him the more fit to be its martyr. Above all, he had been the means of bringing many hundred men into the field, who, without him, would never have broke the peace of the country.

"I repeat it," said the Colonel, "though heaven knows with a heart distressed for him as an individual, that this young gentleman has studied and fully understood the desperate game which he played. He threw for life or death, a coronet or a coffin; and he cannot now be permitted, with justice to the country, to draw stakes because the dice have gone against him."

Such was the reasoning of these times, held even by brave and humane men towards a vanquished enemy. Let us devoutly hope, that, in this respect at least, we shall never see the scenes, or hold the sentiments, that were general in Britain Sixty Years since.

Chapter Twenty-One

"To-morrow? O that's sudden!—Spare him, spare him."
SHAKSPEARE

EDWARD, attended by his former servant Alick Polwarth, who had re-entered his service at Edinburgh, reached Carlisle while the Commission of Oyer and Terminer on his unfortunate associates was yet sitting. He had pushed forwards in haste, not, alas! with the most distant hope of saving Fergus, but to see him for the last time. I ought also to have mentioned, that he had furnished funds for the defence of the prisoner in the most liberal manner, as soon as he heard that the day of trial was fixed. A solicitor, and the first counsel, accordingly attended. But it was upon the same footing on which the first physicians are usually summoned to the bed-side of some dying man of rank—the doctors to take the advantage of some incalculable chance of an exertion of nature—the lawyers of the barely possible occurrence of some legal flaw. Edward pressed into the court, which was extremely crowded; but by his arriving from the north, and his extreme eagerness and agitation, it was supposed he was a relation of the prisoners, and people made way for him. It was the third sitting of the court, and there were two men at the bar. The verdict of GUILTY was already pronounced. Edward just glanced at the bar during the momentous pause which ensued. There was no mistaking the stately form and noble features of Fergus Mac-Ivor, although his dress was squalid, and his countenance tinged with the sickly yellow hue of long and close imprisonment. By his side was Evan Maccombich. Edward felt sick and dizzy as he gazed on them, but was recalled to himself as the Clerk of Arraigns pronounced the solemn words: "Fergus Mac-Ivor of Glennaquoich, otherwise called Vich Ian Vohr, and Evan Mac-Ivor, in the Dhu of Tarrascleugh, otherwise called Evan Dhu, otherwise called Evan Maccombich, or Evan Dhu Maccombich— you, and each of you, stand attainted of high treason. What have you to say for yourselves why the court should not pronounce judgment against you, that you die according to law?"

Fergus, as the presiding judge was putting on the fatal cap of judgment, placed his own bonnet upon his head, regarded him with a stedfast and stern look, and replied, in a firm voice, "I cannot let this numerous audience suppose that to such an appeal I have no answer to make. But what I have to say, you would not bear to hear, for my defence would be your condemnation. Proceed, then, in the name of God, to do what is permitted to you. Yesterday, and the day before, you have condemned loyal and honourable blood to be poured out like water—spare not mine—were that of all my ancestors in my veins, I would have peril'd it in this quarrel." He resumed his seat, and refused again to arise.

Evan Maccombich looked at him with great earnestness, and, rising up, seemed anxious to speak, but the confusion of the court, and the perplexity arising from thinking in a language different from that in which he was to express himself, kept him silent. There was a murmur of compassion among the spectators, from the idea that the poor fellow intended to plead the influence of his superior as an excuse for his crime. The judge commanded silence, and encouraged Evan to proceed.

"I was only ganging to say, my lord," said Evan, in what he meant to be an insinuating manner, "that if your excellent honour, and the honourable court, would let Vich Ian Vohr go free just this once, and let him gae back to France, and no to trouble King George's government again, that ony six o' the very best of his clan will be willing to be justified in his stead; and if you'll just let me gae down to Glennaquoich, I'll fetch them up to ye mysell, to head or hang, and you may begin wi' me the very first man."

Notwithstanding the solemnity of the occasion, a sort of laugh was heard in the court at the extraordinary nature of this proposal. The judge checked this indecency, and Evan, looking sternly around, when the murmur abated, "If the Saxon gentlemen are laughing," he said, "because a poor man, such as me, thinks my life, or the life of six of my degree, is worth that of Vich Ian Vohr, it's like enough they may be very right—But if they laugh because they think I wad not keep my word, and come back to redeem him, I can tell them they ken neither the heart of a Hielandman, nor the honour of a gentleman."

There was no farther inclination to laugh among the audience, and a dead silence ensued.

The judge then pronounced upon both prisoners the sentence of the law of high treason, with all its horrible accompaniments. The execution was appointed for the ensuing day. "For you, Fergus Mac-Ivor," continued the judge, "I can hold out no hope of mercy. You must prepare against to-morrow for your last sufferings here, and your great audit hereafter."

"I desire nothing else, my lord," answered Fergus, in the same manly and firm tone.

The hard eyes of Evan, which had been perpetually bent on his Chief, were moistened with a tear. "For you, poor ignorant man," continued the judge, "who, following the ideas in which you have been educated, have this day given us a striking example how the loyalty due to the king and state alone, is, from your unhappy ideas of clanship, transferred to some ambitious individual, who ends by making you the tool of his crimes—for you, I say, I feel so much compassion, that if you can make up your mind to petition for grace, I will endeavour to procure it for you—otherwise"——

"Grace me no grace," said Evan; "since you are to shed Vich Ian Vohr's blood, the only favour I would accept from you, is to bid them loose my hands and gie me my claymore, and bide you just a minute sitting where you are."

"Remove the prisoners," said the judge; "his blood be upon his own head."

Almost stupified with his feelings, Edward found that the rush of the crowd had conveyed him out into the street, ere he knew what he was doing. His immediate wish was to see and speak with Fergus once more. He applied at the castle where his unfortunate friend was confined, but was refused admittance. "The High Sheriff," a non-commissioned officer said, "had requested of the governor that none should be admitted to see the prisoner, excepting his confessor and his sister."

"And where was Miss Mac-Ivor?" They gave him the direction. It was the house of a distinguished catholic family near Carlisle.

Repulsed from the gate of the castle, and not venturing to make application to the High Sheriff or Judges in his own unpopular name, he had recourse to the solicitor who had come down on Fergus's behalf. This gentleman told him, that it was thought the public mind was in danger of being debauched by the accounts of the last moments of these persons, as they were given by the friends of the Pretender; that there had been a resolution therefore to exclude all such persons as had not the plea of near kindred for attending upon them. Yet he promised (to oblige the heir of Waverley-Honour) to get him an order for admittance to the prisoner the next morning, before his irons were knocked off for execution.

"Is it of Fergus Mac-Ivor they speak thus," thought Waverley, "or do I dream? Of Fergus, the bold, the chivalrous, the free-minded? The lofty chieftain of a tribe devoted to him? Is it he, that I have seen lead the chase and head the attack,—the brave, the active, the young, the noble, the love of ladies, and the theme of song,—is it he who is ironed like a malefactor, who is to be dragged on a hurdle to the common gallows to die a lingering and cruel death, and to be mangled by the hands of the most outcast of wretches? Evil, indeed, was the spectre that boded such a fate as this to the brave Chief of Glenna-quoich."

With a faultering voice he requested the solicitor to find means to warn Fergus of his intended visit, should he obtain permission to make it. He then turned away from him, and, returning to the inn, wrote a scarce intelligible note to Flora Mac-Ivor, intimating his purpose to wait upon her that evening. The messenger brought back a letter in Flora's beautiful Italian hand, which seemed scarce to tremble even under this load of misery. "Miss Flora Mac-Ivor," the letter bore, "could not refuse to see the dearest friend of her dear brother, even in her present circumstances of unparalleled distress."

When Edward reached Miss Mac-Ivor's present place of abode, he was instantly admitted. In a large and gloomy tapestried apartment, Flora was seated by a latticed window, sewing what seemed to be a garment of white flannel. At a little distance sat an elderly woman, apparently a foreigner, and of a religious order. She was reading in a book of catholic devotion, but, when Waverley entered, laid it on the table and left the room. Flora rose to receive him, and stretched out her hand, but neither ventured to attempt speech. Her fine complexion was totally gone; her person considerably emaciated; and her face and hands, as white as the purest statuary marble, forming a strong contrast with her sable dress and jet-black hair. Yet, amid these marks of distress, there was nothing negligent or ill-arranged about her dress —even her hair, though totally without ornament, was disposed with her usual attention to neatness. The first words she uttered, were, "Have you seen him?"

"Alas! no," answered Waverley, "I have been refused admittance."

"It accords with the rest," she said, "but we must submit. Shall you obtain leave, do you suppose?"

"For—for—to-morrow," said Waverley, but muttering the last word so faintly that it was almost unintelligible.

"Aye, then or never," said Flora, "until"—she added, looking upward, "the time when, I trust, we shall all meet. But I hope you will see him while earth yet bears him—he always loved you at his heart— though—but it is vain to talk of the past."

"Vain indeed!" echoed Waverley.

"Or even of the future, my good friend, so far as earthly events are concerned; for how often have I pictured to myself the strong possibility of this horrid issue, and tasked myself to consider how I could support my part, and yet how far has all my anticipation fallen short of the unimaginable bitterness of this hour."

"Dear Flora, if your strength of mind"——

"Ay, there it is," she answered, something wildly; "there is, Mr Waverley, there is a busy devil at my heart, that whispers—but it were madness to listen to it—that the strength of mind on which Flora prided herself has—murdered her brother!"

"Good God! how can you give utterance to a thought so shocking?"

"Ay, is it not so? but yet it haunts me like a phantom: I know it unsubstantial and vain; but it *will* be present; will intrude its horrors on my mind; will whisper that my brother, as volatile as ardent, would have divided his energies amid an hundred objects. It was I who taught him to centre them, and to gage all on this dreadful and desperate cast. Oh that I could recollect that I had but once said to him, 'He that striketh with the sword shall perish by the sword;' that I had but once said, Remain at home, spare yourself, your vassals, your life, for enterprises within the reach of man. But O, Mr Waverley, I spurred his fiery temper, and half of his ruin at least lies with his sister!"

The horrid idea which she had intimated, Edward endeavoured to combat by every incoherent argument that occurred to him. He recalled to her the principles on which both thought it their duty to act, and in which they had been educated.

"Do not think I have forgotten them," said she, looking up, with eager quickness; "I do not regret his attempt, because it was wrong—O no, on that point I am armed—but because it was impossible it could end otherwise than thus."

"Yet it did not always seem so desperate and hazardous as it was; and it would have been chosen by the bold spirit of Fergus, whether you had approved it or no; your counsels only served to give unity and consistence to his conduct; to dignify, but not to precipitate his resolution." But while he urged these and similar arguments, Flora had ceased to listen, and was again intent upon her needle-work.

"Do you remember," she said, looking up with a ghastly smile, as he paused in his discourse, "you once found me making Fergus's bride-favour, and now I am sewing his bridal-garment; our friends here," said she, with suppressed emotion, "are to give hallowed earth in their chapel to the bloody reliques of the last Vich Ian Vohr. But they will not all rest together—no—his head!—I shall not have the last miserable satisfaction of kissing the cold lips of my dear, dear Fergus!"

The unfortunate Flora here, after one or two hysterical sobs, fainted in her chair. The lady, who had been attending in the anti-room, now entered hastily, and begged Edward to leave the room, but not the house.

When he was recalled, after the space of nearly half an hour, he found that, by a strong effort, Miss Mac-Ivor had greatly composed herself. It was then he ventured to urge Miss Bradwardine's claim, to be considered as an adopted sister, and empowered to assist her plans for the future.

"I have had a letter from my dear Rose," she replied, "to the same kind purpose. Sorrow is selfish and engrossing, or I would have written to express, that, even in my own despair, I felt a gleam of pleasure at learning her happy prospects, and at hearing that the good old Baron has escaped the general wreck. Give this to my dearest Rose; it is her poor Flora's only ornament of value, and was the gift of a princess." She put into his hands a case, containing the chain of diamonds with which she used to decorate her hair. "To me it is in future useless. The kindness of my friends has secured me a retreat in the convent of the Scottish Benedictine nuns at Paris. To-morrow—if indeed I can survive to-morrow—I set forward on my journey with this venerable sister.—And now, Mr Waverley, adieu—may you be as happy with Rose as your amiable dispositions deserve; and think sometimes on the friends you have lost. Do not attempt to see me again; it would be mistaken kindness."

She gave her hand, on which Edward shed a torrent of tears, and, with a tottering step, withdrew from the apartment, and returned to the town of Carlisle. At the inn, he found a letter from his law friend, intimating, that he would be admitted to Fergus next morning, as soon as the Castle-gates were opened, and permitted to remain with him till the arrival of the Sheriff gave signal for the fatal procession.

Chapter Twenty-Two

—————A darker departure is near,
The death-drum is muffled, and sable the bier.
                                        CAMPBELL

AFTER A sleepless night, the first dawn of morning found Waverley on the esplanade in front of the old Gothic gate of Carlisle Castle. But he paced it long in every direction, before the hour came when, according to the rules of the garrison, the gates were opened, and the drawbridge lowered. He produced his order to the serjeant of the guard, and was admitted. The place of Fergus's confinement was a gloomy and vaulted apartment in the central part of the castle; a massive old tower, supposed to be of great antiquity, and surrounded by outworks, seemingly of Henry VIII.'s time, or somewhat later. The grating of the huge old-fashioned bars and bolts, withdrawn for the purpose of admitting Edward, was answered by the clash of chains, as the unfortunate Chieftain, strongly and heavily fettered, shuffled along the stone floor of his prison, to fling himself into his friend's arms.

"My dear Edward," said he, in a firm and even chearful voice, "this is truly kind. I heard of your approaching happiness with the highest pleasure; and how does Rose? and how our old whimsical friend the Baron? Well, I am sure, from your looks—and how will you settle precedence between the three ermines passant and the bear and boot-jack?"

"How, O how, my dear Fergus, can you talk of such trifles at such a moment?"

"Why, we have entered Carlisle with happier auspices, to be sure—on the 16th of November last, for example, when we marched in, side by side, and hoisted the white flag on these ancient towers. But I am no boy, to sit down and weep, because the luck has gone against me. I knew the stake which I risqued; we played the game boldly, and the forfeit shall be paid manfully. And now, since my time is short, let me come to the questions that interest me most—the Prince? has he escaped the bloodhounds?"

"He has, and is in safety!"

"Praised be God for that! Tell me the particulars of his escape."

Waverley communicated that remarkable history, so far as it had then transpired, to which Fergus listened with deep interest. He asked after several other friends; and then made many minute enquiries concerning the fate of his own clansmen. They had suffered less than other tribes who had been engaged in the affair; for having, in a great measure, dispersed, and returned home after the captivity of their Chieftain, as was an universal custom among the Highlanders, they were not in arms when the insurrection was finally suppressed, and consequently were treated with less rigour. This Fergus heard with great satisfaction.

"You are rich," he said, "Waverley, and you are generous; when you hear of these poor Mac-Ivors being distressed about their miserable possessions by some harsh overseer or agent of government, remember you have worn their tartan, and are an adopted son of their race. The Baron, who knows our manners, and lies near our country, will apprize you of the time and means to be their protector. Will you promise this to the last Vich Ian Vohr?"

Edward, as may well be believed, pledged his word; which he afterwards so amply redeemed, that his memory still lives in these glens by the name of the Friend of the Sons of Ivor.

"Would to God," continued the Chieftain, "I could bequeath to you my rights to the love and obedience and affection of this primitive and brave race:—or at least, as I have striven to do, persuade poor Evan to accept of his life upon their terms; and be to you, what he has been to me, the kindest,—the bravest,—the most devoted——"

The tears which his own fate could not draw forth, fell fast for that of his foster-brother.

"But," said he, drying them, "that cannot be. You cannot be to them Vich Ian Vohr; and these three magic words," said he, half smiling, "are the only *Open Sesamum* to their feelings and sympathies, and poor Evan must attend his foster-brother in death, as he has done through his whole life."

"And I am sure," said Maccombich, raising himself from the floor, on which, for fear of interrupting their conversation, he had lain so still, that, in the obscurity of the apartment, Edward was not aware of his presence,—"I am sure Evan never desired nor deserved a better end than just to die with his chieftain."

"And now," said Fergus, "while we are upon the subject of clanship —what think you now of the prediction of the Bodach glas?"—then before Edward could answer, "I saw him again last night—he stood in the slip of moonshine which fell, from that high and narrow window, towards my bed. Why should I fear him, I thought—to-morrow, long ere this time, I shall be as immaterial as he. 'False Spirit,' I said, 'art thou come to close thy walks on earth, and to enjoy thy triumph in the fall of the last descendant of thine enemy?' The spectre seemed to beckon and to smile, as he faded from my sight. What do you think of it?—I asked the same question at the priest, who is a good and sensible man; he admitted that the church allowed that such apparitions were possible, but urged me not to permit my mind to dwell upon it, as imagination plays us such strange tricks. What do you think of it?"

"Much as your confessor," said Waverley, willing to avoid dispute upon such a point at such a moment. A tap at the door now announced that good man, and Edward retired while he administered to both prisoners the last rites of religion, in the mode which the church of Rome prescribes.

In about an hour he was re-admitted. Soon after three files of soldiers entered with a blacksmith, who struck the fetters from the legs of the prisoners.

"You see the compliment they pay to our Highland strength and courage—we have lain chained here like wild beasts, till our legs are cramped into palsy, and when they free us they send six soldiers with loaded muskets to prevent our taking the castle by storm."

Edward afterwards learned that these severe precautions had been taken in consequence of a desperate attempt of the prisoners to escape, in which they had very nearly succeeded.

Shortly afterwards the drums of the garrison beat to arms. "That is the last turn-out," said Fergus, "that I shall hear and obey. And now, my dear, dear Edward, ere we part let us speak of Flora,—a subject which awakes the tenderest feeling that yet thrills within me."

"We part not *here?*" said Waverley.

"O yes, we do, you must come no farther.—Not that I fear what is to follow for myself," he said proudly; "Nature has her tortures as well as art, and how happy should we think the man who escapes from the throes of a mortal and painful disorder, in the space of a short half hour? And this matter, spin it out as they will, cannot last longer. But what a dying man can suffer firmly, may kill a living friend to look upon.—This same law of high treason," he continued, with astonishing firmness and composure, "is one of the blessings, Edward, with which your free country has accommodated poor old Scotland—her own jurisprudence, as I have heard, was much milder. But I suppose one day or other—when there are no longer any wild Highlanders to benefit by its tender mercies—they will blot it from their records, as levelling them with a nation of cannibals. The mummery, too, of exposing the senseless head—they have not the wit to grace mine with a paper coronet; there would be some satire in that, Edward. I hope they will set it on the Scotch gate though, that I may look, even after death, to the blue hills of my own country, that I love so well. The Baron would have added,

> Moritur, et moriens dulces reminiscitur Argos."

A bustle, and the sound of wheels and horses' feet, was now heard in the court-yard of the castle. "As I have told you why you must not follow me, and as these sounds admonish me my time flies fast, tell me how you found poor Flora?"

Waverley, with a voice interrupted by suffocating sensations, gave some account of her state of mind.

"Poor Flora!" answered the Chief, "she could have borne her own death, but not mine. You, Waverley, will soon know the happiness of mutual affection in the married state—long, long, may Rose and you enjoy it!—but you never can know the purity of feeling which combines two orphans, like Flora and me, left alone as it were in the world, and being all in all to each other from our very infancy. But her strong sense of duty, and predominant feeling of loyalty, will give new nerve to her mind after the immediate and acute sensation of this parting has passed away. She will then think of Fergus as of the heroes of our race upon whose deeds she loved to dwell."

"Shall you not see her then? She seemed to expect it."

"A necessary deceit will spare her the last dreadful parting. I could not part from her without tears, and I cannot bear that these men should think they have power to extort them. She was made to believe she would see me at a later hour, and this letter, which my confessor will deliver, will apprize her that all is over."

An officer now appeared, and intimated that the High Sheriff and his attendants waited before the gate of the castle, to claim the bodies of Fergus Mac-Ivor and Evan Maccombich: "I come," said Fergus. Accordingly, supporting Edward by the arm, and followed by Evan Dhu and the priest, he moved down the stairs of the tower, the soldiers bringing up the rear. The court was occupied by a squadron of dragoons and a battalion of infantry, drawn up in hollow square. Within their ranks was the sledge, or hurdle, on which the prisoners were to be drawn to the place of execution, about a mile distant from Carlisle. It was painted black, and drawn by a white horse. At one end of the vehicle sate the executioner, a horrid looking fellow, as beseemed his trade, with the broad axe in his hand; at the other end, next the horse, was an empty seat for two persons. Through the deep and dark Gothic arch-way that opened on the drawbridge, were seen on horseback the High Sheriff and his attendants, whom the etiquette betwixt the civil and military powers did not permit to come farther. "This is well GOT UP for a closing scene," said Fergus, smiling disdainfully as he gazed around upon this apparatus of terror. Evan Dhu exclaimed with some eagerness, after looking at the dragoons, "These are the very chields that galloped off at Gladsmuir, ere we could kill a dozen o' them. They look bold enough now, however." The priest entreated him to be silent.

The sledge now approached, and Fergus turning round embraced Waverley, kissed him on each side of the face, and stepped nimbly into his place. Evan sate down by his side. The priest was to follow in a carriage belonging to his patron, the catholic gentleman at whose house Flora resided. As Fergus waved his hand to Edward, the ranks closed around the sledge, and the whole procession began to move forward. There was a moment's stop at the gateway, while the governor of the castle and the High Sheriff went through a short ceremony, the military officer there delivering over the persons of the criminals to the civil power. "God save King George!" said the High Sheriff. When the formality concluded, Fergus stood erect in his sledge, and, with a firm and steady voice, replied, "God save King *James!*" These were the last words which Waverley heard him speak.

The procession resumed its march, and the sledge vanished from beneath the portal, under which it had stopped for an instant. The dead march, as it is called, was instantly heard, and its melancholy sounds were mingled with those of a muffled peal, tolled from the neighbouring cathedral. The sound of the military music died away as the procession moved on; the sullen clang of the bells was soon heard to sound alone.

The last of the soldiers had now disappeared from under the vaulted archway through which they had been filing for several minutes; the court-yard was now totally empty, but Waverley still stood there as if stupified, his eyes fixed upon the dark pass where he had so lately seen the last glimpse of his friend.—At length, a female servant of the governor, struck with surprise and compassion at the stupified misery which his countenance expressed, asked him, if he would not walk into her master's house and sit down? She was obliged to repeat her question twice, ere he comprehended her, but at length it recalled him to himself.—Declining the courtesy, by a hasty gesture, he pulled his hat over his eyes, and, leaving the castle, walked as swiftly as he could through the empty streets, till he regained his inn, then threw himself into an apartment and bolted the door.

In about an hour and a half, which seemed an age of unutterable suspense, the sound of the drums and fifes, performing a lively air, and the confused murmur of the crowd which now filled the streets, so lately deserted, apprized him that all was over, and that the military and populace were returning from the dreadful scene. I will not attempt to describe his sensations.

In the evening the priest made him a visit, and informed him that he did so by directions of his deceased friend, to assure him that Fergus Mac-Ivor had died as he lived, and remembered his friendship to the last. He added, he had also seen Flora, whose state of mind seemed more composed since all was over. With her, and sister Theresa, the priest proposed next day to leave Carlisle, for the nearest sea-port, from which they could embark for France. Waverley forced on this good man a ring of some value, and a sum of money to be employed (as he thought might gratify Flora) in the services of the catholic church, for the memory of his friend. "*Fungarque inani munere*," he repeated as the ecclesiastic retired. "Yet why not class these acts of remembrance with the other honours, with which affection, in all sects, pursues the memory of the dead?"

The next morning ere day-light he took leave of the town of Carlisle, promising to himself never again to enter its walls. He dared hardly look back towards the Gothic battlements of the fortified gate under which he passed, for the place is surrounded with an old wall. "They're no there," said Alick Polwarth, who guessed the cause of the dubious look which Waverley cast backward, and who, with the vulgar appetite for the horrible, was master of each detail of the butchery. "The heads are ower the Scotch yate, as they ca' it. It's a great pity of Evan Dhu, who was a very weel-meaning good-natured man, to be a Hieland-man; and indeed so was the Laird o' Glennaquoich, for that matter, when he was na in ane o' his tirrivies."

Chapter Twenty-Three

DULCE DOMUM

THE IMPRESSION of horror with which Waverley left Carlisle, soft-ened by degrees into melancholy, a gradation which was accelerated by the painful, yet soothing, task of writing to Rose, and, while he could not suppress his own feelings of the calamity, endeavouring to place it before her in a light which might grieve her, without shocking her imagination. The picture which he drew for her benefit he gradu-ally familiarized to his own mind, and his next letters of course referred to the prospects of peace and happiness which lay before them. Yet, though his first horrible sensations had sunk into melancholy, Edward had reached his native county before he could, as usual upon former excursions, look round for enjoyment upon the face of nature.

He then, for the first time since leaving Edinburgh, began to experience that pleasure which almost all feel who return to a verdant, populous, and highly-cultivated country, from scenes of waste desolation, or of solitary and melancholy grandeur. But how were those feelings enhanced when he entered on the domain so long possessed by his fore-fathers; recognized the old oaks of Waverley Chace; thought with what delight he would introduce Rose to all his favourite haunts; beheld at length the towers of the venerable Hall arise above the woods in which they were embowered, and finally threw himself into the arms of the venerable relatives to whom he owed so much duty and affection!

The happiness of their meeting was not tarnished by a single word of reproach. On the contrary, whatever pain Sir Everard and Mrs Rachael had felt during Waverley's perilous engagement with the young Chevalier, it assorted too well with the principles in which they had been brought up, to incur reprobation, or even censure. Colonel Talbot also had smoothed the way, with great address, for Edward's favourable reception, by dwelling upon his gallant behaviour in the military character, particularly his bravery and generosity at Preston; until, warmed at the idea of their nephew's engaging in single combat, making prisoner, and saving from slaughter, so distinguished an officer as the Colonel himself, the imagination of the Baronet and his sister ranked the exploits of Edward with those of Wilibert, Hildebrand, and Nigel, the vaunted heroes of their race.

The appearance of Waverley, embrowned by exercise, and dignified by the habits of military discipline, had acquired an athletic and hardy character, which not only verified the Colonel's narrative, but surprised and delighted all the inhabitants of Waverley-Honour. They crowded to see, to hear him, and to sing his praises. Mr Pembroke, who, it will readily be believed, secretly extolled his spirit and courage in embracing the genuine cause of the Church of England, censured his pupil gently nevertheless for being so careless of his manuscripts, which indeed he said had occasioned him some personal inconvenience, as, upon the Baronet being arrested by a king's messenger, he had deemed it prudent to retire to a concealment called the "priest's hole," from the use it had been put to in former days; where, he assured our hero, the butler had thought it safe to venture with food only once in the day, so that he had repeatedly been compelled to dine upon victuals either absolutely cold, or, what was worse, only half warm, not to mention that sometimes his bed had not been arranged for two days together. Waverley's mind involuntarily turned to the Patmos of the Baron of Bradwardine, who was enchanted with Janet's fare, and a few bunches of straw stowed in a cleft in the front of a sand-cliff; but he made no remarks upon a contrast which could only mortify his worthy tutor.

All was now in bustle to prepare for the nuptials of Edward, an event to which the good old Baronet and Mrs Rachael looked forward as if to the renewal of their own youth. The match, as Colonel Talbot had intimated, seemed to them in the highest degree eligible, having every recommendation but wealth, of which they themselves had more than enough. Mr Clippurse was, therefore, summoned to Waverley-Honour, under better auspices than at the commencement of our story. But Mr Clippurse came not alone, for, being now stricken in years, he had associated with him a nephew, a younger vulture (as our English Juvenal, who tells the tale of Swallow the attorney, might have called him,) and they now carried on business as Messrs Clippurse and Hookem. These worthy gentlemen had directions to make the necessary settlements on the most splendid scale of liberality, as if Edward were to wed a peeress in her own right, with her paternal estate tacked to the fringe of her ermine.

But, ere entering upon a subject of proverbial delay, I must remind my reader of the progress of a stone rolled down hill by an idle truant boy (a pastime at which I was myself expert in my more juvenile years:) it moveth at first slowly, avoiding by inflection every obstacle of the least importance; but when it has attained its full impulse, and draws near the conclusion of its career, it smokes and thunders down, taking a rood at every spring, clearing hedge and ditch like a Yorkshire huntsman, and becoming most furiously speedy in its course when it is nearest to being consigned to rest for ever. Even such is the course of a narrative, like that which you are perusing; the earlier events are studiously dwelt upon, that you, kind reader, may be introduced to the character rather by narrative, than by the duller medium of direct description; but when the story draws near its close, we hurry over the circumstances, however important, which your imagination must have forestalled, and leave you to suppose those things, which it would be abusing your patience to narrate at length.

We are, therefore, so far from attempting to trace the progress of the dull labours of Messrs Clippurse and Hookem, or that of their worthy official brethren, who had the charge of suing out the pardons of Edward Waverley and his intended father-in-law, that we can but touch upon matters more attractive. The mutual epistles, for example, which were exchanged between Sir Everard and the Baron upon this occasion, though matchless specimens of eloquence in their way, must be consigned to merciless oblivion. Nor can I tell you at length, how worthy Aunt Rachael, not without a delicate and affectionate allusion to the circumstances which had transferred Rose's maternal diamonds to the hands of Donald Bean Lean, stocked her casket with a set of jewels that a duchess might have envied. Moreover, the reader will have the goodness to imagine that Job Houghton and his dame were suitably provided for, although they could never be persuaded that their son fell otherwise than fighting by the young squire's side; so that Alick, who, as a lover of truth, had made many needless attempts to expound the real circumstances to them, was finally ordered to say not a word more upon the subject. He indemnified himself, however, by the liberal allowance of desperate battles, grisly executions, and raw-head and bloody-bones stories, with which he astonished the servants' hall.

But although these important matters may be briefly told in narrative, like a newspaper report of a chancery suit, yet, with all the urgency which Waverley could use, the real time, which the law proceedings occupied, joined to the delay occasioned by the mode of travelling at that period, rendered it considerably more than two months ere Waverley could leave England and alight at the mansion of the Laird of Duchran to claim the hand of his plighted bride.

The day of his marriage was fixed for the sixth after his arrival. The Baron of Bradwardine, with whom bridals, christenings, and funerals, were festivals of high and solemn import, felt a little hurt, that, including the family of the Duchran, and all in the immediate vicinity who had title to be present on such an occasion, there would not be above thirty persons collected. "When he was married," he observed, "three hundred horse of gentlemen born, besides servants, and some score or two of Highland lairds, who never got on horse-back, were present on the occasion."

But his pride found some consolation in reflecting, that he and his son-in-law having been so lately in arms against government, "it might give matter of reasonable fear and offence to the ruling powers, if they were to collect together the kith, kin, and allies of their houses, arrayed in effeir of war, as was the ancient custom of Scotland on these occasions—And, without dubitation," he concluded with a sigh, "many of those who would have rejoiced most freely upon these joyful espousals, are either gone to a better place, or are now exiles from their native land."

The marriage took place on the appointed day. The Reverend Mr Rubrick, kinsman to the proprietor of the hospitable mansion where it was solemnized, and formerly chaplain to the Baron of Bradwardine, had the satisfaction to unite their hands; and Frank Stanley acted as bridesman, having joined Edward with that view soon after his arrival. Lady Emily and Colonel Talbot had proposed being present, but her health, when the day approached, was found inadequate to the journey. In amends, it was arranged that Edward Waverley and his lady, who, with the Baron, proposed an immediate journey to Waverley-Honour, should, in their way, spend a few days at an estate which Colonel Talbot had been tempted to purchase in Scotland as a very great bargain, and at which he proposed to reside for some time.

Chapter Twenty-Four

"This is no mine ain house, I ken by the biggin o't."
OLD SONG

THE NUPTIAL PARTY travelled in great style. There was a coach and six upon the newest pattern, that dazzled with its splendour the eyes of one half of Scotland, which Sir Everard had presented to his nephew; there was the family coach of Mr Rubrick;—both these were crowded with ladies; and there were gentlemen on horseback, with their servants, to the number of a round score. Nevertheless, without having the fear of famine before his eyes, Baillie Macwheeble met them in the road, to entreat that they would pass by his factor's house at Little Veolan. The Baron stared, and said his son and he would certainly ride by Little Veolan, and pay their compliments to the Baillie, but could not think of bringing with them the "hail *comitatus nuptialis*, or matrimonial procession." He added that, as he understood the Barony had been sold by its unworthy possessor, he was glad to see his old friend Duncan had regained his situation under the new *Dominus*, or proprietor. The Baillie ducked, bowed, and fidgetted, and then again insisted upon his invitation; until the Baron, though rather piqued at the pertinacity of his instances, could not nevertheless refuse to consent, without making evident sensations which he was anxious to conceal.

He fell into a deep study as they approached the top of the avenue, and was only startled from it by observing that the battlements were replaced, the ruins cleared away, and (most wonderful of all) that the two great stone Bears, those mutilated Dagons of his idolatry, had resumed their posts over the gateway. "Now this new proprietor," said he to Edward, "has shewn mair *gusto*, as the Italians call it, in the short time he has had this domain, than that hound Malcolm, though I bred him here mysell, has acquired *vita adhuc durante*.—And now I talk of hounds, is not yon Ban and Buscar, come scouping up the avenue with Davie Gellatley?"

"And I vote we should go to meet them, sir, for I believe the present master of the house is Colonel Talbot, who will expect to see us. We hesitated to mention to you at first that he had purchased your ancient patrimonial property, and even yet, if you do not incline to visit him, we can pass on to the Baillie's."

The Baron had occasion for all his magnanimity. However, he drew a long breath, took a long snuff, and observed, since they had brought him so far, he could not pass the Colonel's gate, and he would be happy to see the new master of his old tenants. He alighted accordingly, as did the other gentlemen and ladies;—he gave his arm to his daughter, and as they descended the avenue, pointed out to her how speedily "the *Diva Pecunia* of the Southron—their tutelary deity, he might call her—had removed the marks of spoliation."

In truth, not only had the felled trees been removed, but, their stumps being grubbed up, and the earth round them levelled and sown with grass, it was evident that the marks of devastation, unless to an eye intimately acquainted with the spot, were already totally obliterated. There was a similar reformation in the outward man of David Gellatley, who met them, every now and then stopping to admire the new suit which graced his person, in the same colours as formerly, but bedizened fine enough to have served Touchstone himself. He danced up with his usual ungainly frolics, first to the Baron, and then to Rose, passing his hands over his clothes, and crying, *"Bra', bra' Davie,"* and scarce able to sing a bar to an end of his thousand-and-one songs, for the breathless extravagance of his joy. The dogs also acknowledged their old master with a thousand gambols. "Upon my conscience, Rose, the gratitude o' thae dumb brutes, and of that puir innocent, brings the tears into my auld een, while that schellum Malcolm—but I'm obliged to Colonel Talbot for putting my hounds into sick good condition, and likewise for puir Davie. But, Rose, my dear, we must not permit them to be a life-rent burden upon the estate."

As he spoke, Lady Emily, leaning upon the arm of her husband, met the party at the lower gate, with a thousand welcomes. After the ceremony of introduction had been gone through, much abridged by the ease and excellent breeding of Lady Emily, she apologized for having used a little art to wile them back to a place which might awaken some painful reflections—"But as it was to change masters, we were very desirous that the Baron"——

"Mr Bradwardine, madam, if you please," said the old gentleman.

"Mr Bradwardine, then, and Mrs Waverley, should see and approve of what we have done to restore the mansion of your fathers to its former state."

The Baron answered with a low bow. Indeed, when he entered the court, excepting that the heavy stables, which had been burned down, were replaced by buildings of a lighter and more picturesque appearance, all seemed as much as possible restored to the state in which he had left it, when he assumed arms some months before. The pigeon-house was replenished; the fountain played with its usual activity, and not only the Bear who predominated over its bason, but all the other Bears whatsoever were replaced upon their stations, and renewed or repaired with so much care, that they bore no tokens of the violence with which they had so lately descended from them. While these minutiæ had been so heedfully attended to, it is scarce necessary to add, that the house itself had been thoroughly repaired, as well as the gardens, with the strictest attention to maintain the original character of both, and to erase, as far as possible, all appearance of the ravage they had sustained. The Baron gazed in silent wonder; at length he addressed Colonel Talbot.

"While I acknowledge my obligation to you for the restoration of these images of bears as being the ancient badge of our family, I cannot but marvel that you have no where established your own crest, Colonel Talbot, whilk is, I believe, a mastiff, anciently called a talbot; as the poet has it,

> A talbot strong—a sturdy tyke.

At least such a dog is the crest of the martial and renowned Earls of Shrewsbury, to whom your family are probably blood relations."

"I believe," said the Colonel, smiling, "our dogs are whelps of the same litter—for my part, if crests were to dispute precedence, I should be apt to let them, as the proverb says, 'fight dog, fight bear.' "

As he made this speech, at which the Baron took another long pinch of snuff, they had entered the house, that is the Baron, Rose, and Lady Emily, with young Stanley and the Baillie, for Edward and the rest of the party remained on the terrace, to examine a new green-house stocked with the finest plants. The Baron resumed his favourite topic: "However it may please you to derogate from the honour of your burgonet, Colonel Talbot, which is doubtless your humour, as I have seen in other gentlemen of birth and honour in your country, I must again repeat it is a most ancient and distinguished bearing, as well as that of my young friend Francis Stanley, whilk is the eagle and child."

"The bird and bantling they call it in Derbyshire, sir," said Stanley.

"Ye're a daft callant, sir," said the Baron, who had a great liking to this young man, perhaps because he sometimes teazed him.—"Ye're a daft callant, and I must correct you one of these days," shaking his great brown fist at him. "But what I meant to say, Colonel Talbot, is, that yours is an ancient *prosapia*, or descent, and since you have law-fully and justly acquired the estate for you and yours, which I have lost for me and mine, I wish sincerely it may remain in your name as many centuries as it has done in that of the late proprietors."

"That's very handsome, Mr Bradwardine."

"And yet, sir, I cannot but marvel that you, Colonel, whom I noted to have so much of the *amor patriæ*, when we met at Edinburgh, as even to vilipend other countries, should have chosen to establish your lares or household gods, *procul a patriæ finibus*, and in a manner to expatriate yourself."

"Why really, Baron, I do not see why, to keep the secret of these foolish boys, Waverley and Stanley, and my wife, who is no wiser, one old soldier should continue to impose upon another. You must know then, I have so much of that same prejudice in favour of my native country, that the sum of money which I advanced to the seller of this extensive barony, has only purchased for me a box in ——shire, called Brere-wood Lodge, with about two hundred and fifty acres of land, the chief merit of which is, that it is within a very few miles of Waverley-Honour."

"And who then, in the name of Heaven, has bought this property?"

"That," said the Colonel, "it is this gentleman's profession to explain."

The Baillie, whom this reference regarded, had all this while shifted from one foot to another with great impatience, "like a hen," as he afterwards said, "upon a het girdle," and chuckling, he might have added, like the said hen in all the glory of laying an egg,—now pushed forward. "That I can, that I can—your honour;" drawing from his pocket a formidable budget of papers, and untying the red tape with a hand trembling with eagerness. "Here is the Disposition and Assignation by Malcolm Bradwardine of Inch-Grubbit, regularly signed and tested in terms of the statute, whereby for a certain sum of sterling money presently contented and paid to him, he has disponed, alienated, and conveyed the whole estate and barony of Bradwardine, Tully-Veolan, and others, with the fortalice and manor"——

"For God's sake to the point, sir; I have all that by heart," said the Colonel.

"To Cosmo Comyne Bradwardine, Esq." pursued the Baillie, "his heirs and assignees, simply and irredeemably—to be held either *a me vel de me*"——

"Pray read short, sir."

"On the conscience of an honest man, Colonel, I read as short as is consistent with Stile.—Under the burden and reservation always"——

"Mr Macwheeble, this would outlast a Russian winter—give me leave. In short, Mr Bradwardine, your family estate is your own once more in full property, and at your absolute disposal, but only burdened with the sum advanced to re-purchase it, which I understand is utterly disproportioned to its value."

"An auld sang, an auld sang, if it please your honours," cried the Baillie, rubbing his hands, "look at the rental book."

"Which sum being advanced by Mr Edward Waverley, chiefly from the price of his father's property which I bought from him, is secured to his lady your daughter and her family by this marriage."

"It is a catholic security," shouted the Baillie, "to Rose Comyne Bradwardine, alias Waaverley, in life-rent, and the children of the said marriage in fee; and I made up a wee bit jotting of an ante-nuptial contract, *intuitu matrimonij*, so it canna be subject to reduction here-after as a *donatio inter virum et uxorem*."

It is difficult to say whether the worthy Baron was most delighted with the restitution of his family property, or with the delicacy and generosity that left him unfettered to pursue his pleasure in disposing of it after his death, and which avoided, as much as possible, even the appearance of laying him under pecuniary obligation. When his first pause of joy and astonishment was over, his thoughts turned to the unworthy heir male, who, he pronounced, had sold his birth-right like Esau, for a mess o' pottage.

"But wha cookit the parridge for him?" exclaimed the Baillie, "I wad like to ken that;—wha, but your honour's to command, Duncan Macwheeble? His honour, young Mr Waaverley, pat it a' in my hand frae the beginning—frae the first calling o' the summons, as I may say. I circumvented them—I played at bogle about the bush wi' them—I cajolled them; and if I have na gien Inch-Grubbit and Jamie Howie a bonnie begunk, they ken themselves. Him a writer! I did na gae slapdash to them wi' our young bra' bridegroom, to gar them haud up the market; na, na; I scared them wi' our wild tenantry, and the Mac-Ivors, that are but ill settled yet, till they durst na on ony errand whatsoever gang ower the door-stane after gloaming, for fear John Heatherblutter, or some siccan dare-the-deil, should take a baff at them: than, on the other side, I beflum'd them wi' Colonel Talbot—wad they offer to keep up the price again the Duke's friend? did na they ken wha was master? had na they seen aneuch, by the example of mony a poor misguided unhappy body"——

"Who went to Derby, for example, Mr Macwheeble?" said the Colonel to him, aside.

"O whisht, Colonel, for the luve o' God! let that flee stick i' the wa'. —There were mony gude folk at Derby; and it's ill speaking of hal-ters,"—with a sly cast of his eye toward the Baron, who was in deep reverie.

Starting out of it at once, he took Macwheeble by the button, and led him into one of the deep window recesses, whence only fragments of their conversation reached the rest of the party. It certainly related to stamped paper and parchment; for no other subject, even from the mouth of his patron, and he once more an effective one, could have arrested so deeply the Baillie's reverend and absorbed attention.

"I understand your honour perfectly; it can be done as easy as taking out a decreet in absence."

"To her and him, after my demise, and to their heirs-male,—but preferring the second son, if God shall bless them with two, who is to carry the name and arms of Bradwardine of that ilk, without any other name or armorial bearings whatsoever."

"Tut, your honour; I'll mak a slight jotting the morn; it will cost but a charter of resignation *in favorem;* and I'll hae it ready for the next term in Exchequer."

Their private conversation ended, the Baron was now summoned to do the honours of Tully-Veolan to new guests. These were, Major Mellville of Cairnvreckan, and the Reverend Mr Morton, followed by two or three others of the Baron's acquaintances, who had been made privy to his having again acquired the estate of his fathers. The shouts of the villagers were also heard beneath in the court-yard; for Saunders Saunderson, who had kept the secret for several days with laudable prudence, had unloosed his tongue upon beholding the arrival of the carriages.

But, while Edward received Major Mellville with politeness, and the clergyman with the most affectionate and grateful kindness, his father-in-law looked a little awkward, as uncertain how he should answer the necessary claims of hospitality to his guests, and forward the festivity of his tenants. Lady Emily relieved him, by intimating, that, though she must be an indifferent representative of Mrs Edward Waverley in many respects, she hoped the Baron would approve of the entertainment she had ordered, in expectation of so many guests; and that they would find such other accommodations provided, as might in some degree support the ancient hospitality of Tully-Veolan. It is impossible to describe the pleasure which this assurance gave the Baron, who, with an air of gallantry, half appertaining to the stiff Scottish laird, and half to the officer in the French service, offered his arm to the fair speaker, and led the way, in something between a stride and a minuet step, into the large dining parlour, followed by all the rest of the good company.

By dint of Saunderson's directions and exertions, all here, as well as in the other apartments, had been disposed as much as possible according to the old arrangement; and even where new moveables had been necessary, they had been selected in the same character with the old furniture. There was one addition to this fine old apartment, however, which drew tears into the Baron's eyes. It was a large and animated painting, representing Fergus Mac-Ivor and Waverley in their Highland dress, the scene a wild, rocky, and mountainous pass, down which the clan were descending in the back-ground. It was taken from a spirited sketch, drawn while they were in Edinburgh by a young man of high genius, and had been painted on a full length scale by an eminent London artist. Raeburn himself, (whose Highland chiefs do all but walk out of the canvas) could not have done more justice to the subject; and the ardent, fiery, and impetuous character of the unfortunate Chief of Glennaquoich was finely contrasted with the contemplative, fanciful, and enthusiastic expression of his happier friend. Beside this painting were hung the arms which Waverley had borne in the unfortunate civil war. The whole piece was generally admired.

Men must however eat, in spite both of sentiment and vertu; and the Baron, while he assumed the lower end of the table, insisted that Lady Emily should do the honours of the head, that they might, he said, set a meet example to the *young folk*. After a pause of deliberation, employed in adjusting in his own brain the precedence between the presbyterian kirk and episcopal church of Scotland, he requested Mr Morton, as the stranger, would crave a blessing, observing, Mr Rubrick, who was *at home*, would return thanks for the distinguished mercies it had been his lot to experience. The dinner was excellent. Saunderson attended in full costume, with all the former inferior servants, excepting one or two, who had not been heard of since Culloden. The cellars were stocked with wine which was pronounced superb, and it had been contrived that the Bear of the fountain, in the court-yard, should (for that night only) play excellent brandy punch, for the benefit of the lower orders.

When the dinner was over, the Baron, about to propose a solemn toast, cast somewhat a sorrowful look upon the side-board, which however exhibited much of his plate that had either been secreted, or purchased by neighbouring gentlemen from the soldiery, and by them gladly restored to the original owner.

"In the late times," he said, "those must be thankful who have saved life and lands; and yet when I am to pronounce this toast, I cannot but regret an old heirloom, Lady Emily—a *poculum potatorium*, Colonel Talbot"——

Here the Baron's elbow was gently touched by his Major Domo, and turning round, he beheld, in the hands of Alexander ab Alexandro, the celebrated cup of Saint Duthac, the Blessed Bear of Bradwardine! I question if the recovery of his estate afforded him more rapture. "By my honour," he said, "one might almost believe in brownies and fairies, Lady Emily, where your ladyship is in presence."

"I am truly happy," said Colonel Talbot, "that, by the recovery of this piece of family antiquity, it has fallen within my power to give you some token of my deep interest in all that concerns my young friend Edward. But, that you may not suspect Lady Emily for a sorceress, or me for a conjuror, which is no joke in Scotland, I must tell you that Frank Stanley, your friend, who has been seized with a *tartan* fever ever since he heard Edward's tales of old Scotch manners, happened once to describe to us at second hand this remarkable cup. My servant, Spontoon, who, like a true old soldier, observes every thing and says little, gave me afterwards to understand, that he thought he had seen the piece of plate Mr Stanley mentioned in the possession of a certain Mrs Nosebag, the wife of an adjutant of dragoons, who, having been originally the helpmate of a pawnbroker, had found an opportunity, during the late unpleasant scenes in Scotland, to trade a little in her old line, and accordingly, by dint of a little ready money, had become the depositary of the more valuable part of the spoil of half the army. You may believe the cup was speedily recovered, and it will give me very great pleasure if you can allow me to suppose that its value is not diminished by having been restored through my means."

The tear mingled with the wine which the Baron filled, as he proposed a cup of gratitude to Colonel Talbot and the prosperity of the united Houses of Waverley-Honour and Bradwardine.

It only remains for me to say, that as no wish was ever uttered with more affectionate sincerity, there are few which, allowing for the necessary mutability of human events, have been, upon the whole, more happily fulfilled.

Chapter Twenty-Five

A POSTSCRIPT, WHICH SHOULD HAVE BEEN A PREFACE

OUR JOURNEY is now finished, gentle reader, and if your patience has accompanied me through these sheets, the contract is, on your part, strictly fulfilled. Yet, like the driver who has received his full hire, I still linger near you, and make, with becoming diffidence, a trifling additional claim upon your bounty and good nature. You are as free, however, to shut the volume of the one petitioner, as to close your door in the face of the other.

This should have been a prefatory chapter, but for two reasons: First, that most novel readers, as my own conscience reminds me, are apt to be guilty of the sin of omission respecting that same matter of prefaces. Secondly, that it is a general custom with that class of students, to begin with the last chapter of a work; so that, after all, these remarks, being introduced last in order, have still the best chance to be read in their proper place.

There is no European nation which, within the course of half a century, or little more, has undergone so complete a change as this kingdom of Scotland. The effects of the insurrection of 1745,—the destruction of the patriarchal power of the Highland chiefs, and the abolition of the heritable jurisdictions of the Lowland nobility and barons, the total eradication of the Jacobite party, which, averse to intermingle with the English, or adopt their customs, long continued to pride themselves upon maintaining ancient Scottish manners and customs,—commenced this innovation. The gradual influx of wealth, and extension of commerce, have since united to render the present people of Scotland a class of beings as different from their grandfathers, as the existing English are from those of Queen Elizabeth's time. The political and economical effects of these changes have been traced by Lord Selkirk with great precision and accuracy. But the change, though steadily and rapidly progressive, has, nevertheless, been gradual; and, like those who drift down the stream of a deep and smooth river, we are not aware of the progress we have made until we fix our eye on the now-distant point from which we set out. Such of the present generation as can recollect the last twenty or twenty-five years of the eighteenth century, will be fully sensible of the truth of this statement; especially if their acquaintance and connexions lay among those who, in my younger time, were facetiously called, "folks of the old leaven," who still cherished a lingering, though hopeless attachment, to the house of Stuart. This race has now almost entirely vanished from the land, and with it, doubtless, much absurd political prejudice; but, also, many living examples of singular and disinterested attachment to the principles of loyalty which they received from their fathers, and of old Scottish faith, hospitality, worth, and honour.

It was my accidental lot, though not born a Highlander, (which may be an apology for much bad Gaelic) to reside, during my childhood and youth, among persons of the above description; and now, for the purpose of preserving some idea of the ancient manners of which I have witnessed the almost total extinction, I have embodied in imaginary scenes, and ascribed to fictitious characters, a part of the incidents which I then received from those who were actors in them. Indeed, the most romantic parts of this narrative are precisely those which have a foundation in fact. The exchange of mutual protection between a Highland gentleman and an officer of rank in the king's service, together with the spirited manner in which the latter asserted his right to return the favour he had received, is literally true. The accident by a musket-shot, and the heroic reply imputed to Flora, relate to a lady of rank not long deceased. And scarce a gentleman who was "in hiding," after the battle of Culloden, but could tell a tale of strange concealments, and of wild and hair's-breadth 'scapes, far more extravagant than any I have ascribed to my heroes. Of this the escape of Charles Edward himself, as the most prominent, is the most striking example. The account of the battle of Preston, and skirmish at Clifton, is taken from the narrative of intelligent eye-witnesses, and corrected from the History of the Rebellion by the late venerable author of Douglas. The Lowland Scottish gentleman, and the subordinate characters, are taken not from any individual portrait but from the general habits of the period, of which I have witnessed some remnants in my younger days, and partly gathered from tradition.

It has been my object, certainly, to describe these persons, not by a caricatured and exaggerated use of the national dialect, but by their habits, manners, and feelings; so as, in some distant degree, to emulate the admirable Irish portraits drawn by Miss Edgeworth, so different from the "dear joys" who so long, with the most perfect family resemblance to each other, occupied the drama and the novel.

I feel no confidence, however, in the manner with which I have executed my purpose. Indeed, I was so little satisfied with my production, that I laid it aside in an unfinished state, and only found it again by mere accident among other waste papers, after it had been forgotten and mislaid for several years. Two works upon similar subjects, by female authors, whose genius is highly creditable to their country, have appeared in the interval; I mean Mrs Hamilton's Glenburnie, and the late Account of Highland Superstitions. But the first is confined to the rural habits of Scotland, of which it has given a picture with striking and impressive fidelity; and the traditional records of the worthy and ingenious Mrs Grant of Laggan are of a nature distinct from the fictitious narrative which I have attempted.

I would willingly persuade myself, that the preceding work will not be found altogether uninteresting. To elder persons it will recall scenes and characters familiar to their youth; and to the rising generation the tale may present some idea of the manners of their forefathers.

Yet I heartily wish that the task of tracing the evanescent manners of his own country had employed the pen of the only man in Scotland who could have done it justice,—of him so eminently distinguished in elegant literature, and whose sketches of Colonel Caustic and Umphraville are perfectly blended with the finer traits of national character; I should in that case have had more pleasure as a reader, than I shall ever feel in the pride of a successful author, should these sheets confer upon me that envied distinction. And as I have inverted the usual arrangement, placing these remarks at the end of the work to which they refer, I will venture on a second violation of form, by closing the whole with a Dedication;

THESE VOLUMES
BEING RESPECTFULLY INSCRIBED
TO
OUR SCOTTISH ADDISON,
HENRY MACKENZIE,
BY
AN UNKNOWN ADMIRER
OF
HIS GENIUS.

THE END

HISTORICAL NOTE

Chronology. The main events in *Waverley* take place at the time of the Jacobite rising of 1745–46, with its hero's private adventures interconnecting at various points with this last main effort to restore the Stuart family as monarchs. Through Waverley's upbringing at Waverley-Honour, and his first-hand experiences of two main motor forces of Jacobite opposition in Scotland, the novel also offers a wider overview of Jacobitism as a cultural and historical phenomenon.

In the case of the English Waverley family, loyalty to the Stuarts begins with the accession to the English throne of James VI of Scotland and the union of the two Crowns in 1603. This involves their taking the side of the monarchy during the English Civil War, followed by support for the invasion of England by Charles II with a Scottish army in 1651, leading to the battle of Worcester, in the wake of which the family members take an active role in securing the King's escape. The pattern of monarchical loyalism, however, would have been broken by James VII and II vacating the throne in 1688, having openly avowed Catholicism, to be succeeded by William of Orange and his wife Mary, James's daughter. William was then succeeded by Anne (Mary's sister) in 1702, whose reign saw the dominance of the Tory party but also a series of measures obstructing a succession by the Catholic James VIII and III, exiled in France, these including the Act of Settlement of 1701, providing for a Protestant succession, and the Act of Union of 1707, amalgamating England and Scotland, and aimed partly at closing off the possibility of French invasion through Scotland. The career of Sir Everard Waverley, who appears to have been born in about 1673,[1] reflects that of a country party Tory loyalist during the early eighteenth century. In Queen Anne's reign he has attended parliament, registering 'zealous Noes' (21.24) during the Tory administration (1702–1710) of Sidney Godolphin to measures brought in at a time when the Whig party was becoming stronger; and then resigning on Anne's death in 1714, just before the accession of George I and the coming of the Protestant Hanoverian dynasty. In 1715 he has offered at least tacit support for the Jacobite rising of that year, with rumour suggesting a connection with Sir William Wyndham (the leader of the Tories: see note to 22.43), his own sympathies being made evident through financial support for the Scots and Northumbrian Jacobites captured at Preston, an involvement which also provides the starting-point for the family alliance with the Baron of Bradwardine.

In contrast to the 'sullen opposition' exhibited by 'wealthy country gentlemen' such as his elder brother, with their looks of 'mingled regret and hope' (7.21–26) to the exiled Jacobite court, Richard Waverley, the hero's father, takes an opposite path, opportunistically embracing the new Protestant Whig political establishment. Mention of his distinguishing himself in the Excise Bill, a key measure of the Whig Prime Minister Sir Robert Walpole in 1733, and more generally reference to the minister patronising him as the 'great man', strongly associate him not only with Walpolian politics but also arguably with Sir Robert personally. The political events which take place in the story's immediate present, with Richard suffering disgrace after an attempted coup against his patron, are harder to decipher in these terms, since Walpole had already been forced to resign in 1742. But such intrigues could be related to struggles within the so-called Broad Bottom administration that followed Walpole, which included some of the most persistent Whig opponents of Walpole, who themselves were eventually removed in 1746 in favour of Henry Pelham, one of the old Walpole faction. Meanwhile Sir Everard's own Jacobitism reaches the point of near extinction in practical terms through his acceptance of Edward's taking a commission in the government army. A link with one of the main ideological supports of the movement nevertheless remains in the person of the non-juring Mr Pembroke, Edward's tutor, a remnant of the High Church of England party, which had refused to take oaths of allegiance to William III, and then to the Hanoverians. A visit by him to the book trade in Little Britain also offers a snap-shot view of Tory/Jacobite opposition to Walpolian government in the book trade at the time of Nicholas Amhurst and *The Craftsman* (see notes to 30.28 and 31.21).

In Scotland the Jacobite movement had proved a militant force virtually since the ousting of James VII and II and the accession of William and Mary to the Scottish throne in 1689. Among key years of opposition can be counted: 1689, when a Jacobite army, consisting mainly of Highland clansmen and led by Viscount Dundee (Claverhouse), gained a Pyrrhic victory at Killiecrankie; 1708, in the immediate aftermath of the Union, when a French fleet with James VIII and III aboard approached the Firth of Forth, but returned to open sea at the sight of a larger English fleet; 1715, when James VIII finally landed, joining the insurgents at Perth, but only after the main Jacobite advance under the Earl of Mar had stalled at the battle of Sheriffmuir, fought inconclusively near Stirling; and 1719, when a Spanish-backed rising in the western Highlands was crushed at Glenshiel. Bradwardine and Fergus Mac-Ivor in the novel represent two of the main elements of support for Jacobitism within Scotland: the Episcopalian Perthshire and North-east gentry, and the Highland clans (especially, though not exclusively, those with Catholic chiefs). In Bradwardine's case, loyalty to the Stuarts is an integral part of a commitment to an indigenous Scottish monarchy and national feudal structure, with tradition dating his family back to King Duncan (d. 1040), and the granting of its charter of free barony originating from David I (d. 1153), the reign of the Stuarts (descended from the High Stewards of Scotland) only arriving in the later fourteenth century. Prohibited from entering into the main currents of the Whig Presbyterian Scotland, and practising in the legal profession, Bradwardine has served overseas under James FitzJames, Duke of Berwick (1670–1734), the natural son of

James VII and Arabella Churchill (sister of the Duke of Marlborough), who was created a Marechal of France in 1706, and played a distinguished part in the War of Spanish Succession (1701–14). Bradwardine is described as having been honoured by him for being 'the first to mount the breach of a fort in Savoy during the memorable campaign of 1709' (62.41–42), and his continuing affection for the Marechal is also apparent in the naming of his horse as Berwick. After his active engagement in the 1715 rising, and near escape from committal as a traitor, he has lived almost exclusively in his own neighbourhood, subject to two government disarming acts in 1716 and 1725, and limited to a society defined by the boorishness of Killancureit and the muddled vindictive Jacobitism of Balmawhapple. Bradwardine also has a counterpart of Mr Pembroke in the non-juring Mr Rubrick, of the Episcopalian Church of Scotland (which had been replaced as the established Church in 1690 by the Presbyterian Kirk), and whose meeting-house was attacked by a Whig mob in 1715, when clergy of his persuasion became subject to penalty of imprisonment for non-compliance with the oaths of Allegiance and Abjuration (see note to 47.18–20).

Fergus Mac-Ivor's clan are described as having settled in Perthshire, 'about three centuries before' (97.31), as a splinter group from the main body in the North. Fergus's father, after engaging 'heart and hand in the insurrection of 1715' (98.17), had been forced into exile in France, where he married a lady of rank. Having been born there, Fergus and Flora are cultivated by Maria Clementina Sobieska (1702–35), who married James VIII and III in 1719, and was the mother of Prince Charles Edward Stuart. Commentators have questioned in particular the chronology of Scott's later reference to Flora having witnessed the 'grand airs' of 'the mock court of St Germains' (262.35–36), on the grounds that the Stuarts had been obliged to leave the palace there in 1713, which would place Flora well into her forties at the time of the main action of the novel. It is worth noting however that this forms part of a commentary by the Francophobic Colonel Talbot, and also that the phrase 'court of St Germains' continued to be used of the Jacobite court well after it had left France. Since his upbringing abroad, Fergus has regained his clan's domains, been granted an earl's patent by James VIII and III, and headed one of the Independent Companies of 'loyal Highlanders' formed by the British government as a means of policing the Highlands: actions which are as plausible together on one level as they might seem contradictory on another. Underlying all this is his assiduous cultivation of the clan as a war machine.

From the point of Waverley's arrival in Scotland the novel's fictional events intermesh in a variety of ways with actual historical events relating to the 1745 rising. To comprehend these connections fully it is necessary to bear in mind the exact chronology of Prince Charles Edward's landing in Scotland, and the main events leading up to the defeat of the government army at Prestonpans, near Edinburgh. Dates in the following table (as elsewhere for 1745–46) reflect the old-style Julian calendar, which was used in Great Britain until 1752, these dates lagging

11 days behind the new-style Gregorian calendar, introduced on the Continent by Pope Gregory XIII in 1582.

22 June 1745. Prince Charles Edward embarks at Nantes in France on board the *Doutelle*.

25 July. Prince lands on West coast of Highlands at Loch nan Uamh ('the Loch of the Caves') near Moidart, accompanied by the 'Seven Men of Moidart' (see note to 207.20). Appeals made to clan leaders.

16 August. First outbreak of hostilities. Donald MacDonnell of Tirnadris (of MacDonnell of Keppoch's clan) assisted by Mac-Donnell of Glengarry's men take prisoner near Loch Lochy two companies of Royal Scots marching to reinforce Fort William.

18–19 August. The Prince spends the night at Glenaladale, half-way along Loch Shiel, before proceeding by boat to the head of the loch at Glenfinnan, where the royal standard is raised (19 August) by William Murray, titular Duke of Atholl. In the after-noon he is joined by Cameron of Lochiel and his clansmen, and later by Keppoch with his MacDonnells.

22–29 August. The Prince's force marches East, passing between Forts William and Augustus towards Corrieyairack Pass. General Sir John Cope, commander of government troops in Scotland, marches with his force north from Stirling (20 August) for Fort Augustus, but on hearing (26 August) that the Jacobites hold Corrieyairack doubles back and turns northward towards Inver-ness, leaving Perth and the Lowlands open to the Jacobite army, itself augmented by the Glengarry MacDonnells and MacDonalds of Glencoe.

31 August–4 September. The Prince marches to Blair Castle in Atholl, seat of the Duke of Atholl, visits the nearby House of Lude, then proceeds via Dunkeld to Perth.

4–10 September. The Prince remains in Perth, where he is joined by Lord George Murray, the Duke of Perth, Lord Ogilvy, Laur-ence Oliphant of Gask, and other Perthshire gentry.

11–15 September. On successive days, the Prince and his army march to Dunblane, Doune, cross the Forth at the Fords of Frew, and pass by Stirling Castle, where they are fired on by the garrison, reaching Linlithgow early on 15 September.

17 September. The army takes Edinburgh, but the Castle remains in government hands. James VIII and III proclaimed at Market Cross; the Prince occupies Holyrood Palace, and the army is encamped in the King's Park.

19–22 September. The army moved to Duddingston, from where the Prince marches on the 20 September by Musselburgh and Tranent to meet Sir John Cope, who had landed at Dunbar on the 17th, and proceeded via Haddington towards Edinburgh. The battle of Prestonpans (or Preston or Gladsmuir) is fought early on 21 September, with the government forces being routed. The Prince spends the night at Pinkie House, and returns to Holyrood next day, where he remains until 31 October.

As suggested, Waverley's early experiences in Scotland are closely connected with the above events, though Waverley himself and to some extent the reader also are often oblivious to this. With the 'arrival of summer' (34.12), he takes leave of absence, and has been a guest at Tully-Veolan for 'nearly six weeks' (72.15), when the cattle-raid takes place which leads to his visiting Glennaquoich and the Mac-Ivors. Hints that the earliest events of the Rising have already taken place are contained in Mac-Murrough's 'Celtic verses', as translated by Flora, especially verses 4 and 5, which refer to Glenaladale, Glenfinnan, and the raising of 'the Standard' (115.31–34). Waverley then undertakes to stay a further fortnight to attend the hunting party, which in the event is delayed for 'about three weeks' (122.18–19). After taking leave of the injured Waverley, after the hunt, Fergus returns on 'the sixth morning' in 'the highest spirits' (127.26–29), having evidently met Charles Edward and undertaken to join the Rising (points later asserted by Major Mellville at 168.29–31). This would tally with Fergus going westward to meet the Prince in late August, and returning with the intention of uniting with the Jacobite army on its entering Perthshire. On returning to Glennaquoich Waverley receives family letters concerning his father's political disgrace, as well as one from Colonel Gardiner admonishing him for his behaviour 'at the present crisis' (132.25), and learns too from the *Caledonian Mercury* of his replacement in the regiment. Fergus and Flora are now apparently ultra-active in the cause of the Rising: Flora preparing white cockades ('what appeared to Waverley to be white bridal favours' (136.31–32)), and Fergus preoccupied with 'guns, broad-swords, bonnets, cantines, and tartan hose' (139.38). 'In the morning' (146.3) Waverley is awoken by Davie Gellatley, who hands him Rose's letter, describing how her father and Mr Falconer [Balmawhapple] 'with a body of about forty horsemen' (147.23) have gone off northwards, and informing him that Tully-Veolan is now garrisoned by a small body of government troops.

Waverley's resolution 'instantly to go to Edinburgh' (149.39–40) initiates a fresh sequence of events, in which his own movements criss-cross with Charles Edward's actual progress to Edinburgh. Arriving in Cairnvreckan, he finds the people there abuzz with news: 'The names of Lochiel, Clanronald, Glengary, and other distinguished Highland Chiefs . . . were familiar in men's mouths as household words; and from the alarm generally expressed, he easily conceived that their descent into the Lowlands, at the head of their armed tribes, had either already taken place, or was instantly apprehended' (160.16–22). After Waverley's interrogation, Mellville discloses to Morton how he has just heard of Cope's retreat from Corrieyairack Pass, and consequent march to Inverness [where Cope arrived on 29 August], leaving the Lowlands exposed (see 175.11–18). Waverley's rescue next day from Gilfillan's band and semi-imprisonment in Janet's 'hovel' effectively puts him out of action for another seven days (see 192.43), after which he is taken overnight to Doune Castle [which Charles Edward had reached on 12 September], now garrisoned by the Jacobites. Escorted next day by Balmawhapple and his troop, he makes one further overnight stop on the way to Edinburgh, on approaching which he finds the Castle under blockade 'by the northern insurgents, who had already occupied the town for two or three days' (203.41–42). In view of the seizure of Edinburgh on 17 September, this would place his arrival *circa* 19 September, allowing just about enough time (though the schedule is increasingly hectic) for him to be presented to Charles Edward, get fitted up and attend the Holyrood ball, before on the next day viewing the assembly of the Highland army near Duddingston [20 September]. The battle of Prestonpans is fought early on the following morning; the ceremony involving Brad-wardine (which Waverley misses in attending to Colonel Talbot) is performed at Pinkie House that evening; and the 'triumphant entrance' (256.11) of Charles Edward into Edinburgh, where the accidental wounding of Flora happens, takes place the following day [22 September].

Waverley's adventures from this point, until separation at Clifton, run chronologically parallel with the movement of the Jacobite army. The setting out of Charles Edward with his small army 'about the beginning of November' (280.19–20) is duly noted by the main narrat-ive, as is the capture of Carlisle, which Fergus later recalls having entered on 16 November (see note to 346.32 for exact dates). The council of war at Derby where the decision to return northward was taken is accurately placed on 5 December (292.4); and the manuscript version correctly places the events in the story leading up to the skirm-ish at Clifton on '18th of December' (see 292.20). With Waverley's detach-ment from the army at Clifton, public events appear more sporadically and at second hand. In refuge at Fasthwaite, after being bound in by snow for 'more than ten days' (300.42), he successively hears of the retreat into Scotland [20 December], Cumberland's besieging of Car-lisle [21 December], and the surrender of the Jacobite garrison there [30 December].

Having attended the marriage of Ned Williams and Cicely Jopson, at the 'end of January' (302.3), Waverley reads in a newspaper report of the death of his father 'upon the 10th inst.' (302.21–22). Determin-ing to go to London, he crosses the country to Boroughbridge (presum-ably on foot), with some 'vexatious delays' (303.28). He there takes the Northern Diligence, which is described as taking 'three weeks' (303.25) to go from Edinburgh to London—indicating that 10 or 11 days would be required from the equidistant Boroughbridge. These procedures would be likely then to bring him to London about mid/late February 1746. As Colonel Talbot's guest, he learns from the Colonel of Donald Bean Lean's hanging at Stirling 'after the rebels raised the siege [1 February]' (308.26). Reaching again the 'borders of Scotland' (312.27), he hears of the 'decisive battle of Culloden' [16 April], and in Edinburgh from Mrs Flockhart that Fergus is 'to be tried, and to suffer wi' them that were ta'en at Carlisle' (314.14). On his way back south from Tully-Veolan, after a stay long enough to secure the free-ing of the Baron and his own engagement to Rose, and a stopover at Edinburgh to meet Talbot, Waverley reaches Carlisle while the Court is still sitting and sentence is being pronounced. According to the *Caledonian Mercury*, Major Donald MacDonnell of Tirnadris, who is often cited as a model for Fergus (see also below), was tried in September, and executed on 18 October 1746. While Scott for fictional reasons is perhaps guilty of telescoping these two parts of the process, it is entirely in keeping with overall chronology that Waverley should be able to assure Fergus (347.1–2) on the day of his execution of Charles Edward's escape to France [20 September 1746].

In the closing stages of the story chronology tends to collapse in the face of other priorities. A combination of the law's 'proverbial delay' (353.18) and the slowness of travel at the time means that it is 'considerably more than two months' before Waverley can return from England to Tully-Veolan (see 354.12–18). This would seem to push the final events in the story, culminating in Waverley's marriage six days after his arrival (354.19), well into the year 1747. By this point, however, Scott's own sense of time seems to have virtually collapsed. Such is apparent in the reference to Bradwardine having 'assumed arms some months before' (357.1): an event which must actually have taken place about a year and a half ago. From Macwheeble's late mention of papers being made ready 'for the next term in Exchequer' (360.13–14), it seems likely that Bradwardine wishes his new entail to be presented for approval by that Court between 1 June and 31 July 1747.

Sources. A wide array of sources can be found at work in *Waverley*, most of these falling into one of three categories: anecdotal records; historical literary sources; and more contemporary influences.

One central element, belonging to the first category, is partly revealed by Scott in the novel's concluding Postscript: 'The exchange of mutual protection between a Highland gentleman and an officer of rank in the king's service, together with the spirited manner in which the latter asserted his right to return the favour he had received, is literally true' (363.42–364.2). Scott is here referring to the account told him by Alexander Stewart of Invernahyle of the reciprocal aid provided between himself and a government officer, Lieutenant-Colonel Charles Whitefoord, which had begun with the latter's rescue by Invernahyle at Prestonpans, and ended with Whitefoord securing a pardon for his rescuer in the aftermath of the Rising. Scott went on to supply further details relating to this core story on a number of occasions, beginning with his self-review of the first series of *Tales of my Landlord* in the *Quarterly Review* for January 1817. This account describes how four field pieces were stormed by the Camerons and Stewarts of Appin at Prestonpans; how Invernahyle had commanded Whitefoord to surrender, this being first met by a sword thrust, and the appeal then proving successful as the battle-axe of a Highlander was about to descend; and how Invernahyle had subsequently protected his prisoner, 'and finally obtained him liberty on his parole'. With the tables turned, Whitefoord had then pleaded unsuccessfully for a pardon from the Scottish legal authorities and from the Duke of Cumberland, limiting his appeal then to protection for the family and property, again unsuccessfully, but had ultimately achieved his purpose with the Duke by threatening to resign his own commission. Scott in this account also describes Invernahyle's hiding in a cave on his own estate after Culloden, where food was brought to him by his daughter, and also adds a story concerning his being fired at one morning after returning from his own house, and an old woman's ruse to cover for him (involving a deaf shepherd).[2] Reference to other sources, such as the *Dewar Manuscripts*, which contains a version from oral record apparently unrelated to Scott,[3] tends in the main to corroborate the above account, though Scott wrongly calls the Colonel '*Allan* Whitefoord', and gives the misleading impression that Invernahyle was a veteran of both 1715 and 1745. The transformation of Whitefoord into Colonel Talbot, as an English gentleman with a residence in the West End of London, so important to the novel thematically, also overrides the fact that Whitefoord was a Scotsman, with an estate at Ballochmyle in Ayrshire (strangely close to where the apparently entirely fictional Gilfillan's lands are placed in the story).

Another incident for which Scott claims an anecdotal origin is the accidental wounding of Flora Mac-Ivor, which the Postscript describes as relating 'to a lady of rank not long deceased' (364.3–4). According to other sources, this actually happened to Mary Nairne, sixth daughter of Baron Nairne, whose son, the 3rd Baron, had joined the Prince at Holyrood on 18 September 1745, and was closely connected with other Perthshire Jacobite families, including the Oliphants of Gask (see further below). Mary died unmarried at Gask in 1774, which sits uneasily with the Postscript's 'not long deceased', and it is possible that Scott was thinking (mistakenly or not) of the youngest Nairne daughter, Henrietta, who died also at Gask in 1802 aged 89. First-hand evidence of such an incident occurring is found in a surviving letter of Magdalen Pringle, herself belonging to a Whig family, to her sister Isabella, describing an incident in the wake of the entry of Highland troops into Edinburgh: 'On ye other side of the street there was a Highland Man and a Boy standing with a Gun in his hand which Gun went off and shot in at ye Window and ye Bullet went in at Mady [*sic*] Nairn's head'.[4]

Through his personal connections, Scott could easily have heard of such stories either through Whig or ex-Jacobite sources, or indeed from both. One person who had witnessed the events immediately leading up to Prestonpans was the Rev. Alexander Carlyle of Inveresk, who as a young man had been a volunteer in the College company formed to defend Edinburgh and had attempted to aid General Cope's force in the field by acting as an observer from his father's nearby manse and church. His worm's-eye-view account was eventually published in *The Autobiography of Dr Alexander Carlyle* (1910), but Scott elsewhere gives the impression of having heard the narrative of the volunteers' activities directly from the mouth of Carlyle.[5] Among other possible first-hand informants of Scott's can be counted: William Curle, his paternal aunt's husband, who had been at the Carlisle executions; Alexander Campbell, his music tutor, whose wife was the widow of Ronald Macdonald of Keppoch; and George Constable, a lawyer and another witness of the '45, whom Scott first met when exploring Prestonpans as a young man.[6]

Prominent among historical literary sources used is John Home's *The History of the Rebellion in the Year 1745* (1802), which Scott cites in the Postscript as his main authority for 'correcting' eye-witness accounts. Home's record is supported by his own recollections as a youthful volunteer on the government side, which involved him in activities comparable to those of Carlyle in Edinburgh, and also led to imprisonment at (and escape from) Doune Castle after the Battle of Falkirk. The publication of the *History* helped break something of a taboo in giving a formal account of its subject, made possible partly by its Dedication to George III. The *History* nevertheless broke new ground by incorporating recollections of Jacobite witnesses, and also comes to life (in a way Scott would have fully recognised) in those areas where Home had been personally involved. A notable instance is Home's account of the size and condition of the Jacobite army as it lay encamped in the King's Park outside Edinburgh, which is given in the form of a report by a 'volunteer' (probably Home himself) to General Cope, and which Scott feeds on extensively in his picturesque account of the army assembling and marching out prior to Prestonpans. Another place where Scott seems especially indebted to Home is the skirmish at Clifton, where details such as the shouting out of 'Claymore!' and the transitory state of the moonlight are common to both accounts. Scott also appears to have been generally indebted to Home's account for a number of points concerning Highland life and culture.

Two other major historical literary sources remain comparatively hidden. In an early notice of *Waverley* the *Monthly Review* recorded its discovery 'that most of the descriptions of local manners and customs, and some strong touches of character, to be found in these volumes, may be traced to the publication intitled "Letters from a Gentleman in the North of Scotland to his Friend in London", printed in the year 1754, but professing to be written several years sooner'. It also added that the same source had been used in the notes of *The Lady of the Lake* (1810), which of course had appeared under Scott's name.[7] The originally anonymous author of *Letters from a Gentleman in the North of Scotland* was Edmund Burt, who was appointed in 1725 as a receiver-general and collector of unsold forfeited estates in Scotland, and appears to have been mainly stationed at Inverness. Scott was already aware of the work by the time of his review of Sir John Carr's *Caledonian Sketches* in the first number of the *Quarterly Review* (February 1809); and his attention may have been drawn or re-directed to it by the sizeable extracts given in Appendix B to the Earl of Selkirk's *Observations on the Present State of the Highlands of Scotland* (1805), these including a listing by Burt of the various followers of a Chief, which in turn is absorbed largely unmediated into Evan Dhu's description to Waverley within the novel (see present text 81.11–23). As a whole Scott uses this source extensively in the novel for Highland 'manners', especially of the common folk, and as such it helps provide a markedly unromantic element in the depiction of Highland life. Other instances of indebtedness are found in the early account of clothes-washing 'in a spacious tub' (40.18), Evan Dhu's remarks on the gallows being preferable for Bean Lean to death like a 'mangy tyke' (92.14), as well as in both Callum Beg's concealed '*skene-occle*' (155.19) and his likening by Colonel Talbot to a 'little cockatrice' (279.34). Invaluable help in the presentation of Gaelic speech in equivalent English terms came from Donald Macintosh's *Collection of Gaelic Proverbs, and Familiar Phrases* (1785), which provides parallel Gaelic and English versions on facing pages of openings, and a copy of which was owned by Scott.[8] Born in 1743 in Blair Atholl, Macintosh had come to Edinburgh and worked as a penny postman, before receiving help from Henry Mackenzie and being appointed as translator of Gaelic to the Highland Society of Scotland and placed on the committee that produced the 1805 Report on *Ossian*. On his death in 1808 he was the last survivor of the Scottish non-juring clergy. The input from his *Gaelic Proverbs* first comes into view with the appearance of Evan Dhu after the cattle-raid (present text, starting 79.28), where five rapid near 'citations' occur. In all, there are some twenty cases where Scott can be found placing Macintosh's English version of proverbs (or near equivalents) in Gaelic mouths.

For the broader political context of the work Scott calls on the knowledge gained through his work on three extensive projects, his editions of the *Works* of Dryden (contracted 1805, published 1808) and Swift (contracted 1808, published 1814), and of a second edition of *A Collection of Scarce and Valuable Tracts* (the Somers Tracts), published 1809–15. Of these the Swift edition, finally completed just as Scott returned to finish the novel in summer 1814, is perhaps most invasively present, relatively clear markers here being Sir Everard's 'zealous Noes' (21.24) and a smattering of pseudo-Gaelic (actually Irish) in '*ceade millia molighiart*' at 125.21 (see also note). With the Somers Tracts, Scott's indebtedness is particularly noticeable in the account of Mr Pembroke's visit to Little Britain, a number of figures and works alluded to there relating to polemical tracts included in the collection from the period of William and Mary and Queen Anne, their shadowy presence in the novel indicative arguably of how backward-looking Pembroke's concerns are. In the case of Dryden, allusions to passages in his poems and his plays are found on at least ten occasions, as illustrated by the following Explanatory Notes.

With regard to Scottish Jacobitism, Scott was an inveterate collector of materials relating to the 1745 rising, and by the time of his writing the Notes for the Magnum Opus edition (1829) had become a major authority on the subject, as is also evident from the maturity of the historical account given in his *Tales of a Grandfather* (3rd series, 1830), and his active participation in the reproduction of manuscript sources by historical societies such as the Bannatyne Club. It should be noted, however, that not all of this material was available to him at the time of the composition of *Waverley*, leading sources such as the personal records of Lord Elcho, James Maxwell of Kirkconnell, and the Chevalier de Johnstone, probably first coming to him at a later stage.[9] Scott may nevertheless have known about some relevant first-hand accounts, such as John Murray of Broughton's *Memorials*, which was preserved by his descendants before publication by the Scottish History Society in 1898; and the *Woodhouselee MS* (eventually published in 1907), a detailed eye-witness account of events in Edinburgh by the Whiggish Presbyterian Patrick Crichton, from the arrival of the Jacobite army to its march south early in November.[10]

Scott would at the same time have been fully aware of a species of 'topical' works published in the immediate wake of the Rising, usually written and compiled from a strong Hanoverian position, and which he was well-equipped to read as a gauge for judging the attitudes of the times. A good number of these are found in the Abbotsford Library, sometimes with marginal annotations by Scott. Prominent titles include: *Genuine Memoirs of John Murray, Esq.* (London, 1747), a scathing anti-Papist account of its subject, written about Murray after he had turned king's evidence, and describing among other things his various missions in disguise; *A Compleat History of the Rebellion* (York, 1749), by James Ray of Whitehaven, some of which appears to be based on first-hand knowledge, including the account of Clifton, even though the dragoons are shown there as forcing the Jacobites to leave the field;[11] *The Edinburgh History of the Late Rebellion*, by Andrew Henderson (4th edn; London, 1752), which provides a close-up view of Charles Edward's arrival at Holyrood, and a reasonably accurate account of Prestonpans; *A Journey through Part of England and Scotland along with the Army under the Command of His Royal Highness the Duke of Cumberland* (2nd edn; London, 1747), 'by a Volunteer', a largely pastiche work, but with some valuable glimpses at points; and Michael Hughes, *A Plain Narrative or Journal of the Late Rebellion begun in 1745* (London, 1746), which describes the female admiration for the Prince in Edinburgh, General Preston ordering cannon to be fired from the Castle, and the destruction by Cumberland's forces of Lochiel's house at Achnacarry. Additionally the Abbotsford Library contains a set of issues of the *Caledonian Mercury* from 23 September 1745 to 30 April 1747, a period during which that newspaper exhibited a strong Jacobite tone, most palpably in a key issue on 23 September 1745, which featured a report 'From the Head Quarters of his Royal Highness the Prince, Sept. 21'. Among other elements this is the root source of Charles Edward's supposed words at Duddingston, on placing himself at the head of his army ('presenting his Sword, said, *My Friends, I have flung away the Scabbard*'). The same paper also provided regular reports of the Carlisle trials, in which a seething sense of injustice and disapproval at barbarous severity is barely hidden under the outer guise of objectivity.

Scott also brings in materials from other periods, most noticeably in the meeting of Fergus and other Perthshire chiefs in anticipation of the outbreak of the Rising, this relating not to any known incident in 1745, but clearly paralleling the assembly of Jacobite nobles and gentry at Braemar, in Aberdeenshire, under the guise of a hunt (known later as the 'Hunting of Braemar') at the onset of the rising of 1715. At the beginning of Volume 2, in fact, Scott brings together a whole panoply of sources relating to earlier huntings in Braemar, from the early 16th century on, almost as if consciously filling in the void with regard to 1745. Signs of indebtedness, again representing an overspill from 1715 to 1745, are also traceable in John Master of Sinclair's *Memoirs of the Insurrection in Scotland in 1715*, which was eventually published with annotations by Scott by the Abbotsford Club in 1858.[12] In particular one might point to elements of Sinclair's bitter account of a sally through Fife proclaiming James VIII, with little response from locals, and a troop of followers more intent on getting drunk than regime change, in both Balmawhapple's journey escorting Waverley from Doune to Edinburgh and (converted to the opposing side) Gilfillan's abortive march from Cairnvreckan to Stirling.

Additionally, a number of more contemporary sources are absorbed into the text, many of these being interestingly positioned in the years of composition. Though comparable case histories are by no means uncommon, the circumstances of Bradwardine's later misfortunes may have been partly suggested by Henry Mackenzie's story of Albert Bane in *The Lounger* (no. 61, 1 April 1786), concerning a servant who aids his master in hiding on his estate (in a cave) after Culloden.[13] For the scenery at Glennaquoich, especially that providing a backdrop for Flora's song, Scott undoubtedly drew on Patrick Graham's *Sketches Descriptive of Picturesque Scenery on the Southern Confines of Perth-shire* (Edinburgh, 1806), particularly descriptions of two waterfalls there. One source for Flora's singing to the harp is almost certainly John Gunn's *An Historical Enquiry respecting the Performance on the Harp in the Highlands of Scotland* (1807), published by direction of the High-land Society, which gives a description with illustrations of two small harps, 'The Caledonian Harp' and 'Queen Mary's Harp', found in the possession of the Robertsons of Lude. As well as a more general disser-tation on Highland music, this also gives an account of the blind harper Roderick Morison ('Rory Dall'), who is supposed to be Flora's teacher in the novel (present text 114.6). For other Gaelic materials, in addition to the contributions sent by the Clephanes of Mull in the years from 1809, Scott would have benefited through contact with Alexander Campbell, whose *Grampians Desolate* (a long elegiac poem with copious notes) appeared in 1804, in the wake of a two-volume *Journey from Edinburgh through part of Great Britain* (1802), which might have pro-vided a supplementary source to Graham for the Perthshire scenery. Scott later contributed several Highland songs to Campbell's *Albyn's Anthology* (2 vols; Edinburgh, 1816–1818), including (in Vol. 1) 'Pib-roch of Donuil Dhu' (a call to arms) and 'The Macgregors Gathering'.

For Fergus's last hours in Carlisle, in addition to any anecdotal accounts available, Scott appears to have turned to his own memory of the trial and execution (involving beheading) in Edinburgh of Robert Watt for sedition in 1794, the novel's description of the execution procession showing a number of clear resemblances to the contempor-ary account given in *The Scots Magazine*. Another fertile source, whose effects can only be touched on here, is found in Scots law. David

Marshall notes four cases dealing with the law of entail, between 1807 and 1812, when Scott was a Clerk of Court.[14] More broadly the legal allusions in the novel show close familiarity with the main works of Scottish law, with Macwheeble in particular mouthing whole extracts almost verbatim, not least from George Dallas's *System of Stiles As now Practicable within the Kingdom of Scotland* (Edinburgh, 1697; 2nd edn, 2 vols, 1774), a main reference source for framing legal documents, which was undoubtedly used by Scott's own clerk when Scott officiated as Sheriff-Substitute of Selkirkshire.

Topography. As Franco Moretti suggests,[15] the broader topographical and historical aspects in *Waverley* tend to run parallel with each other, as the main narrative (through its peripatetic 'observing' hero) moves from the somnambulant English country-house situation of Waverley-Honour, to a more threadbare Scottish counter-version in Tully-Veolan, at the outer fringes of the Lowland society, and beyond that into the Highlands of Scotland proper. At the same time, there is a danger of underestimating the relative precision of detail found in certain settings, as too in the geography of Waverley's journeying.

Of all the main settings, that of Waverley-Honour has traditionally proved most resistant to identification. Arguments as to whether Scott visited Waverley Abbey, the 12th-century Cistercian foundation near Farnham in Surrey, have generally proved inconclusive. The main opportunity for such a visit would have been in April 1807, when Scott was the guest of William Stewart Rose at Cuffnells in Hampshire, and when he was in the process of writing *Marmion*; though surviving records of that occasion point to more southerly excursions, to the New Forest and Isle of Wight.[16] There is some possibility that Scott was aware of the Abbey through its connection with Charlotte Smith: both through her choice of Waverley as the surname for one of the characters in her novel *Desmond* (1792), and by virtue of her own residence at Tilford, near Farnham, in later life. Scott also owned a copy of *Historiae Anglicanae Scriptores Quinque* (1687), edited by Thomas Gale, which includes 'Annales Waverleiensis', a Latin record of events in the Abbey's history, which he might have known and consulted as an antiquary. In terms of *location* however a situation relatively so close to London seems wrong in view of the novel's overall spatial organisation, and quite possibly there is no need for any greater specificity than is due in the case of a host of eighteenth-century novels where West of England settings counterbalance the metropolitan culture of London. One possible clue nevertheless might be found in the similarity in names of Brere-wood Lodge, Richard Waverley's seat close to Waverley-Honour (see 11.6), and Brewood in south Staffordshire, some 12 km NNW of Wolverhampton, which featured prominently in the escape of Charles II after the battle of Worcester in 1651, a sequence of events in which the Waverley family is described as having been crucially involved. An ancient community noted in the Domesday Book, Brewood was once surrounded by a Royal Forest;

and it was the local family of the Giffards (whose ancestor had been standard-bearer to William the Conqueror at Hastings in 1066) who played a vital part in the aftermath of the defeat, with Charles being taken to Boscobel House, a Giffard hunting lodge, near where he hid in the 'Royal Oak' with Colonel Carless, a Brewood man. Interestingly an outline map provided by Moretti tentatively places Waverley-Honour in just such a position, though for reasons that are not fully disclosed.[17]

With Waverley's movement northward as a newly-commissioned officer, the topographical guidelines become clearer, and there are also references to actual locations. Waverley and his troop are placed in quarters as part of Gardiner's dragoons 'at D—— in Scotland' (22.32–33), the place name being later expanded by Scott in the Interleaved Set and Magnum Opus edition to Dundee. There is no evidence that Gardiner's regiment was ever stationed at Dundee in the build-up to the 1745 rising, and it would seem reasonable to assume that Scott has chosen the location at least partly for its proximity to Perthshire, where the main Scottish scenes in the novel are set. On his way to visit the Baron of Bradwardine, Waverley stops one night at an inn before next day approaching 'the Highlands of Perthshire' (34.23), the Baron's house at Tully-Veolan itself lying near the bottom of 'this stupendous barrier, but still in champaign country' (34.26–27). A number of possible prototypes for this country estate and its satellite village have been suggested, one of the most convincing of these being Craighall Castle, home of the Rattray family since 1533, which stands in woodland above the River Ericht, about 3 km N of Blairgowrie, itself approximately 30 km NW of Dundee. Scott visited Craighall with William Clerk (a relation of the Rattrays) on his tour of Stirlingshire and Perthshire in Spring 1793, and according to Lockhart's testimony Clerk was later to recognise instantly this locale in Scott's description. (It is perhaps significant that the fold-out map at the beginning of John Home's *History of the Rebellion in the Year 1745* (1802) places the 'Highland line' as running straight through Blairgowrie and Craighall.) In terms of the intricacy of architecture and garden terracing described by Scott, Craighall is not such an obvious model, though Murthly Castle, about 12 km SW of Blairgowrie, which came into the possession of the Stewarts of Grandtully in 1615, does offer parallels on both counts. The similarity of the Dutch-style gardens there to the landscaping of Tully-Veolan is noted in an article in the *Edinburgh Magazine* for October 1817: 'The dovecot adjoining the house, the fountain, gate, and, in short, every particular, entirely coincide' (1.230). Another, more specific feature of the house might also help throw light on the nature of the 'bartizan, or projecting gallery' (63.26) which forms part of Rose's apartment in the novel. One peculiar feature of the four-storeyed Murthly Castle, as noted by Nigel Tranter, is 'the little ornamental corbelled-out projection like another tiny angle-turret at the north-west angle, obviously original—something that I have not noted elsewhere'.[18]

In other respects Tully-Veolan can be seen as an amalgam of semi-fortified houses from a variety of locations in Scotland. Scott in his later Magnum note (1.82n.) refers to three houses on the outskirts of Edinburgh in his own day: Bruntsfield House, old Ravelston House, once in possession of the Foulis family, who forfeited the estate after the 1745 rising, and the House of Dean. More especially, the two bears standing at the head of the avenue at Tully-Veolan have long been held to be modelled on those which guard the disused avenue at Traquair House, in Peeblesshire, in Scott's own Border country.[19] In terms of locality, however, the neighbourhood of Tully-Veolan is unequivocally placed in Perthshire, with some indications of a proximity to the border with Angus. A hitherto unnoticed marker here could lie in 'the piper o' Cupar' (52.1–2, 69.38–39), whose denomination might well stem from Coupar Angus (on the way from Blairgowrie to Dundee) rather than Cupar in Fife.

Evidence concerning the whereabouts and possible origins of Fergus's estate at Glennaquoich is more varied and problematical. Waverley's journey there involves an overnight stay at Donald Bean Lean's cave, Uaimh an Ri ('the King's cavern'), and is punctuated with estimations of distances travelled which build up into a kind of running joke, playing on the disparity between the Scottish and English computation of miles and the different attitudes to the terrain covered by Waverley and his Highland guides. Insofar as it is possible to calculate any clear distance, it would seem that Waverley travels up to 50 km between Tully-Veolan and Glennaquoich, presumably in a north-westerly direction towards the Grampian Mountains. The name Glennaquoich most obviously derives from the Gaelic *Gleann Cuaich*, and is also matched by two actual Highland locations: Glenquoich, an estate next to Glengarry, stretching westward from the Great Glen, in the NW Highlands; and Glen Quaich in W Perthshire, through which the River Quaich runs from the west towards Amulree. In terms of historical associations the first of these is the more fitting, not least in view of the leading participation of the Glengarry regiment in the 1745 rising; *geographically* the second seems more appropriate, one factor here being its position north of Crieff (see further below). While there may be a temptation to move Fergus further westward towards the epicentre of the rising in its crucial early weeks, there are a number of clear references in the novel to him and his clan belonging to Perthshire, a positioning which allows easier linkage with events relating to Tully-Veolan, and which no doubt also reflects Scott's preference for an area familiar to him when undertaking the novel.

A more general Highland setting is nevertheless suggested by a number of references to other locations, some supposedly on Fergus's own territory, others indicative of a wider expanse of territory. The pass of Bally-Brough, which is mentioned on several occasions as the point of entry into Fergus's domain, was identified by one early commentator (*Edinburgh Magazine*, 1 (1817), 230) as the pass of Strathtay above Dunkeld: that is, where the Highland army of Viscount Dundee had tried to force their way into the Lowlands after the battle of Killiecrankie in 1689, and through which Prince Charles and his small army proceeded early in September 1745 on their way from Blair

Atholl to Perth. Evan Dhu, on leaving Uaimh an Ri with Waverley, mentions Ben-Lawers as lying on the horizon (see 92.23), this evidently referring to the mountain of that name in the far west of Perthshire. He also maps out the places of retreat open to Bean Lean should he be pursued with vigour, these stretching as far as Rannoch (see 93.27), alluding no doubt to the area around Loch Rannoch in NW Perthshire, and beyond that Rannoch Moor, still considered today to be one of the most remote places in Scotland. Further possibilities (and some ambiguities) occur later when, in the vicinity of the Lake District, Fergus recalls three defining landmarks of his own country (294.12–14). Of these 'Benmore' (also mentioned at 210.41) most obviously relates to Ben More in W Stirlingshire, 5 km E of Crianlarich, though the name (meaning 'big hill') is not uncommon throughout the Highlands. Loch Tay is clearly the large loch of that name in W Perthshire. Loch an Ri on the other hand, which Fergus distinguishes as 'my own', is presumably a fictional 'King's Loch', though there may be remnants in the sound of the name of Loch Ericht (*Eireachd* in Gaelic), NNW of Loch Tay. While clearly intending a Perthshire setting for Glennaquoich, Scott appears to have left himself a good deal of room in the execution, allowing a flexible movement between indications of specific locations and more general representations of the Highlands as a whole.

Waverley's return southward, concluding at Edinburgh, involves a similar kind of mixture, with apparently fictional locations and indistinct circuitous movements in the earlier stages, and graphically linear movements through an historically-charged landscape nearer the end. The process starts with Fergus's instruction that Callum Beg should attend Waverley 'as far as —— (naming a small town,) where he can have a horse and guide to Edinburgh' (150.40–41). Fergus then accompanies the party to 'the top of the pass of Bally-Brough' (151.15–16), after which Waverley and Callum proceed without apparent break to the still unnamed 'market town of ——' (152.24–25), where Mr Ebenezer Cruickshanks offers himself as a guide 'as far as Perth' (158.1). Colonel David Stewart was later to associate Cruickshanks' inn with Crieff,[20] and certainly if Fergus and his clan are placed in Glen Quaich, below Aberfeldy, the circumstance would fit; though if one retains the idea of Strathtay leading to the clan heartlands, then Dunkeld would make more sense. There are moreover signs of uncertainty on Scott's own part at this juncture: in the manuscript he vacillates at one point between Perth and Stirling as the place to which Waverley is next bound; and at 158.33 it is a village rather than a town that is left behind as the two set out. The 'village of Cairnvreckan' (159.30), which is apparently reached on the same long day, has been associated with Auchterarder in SW Perthshire, which would tally with a progress from Crieff, but not a situation where Perth (some 25 km to the NE) has still to be reached. Certain features of Auchterarder, such as its long main street, and associations with the rising of 1715, might have helped draw Scott's attention. Equally the unusually clear marker of Stirling being 'eighteen miles distant' (185.15), given as Waverley is about to be escorted there by Gilfillan and his troop, matches Auchterarder well—considerably better than Methven, 10 km W of Perth, which has also been suggested as a possible prototype. At the same time, one senses that Scott is compressing landscape in anticipation of two main ensuing topographical movements: the first involving Waverley's 'rescue' and rapid transportation to what transpires later to be Janet's cottage on the Tully-Veolan estate; the second entailing a similarly swift reverse journey (again mainly overnight) which terminates with his arrival at Doune, itself just 12 km NW of Stirling.

With Doune and its castle, which Scott had himself visited on a number of occasions, the narrative enters into much firmer territory, and the subsequent journey to Edinburgh accompanied by Balmawhapple and his troop involves a number of distinct locations while following a clear chronological procedure. It is also a highly significant journey in terms of its historical associations, shadowing most immediately the march only days earlier of Charles Edward and his army between Doune and Edinburgh, while at the same time bringing to mind some of the most significant moments in Scotland's early struggles for independence. Just as Prince Charles, having crossed the Forth at the Fords of Frew, had marched his army by Stirling, where he was fired on by the garrison of the Castle, so Balmawhapple has an equivalent experience, though without showing any of the sang-froid accredited to the Prince. Again following the progress of the main Jacobite army, Waverley and his party pass 'the memorable field of Bannockburn' (203.5), followed by Torwood forest (where William Wallace once took refuge), before proceeding to Falkirk (the site of Wallace's battle against the English in 1298), where they stop overnight. The next morning they pass Linlithgow, with its royal Stuart palace, skirt Edinburgh from the south (as had Charles Edward), and arrive at 'the ancient palace of Holy-Rood' (204.15).

The novel's Edinburgh scenes and the description of terrain relating to the battle of Prestonpans are both supported by first-hand knowledge. In one instance, however, there are some signs of Scott having manipulated his materials for aesthetic effect. Mrs Flockhart's lodgings are evidently in a close near the foot of the Canongate, and it is from there that on the day prior to the battle Waverley goes to St Leonard's Hill, from where he views the Jacobite army in the King's Park (now known as Holyrood Park) preparing to march off. The vista is impressive, with its background setting of Arthur's Seat, and it is also true that the main part of the Jacobite army encamped in a hollow area in the King's Park on its arrival in Edinburgh. However, Charles Edward moved his army to new bivouacs at Duddingston, at the far eastern end of the King's Park, a day before the army set off to confront General Cope. Not only would it be impractical to view an assembly at this new venue from St Leonard's Hill, but the effect even if visible would be less stunning, with Samson's Ribs forming the overhanging cliffs rather than the more distantly impressive Salisbury Crags (see 229.40 and note). The account of the landmarks and settlements directly relating to the battle, such as the old villages of Seaton and Preston,

on the other hand is remarkably accurate, and reflects a strong awareness of the situation as it stood in 1745 as well as a youthful first-hand
experience of the terrain.

With the departure of the Jacobite army on its ill-fated expedition
to England, the novel enters into a more hectic perambulatory mode,
with much of Scott's attention being devoted to orchestrating his hero's
movements by foot, wagon, post-horses, and carriage, as his fortunes
vary. Nevertheless a surprising accuracy of detail can be found in some
of Waverley's more stationary moments. After his separation from the
Jacobite army at Clifton, just south of Penrith, Scott might seem to
refer to the counties involved indiscriminately (an element that was
to engage subsequent editions). But closer examination suggests that
Waverley moves from his first-found refuge close to Clifton, just within
the old boundary of Westmorland, to a farm (Fasthwaite in the novel)
based on Waterfoot, at the NW tip of Ullswater, just within the old
Cumberland border (see note to 299.17). London is largely an indistinct entity, apart from the mention of Richard Waverley's address as
Hill Street, Berkeley Square, which Scott probably chose as a result
of his correspondence with one of the occupants of his own day, Lord
Somerville, concerning an edition of the *Memorie of the Somervilles*
(1815). The Carlisle scenes involving Fergus's last hours on the other
hand clearly gain strength from direct knowledge, most obviously in
the accurate description of the Castle and its outworks, while the incidents involving Flora in the refuge of a nearby Catholic household are
almost certainly informed by personal acquaintance with Corby Castle
(home of the Howard family) and its proprietor.

Character Prototypes. Broadly speaking, relevant characters can be
divided into three categories: actual historical figures, those who appear
to be mostly fictitious though representative of the period, and generic
characters who combine attributes relating to a number of persons
Scott knew about. Of these the last category has generally received the
most attention from commentators, with a particular focus on the figures of the Baron of Bradwardine and Fergus Mac-Ivor.[21]

Baron Cosmo Comyne Bradwardine can be associated with a number of members of the Jacobite aristocracy and gentry who joined in the
1745 rising at an early stage, notably Alexander Forbes, 4th Lord of
Pitsligo (1678–1762), Laurence Oliphant of Gask (1691–1767), and
Alexander Robertson of Struan (c. 1670–1749). Lord Pitsligo, whose
estate lay on the Buchan coast of Aberdeenshire, was a veteran of the
1715 rising, when he commanded a troop of horse at Sheriffmuir.
Noted for his strong nationalist feelings and philosophical interests,
he also spent several spells in semi-exile on the Continent, eventually
returning to his estate in 1720. In 1745 he joined Charles Edward's
army shortly after Prestonpans at the head of a body of cavalry mustered
in his own territory, was appointed general of horse by the Prince, and
though well into his sixties played a prominent part in the campaign
into England, as well as being at both the battles of Falkirk and Culloden. The similarity to Bradwardine is perhaps most marked in the

aftermath of defeat, when Pitsligo went into hiding on his own estate, sustained by support from his family and the local people, one of his main hiding places being a cave on the Buchan coast (still known as 'Lord Pitsligo's Cave'). It is perhaps also significant that the supporters of the arms of the family of Forbes of Pitsligo are two bears (see note to 37.6–7), and that the Pitsligo lands were once held by the Comyns of Buchan, a branch of the powerful family that had first come to Scotland in the reign of David I. Attempts to derive any such connection from the Baron's main name, on the other hand, are likely to prove less productive: the most obvious forerunner here being Thomas Bradwardine (c. 1290–1349), English scholar and (briefly) Archbishop of Canterbury, who is mentioned in Chaucer's *Nun's Priest's Tale*. Bra/edwardine is also a settlement and parish in Herefordshire, about 20 km W of Hereford, though no evidence of a connection with Scott has been discovered.

One of the qualities absent in Lord Pitsligo as a prototype is a clear Perthshire origin, a deficiency amply supplied in the case of Laurence Oliphant of Gask and Alexander Robertson of Struan. The Oliphants of Gask were descended from William Oliphant of Newton, Perthshire, who was slain at the battle of Flodden, and held lands in the region of Findo Gask, some 10 km SW of Perth. Laurence Oliphant, who had been present at the battle of Sheriffmuir, as part of the Perthshire horse, succeeded to the Gask estates in 1732; like the Baron he also had keen antiquarian interests, and was fluent in the Classical languages. After some deliberation, both he and his son (also Laurence) decided to enter into the 1745 rising, joining the Prince at Blair Atholl on 31 August. In September the two helped raise two troops of Perthshire horse, which were present at Prestonpans, Gask senior holding the rank of lieutenant-colonel, while apparently not directly participating in the action, though his son served as an aide-de-camp to the Prince. According to one account, the elder Gask in Edinburgh challenged four dragoons in flight from Prestonpans who were attempting to enter the safety of the Castle, narrowly escaping with his life when two who had dismounted fired at him.[22] The younger Gask followed Charles Edward on his campaign into England, while his father served as governor of Perth. Both were at Culloden, where Laurence senior was with the Perthshire horse, and both went into hiding afterwards, enduring hardships for over six months in a number of locations. According to one family historian, it is likely that Scott had heard of the Oliphants' history through his friendship with William Erskine, whose father, the Rev. William Erskine of Muthill (5 km S of Crieff), had attended to Laurence senior in the last years of his life.[23]

Alexander Robertson, 13th holder of the barony of Struan (in N Perthshire), was the longest-serving Jacobite in the present grouping, and also stands out as a skilful poet (as alluded to in the text: see 219.24 and note), his output including a number of imitations from Classical models. Educated at the University of St Andrews, Robertson had brought out his clan in 1689 in support of Viscount Dundee, and again in 1715, when he was captured at Sheriffmuir, though later escaping. After both these events, he had spent time in France, serving on the second occasion as a colonel in the Scots brigade. In the 1745 rising he joined Charles Edward in Perth early in September with a battalion of about 200 men, which fought with the Atholl brigade at Prestonpans, where Robertson (then in his seventies) appears to have been just a spectator. After the battle he returned to his homeland in General Cope's carriage and wearing his wolfskin coat, both gifts from the Prince; and there is evidence that he continued to aid the Jacobite cause till the end, spending his last few remaining years in the remote region of Rannoch as a semi-outcast.[24] While none of the prototypes mentioned above fit Bradwardine's circumstances fully, there is a clear preponderance of elements in the following respects: a) Classical education; b) service overseas; c) participation in the 1715 rising; d) strong feudal prejudices; d) engagement in the rising of 1745–46, as a leader of cavalry; e) hiding after Culloden, aided by local tenantry. Seen in this light, some of the main characteristics of the Baron are less idiosyncratic than modern commentators have allowed.

In a similar way, the character of Fergus Mac-Ivor incorporates a number of attributes belonging to chiefs of the Jacobite clans during the 1745 rising. Though his full patronymic (see 73.19–20 and note) and clan history are for the most part fictional, it is worth noting that the MacIvers were once a distinct clan, and that one of its remnants in the eighteenth century inhabited Perthshire, though largely absorbed by then into the Robertson clan. According to their clan historian, another body of MacIvers, in Lochaber, were allied to MacDonnells of Keppoch, and had insisted on maintaining their own identity when joining with Keppoch in the rising.[25] Insofar as individual clan-leaders are concerned, it is possible to trace elements of Fergus Mac-Ivor's character in both Donald Cameron of Lochiel (c. 1700–48), chief of the clan Cameron, and Simon Fraser, 11th Lord Lovat (1667/8–1747), a pairing which Scott later, in his *Tales of a Grandfather*, presented as offering models of good and bad clan leadership generally. Cameron of Lochiel matches Fergus in his family history (an exiled father), commitment to the Jacobite cause (albeit in his case with reservations at the onset of the '45), and the efficiency of his regiment—in the maintenance of which latter an element of ruthlessness is sometimes apparent, sitting uneasily with an image of 'the Gentle Lochiel', though it helps extend the connection with Fergus. In particular Fergus's callous pistol-whipping of Callum Beg (287.4–7) might possibly originate from an occasion when Lochiel shot one of his clansmen in the shoulder for carrying off a sheep.[26] In Simon Fraser, Lord Lovat— though an older and considerably more scandalous figure—one might trace some of Mac-Ivor's duplicity (both had held government commissions), cynical cultivation of the clan as a war machine, and agenda of personal advancement (Fergus's Earl's patent is matched by a Jacobite 'patent to be Duke of Fraser' held by Lovat).[27] In particular, there is a strong resemblance between Fergus's feast and a similar occasion presided over by Lord Lovat (see note to 103.20); while a broader overlap might be claimed in the case of Burt's *Letters from a Gentleman in the North of Scotland* (1754), where Lovat is invasively present if rarely named.

Elements of Fergus Mac-Ivor might also be sought in other officers of clan regiments in the Jacobite army of 1745. Especially notable here is Ewan MacPherson of Cluny (1706–1764), who had accepted command in a government Highland regiment shortly before the outbreak of hostilities, and was held captive by the Jacobites before accepting a commission as a colonel in the Prince's army. His Cluny regiment excelled itself in the action at Clifton, leading the successful charge against the enemy dragoons, though losing in the action a sergeant and twelve men.[28] MacPherson himself survived, fighting again with distinction at Falkirk, and, having narrowly missed Culloden, remaining an outlaw for nine years in his refuge known as the 'cage' (which itself might have fed into the account of Bradwardine's survival). In the description of the action at Clifton in particular Fergus and the Mac-Ivors might well have combined closely in Scott's imagination with Cluny of MacPherson and his regiment, who are specifically mentioned in the novel as being then with 'Fergus's people' (296.13–14). When Fergus is later imprisoned at Carlisle, the focus is likely to have shifted to another Jacobite officer, Major Donald MacDonnell of Tranadris, who was executed at Harraby, about a mile from Carlisle, on 18 October 1746. A cousin of MacDonnell of Keppoch, Tirnadris had been engaged in one of the earliest actions of the Rising, participating fully thereafter, before capture at the battle of Falkirk. After imprisonment in Edinburgh, he was taken to Carlisle with a body of other prisoners in August 1746, and kept there strongly ironed prior to being tried and found guilty in September. The speech that Tirnadris prepared for his execution was later published in *The Lyon in Mourning*, where a footnote states that 'He is said to be the original of Sir Walter Scott's Fergus MacIvor'.[29] Interestingly one of the two marginal interventions in the Abbotsford copy of John Home's *History of the Rebellion* concerns Tirnadris, with Scott adding that he was 'Major in the Princes service, and afterwards executed at Carlisle 18 October 1746' [right column of page 47]. Also sometimes mentioned as a model for Fergus Mac-Ivor is Scott's immediate contemporary Alasdair Ranaldson Mac-Donnell of Glengarry (1771–1828), whose carefully-cultivated image as a latter-day Highland chieftain is so strongly captured in a full-length painting by Sir Henry Raeburn, first exhibited in 1812 (see also note to 361.8).[30]

A number of origins can also be suggested for two other characters who inhabit the regions of Tully-Veolan and Glennaquoich, David Gellatley and Donald Bean Lean. The figure of David Gellatley has attracted a good deal of commentary, though the results arguably have not been commensurately helpful. Scott as early as his 1817 review of *Tales of my Landlord* in the *Quarterly* intervened to draw attention to the late survival of the custom of noblemen keeping fools in the remoter parts of Scotland, with particular reference to the Earls of Strathmore and Glamis Castle.[31] Other commentators have pointed to a number

of individual figures of Scott's own acquaintance, including Daft Jock
Gray of Gilmanscleugh in Ettrick, Selkirkshire, who reportedly visited
Scott at Ashestiel, and David Hinves (d. 1838), the valet of his friend
William Stewart Rose, whose residence at Cuffnells Scott had visited
in 1807.[32] Relatively unnoticed however has been the fact that a real-
life David Gellatly [sic] studied alongside Scott at the University of
Edinburgh, the two both being enrolled in John Bruce's Logic Class
in 1785.[33]

In the case of Bean Lean, Colonel David Stewart identifies a namesake and prototype in 'Donald Cameron, or Donald Bane Leane, [who]
was tried in Perth for cattle stealing, and executed at Kinloch Rannoch
in 1752, in order to strike terror into his band in that district'.[34] It is
also possible that Scott's attention was first drawn to the name by an
example of patronymics in Burt's Letters: 'Donald Bane, i.e. White
hair'd Donald' (2.111). He may also have known about a broadside
ballad, entitled 'The Highland Man's Lament, for the Death of Donald
Bayn . . . who was Execute at the Grass Market of Edinburgh on
Wednesday the 9th day of January 1723', where the speaker, a clansman
vowing vengeance against the enemies of his companion, laments that
the execution was not on 'kind Gallows at the Crief' (see also note to
92.8–9).[35] Among other Highland characters, it is worth noting that
the first part of Evan Dhu Maccombich's name (meaning 'Evan the
Dark') reflects that of Sir Ewen Dubh Cameron (1629–1719), chief
of the Camerons of Lochiel, who took part in Glencairn's rising in
1653–54 and led his clan at Killiecrankie in 1689, and whose deeds
were to be emulated by his equally celebrated grandson in 1745.

Among the more purely historically-based characters in the novel,
that of Waverley's commander Colonel Gardiner (truncated to Colonel
G—— in the early editions, as in the present) is guided by both an
established public image on the one hand, and direct anecdotal information on the other. His reputation for moral probity at Waverley-
Honour (pace his Presbyterianism: see 27.20) and for Calvinistical
bigotry at Glennaquoich (135.34) reflects the image of Gardiner
as a religious convert from dissolute living, as propagated through the
hymn-writer Philip Doddridge's Some Remarkable Passages in the Life
of the Honourable Colonel James Gardiner (1747), much reprinted as a
religious tract in the later eighteenth century. The account of his last
moments at Prestonpans in Waverley is undoubtedly vivified by Scott's
knowledge of the terrain (Gardiner's own house at Bankton adjoined
the battlefield), as well as information derived from first-hand witnesses such as Alexander Carlyle.[36]

As noted previously, the character of Colonel Talbot is drawn to a
significant degree from the Hanoverian officer Colonel Charles Whitefoord, whom Scott probably first heard about from Stewart of Invernahyle. The name Talbot itself also has a precedent: a Major Talbot
('of Murray's Regiment') is to be found in a list of prisoners taken at
Gladsmuir [i.e. Prestonpans] in the Caledonian Mercury for 23 September 1745, as too in Ray's Compleat History of the Rebellion,[37] and
also (as a witness in the defence) in A Report of the Proceedings and

Opinion of the Board of General Officers, in their Examination into the Conduct, Behaviour, and Proceedings of Lieutenant-General Sir John Cope (1749), of which Scott likewise owned a copy. Scott also in the course of the novel uses the name Talbot to establish a link for his character with the Earls of Shrewsbury (see 357.18–20, and notes).

In some other instances, a predominantly literary foundation seems to underlie Scott's characterisation. In the pairing of the Rev. Mr Morton and Major Mellville, though both surnames have strong associations with Scottish history, one senses a conscious reworking of the characters of the sentimental Umphraville and worldly-wise Colonel Caustic in Henry Mackenzie's *The Mirror* and *The Lounger*, and more particularly of the depiction of the clergyman in Caustic's parish in *The Lounger*, no. 40, 5 Nov. 1785. As several modern critics have observed, the description of Flora Mac-Ivor shows a number of affinities with the portrayal of the harp-playing Glorvina in Sydney Owenson's *The Wild Irish Girl* (1806), an image sharpened in Scott's case possibly through his personal relationship with the Gaelic song-translating Clephane sisters from the Isle of Mull; though on another level Scott is clearly attempting to embody actual characteristics belonging to a number of committed female supporters of the 1745 rising, such as 'Colonel' Anne Mackintosh.[38] According to an article in *The Border Magazine*, reporting material found in the Lundie family papers, a namesake of Flora's witnessed Charles Edward's entry into Edinburgh: 'In a frenzy of excitement and enthusiasm, Jean M'Ivor writes from Edinburgh, September 1745:—"The Prince is in the Abbey (Holyrood), and yesterday at 1 o'clock, the King was proclaimed over the Cross by the heralds. Thank God, there was not a sword drawn against them. The town is half mad, and no one can settle."'[39] Flora's Christian name matches both that of Flora MacDonald, the celebrated preserver of Charles Edward in hiding, and of the sister of the Laird of Staffa in his own day, whom Scott had visited in 1810. A range of (mainly male) burlesque character names stand more in the tradition of the comic novels of Fielding and Smollett, though Scott's linguistic range often adds a special flavour. Some etymologies, as in the case of 'Killancureit' for a boorish if locally ambitious cattle farmer, should be self-evident. Other combinations, involving several languages or idioms, require disentangling; and individual explanations, wherever possible, are offered for these in the following Explanatory Notes.

NOTES

For standard abbreviations in references, see 393–94

1   He is described as having remained 'a bachelor at seventy-two', apparently from a vantage-point of 'sixty years since', his brother being 'ten years younger' (see present text, 6.39–7.1, 6.25).

2   *Quarterly Review*, 16 (Jan. 1817), 430–80 (433–34). The connection with Bradwardine at this point, as opposed to the parallelism with Waverley and Talbot earlier, is made explicit in a sentence in Scott's original holograph omitted by the published review: 'A similar incident is related of the Baron of Bradwardine . . . in which Davie Gellatley appears as his

polygraph' (NLS, MS 42540, f. 8v). Scott returned to the core story in the Introductions to *The Chronicles of the Canongate* (see EEWN 20, 7–8) and the Magnum Opus edition of *Waverley* (1.xcvii–cii).

3 *The Dewar Manuscripts. Volume One*, ed. Rev. John Mackechnie (Glasgow, 1964), Item 35, 'The Battle of Gladsmuir', 228–29.

4 *A Jacobite Miscellany*, ed. Henrietta Tayler (Oxford, 1948), 39. Magdalen Pringle, 18 at the time, later married Sir John Hall of Dunglass, 3rd baronet (1710/11–76), and was the mother of Sir James Hall of Dunglass, 4th baronet (1761–1832), chemist and geologist, whom Scott succeeded as President of the Royal Society of Edinburgh. Sir James's own wife was Helen Douglas, daughter of the 4th Earl of Selkirk, and so a brother of Thomas Douglas, 5th Earl of Selkirk (1771–1820), the author of *Observations on the Present State of the Highlands of Scotland* (1805), also mentioned in Scott's 'Postscript'. It was one of their sons, James Hall (1800–1854), who later purchased the manuscript of *Waverley*.

5 See Scott's article in the *Quarterly Review* for June 1827 on the *Life and Works* of John Home: *Prose Works*, 19.283–367, where he mentions 'our narrator (a clergyman)' (301). Scott possibly might also have had sight of Carlyle's papers when held by trustees after his death in 1805: see *The Autobiography of Dr Alexander Carlyle of Inveresk 1722–1805*, ed. John Hill Burton (London and Edinburgh, 1910; facsimile edn, Thoemmes Press, Bristol 1990), Introduction by Richard B. Sher, xivn.

6 *Scott on Himself*, ed. David Hewitt (Edinburgh, 1981), 13, 38, 17–18.

7 *Monthly Review*, 2nd series 75 (Nov. 1814), 275–89 (p. 280).

8 See 'A Note on Gaelic Proverbs in Waverley', *Notes and Queries*, 220 (1975), 64–66. The following biographical details are partly taken from Alexander Campbell's Preface to the 1819 edition of the *Collection of Gaelic Proverbs*.

9 The manuscripts of David Wemyss, Lord Elcho (1721–87), and of James Maxwell of Kirkconnell (1708–62) are both in the Abbotsford Library: *CLA*, 23. Maxwell's manuscript was sent to Scott in October 1828: see *Letters*, 12.459n., and was published by the Maitland Club in 1841. *A Short Account of the Affairs of Scotland in the Years 1744, 1745, 1746*, by David, Lord Elcho, was published in 1907. The Chevalier de Johnstone's *Memoir of the Rebellion in 1745 and 1746* was first published in London in 1820, with two further editions in 1821 and 1823: the editor takes issue with 'the author of Waverley' at several points in his footnotes. James Johnstone (born 1719), the son of an Edinburgh merchant, went to Perth to join the Rising, and was aide-de-camp to Lord George Murray, and for a time assistant aide-de-camp to the Prince; he entered service in France afterwards, spent time in Canada, and died about 1800.

10 Robert Fitzroy Bell, the editor of *Memorials of John Murray of Broughton* (Edinburgh, 1898), suggests in his Introduction that 'Sir Walter may have seen them' (xxxiii). The work as a whole gives detailed first-hand accounts of secret negotiations, including a trip in disguise to the Highlands prior to the Rising. See also *The Woodhouselee MS*, ed. Archibald Francis Steuart (London, 1907), Introduction, 6.

11 A note by Scott at the beginning of the Abbotsford copy (press mark M: 16) reads: 'The writer may be trusted in what he says he saw allowing for party heat & violence but his information from *report* is terribly inaccurate'.

12 Scott evidently had access to this from an early stage, referring to it in a footnote to 'The Battle of Philiphaugh' in his *Minstrelsy of the Scottish Border* (ed. Henderson, 1902, 2.206n.). According to the Preface to the 1858 edition of the *Memoirs*, Scott at some point had a copy made and began annotating.

13 The connection was later noted by John Galt in introducing the 1824 *Works of Henry Mackenzie, Esq.* 'It is indeed, worthy of remark, that one of the most interesting passages in that popular romance, the concealment of the Baron Bradwardine, has been anticipated in Albert Bane by Mr. Mackenzie' (16).

14 *Sir Walter Scott and Scots Law* (Edinburgh and London, 1932), 23.

15 *Atlas of the European Novel, 1800–1900* (London, 1999), 37–38.

16 See *Letters*, 12.104–06; Lockhart, *Life*, 2.118–19.

17 *Atlas of the European Novel*, 41.

18 *The Fortified House in Scotland. Volume Two: Central Scotland* (Edinburgh, 1986), 140 (see also illustration on 141). For Scott's understanding and use of the term bartizan, see Clive Wainwright, *The Romantic Interior: The British Collector at Home 1750–1850* (New Haven and London, 1989), 157–58.

19 For traditional explanations for the closing of the great gate, one of which is the Earl's vow that it should not be opened till a Stuart was restored, see W. S. Crockett, *The Scott Country* (London, 1902), 185–86.

20 *Sketches of the Character, Manners, and Present State of the Highlanders of Scotland*, 2 vols (Edinburgh, 1822). A footnote refers to 'his rencontre with the landlord of the Seven-branched Golden Candlesticks [*sic*] at Crieff' (1.104n.).

21 See Robert Chambers, *Illustrations of the Author of Waverley* (2nd edn, Edinburgh, 1825), 1–34; *Waverley Anecdotes*, Vol. 1 (London, 1833), *passim*; W. S. Crockett, *The Scott Originals* (London and Edinburgh, 1912), 3–41.

22 John Sibbald Gibson, *Edinburgh in the '45* (Edinburgh, 1976), 29.

23 L. Kington Oliphant, *The Jacobite Lairds of Gask* (London, 1870), 350–51; see also E. Maxtone Graham, *The Oliphants of Gask. Records of a Jacobite Family* (London, 1910).

24 Collection of Robertson's poetry published posthumously in Edinburgh in 1751 or 1752 and 1775. The latter of these also includes *The History and Martial Atchievements of the Robertson's of Strowan*, which states of him 'It was alleged he joined the young pretender in 1745, but no act of rebellion could be proved upon him before the courts of Oyer and Terminer. He died in April 1749 in the 81st year of his age' (22).

25 Peter C. Campbell, *Account of the Clan-Iver* (Aberdeen, 1873), 4, 12.

26 Amelia Georgiana Murray MacGregor, *The History of the Clan Gregor*, 2 vols (Edinburgh, 1898–1901), 2.366. Lochiel had set out with Robert MacGregor of Glencarnock, with the dual intention of shooting any of their clansmen killing sheep.

27 John Home, *The History of the Rebellion in the Year 1745* (London, 1802), 131.

28 According to MacPherson in a letter of 20 December 1745 given in Home's *History*, 341–43, 'I had twelve men and a serjeant killed on the

spot, and three private men wounded' (342). See also Alan Gibson Macpherson, *A Day's March to Ruin. The Badenoch Men in the Forty-Five and
biography of Col. Ewan Macpherson of Cluny* (Clan Macpherson Association, 1996), 101.

29   Norman H. MacDonald, *The Clan Ranald of Lochaber. A History of the
MacDonalds or MacDonells of Keppoch* (Edinburgh, [1972]), 41–42;
'The Speech of Donald MacDonell of Tiendrish, of the Family of Keppoch', *The Lyon in Mourning*, Scottish History Society, 3 vols (Edinburgh,
1895–96), 1.34–36, 34n. The footnote in the latter adds: 'His sword, a
genuine *Andrew Ferrara*, afterwards came into the possession of the
Howards of Corby Castle'.

30   See *Letters*, 4.198n. Further details are to be found in John Prebble, *The
King's Jaunt* (London, 1988), 112–15, which at one point notes how
MacDonnell 'often went alone into the hills of Glen Quoich where he
allowed no one to hunt but himself' (114).

31   *Quarterly Review*, 16 (Jan. 1817), 437–38.

32   Chambers, *Illustrations*, 7–29; Crockett, *Scott Originals*, 32–41. A similarity to Hinves was pointed out by J. B. S. Morritt in a letter to Scott of 14
July 1814: 'Davie Gellatly who I take to be a transcript of William Rose's
motley follower commonly yclept Caliban' (NLS, MS 3885, f. 134r). This
however is discounted by Crockett, *Scott Originals*, 32–33.

33   'Matriculation Roll of the University of Edinburgh, Vol. 2 1775–1810'
(unpublished typescript, Edinburgh University Library), 440. Gellatly
was enrolled in two other classes in 1786 (452, 453); nothing else has
been discovered about him.

34   *Sketches of the Character, Manners, and Present State of the Highlanders of
Scotland*, 1.42.

35   A copy survives in the National Library of Scotland, Ry.III.a.1. See also
William Donaldson, 'Bonny Highland Laddie: The Making of a Myth',
Scottish Literary Journal, 3:2 (Dec. 1976), 30–50 (32–33), which
interprets the broadside as an ironic take on Highlanders' narrowness of
vision.

36   In the printed *Autobiography* (see above) Carlyle mentions visiting Gardiner for a 'third time' on the eve of the battle, 'I . . . found him grave, but
serene and resigned; and he concluded by praying God to bless me, and
that he could not wish for a better night to lie on the field; and then
called for his cloak and other conveniences for lying down' (149–50).

37   James Ray, *A Compleat History of the Rebellion* (York, 1749), 56, 'A List
of the Officers killed, wounded and Prisoners, at the Battle of Glaidsmuir,
September 21, 1745'.

38   A direct claim for the latter providing a historical basis is made by John
Sibbald Gibson, *Lochiel of the '45* (Edinburgh, 2004), 50; though it
should added that the Flora of the novel is not herself a militant activist.
For possible connections with Glorvina in *The Wild Irish Girl*, see Peter
Garside, 'Popular Fiction and National Tale: Hidden Origins of Scott's
Waverley', *Nineteenth-Century Literature*, 46 (1991), 30–53 (50–51).

39   'An Old Literary Border Circle', *Border Magazine*, 30 (Jan.–Dec. 1915)
246–48 (246).

EXPLANATORY NOTES

In these notes a comprehensive attempt is made to identify Scott's sources, and all quotations, references, historical events, and historical personages, to explain proverbs, and to translate difficult or obscure language. (Phrases are explained in the notes while single words are treated in the glossary.) The notes are brief; they offer information rather than critical comment or exposition. Gaelic phrases are first transliterated into modern Gaelic, and then translated. When a quotation has not been recognised this is stated: any new information from readers will be welcomed. References are to first editions, standard editions, or to the editions Scott himself used. Books in the Abbotsford Library are identified, where significant, by reference to the appropriate page of the *Catalogue of the Library at Abbotsford*. When quotations reproduce their sources accurately, the reference is given without comment. Verbal differences in the source are indicated by a prefatory 'see', while a general rather than a verbal indebtedness is indicated by 'compare'. Biblical references are to the Author-ised Version. Plays by Shakespeare are cited without authorial ascription, and references are to *William Shakespeare: The Complete Works*, edited by Peter Alexander (London and Glasgow, 1951, frequently reprinted). Manuscripts referred to with the prefix MS or MSS alone are in the National Library of Scotland. Specific dates relating to the 1745–46 rising reflect the old-style (O S) Julian calendar which was used in Great Britain until 1752. Ed1/Ed3/Ed6 refer respectively to the first, third (1814) and sixth (1816) editions of *Waverley*.

The following works are also distinguished by abbreviations.

Blaikie   Walter Biggar Blaikie, *Itinerary of Prince Charles Edward Stuart*, Scottish History Society, Vol. 23 (Edinburgh, 1897).

Burt   Edmund Burt, *Letters from a Gentleman in the North of Scotland*, 2 vols (London, 1754): *CLA*, 19.

Child   Francis James Child, *The English and Scottish Popular Ballads*, 5 vols (Boston and New York, 1882–98).

CLA   [J. G. Cochrane], *Catalogue of the Library at Abbotsford* (Edinburgh, 1838).

Duffy   Christopher Duffy, *The '45* (London, 2003).

EEWN   The Edinburgh Edition of the Waverley Novels (Edinburgh, 1993–2012).

Grose   Francis Grose, *A Classical Dictionary of the Vulgar Tongue*, 3rd edn (London, 1796): *CLA*, 156.

Herd   David Herd, *Ancient and Modern Scottish Songs, Heroic Ballads, Etc.*, 2nd edn, 2 vols (Edinburgh, 1776): *CLA*, 171.

Home   John Home, *The History of the Rebellion in the Year 1745* (London, 1802): *CLA*, 4.

ISet   Interleaved Set, *Novels and Tales of the Author of Waverley*, 12 vols (Edinburgh, 1822): Vols 1 and 2, MSS 23001–02.

Kinsley   *The Poems and Songs of Robert Burns*, ed. James Kinsley, 3 vols (Oxford, 1968).

Letters   *The Letters of Sir Walter Scott*, ed. H. J. C. Grierson and others, 12 vols (London, 1932–37).

Life   J. G. Lockhart, *Memoirs of the Life of Sir Walter Scott, Bart.*, 7 vols (Edinburgh, 1837–38).

Macintosh   Donald Macintosh, *A Collection of Gaelic Proverbs, and Familiar*

Phrases (Edinburgh 1785): *CLA*, 175.

Magnum   Walter Scott, *Waverley Novels*, 48 vols (Edinburgh, 1829–33).

Minstrelsy   Walter Scott, *Minstrelsy of the Scottish Border*, ed. T. F. Henderson, 4 vols (Edinburgh, 1902).

ODEP   The Oxford Dictionary of English Proverbs, 3rd edn, rev. F. P. Wilson (Oxford, 1970).

OED   The Oxford English Dictionary, 2nd edn, 20 vols (Oxford, 1989).

Pennant   Thomas Pennant, *A Tour in Scotland*, 5th edn, 3 vols (London, 1790): *CLA*, 4.

Percy   *Reliques of Ancient English Poetry*, ed. Thomas Percy, 3 vols (London, 1765): see *CLA*, 172.

Poetical Works   The Poetical Works of Sir Walter Scott, Bart., ed. J. G. Lockhart, 12 vols (Edinburgh, 1833–34).

Prose Works   The Prose Works of Sir Walter Scott, Bart., 28 vols (Edinburgh, 1834–36).

Ramsay   Allan Ramsay, *A Collection of Scots Proverbs* (1737), in *The Works of Allan Ramsay*, 6 vols, Vol. 5, ed. Alexander M. Kinghorn and Alexander Law (Edinburgh and London: Scottish Text Society, 1972), 59–133.

Ray   J[ohn] Ray, *A Compleat Collection of English Proverbs*, 3rd edn (London, 1737): *CLA*, 169.

SMM   The Scots Musical Museum, ed. James Johnson, 6 vols (Edinburgh, 1787–1803).

SND   Scottish National Dictionary, ed. William Grant and David D. Murison, 10 vols (Edinburgh, 1931–76).

Tom Jones   Henry Fielding, *The History of Tom Jones, a Foundling*, 6 vols (London, 1749).

Information derived from the notes of the late Dr J. C. Corson is indicated by 'Corson' or '(Corson)'. In legal matters the notes (MS 23070, loose slips; MS 23095, notebook) of the late Lord Normand '(Normand)' have been informative. MS 743, ff. 27–36, consisting of incomplete proofs of *The Poetry of the Novels, Tales, and Romances, of 'The Author of Waverley'* (Edinburgh, 1822), annotated by Scott, have helped identify authorship of verse in the novel. The following editions of *Waverley* have proved most helpful: Dryburgh Edition, 25 vols (London, 1892–94), Vol. 1; The Border Edition, ed. Andrew Lang, 24 vols (London, 1901) ('Lang'), Vol. 1; ed. Andrew Hook (Harmondsworth, 1972); ed. Claire Lamont (Oxford, 1981) ('Lamont'). Useful information has also been found in Henry Weston Eve, *Notes to Scott's Waverley* (London, 1875), and Victor H. Allemandy, *Notes on Scott's Waverley* (London, n.d.).

title-page epigraph   *2 Henry IV*, 5.3.112–13.

3.16   Howard, Mordaunt, Mortimer, or Stanley   aristocratic family names, that of Stanley (the family name of the Earls of Derby) being used later in the novel for the character of Frank Stanley. The combination also echoes Henry Mackenzie when discussing stereotypical names for the hero of a novel or play: 'those of Mordaunt, Montague, or Howard' (*The Mirror*, no. 7, 16 Feb. 1779).

3.17–18   Belmour, Belville, Belfield, and Belgrave   stereotypical assonant names in sentimental and domestic fiction of the later 18th and early 19th centuries. Belfield features as a name in Smollett's *The Expedition of Humphry Clinker* (1771), Frances Burney's *Cecilia* (1782), Hannah More's *Coelebs in Search of a Wife* (1808), and Henry Kett's *Emily, A Moral Tale* (1809–11). Compare *The Antiquary* (1816): 'Lovel or Belville are just the names which youngsters are apt to assume on such occasions' (EEWN 3, 17.28–29).

3.21–22   maiden knight . . . white shield   matching the setting out of

Don Quixote: 'he also considered, that though he was already knighted, it would become him to wear white armour, and not to adorn his shield with any device, until he had deserved one by some extraordinary demonstration of his valour' (*Don Quixote*, Part 1 (1605), Bk 1, Ch. 2). The passage quoted is from J. G. Lockhart's revised version of Motteux's translation: *The History of the Ingenious Gentleman, Don Quixote of La Mancha*, 5 vols (1822), 1.24–25. Scott used the metaphor again with regard to his fourth work of fiction, *Tales of my Landlord* (1816): 'I have changed my publisher, and come forth like a maiden knight's white shield (there is a conceit!)': *Letters*, 4.288.

3.22   Waverley the name has historical associations with Waverley Abbey, the first English Cistercian abbey, founded in 1128 by William Giffard, bishop of Winchester. It is situated about 4 miles south of Farnham, Surrey, and was visited by King John in 1208 and Henry III in 1225. By the time of its suppression at the Reformation, in 1536, there were only 13 monks in the community. The 'Annales Waverleienses' (in Latin) are printed in Thomas Gale, *Historiae Anglicanae Scriptores . . .* (Oxford, 1687; *CLA*, 27), 129ff. For the use of the name in fiction, notably Charlotte Smith's *Desmond* (1792) and Jane West's *The Loyalists* (1812), see Wilbur L. Cross, 'An Earlier Waverley', *Modern Language Notes*, 17:2 (Feb. 1902), 44–45, and Peter Garside, 'Walter Scott and the "Common" Novel, 1808–1819', *Cardiff Corvey: Reading the Romantic Text*, 3 (Sept. 1999) ⟨www.cardif.ac.uk/encap/journals/corvey/articles/cc03_no2.html⟩.

3.27   frontispiece used in the older sense of a title-page, rather than illustration facing the title-page.

4.1   Udolpho referring to Ann Radcliffe's *The Mysteries of Udolpho* (1794), probably the most influential of English Gothic romances of the period. For a commentary on the different types of contemporary fiction outlined by Scott, see Peter Garside, 'Popular Fiction and National Tale: Hidden Origins of Scott's *Waverley*', *Nineteenth-Century Literature*, 46 (1991), 30–53 (37–40).

4.5   owl have shrieked compare *Macbeth*, 2.2.3.

4.14   Rosycrucians and illuminati members of secret philosophical societies reputed to deal in the occult, such as feature in several German and pseudo-German novels of the period.

4.16   dark lanterns lanterns with a slide or arrangement for concealing the light.

4.23   blowzy meaning red and coarse-complexioned, and not in the present sense of 'buxom'.

4.28   Grosvenor Square fashionable residential square in the West End of London; used as a testing-ground for the young heroine by a variety of novelists, including Frances Burney.

4.28–29   Barouche Club or the Four-in-Hand names for two clubs of fashionable young men skilled in riding coaches with four horses single-handedly at breakneck speed. Reports on the meetings of both can be found in *The Sporting Magazine* for Feb. 1810, Vol. 35, 201, which also includes a frontispiece illustration of 'Four in Hand' (showing a coach with four horses, with two men at both back and front). The report on the Barouche Club there states that 'This society of Charioteers takes precedence of the Four-in-Hand Club, its having been formed in the early part of the year 1807' (201). The first account of the Four-in-Hand club found in the *Sporting Magazine* is in the issue for June 1809 (Vol. 34, 142–44). An account of an assembly of the same club on 1 May, starting in Cavendish Square, is given in the *Edinburgh Annual Register* for 1811 (Vol. 4, Part 2, 90–91). The activity also features in a number of scandal novels of the period, including Charles Sedley's *The Barouche Driver and his Wife* (1807), and Alicia Tyndal Palmer's *The Sons of Altringham* (1811), the second of whose three volumes contains 'Mortimer; or, the Election and the Four-in-Hand Club'.

4.30　Queen Anne Street East　the eastern section of Queen Anne Street in London, close to Cavendish Square, this part later being renamed Foley Street.

4.30–31　Bow-Street Office　home of the Bow Street Runners, London's only police force in the later 18th and early 19th centuries. A coloured engraving of the 'Bow-Street Office', by Ackermann, showing the interior with figures, can be found in William Pyne's *Microcosm of London* (1808). According to the accompanying text: 'This office has the largest jurisdiction of any in the metropolis, its authority extending to every part of his majesty's dominions, except the city of London, which is governed by its own magistrates' (facsimile edn, 3 vols (London, 1904), 1.82).

4.41–42　iron on his shoulders . . . heels of his boots　i.e. wearing neither armour nor spurs.

5.1　in purple and in pall　this phrase is found in 'Sir Cauline', in Percy, 1.47. The heroine there, however, is called Christabelle and not Lady Alice. See also 'The Cherry-Tree Carol', Child, 54B, stanza 11 ('in purple nor in pall'), taken from a later text, though Child refers to an 18th-century broadside. As Lamont points out, Scott's ballad imitation, 'Alice Brand', in Canto 4 of *The Lady of the Lake* (1810), contains the line 'If pall and vair no more I wear' (*Poetical Works*, 8.175).

5.2　a route　a fashionable gathering or large evening party, in vogue in the 18th and early 19th centuries. Compare J. G. Lockhart, referring to Edinburgh society in *Peter's Letters to his Kinsfolk* (1819): 'There is at least one regular ball every evening, and besides this, half the routs are in their waning hours, transferred into carpet-dances' (3rd edn [actually the 2nd], 1819, 1.220).

5.12–13　George the Second's reign　1727–60.

5.16–18　table garnished . . . fictitious description　the description here echoes Scott's summarising Conclusion to Joseph Strutt's antiquarian romance, *Queenhoo-Hall* (1808): 'There is a prolix account of the marriage-feast, of which we can pick out the names of a few dishes, such as peterel, crane, sturgeon, swan, &c. &c. with a profusion of wild-fowl and venison' (4.78; reprinted in Magnum, 1.lxxxix).

5.20　Mirror of Fashion　heading of a regular gossip column in *The Morning Chronicle* in the early 19th century.

5.31　brocaded coat　coat made of a fabric variegated with silver and gold, or enriched with a raised pattern.

6.3　book of Nature　the phrase, indicative of the Augustan belief in an uniform human nature and the mimetic qualities of art, is employed in a similar way in *Tom Jones*: 'it is the Part of the learned and sagacious Reader to consult that original Book of Nature, whence every Passage in our Work is transcribed' (Bk 7, Ch. 12: 3.102).

6.4　black letter　term originating from about 1600, and referring to the heavy 'gothic' type-face in early English printing, used usually for vernacular and religious literature, whereas the Roman font was used for Latin texts.

6.4　wire-wove and hot-pressed　referring to modern methods in producing paper. According to Philip Gaskell, 'wove paper' (produced in moulds of which the wire mesh was woven like cloth) was developed in the mid-18th century, but 'it was not until the last decade of the century that it was used in any quantity by printers'; however, 'by about 1805 nearly all British printing paper was made in wove moulds' (*A New Introduction to Bibliography* (Oxford, 1972), 65–66, 214). Hot-pressing refers to a process of pressing sheets of paper through hot cylinders, ensuring an extra smoothness. As a combination this appears to have been a set phrase in Scott's time. See, e.g., Mary Brunton, referring to her second novel *Discipline* (1814), in a letter of 9 September 1813: 'I mean to do my very best for my second daughter; and if I live and thrive till this time next year, we shall try how she looks in "wire-wove and hot-pressed"' (in *Emmeline, With Some Other Pieces* (1819), lxx). Compare also the 'Advertisement' to the satirical poem, *An Heroic Epistle to Mr. Winsor* (London, 1808; *CLA*, 186): 'I intend to print the Text upon a fine wire-woven hot-pressed paper' ([i]).

6.14 Waverley-Honour the term 'Honour', as used here, denotes a seigniory of several manors held under one baron or lord paramount (*OED*, noun 7).

6.20 presumptive heir nearest heir in succession, who it is presumed will inherit; as opposed to the 'heir apparent' (e.g. a first son who will undoubtedly inherit).

6.27 Will Wimble 'younger brother to a Baronet, and descended from the ancient family of *Wimbles*': the subject of Joseph Addison's *The Spectator*, no. 108 (4 July 1711).

6.35–36 Passive obedience ... non-resistance see 'The Vicar of Bray', an anonymous 18th-century song about a vicar who accommodates himself to religious and political changes during five reigns, and here referring to that of William III (reigned 1689–1702) and the overturning of slogans of the later Stuart period: see Joseph Ritson, *A Select Collection of English Songs*, 3 vols (London, 1783; *CLA*, 174), 2.126.

7.6 country interest a party in the House of Commons consisting largely of independent country gentlemen, often opposed to the current 'court' administration.

7.15 house of Stuart the Scottish dynasty which succeeded to the throne of England in 1603 after the death of Elizabeth. Its rule ended in 1688 when James VII of Scotland and II of England vacated the throne. See also following note and Historical Note, 367.

7.17 Hanover succession the succession of the Protestant Hanoverian royal family was established by the Act of Settlement of 1701 to prevent that of the Catholic Stuarts, with George, Elector of Hanover (1660–1727), consequently acceding to the throne in 1714 as George I, as opposed to the exiled James Francis Edward Stuart (1688–1766). The latter was proclaimed King James VIII of Scotland and III of England during the Jacobite risings of 1715 and 1745. See also Historical Note, 367–68.

7.25 Bar le Duc in NE France, capital of the (before 1760) nominally independent Duchy of Lorraine. In 1713 the Treaty of Utrecht obliged the King of France to expel James VIII and III from France, so the Jacobite court was established instead in Bar-le-Duc, where it existed until 1715: see Bryan Bevan, *King James the Third of England: A Study in Kingship in Exile* (London, 1967), 64. In all previous editions of *Waverley*, this is given as 'Bois le Duc', evidently a misreading.

7.26 Avignon, and Italy James VIII and III twice resided in Avignon, from 1716–17 and in 1727, while between 1717–18 he was at Urbino in Italy; a more permanent Jacobite court was then set up in Rome at the Palazzo Muti-Papazurri after his marriage to Maria Clementina Sobieska in 1719.

7.33 News Letter see note to 8.2.

7.36 Excise Bill in 1733 Sir Robert Walpole introduced measures for imposing an excise duty on wine and tobacco, but was forced to withdraw, in the face of an intense campaign which united the gentry and mercantile interests: see M. J. Daunton, *Progress and Poverty* (Oxford, 1995), 510.

7.40 once a quarter apparently referring to quarterly payments of government salaries and pensions, as received by placemen politicians in the Walpolian era.

8.2 Dyer's Weekly Letter for an account of these manuscript newsletters, produced under the supervision of John Dyer (*c.*1653–1713), distributed by

398   EXPLANATORY NOTES

penny post in the early 18th century, see Henry L. Snyder, 'Newsletters in
England, 1689–1715', in *Newsletters to Newspapers: Eighteenth-Century Journal-
ism*, ed. D. H. Bond and W. R. McLeod (Morgantown, West Virginia, 1977),
3–16. Snyder observes that Dyer was reputed by some to be a Jacobite and
notes the 'blatant, Tory tone of his letters' (13). The Tory newsletter genre
persisted well after Dyer's death in 1713. Joseph Addison refers to these
newsletters in satirising the mentality of the '*Fox-hunters*' in *The Freeholder*, no.
22, 5 March 1716: 'Sir, says he, I make it a Rule never to believe any of your
printed News. We never see, Sir, how Things go, except now and then in
Dyer's Letter, and I read that more for the Style than the News'. The spurned
alternative here is the government's printed newspaper *The London Gazette*.
8.3 mail-coaches proposed by John Palmer in 1782 as the means of
distributing mail, and adopted by William Pitt, the Prime Minister, in 1784.
8.4 six-penny club evidently referring to working-men's reading clubs,
in Scott's own day, which provided access to newspapers and periodicals for a
small (often monthly) subscription.
8.6 weekly post referring to the service conducted by messengers carrying
letters on horseback by stages or otherwise.
8.6–7 Weekly Intelligencer the term 'Intelligencer' (informant, messenger) was used in the title of a number of early newspapers and other publications, a notable instance being Jonathan Swift and Thomas Sheridan's *The
Intelligencer*, first published in Dublin in weekly numbers in 1728. See also
note to 8.2 above.
8.21 fettered by no entail an entail specified which descendants could
inherit heritable or real property, and prevented heirs from selling or giving
away the whole or any part of it. In this case, no such limitation applies, for
reasons stated.
8.33 com. Hants i.e. Hampshire, *com.* signifying 'comitatus' (county).
8.39 Bradshawe the regicide John Bradshaw (1602–59), who was president of the court which condemned Charles I to death in 1649.
9.14 borne in the field of Hastings according to E. A. Greening Lamborn, in 'Sir Walter's Heraldry', no coats of arms were borne at the battle of
Hastings in 1066: *Notes and Queries*, 190 (18 May 1946), 208.
9.14–15 three ermines passant the ermine is an animal of the weasel
family, noted in heraldry for its black-spotted fur. A field of ermine in heraldry
is normally white with black spots of a particular shape. Though E. A. Greening
Lamborn (see previous note) comments that no ermines are recorded as a
heraldic charge, the spots as mentioned above can have the function or meaning
of figures. According to Alexander Nisbet, 'The spots are in place of figures,
and so make a complete armorial bearing; and, as such, *ermine* has been
carried by the Dukes of Bretagne, which we blazon only *ermine . . .*': *A System
of Heraldry*, 2nd edn, 2 vols (Edinburgh, 1804; *CLA*, 11), 1.18. Scott's addition
of *passant* (walking, usually with the right forepaw raised), however, would
seem to imply the actual depiction of animals.
9.15 argent, in a field azure *argent* (silvery white) is one of the armorial
colours or 'tinctures' used in heraldry, with *azure* signifying bright blue, while
the *field* is the surface of the shield on which figures are depicted. The description here echoes Scott's *Marmion* (1808): 'E'en such a falcon, on his shield;/
Soar'd sable in an azure field' (Canto 1, stanza 6; *Poetical Works*, 7.48).
9.15 sans tache *French* spotless, stainless.
9.20 mend his pen i.e. trim or sharpen his quill pen.
11.6 Brere-wood Lodge possibly suggested by the ancient village of Brewood in SW Staffordshire and the surrounding Royal Forest of Brewood. See
also Historical Note, 379–80; and note to 17.36.
11.12 a Welch-woman or a Scotch-woman intimating a concern for

family genealogy. Compare Scott in his Ashestiel 'Memoirs': 'Every Scotishman has a pedigree. It is a national prerogative as unalienable as his pride and his poverty': *Scott on Himself*, ed. David Hewitt (Edinburgh, 1981), 2.

11.24 Garter or Blue-mantle Garter King-at-Arms, the principal King-at-Arms in England, by whom arms are granted under the authority of the Earl Marshal; and Bluemantle, one of the pursuivants in the College of Arms.

12.26 an Oxonian i.e. a graduate or member of Oxford University, noted in the 18th century for its High Church and Tory leanings.

12.27 oaths at the accession of George I. oaths of allegiance to the House of Hanover in 1714, with those refusing (non-jurors) being excluded from official clerical posts, which included College fellowships.

12.39 Alma ... arms and legs see Matthew Prior, 'Alma: or, the Progress of the Soul' (1718), Canto 1, lines 251–56. Alma is conventionally the mind or spirit, which Prior facetiously seats in various motor parts of the growing body.

13.20 Scaliger or Bentley there were two Scaligers, Julius Caesar (1484–1558), physician and scholar, noted for his scientific and philosophical works, and his son, Joseph Justus (1540–1609), a philologist and historian noted for his work on chronology. Richard Bentley (1662–1742) was an English Classical scholar.

13.28 Tasso's infusion of honey such a metaphor is employed by the Italian poet Torquato Tasso (1544–95), in *Gerusalemme liberata*, Bk 1, stanza 3.

13.36 Royal Game of the Goose a board game popular in the period, used as a means of teaching children ready reckoning, in which a goose was displayed at every fourth or fifth compartment, allowing a doubling of the number thrown. It features in Henry Mackenzie's *The Mirror*, no. 10 (27 Feb. 1779), and is described in Joseph Strutt's *The Sports and Pastimes of the People of England* (London, 1801; *CLA*, 154), 249–50.

14.21 learned ease possibly echoing Marcus Tullius Cicero (106–43 BC), *Tusculan Disputations*, 5.105 (*otio litterato*, 'literary leisure'). Compare also Anna Lætitia Aikin [afterwards Barbauld], 'Ovid to his Wife', in *Poems* (London, 1773; *CLA*, 174), 91: 'I fondly hop'd, content with learned ease,/ To walk amidst cotemporary [*sic*] trees'.

14.40–41 epicure ... peach compare Scott in a letter of 4 April 1812 to Joanna Baillie: 'I have seldom felt myself so fastidious about books as in the midst of a large library where one is naturally tempted to imitate the egregious epicure who condescended to take only one bit out of the sunny side of a peach' (*Letters*, 3.98). No single 'egregious epicure' has been discovered.

15.8 Spenser, Drayton the English poets, Edmund Spenser (*c.* 1552–99), and Michael Drayton (1563–1631). Scott describes the significance of Spenser on his own early reading in his Ashestiel 'Memoirs': see *Scott on Himself*, ed. David Hewitt (Edinburgh, 1981), 26. Drayton wrote a series of poems on legendary and historical figures and a great topographical work, *Poly-Olbion*, completed in 1622.

15.14 Pulci Luigi Pulci (1432–84), Florentine poet, whose chief work was the burlesque romance *Il mogante maggiore*: 'sire of the half-serious rhyme', according to Byron in *Don Juan*, Canto 4 (1821), stanza 6. He is mentioned in Scott's Ashestiel 'Memoirs' as part of his early reading: 'I now acquired ... intimacy with the works of Dante, Boiardo, Pulci and other eminent Italian authors': *Scott on Himself*, ed. David Hewitt (Edinburgh, 1981), 33.

15.17 the Decameron the famous collection of stories, supposedly narrated by Florentines secluded from the plague, by Giovanni Boccaccio (*c.* 1313–75).

15.22 Froissart Jean Froissart (*c.* 1337–*c.* 1410), the French writer and historian, whose *Chroniques* provide dazzling accounts of the chivalric exploits of the nobles of England and France 1325–1400, while also alluding to a succession of brutal events.

15.24   Brantome and De La Noue   Pierre de Bourdeille, Seigneur de Brantôme (*c.* 1539–1614), French soldier, courtier, and chronicler; and François de la Noue (1531–91), French Protestant soldier and author of *Discours politiques et militaires* (1587). Both writers describe the bitter religious war between the Huguenots and the Catholic League in France, from opposing sides.

16.14–15   Isaac Walton's ... angle   Isaac Walton's *The Compleat Angler* (1653). The quotation ('I am a Brother of the Angle [i.e. fishing-rod]') appears in the first chapter (4).

16.25   death of Queen Anne   in 1714, followed by the Hanoverian accession.

17.20–21   three ermines passant   as on the Waverley coat-of-arms: see note to 9.14–15.

17.22–23   bitterness of Hotspur   see *1 Henry IV*, 3.1.148–55, though the subject there is prophecy rather than heraldry.

17.25–30   Wilibert of Waverley ... passeth not away   such a story concerning the family of Bradshaigh, of Haigh Hall in Lancashire, was told to Scott by Lady Balcarres, a descendant of the family. See Magnum note, 1.38n., which also mentions the German ballad of 'The Noble Moringer', translated by Scott in 1819, but known to him earlier; and the Magnum Introduction to *The Betrothed* (37.viii–xvi), which describes both the plot of 'The Noble Moringer' and the Haigh Hall legend. For 'passeth not away' compare Philippians 4.7.

17.36   field of Worcester   where Charles II was defeated by Cromwell in 1651, having entered England from Scotland with an army.

17.36   day's refuge   after the battle, Charles first fled north to Staffordshire, attempted to cross the Severn into Wales, and then made his way to the south coast, seeking protection in the homes of sympathisers. His early escape was aided by the Giffard family of Chillington, in Staffordshire, who also had strong links with Brewood (see note to 11.6); and it was near Boscobel House, in Brewood Forest, that Charles hid in the famous Royal Oak. See Richard Ollard, *The Escape of Charles II after the Battle of Worcester* (London, 2002), 25–38.

18.7   St Aubin   the surname of a Cornish family with strong royalist leanings; the third baronet, Sir John Aubyn (1696–1744), M.P. for Cornwall from 1722, was one of the strongest opponents of Walpole's Whig government, and held in high regard by the exiled Jacobite court.

19.27   wars of York and Lancaster   the Wars of the Roses, fought in 1455–85 for the possession of the English crown between the houses of York and Lancaster.

19.27–28   adherents of the Red Rose   i.e. the Lancastrian supporters.

19.29–30   reduced ... Richard of Gloucester   perhaps after the battle of Tewkesbury (1471), in which the Lancastrians were defeated by Yorkists led by Richard, Duke of Gloucester (1452–85), who subsequently came to the throne as Richard III.

19.33–34   chew the cud of sweet and bitter fancy   see *As You Like It*, 4.3.100. Apparently all editions of Shakespeare up to Scott's day read here 'food of sweet and bitter fancy', with Howard Staunton in his 1859 edition being first to emend 'food' to 'cud' (with its enhanced image of ruminating mentally). Either Scott adjusted the quotation spontaneously, or he is silently amused at the failure of previous editors to make what he considered an obvious emendation.

20.6 romance of Cervantes i.e. *Don Quixote* (1605, 1615), by Miguel de Cervantes Saavedra, in which the eponymous hero suffers mental delusions through chivalric suppositions.

20.31–32 merest accident in the world apparently a phrase from common speech rather than a quotation from literature.

20.33 malice prepense malice aforethought, as applied to wrongful acts carried out intentionally; *prepense* is English Law French.

21.1 Jeweller and Dervise in the oriental tale referring (as Scott's footnote partly explains) to the 'The Seven Lovers', the fourth tale in John Hoppner's *Oriental Tales, translated into English verse* (London, 1805), [39]–59. In this a Derwish [*sic*], Jeweller, Tailor, and 'Carver skill'd' rest in the desert, where the carver manufactures a beautiful female figure from wood, for which all jealously contend, the Jeweller adding jewellery to the figure, the Derwish praying for the maid, before all agree that she should go to the next passer-by. After the intervention of three other characters, the figure is finally repossessed by a mystical tree ('To their first state all things return!'). Hoppner's original frontispiece illustration, depicting this tale, showed a nude female figure, which in the second edition (1806) was partly concealed by a veil. Scott wrote to the publisher John Murray on 16 April 1806 asking for 'a copy of the *cancelled* print to Hoppners tales' (see *Letters*, 2.45). The copy of the second edition in the Abbotsford Library (*CLA*, 227) has two frontispieces, one of these from the first edition.

21.5 saint her namesake Saint Cecilia, the early Christian martyr, patroness of church music, and often celebrated in art and poetry.

21.23 St Stephen's chapel in the Palace of Westminster, where the House of Commons sat until it was burned down in 1834.

21.24 zealous Noes i.e. in expressing disagreement to government measures in parliamentary debates. Compare Jonathan Swift's poem 'Tom Mullinex and Dick', lines 37–38 ('Dick with zealous noes and ayes,/ Could roar as loud as Stentor'): *The Life and Works of Jonathan Swift*, ed. Walter Scott, 19 vols (Edinburgh, 1814), 10.512.

21.25–26 Godolphin's administration Sidney Godolphin, first Earl of Godolphin (1645–1712), was Lord High Treasurer under Queen Anne, and the manager of her administration from 1702 until 1710, in conducting which he was increasingly reliant on Whig support.

21.36 the minister Lamont comments that if an individual is meant it must be Henry Pelham (1696–1754), who by 1744 had become the most influential of the divided collection of ministers who came to office after Sir Robert Walpole's fall in 1742. However, the following 'great man' suggests another possibility in Walpole himself: see also note to 130.17, and Historical Note, 367–68.

21.43 Hoppner's tale see note to 21.1.

22.1 Pretender and his sons the Pretender (originally from the French *prétendre*, 'to claim') was the name given to James VIII and III by his Hanoverian opponents. The sons were Charles Edward (1720–88), 'The Young Pretender', and Henry Benedict, nominal Duke of York, later Cardinal (1725–1807).

22.6 from Flanders as part of the War of Austrian Succession, in which Britain and her allies opposed France and Spain, a large military force was sent to Flanders in 1742, and a presence was maintained there until 1748. The Jacobite rising under Prince Charles Edward, however, necessitated the recall of a substantial part of these forces during 1745–46, though this occurred after the regimental return suggested by the narrative.

22.31–32 the —— regiment Scott in the ISet (followed by the Magnum) replaces this with 'Gardiner's regiment'. James Gardiner (*c.* 1686–1745) became lieutenant-colonel in Stair's dragoons (6th Iniskillings) in 1730, and

succeeded to the command of Bland's dragoons (13th Hussars), based in
Haddingtonshire (East Lothian), 1743.

22.32–33   quarters at D—— expanded to Dundee in the ISet and Magnum. Whereas Gardiner's dragoons were quartered at various places in Scotland in 1745, including Stirling and Linlithgow, there is apparently no evidence
of their being at Dundee: see Blaikie, 89. In the early days of the Rising,
Gardiner was obliged to retreat at the approach of the Jacobite army, withdrawing towards Edinburgh.

22.36   memorable year 1715 the time of the first major Jacobite rising of
the 18th century; see also Historical Note, 367–68.

22.40–41   riding officer of the excise mounted customs officer, whose
function was to patrol a stretch of coastline in search of smugglers.

22.43   Sir W—— W—— identified more fully in the ISet and Magnum,
as 'Sir William Wyndham' (c. 1688–1740), M.P. for Somerset from 1710,
and long-standing leader of the Tories in the House of Commons. In 1715 he
was allegedly involved in plans for a rising in the West of England in favour of
the Stuarts, planned to coincide with the Earl of Mar's rebellion in Scotland.
He was arrested in September 1715 and sent to the Tower of London, but
was released in the following July and never faced trial.

23.9   Preston in Lancashire held by the Jacobites in 1715; its surrender
on 14 November marked the end of the rising in England.

23.10   Newgate and the Marshalsea Newgate prison on the site of the
Old Bailey in Newgate Street, in the City of London; and Marshalsea prison,
in Southwark, S of the Thames.

23.20   quarter-sessions in England, a court of limited criminal and civil
jurisdiction, held four times a year by the justices of peace in the counties.

23.23   Brunswick dynasty the electors of Hanover were also dukes of
Brunswick (Braunschweig).

23.28   Army List an official list of all the commissioned officers in the
Army; the first Army List was published in 1740.

23.29–30   Mordaunts, Granvilles, and Stanleys two of these names
match those in the opening chapter (see note to 3.16).

23.32–35   like Falstaff's . . . rebellion could make it see 2 Henry IV,
1.2.68–73.

23.43   like a fire to heather set from the ballad imitation 'Hardyknute'
by Elizabeth, Lady Wardlaw (1677–1727), published on folio sheets in 1719,
and then included in a number of collections of old verse, including Allan
Ramsay's Evergreen (1724) and Percy's Reliques of Ancient English Poetry (1765).
In the poem, which concerns the battle of Largs between the armies of the
Scots and Norwegian kings, the metaphor describes the charge of a warrior
('Quhair lyke a Fyre to Hether set/ Bauld Thomas did advance', stanza 33).
Scott quoted the same words in a note to The Lady of the Lake (1810); while
the metaphor itself probably derives more mundanely from the practice of
burning the old heather on hillsides to provide healthier food for sheep. Scott's
copy of the 13th edition of the Tea-Table Miscellany (Edinburgh, 1762; CLA,
171) has a MS note by him: 'This book belonged to my grandfather, Robert
Scott, and out of it I was taught Hardiknute by heart before I could read the
ballad itself. It was the first poem I ever learnt—the last I shall ever forget'
(Corson).

24.19–25.13   Late, when the Autumn . . . to arms! these verses are
annotated by Scott as 'Original' in MS 743, f. 29. They do not appear in the
surviving MS of the novel.

24.46   the spirit-stirring change see Othello, 3.3.356 ('the spirit-stirring
drum').

25.29–32   His heart . . . to move see 'Lord Henry and Katharine', lines

5-8, in Allan Ramsay's *Tea-Table Miscellany*, 13th edn (Edinburgh, 1762; *CLA*, 171), 410.

25.36-39 Yet did ... steward's son a comic adaptation of *A Midsummer Night's Dream*, 2.1.165-68.

26.4 article of their gentry matter of their rank. See *The Merry Wives of Windsor*, 2.1.45-46 ('the article of thy gentry').

26.20-21 drawn by hippogriffs in Ludovico Ariosto's *Orlando furioso* (1516), the hero Rogero is transported by a hippogriff (a fabulous animal, in the shape of a winged horse, with the head of a griffin).

26.24-25 Prince Hussein's tapestry ... Malek the Weaver's flying sentry-box see Henry Weber's compilation, *Tales of the East*, 3 vols (Edinburgh, 1812; *CLA*, 43). The flying 'tapestry' features in 'The Story of Prince Ahmed and the Fairy Pari Banou' (1.432-54); the 'sentry-box' (an oblong chest) in 'The History of Malek and the Princess Schirine' (2.428-35). In the latter story, after his downfall, Malek lives with a weaver in Cairo and takes up his trade.

26.36 guards of the broad-sword the various formal postures of defence for the broad-sword, a long, wide-bladed weapon.

27.1-2 Bucephalus the horse of Alexander the Great (356-323 BC); also used as a generic name for any powerful mount.

27.2-3 robes of the Bath as worn by those who held this order of knighthood.

27.20 for a presbyterian James Gardiner, the commander of the regiment which Waverley is about to join (see note to 22.31-32), experienced a religious conversion after living a dissolute life as a young man, and was noted for his abstemious behaviour in later years. Presbyterianism had been the established religion in his native Scotland from 1690, and would have been inimical to the High Church Anglican Sir Everard, both for its system of church government (a series of church courts rather than bishops) and general emphasis on faith and revelation rather than works and ritual.

27.24 de facto ... de jure *Latin* in fact; by right. Sir Everard knows that George II is in fact the King, but believes that the title by right belongs to James VIII and III.

27.28 the regimental colour no evidence has been found to indicate that the regimental colour of Colonel Gardiner's 13th Hussars (see note to 22.31-32) was black. However, Colonel Gardiner reportedly rode a 'black and finely bred' horse, later commandeered for Charles Edward's use: see Duffy, 205. The Hanoverian forces in the '45 also wore the black cockade.

27.42 chain of attachment a common expression among the Five Nations of Canada (Corson). See Cadwallader Colden, *The History of the Five Indian Nations of Canada* (2nd edn, London, 1750; *CLA*, 31), where the metaphor of a 'chain' is used frequently in dealings between the British army and the indigenous tribes (e.g. see 45, 51, 56, 117). Scott also uses the term on several occasions in his correspondence (e.g. see his letter to John Leyden, 25 August 1811, in *Letters*, 2.535).

28.7-8 Cosmo Comyne Bradwardine for possible prototypes, and the significance of the name, see Historical Note, 384-86.

28.8-9 Tully-Veolan a fictitious location, though similarities have been noted to a variety of country houses and estates. See also Historical Note, 380-81.

28.26 Titus Livius Livy (*c.* 59 BC-AD 17), author of a History of Rome (*Ab Urbe Condita*), from its foundation to the reign of Augustus, based partly on legend, and of which only parts survive.

28.31 Patavinian Livy came from Padua (Patavium).

28.32-33 Sweynheim and Pannartz Conrad Sweynheim and Arnold

Pannartz, German printers, who set up in Rome in 1467, where they printed editions of Classical authors from manuscript. Their 1469 edition of Livy's *History of Rome* was highly prized by book collectors as an 'editio princeps' (first printed edition of a work previously only known in manuscript). According to Lang, a copy was sold for £472 10*s*. at the sale of the library of Sir Mark Masterman Sykes, whom Scott succeeded as a member of the Roxburghe Club. It is described in the 1824 sale *Catalogue* as 'one of the most magnificent productions of the XV Century'. Scott himself owned a Latin edition, published in Amsterdam 1678–79 (*CLA*, 226).

28.38–39   Baron of Bradwardine   for the significance of the title of Baron, see note to 44.43.

28.41   Tully   Scottish landowners were traditionally known by the name of their estate. The abbreviated form 'Tully' also possibly puns on the name by which Cicero, Marcus Tullius Cicero (106–43 BC), was commonly known in the 18th century.

28.41   rectus in curia   *Latin literally* upright in court; one who stands at the bar of a court but against whom no charge is made.

29.10   pounds Scotch   the Scots pound was worth one-twelfth of an English pound in 1707 when the Scots currency was abolished. Many continued to refer to pounds Scots well into the 18th century.

29.12   baron baillie   a deputy appointed by a baron (see also note to 44.43) to exercise the jurisdiction of the baron, both civil and criminal; the judicial officer of a barony.

29.23   Woe, woe . . . for me   see *Richard III*, 3.4.82 ('England' in the original).

30.7–8   scoffers and latitudinarians   those who mock at religion or morality, and clergy tolerant of a wide range of belief. In Mr Pembroke's mouth the latter is used pejoratively, in the sense of lax in belief, eroding the established order.

30.10   in 1642   alluding to the outbreak of the English Civil War, and more particularly to the Scots' support of Parliament against Charles I, leading to the decision in 1643 to send an army into England.

30.12–13   candlestick . . . place   see Revelation 2.5.

30.16   Sancroft and his brethren   William Sancroft (1616–93), Archbishop of Canterbury, was one of seven bishops who protested against James VII's and II's Declaration of Indulgence, permitting people to worship other than in the established Church of England; he subsequently headed the High Church party who refused to take the oath of allegiance to William III, becoming in the process non-jurors.

30.17   some of the principal petitions   Lamont identifies, as likely to be most offensive to Mr Pembroke, the prayers for the King's Majesty (in 1745 George II) and the Royal Family, to be said after the Third Collect at Morning and Evening Prayer.

30.18–19   persecuted remnant   Episcopal church government was abolished in Scotland and Presbyterianism established in its place in the Act of 1690, and confirmed by the Act of Union of 1707. All ministers were required to take the oaths of Allegiance to the Crown and Abjuration of James VII and II and his descendants. Those Episcopalian ministers who refused to take the oaths were ejected from their parishes and forbidden to conduct religious services in public. In the early 18th century many Episcopalians in Scotland were Jacobites (i.e. supporters of James VII and II and his descendants).

30.28   Little Britain   an important centre of the London book trade in the later 17th and early 18th centuries, between West Smithfield and St Paul's; the imprint of *The Spectator* states that it is printed in 'Little Britain'. The following sequence is clearly indebted to Parson Adams's interview with a bookseller in Fielding's *Joseph Andrews* (1742), Bk 1, Ch. 17.

30.32   the Shibboleth   the password; originally a word which non-native speakers of a language have difficulty in pronouncing, hence used for detecting enemies or foreigners: see Judges 12.5–6.

30.36   under the rose   in confidence. Lamont adds that the phrase has an additional nuance as a result of the Jacobite use of the white rose as an emblem.

30.37   Hanoverian rat   referring to the Elector of Hanover and his followers, and common in Jacobite toasts of the period. The name 'Hanoverian rat' was also used to describe the common or brown rat, which arrived in Britain by ship and by early Georgian times had begun to oust the black rat. Compare Squire Western in *Tom Jones*: 'I am no Rat. I am a true *Englishman*, and not of your *Hanover* Breed, that have eat up our Nation' (Bk 7, Ch. 3: 3.22).

30.38   over the water   phrase used by Jacobites to refer to the Jacobite court in exile.

30.39   King of France   Louis XV (reigned 1715–74).

30.39   from Rome   a permanent Jacobite court was set up in Rome in 1719: see note to 7.26.

31.5   Comprehension Confuted   *Comprehension* refers to proposals (soon after the Restoration in 1660, then again at the beginning of Queen Anne's reign) to make such alterations in the liturgy and canons of the Church of England as might allow Dissenters to join in. As a sub-title this offers a negative version of *Comprehension Promoted* (1673 and 1704) by John Humfrey (1621–1719). The issue seems somewhat outdated in the present setting.

31.7–8   Fathers of the Church   eminent Christian teachers of the early centuries whose writings remained as a court of appeal for their successors.

31.10   small pica   medium size of type in the early period, in which 20 lines set solid took about 72mm; roughly equivalent to modern 11-point type.

31.13   the martyrdom   of Charles I, through his beheading in 1649; he was commemorated as the Martyr King in the Anglican Book of Common Prayer until Victorian times.

31.13   twelve-penny touch   i.e. an article which will 'touch' or move purchasers to the extent of such a price. Compare Scott to J. B. S. Morritt on 2 October 1815: 'I think . . . the poems of David [Hume] would make a decent twelve Shilling touch' (*Letters*, 4.101).

31.17   letter-press   normally meaning printed material, but here (the cost of) typesetting, imposition, and printing on a hand-press.

31.20   Drake   James Drake (*c.* 1666–1707), political and medical writer. His pamphlets, *The History of the Last Parliament* (1702) and *The Memorial of the Church of England* (1704), both offended the authorities, and the latter was burnt by the common hangman, after the printer had surrendered with a promise of a pardon, Drake himself narrowly avoiding punishment on a legal technicality. Tracts by Drake were published in Scott's edition of the Somers Tracts, where a note by him describes him as figuring 'as a Tory, or indeed a Jacobite pamphleteer': *A Collection of Scarce and Valuable Tracts*, 2nd edn, ed. Walter Scott, 13 vols (London, 1809–15), 12.198.

31.21   Charlwood Lawton   (1660–1721), topical writer, whose pamphlets included *The Jacobite Principles Vindicated* (1693), which was republished in the Somers Tracts (see previous note). Scott's note in the latter describes the pamphlet as, for its time, 'a very moderate and accommodating statement of the principles of the Jacobites', while acknowledging that the air of moderation probably made it more dangerous to the government: *A Collection of Scarce and Valuable Tracts*, 10.523.

31.21   Amhurst . . . Caleb   Nicholas Amhurst (1697–1742), the satirist and political writer. Notwithstanding earlier Whig sympathies, Amhurst edited from 1726 the anti-Walpole newspaper, *The Craftsman*, a satire which in 1737 led to his arrest for libel, and the imprisonment of its then printer (Henry Haines) for two years. According to Thomas Davies, as quoted in Scott's Magnum note (1.67), Amhurst is supposed to have died 'of a broken heart; and was buried at the charge of his honest printer, Richard Francklin [first printer of *The Craftsman*]'. He conducted *The Craftsman* under the pseudonym of Caleb D'Anvers.

31.27 windy side situated towards the wind, figuratively meaning so as not to be 'scented' and attacked, i.e. clear of trouble. Compare *Twelfth Night*, 3.4.156 ('Still you keep o' th' windy side of the law').

31.27–28 Old Palace Yard in Westminster, where the pillory stood.

31.28 Williamites adherents of William III.

31.29 Hanoverian rats see note to 30.37.

31.33 the plantations in America; transportation to the colonies there (e.g. to the Carolinas to work in the rice and cotton plantations) was the punishment for a large number of non-capital offences. See Gwenda Morgan and Peter Rushton, *Eighteenth-Century Criminal Transportation* (Basingstoke, 2004).

31.35 Trimnel not identified and perhaps fictitious, with a pun on 'trim', meaning 'to accommodate to the political mood of the times'. It is just possible, however, that Scott was thinking of Charles Trimnell (1663–1723), bishop of Norwich in 1708, and bishop of Winchester in 1721, who wrote several pamphlets, though in his case *against* High Church doctrines.

32.24–25 gold pieces ... of late in 1797 the Bank Restriction Act limited the Bank of England's obligation to convert bank notes into gold, leading to a reduction of gold coins in Scott's day.

33.2 to ——, a sea-port town i.e. Dundee (see note to 22.32–33).

33.5 Colonel G—— expanded to Gardiner in the 1Set and Magnum. For the historical Colonel Gardiner, see notes to 22.31–32 and 27.20 above; also Historical Note, 388.

33.24 fable of the Centaur the Centaurs were Greek mythical creatures, combining a human upper part and a lower part like a horse.

33.31–32 pomp and circumstance compare *Othello*, 3.3.358 ('Pride, pomp, and circumstance of glorious war!'). Scott uses the phrase 'pomp and circumstance of war' in letters to Anna Seward in Summer 1803 and Joanna Baillie (10 December 1813): see *Letters*, 1.188 and 3.389.

34.30 gracious King Duncan Duncan I, King of Scots, killed by Macbeth in 1040; 'gracious' is a traditional epithet.

35.15 Caledonia the traditional Latin name for Scotland.

35.16–17 chevaux de poste *French* post or mail horses.

35.21 Mr Dent's dog-taxes alluding to the dog tax of 1796, proposed by John Dent (*c.* 1761–1826), a banker and M.P. for Lancaster 1790–1812. Dent's speech in the Commons was marked by its bitterness against the nuisance of dogs, and earned him the nickname 'Dog' Dent. The distinction between dogs that were to be taxed, and those which were to be exempt, was especially a source of satire.

35.31–32 Italian forms of landscape referring to the landscape paintings of French-Italian artists such as Claude Lorraine (1600–82) and Nicolas Poussin (1594–1665), in which human figures (often rustic in character) are seen in spectacular natural settings.

35.39 quantum sufficit *Latin* a sufficient quantity, as much as is needed.

36.10 Minerva Roman goddess of wisdom and handicrafts.

36.19 canine Cossacks the Cossacks were horse-raising tribesmen in S and SW Russia and the Ukraine, famous for their prowess as irregular cavalry, as illustrated in their harrying of Napoleon's retreat from Moscow in 1812.

36.33 cultivated alternate ridges referring to the 'run-rig' system, an early form of cultivation where the land was divided into strips to ensure a fair distribution of productive and less productive ground between tenants. In Scott's edition of *Memorie of Somervilles* (1815), a footnote to 'rune rig' reads: 'That is, lying by alternate ridges, a very inconvenient state of property' (2.115n.).

37.6–7 two rampant bears, the supporters of the family Alexander Nisbet, in his *A System of Heraldry*, under 'Of the Bear', notes that the family of Lord Forbes of Pitsligo has as 'supporters, two bears, proper', and also that the cadet families nearly all have bears incorporated in their arms: 2nd edn, 2 vols (Edinburgh, 1804; *CLA*, 11), 1.320–23. (For Alexander, 4th Lord of Pitsligo (1678–1762), as one of the suggested prototypes of the Baron of Bradwardine, see Historical Note, 384–85.) A *supporter* in heraldry is a figure on each side of a shield, as found in coats of arms. In its review of the novel, *The Monthly Review* adds 'arms' after 'family' when quoting this passage: 75 (Nov. 1814), 281. The passage might well also recall the two bears on columns in the gateway to the old avenue at Traquair House, in Peeblesshire (see Historical Note, 381).

38.17 Arthur's Oven dome-shaped Roman building near Falkirk, Stirlingshire, demolished in 1743 by its owner, Sir Michael Bruce, who used its stones to repair a mill-dam, as is described in Pennant, 1.263 (with facing illustration). It is also referred to in *Ivanhoe*, EEWN 8, 13.21.

38.20 columbarium derived from the Latin word *columba*, meaning 'dove'; a Roman *columbarium* appears to have been more of a nesting-box than a dovecot.

38.20–21 resource to a Scottish laird the keeping of pigeons was originally encouraged by Church and Parliament as a means of increasing the supply and variety of food, but became offensive to neighbours by injury to their crops. The Act 1617, c. 19, placed restrictions on the building of dovecotes, including the provision that they should be surrounded by a certain amount of land.

39.12–19 Orgoglio ... white as snow see Edmund Spenser's *The Faerie Queene* (1590–96), Bk 1, Canto 8, where Prince Arthur slays the giant Orgoglio, and enters his castle. The inset quotation derives from stanza 29, and the 'old, old man' features in the following stanza.

40.15–16 gardens of Alcina alluding to the enchanted garden of Alcina, a witch in Lodovico Ariosto's *Orlando furioso* (1516), Bk 6.

40.16 due donzelette garrule *Italian* two talkative maidens. See also note to 40.19–10.

40.17–18 each standing in a spacious tub a method of washing described and illustrated in Burt, 1.52.

40.19–20 maidens of Armida Armida is an enchantress in Torquato Tasso's *Gerusalemme liberata* (1581), who lures men into her garden and to a life of indolence with a magic girdle. It is here, in Canto 15, stanza 58, that two talkative maidens as at 40.16 above appear ('due donzellette garrule e lascive').

40.24 Eh sirs! Scots exclamation, meaning 'Eh God preserve us!'.

40.34 mister wight a phrase found invasively in Spenser's *The Faerie Queene*, and used there in the sense of 'kind of person'.

40.34–35 Indian Jogue Indian ascetic who practises the system of yoga.

40.37 hackney coachman driver of a carriage kept for hire.

41.12–19 False love ... other men see Herd, 2.6. A version of these verses in Scott's hand is found in a MS volume entitled 'Scottish Songs Walter Scott 1795' in the Abbotsford Library (*CLA*, 104), at f. 69.

41.26–27 still his speech was song see Robert Southey, *Thalaba the*

Destroyer, 2 vols. (London, 1801; *CLA*, 246), Bk 8; 2.128–29.

41.28–35   The Knight's . . . and sure   annotated by Scott as 'Original' in MS 743, f. 30v; but see also following two notes.

41.32   Burd Ellen   see 'Burd Ellen and Young Tamlane' (Child, 28), beginning 'Burd Ellen sits in her bower windowe'.

41.34   Lord William   compare 'Lord William, or, Lord Lundy' (Child, 254).

41.43   roynish clowns   roynish in the sense of 'scurvy, coarse'. See *As You Like It*, 2.2.8 ('the roynish clown, at whom so oft/ Your Grace was wont to laugh').

42.6   Old Adam's . . . garden   *Richard II*, 3.4.73.

42.7   major domo   house-steward, head attendant.

42.22   amusing the time   causing the time to pass pleasantly.

42.29   Davie Gellatley   first mentioned here by name. For possible prototypes, see Historical Note, 387–88.

42.34   more knave than fool   *King Lear*, 1.4.315.

42.41   far ben   normally referring to the innermost room of the house, though here signifying 'in favour, on intimate terms'. The glossary to *The Antiquary* (1816) states that '"To bring far ben," proverbially signifies to pay attention greater than is expected to any one'.

43.7   at an orra time   occasionally, every now and then.

43.11–12   Rose Bradwardine . . . end of a chapter   compare *Tom Jones*, at the end of Bk 3, Ch. 10, and that of the original first volume: 'But this being the intended Heroine of this Work . . . it is by no Means proper she should make her Appearance at the End of a Book' (1.213–14).

43.20   round of beauties   possibly relating to the old custom of proposing 'rounds of toasts' at public dinners: see Henry Cockburn, *Memorials of His Time* (Edinburgh, 1856), 38.

43.20   Bumperquaigh   evidently a facetious name, with *quaich* in Scots referring to a bowl-shaped drinking cup.

43.21–22   More to the pledge   i.e. commanding more wine to accompany the toast; equivalent to 'Let's have it again'.

43.29–30   fallen . . . weltering   parodying John Dryden, 'Alexander's Feast; or The Power of Musique; An Ode in Honour of St Cecilia's Day' (1697), lines 77–79 ('Fallen, fallen, fallen, fallen,/ Fallen from his high estate,/ And weltering in his blood'): in *Works*, ed. Scott (1808), 11.186.

44.15–16   on hospitable thoughts intent   John Milton, *Paradise Lost* (1667), 5.332.

44.17–18   seven-leagued boots   allowing the wearer to cover seven leagues at each step, now found in several fairy stories, such as 'Hop o' my Thumb'. See Stith Thompson, *Motif-Index of Folk-Literature*, 6 vols (Copenhagen, 1955–58), motif D1521.1.

44.23   Swiss officer of the guards   evidently referring to the Swiss mercenary guards employed by the Kings of France, rather than the Papal Swiss Guard. By the 18th century they had gained a reputation for discipline and steadiness both as bodyguards and for service during foreign campaigns. They were famous in Scott's day for their defence of the Tuileries Palace during the French Revolution, as a result of which more than 600 were killed.

44.36   zealous volunteer service   companies of volunteers to protect the country from invasion were established soon after the beginning of the war with France in 1793; the Royal Edinburgh Volunteers were incorporated in 1794, and the Royal Edinburgh Light Dragoons in 1797. Scott was Quartermaster of the latter.

44.37   bar-gown . . . blazing uniform   many of the officers and men of the Royal Edinburgh Light Dragoons were advocates, whom Scott remembers wearing their black court gowns over the red uniform of the regiment.

44.43   free barony   in Scots law, a barony is an estate created by a direct grant from the Crown. A grant of free barony carried with it both criminal and civil jurisdiction: the baron court was competent to try all crimes except the most serious (murder, robbery, rape and fire-raising), and had power to settle disputes between feudal superior and vassal, landowner and tenant, etc.

44.43   David the First   of Scotland (c. 1084–1153; succeeded 1124). The oldest Scottish charter still extant, granting lands to St Cuthbert's Church, Edinburgh, belongs to his reign; Normand, however, comments that free baronies were probably not created as early as David I.

45.1–3   cum liberali . . . bak-barand   the wording is in the manner of a Latin charter granting land in free barony (see note to 44.43 above). The charter gives the right of freely holding courts with rights of pit and gallows (fossa et furca), to hold courts where vassals have to offer suit (sok), to have freedom from custom (sak), to deal with theft committed on the barony (infangthief) by his own men, to deal with theft elsewhere or committed by outsiders (outfangthief). Outfangthief was highly unusual for a barony. 'Handhabend' means being caught in the act of stealing; 'bak-barand' means carrying away stolen goods; 'thol' and 'theam' refer to authority and jurisdiction over serfs. The sequence 'Sok, Sak, Infangthief, Outfangthief' appears in block capitals at 2.3.31 in Thomas Craig's *Jus Feudale* (1655; 3rd edn, 1732, *CLA* 12), which Scott might have been consulting on the structure and contents of charters (see also note to 245.5).

45.1–2   L I E pit and gallows   'pit and gallows' reflects the traditional practice whereby female malefactors were drowned in a water-filled trench, while males were hanged; 'L I E' was used as a prefix in charters when switching from Latin to the vernacular.

45.6–8   James the First . . . prerogative   alluding to James VI and I and his fondness for talking about the Divine Right of Kings. Compare *The Heart of Mid-Lothian*: 'like gentle King Jamie, he was fonder of talking of authority than really exercising it' (EEWN 6, 38.21–22).

45.22   à-la-mode Françoise   in the French manner.

45.27–28   spes altera, as Maro hath it   'a second hope' as Virgil (Publius Vergilius Maro, 70–19 BC) puts it. The phrase comes from Bk 12 of the *Aeneid*, where Aeneas's son Ascanius is praised as *magnae spes altera Romae*, 'great Rome's other hope' (line 168).

45.29–30   mais cela viendra avec le tems   *French* but that will come with time.

45.30   Baron Kikkitbroeck   apparently a burlesque name; *broek* is modern Dutch for breeches.

45.31   sagesse de Madame son epouse   *French* the wisdom of his lady wife.

45.31–32   the cockade   a knot of ribbon, usually worn in the hat: the Hanoverian cockade was black, the Jacobite white.

45.37   et singula prædantur anni   the years steal one thing after another. Compare Horace (Quintus Horatius Flaccus, 65–8 BC), *Epistles*, 2.2.55 ('Singula de nobis anni praedantur euntes', 'the years steal one thing after another as they pass by').

45.40   Alexander Saunderson   as Saunders is a diminutive of Alexander, the butler is called 'Alexander son of Alexander'. See also note to 48.37.

45.40   Chateau Margoux   Margaux claret, a notable wine from the Bordeaux region in SW France.

46.4   epulæ lautiores   *Latin* more lavish fare; compare Statius, *Silvae*, 1.6.32, 'epulasque lautiores'.

46.6–7   Epulæ ad . . . populum attinet   *Latin* a banquet is appropriate for the senate, but an ordinary meal for the people. See also following note.

46.7   Suetonius Tranquillus   Roman historian and biographer (*c*. AD 70–140), author of *Lives of the Twelve Caesars*, which Scott owned both in Latin and in English translation: *CLA*, 227, 228. The passage quoted as his matches two possible sources in Suetonius, which Scott may have linked together: *epulum senatui* ('a banquet for the senate') at *Caligula* 17.2, and *prandium populo* ('an ordinary meal for the people') at *Tiberius* 20.1. Compare also *Domitian* 4.5, where Suetonius says that on one occasion Domitian 'gave a very lavish banquet (*epulum*), distributing large baskets of food to the senate and the knights, and smaller ones to the common people'.

46.8   c'est des deux oreilles   *French literally* it's of two ears. Several commentators, including Lang and Lamont, have suggested that the expression should properly be *c'est d'une oreille*, this being a traditional phrase denoting good wine. Ozell in *The Works of Francis Rabelais*, 4 vols (London, 1807; *CLA*, 121) says: 'to return to *Wine of one ear*, it is a proverbial expression for exceeding good wine' (1.143n.). However, an interpretation of *vin de deux oreilles* (one apparently matching Scott's own intentions) is offered by a correspondent to *The Gentleman's Magazine* in a letter headed 4 June [1812]: 'The saying has been, I think, ingeniously supposed to have originated in that shake of the head, by which approbation of a well-flavoured liquor is commonly denoted: disapprobation on the contrary is well marked by only turning the head to one side, and thus a thing was said to be *d'une oreille*' (Supplement to Vol. 82, Part 1, Jan.-June 1812, 629). This concluded a correspondence initiated in a letter in the issue of *The Gentleman's Magazine* for January 1812 (Vol. 82, 38).

46.8   Vinsauf   echoing the name of Geoffrey de Vinsauf (*fl.* 1200), poet and historian of the Crusades; but also used here perhaps as a comic name suitable for a wine cellarer (from the French *vin* (wine) and *sauf* (safe)).

46.9   Vinum primæ notæ   *Latin* wine of the first class.

46.9   St Andrews   the University of St Andrews, Scotland's oldest university, founded early in 1413. A number of the Jacobite leaders in the 18th century had been educated at St Andrews.

46.17–18   In an old . . . shrewd blows   see 'The Old and Young Courtier', lines 17–18, in Percy, 2.319.

46.26   gala days   days of festivity, festive occasions.

46.30   Balmawhapple   comical name, probably related to 'the young laird of Ballymawhawple', as found in Tobias Smollett's *The Expedition of Humphry Clinker* (1771), J. Melford to Sir Watkin Phillips, 8 Aug.; ed. Thomas R. Preston (Athens and London, 1990), 217.

46.32   gaudet equis et canibus   *Latin* rejoices in horses and dogs. See Horace, *Ars Poetica*, 162: 'gaudet equis canibusque et aprici gramine Campi' (he rejoices in horses and dogs and in the grass of the sunny plain).

46.36–37   Damnonia . . . Robert of Cirencester   probably referring to Richard of Cirencester, a 14th-century monk and chronicler. The tract on Roman Britain alluded to here ('De situ Britanniae'), however, is a forgery in *Britannicarum Gentium Historiae Antiquae Scriptores Tres* (1757), by Charles Bertram (1723–65), a copy of which is in the Abbotsford Library (*CLA*, 257). In this the present Devon is give as 'Danmonij' on a fold-out map. The Abbotsford copy includes an inscription in Scott's hand: 'This is a very rare little book having been printed at the Editor's expence and never publicly sold. It is also intrinsically valuable for the geographical tract of Ricardus Corinensis with the map of Roman Britain is a valuable treasure to historical antiquaries.' Bertram's forgery was not fully exposed until 1866.

46.38   servabit odorem testa diu   *Latin* the cask will long retain the odour (Horace, *Epistles*, 1.2.69–70).

46.40   one Bullsegg   a *bull-seg* is a bull gelded when past his prime.

47.4   unrecorded taillie   a *taillie* was a deed of entail settling property on a specified line of (normally male) heirs. By an Act of 1685 strict entails had to be recorded in a special register of 'tailzies', and any deed involving entailed land had to refer to the entail; in this case the rights of the heir of entail have apparently been jeopardised by non-recording.

47.8   Highland Black Watch   six Independent Companies of 'loyal High-landers' were incorporated in 1739 as the first Highland regiment of the line in the British army, this being known as the Black Watch or 43rd (later 42nd) Regiment of Foot.

47.17   vix ea nostra voco, as Naso saith   *Latin* I scarcely call these things ours (referring to families and inheritances which the speaker has not created for himself): Ovid (Publius Ovidius Naso), 43 BC–AD 17, *Metamorph-oses*, 13.141.

47.18–20   episcopal church of Scotland … meeting-house   Episcopal church government was abolished in Scotland after the accession of William and Mary and Presbyterianism established in its place in an Act of 1690, and confirmed by the Act of Union of 1707. Episcopal meeting-houses ministered to by clergy who refused to take the Oath of Allegiance were nevertheless kept up in several areas of Scotland. After 1715 the penalty for non-compliance to the oaths of Allegiance (to the Crown) and of Abjuration (of the Pretender) was 6 months' imprisonment and the closure of the meeting-house.

47.28–29   As thus … they came   see Oliver Goldsmith, 'The Haunch of Venison: A Poetical Epistle to Lord Clare', lines 79–80: *Collected Works*, ed. Arthur Friedman, 5 vols (Oxford, 1966), 4.317.

48.14   turnspit walking upon its hind legs   *turnspit* here evidently refers to a kind of short-legged dog used for driving a treadmill by which roasting-spits were turned; for a later use of the image, see also 215.40 and note.

48.15   nonjuring clergyman   an Episcopalian clergyman who refused to take the Oath of Allegiance to the established monarch (see note to 47.18–20).

48.19   Who, undeprived, their benefice forsook   see John Dryden, 'The Character of a Good Parson; Imitated from Chaucer, and Inlarg'd' (1699), line 126: in *Works*, ed. Scott (1808), 11.399.

48.29   de facto or de jure   *Latin* 'in fact' or 'by right''; see also note to 27.24.

48.37   Alexander ab Alexandro   *Latin* Alexander from Alexander, i.e. 'Alexander son of Alexander'. Scott might also have been thinking of Alexander ab Alexandro (1461–1523), a Neapolitan jurist, who published a dissertation on the marvellous, *De Rebus Admirabilibus*, in which are described various prodigies supposedly verified or personally witnessed.

49.3   Tom Otter   a 'land, and sea-Captaine' in Ben Jonson's *Epicoene, or The Silent Woman* (performed 1609, published 1616), who is described as using such a 'witty denomination of his chief carousing cups': 'One he calls his bull, another his bear, another his horse' (2.6.56–57).

49.10   in actu ferociori   *Latin literally* in a more ferocious mode of action.

49.12   honourable atchievement   with *atchievement* here used primarily in the heraldic sense, as denoting a heraldic device or composition.

49.13   Frederick Red-beard   Friedrich I, Barbarossa ('red-beard') (*c.* 1123–1190), German King and Holy Roman Emperor.

49.18–19   Mutemus … Aptemus   Virgil, *Aeneid*, 2.389–90 ('Let us (ex)change our shields and put on the insignia of the Greeks'). The passage refers to Aeneas and his men disguising themselves in slain Greeks' armour after the fall of Troy. The allusion possibly includes a pun on the similarity between *Danaum* ('of the Danai', one of Virgil's many names for the Greeks) and Dane.

49.21　Saint Duthac, abbot of Aberbrothock　St Duthus or Duthac (*c.* 1000–1065); though he was evidently never Abbot of Aberbrothock (Arbroath) Abbey, itself founded in 1178. Lamont however notes that a chapel was dedicated to him in the Abbey in 1524.

49.25　Ursa Major　*Latin* Great Bear; and the constellation of that name.

49.28　anilia　*Latin* matters to do with old women, i.e. old wives' tales: for an adjectival use see Ovid (43 BC–AD 17), *Metamorphoses*, 14.765.

49.43　Then change ... bear　John Dryden, *Virgil's Aeneis* (1697), Bk 2, line 526: in *Works*, ed. Scott (1808), 14.279.

50.6　symptoms of innovation　compare *Othello*, 2.3.36.

50.6–7　the good wine ... office　see Robert Southey, *Madoc* (1805), 2.4.121–22.

50.12　grace cup　cup from which the last drink is taken at the end of a meal.

50.14　Bacchus　the god of wine in Classical mythology.

50.24　doch an dorroch　*Gaelic deoch an doruis* stirrup-cup, parting drink. The phrase is an anglicised form of the Gaelic original.

50.24–25　honour of the Baron's roof tree　Burt records that a Highlander in drinking to his friend says, 'To your *Roof Tree*, alluding to the Family's Safety from Tempests' (2.41). A roof tree is the main beam or ridge of a house, with the meaning of home or house in such toasts.

50.35　leges conviviales　*Latin* laws of the festivities.

50.37　merry bout　a drinking session. See Sir Charles Sedley, *The Mulberry-Garden: A Comedy* (1668): 'like small Beer in the Morning after a Merry Bout over night' (1.2).

51.1　sweet of the night　compare Falstaff in *2 Henry IV*, 2.4.354 ('Now comes in the sweetest morsel of the night').

51.15　tappit hen　decanter or mug, usually made of pewter, with a lid knob resembling the crest of a hen.

51.19–20　gaily circling glass　perhaps alluding to the drinking song 'By the gayly circling glass', which was popular in the later 18th century. See George Colman, *Comus: A Masque* (1772), 1.1; also *Calliope; or the Musical Miscellany* (London, 1788), 204.

51.24　top-dressing and bottom-dressing　methods of manuring and preparing soil.

51.25–26　proposed turnpike-act　referring to the Acts of Parliament which sanctioned roads built by trustees and representing local landed interests, the trustees being entitled to charge tolls. The development of the Scottish road system was greatly helped by the large number of turnpike acts passed, especially in the later half of the 18th century.

51.31–32　Marechal Duc de Berwick　James FitzJames (1670–1734), Duke of Berwick, natural son of James VII and II, who fought for the French forces against Britain in Flanders and Spain. *Maréchal* is a French military title, equivalent to field marshal in the British army.

51.34–43　Mon coeur volage ... Laridon　*French* 'My fickle heart, she says, is not for you, boy; it's for a man of war, who has a beard on his chin, Lon, Lon, Laridon. Who wears a plumed hat, shoes with red heels, and plays a flute and a violin, Lon, Lon, Laridon.' Taken (with some omissions) from 'La Belle', stanzas 4–6, in *Sammlung Deutscher Volkslieder* (Berlin, 1807; *CLA*, 47), 346, and described by Scott in MS 743, f. 31, as 'Old french Chanson accommodated'.

52.2　piper o' Cupar　Cupar is the old county town of Fife, about 19 km W of St Andrews. However, the setting of the incidents in the novel suggests that the place in question is actually Coupar Angus, in E Perthshire, about 22 km NW of Dundee. Scott refers to it as 'Coupar' in a letter of 1803 (*Letters*,

1.187); it also appears as 'Couper' on a map of 'The North P[art] of Perthshire' [London, 1745].Town pipers were a feature of Scottish boroughs until the late 18th century, and it is also possible that Scott was thinking of the traditional song 'The Piper o' Dundee'. For a version of this song, and an indication of Scott's involvement with it, see James Hogg, *The Jacobite Relics of Scotland*, 2nd series (1821), ed. Murray G. H. Pittock (Edinburgh, 2003), 43–44, 283, 490–91.

52.3–6, 12–15 It's up Glenbarchan's ... I fail identified by Scott in a Magnum note as by 'Andrew MacDonald, the ingenious and unfortunate author of Vimonda' (1.109n.). Macdonald (born *c.* 1755), the author of *Vimonda*, a tragedy (produced in London 1787), and also of two novels, *The Independent* (1784) and *Laura* (1791), died in poverty in 1788. These verses have not been identified as his. Scott's annotation in MS 743, f. 31v is: 'partly from Andw Macdonald partly orig[ina]l'. Scott in his 'Memoirs' recalls seeing 'the unfortunate Andrew Macdonald, author of Vimonda', in James Sibbald's circulating library in Edinburgh (*Scott on Himself*, ed. Hewitt, 34).

52.14 lunzie string cord of a wallet or knapsack hung at the hip.

52.18 derry-dongs probably here indicating meaningless words used, often together, in the choruses of popular songs from the 16th century onwards; also possibly an echo of 'derring-do', referring to chivalric exploits (with the connotation of their pointlessness).

52.19 to the boot of in addition to.

52.25 Dutch concert 'Where every one plays or sings a different tune' (Grose).

52.30 Stentor a Greek herald in the Trojan War, noted for his loud voice; origin of 'Stentorian'.

52.30–31 gentleman in black velvet i.e. the mole over whose mole-hill William III's horse stumbled early in 1702, resulting in a broken collar-bone that caused his death: a common subject of Jacobite toasts.

52.31–32 white horse an emblem of the House of Hanover, the coat of arms incorporating a running white horse on red; part of the royal coat of arms of the United Kingdom from 1714–1800.

52.39 tanquam privatus *Latin* in a private capacity.

52.43 sacramentum militare *Latin* military oath, as taken by Roman soldiers to the emperor.

53.1 Titus Livius i.e. Livy: see note to 28.26.

53.2 exuere sacramentum *Latin* to renounce the oath. The phrase has not been found in Livy, but Tacitus uses it at *Historiae* 3.42.

53.5 solemn league and covenant made between the Scottish Covenanters and the English Parliament in 1643. Under this treaty it was agreed that Presbyterianism—the form of church government favoured by the Covenanters—would become the established form of religion throughout the British Isles; and by a separate treaty, the Scots undertook in return to provide military assistance to the parliamentary side in the English Civil War.

53.15 sui juris *Latin literally* of one's own right: a term of Roman law referring to those who are not under the authority of their father, and can make legally binding transactions.

53.15 being foris-familiated i.e. outside of the family; a term of Scots law, referring to a minor living independently of parental authority.

53.18 tacit relocation *Scots law* the assumed continuance of a lease on the same terms when a landlord has failed to take action at the date of expiry.

53.18 tenant at will a tenant who holds at the will or pleasure of the landholder, without any fixed lease, until the latter gives appropriate notice.

53.18 in loco parentis *Latin* in the position of a parent.

53.25 crop-eared ... black ribband crop-eared means primarily 'short-haired', with ears exposed, according to the manner associated with Puritans or 'Round-heads'; but also, as used by opponents, can allude to the cropping of ears as a punishment. The 'black ribband' then could either be a bow or a bandage; while, as Lamont suggests, there may also be a glance at Waverley's black (Hanoverian) cockade.

53.30 other gates than he did *Twelfth Night*, 5.1.185–86, of the drunken Sir Toby Belch ('if he had not been in drink he would have tickl'd you other-gates than he did').

53.43–54.1 Boston's Crook of the Lot *The Crook in the Lot; or the Sovereignty and Wisdom of God Displayed in the Afflictions of Man*, a work of theology by the evangelical Presbyterian Thomas Boston (1677–1732). Originally published along with Boston's *Human Nature in its Fourfold State* [1729], as 'the substance of several sermons', it went through numerous editions singly in Scotland in the later 18th century, either as *The Sovereignty and Wisdom of God Displayed* or as *The Crook in the Lot*. The phrase itself, indicating that there are afflictions ('crooks') in every life, is proverbial (see *ODEP*, 155).

54.5–6 flinging her plaid ... weapons the wife of Thorarin and her attendants stop a fight in this way, albeit with the loss of a hand, in the Eyrbiggia-Saga, as recorded in Scott's abstract in *Illustrations of Northern Antiquities*, ed. Robert Jamieson and Henry Weber (Edinburgh, 1814), 485 (*Prose Works*, 5.386).

54.11 John-o'-Groat's to Land's End i.e. from the most northerly point of Scotland to the south-westerly extreme of England.

54.16–17 Centaurs and the Lapithæ alluding to feuding in Greek mythology between the Lapiths and Centaurs (half men, half horse). The incident Bradwardine probably has in mind is given as an example of the bad effects of wine in Homer's *Odyssey*, 21.295–303: 'Remember Eurytion the Centaur! It was the wine that got at *his* wits, in King Peirithous' house, when he was visiting the Lapithae. Fuddled with drink, what must he do but run amuck in the palace? His hosts leapt up in anger, dragged him to the porch, and threw him out of doors ... and so the feud started between Centaurs and men' (trans. E. V. Rieu, Penguin Classics (1946; reprinted 1954), 323).

54.27 laws of Heaven ... his country besides the sixth commandment ('Thou shalt not kill': Exodus 20.13) and Romans 12.19 ('Vengeance is mine'), there was a long tradition of Christian homily against duelling. An Act of 1600 made fighting a duel a capital offence in Scotland, even if no death resulted; an Act of 1696 made giving or accepting a challenge to a duel an offence punishable by banishment and confiscation of moveable goods. However, duelling between soldiers was permitted in Britain until 1844.

55.2 flour and barley *flour* refers to wheat flour, which was comparatively scarce in Scotland.

55.4 rein-deer ham reindeer were indigenous to Scotland, but disappeared in the 9th century through over-killing. Although attempts were made in the 18th century to reintroduce them, they were unsuccessful and the ham was probably imported. (Lamont)

55.5–6 even Johnson ... Scotch breakfast 'Not long after the dram, may be expected the breakfast, a meal in which the Scots, whether of the lowlands or mountains, must be confessed to excel us. The tea and coffee are accompanied not only with butter, but with honey, conserves, and marmalades. If an epicure could remove by a wish, in quest of sensual gratifications, wherever he had supped he would breakfast in Scotland': Samuel Johnson, *A Journey to the Western Islands of Scotland* (1775), ed. J. D. Fleeman (Oxford, 1985), 45. The 'even' stems from Johnson's reputation for deriding Scottish characteristics.

56.3 dans son tort *French* in the wrong.

56.4 Mons. Le Bretailleur fictional name: *brétailleur* in French means a swashbuckler, a bully.

56.7 mavortia pectora, as Buchanan saith *Latin* warlike hearts; George Buchanan (1506–82), Scottish historian and humanist. The phrase originates from an Epithalamium by Buchanan on the marriage between Mary Queen of Scots and the Dauphin of France, and is found in his *Opera Omnia*, 2 vols (Edinburgh, 1715; *CLA*, 10), 2.55: 'Ampla si dote moveris,/ Accipe dotales Mavortia pectora Scotos' ('If you are swayed by a lavish dowry, accept as your dowry the Scots, with their warlike hearts').

56.16–21 ebrius ... ebriosus *Latin* 'drunk(en)' and 'drunkard'. Compare Sir George Mackenzie, *The Laws and Customes of Scotland, in Matters Criminal* (Edinburgh, 1678): 'in this case the Law distinguisheth *inter ebrios*, who are rarely drunk, & *ebriosos*, who are habitually drunk: for these last should be most severely punisht, both for their drunkennesse, and for the Crimes occasioned by it' (15). Scott as a young advocate differentiated between these terms in his defence of the Rev. John M'Naught before the General Assembly of the Church of Scotland in 1793, 'the distinction between *ebrius* and *ebriosus* being founded on common sense, and recognized by law' ('Case for the Reverend Mr M'Naught', p. 11, in MS 1627). For an account, see also *Life*, 1.223–27.

56.20 vinum locutum est *Latin* it is the wine that has spoken.

57.8 ebrii ... ebrioli *Latin* plural forms of *ebrius* ('drunk') and *ebriolus*, the latter meaning 'a little drunk, tipsy, fuddled', and forming with *ebriosus* (see note to 56.16–21) three adjectives relating to drunkenness and its intensity.

57.10 half-seas over i.e. pretty far gone. The phrase appears in Jonathan Swift's 'A Complete Collection of Genteel and Ingenious Conversation' (1738): 'when I left you, you were half seas over' (*Works*, ed. Scott (1814), 11.341). It was also used by James Hogg in a letter to Scott of 24 December 1803: 'I am afraid that I was at least half-seas over' (*Collected Letters of James Hogg*, ed. Gillian Hughes, Vol. 1 (Edinburgh, 2004), 39).

57.20 not only ebriolus see note to 57.8.

57.26 gulæ causa *Latin* for the sake of the gullet. Scott may have got this expression from the elder Pliny's *Historia Naturalis*: 'nec gulae causa, sed avaritiae' (9.168). See also note to 57.29.

57.27 Pittacus of Mitylene (*c.* 650–570 BC), one of the Seven Sages of Greece. According to Diogenes Laertius, 'he made a law that if a man committed a crime while drunk, he should have double punishment; in the hope of deterring men from getting drunk' (*Lives of the Philosophers*, Life of Pittacus, 3).

57.28–29 Liber Pater the Roman god of wine and pleasure (alternative name for Bacchus).

57.29 younger Plinius actually Pliny the Elder, Gaius Plinius Secundus (AD 23–79), was the author of the *Historia Naturalis*. See 14.137–48, where Pliny says much about drunkenness, though there is no 'objurgation' nor any reference to legal punishment.

57.31 wine ... maketh glad see Psalm 104.15.

57.32 Flaccus, recepto amico see Horace, *Odes*, 2.7.27–28 ('recepto/ dulce mihi furere est amico', 'dear to me is the revelry when welcoming a friend').

57.42 pride of grease fat and fit for killing.

58.5 nec naturaliter idiota *Latin* nor a natural idiot. The phrase in context echoes the expression 'fatuus et naturaliter idiota' as used in brieves of idiotry (i.e. idiocy) in Scots law (see next note).

58.6 brieves of furiosity warrants authorising an inquiry into someone's mental state under Scots law. A *brieve* was a letter from the Chancery in the name of the monarch leading to an inquiry by a jury; *furiosity* signifies madness.

58.7   jumped with his own humour   suited his own inclination. See *1 Henry IV*, 1.2.68 (Falstaff).

58.11   eat of our bread and drink of our cup   see Proverbs 9.4–5: 'Whoso is simple, let him turn in hither: as for him that wanteth understanding, she saith to him, Come, eat of my bread, and drink of the wine which I have mingled.'

58.32–33   Negroes ... monkies   Corson locates an example of such a belief in Joano dos Santos, an early Portuguese traveller, concerning the 'Caffres': 'They, moreover, implicitly believe that monkeys have formerly been human beings, endowed with reasoning faculties equal to those of the human species, and that even now they are dumb merely from apprehension that if they should talk they would be made to work' ('History of Eastern Ethiopia', translation in John Pinkerton, *A General Collection of the Best and Most Interesting Voyages and Travels in All Parts of the World*, 17 vols (London, 1808–1814), 16.687).

58.37–38   windy side of insanity   compare *Much Ado About Nothing*, 2.1.283 ('it keeps on the windy side of care'); see also note to 31.27.

59.2–13   Hie away ... hie away   annotated by Scott as 'Original' in MS 743, f. 31v.

59.6   lady fern   British fern (*Athyrium filix-femina*), common in woods and shaded rocks, imagined by early herbalists to be the female of the male fern.

59.20   from our ground   indicating that Davie's brother could not get a position as a minister in the Church of Scotland, owing to his having come from the estate of a Jacobite family of Episcopalian persuasion.

59.40–41   chasseur of Louis Quatorze   huntsman of Louis XIV, King of France from 1643–1715.

59.42–43   Pour la chasse ... debout   *French* 'For an orderly hunt it is necessary to prepare everything ... Quickly! Get up quickly'. From Molière, *La Princesse D'Élide* (1664), Prologue, Scene 2.

60.7   brigadier wig   wig tied back in two curls.

60.11–12   low down in a grassy vale   see Lady Wardlaw, 'Hardyknute' (1719), stanza 9, line 3.

60.23   gillie-white-foots   apparently an English version of the Gaelic *gille-cas-fliuch*, more usually and accurately rendered as 'gillie-wet-foot', meaning a Highland attendant who carries his chieftain over streams; also used contemptuously among Lowlanders for the followers of a Highland chief.

60.26   Earl Percy of yore   compare the ballad 'Chevy Chace' (Child, 162B), in Percy, 1.231–46, stanza 17, though it is Lord Percy's enemy the Earl of Douglas who rides 'a milke-white steede'. Percy however is present as a hunter at the slaughter of deer (stanza 11).

60.28   faire la curée   French hunting term, referring to the flaying and opening up of the carcase of the deer and distribution of the entrails to the hounds. Scott explains the process in a note to his edition of *Sir Tristrem* (1804): 'To the forester he gave his rights, the left shoulder for himself, and the heart, liver, *lights* (lungs), and blood, which, being arranged on the hide, and eaten there by the hounds, formed the *quirré*, or quarry. This operation was called by French huntsmen *faire la curee*' (261).

60.29   couteau de chasse   *French* hunting knife.

61.8–9   Stately stepp'd ... west   see Lady Wardlaw, 'Hardyknute' (1719), stanza 1, lines 1–2.

61.11   Epithalamium   'Francisci Valesii & Mariæ Stuartæ, Regum Franciæ & Scotiæ, Epithalamium', a wedding song for the first marriage of Mary Queen of

Scots, by George Buchanan (1506–82), in his *Opera Omnia*, 2 vols (Edinburgh, 1715; *CLA*, 10), 2.52–57; see also note to 56.7.

61.11–12 Arthur Johnstoun's Psalms *Paraphrasis Poetica Psalmorum Davidis* (Aberdeen, 1637), a Latin translation of the Psalms by Arthur Johnstoun (1587–1641).

61.12 Deliciæ Poetarum Arthur Johnstoun, *Delitiae poetarum Scotorum hujus aevi illustrium*, 2 vols (Amsterdam, 1637; *CLA*, 11), an anthology of contemporary Latin verse. The relative poetical abilities of Johnstoun and Buchanan (see notes above) were a matter of debate.

61.12–13 Sir David Lindsay's Works individual works by Sir David Lindsay (*c.* 1486–1555), herald and court poet, include *The Complaynt to the King* (1529) and *Ane Pleasant Satyre of the Three Estaitis* (1540). His collected *Workes*, including initially only *Ane Satyre of the Three Estaitis*, were first published in 1604; the Abbotsford copy (*CLA*, 21) was published in Glasgow, 1696.

61.13 Barbour's Bruce *The Bruce* (written *c.* 1372–86), by John Barbour (*c.* 1320–95), Archdeacon of Aberdeen. The poem, written half a century after the events it describes, becomes a national epic celebration of Robert Bruce's successful struggle for Scottish independence.

61.13 Blind Harry's Wallace *Wallace* (*c.* 1477), by Blind Harry or Hary (*c.* 1440–92), a long narrative poem in 12 Books describing the heroic career of Sir William Wallace (*c.* 1270–1305) in leading the resistance to Edward I's attempt to subjugate Scotland; see also note to 320.18.

61.14 the Gentle Shepherd title of the popular pastoral drama (1725) by Allan Ramsay (1684–1758), poet and bookseller, who played an important role in the 18th-century revival of poetry in Scots.

61.14 the Cherry and the Slae title of the allegorical work (1597) by the Scottish poet Alexander Montgomerie (*c.* 1545–*c.* 1598).

61.15 sacrificed . . . the muses echoing the expression 'let us sacrifice to the muses', as attributed to Solon in Plutarch's 'The Banquet of the Seven Wise Men' (*Moralia* 164D).

61.20 vain and unprofitable art of poem-making similar wording is found in a 'Biographical Sketch of John Wilson' in *Scotish Descriptive Poems; with some illustrations of Scotish Literary Antiquities*, ed. John Leyden (Edinburgh, 1803; *CLA*, 162): 'the Magistrates and Minister of Greenock, before they admitted Mr. Wilson to the superintendance of the grammar school, stipulated that he should abandon "the profane and unprofitable art of poem-making"' (8). Wilson's poem 'The Clyde' is the first in the collection. This passage is cited by Scott in a note to 'The Battle of Philiphaugh' in *Minstrelsy*, 2.213n.2. He also uses the phrase in a letter to George Ellis of 25 January 1806: 'As I have suffered in my professional line by addicting myself to the profane and unprofitable art of poem-making . . .' (*Letters*, 1.274).

61.21–22 Allan Ramsay the periwig maker Allan Ramsay (1684–1758), author of *The Gentle Shepherd* (see note to 61.14) and other works and collections, was apprenticed in 1704 for five years to a wig-maker in Edinburgh, and for a time carried out that trade in addition to his bookselling and literary career.

61.23 toto cœlo *Latin literally* by the whole sky; entirely, utterly.

62.4–5 puer . . . magnæ indolis *Latin* a boy (or rather young man) of high promise and great talents.

62.13 Troisieme Etage *French* third floor; see also note to 316.43.

62.22 sanctum sanctorum *Latin* holy of holies. Originally the Vulgate (Latin Bible) name for the inner part of the temple in Jerusalem, it came in the 18th century to signify a private retreat, where someone could be free from intrusion.

62.36   Dutch auxiliaries   Dutch troops were sent for to help suppress the Jacobite rising of 1715. They joined the government forces of the Duke of Argyll only after the battle of Sheriffmuir, and so were not engaged in any major action.

62.38   Marechal Duke of Berwick   see note to 51.31–32.

62.41–42   Savoy . . . 1709   during the War of Spanish Succession (1701–14), the Duke of Berwick campaigned against Prince Eugene of Savoy in defence of the SE frontier of France.

63.18–19   married to immortal verse   John Milton, *L'Allegro* (1631), line 137.

64.9   quoted by Edgar   probably the verses beginning 'Swithold footed thrice the 'old', in *King Lear*, 3.4.118–22.

64.11–12   Who, noteless . . . unsung   see John Leyden, *Scenes of Infancy* (Edinburgh, 1803; *CLA*, 193), 22.

64.19   St Swithin's Chair   the following verses are annotated by Scott as 'Original' in MS 743 (f. 32v). St Swithin was Bishop of Winchester, and died in 862; St Swithin's Day, traditionally believed to forecast the next 40 days' weather, is on 15 July.

64.20   Hallow-Mass Eve   31 October, the eve of All Saints' Day; more commonly known as Halloween, and associated in folklore with the supernatural.

64.25   her nine-fold   compare *King Lear*, 3.4.119: 'He met the nightmare and her nine-fold', the latter probably referring to the demon's nine offspring or familiars.

65.19   little work compiled by Julius Obsequens   *Julii Obsequentis de Prodigiis Liber, cum annotationibus J. Schefferi* (Amsterdam, 1679; *CLA*, 146). The work has a dedication to 'Benedicto Skytte Libero Baroni in Duderhoff [*sic*]', signed 'Joannes Schefferus'. An account of portents in ancient Rome, the volume is indeed small, consisting of 156 pages plus an index. Little is known about Julius Obsequens (*c*. 4th century AD), the original compiler.

65.31   sin of witchcraft   the most notable biblical statement regarding the 'sin' of witchcraft is in Exodus 22.18 ('Thou shalt not suffer a witch to live'). The law on witchcraft in Scotland was regulated by the Act 1563 c. 9, which provided for the penalty of death for those practising witchcraft, sorcery, and necromancy and for those who consulted them. The law had later been allowed to fall into disuse, because the legal establishment did not believe in it, although the last execution was in 1727; it was not fully repealed until 1736.

65.37   no conjurors   used here in the sense of 'far from clever' (see *OED*, conjurer 3), though with a punning reference to *conjuror* in the sense of one who conjures up spirits.

65.40   the enemy   of mankind, i.e. Satan.

65.42   Apollyon's taste   Apollyon, 'the angel of the bottomless pit', is named in Revelation 9.11; an alternative name for the devil.

66.3   Evil One   another name for the devil.

66.9   Risu solvuntur tabulæ   the case is laughed out of court: echoing Horace, *Satires*, 2.1.86, which reads *solventur risu tabulae* ('the case will be laughed out of court').

66.10–11   wakening of the process   technical term in Scots law, used to describe a procedure to revive an action after it has 'fallen asleep', i.e. no step has been taken in it for a year and a day after it was raised.

66.13–16   All those . . . and lies   see Spenser, *The Faerie Queene* (1590–96), 2.9.51.

66.28   an old ballad   in fact probably by Scott: annotated as 'Original' in MS 743, f. 33v.

67.9   Sumack and Co.   probably a fictional concern; *sumach* is a name for shrubs and trees of the genus *Rhus*, the leaves of which were used in the process of tanning.

67.34 Archibald Simson (1564–1628), Church of Scotland minister at Dalkeith from 1590, and an opponent of attempts to impose royal authority on church government. His *Hieroglyphica animalium terrestrium, volatilium, natatilium, reptilium, insectorum [etc.]* (Edinburgh, 1622–24), a treatise in Latin, contains a section headed 'De Urso', concerning the Bear, 1.53–57. The Abbotsford copy (*CLA*, 72) contains a MS note by Scott describing Simson's protests and punishments as 'one of the recusant ministers' opposing James VI and I.

68.3–5 armoiries parlantes . . . arma cantantia . . . canting heraldry French, Latin, and English terms relating to a form of allusive or punning arms in heraldry, in which the charges (i.e. heraldic devices) suggest the bearer's name or title, e.g. a falcon for Falconer.

68.19 boast of heraldry Thomas Gray, 'Elegy Written in a Country Churchyard' (1751), line 33.

68.28 Nisbett Alexander Nisbet (1657–1725), whose *System of Heraldry* first appeared in 2 vols (Edinburgh, 1722–42); Scott owned the 2nd edn, also in two large volumes (Edinburgh 1804; *CLA*, 11).

68.28–29 apple of her father's eye proverbial expression, from the pupil appearing to be round like an apple, and figuratively expressing affectionate partiality; see also Proverbs 7.2, and Deuteronomy 32.10.

68.38 an old settlement i.e. the deed of entail under which the property had to be inherited by the nearest male heir. After the Baron's death the property was destined by the entail in default of direct heirs male to pass to a distant relation.

68.43 personal succession referring to moveable property (such as money) as opposed to heritable property (land and houses etc.), the former in this case to be inherited by Rose as the only child.

69.3 settlement on the male line see note to 68.38 above.

69.11 Les coustusmes de Normandie *Old French* the customs of Normandy. These had an influence on early Scots law through the adoption of English forms originating from Normandy.

69.12 C'est L'Homme . . . ki conseille *Old French* it is the man who fights and advises.

69.19–20 in servitio . . . battaliam *Latin* in the service of removing or pulling off the king's boots after a battle.

69.22–23 procul dubio *Latin* far from doubt.

69.27 Inch-Grubbit probably a fictitious name: *grub* in Scots can mean to grasp (at money etc.) in a parsimonious manner.

69.38 Jinker another fictitious name: *jinker* in Scots means libertine, and is also used figuratively of a high-spirited nimble animal.

69.38–39 piper o' Cupar see note to 52.2.

69.39–41 mend . . . sour ale in summer proverbial: see Ramsay, 82; Ray, 202; *ODEP*, 526.

70.5–6 belles lettres *French literally* fine letters; elegant or polite literature.

70.22–23 those of the house of Bourbon or Austria . . . clouds of passion alluding probably to the political marriages between these two powerful European dynasties, and possibly in particular to that in 1615 of Anne of Austria, the daughter of Habsburg parents, to King Louis XIII of France, one of the Bourbon dynasty.

70.35–36 mental legend of Saint Cecilia for the early Christian martyr of that name, see note to 21.5; here, as earlier, the association in Waverley's mind is with Miss Cæcilia Stubbs.

71.2 mend her pen see note to 9.20.

71.2–3 stanza in Tasso referring to the Italian poet Torquato Tasso (1544–95); see earlier notes to 13.28 and 40.19–20.

71.11 le beau ideal *French* the ideal beauty.

71.39–40 the royal prerogative in things sacred as asserted by Charles II and James VII and II, both of whom claimed to be the supreme governor of the Church in matters spiritual as well as temporal. This was the principal cause of civil dissension in the later 17th century, for to Presbyterians who constituted the majority in Scotland the only Head of the Church was Christ.

72.21 the celebrated Belides more commonly called the Danaids (the daughters of Danaus), punished in Hades for the murder of their husbands by being compelled everlastingly to pour water into vessels filled with holes. They are also known by the name of Belides, from their grandfather Belus.

72.34 Diogenes at Sinope the Greek philosopher, Diogenes of Sinope (*c*. 400–*c*. 325 BC), principal representative of the Cynic school of philosophy. He supposedly lived in a tub, and Lucian records that when his fellow citizens were busily preparing for battle he rolled his tub up and down so as to compensate for his inaction (*Quomodo historia conscribenda sit*, 3). Most accounts place this incident at Corinth, though Diogenes was a native of Sinope on the Black Sea.

72.38 Our gear's a' gane see the refrain in the song 'The Fray of Suport', *Minstrelsy*, 2.161–65.

73.19 black-mail as paid to neighbouring Highlanders to ensure that farms would not be raided and cattle driven off, a fairly common eventuality for those living adjacent to the Highlands, not least for those who refused. An account of this practice is found in Burt, 2.228–35; and in Pennant, 1.225.

73.19–20 Fergus Mac-Ivor Vich Ian Vohr as Lamont notes, Vich Ian Vohr is probably a transliteration of the Gaelic *Mhic Iain Mhóir*, son of John the Great. The full name then would mean Fergus son of Ivor son of Big John. '*Vic ean*, Great Grandson of *John*' appears as part of a list explaining patronymics in Burt (2.111). In Gaelic 'Ivor' is properly 'Iomhair'. For possible historical prototypes of the character, see Historical Note, 386–87.

73.24 by the strong hand i.e. by force.

73.27 taken all our arms referring to the disarming acts of 1716 and 1725, making it illegal to have or use warlike weapons within the Highland line; while the first of these proved largely ineffectual, a significant number of weapons were confiscated after the 1725 act.

74.16–17 lapis offensionis, et petra scandali 1 Peter 2.8 in the Vulgate (Latin Bible). In the Authorised Version this reads 'a stone of stumbling, and a rock of offence'.

74.20 sixteen hundred forty and two it is not clear to what Scott refers. The English Civil War began in 1642, and might be taken as a date representative of the civil unrest of the times. It is unlikely to be an error for 1644 when Highlanders under Montrose descended on the Lowlands, in that no one put any part of Montrose's army to flight before its eventual defeat at Philiphaugh in 1645.

74.27 theft-boot, or composition of felony *theft-boot* (or *-bote*) in Scots law was a crime where a person who had been robbed colluded with the thief to get back the goods on agreeing not to prosecute the thief for the theft. As such it could be classed as a type of composition of felony, i.e. a compounding with a crime, or conniving at it.

74.41–42 restitution in integrum matching the Latin legal term *restitutio in integrum*, signifying the restoration of a person to the condition or position formerly enjoyed (in this case to the original state of possession).

74.43 Malcolm Canmore Malcolm III, King of Scots, reigned 1057–93.

75.1   still for war   Joseph Addison, *Cato* (1713), 2.1 ('My voice is still for war').

75.4   nebulones nequissimi   *Latin* worthless rascals.

75.4   Leslæus   John Leslie (1527–96), Bishop of Ross, historian, and close supporter of Mary Queen of Scots. His *De Origine, moribus et rebus gestis Scotorum*, a Latin history of Scotland, was first published in Rome in 1578 (see *CLA*, 6).

75.5   Cacus   a fire-breathing giant who stole oxen from Hercules, who in turn pursued him home to his cave and killed him, as told in Virgil, *Aeneid*, 8.190–305.

75.6   Elisos oculos ... guttur   Virgil, *Aeneid*, 8.261 (eyes squeezed out and throat drained dry of blood).

75.10   Bally-Brough   not located as a place, though according to the *Edinburgh Magazine* in 1817 'the Pass of Ballybrough ... can be no other than that immediately above Dunkeld, leading into the Highlands': 1 (Oct. 1817), 230. The name itself echoes Ballybrough in Ireland, a pass where Brian Boru defeated the Danes at the battle of Clontarf in 1014. See also Historical Note, 381–82.

75.32   commission of peace   the body of justices of the peace, who were usually local landowners appointed to administer justice in minor criminal cases.

76.5   Jonathan Wild   notorious leader of a gang of thieves, born *c*. 1682 and hanged at Tyburn 1725: the ostensible subject of Henry Fielding's *The Life and Death of Jonathan Wild the Great* (1743).

76.11   towering passion   *Hamlet*, 5.2.79.

76.23   Glennaquoich   the name is close to Glenquoich, to the N of Loch Quoich, in the W Highlands: see Edward C. Ellice, *Place-names in Glengarry and Glenquoich, and their origin* (London, 1898), 'The Glenquoich District', 108–24. Compare Hogg's song 'Bauldy Fraser', in his *Jacobite Relics of Scotland*, 2nd series (1821), ed. Murray G. H. Pittock (Edinburgh, 2003), 416 ('Te men of Muideart an' Glenquoich', mentioned there as absentees at Culloden). There is also a Glen Quaich in Perthshire, W of the village of Amulree, itself between Aberfeldy and Crieff. See also Historical Note, 381.

77.1–2   bodies ... bloody tartans   Scott had a similar recollection, of seeing as a child the bodies of Highlanders killed in a mutiny at Leith: 'I saw nothing for ten days after but the highlanders lying stiff and stark' (*Letters*, 11.378–79).

77.3–4   Lord Justice Clerk   President of the High Court of Justiciary, the supreme criminal court in Scotland.

77.14   I do not ... jade me   *Twelfth Night*, 2.5.144–45.

77.30   charge of horning   relating to the process by which the court required a debtor to pay his debts, leading ultimately in case of non-compliance to the debtor's imprisonment. In the event of a failure to pay, letters of horning were read at the Market Cross of Edinburgh, denouncing the debtor, accompanied by three blasts of the horn, with the letters being attached to the Cross.

77.36   goods and gear   worldly possessions; money and property. These and the following terms match a similar listing found under 'Horning and Poinding' in George Dallas, *System of Stiles As now Practicable within the Kingdom of Scotland* (Edinburgh, 1697; 2nd edn, 2 vols, 1774): 'their readiest goods, gear, corns, cattle, insight, plenishing, horse, nolt, sheep, debts, sums of money, and others whatsomever' (1.15). For Dallas's work, widely used in Scotland for framing legal documents, see note to 331.25–26.

77.36–37   outsight and insight plenishing   moveable property: respectively, horses, cattle, etc. (outdoor), and furniture, bedding, etc. (inside).

77.40–41   one thousand five hundred and sixty-seven   the Act 1567

c. 27 of the Scottish Parliament makes blackmail a capital offence as a type of treason, but the Baillie's language and concerns are more obviously reflected in the Act 1587, c. 59, which specifically deals with the Highlands. The crimes listed are also covered in many other acts of the period, such as Act 1581, c.16, Act 1585, c. 13, etc.

78.2 raptus mulierum *Latin* abduction or rape of women.

78.25–26 as if ... in a sheep's skin Scott describes such an attitude as being held by the MacDonnells of Keppoch in a note to his edition of the *Works* of Jonathan Swift: 'This family suffered, from a wild strain of pride in one of their ancestors, who refused to take out a charter for his lands, disdaining, as he said, to hold them by a sheep's-skin' (*Works*, ed. Scott (1814), 10.164n.–65n.). The note goes on to describe how as a result the clan failed to have restored to them lands forfeited in the 1715 and 1745 risings. Scott also refers to this in his review of the *Culloden Papers* for the *Quarterly Review* (Jan. 1816): see *Prose Works*, 20.55.

78.30 patriarchal race Scott as a social historian uses the term *patriarchal* to denote a stage of society prior to and distinct from the feudal, and in which power is centred on a single male tribal leader. The word also can carry with it the broader meaning of 'characteristic of the ancient world, as in the time of the biblical Patriarchs'.

79.14–15 Spanish fowling-piece Spanish guns were brought over to support the planned Jacobite rising of 1719. Corson notes that 'Scott himself possessed a Spanish double-barrelled flint-lock gun (Armoury, no. 142)'.

79.19 Evan Dhu Maccombich the first part of the name most obviously means 'Evan the Dark' (from the Gaelic *dubh*, 'black'). In his story 'The Two Drovers' in *Chronicles of the Canongate* (1827) Scott explains McCombich as meaning 'son of my friend' (see EEWN 20, 126.17–18), a derivation which might come from Gaelic *mac*, son, and *companach*, a companion. George F. Black derives the name, however, from the Gaelic 'MacThomaidh, "son of Tommie" (diminutive of Thomas)': *The Surnames of Scotland* (New York, 1962), 474. Both of these derivations, it should be noted, are at best possibilities. See also Historical Note, 388.

79.28–29 egg between ... a sword *proverbial* 'A stone in place of an egg, and a knife in place of a sword' (Macintosh, 19).

79.31–32 never struck ... the sword *proverbial* 'They never provoked with the scabbard, who did not receive with the sword' (Macintosh, 21).

79.32–33 woe to him ... spring morning *proverbial* 'Woe to him who would lose his friend for the stormy appearance of a spring morning' (Macintosh, 19).

79.38–39 when folks ... no brother *proverbial* 'Feeble is the arm of the man who has not a brother,/ At the time that folks are banding together' (Macintosh, 39).

80.1 turned down drank down, tossed off (*OED*, *turn*, verb 72e).

80.17–18 broken the bone ... marrow *proverbial* 'Though you broke the bone, you did not suck the marrow' (Macintosh, 34).

80.31 Highland Cacus see note to 75.5.

81.3 Lochaber axe weapon combining spear and battle-axe with a hook behind, named after a district of the Highlands.

81.8 foster-brother Evan Dhu's situation as such reflects the once common custom of chiefs fostering their offspring on trusted members of the clan. The practice is described in Burt, 2.156–57: 'the Foster-brother having the same Education as the young Chief, may besides that, in Time become his *Hanchman* ...' (156). See also following note.

81.13–14 officers of his chief's retinue the list of the chief's followers, and much of the spelling of Gaelic terms, comes from the account in

Burt (2.158–59). Unlike the others, *hanchman* (denoting a 'right-hand-man') is an English/Scots term, the nearest Gaelic equivalent being *gille-tòine* (literally, 'bum-man'). *Bladier* possibly derives from the Gaelic word *bladair*, 'babbler, flatterer'; and *gilly-more* from *gille-mór*, 'big lad'. For the remaining individual terms, see Glossary.

81.22 boys of the belt lads ready to execute the will and pleasure of the leader.

82.1 pass of Bally-Brough see note to 75.10.

82.2 clan Donnochie the Robertsons, also referred to as the Clan Donnachie, or Clann Donnchaidh, a name traditionally traced back to Donnchadh Reamhar ('Stout Duncan'), who led the clan at the battle of Bannockburn. The clan's territory was concentrated round Struan near Blair Atholl in N Perthshire, though at one time they also had wide possessions on the banks of Loch Tay and Loch Rannoch.

82.42 Serbonian bog as in Milton, *Paradise Lost*, 2.592–94 ('Where Armies whole have sunk'); usually identified as a morass near the Egyptian coast.

83.16 Donald Bean Lean the last two words effectively meaning 'fair-haired' and (inappropriately it might seem) 'broad[-shouldered]' (from the Gaelic *bàn* and *leathann*). For possible prototypes of this character, see Historical Note, 388.

83.24 sidier roy *Gaelic saighdear ruadh* red (i.e. government) soldier, from their scarlet uniforms. The term is found as here in Burt, 1.244.

83.25 in jockey phrase i.e. in the idiom of jockeys.

83.25 trotted out trotted with extended action (as distinct from trotted short), terms used of horses.

84.6–7 perfume . . . birch trees Scott is evidently thinking of the Downy Birch (*Betula pubescens*), as opposed to the Silver Birch (*Betula pendula*).

84.12 Robin Hood the English outlaw of the ballads and chapbooks.

84.13 Adam o' Gordon see 'Edom o' Gordon', in Percy, 1.99–106; Child, 178D.

85.7 Evil Genius of an oriental tale referring to the genii (more properly *djins* or *jinnees*) as found in popular oriental tales such as the *Arabian Nights Entertainments* and James Ridley's *Tales of the Genii* (1764).

85.20–21 shipping their oars i.e. bringing their oars into the boat.

86.7 Salvator Salvator Rosa (1615–73), Italian painter, noted for his wild landscapes featuring bandits and beleaguered travellers.

86.11 agnomen of Bean see note to 83.16.

87.6 Where there are no bushes . . . nuts proverbial (Macintosh, 33).

87.9 Donnacha an Amrigh interpretable in Gaelic as *Donnacha an iom-raidh*, meaning 'Duncan of the Gift of Speech'. No explanation has been found for Scott's following 'Duncan with the Cap', though it may be that 'amrigh' is a corrupt form of *abhra*, sometimes meaning 'veil, curtain, fringe'; and a fainter possibility still that some kind of corruption of the slang word *gab* (as in 'gift of the gab') might be involved.

87.10 second sight the facility of 'seeing' things distant in time or place, commonly associated with Gaelic prophets.

87.15 Shemus Beg from the Gaelic *beag* (little), so 'Little James'.

88.22 Uaimh an Ri *Gaelic Uamh an Righ*; Scott's translation is correct.

90.1 Scythian camp the Scythians were 'barbaric' nomadic tribes of N Europe and of Asia beyond the Black Sea.

90.6 of scanty longitude compare Robert Burns, 'Tam o' Shanter' (1791), line 173.

90.8 called the snood matching Burt's 'a Fillet of red or blue course [*sic*] Cloth, of which they are very proud' (2.194), mentioned as an exception to the rule that unmarried women should go bare-headed (see note to

106.37–38). Compare *The Lady of the Lake* (1810), Canto 3, stanza 5: 'The virgin snood did Alice wear' (*Poetical Works*, 8.122). The word snood (or *snuid*) is apparently a Scots rather than Gaelic word.

90.29 **cran-berries** probably referring to the cowberry or whortleberry, called in Scotland the cranberry, but unlike other species of cranberry pleasant to the taste uncooked (Lamont).

91.4–5 **scallop shell ... whisky** as mentioned in Burt: ' ... *Usky*; which, tho' a strong Spirit, is to them like Water. And this I have often seen 'em drink out of a Scollop Shell' (2.43).

91.36–37 **too hot or too heavy** echoing Scott's comment on Walter Scott of Harden and his followers in *Minstrelsy*, 1.154n: 'In short, as Froissart says of a similar class of feudal robbers, nothing came amiss to them, that was not *too heavy, or too hot.*'

91.39 **never lifted** compare Burt: 'and the stealing of Cows they call *Lifting*, a soft'ning Word for Theft' (2.229–30).

92.1 **gentleman-drover** compare Burt, regarding a Highlander accused of stealing, and hearing himself in Court called 'a common Thief': 'Common Tief, Common Tief! Steal ane Cow, twa Cow dat be Common Tief: Lift hundred Cow, dat be Shentilmans Trovers' (2.237).

92.1–3 **tree from the forest ... shame upon** *proverbial* 'A fish from the river, a tree from the forest, and a deer from the mountain, are thefts no man was ever ashamed of' (Macintosh, 9).

92.8–9 **kind gallows of Crieff** in a Magnum note (1.199), Scott states: 'This celebrated gibbet was, in the memory of the last generation, still standing at the western end of the town of Crieff, in Perthshire'. He also speculates about the meaning of 'kind', with the suggestion that it expressed an affinity between executed and living Highlanders. The expression is also found in a broadside ballad entitled 'The Highland Man's Lament', concerning the execution in 1723 of Donald Bayn at the Grassmarket in Edinburgh, which refers to his passing 'Not on kind Gallows at the Crief'. In a letter to Anna Seward of 29 June 1802, Scott refers to 'the *kindly* gallows of Elibank', indicating an element of transferability in the term, which may well be at least partly ironical in usage (see *Letters*, 1.145).

92.14 **wet straw ... mangy tyke** compare Burt, concerning a Highland woman who had had three husbands: 'she said the two first were honest Men, and very careful of their Family; for they both *died for the Law*: That is, were hang'd for Theft. Well, but as to the last? *Hout!* says she, *a fulthy Peast! He dy'd at Hame, lik an auld Dug, on a* Puckle *o' Strae*' (2.232–33).

92.23 **Ben-Lawers** to the N of Loch Tay, Ben Lawers (1214 m) is the highest mountain in Perthshire.

92.33 **five bits of miles** five short miles, but here effectively indicating something longer. The Scottish mile was 1.8 km or nearly one-eighth longer than the English mile.

93.25 **Letter-Scriven** not identified as a location, but interpretable in Gaelic as *Leitir Sgrìbhinn*, meaning 'Slope of Rocky Hill'.

93.27 **I'se warrant** I'll bet, I'll be bound.

93.27 **Rannoch** the area round Loch Rannoch in NW Perthshire. Further to the west lies Rannoch Moor, an upland plateau, now considered one of the last truly wild places in Scotland.

93.31–32 **Sidier Dhu** *Gaelic saighdear dubh* black soldier. Alluding here to the Independent Companies first raised from Highland clans as a militia in 1725, later incorporated into the Black Watch (see note to 47.8), so called because of the dark tartans worn, contrasting with the scarlet uniforms of the regular army troops. The term is found (as 'Sidier Dou') in Burt, 1.244; see also note to 83.24.

94.9   inside plenishing   see note to 77.36–37.

94.13   five hundred marks   about £27.80 sterling. A *mark* or *merk* was worth 13s. 4d. Scots, and in 1707 when the Scots currency was replaced a pound Scots was worth one-twelfth of a pound sterling.

94.15   howe o' the Mearns   the plain of Kincardineshire, S of Aberdeen.

94.17   heirship and moveables   representing the main division of property in Scots law, between heritable property, which passed by succession to an heir and included lands, and moveables (such as furniture and jewellery), which could be left independently (with children and a wife being able to claim a proportion).

94.22   malt rather above the meal   proverbial and indicating drunkenness (see Ramsay, 112; Ray, 69; *ODEP*, 503).

94.25   old to do   an anglicised form of 'auld to do', meaning a great fuss or trouble.

94.28   Punds Scottish   a Scots pound was worth one-twelfth of an English pound (see also note to 29.10).

94.30   Black Watch   see note to 47.8.

94.35   ye'll not hinder   emphatic idiomatic Scots expression, roughly meaning here 'it did not prevent (him)'.

94.41–42   open air . . . fresh whey   see note to 339.40.

94.42   deil an   *literally* devil if; an emphatic way of expressing surprise.

95.9   be the evidence what it liked   whatever the evidence.

95.10   be on Donald's inquest   i.e. be a member of the jury at Donald's trial.

95.11   wilful arson, or murder under trust   both capital offences, treated as equivalents to treason in Scots law, and for which a single witness might suffice to obtain a conviction. The underlying implication is that Gilliewhackit would only testify granted the certainty of Donald Bean Lean being executed (and so not able to retaliate).

95.12   bald and disjointed chat   compare *1 Henry IV*, 1.3.65 ('This bald unjointed chat of his'). The same expression, as 'bald disjointed chat', is found in a letter of Scott's to Joanna Baillie, 23 November 1810 (*Letters*, 2.405).

95.18–20   large measure . . . pint stoup   this sequence appears to derive from a similar incident in Burt: 'Says the *English* Fellow, ye sorry Dog, your Shilling is but a Penny. Aye, says *Sawny* (who it seems was a Lover of Ale) 'tis true, but the Deel tak him that has the least *Pint-Stoup*' (1.189). The old Scots pint was about 3 imperial pints (1.696 litres). For the Scottish computation of money and distance, see notes to 29.10 and 92.33.

95.22   Shogh   interpretable as an equivalent of the Gaelic *Seadh*, meaning 'Yes, indeed'.

95.29   Callum Beg   from the Gaelic *beag* (little), so 'Little Callum' or 'Little Malcolm'.

95.31   Qu'il connoit bien ses gens   *French* that he knew his people well.

96.7   trews, or close trowsers   as worn by Highland gentlemen, especially for riding, with the legs extended to cover the feet. The cloth, generally of a tartan pattern, was cut so as to ensure close-fitting and elasticity.

96.10   claymore   from the Gaelic, *claidheamh-mór*, a great sword; originally a large two-handed sword, but by the 18th century it was a basket-hilted Highland broadsword.

96.12–13   close-time was then unknown   in fact legislation for the preservation of game in Scotland dates from the 15th century. The Act 1707 c. 91 fixed the close season for moor-fowl at 1 March to 20 June, though it is likely that this was not observed by the Highland Chiefs.

96.21   Bond-Street   fashionable London street, with shops including barbers and wig-makers; see also note to 263.31–32.

97.13 licentiate Francisco de Ubeda Francisco López de Úbeda, putative author of *La Pícara Justina* (1605). The true author was later identified as Andrés Pérez, a Leonese Dominican friar, though one modern study re-establishes de Úbeda, probably a physician, as the true author (see Bruno M. Damiani, *Francisco López de Úbeda* (Boston, 1977)). The term 'licentiate' (most obviously referring to the author being licenced, or a graduate, but possibly with underlying suggestions of licentiousness) features on the title-page of the Spanish original, which reads: *Compvesto por el Licenciado Francisco de Vbeda, natural de Toledo* ('Composed by the licentiate Franisco Ubeda, native of Toledo'). An English translation appeared in 1707 under the lead title *The Spanish Libertines*. Scott owned an Italian translation, *Vita della Picara Giustina Diez*, published in Venice in 1624–25 (*CLA*, 55). The passage alluded to appears at the beginning of the 'General Introduccion'.

97.20–21 to one thing constant never *Much Ado About Nothing*, 2.3.60.

97.29 like Dogberry see *Much Ado About Nothing*, 3.5.56.

97.36–37 second Æneas alluding to Virgil's Aeneas, the Trojan who founded Rome.

98.10 Ian nan Chaistel actually meaning in Gaelic 'John of the Castles', *nan* generally being the plural article; the correct singular form would be *Iain a' Chaisteil*.

98.12–13 Vich Ian Vohr, i. e. the son of John the Great for this title and translation see note to 73.19–20.

98.14–15 Sliochd nan Ivor, the race of Ivor more correctly translated 'race of the Ivors'.

98.34 Castruccio Castrucani (1284–1328), Italian adventurer and Duke of Lucca, leader of the Ghibelline party in the political wars in early 14th-century Italy. A translation of his life, as written by Machiavelli, can be found in Mrs Haywood's *Select Collection of Novels and Histories*, 6 vols, 2nd edn (London, 1729; *CLA*, 139), 6.1–35 (Corson).

98.39 stretched his means to the uttermost compare *The Merchant of Venice*, 1.1.181 ('rack'd, even to the uttermost').

99.7 like Poins see *2 Henry IV*, 2.2.64 ('I am a proper fellow of my hands').

100.22 louis-d'ors *French* (strictly, in the plural, 'louis d'or') golden French coins, roughly equivalent to English gold guineas.

100.24 earl's patent i.e. letters patent, a document issued by a monarch conferring some right or title, here an earldom.

100.38 lofted house compare Burt, on the subject of stone houses in the Highlands: 'if any one has a Room above, it is, by way of Eminence, called a *lofted* House; but in the inner Part of the Mountains there are no Stone Buildings that I know of, except the Barracks' (2.205).

100.41 Highland Host Highlanders were quartered in the West of Scotland in 1678, during the Royalist administration of the Duke of Lauderdale, in an effort to disarm and intimidate the Presbyterian Covenanters, or, as some people believed, to incite them into open rebellion; they were authorised to take free quarters and horses as needed, and were indemnified from legal action.

101.19 Stow or Blenheim two of the grandest English country houses in the Classical manner. Stow or Stowe in Buckinghamshire, formerly the family seat of the Temples, was built in 1676 and expanded over the next 150 years by a succession of remarkable architects including Vanbrugh, Adam, and Sloane. It is notable for its landscape gardens and ornaments. Blenheim Palace, in Oxfordshire, was designed by Vanbrugh, and built 1705–22. The royal manor of Woodstock, together with £240,000 for the building of Blenheim,

was given by Queen Anne (and confirmed by Parliament) to the Duke of
Marlborough for his victories in the War of Spanish Succession (see note
to 183.12).

101.39–40 all the current of a heady fight see *1 Henry IV*, 2.3.52.

101.42 pitching the bar contest to see who could throw a thick rod of
wood or iron the farthest.

102.8 five hundred claymores possibly echoing a passage in Home:
'About the year 1740, some Low Country gentlemen made a party to visit the
Highlands, where they were entertained at the house of one of the chiefs with
great hospitality, and a profusion of game, fish, and French wine. One of the
guests asked their landlord, somewhat bluntly, What was the rent of the estate?
He answered he could raise 500 men. This story is told of M'Donald of
Keppoch, who was killed at the battle of Culloden' (20n.).

102.9 disarming act see note to 73.27.

102.19 General Blakeney William Blakeney (1672–1761), Irish-born
army officer, promoted to major-general on 20 July 1745, and lieutenant-
governor of Stirling Castle at the time of the Jacobite rising of 1745–46, during
which he withstood a long siege.

102.31 To chafe . . . fragrant oil possibly alluding to Bk 6 of Homer's
Odyssey, where Nausicaa, daughter of Alcinous, with her attendants washes
her nuptial robes and then offers succour to Ulysses; and, more specifically,
to Alexander Pope's translation (1725–26), especially line 110: 'And o'er their
limbs diffuse ambrosial oil'. In other respects, the situation is closer to Ulysses'
account of his bathing by the handmaidens of Circe (Bk 10).

102.34–35 Our fathers' herds . . . service proverbial: compare 'Your
grandfather's flocks and mine were far asunder' (Macintosh, 46).

102.38 Gaelic proverb not found in Macintosh; but what follows is close
to *An làmh a bheir, 's igheibh* ('The hand that gives is the one that will get').
For a similar version, see *Gaelic Proverbs*, ed. Alexander Nicolson (3rd edn;
1951; reprinted Edinburgh, 1996), 32.

103.6 wadsetters and tacksmen the first term refers to a holder of a
wadset, in Scots law a conveyance of land by a debtor to his creditor as a
security for the repayment of the debt (the debtor had power to compel the
reconveyance to him of the land on payment of the debt). Home notes how
'The creditor who lends the money and receives the pledge is called the
wadsetter' (128n.). A *tacksman* holds a tack or lease from a superior landholder.
In the Highlands this customarily meant a superior tenant of a clan chief,
often one of his close kin, who acted as a kind of agent for the chief in dealings
with clansmen.

103.18 curs of low degree Oliver Goldsmith, 'An Elegy on the Death of
a Mad Dog' (1766), lines 15–16 ('mongrel, puppy, whelp and hound/ And
curs of low degree').

103.20–21 hospitality . . . line of economy the description of the feast is
close to an account of a similar occasion presided over by Lord Lovat, as given
in *Memoirs of the Life and Gallant Exploits of the Old Highlander, Sergeant
Donald Macleod* (London, 1791; *CLA*, 80). In particular this notes how Lovat,
lacking a fortune, 'was obliged to regulate his unbounded hospitality by rules
of prudent œconomy' (47), the account then going on to relate the granting
of different positions at table and qualities of food and drink according to
rank, the full perspective ending with those 'without the door of the hall' (48).
See also Coleman O. Parsons, 'The Highland Feasts of Fergus MacIvor and
Lord Lovat', *Modern Language Notes*, 49 (May 1934), 287–90.

103.24 absence of pork the Highlanders did not eat pork, an aversion
also found more generally in Scotland. Scott's Magnum note (1.219) relates
how James VI and I 'carried this prejudice to England', and there are several

references in *The Fortunes of Nigel* (1822) to the Scots' disdain for pork. See also Donald A. Mackenzie, *Scottish Folk-lore and Folk Life* (London, 1935), 'Scottish Pork Taboo' (41–55).

103.26 Penelope's suitors those who courted Penelope, wife of Odysseus, during his absence at Troy; they abused her hospitality with lavish feasting and were eventually slain by Odysseus on his unexpected return home (see *Odyssey*, Bks 20–22).

103.27 a hog in harst a young sheep, smeared at the end of harvest, when it ceases to be a lamb and is called a hog.

104.6 Babel of noises see Genesis 11.1–9.

104.15 every thing will keep after its kind *proverbial* everything will obey its own nature: compare 'cat after kind' (Ramsay, 73; Ray, 198; *ODEP*, 107).

104.21–22 Better an ... belted brands not found in this form as a Gaelic proverb, but similar to 'Better a mother with a sackful of victuals, than a father with a sword at his side' (Macintosh, 43).

104.30 fraud in a Comyne alluding to the Comyn Clan, and more specifically no doubt to John Comyn, 'the Red Comyn', claimant to the Scottish throne, who was killed by Robert Bruce in a church in Dumfries in 1306, supposedly for acting in concert with Edward I of England.

104.37 Ballenkeiroch the name, appropriate for someone with the status of a tacksman (superior tenant of a chief), can be derived from the Gaelic *Baile (n)an Caorach* ('Holding of the sheep').

104.39 Proud Preston Preston, in Lancashire, which was held for a while by the Jacobites during the 1715 rising. The epithet is explained in Daniel Defoe, *A Tour Thro' the Whole Island of Great Britain*, 3 vols (1724–27; *CLA*, 125): 'Here's no Manufacture; the Town is full of Attorneys, Proctors, and Notaries ... The People are gay here, though not perhaps the richer for that; but it has by that obtained the Name of *Proud Preston*' (3.221). Compare James Ray: 'It is vulgarly called *Proud Preston*, on Account of its being a Place of the best Fashion' (*A Compleat History of the Rebellion* (York, 1749; *CLA*, 89), 142). Another explanation is that the name originates from the town's badge carrying the letters PP, standing for *Princeps Pacis* (Prince of Peace), this being reinvented after the Reformation as Proud Preston: see *Dictionary of Lancashire Dialect, Tradition and Folklore*, ed. Alan G. Crosby (Otley, 2000).

105.8–9 Where is the song ... find it? proverbial: compare 'Where was the music, that the harpers could not find it' (Macintosh, 22).

105.9 Mac-Murrough, the family bhairdh the Mac-Murroch (more properly MacMhuirich) family represented the premier bardic dynasty in the Highlands, having served the MacDonalds of the Isles and then their successors for nearly 600 years. In the early 18th century they served in South Uist as bards to the MacDonalds of Clanranald. Though they could seek patronage where they wished, it is unlikely that Fergus or his family would have secured a MacMhuirich as their bard.

105.33–34 nan Fonn (i. e. of the songs) Scott's translation is roughly correct, though 'of the tunes' would be closer to the original Gaelic meaning, and *nam* would be more correct than *nan*.

106.25 Flora Mac-Ivor for possible origins of the character, see Historical Note, 389.

106.37–38 woman's head ... before wedlock see Burt, 2.194: 'The ordinary Girls wear nothing upon their Heads until they are married or have a Child'. The custom is also noted in Macintosh: 'Young women in the Highlands never used to wear linen upon their heads till after they were married, or had connection with men' (15n.).

107.1 Viola and Sebastian brother and sister in *Twelfth Night*, whose likeness is noted at their reunification near the end of the play: 'An apple cleft in two is not more twin/ Than these two creatures' (5.1.215–16). See also following note.

107.2–3 Mrs Henry Siddons and her brother Harriet Siddons (1783–1844) and William Henry Murray (1790–1852). Harriet, an established actress of Shakespearean parts at Covent Garden and Drury Lane, was married to Henry Siddons, the manager of the Theatre Royal Edinburgh from 1809–1815. Her brother was also closely associated with the Edinburgh stage, first appearing there on 20 November 1809. In a letter to Joanna Baillie of 10 January 1813, Scott describes having watched the pair playing Viola and Sebastian (see previous note): 'The night before we left Edinbr. I saw Twelfth Night acted very well indeed. [Daniel] Terry was the very Malvolio of Shakespeare and Mrs. Henry Siddons and her brother Murray from their good playing as well as their extreme likeness and also (which is always natural and pleasing) from the circumstance of their real relation to each other were most interesting in the characters of Viola and Sebastian' (*Letters*, 3.223–24). James C. Corson observes that Scott must have attended the performance on 2 January 1813: *Notes and Index to Sir Herbert Grierson's Edition of the Letters of Sir Walter Scott* (Oxford, 1979), 92, note to 223 (f).

107.13–14 whose voice . . . silver sound John Dryden, 'Palamon and Arcite', 3.84–85: in *Works*, ed. Scott (1808), 11.294. Emetrius is the King of Inde from the source 'The Knight's Tale' by Chaucer.

107.15–16 an excellent thing in woman *King Lear*, 5.3.272–73.

107.30 Chevalier St George French courtesy title for James VIII and III, 'the Old Pretender'.

108.6 his princess Maria Clementina Sobieska (1702–35), granddaughter of John III, King of Poland; she married James VIII and III in 1719, and was the mother of Charles Edward Stuart.

108.41 Princess Sobieski see previous note.

109.8–9 fairest apple . . . highest bough *proverbial* 'The fairest apple is on the highest bough' (Macintosh, 8).

109.11 Parnassus the Muses in Classical mythology were said to inhabit the Greek mountain of Parnassus.

109.11 Bard's croft later echoed in Scott's *The Tale of Old Mortality* (1816), where Niel Blane, as town piper, possesses the Piper's Croft, 'a field of about an acre in extent' (EEWN 4b, 26.21).

109.28 Lindor and Cloris fanciful pastoral names, not discovered as a pairing, though echoing Goethe's 'alle Lindors und Leanders im Busen' in *Wilhelm Meisters Lehrjahre* (1794). See also note to 117.39–40.

109.29 Louis le Grand Louis XIV, King of France 1643–1715.

110.25 cour plénière *French* full court. The term was especially used in relation to the French monarchy, and represents here one of several such indications of Fergus's foreign upbringing.

110.26–27 When the hand . . . utterance not identified as a Gaelic proverb, though the sentiment is characteristic.

110.37 blow for blow, as Conan said to the devil *proverbial* 'Conan never got a stroke but he returned a stroke' (Macintosh, 20). Conan, frequently found in Gaelic tales and proverbs, was noted for being rash and headstrong. A footnote in Macintosh elucidates the present proverb: 'Conan was under a vow not to receive a blow from any without returning the compliment, which obliged him to fight the devils, i.e. to give them as good as they brought, or stroke about' (20n.).

111.13–14 deep and general sensation Flora appears to be prophesying James Macpherson's publication of the 'Ossian' poems, commencing with *Fragments of Ancient Poetry* (1760), which created a sensation all over Europe.

111.41 Mavourneen Celtic expression, meaning 'my darling' (in Irish *Mo mhúirnín*, and in Gaelic *Mo mhùirnean*). It features in line 40 (the last) of Thomas Campbell's 'The Exile of Erin' (written 1800): 'Erin mavournin—Erin go bragh!' ('Ireland my darling—Ireland for ever!)'. In a letter to Lady Louisa Stuart, 6 July 1827, Scott recalled Alexander Stewart of Invernahyle's saying: '"Troth Gurdie mavourneen" (Walter my darling)': see *Letters*, 10.238.

112.2 Dragoman normally meaning an interpreter or guide where Arabic, Persian, or Turkish are spoken. The term was later used by Margaret Clephane in a letter of 11 September 1814, asking of Scott 'why the Author did not allow me to be his Gaelic dragoman?' (MS 3885, f. 180).

113.3 rustic bridge among a number of suggested origins for this bridge, that of the Bridge of Bracklinn, near Callander, on the fringe of the Trossachs, is most commonly mentioned. Scott refers to it in a note to *The Lady of the Lake* (1810): 'There is a beautiful cascade made at a place called the Bridge of Bracklinn, by a mountain stream called the Keltie, about a mile from the village of Callander, in Menteith' (see *Poetical Works*, 8.82n.). Accounts of the bridge itself, emphasising the location's spectacular qualities, can be found in Alexander Campbell's *A Journey from Edinburgh through Parts of North Britain*, 2 vols (London, 1802; *CLA*, 14), 1.102–03, and Patrick Graham's *Sketches Descriptive of Picturesque Scenery on the Southern Confines of Perthshire* (Edinburgh, 1806; see *CLA*, 17), 4–5. As Campbell correctly notes, however, the 'giddy height' for those looking down from the bridge is actually about fifty feet.

113.31–35 natural basin . . . second fall Scott in a Magnum note (1.24) later claimed that his description of the waterfall was 'taken from that of Ledeard, at the farm so called on the northern side of Lochard'. In the process he was perhaps acknowledging his indebtedness to the account in Patrick Graham's *Sketches* (see previous note): 'The stream, which is considerable, falls in one sheet, over a height of 10 or 12 feet, into a beautiful bason, formed of the solid rock; and so transparent, that, at the depth of ten feet, the smallest pebble may be seen: From this bason, dashing over a ledge of rock, it precipitates itself again, over an irregular slope of more than 50 feet, finely skirted with wood' (56). The actual location, on the west shore of Loch Ard just past the farm of Ledard, is now difficult to access and is somewhat less spectacular than in Graham's account, the main feature being a waterfall of about 8 feet falling into a pool. Another possible influence is the Deil's Caldron waterfall, at Comrie, which Scott saw in 1796 (*Letters*, 1.46).

114.3–4 landscapes of Claude Claude Lorraine (1600–82), French painter working in Italy, noted for his Classical pastorals and incandescent use of light. At the suggestion of J. B. S. Morritt, who argued the inferior nature of Claude's figures, Scott authorised the substitution of [Nicolas] Poussin for Claude with the 3rd edn of *Waverley*, thereby arguably losing the potency of the original allusion, with its suggestion of an alluringly 'ideal' landscape.

114.5 small Scottish harp Scott is probably drawing here on John Gunn's *An Historical Enquiry respecting the Performance on the Harp in the Highlands of Scotland* (Edinburgh, 1807), prepared for the Highland Society of Scotland, and published by Archibald Constable and Co., with James Ballantyne being the printer. Gunn describes and provides illustrations of two small harps, 'The Caledonian Harp' and the 'Queen Mary's Harp', both found in the possession of the Robertsons of Lude in Perthshire.

114.6 Rory Dall Roderick Morison (*Ruaidhri MacMhuirich*) (*c.* 1656–*c.* 1714), bard and harper to the Chief of MacLeod at Dunvegan, Skye, who was blind (Gaelic *dall*). He is described in Gunn's *Historical Enquiry* (see previous note) as 'the last person in this country who possessed the talents of Bard and Harper, of Poet and Composer of Music, in an eminent degree'

(99). See also *The Blind Harper: The Songs of Roderick Morison and his Music*, ed. William Matheson (Edinburgh, 1970).

114.16–17 Boiardo or Ariosto Matteo Boiardo (*c.* 1441–94), author of *Orlando innamorato*; and Ludovico Ariosto (1474–1533), author of *Orlando furioso*. For Scott's early reading of the same, see *Scott on Himself*, ed. David Hewitt (Edinburgh, 1981), 33, 267 (n. 78).

115.15 following verses Flora's long Highland song is marked by Scott as 'Original' in MS 743 (f. 34). James C. Corson, however, is convinced that these verses are dependent on a translation of a Gaelic song 'Agus O Mhòrag', which was sent by Margaret Clephane to Scott (at his prompting) in a letter of 9 November 1813: see *Notes and Index to Sir Herbert Grierson's Edition of the Letters of Sir Walter Scott* (Oxford, 1979), 96, note to 285 (b). This translation was later published in Clephane's *Irene, A Poem . . . Miscellaneous Poems* (London, 1833), 170–71, where it is dated November 1813. On the other hand parallels can be seen with other materials sent to Scott by the Clephane family, one of which by April 1809 he had translated in verse as 'War-Song of the Macleans' (see *Letters*, 2.190). More generally, there are affinities with a number of surviving Gaelic songs relating to the 1715 and 1745 risings. See, for example, the songs titled 'Oran nam Fineachan' / 'The Song of the Clans' in *An Lasair: Anthology of 18th Century Scottish Gaelic Verse*, ed. Ronald Black (Edinburgh, 2001), 38–47; and *Highland Songs of the Forty-Five*, ed. John Lorne Campbell (Edinburgh, 1984), 72–85.

115.31–32 Glenaladale's peaks . . . Glenfinnan after his landing in Moidart, Prince Charles spent the night of 18 August at Glenaladale, half-way along Loch Shiel, before proceeding next day to the head of the loch at Glenfinnan, where the royal standard was raised (Blaikie, 7–8). These markers might seem to indicate that the earliest stages of the rising are already proceeding.

115.33 high-minded Moray evidently William Murray, Marquess of Tullibardine (1689–1746), one of the 'seven men of Moidart', who landed in Scotland with Prince Charles. He was titular Duke of Atholl, having been 'succeeded' by his brother James ('the Whig Duke'), with Lord George Murray (the most eminent Jacobite military leader of the campaign) being younger brother to both. At Glenfinnan (see previous note) he unfurled the royal standard on 19 August 1745, and read James VIII's manifesto declaring a regency in favour of Prince Charles.

115.36 Like the sun's . . . is nigh! this line (and the context of the raising of a standard) closely matches Scott's song 'The Return to Ulster', prepared by him in November 1811 (see *Letters*, 3.18, 24) and first published in *A Select Collection of Original Irish Airs*, ed. George Thomson, Vol. 1 [1814]: 'And the standard of Fion flash'd fierce from on high,/ Like a burst of the sun when the tempest is nigh' (p. 1; lines 19–20). Scott in a note there comments: 'In Irish ancient poetry, the standard of Fion, or Fingal, is called the *Sun-burst*, an epithet feebly rendered by the *Sun-beam* of [James] Macpherson.' For 'Fion, or Fingal', the hero of James Macpherson's 'Ossian' poems, see note to 117.9.

115.41 Kings who in Islay Islay is an island of the Inner Hebrides, off the coast of Argyllshire. The ancient Lords of the Isles carried the title 'of Islay'.

115.42 Clan Ranald, Glengary, and Sleat three branches of the Mac-Donald/MacDonnell clan, all of whom claimed descent from the Lords of the Isles. The MacDonalds of Clanranald, commanded by Colonel Ranald Mac-Donald, Younger of Clanranald, were the first body to rally to Prince Charles, and were prominent throughout the Rising. The MacDonnells of Glengarry, whose clan leader John MacDonnell failed to come out, joined the Prince's forces shortly after Glenfinnan (see note to 115.31–32), initially under the command of his second son, Angus MacDonnell, participating then in all the main engagements of the campaign. Sir Alexander MacDonald of Sleat, one of two main chiefs on Skye, refused to join the Rising, and the MacDonalds of Sleat later aided the government forces.

116.1   undaunted Lochiel   Donald Cameron of Lochiel (*c.* 1700–48), who (in spite of personal reservations) joined Prince Charles with 800 of his clansmen at Glenfinnan, effectively making an armed rising possible, and supported him throughout the campaign, accompanying him into exile after its failure. His grandfather, Sir Ewen [Evan] Dubh (1629–1719), a notable Highland chief and Stuart supporter, had fought at the battle of Killiecrankie in 1689; while his father, John, was in exile as a result of having participated in the 1715 Jacobite rising.

116.3   Rough Keppoch   Alexander MacDonnell of Keppoch, who rallied to Prince Charles at the beginning of the Rising. In the earliest stages Keppoch and his cousin, Donald MacDonnell of Tirnadris, with members of the clan, had defeated a detachment of government troops who had set out from Fort Augustus. Keppoch was later killed at Culloden. The epithet 'Rough' possibly derives from his clan's notoriety as cattle thieves, and their reputation as one of the more ill-disciplined units in the Jacobite army.

116.4   Coryarrick   Corrieyairack Pass, 10 km SE of Fort Augustus, reaching a height of 746 m, and through which General Wade's military road ran; also Corrieyairack Hill, to the N of the Pass, which rises to 896 m. See also note to 175.15.

116.5   son of Lord Kenneth   alluding perhaps in particular terms to William Mackenzie, 5th Earl of Seaforth (d. 1740), who played a significant part in the 1715 and 1719 Jacobite risings. In the first instance he attended the hunt which the Earl of Mar used as a cover to plan the Rising (see Historical Note, 377–78). His father Kenneth, the 4th Earl, also had strong Jacobite leanings. Kintail in Wester Ross is the traditional homeland of the Mackenzies. The clan patronymic (more correctly *MacCoinnich*) indicates 'son of Kenneth', while the crest of the Mackenzies of Seaforth shows a stag's antlers, supposedly deriving from an incident in the 13th century in which a Kenneth of Kintail saved the King from a stag charge. In the 1745 rising, however, the 5th Earl's successor, Kenneth, Lord Fortrose, declared for the government, though several other Mackenzies did join the Prince's army. The exile into France of the 5th Earl is the subject of Scott's 'Farewell to Mackenzie' (written 1815?, published 1820), the first stanza of which ends: 'Farewell to Mackenzie, high Chief of Kintail'.

116.7   Clan Gillean   referring to the Maclean clan, whose Gaelic surname is *MacGilleathain*, son of the servant of [St] John. The Macleans fought at the battles of Harlaw (1411), Glenlivet (1594), and (under Viscount Dundee) Killiecrankie in 1689. The name 'Clan Gillian' also features in Scott's 'War-Song of Lachlan, High Chief of Maclean. From the Gaelic' (1815?, published 1820), which can be found with only minor differences as part of a letter of Scott's to Mrs Clephane in 1809: see *Letters*, 2.190. In a footnote to the song in his *Poetical Works* (1820) Scott refers to 'The clan of Maclean, literally the race of Gillian' (12.155n.).

116.9   clan of grey Fingon   the Mackinnon clan, whose Gaelic name is *MacFhionghuin*, and who claimed descent from Fionghuin or Fingon, the 'fair-born' (possibly from *fionn*, 'white, pale').

116.11   Rorri More   probably referring to Sir Ruairidh Mac Leòid [Roderick MacLeod] (*c.* 1562–1626), 15th chief of the MacLeod clan, and called *Mòr* (great), apparently on account of his strength. His successor, Norman MacLeod of Dunvegan, like MacDonald of Sleat (see note to 115.42), failed to join the Rising.

116.13 Mac-Shimei i.e. son of Simon, in Gaelic *Mac Shimidh*: the clan name of the Frasers of Lovat, after the progenitor of the family, Sir Simon Fraser (d. 1332). The badge of clan Fraser of Lovat is the yew. Lord Simon Fraser of Lovat (1667/8–1747), who played a deep and underhand part in the 1745 rising, was beheaded for treason.

116.15 wrong'd Alpin referring to the MacGregor clan, who claimed descent from Griogar, son of Alpin, in the 8th century. After a succession of feuds an edict was issued by James VI and the Privy Council of Scotland banning the use of the name, and the clan leader was hanged in Edinburgh in 1604. The clan's traditional lands were in the Trossachs, between Loch Lomond and Loch Katrine. The MacGregors fought in the Jacobite army, sometimes attached to other bodies, and in 1745 sixty men remained under Gregor MacGregor of Glengyle as a garrison at Doune (see also note to 198.13), while the main force joined the invasion of England.

116.15 murder'd Glencoe referring to the MacDonalds of Glencoe, massacred in 1692.

116.17 sons of brown Dermid the Campbells, also known as Clan Diarmid, after the Celtic hero from whom the clan is allegedly descended. According to legend, Diarmid O'Duibhne died from an injury received as a result of killing a wild boar which had ravaged Kintyre. The Gaelic adjective *donn* (brown-haired) is applied sometimes as a term of endearment as well as of hair-colour. As a whole the Campbells, as Whigs and supporters of the Hanoverians, were unlikely converts to Jacobitism, as the song recognises.

116.18 Callain-More in Gaelic the chief of Clan Campbell is known as *MacCailein Mòr*, meaning 'the great *MacCailein*'. *MacCailein* itself means 'son of Colin', from Sir Colin Campbell of Lochawe, who was killed in 1296.

116.19 Mac-Neil of the Islands Roderick MacNeil of Barra, 39th chief, brother-in-law of the banker Aeneas MacDonald, who had accompanied Prince Charles to Scotland. His father, Roderick Dhu, the 38th chief, had led the MacNeil clan into battle in the 1715 rising. The 39th chief evidently played no active part in the 1745 campaign, though he was arrested in 1746 by troops in search of Prince Charles, and not discharged until 1747.

116.19 Moy of the Lake the chief of the MacKintosh clan, whose original castle stood on an island in Loch Moy, and who now resided at Moy Hall on its banks, 14 km SE of Inverness. Aeneas MacKintosh, the current chief (as a serving officer in the Black Watch) stayed out of the Rising, though his wife Anne played a heroic part, raising two battalions of the clan early in 1746.

116.28–29 Our bootless ... Mac-Gregors see *An Imitation of the Prophecy of Nereus: from Hor. L. I. Od. 15* [Edinburgh, 1715], a broadside lampoon on the Earl of Mar attributed to Thomas Tickell, lines 35–36.

117.9 Fin's referring to Fionn mac Cumhaill, hero of early Celtic history and legend, and the Fingal of James Macpherson's 'Ossian' poems.

117.16 Bran also the name of Fionn's (Fingal's) dog.

117.17–18 jet d'eau at Versailles fountain at Versailles, the French royal palace near Paris, notable for its formal gardens with fountains and statues. Jonathan Swift alludes to 'the great *jet d'eau* at Versailles' in his *Gulliver's Travels* (1726), Part 2, Ch. 5 (*Works*, ed. Scott, 12.155).

117.19–20 Parnassus ... Helicon mountains in Greece, associated in Classical mythology with Apollo and the Muses. The two are found in close proximity in Robert Fergusson, 'The King's Birth-Day in Edinburgh' (1772): 'O *Muse* be kind, and dinna fash us/ To flee awa' beyont Parnassus,/ Nor seek for *Helicon* to wash us,/ That heath'nish spring' (lines 13–16). The fountains of Hippocrene and Aganippe are on the slopes of Mount Helicon.

117.26–29 O Lady ... grass or corn compare Joseph Warton, 'Ode to Fancy' (1746), lines 21–24.

117.31   **Allons, courage**   *French* onward! courage.

117.32–37   **O vous . . . sans sabots**   *French* you who drink a full cup at this happy fountain, where all one can see on the bank are but a few wretched flocks, followed by the village nymphs, who drive them on without shoes. 'This is a parody but of what I cannot now remember' (Scott's note in MS 743, f. 36v).

117.39   **Arcadia**   mountainous region in the central Peloponnese in Greece, developed in pastoral poetry as an ideal region of pastoral contentment, notably in Virgil's *Eclogues* (42–37 BC), where his shepherds are called *Arcades* (*Eclogues*, 7.4, 10.31, and 10.33).

117.39–40   **Coridon and Lindor**   Corydon is the name of a shepherd in Virgil's *Eclogues* (see previous note), 2, 5, and 7; Lindor is not a Classical name, though sometimes found in later pastoral poetry as the name of a nymph (see also note to 109.28). There is a piece addressed 'To Corydon' in the Jacobite poet Alexander Robertson of Struan's *Poems* (1751/52), 107–08; see also note to 219.27–28.

117.41   **la houlette et la chalumeau**   *French* the shepherd's crook and reed pipe (tokens of the ideal pastoral world).

118.3   **ma belle demoiselle**   *French* my pretty young lady.

118.6–8   **Io d'Elicona . . . mi spiacque!**   from *Orlandino* (1526), a burlesque poem on the birth and youth of Roland by Teofilo Folengo (1491–1544), Canto 1, lines 6–8. The Italian has been translated as: 'I quite honestly care nothing for Helicon, for the drinking of water (let him drink who so desires) was always unpleasant for me!': see R. D. S. Jack, *The Italian Influence on Scottish Literature* (Edinburgh, 1972), 218.

118.10   **Drimmindhu**   name of an Irish air, *Druimin Dubh*, the words of which lament the loss of a cow, comparing it to the mythological Irish cow which could never be fully milked. Also used as a political song, in which the cow serves as a metaphor for the exiled Stuart monarch. In Sydney Owenson's *The Wild Irish Girl* (1806), there is a scene involving a peasant and his cow, whom he addresses as Driminduath, this apparently alluding to the song of that name (meaning 'the black white-backed cow'): see ed. Claire Connolly (London, 2000), 22–25, and 281 (n. 51). The loss of a cow is also a common theme in Gaelic verse, and a burlesque elegy is quite possible as a subject, as would be any underlying political connotations.

118.10   **astore**   this expression appears in the first line of 'A Ballad' by Jonathan Swift: 'Patrick astore . . .': *Works*, ed. Scott (1814), 10.564. Harold Williams in his *Poems of Jonathan Swift* (Oxford, 1937) glosses it as meaning literally 'O treasure', the equivalent of darling.

118.11   **Cean-kinné**   *Gaelic ceann-cinnidh* chief, 'head of the kin'. The term is found in Home: 'Each of these districts, called by the natives a country, was the residence of a clan or kindred, who paid implicit obedience to the Cean Cinne or head of the kindred' (8).

118.12–13   **burlesque elegy**   for an Irish equivalent, see note to 118.10. In a Magnum note (1.244n.), Scott refers to a version of this song being 'published . . . under the auspices of the facetious Tom D'Urfey, by the title of "Colley, my Cow"'. Scott might then also have been thinking of Sancho's remark in *Don Quixote*, Part 2 (1615), Ch. 9: 'what is the rout of Roncesvalles to us? it concerns us no more than if he had sung the ballad of *Colly my Cow*' (ed. Lockhart, 5 vols (1822), 3.221).

119.23   **en attendant**   *French* in the meantime.

120.4   **steak-raid . . . collop of the foray**   the custom of exacting 'the *Stike Creich* or *Road Collop*, being a certain part of the booty', from those with stolen cattle passing through another chieftain's territory, is described in Pennant, 1.209.

120.21   la belle passion   *French* fine love.

120.24–25   a kinsman ... his heart   *proverbial* 'A man's kinsman is dear, but his foster brother is a part of his heart' (Macintosh, 21). For the significance of 'foster-brother', see note to 81.8.

121.14   Exchequer   the Court of Exchequer in Scotland, which was retained after the Union of 1707, dealt with the collection of taxes. In England the Exchequer was one of the main old courts of justice, along with Chancery, King's (or Queen's) Bench, and Common Pleas.

121.18   Lindsay of Pitscottie   Robert Lindsay of Pitscottie (*c.* 1532–*c.* 1586), Scottish historian. The quotations that follow are taken, with some minor variations, from an account of a hunting feast prepared by the Earl of Atholl *c.* 1530 for James V in his *History of Scotland, from 21 February, 1436 to March 1565* (Edinburgh, 1728). Scott owned a copy of the 3rd edn (1778; *CLA*, 259), where the account appears at 227–28.

122.2   latter end of the world   the relevant passage from Lindsay of Pitscottie's *History* (see previous note) reads: 'The ambassador of the pope, seeing this great banquet and triumph, which was made in a wilderness, where there was no town near by twenty miles, thought it a great marvel, that such a thing could be in Scotland, considering that it was named, The Arse of the World, by other countries' (3rd edn, 1778, 228).

122.3–4   Taylor the Water Poet's ... braes of Mar   John Taylor (1578–1653), English poet, who worked as a water man on the Thames. For the passage quoted, which occurs in an account of a hunting party in the Highlands at Braemar, see 'The Pennyles Pilgrimage' (1618), in *All the Workes of John Taylor the Water Poet* (London, 1630; *CLA*, 208), 136. The most famous hunting at Braemar, Aberdeenshire, was in late August 1715 before the rising of that year (see Historical Note, 377–78), and the reference here must recall this event.

122.13   at Lude   the incident alluded to is described in the relevant accounts as taking place in Atholl, rather than more specifically in Lude in N Perthshire. Scott here is possibly conflating the main topic of his source (John Gunn), i.e. the two harps discovered in the possession of the Robertsons of Lude (see note to 114.5), and the 'single incident' described in an extensive quotation there (see following note). Atholl and Lude, anciently incorporating the parishes of Blair and Lude, is presently considered as a single hunting area.

122.14   Mr Gunn's Essay on the Caledonian Harp   John Gunn's *An Historical Enquiry respecting the Performance on the Harp in the Highlands of Scotland* (Edinburgh, 1807), reporting on two recently-discovered harps, 'The Caledonian Harp' and the 'Queen Mary's Harp' (see also note to 114.5). The account of a Highland hunt in 1563, which originates from the first-hand account of William Barclay in *De Regno et Regali Potestate* (Paris, 1600), is quoted in translation in Gunn's *Historical Enquiry*, 78–81. Gunn shows an awareness of a previous translation in Pennant, 3.64–65, and is indebted to it, though variants between the texts and two footnote observations in Gunn (80n, 81n–82n) indicate a reference back to the Latin original.

123.11   joys of the shell, as Ossian has it   as found in James Macpherson's *Fingal: An Ancient Epic Poem* (London, 1762; *CLA*, 14). See *The Poems of Ossian and Related Works*, ed. Howard Gaskill (Edinburgh, 1996), *Fingal*, Bk 2, 'the hall of shells is silent' (67), and Macpherson's note: 'The ancient Scots, as well as the present highlanders, drunk in shells; hence it is that we so often meet, in the old poetry, with the *chief of the shells*, and the *halls of the shells*' (426). Compare also *Fingal*, Bk 6: 'But often did they feast in the hall; and send round the joy of the shell' (101).

123.12   Others apart ... retired   John Milton, *Paradise Lost* (1667), 2.557.

123.33   like a leafless grove   echoing John Taylor's description of a hunt in Braemar: 'the Deeare appeare on the hills round about us, (their heads making a shew like a wood)': 'Pennyles Pilgrimage', in *All the Workes* (1630; *CLA*, 208), 136.

123.42–43   fling themselves upon their faces   matching William Barclay's account of the hunt in Atholl in 1563, as translated in Pennant: 'they had nothing for it but to throw themselves flat on the heath, and to allow the dee to pass over them' (3.65). This account, which generally parallels Scott's narrative, is also found in John Gunn's *Historical Enquiry*, 79–81 (see note to 122.14).

124.17   tartan frock   a shift-like garment, distinct from trousers or kilt, still worn in the Highlands early in the 18th century.

124.24   making the deasil   moving sunwise, according to the course of the sun. The custom is described in a note to Scott's 'Abstract of the Eyrbiggia-Saga', in *Illustrations of Northern Antiquities*, ed. Robert Jamieson and Henry Weber (Edinburgh, 1814): 'This is an important circumstance. Whatever revolved with the sun was reckoned a fortunate movement. Thus, the highlanders in making the *deasil*, a sort of benediction which they bestow in walking round the party to be propitiated, always observe the course of the sun. And witches, on the other hand, made their circles, *widdershins*, as the Scottish dialect expresses it, ... in opposition to the course of the orb of light' (506n.; *Prose Works*, 5.397).

124.29   Esculapius   Greek and Roman god of medicine; hence a physician.

124.35   Gaspar-Melchior-Balthazar   names of the biblical three kings or magi who bore gifts on Christ's birth day. They feature alongside *prax* and *max* in a prayer, 'Against the biting of a Mad-Dog', in Reginald Scot, *The Discovery of Witchcraft*, 3rd edn (London, 1665; *CLA*, 123), 137.

125.1–8   Hail to thee ... the ground   see Reginald Scot, *The Discovery of Witchcraft*, 3rd edn (London, 1665; *CLA*, 123), 138.

125.3   Mount Olivet   i.e. the Mount of Olives, the hill to the east of Jerusalem to which Jesus retreated prior to his arrest.

125.21   ceade millia molighiart   *Gaelic Ceud mile mallachd ort.* Scott's probable source for this is found in his edition of Swift's *Works* (1814), 10.564–65, as part of verses headed 'A Ballad', where stanza 4, line 4, reads 'Och ma ceade millia mollighart, on the feeders of swine'; and a footnote glosses this 'Means "*my hundred thousand hearty curses* on the feeders of swine"'. Harold Williams in his edition of *The Poems of Jonathan Swift* (Oxford, 1937), 3.841, glosses the line as: '*Mo chéad mile mallacht ort*, meaning "A hundred thousand curses on thee".' Scott's own translation within the narrative incorrectly has a 'hundred curses' in Ed1.

125.33   birch and hazel grey   see 'The Hunting of the Cheviot' (Child, 162A), stanza 57, line 2.

125.36–37   sturdy Gael ... sedan-chairs   Edinburgh sedan chairs were often carried by Highlanders.

125.37   ten routes   see note to 5.2.

126.41–42   When the wind ... falls soft   compare Macintosh: 'When the wind is still, the shower is blunt' (4).

127.7   Tomanrait   possibly matching the Gaelic *Tom an Raith* ('Hill of the Brake [i.e. bracken]'), in which case a territorial designation.

127.18–19   What sent ... full well   *proverbial* 'The thing that sent the messengers to hell:/ Was asking what they knew full well' (Macintosh, 1).

127.22–23   as she was na tat weel   as he was not that well. Gender confusion when moving from Gaelic to English or Scots is a literary device for suggesting Highland speech and is found as early as Richard Holland's *The Buke of the Howlat* (*c.* 1450).

127.34–35   Now he ... a glen   see Lady Wardlaw, 'Hardyknute' (1719), stanza 15, lines 1–2.

127.36 **with his myrmidons** alluding to the warlike tribe led to the Trojan War by Achilles, noted for their obedience and ruthlessness. A similar comparison is made by Captain John Maclean in his contemporary account of the 1745 Jacobite campaign, which describes Prince Charles travelling 'all on foot' at the head of 'his Mirmidons the Highland Clans': see *Witness to Rebellion*, ed. Iain Gordon Brown and Hugh Cheape (East Linton, 1996), 16, 43.

127.42 **Open your gates** the following passage (with its proper names) reflects the words of the countryman accompanying the deluded Don Quixote on his return from his first adventure: *Don Quixote*, Part 1 (1605), Bk 1, Ch. 5 (ed. Lockhart, 5 vols (1822), 1.59).

128.20 **Caledonian Mercury** founded in 1720. In fact two newspapers were published in Edinburgh in 1745, the other being *The Edinburgh Evening Courant* (from 1718); and also one in Glasgow, the *Glasgow Journal* (from 1741). During the 1745–46 rising the *Caledonian Mercury* published Charles Edward's public documents and despatches, and to some extent assumed a pro-Jacobite stance. There is a set of issues of the *Caledonian Mercury* from 23 September 1745 to 30 April 1747 in the Abbotsford Library (*CLA*, 100).

129.5 **post paper** referring to a size of writing paper, normally about 48×39 cm.

129.11 **wet an Englishman** echoing the proverb 'A Scots Mist will weet an Englishman to the Skin' (Ramsay, 68; see also Ray, 202; *ODEP*, 705).

129.17 **addenda, delenda, et corrigenda** *Latin* additions, deletions, and corrections.

129.19 **sop in the pan** a tit-bit, dainty morsel; a piece of bread soaked in dripping.

129.23 **Little Britain** see note to 30.28.

129.36 **two parties** referring to factions within the dominant Whig party: see Historical Note, 368.

130.9 **holiday texture** i.e. fine or well-turned materials.

130.17 **Great Man** the use of initial capitals is reminiscent of the use of the phrase by Henry Fielding and other satirists of the period as an ironical epithet for Sir Robert Walpole (1676–1745). This would also tally with earlier mention of Richard Waverley being a supporter of the Excise Bill (see note to 7.36). Walpole left office in 1742, but continued (as Earl of Orford) to advise his successors and the King until his death in March 1745. See also note to 21.36 and Historical Note, 367–68.

130.32 **Aristides** Aristides (*c.* 530 BC–*c.* 467 BC), Athenian statesman, called 'the Just'; he was ostracised for a time by the Athenians.

131.32 **roundhead parliament** the Parliament during the English Civil War and early Commonwealth period; also known as the Long Parliament, it lasted in all thirteen years, before being dissolved by Oliver Cromwell in 1653.

133.40 **this same Richard ... all this** see *Richard III*, 4.4.287.

134.38 **Huguenot** the Huguenots were French Calvinists of the 16th–18th centuries, noted for their austere lifestyle. Since Colonel Gardiner is likely to have returned as a member of the Presbyterian Church of Scotland after his celebrated religious 'conversion', the term reflects as much on the speaker (the French-educated Fergus) as the subject. But see also note to 135.34.

135.25–27 **Had Richard ... a son** John Dryden, 'The Character of a Good Parson' (1699), lines 112–14: in *Works*, ed. Scott (1808), 11.398. It is possible that Scott was confusing this passage with somewhat similar lines in *3 Henry VI*, 1.1.143–46. Shakespeare is a more likely candidate for Waverley's 'favourite poet'.

135.34 **Calvinistical** i.e. holding the views of John Calvin (1509–64), the Reformation theologian. The term refers particularly to his doctrines of grace and predestination, both of which informed the theology of the Church of Scotland, but was also often applied loosely and pejoratively to describe those considered to hold narrow moral and religious views. See also note to 134.38.

136.32   white bridal favours   a bridal or bride's favour is a ribbon, or cockade, worn at a wedding ceremony. In this case, however, Flora and her attendants seem to be preparing white Jacobite insignia in anticipation of the Rising.

136.38   as Beatrice says   in *Much Ado About Nothing*, 4.1.265.

137.10–11   Because you ... an enemy   *1 Henry IV*, 4.3.36–37.

138.6   Elector of Hanover   George II held the title of Elector of Hanover as well as that of King of Great Britain and Ireland from his accession in 1727. Here Fergus as a Jacobite characteristically denies him the second of these titles.

138.24–25   small still voice   see 1 Kings 19.12.

139.15   a la mort   mortally sick, dispirited, an anglicised French expression, found as *alamort* (Richardson) and *all amort* (Keats).

139.21   evil eye   faculty, superstitiously ascribed to certain individuals, of inflicting injury by a look. This was not a specifically Highland belief: compare the French 'mauvais oeil'.

139.31   en mousquetaire   *French* in a soldier's way, in a cavalier fashion.

140.7   Laissez faire à Don Antoine   *French* let Don Antoine have his way! (said in the sense of 'I'll take care of it'). Scott's probable source is John Dryden's play *Limberham* (1678), 5.1: 'I warrant you: *laissez faire a Marc Antoine*': in *Works*, ed. Scott (1808), 6.97.

140.8   compliment of Conan   see note to 110.37.

140.10–11   will not slip ... a-foot   compare *1 Henry IV*, 1.3.278 ('Before the game is afoot thou still let'st slip'); a hunting metaphor implying that Fergus will not break into rebellion until circumstances are right.

140.22–23   honest gentlemen   *honest* was a favourite catchword of the Jacobites, indicating loyalty to the cause.

140.26   Out, hyperbolical fiend!   *Twelfth Night*, 4.2.25.

140.31   sober earnest   serious intention, as distinct from the more familiar sense of 'in all seriousness' at line 35. For the latter usage, compare Joanna Baillie's *Count Basil* (1798), 4.1 ('Indeed, my Lord, he speaks in sober earnest').

141.2   cela va sans dire   *French* that goes without saying.

141.17   Captain Wogan   Edward Wogan (*c.* 1626–54), born to an old English family, and a member of Cromwell's New Model Army when founded in 1645. He later joined the Royalist cause, took his men to Scotland in 1648 to join forces assembling for an invasion of England, and daringly returned there again with about 100 volunteers in 1653–54, to join the last-ditch resistance by forces in the Highlands raised by William Cunningham, 9th Earl of Glencairn (1610–64). He was wounded in a skirmish, the wound proving mortal, and buried on 10 February 1654 in Kenmore church, near Aberfeldy, being one of the last royalists to lose his life in the Civil War. See also note to 155.41.

141.19   Middleton   John Middleton, later Earl of Middleton (*c.*1608–74), royalist army officer; who took command of the forces raised by Glencairn (see previous note) in late February 1654.

141.25   Alerte à la muraille   *French* up! and storm the rampart.

141.26   Cupid   god of love in Roman mythology.

141.38   deep, and dangerous   compare *1 Henry IV*, 1.3.190 ('I'll read you matter deep and dangerous').

146.5   voice of Selma   see 'The Songs of Selma', from James Macpher-

son's *Fingal* (1762), in *The Poems of Ossian and Related Works*, ed. Howard
Gaskill (Edinburgh, 1996), 166–70. Selma in the Ossianic poems is a place,
possibly originating from the Gaelic *sealladh* ('sight, view') and *math* ('good').
Scott himself evidently considered it a fabrication, commenting in his review
of the Report of the Highland Society on *Ossian* that 'No Highlander ever
heard of *Selma* except through Macpherson': *Edinburgh Review*, 6 (July 1805),
460n. One possibility is that Scott originally wrote or meant to write 'Colma',
the opening female voice within 'The Songs of Selma' ('Hear the voice of
Colma, when she sat alone on the hill!' (Gaskill, 166)).

146.14–17   My heart's . . . wherever I go   from Robert Burns's song,
'My heart's in the Highlands', first published in *SMM*, Vol. 3 (1790), no. 259
(see also Kinsley, no. 301). In his edition of *Notes on Scottish Song By Robert
Burns* (1908), 46, J. C. Dick quotes Burns as commenting: 'The first half-
stanza of this song [matching the lines given by Scott] is old; the rest is mine'.
This corresponds with the Magnum note: 'These lines form the burden of an
old song to which Burns wrote additional verses' (1.296n.).

146.22–25   There's nought . . . comes hame   not identified. In the Magnum (1.297n.) Scott notes that the 'lines are also ancient, and I believe to the
tune of We'll never have peace till Jamie comes hame; to which Burns likewise
wrote some verses'. In fact, Burns's words to this tune begin 'By yon castle
wa' at the close of the day', though his two verses end with 'There'll never be
peace till Jamie comes hame', which Burns acknowledged as the title of the
original 'Jacobite Air' (see Kinsley, no. 326 and note). A correspondent (Thos.
Ratcliffe) in *Notes and Queries*, 11th series, 10 (1914), quotes lines similar to
those in *Waverley*, stating that 'A Scotch Lady used to sing this to quaint
music years ago' (409).

146.30   Scotch foursome reel   or Highland reel, in which groups of four
dancers move together in a pattern, sometimes performing solo steps facing
one another.

146.32   Seid suas   *Gaelic séid suas*, blow up. Lamont cites Alexander Campbell, *The Grampians Desolate* (Edinburgh, 1804; *CLA*, 167), who writes, 'The
imperative *"seid suas"*, (blow up) is addressed to the musical performer, who
is frequently a *bag-piper*' (268).

146.38   Highland fling   a solo dance, danced on the spot and with upheld
arms; this may form part of a foursome reel (see note to 146.30).

146.39   employed in setting   referring to a particular step in Highland
dancing, in which dancers face each other, one moving to the left and the
other to the right and then back again.

147.2   Harlequin in a pantomime   Harlequin was a mime figure, originating from the Italian *commedia dell'arte*, a dramatic entertainment involving
masks, and also central in a species of English pantomime that flourished in
the early decades of the 19th century. According to David Mayer III, 'With
quick quasi-balletic turns, leaps, and gymnastic tricks he eluded Pantaloon
and Clown, escaping each time by a hairbreadth': *Harlequin in His Element:
The English Pantomime 1806–1836* (Cambridge, Mass., 1969), 38.

148.11   the Duchran   Lamont cites Scott's note in *Memoirs of the Insurrection in Scotland in 1715*, by John, Master of Sinclair (Edinburgh, 1858): 'The
Duchroun is in the Forest of Glenartney. It is well known to sportsmen as
famous for moor game, *me teste*' (135n.). Dalchruin is a settlement in Glen
Artney, Perth and Kinross, on the Water of Ruchill, 18 km WSW of Crieff.

149.9–11   James the Second . . . forfeited his own   referring to James
VII and II's flight to France late in 1688, after the landing of William III. The
question is whether James's behaviour, which resulted in his losing the throne,
should imply the disinheritance of his successors. See also Historical Note,
367.

150.1 the lion's mouth biblical and proverbial: see Psalm 22.21; 2 Timothy 4.17; and *ODEP*, 467.

150.6–7 Lord M——, General G—— the names on this occasion are not supplied in the ISet and Magnum. It is possible that General Joshua Guest is meant in the second case: see also note to 256.1 below.

150.10 mists and the crows Scott's Magnum note (1.304n.) refers to a Highland rhyme, relating to the Earl of Glencairn's campaign against Cromwell's forces in 1653, including the line 'We'll bide a while among ta crows'; but no such verse in Gaelic or Highland English has been discovered.

150.15 Oggam character ... Punic hieroglyphic Oggam or Ogham is an ancient British and Irish writing system, in which 25 letters are formed of straight lines. It was the view of Charles Vallancey (*c.* 1726–1812), antiquary and military surveyor, who is mentioned in Scott's Magnum note (1.304n.), that ancient Irish civilisation had an Eastern origin, a view expounded in a series of publications, including *An Essay on the Antiquity of the Irish Language: being a collation of Irish with the Punic Language* (1772). Punic denotes Carthaginian.

150.16–17 un petit pendement bien joli *French* a pretty little hanging. See Molière, *Monsieur de Pourceaugnac*, 3.3 ('un petit pendement pien choly'), where the spelling reflects the pronunciation of the Swiss speaker. Scott uses the expression in a letter probably of late 1812 to James Ballantyne (see *Letters*, 3.203).

150.18 west-country whigs Presbyterians from SW Scotland. Lanarkshire, Ayrshire, and Galloway had been noted for their general resistance to the imposition of episcopacy under Charles II (reigned 1660–85) which culminated in the rising of 1679, and the battle of Bothwell Brig.

150.21 prelatist abjured a *prelatist* is a potentially derogatory term used of those who believe that the Church should be governed by bishops; one who is *abjured* has renounced an oath, here Edward's oath of loyalty to George II.

150.23 cast down Psalm 42.5, 6. The language of this sentence is biblically inflected in mimicry of the speech habits of Scottish Presbyterians in the 17th and 18th centuries.

150.24 fear of the Lord common biblical phrase.

150.28 Wilful will do't proverbial: a form of 'a wilful man will have his way' (*ODEP*, 890).

151.15–16 pass of Bally-Brough see note to 75.10.

151.27–28 coast of Suffolk the SE coast of Britain was considered a strong alternative to Kent and Sussex for an invasion from France at the time of the 1745 rising, with Orford harbour in Suffolk being identified as especially suitable: see Duffy, 371.

151.37 Clelias and Mandanes female characters in *Clélie* (1654–60) and *Artamène ou le Grand Cyrus* (1649–53; see *CLA*, 101, 102), two romances by Madeleine de Scudéry.

152.19 remembered with advantage compare *Henry V*, 4.3.50 ('But he'll remember, with advantages').

152.32 deil burst tem may the devil destroy them; the spelling of *tem* indicates pronunciation of Scots by a Highlander.

153.2 Jabesh Rentowel Jabesh was the father of a king who reigned briefly in Israel; Rentowel is a form of the surname Rintoul, and may be intended to pun on 'owl', traditionally a bird of ill-omen with a harsh voice.

153.3 Goukthrapple evidently a burlesque name, from *gouk*, 'fool', and *thrapple*, 'throat'.

153.4 mickle Sunday term used to describe the Sunday on which the half-yearly Communion was observed in the Presbyterian churches; the dates were set by the kirk session of each parish.

153.4–5 government Sunday fast days were appointed by the authorities in response to national crises; it was assumed that any calamity was an act of God who was punishing the people for their sins.

153.6 Seven-branched Golden Candlestick in Revelation 1.12–20 seven golden candlesticks represent the seven Churches of New Testament times. Its appearance here as the sign of an inn with a Presbyterian landlord also suggests that Exodus 25.31–40 may be apposite, with its instructions for the candlestick to adorn the tabernacle. For a suggestion that this particular inn matches one at Crieff, see David Stewart, *Sketches of the Character, Manners, and Present State of the Highlanders of Scotland*, 2 vols (Edinburgh, 1822), 1.104n.

153.14 Hawick Gill 'a measure of ale or spirits equivalent to half an Imperial pint' (*SND*), named after the town in the Scottish Borders. It features in the traditional song 'Andro and his Cutty Gun' ('And well she loo'd a Hawick gill').

153.14 Ebenezer Cruickshanks evidently a burlesque name, combining the biblical (for Ebenezer, see 1 Samuel 7.12) and vernacular (crook legs).

153.28–29 covenants burnt ... buried referring especially to the National Covenant of 1638 and the Solemn League and Covenant of 1643. The principal objective of the National Covenant was to eradicate episcopacy and to establish Presbyterian church government in Scotland. The Covenant was repudiated by Charles II after the Restoration of the monarchy in 1660, and, in defiance of the hopes of the more extreme Presbyterians, was not reconfirmed by the Scottish Parliament after the Revolution of 1688–89. Cruickshanks implies that the Jacobite rising is a punishment on the people for not having renewed the Covenant.

153.32 what for gangs he not forward why does he not proceed further.

153.38 taxing of reckonings i.e. questioning of the calculation of the bill or account.

154.5 Salique law alluding to the rule of the Salian Franks which excluded females from succession to land, and, by implication, from positions of authority.

154.15 gill stoup drinking-vessel holding a gill of spirits (¼ of a standard pint, *c.* ⅛ of a litre).

154.22 but just Aberdeen-a-way only from the Aberdeen area.

154.33 cares na for that a boddle doesn't care at all about that. A *boddle* was a Scots coin of negligible value.

155.16 teil ane ta wiser *literally* devil one the wiser, i.e. no one at all the wiser. The spelling of *teil* and *ta* indicate pronunciation of Scots/English by a Gaelic-speaking Highlander.

155.18 Her ain sell he himself. In the literary representation of Gaelic English speakers frequently refer to themselves (as well as external objects) in the third person; gender confusion was also a common literary device for suggesting Highland speech.

155.19 skene-occle *Gaelic sgian-achlais*, knife of arm-pit. Scott is possibly indebted to Burt for the spelling, though there the correct end 's' is preserved for the singular: 'some of them carry a Sort of Knife, which they call a *Skeen-ocles*, from its being conceal'd in the Sleeve near the Arm-pit' (2.222).

155.41 Clarendon Edward Hyde, Earl of Clarendon (1609–74), author of *The History of the Rebellion and Civil Wars in England*, 3 vols (Oxford, 1702–04; *CLA*, 24). His account of Wogan's expedition, which Scott appears to follow, is found in Vol. 3 (1704), 395–97.

155.43–156.1 Earl of Glencairn and General Middleton see notes to 141.17 and 141.19.

156.25 oak trees oak trees had a specific Jacobite implication as Charles

II took refuge in an oak tree to escape his pursuers after the battle of Worcester in 1651 in which Cromwell defeated a Scottish army. Oak leaves were, consequentially, used as a Jacobite symbol.

156.26   White's   a leading club at 37–38 St James's Street, London, with origins in White's Chocolate House which opened in 1693. In 1736 White's began to operate as a private club rather than a public chocolate house, and early members included the Duke of Devonshire and the Earl of Chesterfield, while in the Regency period it was a main base for Beau Brummel. By 1814 the membership was 500, and gaming and placing of bets were leading activities.

156.33–157.22   Emblem of England ... Wogan's tomb   evidently Scott's own composition. Apart from the present title and a deleted draft of the first two lines these verses are absent from the MS.

157.7   Albyn's   poetical name for Scotland, particularly the Highlands.

157.21   bound with oak   Romans who had saved the life of a comrade in battle were awarded what was called the 'civic crown', which was a wreath made of oak-leaves; see also note to 156.25.

158.21   double portion   2 Kings 2.9.

158.22   pharisaical leaven   see Matthew 16.6.

158.35   Loss of a Horse's Shoe   echoing the proverbial rhyme, including the line 'For want of a shoe the horse is lost': see Ray, 22; *ODEP*, 865.

159.20–21   Cairnvreckan   for possible prototypes, see Historical Note, 382–83.

159.37   Vulcan   Roman fire-god, god associated with the smithy.

159.39   John Micklewrath   the surname in Scots suggests 'much wrath'.

160.16–17   Lochiel, Clanronald, Glengary   for the clan leaders involved, see notes to 115.42 and 116.1.

160.18–19   familiar ... household words   see *Henry V*, 4.3.52 ('Familiar in his mouth as household words').

160.30–32   Charlie is my darling ... Chevalier   chorus of the song published in *SMM*, Vol. 5 (1796), no. 428: lyric by Robert Burns, probably from a traditional street ballad (see Kinsley, no. 562 and note). The Burns text pre-dates all evidence of the version by Caroline Oliphant, Lady Nairne (1766–1845), as found in *Life and Songs of the Baroness Nairne*, ed. Charles Rogers (London, 1869), 124, though Scott may have known of the latter through mutual personal acquaintances in Edinburgh.

160.35–37   Little wot ... coming   from 'The Chevalier's Muster Roll', probably first written at the time of the Jacobite rising of 1715. Versions appear in Herd, 1.117–18, and *SMM*, Vol. 6 (1803), no. 572.

160.38   Vulcan ... Venus   Vulcan (see note to 159.37) was cuckolded by his wife Venus, the goddess of love.

160.39   exulting Bacchanal   referring to the frenzy of the female priestesses at the festivals of Bacchus, the Roman god of wine.

160.42–43   wine of wrath ... cup of indignation   see Revelation 14.10.

161.1–3   popery and prelacy ... errors of the church   representing a sequence of forms of church government and religious belief inimical to Micklewrath's own strict Presbyterianism. For a definition of some of these individual terms, see Glossary.

161.6–7   yere synods and yere presbyteries   referring to governing bodies in the structure of the Presbyterian church in Scotland. Presbyteries are courts superior to kirk sessions. Until they were discontinued at the end of 1992 synods were courts ranking between presbyteries and the supreme court, the General Assembly.

161.7   buttock-mail ... stool o' repentance   those found guilty of fornication by the Church of Scotland were required either to sit on the cuttystool, the three-legged stool of repentance, in front of the congregation on three or more Sundays, or to pay a fine (i.e. 'buttock-mail').

161.20–21   I'se warrant   I'll bet, I'll be bound.

161.21–22   gallant Gordon   the powerful Gordon clan, with lands in and near Aberdeenshire, nicknamed the 'gey Gordons', with *gey* being translatable as 'gallant' or 'spirited'.

161.40–41   Secretary Murray   John Murray of Broughton (1714/15?–77), Secretary to Prince Charles through the greater part of the 1745–46 rising. His excursions, sometimes incognito, in the Prince's service, make his mention apposite in this context. For instance, the *Genuine Memoirs of John Murray, Esq.* (London, 1747; *CLA*, 91) recounts how he travelled some 80 miles, prior to the battle of Prestonpans, with a letter from the Prince to 'a certain Nobleman', 'disguis'd . . . with a black Periwig . . . muffled up in his Cloak', and taking with him 'only one Servant whom he had lately hired in the *Highlands*' (26).

161.41   Lord Lewis Gordon   (*c.* 1725–54), joined the Jacobite rising in October 1745, became a member of the Prince's council, and raised the Aberdeen and Aboyne battalions in the Jacobite army. He is the subject of the Jacobite song 'Lewis Gordon', attributed to Fr. Alexander Geddes (1737–1802), with the opening line 'Oh! send Lewis Gordon hame'. For versions of this song, see *The Scots Nightingale: or, Edinburgh Vocal Miscellany* (Edinburgh, 1778), 233–34, and James Hogg, *The Jacobite Relics of Scotland*, 2nd series (1821), ed. Murray G. H. Pittock (Edinburgh, 2003), 81–82.

162.9   ten commandments   slang here for finger nails, as in *2 Henry VI*, 1.3.140.

162.14   Amazon   name of the the mythical warrior women of Greek story and legend.

162.16–19   O gin . . . ranting Highlandman   matching the chorus from the traditional song, 'I wish that you were dead, Goodman', as found in Herd, 2.207–08.

162.43   sapient Partridge   character in *Tom Jones*, noted for shrewd observations. The relevant observation comes at the end of Bk 12, Ch. 14: 'A thousand naked Men are nothing to one Pistol; for though, it is true, it will kill but one at a single Discharge, yet who can tell but that one may be himself' (4.312).

163.3   levy en masse   *French levée en masse*, mass conscription; used particularly of the Revolutionary and early Napoleonic period in France.

163.29   Erskine . . . Robertson   respective heads of the Evangelical and Moderate parties in the Church of Scotland in the later 18th century, the latter grouping distinguished by its general acceptance of Patronage in the appointment of ministers and (unlike the Evangelicals) more amenable to the concept of moral law as a basis for Christianity as opposed to the principle of divine Grace. John Erskine (1721–1803) was minister at New Greyfriars 1758–67, Edinburgh; and from 1767 of Old Greyfriars, the latter jointly with William Robertson (1721–93), the celebrated historian and Principal of Edinburgh University from 1762. According to Sir Henry Moncreiff Wellwood's *Account of the Life and Writings of John Erskine, D.D.* (Edinburgh, 1818), 265: 'Two such men officiating together in the same congregation for six and twenty years, can scarcely be mentioned in the history of any other Church'.

163.35   elf locks   matted hair, tangled locks.

164.6   Geneva cloaks and bands   the Geneva cloak was a simple black gown originally worn by the strict Protestant community founded in Geneva by John Calvin (1509–64), and introduced into Scotland by John Knox. Bands, consisting of strips of white linen hanging from the collar in front, were part of clerical dress, and would normally have been worn by a Presbyterian clergyman along with the Geneva gown.

165.11 next quarter-sessions in Scotland, a court of review and appeal held quarterly by the justices of the peace on days appointed by statute.

167.33 non-juring clergyman see note to 48.15.

167.40 Will Ruthven the surname matches Ruthven, in the Badenoch region of the Highlands, which was involved at several points in the 1745–46 rising: see Duffy, 151, 179, 443. There is also a settlement called Ruthven in Angus, about 5 km N of Meigle.

170.41 sorry rheum used literally of troublesome mucous matter, but here presumably tears. See *Othello*, 3.4.48 ('I have a salt and sorry rheum offends me').

171.12–14 North-American Indians … awaken them see William Robertson, *The History of America* (1777), which describes the torments inflicted on prisoners and on young warriors among the American Indians: 'The prisoners are tied naked to a stake … Every species of torture is applied that the rancour of revenge can invent … Nothing sets bounds to their rage but the dread of abridging the duration of their vengeance by hastening the death of the sufferers': 4th edn (London, 1783), 2.140 (see *CLA*, 204). The sleep which occupies the intervals between torments is nowhere explicitly referred to but is perhaps implied by the fact that 'they often prolong this scene of anguish for several days' (2.141). There is also a possibility that Scott had read Peter Williamson's *French and Indian Cruelty* (York, 1757), detailing Williamson's life with the Indians and their customs.

172.35 Marry and amen to be sure indeed (*Romeo and Juliet*, 4.5.8).

172.40 benefit of clergy the exemption accorded to clergy in the Middle Ages from trial in a secular court. The 'benefit' lay largely in the incapacity of the ecclesiastical courts to condemn to death. This ended in Scotland with the Reformation, but benefit of clergy lasted in England until 1827, though the more serious crimes had been excluded from it.

173.16 Habeas Corpus the name of an English act of 1679 requiring prisoners to be brought speedily to trial and allowing them the right to be freed on bail, except in cases of treason and felony. The act never applied to Scotland, but the name was inaccurately used for a comparable Scottish act of 1701.

174.34–35 house of Brunswick see note to 23.23.

174.38–39 Go and do thou likewise Luke 10.37.

174.42 Cavaliero variant spelling of Cavalier ('horseman, knight'), deriving from the Spanish *Caballero* (in Old Spanish *Cavallero*). The term in both forms was used *c.* 1600 to describe a roistering, swash-buckling fellow, and carried over some of this meaning when applied to those who fought for Charles I in the English Civil War.

175.15 at Corryerick referring to the Corrieyairack Pass, on the military road to Fort Augustus. On 27 August 1745 General Sir John Cope had avoided having to force the pass, doubling back and then turning northwards to Inverness, thus leaving the way to the Lowlands open to Prince Charles's forces. See also note to 116.4, and Historical Note, 370.

175.16 John-o'-Groat's House now known as John o' Groats, 26 km N of Wick in Caithness, and considered as the most northerly point of the Scottish mainland. It is named after the 15th-century Dutch settler Jan de Groot.

175.32–33 Cromwell's military saints *saints* is what the Cromwellian soldiers termed themselves and their co-religionists. The early Christians are frequently called 'saints' in the New Testament, and in the 17th century the term was commonly self-applied by those who had a special sense of being God's people.

175.34 Gilfillan, the Cameronian the Cameronians, a sect of Presbyterians so named after their leader Richard Cameron (d. 1680), had been

persecuted during the later Stuart period (1660–88) for their refusal to accept
the royal authority in spiritual matters. On the accession of William III the
regiment later known as the Cameronians was raised amongst its supporters
in 1689, mainly in SW Scotland, and successfully helped defend lowland
Scotland from the Jacobite forces under Viscount Dundee. No source has
been discovered for the character of Gilfillan, but volunteer companies made
up of religious dissenting groups were a feature of attemped opposition in the
early days of the 1745 rising: see *Witness to Rebellion*, ed. Iain Gordon Brown
and Hugh Cheape (East Linton, 1996), 60–63, where a direct comparison
with Gilfillan is made (63).

176.26–28 Unthread the rude ... his feet see *King John*, 5.4.11–13
('Prince Charles' replaces 'King John').

177.1 in the toils a hunting metaphor, referring to the net or nets into
which quarry is driven, or within which game is known to be.

179.14 the governor i.e. Major General William Blakeney (see note to
102.19).

179.22 the Inquisition a tribunal set up in the Roman Catholic Church
in the 13th century for the suppression of heresy and the punishment of
heretics.

179.30 toleration, or indulgence relating to conciliatory measures during the reigns of the two Stuart monarchs mentioned, aimed at tempting ejected
Presbyterian ministers back into the national church. The best-known of these
is the indulgence of 1669, called by the Covenanters the Black Indulgence,
which allowed ministers to return to their parishes and preach on certain
conditions. Other 'indulgences' included that of 1672 (when specified ministers were given licence to preach), of 1679 (when those who had been attending
conventicles were allowed to return), and of 1687 (when James VII offered
general toleration).

179.34 Richard Cameron see note to 175.34.

179.35–36 the Revolution the 'Glorious Revolution' of 1688–89,
whereby William III replaced James VII and II, and which in Scotland resulted
in Presbyterianism becoming the established religion.

179.39 Solemn League and Covenant see note to 53.5.

179.43 the Union the Treaty of Union of 1707, by which the Parliaments
of England and Scotland were united. In 1706, at a time of widespread Jacobite
conspiracy in Scotland, armed Cameronians marched into Dumfries and
burned the Articles of Union at the Market Cross. According to Scott in *Tales
of a Grandfather* (*Prose Works*, 25.81–84), plans had existed to co-ordinate
an uprising in the West of Scotland with another in the Highlands.

180.11 Erastian divine Erastians were so called after the Swiss theologian Thomas Erastus (1524–83), who held that the sins of Christians should
be punished by the secular authorities, rather than by excommunication; the
term was used more broadly and somewhat misleadingly to describe those
who would subordinate church jurisdiction to the state.

180.35–36 in the year 1715 in October 1715 the Earl of Mar and his
Jacobite forces had remained in the neighbourhood of Perth, rather than moving south to attack the Duke of Argyll in his camp at Stirling.

181.6 Blakeney i.e. Major General William Blakeney (see note to 102.19).

182.2–3 point of war a short phrase sounded on an instrument as a
signal; military musical signal.

182.4 Dumbarton's Drums the Quick March of the Royal Scots Regiment. The name is said to come from Lord George Douglas, created Earl of
Dumbarton in 1675, colonel of the regiment. In 1686 the regiment was divided
into two battalions and the second battalion was later involved in the campaign
against Charles Edward culminating in the battle of Culloden. The earliest

references to the tune being called 'Dumbarton's Drums' appear to have been in Alexander Stuart's *Musick for Allan Ramsay's Collection of Scots Songs* (*c.* 1725), 98–99, and in William Thomson, *Orpheus Caledonius* (1733), 2.16–17. It is common in Scottish music books of the later 18th century, and was published in *SMM*, Vol. 2 (1788), no. 161, with anonymous verses beginning: 'Dumbarton's drums beat bonny O'.

182.7 **119th Psalm** the longest and structurally most complex of the Psalms, praising God for his laws and instructions, and consisting in all of 176 verses in 22 sections, the latter reflecting the letters in the Hebrew alphabet.

182.12 **Anderton** not identified as a location; but there is an Anderston, which was a weavers' village in the early 18th century, later becoming a district of western Glasgow.

182.13 **the British Convention** name of the third and last of three general conventions organised by the reformist 'Friends of the People' Society in Edinburgh, and involving delegates from other Scottish and some English corresponding societies, a number from the working classes, with weavers prominent among the trades. The convention, held in Autumn 1793, issued a manifesto demanding universal male suffrage and expressing support for the principles of the French Revolution. It was broken up by the authorities, with several delegates being arrested and tried for sedition.

182.23 **a large flag** such a flag, incorporating the words 'Covenant For Religion, King, and Kingdomes' in large gold letters, was designed by the Lord Lyon King at Arms as new colours for the Life Guards on Charles II's return from the Continent to Scotland in 1650: see J. K. Hewison, *The Covenanters*, 2 vols (Glasgow, 1913), 2.2–3.

183.6 **Pentland, or Bothwell Brigg** battles, fought in 1666 and 1679, in which the Scottish Covenanters were defeated by government forces.

183.11–12 **Roundheads of yore … Marlborough's captains** alluding in turn to the parliamentary forces in the English Civil War under Oliver Cromwell (1599–1658), Lord Protector 1653–58; and the army of John Churchill (1650–1722), first Duke of Marlborough, celebrated English general, who campaigned almost continuously on the Continent during the War of Spanish Succession (1701–14).

183.24–25 **grenadiers of Ligonier's** referring to John Ligonier, Earl of Ligonier (1680–1770), army officer, who served under Marlborough (see previous note), and who in 1745 commanded the government army defending England from the Jacobites, handing over his command to the Duke of Cumberland in November. As an infantry officer, he would have commanded grenadier battalions, often used as assault troops.

183.26–27 **sent … to the right about** i.e. caused to turn and retreat or flee.

183.35 **hungered and were athirst** see Matthew 25.35–46.

184.7–8 **Even thus … children of light** see Luke 16.8.

184.26 **William Earl of Glencairn** William, 13th Earl of Glencairn, d. 1775, governor of Dumbarton Castle.

185.12 **dinner-hour … two o'clock** the hour of dining in Scotland altered significantly during the 18th century: originally at one or two, the hour advanced until five was considered the polite time from around 1806 to 1820. The fashion for later dinner hours was thought to be in imitation of London customs. See Henry Cockburn, *Memorials of His Time* (Edinburgh, 1856), 33–34.

185.15–16 **borrower on the night … hour or two** see *Macbeth*, 3.1.26–27.

185.26 **black indulgence** see note to 179.30.

185.26–27 **dumb dogs that cannot bark** see Isaiah 56.10.

185.33 **Kirk of Scotland … in 1642** though 1642 is not noteworthy in the history of the constitution of the Presbyterian Church of Scotland as such, it is possible that this refers to the onset of the English Civil War that year. Scotland entered on the side of the English Parliament in the following year, one aspect of the alliance being a commitment to preserve the Presbyterian order of the Church of Scotland and to bring religion in England into conformity with reformed principles.

185.35–36   carved work of the sanctuary ... cut down   see Psalm 74.6–7.

186.4   patronage ... oaths and bonds   alluding to the terms offered to ministers willing to return to their parishes (see also note to 179.30); 'patronage' refers to the right of certain landowners to appoint ministers to parishes, which was restored in 1712, and was fiercely contested by covenanting and evangelical Presbyterians.

186.6–7   Babel of iniquity   evidently referring not to Genesis 11.1–9, as at 104.6, but to Revelation 18.1–5, describing the fall of Babylon (the Greek form of Babel) because of its iniquities.

186.7   saint-killing times   referring to the persecution of the Covenanters in the reigns of Charles II and James VII and II. The early Christians are frequently called 'saints' in the New Testament, and the term was commonly applied to the Covenanting martyrs by their supporters, owing to their special sense of being God's people.

186.10   filthy rag   see Isaiah 64.6.

186.12   muckle harlot ... seven hills   i.e. the Church of Rome, depicted as the great harlot, and with reference to Rome and its seven hills; evoking also 'the seven mountains, on which the woman sitteth' of Revelation 17.9.

186.13   cup of abomination   see Revelation 17.4, depicting the whore of Babylon, commonly identified by reformation Protestants with the Catholic Church (see also previous note).

186.13–14   deaf as adders   see Psalm 58.4; also proverbial: see *ODEP*, 172.

186.16   cup of her fornication   see note to 186.13; also Revelation 18.3.

186.19   hill-folk   those who (after 1662) had worshipped at illegal conventicles in the hills under ministers who had been ejected from their parishes for refusing to take the Oath of Allegiance.

186.29–30   backslidings   term used 13 times in Jeremiah about the Israelites falling away from obedience to God's law.

186.30   root of the matter   Job 19.28.

186.36–37   twenty thousand mark   i.e. he is worth about £1100 sterling. For *mark* see note to 94.13.

186.43   the accursed Achan   see Joshua Ch. 7.

187.2   Mauchlin   Mauchline, a village 16 km SE of Kilmarnock, in East Ayrshire; it is now noted for its association with Robert Burns, who farmed near there with his wife, a Mauchline native.

187.3   your lines ... pleasant places   see Psalm 16.6.

187.7   real Lancashire   an ancient breed of cattle superseded in the early 19th century by shorthorns.

187.8   Mains of Kilmaurs   the home farm of the estate of Kilmaurs. Kilmaurs Place was the seat of the Earls of Glencairn (see note to 184.26), and Kilmaurs is a village in Ayrshire, 4 km NW of Kilmarnock.

187.16   Muscovia   denotes Russia.

187.18   maist feck   the greater part.

187.22   Book of Sports   as issued by James VI and I in 1618, and reissued by Charles I in 1633, authorising and promoting the Sunday sports and rural activities denounced by many Puritans as profanations of the Sabbath.

187.23 Engagers, and the Protesters the Engagers entered into a treaty with Charles I in 1647, promising military support in return for a number of promises, including the introduction of a diluted form of Presbyterianism in England; the Protesters were radical Covenanters opposed to this treaty and other forms of accommodation.

187.23 Whiggamores' Raid name given (usually derogatorily) to a march on Edinburgh by 2,000 countrymen from SW Scotland, in support of radical Presbyterianism and in opposition the Engagers (see previous note).

187.24 Assembly of Divines at Westminster originally met to reform the thirty-nine articles of the Church of England, but after the signing of the Solemn League and Covenant in 1643 (see note to 153.28–29) it was joined by a Scottish delegation, subsequently producing the Westminster Confession of Faith, which laid down rules for Presbyterian government in both England and Scotland.

187.24–25 Longer and Shorter Catechism question-and-answer books used for religious instruction, as drawn up by the Westminster Assembly (see previous note), and approved along with the Confession of Faith by the General Assembly of Scotland in 1647–48, and the English Parliament in 1648.

187.25 the Excommunication at Torwood in 1680 the Covenanting minister Donald Cargill, preaching to a large congregation in the Torwood (between Falkirk and Stirling), formally excommunicated Charles II, the Duke of York (later James VII and II), and others: see also note to 203.6.

187.26 Archbishop Sharpe James Sharp, Archbishop of St Andrews, murdered by Covenanters on Magus Moor in 1679.

187.33 James Mitchell Presbyterian preacher and insurgent, who unsuccessfully attempted to murder James Sharp (see previous note) in 1668. He was arrested in 1674, confessed to the privy council on condition that his life would be spared, and was then tried again in 1678 and executed, some claimed through the malevolence of Sharp.

188.12–13 Tobit and his dog ... heathenish and apocryphal see The Book of Tobit, 5.16. This book is part of the Apocrypha, and was often not included in Protestant bibles, though it did appear in the King James Bible.

188.17 poor Bawty *bawtie* in Scots is a dog's name, and is also used generically for a dog.

188.22 The sword of the Lord and of Gideon the war cry of Israel's soldier-hero Gideon as he leads a successful night attack against the Midianites; see Judges 7.18.

188.23–24 good old cause the Puritan or Covenanting cause. The phrase was used by opponents of the restoration of the Stuart monarchy in 1660. See John Milton, *The Ready and Easy Way to Establish a Free Commonwealth* (1660), final paragraph: 'What I have spoken is the language of that which is not called amiss "The good old Cause"'. See also John Dryden, *Absalom and Achitophel* (1681), line 82.

188.24 Drumclog battle in 1679, on a moor in Lanarkshire, in which a group of some 200 armed Covenanters defeated the royalist troops of John Graham of Claverhouse, later Viscount Dundee.

188.35 dropping shots irregular fire, the shots falling detachedly and not continuous.

189.17 Niel Sassenagh ... no English Scott's Gaelic, which is incorrect, possibly derives from Burt: 'they will answer you by *Haniel Sasson Uggit, i.e.* they have, or speak, no *Saxon* (or *English*)' (1.132–33). This itself is apparently a form of *Chan eil Sasann agam*, in which *Sasann* denotes England. In the 8vo 1819 *Novels and Tales* text of *Waverley*, the wording is changed to '"*Cha n'eil Beurl' agam,*" i. e. "I have no English"', which would be normal nowadays.

However, *beurla* originally meant 'tongue, language', and English was often known as *a' Bheurla Shasannach* (the English tongue), to distinguish it from *a' Bheurla Ghallda* (the Scots language).

190.10–11 tartan striped in the mode peculiar to their race although modern experts have argued that this was a later development, Scott was not writing carelessly. See his letter to Mrs Hughes of 12 April 1825: 'I have myself known many old people that were out in 1715 [*sic*] and I have understood that generally speaking the clan tartans were observed by the more numerous & powerful names . . . I must however add that though I am sure I could show that the Clan tartans were in use a great many years before 1745 I do not believe a word of the nonsense about every clan or name having a regular pattern which was undeviatingly adhered to' (see *Letters*, 9.68–70).

190.38–40 Highland Esculapius . . . Tomanrait see notes to 124.29 and 127.7. Scott here is possibly conflating two distinct characters from an earlier part of the narrative.

191.34 Highland Janizary the Janizaries were a body of Turkish infantry, originally drawn from Christian captives. The term was also used to describe any Turkish soldier, especially one who escorted travellers in the East.

191.40–41 our grandmother Eve *Love's Labours Lost*, 1.1.249.

193.17 light usually carried by a miner relating to a situation prior to the invention in 1815 of Sir Humphry Davy's safety lamp.

195.7 setting spaniel a spaniel dog trained to 'set' (i.e. indicate the presence of) game. The name was also applied to a kind of spaniel.

195.40 Homer's, or rather Pope's, benighted peasant the 'blue vault' and situation match Alexander Pope's translation of Homer's *Iliad* (1715–20), 8.698–99.

195.41–42 Mac-Farlane's buat *Gaelic Buat Mhic Phàrlain*, MacFarlane's lantern; used of the moon, because the MacFarlanes were guided by it on their cattle raids in the vicinity of Loch Lomond. Scott's Magnum note refers to the 'celebrated pibroch of *Hoggil nam Bo* [properly *A thogail nam bò*, to lift the cows], which is the name of their [i.e. the MacFarlanes'] gathering tune' (2.81).

196.17 Nancy Dawson a well-known English dance-tune, sometimes labelled a hornpipe; it reportedly gained its name through association with a stage dancer, Nancy Dawson (1728–67), who performed to the tune in England in the 1760s. The version in *The Vocal Magazine* (London, 1781; *CLA*, 160), Song no. 252, begins 'Of all the girls in our town' (67).

196.21 ruse de guerre *French* stratagem of war.

196.40 Duncan Douroch not identified, though the second name probably derives from the Gaelic *dorcha*, 'dark, of dark complexion'.

197.21–23 massive castle . . . oblong square describing Doune Castle, as later given by name at 198.10. A large courtyard-type castle of the early 14th and 15th centuries, with two tall keeps and a quadrangular court, it lies at the junction of the River Teith and Ardoch burn, slightly SE of the settlement of Doune (see next note). It was garrisoned by the Jacobites during Charles Edward's march south towards Edinburgh in September 1745, a journey replicated in some respects by Waverley's present movements. Prisoners later held there included John Home, the playwright and historian, and Scott heard an account of his escape when first visiting Doune in 1793 (see *Life*, 1.207–08). An account of the escape is given in Home, 187–92.

197.31 small and mean village Doune village, 12 km NW of Stirling. Ed1 (unlike the MS) uses the word 'town' here, though for Home it is 'the village of Downe' (188).

198.10–11 Castle of Doune . . . Menteith for the castle, see note to 197.21–23. Menteith is a fertile district in W Stirlingshire.

198.13 Donald Stuart identified in a Magnum note as 'Mr Stewart of Balloch . . . a man of property near Callander' (2.81). However, in his later Introduction (1829) to the Magnum edition of *Rob Roy*, Scott supplies documentation suggesting that the Doune garrison was in fact commanded by Gregor MacGregor of Glengyle (a nephew of Rob Roy) and 'not Stewart of Balloch, as averred in a note on Waverley' (7.cxxxiv–cxxxv). Certainly Gregor MacGregor of Glengyle was appointed governor of the castle by the time of Charles Edward's expedition into England, with a remit to watch the garrison at Stirling and to raise additional men.

199.37–38 uniform . . . French chasseurs the Magnum text specifies the colours, 'blue and red'. A *chasseur* in French is normally a huntsman, though the term is adaptable in military senses. See also note to 59.40–41.

200.3–4 bitted . . . for the use of the sword *bitted* normally signifies being furnished with or having a bit (the mouthpiece of a horse's bridle, to which the reins are attached). No special application of the term to cavalry horses has been discovered.

200.26 Bob of Dumblane name of popular song and well-known tune. *Bob* means 'dance', and Dunblane is a small town 8 km N of Stirling. The song, which can be interpreted in an equivocal way, applying both to marriage celebrations and the sexual act itself, appears in Allan Ramsay's *Tea-Table Miscellany*, 13th edn (1762; *CLA*, 171), 34; and is also in Herd, 2.22–23. Early versions of the tune can be found in Alexander Stuart, *Musick for Allan Ramsay's Collection of Scots Songs* (c. 1725), 64–65; and William Thomson, *Orpheus Caledonius* (1733), 1.101.

200.38 deil burst them may the devil destroy them.

200.39 mak the auld price gude i.e. make the old price stick. Around February each year justices of the peace and farmers in each Scottish county met to set the fiar price (the recommended price of grain) for the year. The lieutenant believes that a good harvest ought to result in lower prices, but cynically suggests that the price would be fixed to benefit producers at the expense of consumers. As grain prices were very stable in this period he was probably justified. See A. J. S. Gibson and T. C. Smout, *Prices, Food, and Wages in Scotland 1550–1780* (Cambridge, 1995).

200.39–40 against them as has horses till keep to the detriment of those who have horses to feed.

201.4 fule's errand profitless undertaking.

201.7 every why has its wherefore proverbial: see Ray, 272; *ODEP*, 886.

201.12 to settle with at Martinmas formerly accounts were settled on a quarter day, of which Martinmas, 11 November, was one.

201.13 auld Fifteen the 15 judges of the Court of Session, the supreme civil court in Scotland; they presided individually in the Outer House, and sat together as a group in the Inner House, a procedure reformed in 1808.

201.16 gae out to go out as a soldier, to take the field; the expression *out* in Scotland being a nuanced way of expressing participation in the Jacobite risings of 1715 and 1745.

201.17–18 St Johnstone's tippet *proverbial* the hangman's noose: see Ramsay, 129; *ODEP*, 694. St Johnstone is another name for Perth, John the Baptist having been in pre-Reformation times the tutelary saint of the town.

201.21 hack and manger a *hack* (or *heck*) is a portable rack for holding fodder, while a *manger* is stationary. Proverbially the expression means to be in comfortable circumstances: see Ray, 207; *ODEP*, 661.

201.22–23 Whitson-tryst Scott in his 'Memoirs' describes how his grandfather, Robert, on taking on the farm of Sandyknowe, 'set off to purchase a stock of sheep at Whitsun-Tryste, a fair held on a hill near Wooler in

Northumberland' (*Scott on Himself*, ed. Hewitt, 4). Wooler is about 28 km due S of Berwick-upon-Tweed.

201.23 Staneshaw-bank cattle-market just north of Carlisle, on the River Eden. In the ballad 'Kinmont Willie', stanzas 26–28, the rescuers cross the Eden at 'the Staneshaw-bank' (see *Minstrelsy*, 2.63). In the MS 'Staneshaw-bank' is the catch-word at the end of one folio, and the different 'Stagshaw-bank' appears at the start of the next folio. Stagshaw-bank is on the Roman Wall in Northumberland, N of Corbridge; and fairs were held there at Whitsun and Midsummer.

201.23 winter fair at Hawick cattle markets were held at Hawick, in the Scottish Borders, in October and November.

201.24 I'se be caution I assure you. *Caution* (which rhymes with 'nation') is legal security in civil matters.

201.29 Caverton-Edge in the parish of Eckford, Roxburghshire, 7 km S of Kelso. Annual horse races took place there, at dates between late July and late October.

201.29 Duk Hamilton's i.e. the Duke of Hamilton's. Scott was possibly thinking here (slightly anachronistically) of Lord Archibald Hamilton (1740–1819), later 9th Duke of Hamilton, who was the most important Northern breeder of race horses in the Georgian period, at his estate of Hamilton Palace. He owned seven St Leger winners between 1786 and 1814.

202.8 union flag incorporating the crosses of St George and St Andrew, as combined after the Union of the Crowns of England and Scotland in 1603, but not then that of St Patrick, which was added after the Union with Ireland of 1801.

202.11 to the left ... royal park referring to the King's Park, once a hunting ground, to the SW of Stirling Castle. Like Charles Edward and his army in September 1745 (see Duffy, 189) Balmawhapple's party on leaving Doune would have approached Stirling from the NW. Thus it would have been necessary to turn left (not right as in previous printed editions) to enter the King's Park and approach nearer the Castle.

202.16 tournaments of old ... rock such a chivalric tournament is described in *The Lady of the Lake*, Canto 5, stanza 24, where the rock is named the Ladies' Rock: 'The vale with loud applauses rang,/ The Ladies' Rock sent back the clang' (*Poetical Works*, 8.245).

202.33–35 cannon-ball ... few yards distance such an incident reportedly occurred as the Jacobite army passed Stirling Castle, with a cannon ball missing Charles Edward by about 20 yards (see Duffy, 191).

202.36 bid the party trudge compare *Romeo and Juliet*, 1.3.34–35 (' 'Twas no need, I trow,/ To bid me trudge'), with *trudge* meaning 'be off, depart'.

202.39 struck a trot an equestrian term in Scott's period, *trot* referring to a gait between walking and running.

203.5 Bannockburn site of the battle in 1314, about 4 km SSE of Stirling Castle, in which King Robert Bruce defeated the English forces of Edward II.

203.6 the Torwood between Stirling and Falkirk, once part of the Caledonian Forest, and at this time 'chiefly composed of Firs and Beech': see *A Journey through Part of England and Scotland along with the Army under the Command of His Royal Highness the Duke of Cumberland*, 2nd edn (London, 1747; *CLA*, 90), 104. William Wallace took refuge there for a night after his defeat by Edward I at Falkirk in 1298; see also notes to 203.9–10 and 320.18.

203.8 Wude Willie Grime according to the Dryburgh edition of the Waverley Novels (1892) 'Wude [i.e. mad] Willie Grime, having, it is said, shot a trespasser on his land, was acquitted by the jury on the ground of madness' (1.494). It is also possible that Scott had in mind a Willie Graeme

with the same sobriquet, who lived near Dunning in Perthshire, 8 km E of
Auchterarder, and about 40 km NNE of Torwood. See 'Description of the
Parish of Dunning Perthshire in 1723', concerning the mansion house of
James Graeme of Garvock, and remains of an old tower in the vicinity: 'the
place is yet called the Hall Tower herein dwelt of Widd Willie Graeme, as
they then term'd him, being so called by reason of his resolution and Boldness
whereby he struck a terror on the countrey about' (Walter Macfarlane,
Geographical Collections Relating to Scotland, 3 vols (Edinburgh, 1906–08),
I.123).

**203.9–10   Falkirk ... formerly famous... soon to be again distin-
guished**   alluding to two battles: the first fought in 1298, at which the English
army of Edward I defeated the Scots led by William Wallace; the second fought
on 17 January 1746, at which the Jacobite forces defeated the government army
under General Hawley but failed to press home the advantage.

203.21   without remorse or mitigation of voice   see *Twelfth Night*,
2.3.87–88.

203.25–29   Linlithgow ... patriotic statesman   Linlithgow, an ancient
burgh in West Lothian, is about 29 km W of Edinburgh. Its royal palace was
rebuilt in the 15th century by James I, and was a favourite residence of the
Scottish Stuart monarchs, James V and his daughter Mary Queen of Scots
both being born there. Early in 1746 it was destroyed by fire as a result of
Hanoverian troops having bivouacked there. The 'patriotic statesman' who
prevented the conversion of the ruins into a barracks was Robert Blair of
Avontoun (born 1741), Lord President of the Court of Session 1808–11,
who died on 20 May 1811. Scott later applauded Blair's action in preserving
the site in his account of the 'Palace of Linlithgow' in his *Provincial Antiquities
and Picturesque Scenery of Scotland*, 2 vols (London, 1826), 2.179.

204.8   the brave man's knell   possibly echoing William Collins's 'Ode,
Written in the Beginning of the Year 1746', lines 1 and 7 ('How sleep the
brave, who sink to rest ... By fairy hands their knell is rung').

204.15   palace of Holy-Rood   the Scottish royal palace, situated at the
foot of the Canongate in Edinburgh, near the ancient Abbey of Holyrood. It
was originally built by James V, and Mary Queen of Scots held court there
later in the 16th century; it was then substantially rebuilt by Charles II, and
was the Scottish residence of his brother James VII and II.

204.21   portraits of kings   referring to a series of 111 portraits of Scottish
kings (mostly legendary), commissioned by Charles II from the Dutch artist
Jacob de Wet or de Witt (1640–97), who agreed to paint 110 portraits within
two years for £120 per annum. The contract is dated 1684, and the surviving
portraits are in the Great Gallery in the Palace of Holyrood House. The
paintings are said to have been deliberately slashed by the Hanoverian troops
quartered in the palace after the 1745 rising, and evidence gained during
conservation corroborates this. The quartering of troops there is noted in
A Journey through Part of England and Scotland along with the Army ..., 2nd edn
(London, 1747; *CLA*, 90): 'above all, the long Gallery is very remarkable, being
adorned with Pictures of all the *Scots* Kings, from *Fergus* I. done by masterly
Hands. This served as a lodging Room for our Soldiers, upon Straw, as were
most of the other Rooms' (92).

205.3   hands of the Philistines   Judges 10.7: 'And the anger of the
Lord was hot against Israel, and he sold them into the hands of the Philistines'.
The *Philistines* were traditional enemies of Israel.

205.19   star on his breast ... embroidered garter   probably the vestments of the Order of the Garter, the highest English chivalric order,
instituted in 1348, the garter being an accessory worn on the left calf by
knights, and the star being an insignium (with a red St George's cross in the

centre) worn pinned to the left breast. Such accoutrements were noted by Magdalen Pringle on a visit to the Highland camp at Duddingston (see note to 229.41) in October 1745: 'On his left shoulder and side were the Star & Garter and over his right shoulder a very rich Broad Sword Belt': *A Jacobite Miscellany*, ed. Henrietta Tayler (Oxford, 1948), 40–41. Another possibility is the star of the Order of the Thistle, the senior Scottish chivalric order, which in the circle features a thistle on a gold field; as Lamont notes, Home describes Charles Edward as wearing 'on his breast the star of the order of St. Andrew' (100).

207.20   district of Moidart . . . seven attendants   Prince Charles Edward landed on the Isle of Eriskay on 23 July 1745, and proceeded to Borrowdale in Moidart in the western Highlands with 7 companions known as 'the Seven Men of Moidart': the Marquess of Tullibardine; Aeneas MacDonald, a banker; Francis Strickland of a Westmorland family; Sir Thomas Sheridan, Charles's old tutor; George Kelly, a non-juring clergyman; and Sir John MacDonald and John William O'Sullivan, both professional soldiers.

207.23   commander-in-chief   i.e. Sir John Cope (1690–1760), commander in Scotland at the onset of the 1745 rising, whose name is supplied in the ISet and Magnum. For the manoeuvrings of Cope as described here, see note to 175.15.

207.27–28   northward to Aberdeen   in fact, Sir John Cope and his forces had marched to Inverness, before later embarking from Aberdeen.

207.30   two regiments of horse   the Magnum supplies the names of 'Gardiner's and Hamilton's' dragoons (the 13th and 14th). Having retreated before the Jacobite advance from Perth, Gardiner's dragoons were met by Hamilton's from Leith on a field near Coltbridge, 2 km W of Edinburgh, where the rearguard took fright, leading to a panicky flight along the coast towards Haddington.

207.34–36   Lochiel . . . entering the gates   referring to the unopposed entry into Edinburgh through the Netherbow Port, as a result of its accidental opening, by Donald Cameron of Lochiel (see note to 116.1) with several hundred picked clansmen on 17 September 1745.

207.38–39   Aberdeen . . . for Dunbar   Sir John Cope and his forces had left Aberdeen by sea on 15 September, and arrived at Dunbar in East Lothian on 17 September; on 19 September they began their march towards Edinburgh (Blaikie, 16).

208.16   throw away the scabbard   anticipating Charles Edward's reported saying before the battle of Prestonpans (see note to 232.20–21).

208.17   God of Battles   *Henry V*, 4.1.285.

208.28   brevet rank   i.e. a nominal rank, conferred on an honorary basis.

208.42   Andrea Ferrara   sword named after the North Italian sword-smith of the late 16th century. It became a byword in the 17th and 18th centuries for any sword of high quality, but the Prince by virtue of his birth and Italian residence presumably possesses a genuine example.

209.16–17   Irish officers   several of the leading Scottish supporters of Charles Edward, including Lord George Murray, were resentful of the influence of Colonel John William O'Sullivan in the Council, and of other Irish advisers (see Duffy, 101).

209.21   C—— and M——   not identified.

209.24   Aberchallader   apparently from the settlement, otherwise spelt Aberchalder, 8 km SW of Fort Augustus. Charles Edward's army gathered there in August 1745, prior to marching towards the Lowlands.

209.25–26   Master of F——   not identified; 'Master' is the title given to the heir apparent to a Scottish barony.

209.30–31   patience, cousin, and shuffle the cards   see Miguel de

Cervantes Saavedra, *Don Quixote*, Part 2 (1615), Ch. 23 (ed. Lockhart, 5 vols (1822), 4.77). This is Durandarte's aphorism when kept by enchantment in the cave of Montesinos. The expression was a favourite of Scott's: see for example his letter to Joanna Baillie of 23 November 1810 (*Letters*, 2.404).

210.7 court, retiring from the street the ISet and Magnum add 'called the Canongate' after 'street', thus identifying the main street between the Edinburgh Netherbow Port and Holyrood, with the court in question being one of the closes connecting with it.

210.8 widow of forty early reference to the character later named as Widow Flockhart: see note to 215.10.

210.13 an Snaht *Gaelic na Snàthaid*, of the needle.

210.14–15 cath d'ath *Gaelic cadadh* tartan; or, more fancifully, *cath dath* battle colour.

210.16 measure of a well-made man compare Macintosh, under the heading 'The Shape of the Trouse': 'Two full nails to the small of the leg; eleven from the haunch to the heel; seven nails round the band; there are few to which it will not answer, well shap'd all over; and three nails to the breech' (26).

210.20 baulder sneck more decisive cut.

210.20 hers ain i.e. his own. For gender confusion in the representation of Gaelic English, see note to 155.18.

210.20 cumadh an truais *Gaelic cumadh an triubhais*, shape [of] the trousers.

210.23 blue bonnet of the Prince's pattern a man's blue bonnet, said to have been worn by Charles Edward, and left at Moy Hall, was exhibited as recently as 1996: see *Culloden: The Swords and the Sorrows* (National Trust of Scotland, 1996), 83. See also note to 255.39.

210.23–24 Mr Mouat's the haberdasher not identified as a person or concern. Ed6 (1816) replaces 'the haberdasher' with 'in the Crames', thus effectively placing Mouat as a holder of one of the open stalls in the Crames (or Krames), formerly a crowded market area on the N side of St Giles' Cathedral and a narrow passage between the Cathedral and the Luckenbooths (see note to 213.25) in the High Street.

210.41 cairn of Benmore while a *cairn* can mean a pyramid of stones, a stony hill is more probable here. See Burt on the Highland usage: 'At the End of about a Mile, there was a steep Ascent, which they call a *Carne*; that is an exceedingly stony Hill' (2.48). The 'stony hill' meaning is apparent in various 'Cairn' names in the North (as in 'Cairn Gorm'). The present name has not been identified as a location, though there are several hills and mountains named Ben More (meaning 'big hill' in Gaelic) in the Highlands, including the mountain (1174 m) in W Stirlingshire, 5 km E of Crianlarich.

212.8–11 in ergastulo ... in carcere in a private prison, in public confinement. The place where a Roman slave-owner kept his slaves was called *ergastulum*, whereas *carcer* was the Roman public prison.

212.35 sacramentum militare see note to 52.43.

212.37 per conjurationem *Latin* by an oath. Literally this means by 'swearing together', indicating that the Baron (or Scott) is perhaps confusing the terms for single and combined oaths.

212.40 colliers, salters ... slaves of the soil workers in coal mines and salt works were in a form of serfdom in Scotland, bound to perpetual service and passing with the works to any new owner. They were released by acts passed in 1775 (15 Geo. III, c. 28) and 1799 (39 Geo. III, c. 56).

212.42 the learned Sanchez possibly referring to Thomas Sanchez, S.J. (1550–1610), author of legal and theological works, notably *Disputationes de sancti matrimonii sacramento* (1602), regarded as among the standard works on marriage. No work by him called *De Jure-jurando* ('On swearing an oath') has been discovered, though the phrase is found elsewhere within the titles of law and ecclesiastical books from the 15th to 18th centuries. Felinus Sand(a)eus (d. 1503) was the author of a work entitled *De Jure Jurando*, published in Milan in 1499.

213.2–3 Memmia lex . . . In Verrem in his *Pro Sex. Roscio Amerino* (not *In Verrem*), 19.55, Marcus Tullius Cicero (106–43 BC) mentions a lex Remmia, whereby a person convicted under the law of false accusation supposedly had the letter K (for Kalumnia) branded on his forehead. The law was also, probably incorrectly, named lex Memmia.

213.25 Luckenbooths named after the 'locked booths', i.e. small generally timber-fronted shops, found on the ground floor of a four-storey block of buildings which occupied an island site in the High Street N of St Giles' Cathedral.

213.26–27 finer than any street the unusual length and breadth of the High Street, then a forum of public life, was commented on by numerous visitors to Edinburgh in the 18th century. See A. J. Youngson, *The Making of Classical Edinburgh 1750–1840* (Edinburgh, 1966; reissued 1993), 52–53.

213.29 Blondel and Coehorn both military engineers. Nicolas-François Blondel (1618–86), architect under Louis XIV, planned the fortifications at Dunkirk and Le Havre. Baron Menno van Coehoorn (1641–1704), Dutch soldier and engineer, was the author of a famous treatise on fortress construction, *Nieuwe Vestingbouw* (1685), and became Master General of the Artillery in 1695; the fortifications at Bergen op Zoom were considered his masterpiece.

213.32 conclamare vasa *Latin* to give the signal for the baggage (to be gathered together).

213.42 a ganging foot is aye getting proverbial: see Ramsay, 64; Ray, 281; *ODEP*, 315.

213.43 Uhlans Polish light cavalry soldiers, armed with lances; in the Napoleonic period they were drafted into the armies of various countries, including France, and proved extremely effective in battle.

214.1 Schmirschitz's Pandours *pandours* or *pandurs* originated as mountaineer troops who served as a militia in Croatia, and were later incorporated into the Austrian army, with the main function of assassinating enemy officers and conducting guerrilla warfare; they were noted for their ruthlessness, one of their commanders being Baron Franz Freiherr von der Trenck (1711–49). *Schmirschitz* is possibly a fictitious name, from the German *schütze*, a marksman, and *schmieren*, to smear, to lubricate, but used in words such as *Schmierenkomödiant*, a ham actor, or *Schmierfink*, a hack writer.

214.2 knight of the mirror most obviously referring here to the pierglass described as having been taken as booty, but also echoing the knight of the mirrors in *Don Quixote*, Part 2 (1615), Chs 12–15.

214.5 ferociores . . . in actu *Latin* more ferocious in appearance, more gentle in behaviour; no 'heathen author' has been identified.

214.8 King's Park SE of Holyrood, used as an assembly area by the Jacobite army after arriving in Edinburgh; now also known as Holyrood Park.

214.11–12 faire la meilleure chère *French* to eat the best fare.

214.14 Good Town sobriquet for Edinburgh.

214.26 Sliochd nan Ivor see note to 98.14.

214.27 targed him tightly stood over him, supervised him closely.

214.30 Fin Macoul Fionn mac Cumhaill, the Fingal of Ossianic legend; see also note to 117.9.

214.33 garb of old Gaul from the first line of the song ('In the garb of old Gaul, wi' the fire of old Rome'), adopted as the Slow March of the 42nd Regiment of Foot, the Black Watch, with words by Sir Harry Erskine and music by General John Reid. For versions, with words apparently originating from the 1760s, see Herd, 1.116–17; and *SMM*, Vol. 3 (1790), no. 210. Scott refers to this song in the context of the Peninsular War in a letter to Joanna Baillie of 23 November 1810: see *Letters*, 2.405.

215.4   Which melted . . . in war   see Thomas Campbell, 'The Wounded Hussar' (1799), line 12.

215.10   Widow Flockhart   first direct naming of this character, introduced as 'a buxom widow of forty' at 210.8. Robert Chambers suggests a prototype in a real-life widowed Mrs Flockhart (nicknamed 'Luckie Fykie'), whose premises in the Potterrow (Bristo) in Edinburgh combined 'a shop, dwelling-house, and hotel': *Traditions of Edinburgh*, 2 vols (Edinburgh, 1825), 2.290–93. There is also a widow Lockhart with whom Matthew Bramble lodges in Smollett's *The Expedition of Humphry Clinker* (1771): Matt. Bramble to Dr Lewis, 18 July; ed. Thomas R. Preston (Athens and London, 1990), 211. Mrs Flockhart's lodging seems to be off the Canongate in the text: see 225.36–37 and note to 210.7.

215.14   cry barley   ask for a truce.

215.20–21   young saints, auld deils   proverbial: see Ray, 153; *ODEP*, 928.

215.27   Claw for claw, as Conan said   for the origins of the expression, see note to 110.37. The phrasing here, however, is closer to that in Scott's Magnum note (1.241) than that earlier occurrence: 'Sometimes the proverb is worded thus:—"Claw for claw, and the devil take the shortest nails, as Conan said to the devil."'

215.31   Saint Phedar   Phedar is a form of the Gaelic *Peadair*, Peter; hence Saint Peter.

215.36   majoring yonder   *major* is used here in the sense of 'to strut, to swagger', though perhaps with an added nuance in view of Waverley's earlier naming as a brevet-major by Charles Edward.

215.39   droghling, coghling   the original Glossary to Scott's *The Antiquary* (1816) defines *Droghling coghling* as 'Wheezing and blowing'; but for other connotations, see also as individual words in the present Glossary.

215.40   Laird o' Kittlegab's   evidently a burlesque name, from *kittle*, 'tickle, stimulate', and *gab*, 'mouth, palate'.

215.40   turnspit doggie   a dog kept to turn a roasting-spit by running within a kind of treadmill constructed with it. See also 48.14 and note.

215.41   hungry as a gled   anglicised form of the Scots phrase 'gleg as a gled', itself meaning 'keen (i.e. hungry) as a kite'.

216.19   sinews of war   i.e. money, reflecting the aphorism *nervi belli pecunia infinita* ('endless money forms the sinews of war'), Marcus Tullius Cicero (106–43 BC), *Philippics*, 5.2.5; see also Plutarch, *Agis and Cleomenes* 27.1. Also found in a variety of post-Classical sources, including Beaumont and Fletcher, *Fair Maid of the Inn* (1625–26), 1.2.29–31 ('Victuals and ammunition/ And money too, the sinews of the war,/ Are stored up'); and Dryden, *The Duke of Guise* (1679), 2.2.78: 'Ordnance, munition, and the nerve of war' (*Works*, ed. Scott (1808), 7.45).

216.20   caisse militaire   *French* military chest, war fund.

216.23   the Doutelle   name for the frigate which brought Charles Edward to Scotland, actually a corruption of 'Le du Teillay', the ship being named after M. du Teillay, Commissaire de la Marine at Nantes: see John S. Gibson, *Ships of the '45* (London, 1967), 8.

217.17   testamentum militare   *Latin* military will or testament.

217.27   mortis causa   *Latin* in contemplation of death. In Scots law a 'mortis causa donation' is an arrangement whereby property is transferred to a grantee on the death of the grantor.

217.33–34 full sorrow ... hungry one proverbial, as in Ray, 106 ('Fat sorrow is better than lean sorrow'). See also Ramsay, 103; *ODEP*, 247.

217.43 earthly mould compare Edmund Spenser, *The Faerie Queene* (1590–96), Bk 5, Proem, stanza 2 ('Of earthly mould, and form'd of flesh and bone').

218.5 wad scroll for a plack the sheet i.e. would copy legal documents at a rate of a plack (a Scots coin of negligible value) per sheet.

218.11 feal and divot effectively the right of a landholder to remove turf from the surface of subordinate tenements, for thatching roofs and other purposes; *feal*, given as *fail* in *OED*, indicates a clod covered with grass.

218.15 evidents and titles documentary proofs and title-deeds relating to land. The legal terms listed up to this point cannot originate from a medieval charter, which would be in Latin, though they match charters belonging to the 17th century, with the Baillie no doubt employing terminology found in documents relating to land rights. Similar wording can be found in James Hogg's *The Private Memoirs and Confessions of a Justified Sinner* (1824; ed. P. D. Garside (Edinburgh, 2002), 124), where the intimation is that the document being read is a forgery. For individual terms involved, see the present Glossary.

218.22–23 rugging and riving tugging and tearing, pulling this way and that (with the strong sense here of open contention, or a free-for-all).

218.23–24 Sneckus Mac-Snackus the 1Set and Magnum (2.122–23) add parenthetically in explanation 'meaning, probably, annexis, connexis', i.e. as in the preceding charter terms.

218.29 Lillibulero, bullen a la refrain of the anti-Catholic ballad attributed to Thomas Wharton, written in an Irish brogue and put into the mouths of two Irishmen, to a traditional tune later set to music by Henry Purcell. It was used for a variety of political purposes, most notably against James VII and II and in favour of William III and the Revolution Settlement of 1688–89. Lillibullero is the tune which Uncle Toby, in Laurence Sterne's *Tristram Shandy* (1759–67), is always whistling, as Scott later noted in his commentary on that novelist: 'The well-known tune of Lillabullero, composed in ridicule of King James, and his Lieutenant in Ireland, Lord Tyrconnel, was highly fashionable in King William's army, and hence become [*sic*] the favourite of uncle Toby' (*Ballantyne's Novelist's Library*, 5 (1823), 29n.). An anti-Jacobite version can be found in *A Collection of Loyal Songs for the Use of the Revolution Club* (Edinburgh, 1748), the opening verse of which reads: 'O, Brother Sandie, hear ye the news? / Lilli Bullero, Bullen a la. / An army's just come without any shoes. / Lilli Bullero, Bullen a la' (13–14). Scott owned a 1770 edition of this collection (*CLA*, 97). According to Percy, 2.358, the refrain was originally a watchword of the Irish Catholics, though a number of alternative explanations have been offered: see James Porter, 'The Cultural Expropriation of "Lillibulero" ', *Scottish Studies Review*, 5:1 (Spring 2004), 19–32.

219.1 episcopal meeting-house see note to 47.18–20.

219.4 Haddo's-hole one of the four churches within St Giles (the Little Kirk, or West Kirk), which is likely to have been the most popular with Covenanting Presbyterians. Fergus facetiously imagines the chanting of the metrical psalms of the Church of Scotland there. It is named after the royalist Sir John Gordon of Haddo, who was imprisoned in a small priest's room there (demolished *c.* 1790), before being tried and beheaded at the Cross of Edinburgh on 10 July 1644.

219.22–23 Nunc insanus ... detinet hostes *Latin* Now mad passion for the harsh war-god keeps me in arms, surrounded by weapons and confronting foes: Virgil, *Eclogues*, 10.44–45.

219.24 Robertson of Struan Alexander Robertson (*c.* 1670–1749), 13th Baron of Struan or Strowan. A veteran of earlier Jacobite campaigns, as far

back as that of Viscount Dundee in 1689, Robertson led the Robertsons to
the battle of Prestonpans, though not engaging in combat himself, and returned
to his Atholl homeland wearing General Cope's wolfskin coat and being pulled
along in the general's coach by his clansmen (Duffy, 569). He was also an
accomplished classical scholar and poet, and has been mentioned as one of
the prototypes for the Baron of Bradwardine: see Historical Note, 385–86.

219.24 clan Donnochy Clan Donnachie, or Clann Donnchaidh, collective
name for the Robertsons: see also note 82.2.

219.25 claims of Lude the Robertsons, in all their branches, belonged
to the Clann Donnchaidh, the founder of the clan being Donnchadh Reamhar
('Stout Duncan'), who was born *c.* 1275 in the reign of Alexander III. Chieftainship of the clan fell upon this man's eldest son, and from their principal
residence the chiefs were distinguished as the Struan Robertsons. The Robertsons of Lude, also in N Perthshire, were descended from his younger
son Patrick. No evidence has been discovered about a dispute between the
Struan and Lude branches over the chieftainship of the clan. After the 1715
rising, when Alexander Robertson of Struan fled to France, the forfeited
estate was granted by the government to his sister Margaret. In 1726 Alexander returned to Scotland and Margaret disponed the estate in life rent to
her brother and conveyed it in trust after his death to the Drumachune (or
Drummachin) branch of the family. When Alexander Robertson died without
an heir in 1749, the succession devolved upon Duncan Robertson of Drumachune, who therefore became Duncan Robertson of Drumachune and
Struan and Chief of the Clann Donnchaidh. However, in the rising of
1745–46 a leading part was played by Charlotte, the widow of John Robertson
of Lude, known as Lady Lude, and it may be that at this stage of the Rising
some doubt existed about who should be the chief of the clan after Alexander
Robertson died.

219.25 primo loco *Latin* in the first place.

219.27–28 For cruel . . . philabeg not identified. Alexander Robertson
of Struan's *Poems, on Various Subjects and Occasions,* published in 1751 or
1752, shortly after his death, does not include these lines, nor is there any
verse translation there of Virgil's *Eclogues.* 'The Fifth Book of Virgil's Aeneis
translated' appears on 301–44, but the language is in a formal 'classical' style.
Several examples are found of Robertson writing in a satirical vein, but there
is no evidence of him using the 'Doric' or Scots language.

219.32–35 She wadna . . . his plaidy from the ballad 'Bonny Lizie
Baillie' (Child, 227).

220.6 long-deserted halls no monarch visited Scotland between the cor-
onation of Charles II in 1651 and the visit of George IV in 1822.

222.5–6 their withers . . . unwrung see *Hamlet,* 3.2.237 ('Let the galled
jade wince, our withers are unwrung'). The underlying image is of a horse,
the *withers* being the part of the back between the shoulder blades, liable to be
rubbed sore by an ill-fitting saddle. 'Wither-rung' is used to describe the
condition of being injured in the shoulder blades; and 'unwrung' apparently
indicates a freedom from being so pinched or galled.

222.9 Bysshe's Art of Poetry Edward Bysshe, *The Art of English Poetry*
(London, 1702). The third part of this is titled 'A Collection of the most
Natural, Agreeable, and Noble Thoughts, viz. Allusions, Similes, Descriptions,
and Characters, of Persons and Things; that are to be found in the best
English Poets'.

222.22–23 O nymph . . . thine own see Anna Seward (1747–1809),
'From thy waves, stormy Lannow, I fly', stanza 2, lines 7–8, in *The Poetical
Works of Anna Seward,* ed. Walter Scott, 3 vols (Edinburgh, 1810; *CLA,* 202),
1.158. A copy of this poem (without the author's name) exists in Scott's hand in a

MS collection entitled 'Scottish Songs Walter Scott 1795' in the Abbotsford library (*CLA*, 104), at f. 66.

223.30–31   mauvaise honte   *French* false shame, bashfulness.

224.15   Burton's Anatomia   Robert Burton's *Anatomy of Melancholy* (1621; see *CLA*, 123). It has not been established whether the terms mentioned occur there: the only citation for *phrenesiac* in *OED* is from this same passage.

224.32   signal for parting   referring to the old tune, played at the end of assemblies and parties, and since largely replaced by 'Auld Lang Syne'. See 'O this is my departing time', in Herd, 2.225, and *Minstrelsy*, 2.156–58; see also *SMM*, Vol. 6 (1803), no. 600, which gives the tune. The final words of the song, 'Good Night and God/Joy be with you all' are apparent in Charles Edward's following words, and the connection is made explicit in a Magnum note by Scott (2.135n.). William Stenhouse in *Illustrations of the Lyric Poetry and Music of Scotland* (Edinburgh, 1853) notes how 'The principal publishers of Scottish music have also adopted it, as their farewell air, in closing their musical works' (510–11).

224.42–43   Audiit . . . in auras   *Latin* Phoebus heard, and decided that part of his prayer should prosper; part he scattered to the flying breezes: Virgil, *Aeneid*, 11.794–95.

225.1–2   my friend Bangour   referring to the Jacobite poet, William Hamilton of Bangour (1704–54), whose *Poems on Several Occasions* appeared in 1760. He wrote a triumphant 'Ode on the Battle of Gladsmuir, 1745', later published in the *Edinburgh Magazine*, 1 (Dec. 1773), 139. Translations of parts of Homer's *Iliad* and Virgil's *Aeneid* by him, written in heroic couplets, can be found in Robert Anderson, *The Works of the British Poets*, 9 (1795), 450–55, but with no matches to the lines attributed to him here (see following note). A Life of Bangour and List of his Poems by James Chalmers can be found in *Archeologia Scotica: or Transactions of the Society of Antiquaries of Scotland*, 3 (1831), 255–66.

225.3–4   Ae half . . . the wind   this couplet is close to the translation by John Dryden: 'Apollo heard, and, granting half his prayer,/ Shuffled in winds the rest, and tossed in empty air' (*Works*, ed. Scott, 1808, 15.137). Compare also Alexander Pope, *The Rape of the Lock* (1712), Canto 2, lines 45–46, and Alexander Strahan, *The Aeneid of Virgil Translated into Blank Verse*, 2 vols (London, 1767), 2.159 (Book 11, lines 1091–92). There is perhaps also a trace of *Othello*, 3.3.266–67 ('I'd whistle her off and let her down the wind/ To prey at fortune'), which in turn is echoed in Scott's letter to J. B. S. Morritt of 24 July 1814, concerning *Waverley* and novel-writing: 'I shall whistle it down the wind to prey on fortune' (*Letters*, 3.479). Almost certainly the Scots translation in the text is Scott's own.

225.12   proud step of the chief piper   not identified as a quotation.

225.20   bang up   get up quickly, rise hastily.

225.21   ahint the clachan . . . King's Park   by 'clachan' (village, settlement round a church) Callum might mean Edinburgh, somewhat risibly in view of its size; or, an alternative possibility, the village of Duddingston, at the end of the King's Park, near where the Jacobite army was encamped (see also notes to 214.8, 226.16–18, and 229.41).

225.26   leather dorlach wi' the lock   perhaps echoing an anecdote in Burt concering a Highlander seeing a portmanteau: 'Out! says he; what Fool was this that put a Lock upon Leather? and immediately ripp'd it open with his Dirk' (2.136). Scott in an ISet note not repeated in the Magnum glosses *dorlach* as 'Portmanteau'; *dorlach* usually refers to a kind of truss or knapsack worn by Highland soldiers.

225.38   deil ane   not one at all (emphatic).

226.6   Luckie Middlemass's   *Luckie* was a name commonly given to hostesses of taverns, one of the more famous being that of Luckie Middlemass in the Cowgate, running south of and parallel to the High Street, and situated where the south pier of the present South Bridge stands (see Marie W. Stuart, *Old Edinburgh Taverns* (London, 1952), 94). The establishment is celebrated in Robert Fergusson's poem 'Caller Oysters' (1772): 'To Luckie Middlemist's loup in' (line 39).

226.16–18   St Leonard's Hill . . . Arthur's Seat   St Leonard's Hill (now built-up) is a rocky area to the W of the King's Park (see note to 214.8) below Arthur's Seat, the striking peak (250 m) S of Holyrood House, Edinburgh. Charles Edward evidently moved his forces to an encampment near Duddingston, at the SE end of the King's Park, before marching out to confront General Cope on 20 September. See also note to 229.41.

226.29–30   like bees . . . their hives   see John Dryden, *The Spanish Friar* (1681), 1.1.52: in *Works*, ed. Scott (1808), 6.387.

226.43   Ganion Coheriga   *Gaelic* properly *Dh'aindeoin cò theireadh e* ('In spite of who would say it'). James Browne's *History of the Highlands and the Highland Clans*, 4 vols (Glasgow, 1838), under 'Armorial bearings' at end of Vol. 4, gives the motto of Clanranald as 'Dhandeon co Heirigha'.

227.1   Loch-Sloy   *Gaelic Loch Slòigh*. This war-cry of the MacFarlanes, is from the name of a loch in their traditional territory in the district of Lennox, to the W of the northern shores of Loch Lomond.

227.1–2   Forth, fortune . . . Tullibardine   'Furth fortune and fill the fetters' was the motto of the Clan Mhoraidh, or the Murrays (see James Logan, *The Clans of the Scottish Highlands*, 2 vols (London, 1845), Vol.1, Part XI, item 2). For William Murray, Marquess of Tullibardine, see note to 115.33.

227.2   Bydand   the motto of the Gordon clan, meaning 'abiding, steadfast'. For Lord Lewis Gordon, see note to 161.41.

227.8–9   red cross upon a white ground   no clear record appears to have survived concerning such a Jacobite standard in the 1745 rising. According to Robert Chambers, in describing the standard raised at Glenfinnan: 'It was a large banner of red silk, with a white space in the centre, but without the motto of "TANDEM TRIUMPHANS", which has been so often assigned to it': *History of the Rebellion in Scotland in 1745, 1746*, 2 vols (Edinburgh, 1827), 1.46–47. According to Home (50n.) 'The standard erected at Glenfinnin [*sic*] was made of white, blue, and red silk'. Other sources describe a red silken flag with a white square inset, sewn by the ladies of Kinlochmoidart, near where Charles Edward landed (see Duffy, 171).

227.9   Tandem Triumphans   *Latin* triumphant at last. Scott also refers to this motto as part of the royal Stuart standard in *Peveril of the Peak*, EEWN 14, 44.7. See also previous note.

227.17   reformed officers, or reformadoes   referring to the situation where an officer is left without command (officially owing to the 'reforming' of his company, but sometimes through disgrace), but retains his rank and seniority.

227.20–21   Circes of the High Street   from *Circe*, an enchantress in Greek mythology, and the bewitcher of Homer's Odysseus; here transposed to the Edinburgh High Street.

228.21   Helots   servants of Spartan families, having a status comparable to serfs in feudal Europe; in warfare, each Spartan heavy-armed soldier was attended to the field by a number of Helots.

228.21–22   the M'Couls . . . Fingal   evidently referring to the MacColl clan, which anciently settled on the shores of Loch Fyne, and whose patronymic is traditionally derived from 'Colla', a mythical ancestor of the MacDonalds. The MacColls were also connected to other clans, including the Stewarts of

Appin (see also note to 228.23 below). Scott here appears to be mistakenly associating this clan with Fin Macoul (Fionn mac Cumhaill), the Fingal of Ossianic legend.

228.23 Gibeonites inhabitants of the city of Gibeon, condemned to be hewers of wood and drawers of water: see Joshua, 9.21–23, 27.

228.23 Stuarts of Appine a relatively small clan, with lands reaching down to the E shore of Loch Linnhe, in Argyll and Bute. The clan was raised in 1745 by Charles Stewart of Ardsheal, a kinsman of the exiled 8th chief, and formed the core of a regiment which distinguished itself in the main engagements of the campaign. Members of the MacColl clan (see note to 228.21–22) who lived in Appin and Ballachulish followed the Stewarts of Appin. The 'Muster Roll' in *No Quarter Given*, ed. Alastair Livingstone, et al. (Glasgow, 2001), 14–15, shows nearly 30 MacColls in the Appin regiment, all under 'Other Ranks'.

228.24–25 Macbeaths ... Morays the clan ancestor of the Macbeths or Macbeaths is Macbeth (*c.* 1005–57), High Steward of Moray, later King of Scots, and the subject of Shakespeare's play of that name. The later history of the name is complicated, apparently overlapping with anglicised forms such as Bethune and Beaton, and no outstanding case of the clan being subject to the Morays/Murrays or to the Robertsons in Atholl has been discovered. Just one MacBeath (Donald MacBeath) is listed in the Muster Roll of Atholl Brigade: see *No Quarter Given*, ed. Alastair Livingstone, et al. (Glasgow, 2001), 27.

228.30 hewed wood and drew water see note to 228.23 ('Gibeonites').

228.32 general disarming act see note to 73.27.

228.43 scythe set straight upon a pole such a weapon is noted in a number of eye-witness accounts, including one in Home: 'a company or two (about 100 men) had each of them in his hand the shaft of a pitch-fork, with the blade of a scythe fastened to it' (104).

229.18–19 an iron gun Scott's Magnum note (2.146) affirms that this circumstance is historical, but offers no direct supporting evidence. Home reports how 'a volunteer' told Sir John Cope that the insurgents 'had no cannon nor artillery of any sort, but one small iron gun which he had seen without a carriage, lying upon a cart, drawn by a little Highland horse' (104).

229.40 remarkable ridge of basaltic rocks either referring to Salisbury Crags, the circle of cliffs to the W of Arthur's Seat (see note to 226.16–18), or to Samson's Ribs, a large cliff of columnar basalt above the way to Duddingston (see next note).

229.41 Duddingston village then outside and about 4 km SE of Edinburgh. See also note to 226.16–18.

230.12 Mar e Bran is e brathair *Gaelic Mur e Bran, is e a bhràthair* ('If it is not Bran, it is his brother'), Bran being the name of Fionn's (Fingal's) dog. The saying is in Macintosh, 55, and is still current.

230.39 Haddington royal burgh 29 km E of Edinburgh. Sir John Cope's forces had marched there on 19 September, having landed at Dunbar two days earlier.

230.39–231.1 Musselburgh ancient burgh 10 km E of Edinburgh.

231.3 Carberry-Hill just SE of Musselburgh, where Mary Queen of Scots surrendered to the Protestant lords in 1567. The location is mentioned in the *Caledonian Mercury* report of 23 Sept. 1745 (*CLA*, 100): 'The Army marched and drew up on Carberry-hill, where we learn'd that General Cope had fallen down into the Low Country, East of Prestonpans.'

232.20–21 My friends ... the scabbard as reported in a number of contemporary and near-contemporary records, but most immediately in that in the *Caledonian Mercury* of 23 Sept. 1745: 'That Morning his Royal Highness the Prince put himself at the Head of the Army at Duddingston, and presenting his Sword, said, *My Friends, I have flung away the Scabbard*'.

232.25–26 garçons apothicaires *French* apothecary's assistants.

232.32 ceade millia molligheart *Gaelic Ceud mile mallachd ort* ('a hundred thousand curses on you'). See also note to 125.21.

233.16 village of Tranent 15 km E of Edinburgh, overlooking the site of the eventual battle, near Prestonpans. Compare *The Woodhouselee MS* (London, 1907): 'The Highlanders had marched in two divisions from Musleburg and fixed one a rising grownd sowthward above Tranent' (33). See also note to 236.3–4.

234.7 Seaton and Cockenzie settlements along the Firth of Forth coastline, E of Prestonpans (see next note). Port Seaton was directly on the coast, with Seaton village slightly inland, to the W of Seaton House. Cockenzie and Port Seton now form a combined burgh.

234.8 Preston then a settlement 2 km to the W of Seaton village, with Prestonpans slightly to the N on the Forth coast, the latter known at this period for its fishing and salt industry. The low road Scott described is visible as 'Road to Dunbar' on 'A Plan of the Battle of Tranent fought Sept 21st 1745' (NLS, Acc. 8392), and passes between Seaton House and the old village of Preston.

234.9 inclosures of Seaton-house i.e. the ground surrounding the house (see note to 234.7) had been enclosed with walls, whereas the area was mostly open country.

235.9 sidier roy red (i.e. government) soldier; see note to 83.24.

235.9 tottering . . . a staff *proverbial* 'As tottering as an egg on a staff' (Macintosh, 24).

235.10 even a haggis *proverbial* 'Even a haggies will run down the hill' (Macintosh, 60).

235.40 tops and yards referring to the spars supporting sails in a square-rigged vessel.

236.3–4 church-yard of Tranent which was occupied by some 50 Lochiel Camerons on the eve of the battle, who suffered a number of casualties through the Hanoverian artillery. The incident is recorded in a number of contemporary accounts of the battle.

236.33 see his winding-sheet such a superstition is described in Martin Martin's *A Description of the Western Islands of Scotland*, 2nd edn (London, 1716; *CLA*, 5): 'When a Shroud is perceiv'd about one, it is a sure Prognostick of Death: The time is judged according to the height of it about the Person . . . and as it is frequently seen to ascend higher towards the head, Death is concluded to be at hand within a few days, if not hours, as daily experience confirms' (302).

237.11–12 Evening Service of the Episcopal Church the liturgy of the Episcopal Church in Scotland was not much different to that of the Presbyterian Church of Scotland, but this detail reflects the fact that many Jacobites from NE Scotland were Episcopalian, and had resisted Presbyterianism in the NE in spite of the Church of Scotland being established by law in 1690.

237.26 Tacitus Roman historian (*c.* 55–c. 119), author of *Histories, Annals*, and other works.

237.26–27 In rebus . . . Fortuna *Latin* in matters of war Fortune is most dominant. Not located in Tacitus. But compare 'fortuna per omnia humana maxime in res bellicas potens' ('fortune [is] powerful in all human affairs, but particularly in matters of war'), in Livy, *Ab Urbe Condita*, 9.17.3.

237.28 Luck can maist in the mellee i.e. luck is most powerful in the confusion of battle: not identified as a saying.

237.29 yon man i.e. General Cope.

237.29 deacon of his craft in Scotland, the president of an incorporated trade, or (more generally) the master of a craft.

237.32 as a toad under a harrow proverbial: see Ramsay, 100; Ray, 299; *ODEP*, 826.

237.39–40 Though it appears... 'Scotchman' see *Henry V*, 4.1.83–84 (with 'Welshman' for 'Scotchman').

238.5–6 point of war... nocturnal duty for 'point of war' see note to 182.2–3. The signal generally used to mark the end of the day in the British army from the 17th century was the Last Post.

238.17 thick as leaves in Valambrosa see Milton, *Paradise Lost*, 1.302–03.

238.33–34 distant village clock... toll three compare *Henry V*, Prologue to Act 4, 15–16 ('the clocks do toll,/ And the third hour of drowsy morning name').

238.38 Courage, my brave friends equivalent of the French phrase 'courage, mes braves', which is used to raise the listeners' spirits.

238.39 faithful friend identified in a Magnum note (2.172–73) as Robert Anderson, junior, of Whitburgh, an East Lothian landholder. The information is also found in Home (114), who notes that Anderson's father had enaged in the Jacobite rising of 1715.

239.30 Hylax in limine latrat *Latin* Hylax barks at the threshold: Virgil, *Eclogues*, 8.107. In Virgil it is a lover, not an army, which is being announced.

239.36 beat the general referring to the beat of the drum for an assembly of all troops prior to a battle or march.

240.15 win silks for our tartans possibly relating to Fergus's ambition for royal reward in the Jacobite cause, with the prospect of court dress replacing the tartans worn on the battlefield.

240.19 a short prayer as mentioned in the *Caledonian Mercury* report of 23 Sept. 1745 (*CLA*, 100): 'and pulling off their Bonnets, looking up to Heaven, made a short Prayer, and run forward.' Scott later recalled Stewart of Invernahyle describing this event: 'our people put up their bonnets to say a bit prayer and then scrug their bonnets doun our their een and set forward' (*Letters*, 10.238–39).

240.33 Camerons will draw the first blood compare *The Lady of the Lake* (1810): 'Which spills the foremost foeman's life,/ That party conquers in the strife' (Canto 4, stanza 6; repeated at Canto 5, stanza 13; *Poetical Works*, 8.168, 224). In the battle, the Camerons formed the left flank of the Jacobite army: Home notes that they were nearest the enemy as the army advanced (118). An underlying implication here perhaps is that Fergus wants luck for his own clan, though inter-clan rivalry seems to be the main spur.

241.29 his house Colonel Gardiner's residence was at Bankton House, formerly Olivestob, between the village of Preston and Tranent Church.

241.37 blow of a scythe in the Abbotford copy of James Ray's *Compleat History of the Rebellion* (York, 1749; *CLA*, 89) Scott has written in the margin of p. 52: 'He was dismounted by the blow of a highlander armed with a scythe straight on a pole'. This presumably is in correction of the statement in Ray that the mortal blow was from 'a *Lochaber* ax'. Scott's Magnum note (2.173–75) quotes from Dr Doddridge's *Some Remarkable Passages in the Life of the Honourable Col. James Gardiner* (Edinburgh, 1747; *CLA*, 97): 'a Highlander advanced towards him with scythe fastened to a long Pole, with which he gave him such a deep Wound on his Right Arm, that his Sword dropped out of his hand'. The same account, as quoted, attributes the giving of the death blow to 'one Mac-Naught, who was executed about a Year after' (186). The trial and execution of John MacNaughton for the murder was a contentious issue in the years following. According to one source, such a deed was 'an impossibility, for Gardiner had been cut down by a Highlander armed with a scythe (supposed to be a Cameron), while Macnaughton was on horseback in another part of the field': Katharine M. Murray, *A Military History of Perthshire 1660–1902*, 2 vols (Perth, 1908), 1.332.

242.12   fate of Balmawhapple   Scott's Magnum note (2.175) indicates a source in the death of a 'gentleman . . . who resembled Balmawhapple in the article of courage only, [who] fell at Preston in the manner described'. This person is identifiable as David Threipland, and the incident was later described by Robert Chambers: 'when he had got to about two miles from the field of battle, one of the dragoons turning around and observing that they had only a single pursuer close to them, drew a pistol and shot him dead' (*The Threiplands of Fingask: A Family Memoir* (London and Edinburgh, 1880), 41).

242.15   took heart of grace   plucked up courage, took heart.

242.20–21   mair tint . . . Sherriff-Muir   apparently proverbial, though the first citation in *ODEP* (500) is from this passage. Scott uses the expression 'Mair Skaith at Sheriffmoor' in a letter to Adam Fergusson of 15 January 1819 (*Letters*, 5.293). He also later applies the expression to the battle of Flodden in *The Monastery* (1820) and *The Fortunes of Nigel* (1822). Sherriff-Muir itself refers to the indecisive battle near Stirling in 1715, which checked the progress of the Jacobite rising under the Earl of Mar.

243.20   want of winding up   a similar incident can be found in James Pettit Andrews, *Anecdotes, &c. Antient and Modern. With Observations* (London, 1789), 16–17. The reviewer in the *Critical Review* (5th series, 1 (March 1815), 294–95) complained about the 'threadbare' nature of the anecdote. Scott nevertheless gave his own version in a note in the 1Set, omitted by the Magnum but later printed in the Dryburgh edition (1892).

243.26   puir Berwick   named presumably after the Duke of Berwick (see note to 51.31–32).

244.3   prœlium equestre   *Latin* equestrian combat; see Julius Caesar, *De Bello Gallico*, 1.18, etc.

244.5   pride and terrour   the same combination (and spelling) is found in 'A Sacred Poem of the Troubles of David' by Abraham Cowley (1618–67): 'So when the pride and terrour of the Wood' (of a lion); and in Samuel Johnson's *Irene* (written 1736, performed 1749): 'The pride and terrour of succeeding days' (2.2).

244.6   far ben   normally referring to the innermost room of the house (see note to 42.41), though here presumably signifying engagement in the heart of the battle.

244.14   Inveraughlin . . . Edderalshendrach   possibly deriving in Gaelic from *Inbhir Adhlainn* ('Confluence of the river Adhlann') and *Eadar Dha Seann Daraich* ('Between the two old oaks'), in which case the names would denote territory. On the other hand, Scott may have been inventing or guessing names.

244.33   black as midnight   see William D'Avenant (1606–68), *The Rivals* (London, 1668), 7 (Act 1): 'Though our Misfortunes are as black as midnight . . .'.

244.37   letters of slains   documents issued by the relations of a person killed in private feud, stating that no further liability for the crime existed, and requesting the sovereign to pardon the offender. This chiefly came as the result of an acceptable satisfaction or reparation having been received.

245.5   blanch   more usually *blench* in modern Scots law; and usually applied to a holding of land for which there is no return or a token one.

245.5   which Craig opines   Thomas Craig (1538?-1608), Scottish lawyer and author of *Jus Feudale* (1655; 3rd edn, 1732, *CLA* 12), in which Craig identifies *blench* holdings with frank ('free') holdings in feudal law (e.g. at 1.10.5). See the translation by James Avon (Lord) Clyde: 'In Scotland frank feus are known under the description of blench-holdings, and were originally granted because of distinguished public service or as the reward of military prowess' (*The Jus Feudale of Thomas Craig of Riccarton*, 2 vols (Edinburgh and London, 1934), 1.145). Later at 2.3.32 Craig describes the returns for various kinds of feudal holdings, including two types of *blench* holding, 'blanca' and 'blanca firma', the dues for the former being nominal and never paid or sought, the latter involving payment of something of value (such as a pound of pepper) which the superior can demand.

245.5–6 blancum, or rather francum *blancus* and *francus* (with the neuter forms *blancum* and *francum*) are not Classical Latin adjectives, but are both found in later Latin, meaning 'white' and 'free' respectively.

245.6 pro servitio... post battalliam *Latin* for the service of pulling off, or removing, the king's boots after battle.

245.12 per expressum *Latin* expressly, distinctly.

245.15 Prince Regent in December 1743 Charles Edward's father had named him Prince Regent, giving him full authority to act in his name. Declarations by the Jacobite council during the 1745 rising refer to him as Charles, Prince Regent, and are generally signed by him as such.

245.16 court of France Philip, Duke of Orleans, was Regent from the death of Louis XIV in 1715 until 1723, the likely period of Fergus's childhood.

245.23 alter ego *Latin* another I; a second self.

245.24 great tenants of the crown those who hold their lands directly from the Crown, as immediate vassals.

245.33–34 It's ill... off a Highlandman not found in traditional proverb books, but possibly an adaptation of 'It is ill getting Breeks aff a bare Arse' (Ramsay, 93; see also Ray, 296, and *ODEP*, 84, 802). However the wording 'Its ill taking a Breek off an Highlandman' is found in a MS 'Collection of Scots Proverbs' in the Abbotsford Library (*CLA*, 169), unfoliated, under 'I', no. 248. As Highlanders wore a plaid, or kilt, the proverb means you cannot do the impossible. Scott also uses the expression in *Rob Roy*, EEWN 5, 220.21, and in *The Fortunes of Nigel*, EEWN 13, 73.37–38.

245.38 lie BOOTS i.e. in the vernacular boots; see also note to 45.1–2.

245.39–40 Caius Cæsar... Caius Tiberius... Caligula Tiberius Caesar Augustus (42 BC–AD 37), Roman emperor, was succeeded by Caius Julius Caesar Germanicus (AD 12–41), nicknamed Caligula, 'little (soldier's) boots'.

245.40–41 a caligulis... patris sui *Latin* from the small boots, or light boots, which he wore as a young child in the army of his father, Germanicus. See Tacitus, *Annals*, 1.41.3; and also compare Suetonius, *Gaius*, 9.

245.43 Rule of St Benedict St Benedict (*c.* 480–*c.* 547) was the founder of the Benedictine Order, the earliest established order in the West. The 'Rule of St Benedict', a basis for the practice of monasticism, was compiled in Italy in about 530, and was distributed in manuscript form widely throughout Europe. Ch. 55 is 'Of the Clothing and Shoes of the Brethren'. Paul Delatte comments, 'It is difficult to identify these coverings of the feet...; antiquaries dispute lengthily about them': *The Rule of St Benedict: A Commentary* (London 1921), 350.

245.43 Abbey of St Amand near Valenciennes in northern France, founded in the 7th century. It was a Benedictine monastery known for the production of manuscripts, though no specific 'Glossarium' has been discovered.

246.4–5 Caligæ dictæ... tantum intromittuntur *Latin* boots are so called because they are tied with straps, whereas slippers are not bound but only slipped on the feet.

246.5 denominated from the ligatures the Baron is wrong in implying that *caligae* are so called because they are tied with straps: the word is derived from the verb *calcare* ('to trample down').

246.8   exuere seu detrahere   *Latin* to remove or to pull off.

246.11   de re vestiaria   *Latin* on what concerns clothes.

246.14   res vestiaria   *Latin literally* a thing to do with clothes; clothing, dress. Fergus wittily switches the Latin from theoretical issues to practical reality (the Highlanders' stripping of the corpses of the slain).

246.20   si petatur tantum   *Latin* only if asked for. This phrase is discussed in Thomas Craig's *Jus Feudale* (1655; 3rd edn, 1732, *CLA* 12), at 2.3.32, in relation to *blench* holdings (see note to 245.5), where the import clearly is that the service is only to be performed if demanded.

246.22–23   Dirleton's Doubts and Queries   Sir John Nisbet, Lord Dirleton (1610–88), *Some Doubts & Questions, in the Law; especially of Scotland. As also, some Decisions of the Lords of Council and Session* (Edinburgh, 1698).

246.23   Grippit versus Spicer   apparently a fictitious case, and not found among the *Decisions* listed in Dirleton (see previous note).

246.24   ob non solutum canonem   *Latin* for not paying the sum due: referring, in Scots law, to a failure to perform the dues for which a feudal holding had been granted.

246.29   schedule of a protest   a *schedule* is a formal document prepared by a notary, with *protest* implying the protecting of one's rights in the face of the action of another.

247.23   au revoir   *French* till we meet again.

248.3   sidier roy   see note to 83.24.

248.4–5   forbad her ... wi' her   for gender confusion in the representation of Gaelic English, see note to 155.18.

248.5   Lochaber axe   the assurance as offered by Dugald here possibly relates to reports in James Ray's *Compleat History of the Rebellion* (York, 1749; *CLA*, 89) and elsewhere that Colonel Gardiner (as opposed to the present officer) had been killed by a blow from such a weapon: see also note to 241.37, and, for the weapon itself, 81.3.

248.22   Pinkie-house   near Musselburgh, on the E side of the River Esk, the seat of the Marquis of Tweeddale, then Secretary of State for Scotland. Compare the *Caledonian Mercury*, 23 Sept. 1745 (*CLA*, 100): 'The Victorious Prince lay that Night at the House of Pinkie, and retired Yesternight to Holy-rood-house'.

249.11   Colonel Talbot   for possible prototypes, and the significance of the name, see Historical Note, 373–74, 388–89.

250.31   king's messenger   messenger employed to deliver documents and arrest individuals for treason and other state crimes.

252.3–4   as plenty as blackberries   compare *1 Henry IV*, 2.4.232 ('If reasons were as plentiful as blackberries').

252.13   Duke of Cumberland   William Augustus, Duke of Cumberland (1721–65), third son of George II, who took over the command of the government forces in southern England in November 1745.

252.14   triumphs at Fontenoy   referring to the battle of Fontenoy, fought in the Austrian Netherlands on 11 May 1745, in which the French forces under Marshal Maurice de Saxe defeated British troops commanded by the Duke of Cumberland. Fergus is clearly being ironic, though it should be added that British foot soldiers (including the Highland Black Watch regiment) performed well, with the Duke himself reportedly showing personal courage, though little tactical skill.

252.16   St James's   St James's Palace, built by Henry VIII, the London residence of the sovereign 1698–1837.

252.17   Whittington ... those of Bow   referring to the traditional story of Dick Whittington (*c.* 1350–1423), who, as an orphan apprentice retreating from London in despair of finding fame and fortune, supposedly heard the

Bow bells (those St Mary-le-Bow, in Cheapside) prophetically chiming 'Turn, again, Whittington, Lord Mayor of London'.

252.20 every wind of doctrine Ephesians 4.14.

252.23 white rose a Jacobite emblem.

252.23 pulling caps snatching or pulling off someone else's headgear, used especially when there is rivalry.

252.23-24 preux chevalier *French* valiant knight.

252.24-25 butter-woman riding to market see *As You Like It*, 3.2.88.

252.34 Andrew Ferrara i.e. sword: compare 208.42 and note.

252.35-36 Westminster-hall the Hall of the old medieval Palace of Westminster in London, and the home of the chief Law Courts of England from the 13th century (to 1882).

254.7 in love with vanity *1 Henry IV*, 5.4.106.

254.10 battle of Gladsmuir Gladsmuir is a village (and parish) in East Lothian, lying 5 km W of Haddington. This name for the battle is used in a number of contemporary documents, substantiating Scott's claim that it was the one chosen by the Jacobites. An explanation is given in the account of the parish of Prestonpans (1793) in *The Statistical Account of Scotland*, ed. Sir John Sinclair, 21 vols (Edinburgh, 1791–99; *CLA*, 84): 'The Highlanders, in their accounts, usually gave it the name of the *Battle of Gladsmuir*; though Gladsmuir is at least 3 miles distant from the scene of action. There was, it seems, a tradition among them, that a battle was to be fought on the *Moor of the Gledes*, which, in the issue, would insure the *rightful Sovereign* the peaceable possession of his throne. They made the application that was most favourable to their views' (ed. Donald J. Withrington and Ian R. Grant, Vol. 2, 'The Lothians' (Wakefield, 1975), 584). A similar explanation is offered in Scott's *Tales of a Grandfather*, in a note tagged to 'the battle of Preston, or of Gladsmuir, as the Jacobites preferred calling it': 'They affected this name to reconcile the victory to some ancient metrical prophecies, which happen to fix on Gladsmuir as a field of battle in which the Scottish should be victorious:— / "On Gladsmuir sall the battle be"' (*Prose Works*, 26.180n.).

254.20-21 evening of the 20th the battle of Prestonpans or Gladsmuir was actually fought on 21 September, so Prince Charles would have been at Pinkie-house that evening.

254.23 of that Ilk *literally* of that place; properly used when a person's name is the same as that of his estate, and a means of distinguishing the main branch of a family from the cadet lines.

254.26 lately named a commissary a *commissary* was a local judge, who, after the Reformation, dealt primarily with minor matters relating to marriage, legitimacy, debt, defamation, and the execution of wills and testaments. Alternatively, the title refers to Macwheeble's appointment as an officer in charge of military stores.

254.26-27 under form of instrument by production of a formal notarial document (compare 246.29 and note).

254.28-29 used and wont i.e. that is usual and customary.

254.29 Charter of Robert Bruce i.e. one granted by Robert Bruce (1274–1329), King of Scots.

254.31 Chancery the Chancery in Scotland was the royal office that issued formal documents in the monarch's name; it carried on after the Union of 1707, with the function of keeping registers and issuing various commissions, though after 1708 there was no Scottish Lord Chancellor. In the present case, however, the recording of the act of homage in one of the registers of the Jacobite Chancery Office is apparently meant.

255.1-2 rite et . . . et peracta *Latin* duly and solemnly carried out and completed: used in legal practice to express the presumption of the regularity of a legal proceeding.

255.2–3 protocol of the Lord High Chamberlain the Lord Chamberlain is a member of the royal household, so presumably a shadow Jacobite office is meant here; *protocol* here indicates a formal record in an official book which has a legal effect. The overall supposition behind the Gazette report appears to be that a full royal court is in presence.

255.11 dexter cantle of the shield the right-hand corner of the shield (but left-hand from the position of the onlooker).

255.17 seamy side *Othello*, 4.2.147.

255.33 presbyterian clergyman according to Scott's Magnum note: 'The clergyman's name was Mac-Vicar; . . . he preached every Sunday in the West Kirk, while the Highlanders were in possession of Edinburgh' (2.199n.). A version of the sermon is given in James Ray's *Compleat History of the Rebellion* (York, 1749; *CLA*, 89): 'Bless the King, thou knows what King I mean; may the Crown sit long easy on his Head, &c. And for this Man that is come amongst us to seek an earthly Crown: We beseech thee in Mercy to take him to thyself and give him a Crown of Glory' (59). The minister in question can be identified as the Rev. Neil M'Vicar (d. 1747), Minister of St Cuthbert's Church (known then as the West Kirk), 1707–47 (see Hew Scott, *Fasti Ecclesiae Scoticanae*, 1 (1915), 101).

255.39 blue caps knitted dark blue bonnets, as worn by the Highland army; also used of the wearers of such caps, e.g. for Scotsmen or for marauders.

256.1 my old commander, Guest General Joshua Guest (1660–1747), barrack-master for north Britain and in a state of half-retirement at the start of the 1745 rising. However, at the time of the battle of Prestonpans Guest became for a period commander-in-chief in the Edinburgh district, with General Preston (1659?–1748), who had held the Deputy-Governorship of the Castle since 1715, under him: see W. B. Blaikie, 'Edinburgh at the Time of the Occupation of Prince Charles', *The Book of the Old Edinburgh Club*, 2 (1909), 17n. The first edition's 'General Guest' was later changed by Scott in the ISet and Magnum to 'General Preston', possibly on account of Preston's greater obduracy in defending the position. Illustrative of contemporary perceptions is Michael Hughes, *A Plain Narrative or Journal of the Late Rebellion begun in 1745* (London, 1746; *CLA*, 93) concerning Preston's ordering a cannon to be fired from Castle Hill: 'It is to be noted, that this Order of Governor *Preston*, was against the Orders of General *Guest*, who was then Lieutenant Governor, and commanded *Preston*' (9).

256.2 North Loch the loch or lake N of the Castle and Old Town of Edinburgh, where Princes Street Gardens now are. It was drained in the later 18th century.

256.17–18 bullet grazed . . . from a balcony Scott's Magnum note (2.202n.) describes such an incident occurring in the case of a Miss Nairne in Edinburgh. This person has been identified as Mary Nairne (1709–74), the 6th daughter and 10th child of the second Lord Nairne. For further information, see Historical Note, 374.

256.38 malice prepense malice planned beforehand; see note to 20.33.

257.1 Italian knight-errant Prince Charles's grandmother, Mary of Modena, was an Italian princess; he was also born (1720) in Rome, at the Palazzo Muti-Papazurri, the main Jacobite centre from 1719, and spent much of his childhood and young manhood in Italy; 'knight-errant' signifies an itinerant knight.

257.33 disaster in Flanders referring to the defeat of the allied forces by the French at Fontenoy during the War of Austrian Succession (see also note to 252.14).

258.12 amende honorable *French* honourable amends, apology or reparation.

258.40 Ruffen *Ruffin* is a cant name for the devil. The name is also interpretable as a phonetic version of Ruthven, itself pronounced 'Riven' (compare note to 167.40).

259.3 Hoy Church and Sachefrel rustic form of a popular call in the street during the trial of Dr Henry Sacheverell (*c.* 1674–1724), a High Church clergyman who had been impeached for a sermon preached on Guy Fawkes Day, 1709, denouncing toleration and the right of resistance. Dissenting chapels were sacked to the cry of High Church and Sacheverell.

259.3 harvest whome harvest home, close of the harvesting.

259.13 poor Gardiner the surname is restored here in full from the MS, making the pun more explicit, while offering a fuller clue than elsewhere available in the original printed text to the identity of Colonel Gardiner (see notes to 22.31–32 and 33.5).

261.18–19 at Berwick Berwick-upon-Tweed, town on the E coast at the border between England and Scotland where the Tweed joins the sea, an English borough after its final capture from the Scots in 1482.

262.36 mock court of St Germains Saint-Germain-en-Laye, near Paris, where the exiled Stuart family held court after the flight of James VII and II in 1688. Although the Stuarts were forced to leave St Germain in 1713 the phrase 'court of St Germains' continued to be in use (as here).

262.42 Mac a standard part of a surname in Gaelic, signifying 'son of'. In 1745 'Mac' names would nearly always indicate a Highlander.

263.3 Miss Mac-Jupiter i.e. Miss son of Jupiter. In Greek mythology Aphrodite, goddess of love, was the daughter of Zeus, chief of the gods; their Roman equivalents, Venus and Jupiter, came to absorb the characteristics of their Greek predecessors.

263.31 David and Jonathan biblical exemplars of male bonding: see 1 Samuel 18.1–4.

263.31–32 two Bond-street loungers possibly echoing *An Heroic Epistle to Mr. Winsor* (London, 1808; *CLA*, 186): 'E'en Bond-street loungers bright ideas gain, / And what is now a blank—becomes a brain' (7). Bond Street (now called Old and New Bond Street) was and is a fashionable shopping street running from Piccadilly to Oxford Street in London.

264.42 of the Mac—— Ed6 (1816) fills out the name to 'Macindallaghers', itself probably a fictitious name.

265.2 Corrinaschian *Gaelic Coire na[n] Sìthean*, Corrie of the Fairy Knoll(s); the latter probably signifying the name of a tack, or farm.

265.3 eldest cadet . . . youngest in the Highland clan system the branch of the clan that had been longest separated from the main stem is called the eldest cadet, and the branch closest to the main stem the youngest cadet, the terms also being used to describe the chieftains of those branches. Home observes that customarily 'The chief was colonel, the eldest cadet was lieutenant-colonel, and the next cadet was major', while noting that in 1745 'In some regiments, the eldest cadet was lieutenant-colonel, and in others the youngest cadet' (9, 9n.). In battle the eldest cadet might command the right wing (traditionally 'the post of honour'), and the youngest the rear.

265.16–17 gun-powder Highlanders compare *1 Henry IV*, 5.4.121 ('gunpowder Percy').

265.26 Lochiel see note to 116.1. The truncated names which follow are not so easily identified.

265.33 Tasso Torquato Tasso (1544–95), author of *Gerusalemme liberata*.

266.24 obsidional crown used to describe a wreath conferred as a mark of honour upon a Roman general who raised a siege.

266.26   paretaria, or pellitory   *pellitory* is used to describe a plant growing on walls; in Latin (*herba*) *parietaria*, from *paries*, a wall.

266.37   ditch ... across the Castle-hill   'On the 1st of Octo[be]r in the forenoon, they began to dig a Trench at the back of the Reservoir; And from other quarters they fir'd some Small shot at the Centries on the wall. This provocked [*sic*] the Garrison to fire upon them with Small arms which killed 3 of the Enemy, wounded their Officer, and made them discontinue their trenching': [Anon], *The History of the Rebellion in the Years 1745 and 1746*, ed. Henrietta Tayler (Oxford, 1944), 81. The Castle Hill reservoir, which served five cisterns in the High Street, was originally built in 1720. Shortly afterwards another trench was formed across Castle Hill Street by soldiers sallying from the Castle, after which a truce was arrived at allowing communication with the Castle (Home, 126).

267.1–2   towering passion   *Hamlet*, 5.2.79.

267.32–33   Highland Ancient   *ancient* here used to signify ensign (or standard-bearer), as in Shakespeare; e.g. Ancient Pistol and Ancient Iago.

268.6   earl's patent   see note to 100.24.

269.6   party per pale   divided by a perpendicular line.

269.6   scutcheon of pretence   a small heraldic shield bearing the arms of an heiress placed in the centre of her husband's shield, instead of being impaled with his arms.

269.35   put your faith in princes   see Psalm 146.3 ('Put not your trust in princes').

270.2–3   curse not ... thy thought   Ecclesiastes 10.20.

270.10   planté la   *French* standing there, fixed to the spot.

270.16–17   Bisogna coprirsi, Signor   *Italian* you must cover (guard), sir; effectively, 'look out for yourself, mister'.

270.24   To one thing constant never   *Much Ado About Nothing*, 2.3.60.

270.31   Warwick, the King-maker   Richard Neville (1428–71), who became Earl of Warwick in 1449; known as the Kingmaker for his part in placing both Henry VI and Edward IV on the English throne.

271.5–9   And then ... she'll die   see *King John*, 3.4.82–86.

271.11   had his eyes   *Julius Caesar*, 1.2.62.

271.32   Ariosto   Ludovico Ariosto (1474–1533), Italian poet, best known for his romantic epic *Orlando furioso* (1516).

272.17   Mercutio   witty nobleman and Romeo's friend in *Romeo and Juliet*.

272.21   Tibbert, or Taggart   Tybalt, pronounced Tibbert, who fatally wounds Mercutio in *Romeo and Juliet*.

272.27   Rosaline   with whom Romeo is infatuated at the start of *Romeo and Juliet*, though his love is unrequited.

272.34   From love's ... lives unharmed   *Romeo and Juliet*, 1.1.209.

272.36   She hath forsworn to love   *Romeo and Juliet*, 1.1.221.

273.4–6   come what ... in her sight   *Romeo and Juliet*, 2.6.3–5.

273.18–20   Mac-Girdie's mare ... poor thing died   according to Brewer, this is an old Greek joke, well known to schoolboys who have been taught the *Analecta Graeca Minora*: see *Dictionary of Phrase and Fable* (1895), under 'MacGirdie's Mare'.

273.28   alors comme alors   *French* time enough when that comes.

273.36–38   the lyrical poet ... in drink   see Alexander Brome, 'The Mad Lover' (line 1), in *Songs and other Poems* (2nd edn, 1664), 47.

274.6   come what come will   proverbial (see *ODEP*, 135), and Shakespearean (see *Macbeth*, 1.3.146). The expression is matched in Horace Walpole, *The Castle of Otranto* (1765), Ch. 3: 'well! Sirs, he held this estate; he held it by his good sword and by the favour of St. Nicholas—so did my father, and so, Sirs, will I, come what come will ...'.

277.12   Leith   the port of Edinburgh.

277.20   camp at Duddingston   in the weeks following the battle of
Prestonpans, a large part of the Jacobite army remained in camp at Duddingston
(see Home, 129n.; also note above to 229.41).

277.23   this passport   for instances of passports and terms of parole
allowed by the Jacobites to their prisoners, see *The Whitefoord Papers*, ed. W.
A. S. Hewins (Oxford, 1898), 60–65.

278.10–11   to the Pretend——   i.e. Talbot cuts short saying 'the Pretender',
the name used for the exiled Stuart claimants by their opponents. Scott expressed his own sensibilities over this in a letter to Margaret Clephane of 13
July 1813: 'I never used the word Pretender which is a most unseemly word
in my life unless when (God help me) I was obliged to take the oaths of
Abjuration and Supremacy at elections and so forth and even then I always
did it with a qualm of conscience' (*Letters*, 3.302).

278.13   Chevalier . . . travelling name   compare Saunders Fairford in
Redgauntlet: 'Thus he spoke sometimes of the Chevalier, but never either of
the Prince, which would have been sacrificing his own principles, or of the
Pretender, which would have been offensive to those of others' (EEWN 17,
126.29–32).

278.34   Berwick or Shields   for Berwick, see note to 261.18–19; (North)
Shields is down river from Newcastle-upon-Tyne, near the mouth of the
Tyne.

278.34   ride post   i.e. ride on post horses, hired for one stage at a time at
inns around 12 to 20 miles (20 to 32 km) apart on the road to London.

279.11–13   Close behind . . . be employed   compare John Dryden, *The
Spanish Friar* (1681), 4.2.34–36: 'And that accursed Bertran/ Stalks close
behind her, like a witch's fiend,/ Pressing to be employed' (in *Works*, ed.
Scott (1808), 6.450). The spelling of Bertram instead of Bertran, possibly a
slip by Scott or by Talbot, has resulted in this passage being wrongly associated
with Charles Robert Maturin's tragedy, *Bertram* (1816).

279.16–17   bate them an ace   make the slightest abatement: proverbial
(see Ray, 176; *ODEP*, 32).

279.18   hang their bonnets . . . moon   see *Coriolanus*, 1.1.210–12.

279.25   sucking devil   i.e. a devil still being suckled, one who is as yet
unweaned. The term is also found in Scott, *Kenilworth* (1821), EEWN 11,
371.26.

279.27   about fourteen in years   Talbot's observation is not necessarily an
exaggeration. The young age of several of the Jacobite prisoners held after the
failure of the Rising is noted in Robert C. Jarvis, *Collected Papers of the Jacobite
Rising*, 2 vols (Manchester, 1971–72): 'This factor of the extreme youth of
some of the prisoners is common to Carlisle, York, and Chester . . . Certainly
many people in England were struck by the very high proportion of young
boys accompanying the invading army. A particular letter from Manchester,
from one private person to another, . . . estimated that the army as it entered
Manchester included as many as three thousand "boys of 10, 12 or 14 years
old"' (2.298–99).

279.28   playing at quoits   game involving throwing metal rings at a target-
pin in the ground; horseshoes were often used in impromptu versions of the
game.

279.31   Beau Clincher   Clincher in George Farquhar's comedy, *The Constant Couple, or a Trip to the Jubilee* (1699), 'A pert London Prentice turn'd
Beau, and affecting Travel'. In Act 3, Scene 1, he boasts how he will defend
himself with his pistol in Rome: 'he whips out his *Stiletto* [rapier], and I whips
out my *Bull-Dog* [pistol]'.

279.32   Gardez l'eau   *French* watch for the water. Well-known street cry of old Edinburgh, announcing the emptying of slops on to the street from the windows above.

279.34   that little cockatrice   the words parallel those found in response to a similar incident recorded in Burt: 'A Youth who was *Hanchman*, not understanding one Word of *English*, imagin'd his Chief was insulted, and thereupon drew his Pistol from his Side, and snap'd it at the Officer's Head; but the Pistol miss'd Fire, otherwise it is more than probable he might have suffer'd Death from the Hand of that little Vermin' (2.157–58).

279.37–38   Justice Shallow . . . marry, good air   the character in 2 *Henry IV*, and the words spoken there by him at 5.3.7–8.

279.41–43   The boat rock'd . . . Berwick Law   see Robert Burns, 'My bony Mary', lines 5–7 (Kinsley, no. 242). Leith is the port of Edinburgh, and (North) Berwick Law is a prominent hill, S of the town of North Berwick, near the entrance of the Firth of Forth. According to Kinsley, 'the ferry' refers to Queensferry, N of Edinburgh.

280.12–13   Que diable . . . cette galere   *French literally* what the devil was he doing in this galley; effectively, 'what business had he in this affair at all'. From Molière's play *Les Fourberies de Scapin* (1671), 2.7, where it is repeated several times. Scott gives a version of the same quotation in a letter to George Ellis of 13 July 1801 (*Letters*, 1.118). In an account of Molière in the *Foreign Quarterly Review* (1828), he later wrote: 'The phrase *Que diable alla-t-il faire dans cette galère?* will live as long as the French language' (*Prose Works*, 17.185).

280.27–28   Field-Marshal Wade . . . took Carlisle   an army based at Newcastle-upon-Tyne, commanded by the veteran Field Marshal George Wade (1673–1748), was unable through severe weather conditions to cross westwards in order to confront the Jacobite army; the surrender of the town of Carlisle was negotiated on 15 November, and the garrison made its way out of the Castle on the following day (see also note to 346.32).

280.34   all air and fire   see *Henry V*, 3.7.21; also compare *Antony and Cleopatra*, 4.10.3.

280.34–35   confident against the world in arms   *1 Henry IV*, 5.1.117.

281.5–6   no man cried, God bless him   see *Richard II*, 5.2.28.

281.9   most sweet voices   *Coriolanus*, 2.3.109, 169.

281.11   White Rose   see note to 252.23.

281.13   feigned themselves sick   compare 2 *Henry IV*, Induction lines 33–37.

281.26–28   King David . . . discontented   see 1 Samuel 22.1–2.

281.29   Vulgate renders bitter of soul   the expression in the Vulgate (Latin Bible) is 'amaro animo' (1 Samuel 22.2).

281.30   mighty men of their hands   i.e. mighty men of valour. 'Mighty men' is biblical; see especially 2 Samuel 23.8–10. 'Men of their hands' is a set phrase meaning 'men of valour, skill, or practical ability', for which see *OED, hand* 30.

283.42   Caranza or Vincent Saviola   two authorities on fencing and duelling. Jeronimo de Carranza, called the father of Spanish fencing, was the author of a treatise *De la philosophia de las armas* (1582); while Vincentio Saviolo was an Italian-born fencing master, who arrived in London in 1590, where was published *Vincentio Saviolo his Practise. In two Bookes. The first intreating of the use of the Rapier and Dagger. The second, of Honor and honorable Quarrels* (1595; *CLA*, 119). The latter publication was illustrated by woodcuts showing fencing positions; while the former includes diagrams illustrating matters such as arm reach.

284.6–7   whirligig of time   *Twelfth Night*, 5.1.363.

284.19–20   Cham of Tartary . . . Grand Seignior . . . Great Mogul

rulers of respectively: a Central Asian region E of the Caspian sea; the Ottoman Empire, notably Turkey; the Moslem-controlled areas of India.

284.21 Lucifer i.e. Satan, thrown out as an angel from heaven for his ambitious pride.

284.23–24 Sancho's jests ... Sierra Morena Sancho and his master Don Quixote enter the Sierra Morena (a wild and isolated area in southern Spain) in *Don Quixote*, Part 1 (1605), Bk 3, Chs 9–11. Scott alludes to the restraint placed on Sancho's imagination on several occasions in his correspondence, e.g. in a letter to J. B. S. Morritt of September 1811: 'there are so many good things which rot in one's gizzard as Sancho pathetically complained during the interval when the Don imposed silence upon him!' (*Letters*, 2.542). The incident referred to here, however, actually takes place in Ch. 7 before entry into the Sierra Morena (Lockhart 1822 edn, 1.236). The prohibition of silence nevertheless continues to operate, with Sancho again complaining about this near the beginning of Ch.11.

284.39 Parmi ... est roi *French* among the blind a one-eyed man is king.

285.9 King Agramant's Camp see Ludovico Ariosto, *Orlando furioso* (1516), Bk 14, stanzas 75–77, where God commands the Archangel Michael to spread discord and strife among the army of the Moorish king Agramant.

285.19 'N aire! signifying in Gaelic 'Careful!', a shortened version of '*N aire ort fhèin* ('Look out for yourself').

285.25 The ne'er be in me the devil be in me.

286.1 that the best revenge ... most safe not found as a proverb with this wording. Previous printed editions supply quotation marks, though these are not in the MS.

286.6 deevil's buckie most perverse person.

286.37–38 auld kirk at Coudingham Coldingham Priory, founded in 1098, whose tower rose to above 90 feet, before falling in the later 18th century. Coldingham is a small town in Berwickshire, close to the North Sea coast, about 5 km NW of Eyemouth.

286.42 Merse-man strictly the Merse is the plain occupying the south of Berwickshire and the eastern part of Roxburghshire in the Scottish Borders, but it was often used synonymously with Berwickshire.

286.42 bow of Cupid Cupid is traditionally depicted shooting arrows at people, causing them to fall in love.

288.14 made no doubt had no doubt; did not hesitate in thinking.

288.16 gare! gare! place à Monseigneur *French* look out! look out! make way for his Royal Highness.

288.18 Fitz-James's foreign dragoons a squadron of heavy cavalry, part of the Irish Brigade in the French army, and originally raised by James FitzJames, Duke of Berwick (see note to 51.31–32). It first arrived in Scotland in February 1746, so the reference here seems slightly anachronistic.

288.20 fell in and formed squadron got into lines and formed a square.

288.29 patriarchal authority of the Chieftains in addition to the broader authority of the clan leader as patriarch (see note to 78.30), heritable legal jurisdictions were also attached to certain chiefdoms. These jurisdictions varied in extent: the most common was the *barony* (see note to 44.43), and the fullest the *regality*, a kind of little kingdom whose jurisdiction covered everything except treason. Although it is not made clear it is probable that Fergus's legal powers matched those of a baron.

288.40–41 court of St Germains see note to 262.36.

288.43 Frederick of Prussia ... trade of royalty Frederick William I (1688–1740), King of Prussia, who created an efficient bureaucracy and army, and carefully marshalled the upbringing of his son, Frederick II (The

Great). Similar phrases have also been associated with Louis XIV of France : see John C. Rule (ed.), *Louis XIV and the Craft of Kingship* (Ohio State University Press, 1969).

289.3 Monsieur de Beaujeu the surname in French (as *beau jeu*) can mean good cards, a fair chance, a good opportunity; and the whole enterprise is called a 'grand jeu' by Charles Edward at 291.38. There may also possibly be a trace in this character of Alexandre-Jean-Baptiste de Boyer, Marquis d'Éguilles, a secret envoy from the King of France, whose presence encouraged Charles Edward to undertake the march into England.

289.6–8 Ayez ... beaucoup de peine *French* have the goodness to form in line those highlanders, as well as the cavalry, and put them back on the march. You speak English so well, that it would not give you much trouble.

289.9 pas de tout *French* not at all.

289.14 gentilmans savages for an account of a similar phrase ('un gentil-homme *sauvage*') being clumsily used by Lord Adam Gordon in introducing a Highland chief to the Comte d'Artois (later Charles X of France), when the latter was living in exile at Holyrood House in the 1790s, see Henry Mackenzie, *Anecdotes and Egotisms*, ed. Harold William Thompson (London, 1927), 236.

289.15 d'arranger vous *French* put yourself in order.

289.19 fort bien *French* very good.

289.20–21 Qu'est ce que vous appellez visage *French* What do you call *visage*.

289.22 Je vous remercie *French* I thank you.

289.24–26 Mais ... comprenez très bien *French* Very good—again, gentlemen, you must march—March then, for God's sake, because I have forgotten the English word—but you are fine fellows, and understand me very well.

289.28 par ma foi *French* upon my word!

289.29–31 Ah, mon dieu ... Monsieur! *French* Oh, my God! it's the commissary who brought us the first news of this unhappy quarrel. I am too vexed, Sir!

289.38 by trees behind the pun lies the fact that marching in a column of three files, which could be turned quickly to form a battle front, was a characteristic of the Jacobite army (see Duffy, 116–17). This procedure is apparent in the description in Home of the march leading up to Prestonpans: 'Next morning the Highland army marched from Duddingston in a column whose front was very narrow, three men in a rank' (109). A footnote adds: 'The Highland regiments, drawn up three men deep, marched off by the flank, which the regulars call marching by files' (109n.)

289.38–40 Et Monsieur ... puis plus *French* And Mr de Bradwardine, have the goodness to put yourself at the head of your regiment, for, by God, I can't do any more.

291.36–38 Beaujeu ... après tout *French* Beaujeu, my dear friend, how wearisome is my trade of wandering-prince, sometimes. But, take heart! great things are at stake, after all.

292.17–18 soaring and ardent ... too narrow compare Prince Harry's lines to Hotspur, *1 Henry IV*, 5.4.89–92; and for the collocation of 'earth' and 'narrow' compare *Julius Caesar*, 1.2.135.

292.20 18th of December on 18 December 1745 the main Jacobite army occupied Penrith after crossing over Shap Fell, with the rearguard arriving at Shap village that morning. Ed1 incorrectly reads '8th of December', imperfectly changed to '12th of December' in subsequent editions; the present edition restores the original MS reading.

292.21 hamlet ... Shap and Penrith Great or Little Strickland would fit the description, the first of these being virtually equidistant between Shap village and the town of Penrith.

292.29   a little river   as Lamont notes, the MS originally read 'by the Emont', with 'the Emont' being deleted and 'a little river in the vicinity' put in its place. As she also observes, the River Eamont, being just below Penrith, is too far north for the present situation.

293.24   think ... as on former occasions   echoing the observations of John, Master of Sinclair, in prognosticating the comparatively light consequences likely to be faced by the Highlanders, as opposed to the Lowlanders, in the event of the failure of the Jacobite rising of 1715: *Memoirs of the Insurrection in Scotland in 1715* (Edinburgh, 1858), 26–27.

293.27–28   to listen ... waters abate   *proverbial* 'Listen to the wind of the mountains till the waters abate' (Macintosh, 31).

293.29   John Bull   a personification of England or the English; a typical Englishman. Proverbial: *ODEP*, 412–13.

293.36   root and branch work   complete removal or destruction; see Malachi 4.1.

294.5   Bodach glas   *Gaelic* grey spectre. As Lamont notes, there are several legends in Highland families relating to such figures. One such concerns the Macleans of Lochbuidhe or Lochbuy, where the death of the chief is announced by the appearance of 'the Ghost of one of their Ancestors killd in battle', an account of which Scott received in a letter from Margaret Clephane of 7 August 1809 (MS 3878, f 105v), and which he relates in a note to Canto 3, stanza 7 in *The Lady of the Lake* (1810), lvii. An adjoining note there, concerning the 'Ben-Shie', also comments how 'Grant of Rothemurcus had an attendant called *Bodach-an-dun*, or the Ghost of the Hill; and many other examples might be mentioned' (lvi; *Poetical Works*, 8.126n.). See also Coleman O. Parsons, 'The Bodach Glas in *Waverley*', *Notes and Queries*, 184 (13 Feb. 1943), 95–97.

294.12   Benmore   see note to 210.41.

294.13   Loch Tay   extensive loch in Perthshire, SW of Aberfeldy.

294.14   Loch an Ri   meaning in Gaelic (where *Righ* would be the correct form) 'King's Loch' (compare note to 88.22). No actual location has been discovered, but see Historical Note, 382.

294.15   Saddleback and Ulswater   peak in the Lake District, in Cumbria, *c.* 6 km N of Keswick; and an extensive lake SW of Penrith.

294.17–18   Ian nan Chaistel   see note to 98.10.

294.20   Halbert Hall   not a historical character, but the name suggests an archetypal Borderer.

294.20   the Cheviots   the line of hills separating Scotland and England.

294.27   Sherriff-Muir   the indecisive battle fought near Stirling in 1715, which irreparably halted the Jacobite rising of that year: see also note to 242.20–21.

296.13–14   fine clan-regiment ... Cluny Mac-Pherson   as raised in Badenoch (SE of Inverness), along the upper reaches of the River Spey by Ewan MacPherson of Cluny (1706–64), one of three clan regiments who fought at the engagement at Clifton (see next note), under the command of Lord George Murray, the other two being the Glengarry regiment and that of the Appin Stewarts. See also Duffy, 332–36.

296.16   village called Clifton   a small settlement consisting of one street, by the E bank of the River Lowther, about 4 km SSE of Penrith, and close to the engagement on the evening of 18 December 1745, in which pursuing government dragoons were temporarily repulsed, with losses. For the enclosures close to the village, see Home, 149–50; and Duffy, 334.

296.18   ides of March   15 March, the day on which Julius Caesar was murdered in 44 BC, as forewarned: see *Julius Caesar*, 3.1.1–2.

296.33–34   calling out "Claymore!"   reportedly the actual cry of Lord George Murray, the commanding officer, who 'immediately drew his sword, and called Claymore' (Home, 150n.).

297.15   What, can the devil speak truth?   see *Macbeth*, 1.3.107.

298.11   houlerying and poulerying   Scott uses these terms, in describing the commotion of a hunt assembling, in a letter to Maria Edgeworth of 4 August 1826: 'And now there is such a *howlering and a powerling* as the Lancashire man says' (*Letters*, 10.85–86). The 'Lancashire man' here probably refers to Thomas ('Tummus') in John Collier, *The Miscellaneous Works of Tim Bobbin, Esq.; containing his View of the Lancashire Dialect* (Manchester, 1775; *CLA*, 175), where *powlering* features in a dialogue with Mary ('Meery'): 'Whau, weh mitch powlering I geete eawt oth' poo' (63) (meaning, roughly, 'Why, with much commotion, I got out of the pool'). A version of this dialogue later appeared in Edgeworth's *Essay on Irish Bulls* (London, 1802), 206.

298.22   Westmoreland statesman's   *statesman* here describing a yeoman farmer in the region. See J. D. Marshall, '"Statesmen" in Cumbria: The Vicissitudes of an Expression', *Transactions of the Cumberland and Westmorland Antiquarian & Archaeological Society*, 72 (1972), 248–73, which argues that the term (an equivalent of *estatesman*) came into general use in the later 18th century.

299.17   near Ulswater   the MS originally read 'at Wateritt near Ulswater', before deletion of the first two words. Scott here was possibly thinking of the farm Waterfoot, at the NW end of Ullswater, just within the border of the county of Cumberland (with Westmorland on the other side of the lake).

299.35   Lord Lonsdale's property   Lowther Hall, Westmorland, near Clifton.

299.41–42   here fell . . . nameless heath   compare Samuel Johnson, *The Vanity of Human Wishes* (1749), lines 219–20 (on Charles XII of Sweden).

300.40   Fasthwaite   a Philip of Fasthwaite appears in Scott's 'The Bridal of Triermain' (1813), Canto 1, stanza 5 (*Poetical Works*, 11.32). The name, especially its suffix, is characteristic of the region, though no such actual location has been discovered. There is however a Finsthwaite parish, at the southern end of Lake Windermere, where a Clementina Douglass (reputed to be an illegitimate daughter of Charles Edward and Clementina Walkinshaw) was buried in 1771: see Hugh Douglas, *Jacobite Spy Wars* (Stroud, 1999), 221.

301.8–9   surrender of Carlisle   the remaining Jacobite garrison at Carlisle surrendered on 30 December 1745.

301.29–30   romance of his life . . . real history   see John Logan (1748–88), 'On the Death of a Young Lady': 'The wild romance of life is done;/ The real history is begun' (stanza 13, lines 3–4). The poem is printed in *English Minstrelsy*, ed. Walter Scott, 2 vols (Edinburgh, 1810), 1.184–88. Scott is clearly alluding to this passage in a letter to Lady Abercorn of 18 September 1811, in referring to Sydney Owenson (shortly to become Lady Morgan): 'I hope the realities of life will not lead her to renounce the "wild romance" with which she has so frequently embellished it' (*Letters*, 3.2).

302.18   Twigtythe   *twig* here possibly in the colloquial sense of 'watch', or 'glance at'; hence an eye on his tithes (church dues, a tenth part of produce in the parish).

302.21   Hill-Street, Berkeley-Square   a residential street in the West End of London, adjoining the fashionable Georgian Berkeley Square, itself laid out in the 1730s. Scott received letters from several correspondents resident in Hill Street; notably at this period John, Lord Somerville (1765–1819), with whom in 1813–14 he was co-operating over the publication of the *Memorie of the Somervilles* (1815): see, e.g., *Letters*, 3.511.

303.4f   battle of Falkirk   fought on 17 January 1746, in which the Jacobite army defeated the pursuing army under General Hawley, but was unable to press home its advantage. See also note to 313.29.

303.20   travelling post   see note to 278.34.

303.21 great north road ran between London and Edinburgh, on the east side of the country, incorporating stretches of Roman road; it was later converted into the A1 highway.

303.21 Boroughbridge in N Yorkshire, approximately half-way on the old stage-coach journey between Edinburgh and London, a major stop.

303.22 Northern Diligence a *diligence* is a public stage-coach; no specific 'Northern Diligence' has been discovered, though the name seems appropriate for a service using the Great North Road (note to 303.21).

303.36 faire les frais de la conversation *French* to pay the expenses of (i.e. keep up) the conversation.

304.4–5 army-list see note to 23.28.

304.7 race at the battle of Preston alluding to the flight of the dragoons at the battle of Prestonpans. 'A Race from Preston Pans to Berwick' is the title of a contemporary cartoon depicting Sir John Cope's flight.

304.16 Ferrybridge W Yorkshire, about 30 km SSW of York, on the Great North Road.

304.20 Corporal Bridoon a *bridoon* is the snaffle and rein of a military bridle.

305.2 fire a slug to 'drink a dram' (Grose).

305.6 slouched hat soft felt hat with a broad brim worn so that the brim hangs over the face.

305.8 gooseberry wig a 'large frizzled wig; perhaps, from a supposed likeness to a gooseberry bush' (Grose).

305.11 Hubble-de-Shuff 'Confusedly. To fire hubble de shuff; to fire quick and irregularly. *Old military term*' (Grose).

305.14–15 stand godfather to act sponsor to, here effectively 'pay for a round'.

305.19 corps de garde *French* small body of soldiers stationed on guard; a guard-post.

306.13 Spontoon a spontoon was a kind of half-pike or halberd carried by infantry officers in the 18th century (from about 1740).

306.25 squeezed to death in their own presses in the hand-press era in printing a lever was used to turn a screw which lowered the platen to press the paper against the inked type. The force generated by the screw could be considerable: see Philip Gaskell, *A New Introduction to Bibliography* (Oxford, 1972), 124. The idea is also evocative of the punishment of pressing to death (in which the victim was pressed to death between boards with heavy weights).

307.9 limb of the devil agent or scion of the devil, mischievous wicked person.

307.15 clack of a mill instrument in a flour mill which struck the hopper and caused corn to fall into the mill stones. The motion and the noise were continuous while the mill was in operation.

307.39 hands of the Philistines see note to 205.3.

308.2 the lion's mouth see note to 150.1.

308.6 extreme unction the anointing with oil when a person is close to death, one the seven sacraments of the Roman Catholic Church. A similar response was later attributed to Rob Roy MacGregor in the Magnum Introduction (1829) to *Rob Roy*, with a reference to its use in *Waverley*: 'Rob did not pretend, when pressed closely on the subject, to justify all the tenets of Catholicism, and acknowledged that extreme unction always appeared to him a great waste of *ulzie*, or oil' (7.lxxxi–lxxxii).

308.23–24 upon the edge of his dirk ... inviolable obligation for the custom, see Burt, 2.244–46.

308.28 gallows more lofty than his friends traditionally a higher gallows was given to the most important malefactor when a whole group was hanged at once. Compare the fate of Allaster MacGregor of Glanstrae, on 20 January 1604, as described in 'The Diarey of Robert Birrel', in [J. G. Dalyell], *Fragments of Scotish History* (Edinburgh, 1798; *CLA*, 4): 'himself being chieff, he was hangit his awin hight above the rest of hes freindis' (61).

308.41   claws of Justice   an expression also found in Sir George Mackenzie, *Aretina* (Edinburgh, 1660), 248.

308.43   First come first served   proverbial (Ramsay, 77; Ray, 107; *ODEP*, 262).

309.32   trade of war   common literary phrase, to be found in *Othello*, 1.2.1, Samuel Butler, *Hudibras*, First Part (1663), 3.607, and in several contexts in Dryden.

309.33–34   Fletcher's Humorous Lieutenant . . . this fighting   *The Humorous Lieutenant*, by John Fletcher (1579–1625), 3.7.20.

309.38–39   Enough . . . good as a feast   proverbial (Ramsay, 76; Ray, 102; *ODEP*, 224).

309.39   plumed troops . . . big war   see *Othello*, 3.3.353.

309.42   dry blows   blows that do not draw blood.

310.3   'tis my vocation, Hal   *1 Henry IV*, 1.2.101.

310.21   pass for the other   presumably intimating 'let's pass to the other', possibly with an element of the French *passer*, 'to pass by, to go over'.

310.24   his brogue   although in the singular *brogue* is normally 'strongly accented speech', and in the plural 'shoes made of untanned hide', Bradwardine's earlier homage to the Prince makes it possible for the word as used here to refer to either.

310.36   land of mountains and floods   see *The Lay of the Last Minstrel* (1805), Canto 6, stanza 2 (*Poetical Works*, 6.188).

310.42–43   as Fluellen says . . . hands   see *Henry V*, 3.6.21–23.

311.4   true as steel   proverbial: *ODEP*, 840.

311.15   ride post as far as Huntingdon   Huntingdon, 90 km N of London, was on the Great North Road, the main post road leading towards Edinburgh, and could be reached from Cambridge, some 30 km away, by a road running NW along the edge of the the fens. For 'ride post', see note to 278.34.

311.20   Secretary of State's office   there were two Secretaries of State at this time, one for the Northern Department (including Scotland), and the other for the Southern Department, both sitting in the British Cabinet.

311.30   for your advantage   for your benefit.

312.8   young Cantab   i.e. student at Cambridge University.

312.8   cela ne tire à rien   *French* that doesn't matter, that amounts to nothing.

312.28   battle of Culloden   the battle near Inverness on 16 April 1746, marking the final defeat of the Jacobite army.

313.21   change o' markets   i.e. transition in circumstances, the metaphor probably relating to a change in the location or time of markets.

313.26   step in bye   Scots expression, with 'in bye' intimating a movement from outside to inside.

313.29   Hawley's dragoons   Lieutenant General Henry Hawley (*c.* 1685–1759) commanded the government forces defeated by the Jacobite army at Falkirk on 17 January 1746; while still nominally Commander-in Chief in Scotland, he led the cavalry under the Duke of Cumberland at Culloden.

314.34   battle at Inverness   i.e. Culloden: see note to 312.28.

314.35   white-iron smith   one who makes goods from white iron (pig-iron or cast-iron); a tin-plate worker, or tinsmith.

314.37   nae fule like an auld fule   proverbial (see Ramsay, 101; Ray, 108; *ODEP*, 276).

315.25–26   sadder and a wiser man   as said of the wedding guest at the end of Coleridge's 'The Rime of the Ancient Mariner' (1798): 'A sadder and a wiser man/ He rose the morrow morn'.

316.10 scorched and blackened the account here matches that of the similar destruction of Cameron of Lochiel's residence at Achnacarry, as found in Michael Hughes, *A Plain Narrative or Journal of the Late Rebellion begun in 1745* (London, 1746; *CLA*, 93), 56–57.

316.21–22 family pictures … served for targets i.e. for target practice; and perhaps echoing the damage caused to the pictures at Holyrood by government troops: see note to 204.21.

316.29–30 two immense horse-chesnut trees Scott's Magnum note refers to a similar destruction of two such trees at 'Invergarry Castle, the fastness of MacDonald of Glengarry' (2.327n.).

316.43 troisième … cinquième étage *French* third … fifth floor. The qualification is perhaps explained by Rose's balcony forming an extra 'floor' in addition to the main ones of the house, comparable to the situation found at Murthly Castle in Perthshire (for which see Historical Note, 380). See also note to 62.13.

317.11–18 They came … his eyes according to Scott's Magnum note, the 'first three couplets are from an old ballad, called the Border Widow's Lament' (2.328n.). Line 1 matches 'The Lady Turned Serving-Man', stanza 5, line 1, in Percy, 3.88; lines 2–6 have equivalents in stanzas 2 and 3 of 'The Lament of the Border Widow' (*Minstrelsy*, 3.112). Child considers both the Percy ballad and the Scott to be versions of 'The Famous Flower of Serving-Men' (Child, 106).

317.29–30 Blondel … Cœur de Lion when Richard I ('the Lionheart'), King of England 1189–99, was imprisoned in Austria on his journey home from the crusades, his French troubadour friend Blondel is supposed to have discovered him by singing half a song to which the king replied.

318.7–15 But follow … dead men's lea evidently Scott's own composition.

319.24–27 forfeited … Baron's attainder after the 1745–46 rising an Act of Attainder listed the most prominent Jacobites, and, if they did not surrender by 12 July 1746, rendered them liable to be attainted of high treason. Attainted persons were put to death; their estates could not be inherited by their heirs and fell to their feudal superior; and their titles and honours were forfeit. However, properties under entail could pass to the person entitled to the succession in spite of forfeiture, because the Act 1690, c. 104, provided that an heir of entail was not to be prejudiced by the forfeiture of his predecessor, provided the entail was properly registered under the act of 1685. In this respect, Malcolm Bradwardine cannot be deprived of his right to the estate (as substitute: see note to 320.5) because of the Baron's attainder.

319.37–38 mails and duties *mail* is rent for a farm; *duty* is payment to a feudal superior.

320.1 Heatherblutter the name matches a form of *heather-bleater*, signifying in Scots the common snipe.

320.3–4 Tullius … effugit Marcus Tullius Cicero (106–43 BC), whose *Oratio in Catilinam*, 2.1.1, actually reads 'Abiit, excessit, evasit, erupit', he departed, he withdrew, rushed off, broke away. Scott's variant *effugit* means 'ran away'.

320.5 last substitute originally reading 'last institute', and altered by Ed3 to 'last substitute'. In Scots law, the person named as inheritor under an entail is the 'institute', while subsequent heirs are 'substitutes'. The last substitute is at liberty as absolute owner to sell or lease the estate as he pleases.

320.9–10 sæcula sæculorum *Latin* ages of ages, permanently.

320.10 humana perpessi sumus *Latin* we have suffered all that is common to humanity.

320.16–17 like a partridge . . . King David see 1 Samuel 26.20.

320.18 valiant Sir William Wallace Sir William Wallace (*c.* 1270–1305), Scottish patriot, the first champion of the Scottish people in their struggle for independence; captured by the English in 1305, taken to London and executed. The wording here reflects the title of *The Acts and Deeds of the Illustrious and Valiant Champion Sir William Wallace*, by Blind Harry or Hary, previously mentioned as forming part of Bradwardine's reading (see note to 61.13).

320.21 a buck of the first head a male deer when it attains its complete set of antlers (compare *Love's Labours Lost*, 4.2.9). The phrase is proverbial (Ray, 52; *ODEP*, 88), and in contemporary slang meant, a 'blood or choice spirit' (Grose).

320.31–32 there . . . roasting of eggs proverbial (see Ray, 150; *ODEP*, 666).

320.34 Him whom . . . idiot boy see Wordsworth, 'The Idiot Boy' (1798), line 41.

321.15 Sawney a 'general nick-name for a Scotchman . . . Sawny or Sandy being the familiar abbreviation or diminutive of Alexander, a very favourite name among the Scottish nation' (Grose). At this period, the term could have a strong derogatory edge.

321.24 heck and manger *proverbial* in comfortable circumstances: see Ray, 207; *ODEP*, 661. See also note to 201.21.

321.24 maist feck the greater part.

321.27 the Duchran see note to 148.11.

321.34 the feifteen i.e. the Jacobite rising of 1715.

322.11 Impiger, iracundus, inexorabilis, acer *Latin* active, irascible, inexorable, keen. From Horace, *Ars Poetica*, 121. The terms indicate how Achilles, the Greek warrior, should be depicted on the stage.

322.12–14 Struan Robertson . . . stieve as steel for Struan Robertson (Alexander Robertson of Struan), Jacobite chief, see note to 219.24. As previously, the quotation has not been located, though there are several short pieces after Horace in his *Poems* (see note to 219.27–28).

323.8 remove next term i.e. move out on the next term day, those for the beginning and ending of tenancies in Scotland normally being Whitsunday (15 May) or Martinmas (11 November).

323.30–31 Gustavus Adolphus . . . Colonel Munro his Expedition Gustavus Adolphus (1594–1632), King of Sweden, led the Protestant forces in the Thirty Years' War. Large numbers of Scots fought in Europe under him, including Colonel Robert Monro (d. ?1675), who described his experiences in *Monro His Expedition with the worthy Scots Regiment (called Mac-Keyes Regiment) levied in August 1626* (London, 1637; *CLA*, 5). Scott later used this work as a major source for *A Legend of the Wars of Montrose*, in particular the character of Dugald Dalgetty (see EEWN 7b, 219–20).

323.34 Marechal Duke of Berwick see note to 51.31–32.

323.35 Fuimus Troes *Latin* we Trojans are no more: from Virgil's *Aeneid*, 2.325.

323.35–36 there's the end of an auld sang proverbial: Ramsay, 114; *ODEP*, 220–21. The phrase was used most memorably, as a 'despising and contemning remark', by the Earl of Seafield on signing the Act of Union of 1707: see *The Lockhart Papers*, 2 vols (London, 1817; *CLA*, 3), 1.223. Subsequent uses have often introduced a more nostalgic tone.

323.38 domus ultima *Latin literally* last home, here effectively meaning the grave.

323.40–42 **conies in Holy Scripture . . . in the rocks** paralleling Proverbs 30.26 ('The conies are but a feeble folk, yet make their houses in the rocks'). *Conies* are a species of rabbit.

323.41 **the great traveller Pococke . . . Jerboa** Richard Pococke (1704–65), author of *A Description of the East, and some other countries*, 2 vols (London, 1743–45). The *jerboa* is a desert rodent, capable of jumping large distances with its hind legs. Pococke does not seem to mention the *jerboa* in the above work.

324.1 **Patmos** island in the Aegean Sea to which St John was banished (see Revelation 1.9), and hence used allusively for a place of banishment or solitude. Scott refers to Abbotsford as his Patmos in a letter to Joanna Baillie of 10 January 1813 (*Letters*, 3.223).

324.8 **long pedigree** Scott, who wrote 'long roll of paper' in the MS, is apparently thinking of a long family tree, on rolled-up paper.

324.12 **reel in a bottle** evidently a children's game involving a cylinder in a bottle; comparable to the now more familiar model ship in a bottle.

324.18 **Titus Livius** see note to 28.26.

324.25 **purpose of recognoscing** to *recognosce* (a rare word) is to reconnoitre. Robert Monro in his *Expedition with the worthy Scots Regiment* (see note to 323.30–31) has a chapter titled 'Of Recognoscing' (2.202–04). This includes, for example: 'we must go recognosce on horse and foot' (2.202).

324.35–36 **the trysting-tree** a trysting place was a location, usually a well-known landmark, employed as a rendezvous.

325.18–19 **reasonable compass** *1 Henry IV*, 3.3.23.

326.3 **roving commission** i.e. authorisation to pursue any inquiry or investigation in whatever quarters may be considered necessary. Evidently a fairly new term in Scott's time.

326.7 **make hay while the sun shone** proverbial (see Ramsay, 99; Ray, 117; *ODEP*, 501).

326.12 **For well . . . was deadly** see John Home, *Douglas: A Tragedy* (Edinburgh, 1757; *CLA*, 10), 1.334.

327.9–10 **a whin bits o' scarted paper** a few small pieces of scribbled (on) paper.

330 **motto** *The Merry Wives of Windsor*, 5.5.27.

330.12–13 **capacious mouth** compare John Gay, *Acis and Galatea* (1732), 2.14: 'To make a Pipe for my capacious Mouth'. Quoted jocularly, as an allusion made by Anna Seward, in James Boswell's *Life of Johnson*, ed. G. B. Hill, 6 vols (Oxford, 1887), 3.242n.

330.33–35 **Syphax . . . love-tale with** Joseph Addison, *Cato* (1713), 2.1.325–26. Syphax is a Numidian general, here responding to having heard from Juba, his leader, that he (Juba) has intimated to Cato his love for Marcia, Cato's daughter. Cato's stern response to Juba, before exiting, had been: 'It is not now a Time to talk of aught/ But Chains, or Conquest, Liberty, or Death'.

331.14 **Pythoness from her tripod** referring to the Priestess of the temple of Apollo, in Delphi, on the slopes of Parnassus; known as *Pythia*, she sat on Apollo's tripod seat to deliver her oracular responses.

331.16–17 **Tullochgorum** a traditional reel or strathspey, for which popular words were later supplied in 1776 by Rev. John Skinner (1721–1807). The intrinsically Scottish nature of the tune, as opposed to foreign imports, was noted by Robert Fergusson in his poem 'The Daft Days' (1772): 'Nor *fortes* wi *pianos* mix—/ Gie's Tulloch Gorum'. Skinner's song includes the repeated line 'Let whig an' tory a' agree'.

331.18–19 **Lady Waaverley!—ten thousand a-year** Mark A. Weinstein suggests that this echoes Mrs Bennet's exclamation on hearing of her daughter

Elizabeth's engagement to Darcy in *Pride and Prejudice* (1813), in *Novels*, ed. R. W. Chapman, 3rd edn (1932), 2.378: 'Mr. Darcy! . . . Ten thousand a year! Oh, Lord! What will become of me. I shall go distracted' (see 'An Echo of Mrs. Bennet in *Waverley*', *Notes and Queries*, 220 (1975), 63–64).

331.24   in the bees   not identified as an expression, but presumably equivalent to having one's head full of bees, i.e. with fancies and unsorted possibilities.

331.25–26   Dallas of Saint Martins' Stiles   George Dallas of Saint-Martins (*c.* 1630–1702), *System of Stiles As now Practicable within the Kingdom of Scotland* (Edinburgh, 1697). The work covers the whole system of legal procedures, documentation and authorisations, and was widely used by lawyers and their clerks for composing legal documents.

331.27   Stair's Institutions   James Dalrymple, Viscount Stair (1619–95), *The Institutions of the Law of Scotland* (Edinburgh, 1681; see *CLA*, 263), in which modern Scots law was first given articulate form.

331.27   Dirleton's Doubts   see note to 246.22–23.

331.27   Balfour's Practiques   Sir James Balfour, Lord Pittendreich (*c.* 1525–83), *Practicks: or, a System of the more ancient Law of Scotland* (Edinburgh, 1754). This work was compiled *c.* 1574–83, and manuscript versions were fairly common before publication in the mid-18th century, the work being much relied on.

331.28–29   Contract of Marriage   'Contracts of Marriage' constitutes a section in Part 5 of Dallas's *System of Stiles* (see note to 331.25–26 above).

331.29–30   sma' minute . . . from resiling   a short written record to prevent parties withdrawing from an agreement or undertaking that is not yet perfected or concluded. However the 'sma' minute' that the Baillie is proposing is probably an actual marriage contract, in the sense of undertakings to marry with property arrangements—the section of Dallas consulted (see previous note) has only such marriage contracts.

332.3   Jock Scriever   i.e. John Writer, referring both to the copying of legal documents that was often the law apprentice's task, and the Scottish word for a solicitor in Scott's day, *writer*.

332.16   I'se be caution   I'll warrant, I'll be the surety; see also note to 201.24.

332.18   fee and life-rent   i.e. both the rights of a proprietor in his estate and the rights of one with a life interest in it (Normand). See also note to 358.34–359.10.

332.23   pannelled for his life   i.e. tried for his life. In Scots law the *panel* is the accused person at the bar of the court.

332.27   masterfu' oppression and spoliation   *Scots law* oppression and depredation through threatening or use of force.

332.30   light come light gane   proverbial (Ramsay, 97; Ray, 129; *ODEP*, 463).

332.32   tarr'd wi' ae stick   proverbial (*ODEP*, 805).

332.33–34   decreet of spuilzie . . . violent profits   decree of a court for the restoration of stolen goods or the value and the profits that might have been made out of them.

332.42   Scotch collops   savoury dish made of sliced veal, bacon, forced meat (a kind of highly seasoned mince used as stuffing) and other ingredients.

334.19   Chevalier Errant   *French literally* wandering knight (with possibly a suggestion of 'erring' or 'erratic' in Talbot's English mouth).

334.26–27   ride quarantine   i.e. as a ship in quarantine rides at anchor outside harbour.

335   motto   matching two lines in *The Paradise of Daintie Deuises* (first published 1576): 'Thrise happie is that woyng,/ That is not long a doyng'

(London, 1810; *CLA* 177), 71. Also found in a form closer to the wording here in James Kelly, *A Complete Collection of Scottish Proverbs* (London, 1721; *CLA*, 169), 153.

335.9 powers that be the existing ruling authorities: originally from Romans 13.1.

335.22 bounden duty bound by the duties of the office. The phrase comes from the Communion Service, in the *Book of Common Prayer* (1549, revised 1662), and the Scottish *Book of Common Order* (1564).

335.24 no that canny 'no canny' in Scots indicates unnatural or supernatural qualities.

335.26–27 sae's seen o't i.e. the consequences are plain enough.

335.27 Sir George Mackenyie Sir George Mackenzie (1636–91), judge and politician, author of the novel *Aretina* (see note to 308.41) and several legal and historical works, including *The Laws and Customes of Scotland, in Matters Criminal* (Edinburgh, 1678) and *Institutions of the Law of Scotland* (Edinburgh, 1684). The sentiments attributed to Mackenzie here reflect the opening of Part 1, Title 10, 'Witchcraft', in the first of the above legal works: 'That there are Witches, Divines cannot doubt, since the Word of God hath ordain'd that no Witch shall live; nor lawyers in Scotland, seing [*sic*] our Law ordains it to be punished with death' (81). The 'y' in Mackenyie in the text reflects an older spelling and pronunciation, and possibly Scott is representing the Baillie's speech here.

335.28 the Bible says Exodus 22.18: 'Thou shalt not suffer a witch to live'.

335.30 punishable by death in the period between 1563 and 1735 witchcraft was a crime punishable in Scotland under statute law by death; the Witchcraft Act 1735 (9 Geo. II, c. 5), which came into force in 1736, finally abolished witchcraft as a criminal offence.

335.31 Leviticus the third book of the Bible which expounds Jewish law and priestly custom. The word as used here seems to represent the whole body of law rather than just what is contained within the book called 'Leviticus'; the most notable biblical statement about the punishment for witchcraft is at Exodus 22.18 (see note to 335.28).

335.34 no to lightly them *lightly* here in the sense of 'to speak lightly of, to disparage', a chiefly Scots usage.

336.2–10 There, in a gloomy ... she espied see Spenser, *The Faerie Queene* (1590–96), 3.7.6.

336.23–24 if I were nae feared the Enemy if I were not afraid that the devil.

336.29 Patmos see note to 324.1.

336.32 beat the tattoo drum beat to call the soldiers back to their quarters in the evening.

336.41 warld's gear worldly goods and property.

337.25 in loco parentis *Latin* in the position of a parent.

337.32 Diva Pecunia *Latin* the goddess Money.

337.36 hurley-house 'a large, tumble-down, half-ruinous house' (*SND*, which states 'only in Scott').

338.18–20 unworthy kinsman ... from the crown as a consequence of the Baron's attainder his estates have passed to the next substitute in the entail, a procedure which is not affected by his subsequent pardon. See also notes to 319.24–27 and 320.5.

338.23 restored in integrum matching the legal Latin *restitutio in integrum*, signifying the return of a person to the condition or position formerly enjoyed.

338.37–38 jet d'eau *French* fountain.

339.40 goat's whey ... recommended as in Tobias Smollett, *The Expedition of Humphry Clinker* (1771): 'the highland air, and the use of goat-milk whey'. Matt. Bramble to Dr. Lewis, 8 Aug.; ed. Thomas R. Preston (Athens and London, 1990), 229.

340.22 draw stakes i.e. withdraw what is staked as a wager.

340 motto *Measure for Measure*, 2.2.83.

340.33 Oyer and Terminer Anglo-Norman name, meaning to hear and determine. Here referring to a special commission of judges to try the Jacobite prisoners.

341.15 Clerk of Arraigns court official who reads out the charge against a prisoner.

341.17 in the Dhu of Tarrascleugh with *Dhu* here presumably meaning 'black or shady place'. There is a Tarras Water in the Scottish Borders, but the present name in context appears to be fanciful.

341.21 die according to law the punishment under the old English Treason Law being hanging, drawing, and quartering. In the MS the Clerk of Arraigns' speech is supplied on a slip of a paper tipped into the volume, with text in another hand, probably William Erskine's, this overriding Scott's previous version (which itself does not include the above words).

341.29–30 poured out like water see Psalm 22.14 ('I am poured out like water').

342.4 to head or hang to be beheaded or hanged.

342.17–18 sentence ... horrible accompaniments such a sentence, given at Carlisle, is reported in the *Caledonian Mercury* for 30 Sept. 1746 (*CLA*, 100): 'You and every one of you, Prisoners at the Bar, return to the Prison from whence you came, and from thence you must be drawn to the Place of Execution, when you come there, you must be hanged by the Neck, but not till you be dead: For you must be cut down alive, then your Bowels must be taken out, and burnt before your Faces; then your Heads must be severed from your Bodies, and your Bodies divided in four Quarters, and these must be at the King's Disposal. And God have Mercy on your Souls.'

342.34 Grace me no grace *Richard II*, 2.3.87.

342.38–39 his blood be upon his own head see Joshua 2.19.

343.6 distinguished catholic family near Carlisle Scott may have been thinking of the Howards of Corby Castle, overlooking the River Eden near Wetheral, 8 km E of Carlisle. Scott was in contact with Mr Howard, the then proprietor, in 1806, and received an invitation from him to visit the castle in a letter of 17 March that year (see MS 3875, f. 148). He also gave an account of a later visit in a letter to J. B. S. Morritt in 1815, which itself points to a knowledge of the original 'old irregular monastic hall with its weather beaten and antique appearance' (see *Letters*, 4.101). Another possibly apposite location is Warwick Hall, on the west bank of the Eden, 7 km E of Carlisle, where Prince Charles was entertained during the siege of Carlisle, by Mrs Warwick and her kinswoman Mrs Howard of Corby Castle (see Duffy, 229).

344.36 shall perish by the sword see Matthew 26.52.

345.36 Scottish Benedictine nuns at Paris no Scottish convent at Paris during this period has been discovered.

346 motto see Thomas Campbell, 'Lochiel's Warning', lines 67–68, in *Gertrude of Wyoming ... And Other Poems* (London, 1809; *CLA*, 195). These words are spoken by a Wizard to Cameron of Lochiel, who is warned not to join the Jacobite rising of 1745, the immediate context here being the predicted execution of the 'iron-bound prisoner' after final defeat.

346.16–17 massive old tower ... surrounded by outworks the Keep of Carlisle Castle was begun in 1122 by Henry I of England, and completed by David I of Scotland, this being followed by the construction of a gatehouse tower ('Captain's Tower') in the 1160s. Works to strengthen the defences were undertaken in the early 1540s, late in Henry VIII's reign, these including the extension of the inner bailey walls to take guns, and the construction of a new stone bulwark to protect the Captain's Tower. Scott's daughter Anne, referring to a visit with her father to the Castle in 1828, reported how the guide had exploited 'the old trick of pointing out Fergus MacIvor's *very* dungeon' (see *Life*, 7.144).

346.32   16th of November last   terms for the capitulation of both the town and castle of Carlisle were negotiatated on 15 November 1745, with Prince Charles entering the town at the head of his troops on 17 November (see Blaikie, 26). The MS here reads '14th of November', when in fact the Prince was still at nearby Brampton, though a white flag was displayed from Carlisle that evening.

346.40   particulars of his escape   Charles Edward, after being a fugitive in the Highlands for several months, finally embarked for France on 20 September 1746.

347.30   Open Sesamum   the magical words used by Ali Baba to open the door of the robbers' den in the *Arabian Nights*. See 'The Story of Ali Baba, and the forty Thieves destroyed by a slave', in *Tales of the East*, ed. Henry Weber, 3 vols (Edinburgh, 1812; *CLA*, 43), 1.402–14. *Sesamum* is the Latin form of *sesame*, the grain used in baking and cooking.

348.13   three files   *file* evidently used here in the sense of two soldiers walking abreast.

348.14–19   fetters . . . loaded muskets   compare the *Caledonian Mercury*, 25 Sept. 1746 (*CLA*, 100): 'Large Bars of Iron are fix'd along the Wall of the Prison of the Castle of Carlisle, and Chains of seven Feet long are made ready, and each Rebel found guilty is to be fastened to one of these Bars with one of the Chains. All the Soldiers lying in the Castle have Orders to Keep their Arms continually loaden.'

348.21–22   attempt of the prisoners to escape   'Scarcely were the trials closed than some of the most notorious prisoners staged an escape effort': Rupert C. Jarvis, *Collected Papers on the Jacobite Rising*s, 2 vols (Manchester, 1971–72), 2.272. This apparently involved attempting to corrupt the sentries and the filing off of irons.

348.34–36   high treason . . . accommodated poor old Scotland   according to the terms of the Act of Union of 1707, Scotland preserved its own legal system. However, after an attempted Jacobite rising in 1708, the new British Parliament passed an Act introducing the English law of treason into Scotland, this embracing the definition of the crime, the procedure for prosecuting, and the mode of punishment (including, for the first time, live disembowelling). Previously those condemned for treason in Scotland had suffered hanging or decapitation, with various kinds of dismemberment after death. For the law of treason, see also notes to 341.21 and 342.17–18; and for an overview of the differences between English and Scottish procedures, in the light of events in the novel, see Joan Garden Cooper, 'Scott's Critique of the English Treason Law in *Waverley*', *Scottish Studies Review*, 4:2 (Autumn 2003), 17–36.

348.39   blot it from their records   as at least partly accomplished by the Act 54 Geo. III c. 146, 27 July 1814, in the same year as the publication of the novel. This states that 'such Person shall not be there hanged by the Neck, but that instead thereof the Head shall be there severed from the Body of such Person whilst alive', and that the death Warrant 'may direct and order how and in what manner the Body, Head and Quarters of such Person shall be disposed of'.

348.42   paper coronet   compare *3 Henry VI*, 1.4.93–95, and *Richard III*, 1.3.175.

348.43   the Scotch gate   the Scottish gate, facing north and about 13 km from the border with Scotland, one of three such gates in the town wall at Carlisle.

349.3   Moritur ... reminiscitur Argos   *Latin* he dies, and dying remembers his beloved Argos [Greece]. A version of Virgil's *Aeneid*, 10.782, referring to the death of Antores.

349.34   place of execution   Harraby Hill.

349.35–37   painted black ... broad axe in his hand   the description here is close to the account in the *Scots Magazine* of the execution of Robert Watt for high treason on 15 October 1794: 'The hurdle painted black (drawn by a white horse), in which were seated the executioner dressed in black, with the axe in his hand, and the criminal drawn backwards, and tied to the hurdle': 56 (Oct. 1794), 651. Watt had been tried along with David Downie, accused of having attempted to foment a revolution in the wake of attending the British Convention meeting in Edinburgh of 1793 (see also note to 182.13). According to the *Scots Magazine* account, 56 (Nov. 1794), 700, the sentence passed by the Lord President had included hanging, drawing, and quartering; though in the event the actual execution of Watt—Downie's sentence being reduced to banishment—was confined to hanging until death, followed by decapitation. Scott witnessed both the trial and execution himself (see *Letters*, 1.34, 37).

349.42   well GOT UP for a closing scene   the term 'got up', meaning 'turned out in a (specified) style in external appearance', was a relatively new one in Scott's days (see *OED, get*, verb 8om), and was used with reference to the mounting of plays, etc.

350.17–18   God save King James   echoing the words reportedly spoken at the execution (by beheading) of William Boyd, Earl of Kilmarnock, and Arthur Elphinstone, Lord Balmerino, at Tower Hill, London, on 18 August 1746. 'When the above Lords came out of the Tower, the Governour, as is usual, said, *God Bless King George*; to which the Earl of Kilmarnock replied, by making a Bow; and Lord Balmerino answered, *God bless K—g J—s*' (*Caledonian Mercury*, 25 Aug. 1746; *CLA*, 100).

350.21   dead march   solemn music played at a funeral procession, especially at a military funeral.

351.11   Fungarque inani munere   *Latin* and I will perform the useless service: see Virgil, *Aeneid*, 6.885–86, on the death of Marcellus, the nephew of Augustus. Waverley, as a Protestant, thinks of Catholic devotions for the dead as an unavailing office.

351.22   the Scotch yate   the Scottish gate: see note to 348.43.

351.27   Dulce Domum   *Latin* sweet home.

352.35–36   priest's hole   name to describe hiding places in the houses of recusant Catholic families, used to conceal forbidden clergy.

352.42   Patmos   see note to 324.1.

353.3   in bustle   in a commotion. Compare Jane Austen, *Pride and Prejudice* (1813), Vol. 2, ch. 4: 'The day passed most pleasantly away; the morning in bustle and shopping': in *Novels*, ed. R. W. Chapman, 3rd edn (1932), 2.152.

353.11–12   our English Juvenal, who tells the tale of Swallow the Attorney   George Crabbe (1754–1832), likewise called 'British Juvenal' in *The Heart of Mid-Lothian*, EEWN 6, 316.9. 'Swallow, a poor Attorney' appears in his *The Borough* (1810), Letter 6, line 200, and 'young Swallow' at line 210; the word 'vulture' occurs at line 257 ('And like a vulture look'd abroad for meat').

353.18   subject of proverbial delay   i.e. the law. See *Hamlet*, 3.1.72.

353.23   smokes and thunders down   see Samuel Johnson, in his 'Life' of Pope: 'Thunders impetuous down, and smokes along the ground', cited as a successful attempt at conveying onomatopoeically the labours of Sisyphus (see

The Works of the English Poets, ed. Alexander Chalmers, 21 vols (London, 1810; *CLA*, 41–42), 12.109).

353.38 matters more attractive compare *Hamlet*, 3.2.106 ('metal more attractive').

354.10 raw-head and bloody-bones stories see Samuel Butler, *Hudibras*, Part 3 (1678), 2.682 ('To Raw-heads fierce and Bloody bones'). Scott also alludes to this passage in *Saint Ronan's Well*, EEWN 16.102.40–41.

354.13 newspaper report of a chancery suit i.e. a quick summary of the proceedings of a case in *chancery*, the court of the Lord Chancellor of England, which considered matters of equity especially when there was no remedy in the common law courts, and which was notorious for the slowness of its deliberations.

354.32 in effeir of war in show of war.

355 motto matching the first two lines of a traditional song, which appears as a love song in Herd, 2.105–06. For a Jacobite version of the song, in which the house apparently represents a Scotland usurped and corrupted by outsiders, see James Hogg, *The Jacobite Relics of Scotland*, 1st series (1819), ed. Murray G. H. Pittock (Edinburgh, 2002), 57–58, 223–24, 445. Charles Edward is supposed to have requested this as the first of several Highland reels to accompany dancing when at the House of Lude early in September 1745: see John Sibbald Gibson, *Edinburgh in the '45* (Edinburgh, 1995), 33.

355.19–20 comitatus nuptialis *Latin* matrimonial retinue.

355.31 Dagons of his idolatry see 1 Samuel 5.1–5.

355.35 vita adhuc durante *Latin* during his life until now.

356.9 Diva Pecunia *Latin* the goddess Money.

356.18 Touchstone the court jester in *As You Like It*.

357.18 A talbot strong—a sturdy tyke see *The Battle of Flodden Field; A Poem of the Sixteenth Century*, ed. Henry Weber (Edinburgh, 1808; *CLA*, 187), line 214 ('A talbot brave, a burly tike'). A footnote here glossing 'talbot' comments: 'Though all the editions concur in spelling Talbot as a proper name, there can be no doubt, that the family name of the Earl of Shrewsbury is not alluded to, but the supporters of the arms, which are two talbots argent. The words "a burly tike", (a rough dog,) leave no doubt that this explanation is the true one, as a talbot, in heraldick language, is a species of hound' (12n.). Weber had been employed as Scott's amanuensis and assistant and it is possible that Scott may have written this note.

357.19–20 Earls of Shrewsbury Talbot is the family name of the Earls of Shrewsbury (see also previous note).

357.23 fight dog, fight bear fight till one be overcome: proverbial (Ramsay, 77; Ray, 190; *ODEP*, 256).

357.33 eagle and child the crest of the Stanley family. For an account of a family legend, concerning the discovery (by the Lathoms, of Lathom House, in Lancashire) of a child and heir in an eagle's nest, see J. A. Picton, 'The House of Stanley and the Legend of the Eagle and Child', *Notes and Queries*, 5th series (1 Jan. 1876), 2–4. A daughter of the house, Isabel, subsequently married Sir John Stanley, who took the eagle and child for his own crest.

357.34 in Derbyshire the Earl of Derby is the head of the Stanley family.

358.3 amor patriæ *Latin* love of one's own country, patriotism; as found in Virgil, *Aeneid*, 6.823.

358.5 procul a patriæ finibus *Latin* far from the bounds of your country.

358.21–22 like a hen . . . upon a het girdle like a hen on a hot griddle (flat iron pan for baking); proverbial (see *ODEP*, 369), usually indicating restlessness or anxiety.

358.26–27 Disposition and Assignation referring to a form of conveyance when the feudal rights to the conveyed were not fully established. Such might apply if Malcolm Bradwardine had not become fully possessed of the barony that he has gained as substitute (see note to 320.5) under the entail on the Baron's attainder. To gain infeftment (effectively, ownership), it was necessary to gain 'entry' from the Crown, via the Barons of Exchequer, which was expensive and time-consuming and often not done. This means that Malcolm Bradwardine cannot dispone (i.e. transfer) ownership, because he is not owner, but he can dispone and assign his right to become owner. This is why there is a Disposition and Assignation.

358.27–28 signed and tested in terms of the statute evidently referring to the Subscription of Deeds Act, 1681, c. 5, which required the grantor to sign in the presence of witnesses who also signed.

358.34–359.10 To Cosmo ... in fee Tully-Veolan has been bought by Waverley with money from the sale of his late father's house to Talbot. The property is then being given by Waverley to Bradwardine (the 'title deeds' are made out to the Baron), and the Baron has full rights as owner to the income generated by the estate through letting farms and holdings to others (the rental book). However the property is mortgaged ('burdened with the sum advanced to re-purchase it'), and Waverley by deed of gift has before his marriage assigned the mortgage to his future children (they have it 'in fee', which involves the full rights of ownership), but given Rose a life-rent of the mortgage (i.e. the income from the mortgage is hers while she lives). This complicated arrangement mimics a normal marriage settlement among the landed classes, in which a father would give a dowry on the marriage of his daughter, the dowry consisting of property or a sum of money sufficient to maintain his daughter should she be widowed, thus allowing ownership of the husband's property to pass to the next generation. The settlement also mimics the workings of an entail, for an entail passed ownership of a property to generations unborn until such time as there were no more heirs as specified by the entail, at which point ownership became absolute (see note to 320.5).

358.35–36 a me vel de me Latin literally by me or from me. In terms of Scots law, 'de me' here effectively means that the Baron holds the property under the person transferring the property, in this case Malcolm Bradwardine, in what was known as a base infeftment. The 'a me' effectively means that gaining infeftment from the Crown will complete this right, and he will come into the grantor's place as the Crown's vassal, so that the base infeftment 'de me' ends. In other terms, the disposition puts him as potentially the disponer's vassal until he gains entry from the disponer's superior. This procedure should be followed by a charter of confirmation from the Crown issued by the Exchequer.

358.39 consistent with Stile in Scots law usage *stile* or *style* refers to the approved form or model for drawing up a legal document. Just possibly the Baillie is also here alluding to George Dallas's *System of Stiles* (1697), widely used as a guide for framing legal documents: see note to 331.25–26.

358.41 outlast a Russian winter compare *Measure for Measure*, 2.1.128 ('This will last out a night in Russia').

359.3 auld sang probably echoing the proverbial statement, with its strong Scottish associations, as described in note to 323.35–36.

359.8 catholic security i.e. the security for the mortgage is the whole barony or estate of Tully-Veolan, and not just part of it. It follows that the Baron cannot sell or alienate any part of the estate without Rose's agreement.

359.11 intuitu matrimonij Latin in prospect of marriage.

359.12 donatio inter virum et uxorem Latin a gift made between a husband and wife. The distinction is that gifts made after marriage were revocable, whereas mutual provisions in an ante-nuptial marriage contract were not.

359.20 Esau, for a mess o' pottage see Genesis 25.29–34. The phrase 'a mess of pottage' comes from the chapter heading to Genesis 25 in the Geneva Bible (Geneva, 1560): 'Esau selleth his birth right for a messe of potage'.

359.21 cookit the parridge cooked the porridge, i.e. arranged matters, smoothed the way.

359.25 bogle about the bush a form of the game hide-and-seek.

359.39 let that flee stick i' the wa' i.e. don't worry about that, let that alone. Also used, in the slightly fuller form of 'let that flee stick i' the wa'— when the dirt's dry it will rub out', in *The Antiquary*, EEWN 3, 222.37. Compare also Tobias Smollett, *The Reprisal* (1757), 2.3; and *Rob Roy* (1818), EEWN 5, 188.38. Listed in *ODEP*, 268, under 'Flea (Fly), stick in the wall', though it should be noted that 'flee' in the present case, as in the other instances cited, is Scots for 'fly'.

360.3 stamped paper and parchment paper and parchment used for deeds. The stamping showed that the tax on certain types of deed had been paid.

360.7 decreet in absence *Scots law* final court judgment given in favour of a pursuer when the defender has not appeared or entered any defences. These could be easily overturned, i.e. cancelled, which is one reason why they could be procured easily, if the defender did not appear.

360.13–14 charter of resignation . . . in Exchequer referring to the procedure whereby the barony is resigned into the hands of the Crown, the Baron's feudal superior, so that it can then be regranted in a different way, which was specified: hence *in favorem*, here in favour of the Baron, then Rose and Waverley and then their heirs male with the preference for the second son, hence re-establishing an entail. The requirement that the second son take the name and arms of Bradwardine was known as a 'name and arms clause', and common in these types of circumstances. This was done through the Court of Exchequer, which looked after Crown affairs in Scotland.

360.13 in favorem *Latin* in favour of (see also previous note).

360.14 term in Exchequer i.e. during the next term of the Exchequer Court. Until 1790 law terms were defined in an Act of 1661 as 1 June to 31 July, and 1 November to 28 February.

361.8 Raeburn himself Sir Henry Raeburn (1756–1823), Scottish portrait artist. One of several large canvases in oil by Raeburn depicting Highland chiefs is that of Alasdair Ranaldson MacDonnell of Glengarry (1771–1828), who is sometimes claimed as a model of Fergus Mac-Ivor: see Historical Note, 387. This portrait was painted in about 1810, and exhibited at the Royal Academy in London in 1812; it is presently in the National Gallery of Scotland.

361.16 sentiment and vertu *vertu* here in the sense of 'a love of, or taste for, works of art'. Compare *Tom Jones*: 'To give them their due, they soar a Step higher than their Predecessors, and may be called Men of Wisdom and Vertù (take heed you do read Virtue)' (Bk 13, Ch. 5; 5.34).

361.23 at home i.e. in his own neighbourhood or place of residence.

361.38 poculum potatorium *Latin* drinking cup.

361.42 Saint Duthac see note to 49.21.

362.6–7 for a sorceress . . . conjuror in Scotland, by the Act 1563 c. 9, the penalty for those practising witchcraft, sorcery, and necromancy, and for those who consulted them, was death. It was not repealed until 1735. See also note to 335.30.

362.22 The tear mingled with the wine compare William Cowper (1731–1800), 'On the Loss of the Royal George', lines 27–28: 'And mingle with our cup/ The tear that England owes'. More generally the phrasing here reflects that of the traditional ballads.

363.10 abolition of the heritable jurisdictions the Heritable Jurisdictions Act (20 George II, c. 43), passed in 1747 and effective from 1748,
abolished the franchise jurisdictions of the baron courts and the Lords of
Regality to try accused persons of crimes committed in the area of their jurisdiction, as well as the heritable office of sheriff. The Act was of the greatest
significance in reducing the power of landowners over their feudal vassals,
and in giving control of the administration of justice to anti-Jacobite lawyers
and politicians in lowland Scotland.

363.19 Lord Selkirk Thomas Douglas, 5th Earl of Selkirk, author of *Observations on the Present State of the Highlands of Scotland* (London, 1805; *CLA*, 17).

363.28 old leaven 1 Corinthians 5.8.

363.43 Highland gentleman ... officer of rank later revealed by Scott
to be Alexander Stewart of Invernahyle (1707–95) and Lieutenant-Colonel
Charles Whitefoord (d. 1753). See also Historical Note, 373–74.

364.3–4 lady of rank see note to 256.17–18.

364.11 late venerable author John Home (1722–1808), playwright and
historian, author of the tragedy *Douglas*, first performed in Edinburgh 1756.
Home served as a volunteer on the government side in 1745–46, and later
published *The History of the Rebellion in the Year 1745* (London, 1802; *CLA*
4), which is used by Scott both as a point of reference and a source of personal
anecdote throughout the novel.

364.19 Miss Edgeworth Maria Edgeworth (1768–1849), Irish novelist,
and author of the Irish tales, *Castle Rackrent, An Hibernian Tale* (London,
1800), 'Ennui' (1809), and 'The Absentee' (1812), the latter two published
in *Tales of Fashionable Life* (London, 1809–12; *CLA*, 334).

364.20 dear joys 'Irishmen; from their frequently making use of that
expression' (Grose).

364.28 Mrs Hamilton's Glenburnie *The Cottagers of Glenburnie, A Tale
for the Farmer's Inglenook* (Edinburgh, 1808; *CLA*, 334), containing Scottish
locations, characters, and dialogue, by Elizabeth Hamilton (1758–1816).

364.29 late Account of Highland Superstitions *Essays on the Superstitions of the Highlanders of Scotland* (London, 1811; *CLA*, 23), by Anne Grant of
Laggan (1755–1838).

364.42–43 Colonel Caustic and Umphraville two key characters from
periodical essays by Henry Mackenzie (1745–1831): the retiring Umphraville
from *The Mirror* (1779–80), and irascible Colonel Caustic of *The Lounger*
(1785–87).

365.10 OUR SCOTTISH ADDISON a title pointing to the cultural prominence
gained by Mackenzie in Scotland through his editorship of and contributions
to *The Mirror* and *The Lounger* (see previous note), and that acquired in early
Augustan England by Joseph Addison (1672–1719), through periodicals such
as *The Tatler* and *The Spectator*. An earlier use of the term, suggesting that it
was already well established, is found in Anne Grant's *The Highlanders, and
other Poems*, 2nd edn (London, 1808), 265.

GLOSSARY

This selective glossary defines single words; phrases are treated in the Explanatory Notes. It includes words in Scots, English dialect, Gaelic, and foreign languages, as well as archaic and technical terms, and occurrences of familiar words in senses that are likely to be strange to the modern reader. The term *Gaelic English* indicates the pronunciation of English by a Gaelic speaker. For each word (or clearly distinguishable sense) glossed, up to four occurrences are normally noted; when a word occurs more than four times in the novel, only the first instance is given, followed by 'etc.'. Orthographical variants of single words are listed together, usually with the most common use first. Often the most economical and effective way of defining a word or expanding a definition is to refer the reader to the appropriate explanatory note.

a' all 54.4 etc.

abjure renounce an oath, retract a position formerly held 150.21 (see note), 155.42, 174.35

aboon above 152.39, 154.19, 154.20, 186.36

abstersion act of wiping clean 102.29

accolade *French* embrace, hug 45.24

accoutre equip, dress 122.36 etc.

adage maxim, proverb 237.28, 319.15

ae one 225.3, 314.20, 321.3, 332.32

æquiponderant of equal weight or value 78.21

aff off 186.34, 313.28, 321.15, 321.34

afore before, in front of 215.36, 226.5, 260.9

again against, in opposition to 164.3, 359.34

agnomen additional name 86.11, 245.40

ahint behind 215.41, 225.21

aich oh 83.40

aid-de-camp military officer who aids a general in his duties by bearing orders etc. 208.29, 209.22, 235.30

ain own 155.18 etc.

aits oats 200.38

alembic distilling apparatus 8.2

alias *Latin* otherwise called or named 311.11, 311.12, 359.9; alternative name 311.12

amaist almost 320.42

amang among 215.32 etc.

amateur person who has a taste for some activity 325.15

ambagitory indirect, roundabout 122.16

ambry repository in a house for keeping utensils, dresser 190.18

an if 94.42 (see note), 215.24, 285.32

an' and 218.23, 321.35

ance, anes once 94.13, 186.42, 314.37

ane one 53.25 etc.

anent concerning, about 184.28, 186.2, 245.13, 246.23

aneuch, aneugh enough 215.15, 321.18, 359.35

angle fishing-rod 16.15

anilia see note to 49.28

annexis *Scots law* appendages, appurtenances (frequently coupled with connex(is)) 218.11

annunciation announcement, declaration 74.4, 159.5, 193.5

antinomianism belief that the moral law is not binding on Christians 161.3

anti-room room before, or leading to, another 62.22, 345.19

apocryphal see note to 188.12–13

apostrophize address rhetorically 105.18

apothegm pithy maxim 61.17

apotheosis deification, canonisation 21.7

appropriated suitable, appropriate 30.32; specially assigned 238.5

aquavitæ strong spirits such as brandy or whisky 121.20

arbitrement settlement of a dispute 283.39

architrave ornamental moulding over an arch or door 39.5

argent *heraldry* silver or white 9.15

ariette *French* little aria or air 51.31

assassinate assassin 320.15

assignation see note to 358.26–27

assoilzie *Scots law* acquit of a criminal charge 246.26

assythment fine for bloodshed, paid to nearest relatives of the slain person 244.37

astore see note to 118.10

at *Gaelic English* that 225.21, 226.5

atchievement heraldic device 49.12 (see note)

atrophy wasting away, emaciation 46.42

attach arrest 164.36

attainder forfeiture of estate and loss of civil rights 319.26 (see note to 319.24–27), 338.19

attainted condemned (for treason) to death and extinction of all civil rights 311.30, 341.19

aught anything 34.28, 69.25, 172.37, 212.24

augur anticipate, foretell 9.26, 123.37, 142.14, 159.35

augury omen 142.19

auld old 94.15 etc.

Ave *Latin, short for* Ave Maria (Hail Mary), the first words of a prayer to the Virgin Mary 64.23

avocation calling away, distraction 44.10

awa' away 225.20, 225.27, 321.3

ay, aye yes 31.15 etc.

aye always, at all times 154.27 etc.; still 335.31

azure *heraldry* blue 9.15 (see note)

backslide fall away from religious faith 153.26, 186.29 (see note)

baff blow, shot 359.32

bagganet bayonet 215.29

bag-wig wig with the back hair enclosed in an ornamental bag 62.27

bailiff agent of a landowner 8.11, 46.40

baillie officer of a barony 29.12 (see note) etc.; town magistrate 87.19, 94.12.

bairn child 162.12 etc.

baith both 216.29, 335.30

ban swear, curse 243.24

band strip for fastening clothing 66.6; for 164.6 see note

banditti robbers, brigands 86.8, 99.16, 120.13, 228.42

banes bones 321.32

bang for 225.20 see note

bantling young or small child, brat 357.34

bar bear 38.31

barley for 215.14 see note

baron baillie, baron-baillie for 29.12 and 47.23 see note to 29.12

barony lands held directly of the Crown 42.8 etc.

barred ornamented with bars, striped 60.6

bartizan projecting turret, overhanging gallery 37.43, 63.26, 317.2

basaltic see note to 229.40

basis bottom, foot 229.39

basket-hilt hilt in which the swordsman's hand is protected by narrow plates of steel curved like a basket 208.40

bate lessen, diminish 279.16 (see note to 279.16–17), 282.41

battled furnished with battlements, crenellated 37.3

bauld bold 210.20 (see note), 314.10

bawbee copper coin originally worth 6 pence Scots, one halfpenny sterling (0.2p) 285.31

baxter baker 121.25

beaufet sideboard or side-table 46.23

beaux *French* fashionable young men 5.9

bedizened decked, dressed up 317.40, 356.18

beflum befool by cajoling language 359.33

begunk trick, deception 359.27

belang belong 337.36

belike probably, perhaps 185.29

belle *French adjective* see notes to 70.5–6, 118.3, 120.21

belle *French noun* beautiful or fashionable young woman 125.36

bell-hoop bell-shaped hoop foundation for spreading out skirt from the hips 62.26

ben for 42.41 and 244.6 see notes

benefice church living 48.19

benempt called, named 159.38

bent slope or ridge of a hill 52.4

beseem fit, suit 349.37

bewar beware 38.30

bhaird, bhairdh *Gaelic bàrd* bard, Highland minstrel and poet 78.21, 81.15, 105.9

bibliopolist bookseller 30.33

bicker bowl 330.9

bickering flashing, glittering 85.36

bieldy sheltered, cosy 320.41

biggin building 355.7

billet short written document, letter 119.35

birlieman rustic judge, minor officer of a town or manor 218.19

bit indicating smallness, familiarity, or contempt 92.33 (see note) etc.; spot, place 320.41

bitted see note to 200.3–4

bivouac camp in the open 123.5, 237.38

black-cock male of the black grouse 52.12, 59.8, 121.23, 285.30

black-fishing poaching of salmon at night 321.4

black-mail for 73.19 etc. see note to 73.19

bladier for 81.15 see note to 81.13–14

blanch see note to 245.5

blank make blank, put out of countenance, disconcert 55.32, 125.30, 139.22

blind out of sight, obscure 219.15

blood-horse thoroughbred or pedigree horse 158.15

blood-wit penalty for bloodshed 244.36

blowzy red and coarse-complexioned 4.23 (see note)

bluid, blude blood 67.7, 187.1, 215.20, 298.39

bluidy bloody 186.7, 314.34

blythe cheerful, joyous 94.14

boddle small copper coin worth 2 pence Scots (0.07p), something that is worthless 154.33 (see note), 201.11, 218.4

body person 94.7 etc.

bogle ghost 359.25 (see note)

bole bowl-shaped part of a tobacco-pipe 42.38

bonnie, bonny fine, dear, beautiful, pretty 52.12 etc

bon-vivant *French* gourmand, one fond of good living 181.21

boot good 125.5; for 52.19, 91.31, and 95.8 see note to 52.19

boot-jack contrivance for pulling off boots 255.10, 255.18, 269.6, 346.27

boot-ketch contrivance for pulling off boots 247.4

borrow surety, pledge 77.38

boune prepare oneself, get ready 64.20

Bourdeaux wine made in Bordeaux, claret 43.22

bower inner chamber 18.37, 39.17; shady recess, arbour 41.32, 317.12

bra' fine, splendid 200.34 etc.

brae bank, hillside, upland 52.3 etc.

brand sword 26.37, 104.22, 117.9; piece of burning wood 18.23, 88.29

brander cook on the gridiron, grill 320.23, 321.36

bravo daring villain, desperado 279.30, 320.15

breeks breeches, trousers 146.23, 146.24, 146.25, 245.34

brent smooth, unwrinkled 267.30

brevet see note to 208.28

bridal wedding, wedding feast 94.14, 136.35, 354.20

bride-favour ribbon or cockade, as worn at a wedding 345.12 (see note to 136.32)

bride's-man, bridesman bridegroom's attendant at a wedding, best man 136.37, 269.17, 354.41

brieve see note to 58.6

brissell-cock a kind of game bird, turkey-cock 121.23

broad-piece large, thin one-pound sterling gold coin 218.30

broadsword, broad-sword, broad sword cutting sword with broad blade 25.28 etc.

brocard pithy legal maxim 212.41

brogue Highland shoe of untanned hide 82.39 etc.; for 310.24 see note

broo' soup, broth 215.42

brownie goblin, benevolent household spirit 362.2

bruckle brittle, uncertain 336.40

bruick enjoy possession of 336.27

brulzie commotion, quarrel 215.15

buckie see note to 286.6

buckler small round shield 46.18

budget pouch, bag 255.9; bundle 358.25

burd woman, young lady 41.32

burgh town in Scotland possessing a charter 121.19, 181.43

burgher citizen of a burgh 186.34

burgonet open-faced helmet with cheek guards, heraldic helmet 357.30

burn stream 82.4

busk prepare, dress a fishing hook 43.6

buttock-mail see note to 161.7

bye see note to 313.26

bye-path side-path (as opposed to the highroad) 299.25, 315.36

ca' call 153.5 etc.

cabal intrigue, conspiracy 148.23, 259.36

cabalistical mysterious, secret 45.4

cabinet small chamber or room, private apartment 9.11

cabriole capriole, high leap made by a horse and throwing out the hind legs 36.18

cadet branch of a clan; son of a chief 265.3 (see note); younger son of a family, gentleman entering an army without a commission 291.32

cadger itinerant dealer 242.28

cailliach Gaelic cailleach old woman 94.40, 217.15

cairn see note to 210.41

caligæ Latin (soldier's) boots 245.36 etc.

callant, callan lad, fellow 146.23, 314.11, 357.35, 357.37

Cameronian see note to 175.34

canna cannot 42.26, 159.15, 320.22

cannily skilfully, carefully 94.21, 242.28

canny careful, cautious, astute 74.28, 91.30, 298.39; for 335.24 see note

Cantab see note to 312.8

canter one who uses the 'cant' of thieves; rogue, vagabond 68.6

canticle little song 162.20

cantine canteen, drinking vessel carried by soldiers on the march 139.38, 291.26

canting using religious language in a jargon-like way, hypocritical

210.43; for 68.4 see note to 68.3–5

cantle see note to 255.11

cantraip trick 158.28

capercailzie wood-grouse 121.23

capon castrated cock 121.22

carabine, carbine gun half-way between pistol and musket 22.39, 104.38, 239.28

carle, carl fellow 82.3 etc.

cartouch-box cartridge-box 141.27

castellated with battlements, like a castle 285.12

catechise ask questions systematically of 324.39

catechism see note to 187.24–25

catheran, cateran Highland marauder 38.5 etc.

cattle [human] beasts 38.10; horses 40.38

cauld cold 321.1

caution for 201.24 and 332.16 see notes

Cavaliero see note to 174.42

cean-kinné see note to 118.11

centinel sentinel 47.8 etc.

cess-money land-tax 76.14

chace unenclosed land reserved for breeding and hunting wild animals 19.7 etc.

champaign level and open 34.27, 203.31

change-house small inn or ale-house 50.16 etc.

chansons-à-boire French drinking songs 51.22

chariot coach, private carriage 311.14

chasseur hunter, huntsman 59.40, 60.28; for 199.38 see note to 199.37–38

chield, chiel lad, fellow 215.25, 322.13, 350.3

chimerical imaginary, visionary 168.15

chlain Gaelic clan clan, tribe 225.12

cholic stomach pains, bilious attack 29.13, 29.34

ci-devant former 252.5

circumbendibus roundabout process or method 122.17

clachan village 225.21 (see note)

clack see note to 307.15

clamhewit blow, drubbing 248.4

claw scrape, curry 53.26

claymore for 96.10 etc. see note to 96.10

cleik hook, seize 94.20

cleugh gorge 320.42

clew clue, guiding thread 261.5

close-time see note to 96.12–13

clour swelling caused by a blow 314.4

coble short flat-bottomed rowing-boat 218.9

cockade for 45.32 etc. see note to 45.31–32

cockatrice serpent-like monster 279.34

cocked *of a firearm* with the cock drawn back, ready for firing when the trigger is pulled 319.7

cocked *of a hat* three-cornered with brim turned up 60.7, 200.25

cock-match cock-fighting match 94.18

cocky-leeky chicken and leek soup 332.42

coghling coughing, gasping 215.39 (see note)

cogue wooden container 86.29

colewort cabbage 36.24

collateral descended from the same stock, but in a different line (as opposed to lineal) 8.24

collie sheep-dog 35.16, 36.20

collop slice of meat 120.4 (see note), 332.42 (see note)

columbarium see note to 38.20

comfortable causing comfort, re-assuring 35.34

commissary for 254.26 etc. see note to 254.26

commodious convenient, ser-viceable 234.12

complacence satisfaction, pleas-ure 49.5, 243.27

compotation drinking together, carousing 50.35

conciliate procure, gain 100.12

conclave private assembly, closet 69.42

concuss force by threats 77.38

concussion shock of impact 158.32

coney rabbit 121.22; for 323.40 see note to 323.40–42

congé bow 42.39, 216.9

conjuror one who conjures spirits, magician 124.16, 362.7; for 65.37 see note

connexis *Scots law* connected items of property, appurten-ances (usually in conjunction with annex(is)) 218.11

construe interpret, put a con-struction on 50.34, 143.31 166.10; analyse grammatically, translate 71.2

conventicle illegal religious assembly or meeting 179.31

cookit cooked 359.21 (see note)

copartment compartment 316.29

cope ecclesiastical long cloak or cape 186.11

coronach *Gaelic corranach* funeral song, dirge 76.41, 217.15

corri *Gaelic coire* hollow on the side of or between mountains 82.4, 93.3

corslet piece of defensive armour covering the body 5.30

costume characteristic or appro-priate mode of dress 44.24, 46.16

cottar tenant or farm-worker who occupies a cottage 91.43, 186.33

couldna couldn't 332.28

countenance *noun* face, expression, 42.16 etc.; support, favour, appro-bation 103.14, 228.5, 269.16

countenance *verb* support, sanc-tion, patronise 120.1, 120.2, 272.3

counter-tenor voice in a higher pitch than a tenor 219.2

countervail match, counterbal-ance 273.5

coup overturn, upset 332.9

coupe-jarret *French literally* cut hamstring (hence professional bandit) 320.15

course hunt 19.12, 60.25

cove cave, cavern 83.36 etc.

cow cut short 160.34

cowl hood or hooded habit 4.15, 157.35

coxcomb showy person, fop 247.16

cracks talk, gossip 160.34

craig neck, throat 201.17, 243.26

cran-berries see note to 90.29

crane large wading bird (now ex-tinct in Britain) 5.17, 121.22

creagh *Gaelic creach* raid, foray 72.14, 77.22, 87.17, 92.11

crest *heraldry* device placed above the shield and helmet in a coat of arms 49.14 etc.

crib pilfer 333.1

croft small piece of arable land, smallholding 109.11, 218.8

crop-eared see note to 53.25

cross-grained difficult, contrary 151.18

croupier one who sits as assistant chairman at a dinner at the lower end of the table 43.21

cud food chewed by an animal at leisure 19.33 (see note to 19.33–34)

cuittle tickle 52.6

cum *Latin* with, together with 26.11

cunzie coin, money 94.20

cupping-glass glass vessel for drawing blood 124.30

curb chain or strap passing under lower jaw of horse 242.25

curious interesting, noteworthy 15.4 etc.

curiously intricately, elaborately 150.16, 208.41

curragh boat (of hide over a wickerwork frame) 83.37, 83.38, 83.41

currant *heraldry* running 49.9

custodier custodian 67.42

cut-lugged crop-eared 161.5 (see note to 53.25)

cygnet young swan 5.17

daft foolish, crazy 56.27 etc.

dainty fastidious, over-nice 16.3; handsome, fine 164.5

dam-dyke wall confining water in a dam 38.19

dare-the-deil dare-devil 359.32

darkening nightfall, dusk 313.25

day's-wark day's-work, work done on or proper to a day 162.36

deacon see note to 237.29

deal plank, plain board 51.5

deasil see note to 124.24

deave deafen, annoy with din 162.12

debauch seduce from allegiance 343.11

debind bind down 212.8

debursement disbursement, expenditure 29.28

decreet *Scots law* decree, court judgment 332.33 (see note to 332.33–34) and 360.7 (see note)

defiance distrust, disregard 65.22

deil, deevil devil 94.42 etc.; for 94.42, 152.32, 200.38, 225.38, and 286.6 see notes

deliver active, nimble 215.14

démêlée quarrel, contention 44.32

demi half-sized, diminutive 38.28

demi-pique *of a saddle* half-peaked, having a peak half the height of the older war-saddle 60.4

depositary person to whom something is committed for safe-keeping 327.6, 362.18

dern secret, hidden 57.38, 93.3, 320.41

derogate detract from 357.29

derry-dongs see note to 52.18

dervise Moslem friar who has taken vows of poverty and austere life 21.1

descry perceive, discover 40.32, 72.16, 89.18, 123.15

destination *Scots law* nomination or sequence of heirs succeeding to property 69.25, 268.17, 287.28

determinate definite, fixed 8.26

device *heraldry* emblematic figure or design 9.13

devoted doomed 99.38

dexter see note to 255.11

diaoul devil 232.32, 266.39

diligence public stage-coach 153.36, 303.22 (see note)

dimity (made of) cotton fabric, with raised stripes or fancy figures 5.31

ding beat 332.17

dingle dell, hollow 19.22, 187.40

dinmont male sheep between its first and second shearing 51.25

dinna don't 216.1, 332.23

dinnle shake, vibrate 225.15

dirk short dagger, worn especially by Highlanders 79.11 etc.

disclamation repudiation, disclaimer 30.33

discomfited defeated, overthrew 74.15, 74.18

discompose agitate, ruffle 45.19 etc.

discussion consumption 43.36

dismissio *Latin* discharge 212.39

dispone *Scots law* legally assign, make over or convey 358.29

disponer *Scots law* one who makes over property to another 47.5

disposition frame of mind, mood, tendency 10.28 etc.; arrangement of troops in preparation for a military operation 236.2, 239.39; for 358.26 see note

disproportioned disproportionate 95.33, 266.19, 359.2

distaff stick used in spinning to hold the unspun fibres 35.3

divers various, several 43.31, 77.34, 77.40, 78.23

divertisement diversion, entertainment 42.25

divot see note to 218.11

doer agent 47.24, 218.18

dog-head hammer of a gun-lock 161.18

doil'd stupid, confused 161.15

dollar four-merk silver coin (first issued in 1676) 74.26.

dominus Latin master, lord superior 355.23

donative donation, gift 28.1, 109.9

doon down 42.20, 161.9, 313.37

door-stane threshold 359.31

dorlach for 215.35 and 225.26 see note to 225.26

dovering slumbering, dozing 94.22

dow term of endearment dove 215.41

dowff dull, spiritless 224.13

dr. abbreviation of debtor (in book-keeping) 129.28

dragoman see note to 112.2

dram measure of spirits, tipple 80.11, 91.6, 154.14, 225.33

drap drop 187.1

drave drove 317.16

drill military drill-master 307.21

droghling walking with short steps 215.39 (see note)

dropping for 188.35, 197.6 and 204.2 see note to 188.35

dubitation doubt, uncertainty 213.26, 245.10, 354.33

duello duel 55.39

duinhé-wassal, duinhé-wassel, duihne wassal, duinhé-wassell Gaelic duin' uasal gentleman 79.13 etc.

Duk Duke 201.29 (see note)

duns demands for payment 218.32

duresse confinement, imprisonment 189.4

durst dare(d) 9.36 etc.

d'ye do ye 160.33 etc.

eal-house-door Cumbrian ale-house-door 298.1

earn eagle 82.6

earnest for 140.31, 140.33, 140.35 see note to 140.31

earth-damp noxious mist near the ground 193.20

ebriety state of being intoxicated, drunkenness 57.6, 57.25

ebriolus Latin see note to 57.8

ebriosus Latin see note to 56.16–21

ebrius Latin see note to 56.16–21

eclaircissement clarification, explanation 136.2

Ecossois French Scottish 289.14

e'en¹ even, just 92.13 etc.

e'en² see even

een eyes 356.25

effeir appearance, show 354.32 (see note)

eh exclamation expressing surprise, dismay, affirmation etc. 30.41 etc.

eld antiquity, people of olden time 34.28

elegante fashionable lady 4.29

embrazure opening to allow a gun to be fired through it 202.32

Embro' Edinburgh 158.2

embrocation liquid for applying to the skin in diseases 124.32, 127.3

emergence emergency, pressing state of affairs 199.37

emolument reward, remuneration 130.15, 130.30

enclosure see inclosure

encomium high praise, eulogy 48.33, 119.7

enough enough 325.11

ensign banner, flag 197.28

ensure warrant, guarantee 215.24

epulæ Latin feast, banquet 46.5

equipage accoutrements, outfit for a journey 158.18

equiponderate equal in weight, equivalent 237.27

Erastian, erastianism for 161.2, 180.11, and 185.25 see note to 180.11

ere before 7.4 etc.

ermine for 9.14 etc. see note to 9.14–15; fur or fur-trimmed garment 353.17

errant itinerant, travelling 334.19 (see note)

esplanade open level space of ground, separating a fortress from the town 346.10

etter-cap spider; bad-tempered, spiteful person 322.13

eulogium eulogy, speech of praise 10.26, 276.8, 320.32

euphonia Latin euphony, pleasantness of sound 271.31

even, e'en evening 323.43, 335.33

evidents *Scots law* documents establishing a right or title 78.25, 218.15 (see note), 245.37

evite avoid, escape from 67.23

ewest near, contiguous 218.40

exeemed released, exempted 56.24

factor agent, estate manager 29.12 etc.

factory jurisdiction of a factor, agency 218.41

fain gladly 64.43; obliged 182.8

faineant sluggard, do-nothing 269.27

fallow fellow 321.17

fallow-deer small yellowish-brownish deer 58.1

fatuous *Scots law* in a state of imbecility and therefore incapable of managing own affairs 58.5

fauld fold, pen 185.29

faultering faltering 306.5, 343.28

feal[1] loyal, faithful 100.25

feal[2] for 218.11 see note

feck for 187.18 and 321.24 see notes

feifteen fifteen 321.34 (see note)

fendy resourceful, good at providing 91.31

fery *Gaelic English* very 248.4

fête festival, large-scale entertainment 5.19

fetched made, took 315.35

feu-duty annual rent paid by a vassal to his superior for tenure of lands held in feu 246.24

feyther *Cumbrian* father 298.13, 298.18, 298.18

fiat decree, command 9.9

fief feudal estate 69.9, 268.17

field-piece light cannon for use on the field of battle 229.25, 234.28, 241.1

fife small wind instrument used to accompany the drum in military music 238.2, 350.40

fille-de-chambre *French* chambermaid, lady's personal maid 4.10, 339.16

fire-drum drum beaten as a fire alarm 181.42

firelock musket in which the powder was ignited by sparks 101.34, 139.17, 188.29, 195.25

fishing-wand fishing-rod 43.6

flang flung 332.29

flee fly 359.39 (see note)

flemit chased, put to flight 43.1

fleyt scolded 321.8

fling for 146.38 and 331.17 see note to 146.38

flour see note to 55.2

flox-silk floss-silk, fine filaments of silk 28.5

fob small pocket in waistband of breeches, used for carrying watch, money, etc. 155.11

folio book made up from sheets of paper folded in half, i.e. a large book 68.25, 68.28; paper of that size 129.16

foment bathe with medication 124.33, 124.36

foot-wobbler *slang* foot-soldier 304.2

forgie forgive 321.22, 332.10

foris-familiated see note to 53.15

fortalice fortress, small fort 64.3 etc.

foun *Cumbrian* fun 298.10

fowling-piece light gun for shooting game birds 79.14, 80.42, 96.10

frae from 154.11 etc.

freebooter plundering adventurer 99.20, 325.34, 328.14

friseur hairdresser 106.34

frith firth, estuary 117.2

frock frock-coat; long coat or coat with long skirts 5.31

frontispiece title-page 3.28 (see note)

fule fool 45.12 etc.

fule-sangs foolish songs 160.42

furiosity see note to 58.6

furze gorse 187.39, 233.11

fusee light musket 123.39, 228.2, 236.25, 240.37

gaberlunzie beggar, tramp 68.6

gad bar of iron 162.22

gae[1] go 162.11 etc.

gae[2] gave 285.32, 321.16

gaed went 52.3 etc.

Gael Scottish Highlander(s) 79.7 etc.

gaffer term for an elderly rustic, or title for rustic below the rank of 'Master' 8.12

gage *noun* pledge, security 177.41

gage *verb* pledge, stake 344.34

gainsay oppose, contradict 226.43

gait, gate way 319.3, 320.27

gala see note to 46.26

gallow's-bird one who deserves to be hanged 296.7

gambado large boot or gaiter 157.39

gane gone 72.38 etc.

gang go 92.29 etc.

gar make (someone do something or something happen) 225.15, 325.9, 335.35, 359.28

gartan'd gartered, bound with a garter 219.27

gat got 94.23, 321.34, 332.9

gate see gait

gaun going 146.23, 185.8

gay addicted to social pleasures and dissipations 33.9; brilliant, showy 43.3; very, considerably 298.39

gear movable possessions, livestock 72.38, 74.1, 317.16; property, possessions in general 77.36 (see note), 336.22, 336.41 (see note)

general for 239.36 see note

generalissimo supreme commander of combined forces 284.18

ghaist ghost 317.33

gie give 155.38 etc.

gill for 153.14 and 154.15 see notes

gillie-trusharnish *Gaelic gille-truis-àirnis* attendant of a Highland chieftain who carries his baggage 81.20

gillie-white-foot see note to 60.23

gilly *Gaelic gille* attendant, lad, servant 83.12 etc.

gilly-casflue *Gaelic gille-cas-fliuch* attendant of a Highland chieftain who carries over streams 81.17

gilly-comstraine *Gaelic gille-comh-sreathainn* attendant of a Highland chieftain who takes care of his horse 81.18

gilly-more for 81.16 see note to 81.13–14

gimlet-eyed having a sharp or piercing eye 305.9

gimmer female sheep between its first and second shearing 51.24

gin if 162.16, 186.7

ginge-bread gingerbread 121.21

girdle see note to 358.21–22

girnel granary, storehouse 38.11

gite *French* lodging, quarters 324.24

gled kite, bird of prey 215.41 (see note)

gleg keen, alert 215.15

glisk glance, glimpse 321.6

gloaming twilight 320.2, 359.31

glossarium commentary, often within the margins of a book 245.43

goud gold 217.26

grandame, grand-dam grandmother 35.2, 201.33

grandsire grandfather 46.39, 74.14, 201.32

graning groaning 161.5

grat wept 314.12

grazier one who grazes or feeds cattle for the market 184.35

gree agree, get on with each other 185.31

greybeard one- or two-handled jug for holding liquor 321.38

grice young pig, suckling pig 121.22

griffin *heraldry* imaginary animal, part eagle, part lion 17.22

grip lay hold of, seize 87.18

gripe grasp, hold 45.23

grippal niggardly, usurious 336.22

grounsill door-sill, threshold 65.13

grub dig up by the roots 316.29, 356.12

gude, guid good 74.1 etc.; God 313.19

gudeman husband, head of household 162.12, 162.16, 162.17, 320.41

gudewife wife, mistress of a household 154.15, 160.41, 162.11

guerdon reward, recompense 327.24

gules *heraldry* red 5.36

gulpin credulous person, simpleton 258.41

gunpowder explosive as gunpowder, easily fired or inflamed 265.16

gusto relish, zest 91.11; taste, style 355.33

ha'¹ have 32.35, 45.33

ha'² hall 42.31

habiliments dress, garments 157.35

habit dress, garment 303.33

hack, heck for 201.21 and 321.24 see notes

hackney-coach carriage kept for hire 305.30

hae have 154.13 etc.

hag portion of wood set aside for cutting 42.20, 42.30, 44.8, 320.41

haggis Scottish dish, made of offal, oatmeal, etc. (boiled in a sheep's stomach, and usually in a round shape) 235.10

ha' house, ha-house, ha'-house manor-house, laird's residence 45.12–13, 320.26, 321.21

haill, hail undamaged, sound 248.3; whole, entire 355.19

hair-brained heedless, reckless 178.27–28

hale sound, healthy 42.4

half-pike small pike, having a shaft about half the length of the full-sized one 62.43

hallan inner wall, erected between the door and the fireplace 53.42, 298.38, 322.18

Hallow-Mass the feast of All Saints (1 November) 64.20 (see note), 64.24

halter hangman's noose 172.33, 359.40; rope for holding a horse 201.17

hame home 94.22 etc.

hanchman personal attendant of a Highland chieftain, bodyguard 81.14 (see note to 81.13–14)

hantle great deal of, much 154.28

harlequin see note to 147.2

harrow spiked instrument for drawing over ploughed land 237.32 (see note)

harry plunder, lay waste 74.19, 101.1

haud hold 359.28

haugh level ground on the banks of a river 40.12

hazy confused with drink 304.31

heading beheading 293.24

heath-cock male of the black grouse 115.24, 127.37

hebdomadal weekly, every seven days 20.28

heck see **hack**

heel crust at bottom of a loaf of bread 321.37

heirship see note to 94.17

hemlock tall poisonous plant, common in ditches 36.26

her *Gaelic English* his, him 155.18 (see note) etc.

heritage *Scots law* property in the form of land and houses 34.29

heritor proprietor, landowner 75.40

hersell, hersel herself 94.16; for 153.4 and 155.3 see note to 155.18

herships armed incursions, predatory raids 77.34

het hot 162.22, 320.28, 358.22

heuch precipice, steep bank 62.35

hie hasten 45.39 etc.

Hieland Highland 314.2, 325.11, 325.11, 332.25

Hielandman Highlander 342.14, 351.23

hight called, named 25.39

hill-folk see note to 186.19

himsell, himsel himself 92.10 etc.

hippocras cordial drink made of wine flavoured with spices 121.20

hippogriff see note to 26.20–21

ho *Cumbrian* thou, you 298.13, 298.32, 298.37

homagium *Latin* homage, acknowledgement of allegiance 245.23

honest for 140.22 and 337.20 see note to 140.22–23

honeycomb wax structure formed by bees and containing honey 89.36

hoop circle of flexible material, such as whalebone, used to expand the skirt of a woman's dress 25.25

horse-couper horse-dealer 69.38, 201.22

hot-pressed see note to 6.4

houlerying see note to 298.11

houndsfoot houndsfoot; scoundrel-like, rascally 243.26

housings coverings, trappings 60.4

hout *exclamation* tut, nonsense 215.20, 215.20, 321.34

howbeit be that as it may, however 183.43

howe plain, vale 94.15 (see note)

hunder hundred 321.20

hurdies haunches 219.28

hurley-house see note to 337.36

hus us 332.13

hyperbolical extravagant, vehement 140.26

hyperborean extremely northern 38.31

hypochondriac affected by melancholy 224.15

i' in 359.39

ilk[1] each, every 321.36

ilk[2] for 254.23, 333.11, and 360.10

see note to 254.23

ilka each, every , 313.37

illuminati members of society claiming special enlightenment 4.14

implant insert, infix 283.40

inclosure, enclosure land marked off by boundaries, encompassing wall or barrier 36.27 etc.

incontinent straight away, immediately 320.4

incumbent bending one's energies to some work, closely occupied with something 13.23

independency system of church polity in which congregations are held to be independent of external authority 161.2

indue endue, put on 59.37

infer imply 67.43, 180.26, 214.7; involve, bring about 141.38

infield arable land nearest the farm-buildings, kept continuously under crop and well manured 218.8

ingenuity ingenuousness, freedom from dissimulation 170.13

ingle fire-side 321.2

ingle-nook side of the room where the fire is, chimney-corner 338.9

inmate inhabitant, resident 12.20, 12.24, 68.15, 72.11

innocent one lacking in ordinary knowledge or intelligence, simpleton 42.40, 43.15, 58.25, 356.25

inrigh *Gaelic eanraich* kind of soup, broth, gravy 86.30

insight for 77.36 see note to 77.36–37

intelligence news, information 8.14 etc.; comprehension, understanding 41.40 etc.

intelligencer informant, messenger 8.7 (see note to 8.6–7)

intercessor mediator 170.17

interdict prohibit, forbid 323.16

interrogation question 30.43, 126.17

interrogatory question, examination 160.16, 166.34

intromit handle another's property, interfere 47.21, 77.35

irritate provoke, excite 269.3, 323.24

I'se I shall 93.27 (see note) etc.

ither other 225.22

jade *noun* hack, worn-out horse 222.1; hussy, minx 305.9

jade *verb* befool, jape 77.14

Janizary see note to 191.34

jerboa see note to 323.41

Jeremiad lamentation, melancholy denunciation 186.1

jer-falcon gerfalcon, large Arctic falcon 321.7

jetty jet-black 106.35

jogue see note to 40.34–35

joint-stool stool made of parts inserted in each other 53.37

joisted with joists, built with timber supports 121.18

jotting something jotted down, brief note 359.10, 360.12

jougs instrument of public punishment consisting of a hinged iron collar attached by a chain to a wall or post and locked round the neck of the criminal 45.11

justified punished with death, executed 342.3

justle jostle 211.29

kale curly cabbage 36.24

keepit kept 248.3, 321.20

kemple Scottish measure of hay or straw (varying between 14 and 19 stones in weight) 320.42

ken *verb* know 53.5 etc.

ken *noun* range of vision 187.43

kettle-drum percussion instrument, consisting of hollow metal hemisphere with a parchment head 236.10, 238.4, 297.22

kilt part of Highland dress, consisting of a skirt reaching from the waist to the knee 79.9 etc.

kin kinsfolk, relations 75.30, 225.39, 354.31

kind for 92.8 see note to 92.8–9

kine cows 73.34

kippage state of excitement or anger 267.29

kirk church, the Presbyterian Church of Scotland 59.19 etc.

kith neighbours, personal acquaintances 75.30, 354.31

kittle *adjective* tricky, difficult 186.27

kittle *verb* tickle 155.19

knap-sack, knapsack bag or case for carrying necessaries, as worn on the back by soldiers and travellers 80.40, 81.20, 278.30

knight-errant knight in search of chivalrous adventures 257.1 (see note)

knot small group, cluster 300.19

kyloes small, black Highland cattle 51.25

lack-a-day shame or reproach to the day, alack 313.20, 313.21

laird lord, landowner 29.12 etc.

lamp-black soot from a lamp, pigment consisting almost of pure carbon 160.26

land-louper roving vagabond, adventurer 212.13

lang long 154.13 etc.; tall 185.8

lang-leggit long-legged 146.23

lanthorn lantern 195.42

lanthorn-jawed lantern-jawed, i.e. with long thin jaw, giving a hollow appearance to the cheek 160.5

lares *Latin* household gods, home 358.5

lass, lassie girl 104.14, 219.20, 314.22

latchet thong used to fasten a shoe 246.1, 254.35

latitudinarian one liberal or lax in religious matters 30.8 (see note to 30.7–8)

latticed made of pieces of wood crossed and joined to each other with spaces in between (for glass) 343.39

lawing tavern-bill, reckoning 154.29

lea tract of open land 318.8, 318.15

leach leech, physician 124.15, 124.24

leaguer camp (especially of a besieging army) 213.31, 266.27

lea-land fallow land, grass-land 54.4

leasing falsehood, lying 66.16

leasing-making *Scots law* making false accusations, verbal sedition 213.1

leaven substance added to dough to produce fermentation 158.22, 363.28

leddy, leddie lady 217.28, 285.29, 318.4, 325.2

letter-press see note to 31.17

levee morning assembly held by an important person 7.32, 277.19, 333.20

libation pouring out of wine in honour of a god 43.23

licentiate see note to 97.13

lie for 45.1 and 245.38 see notes

liege superior to whom one owes feudal allegiance 64.40

life-rent *Scots law* right to receive income from a property till death, but without ownership 332.18 (see note), 356.28, 359.9

lift steal, take by a raid 91.39 (see note), 91.43, 94.5; collect 319.39

ligature tie, bond 246.5

lightly for 335.34 see note

limb agent, scion 307.9 (see note), 330.14

limmer rascal, scoundrel 77.32, 77.43; jade, idle hussy 313.28

lineal in direct line of descent 176.25

livery distinctive uniform or badge worn by retainers or servants, distinguishing dress 9.29 etc.

loathly hideous, disgusting 336.5

lock mechanism by which the charge in a gun is exploded 90.43, 228.43, 296.8

lofted with an upper storey 100.38 (see note), 121.18

loike *Cumbrian* like 298.12, 298.33

loon rascal, scoundrel, fellow 29.20 etc.

lordship (title to) a domain 9.1

louis-d'or, louis d'or for 100.22 etc. see note to 100.22

louping-on-stane leaping-on-stone, mounting-block 158.11

luckie familiar name for an elderly woman, and more specifically for the mistress of an ale-house 50.20 etc.; for 226.6 see note

lucubration product of nocturnal study, literary work showing careful elaboration 31.42, 174.23

lug ear 53.25

lunzie see note to 52.14

luve love 359.39

mae more 285.29, 314.12, 332.11

magnum bottle containing two quarts of wine or spirits 43.36

mails see note to 319.37–38

main-bread white bread of the finest quality 121.21

mains home farm of an estate 75.18 etc.

mair more 45.12 etc.

maist most, mostly 77.31 etc.; for 187.18 and 321.24 see notes

major strut, swagger 215.36 (see note), 321.13

mak make 200.39 etc.

mal-a-propos inappropriate, inopportune 247.23

malvasie malmsey, a sweet wine 121.20

manege training of horses, horsemanship 33.23

manger for 201.21 and 321.24 see note to 201.21

mantle spread, cover 48.39, 182.27; froth 51.16

mantua woman's loose gown 25.26

marechal see note to 51.31–32

mark for 94.13 and 186.37 see note to 94.13

marry name of the Virgin Mary used as an exclamation 172.35, 279.38

mart ox or cow fattened for slaughter (usually salted for the winter) 47.21

martinet *noun* military officer who is a stickler for maintaining discipline 226.33, 338.31

martinet *adjective* characteristic of a martinet, fussily concerned with military discipline 262.2

martingale strap joining horse's noseband to girth 242.24

Martinmas 11 November, a Scottish quarter-day 201.12 (see note), 244.33

mask brew or infuse [tea] 219.6

matins morning song 146.7

maud checked plaid or wrap (as worn by shepherds) 321.11

maugre in spite of 227.31

maun must 154.31 etc.

mayhap perhaps, possibly 339.13

meal-ark meal-chest, wooden bin for storing meal or grain 47.22

meed reward 115.26

meeting-house see note to 47.18–20

meikle see **mickle**

mellee battle, close combat 237.28

memorabilia memorable thoughts, observations 35.15

mend improve, get better 69.39, 69.39, 180.16; for 9.20, 9.20, 71.2, and 331.24 see note to 9.20

mendicant beggar 68.6

mess dish, portion of food 55.7, 359.20 (see note); military

group who take their meal together 33.19, 174.2

methinks it seems to me 102.20

mickle, muckle, meikle much, great, big 81.26 etc.; for 153.4 see note

mien bearing, air 41.5, 205.15

milch yielding milk, kept for milking 73.34, 100.20

mind remember 314.4, 314.7

misgugle spoil by careless handling, mistreat 94.38

moldwarp mole 17.22

mon *Cumbrian* man 298.33, 298.33

monitor adviser 138.22

monomachia duel, single combat 55.39

Monseigneur *French* (your) Grace, (your) Royal Highness 288.16, 288.16–17, 289.4, 289.9

mony many 52.5 etc.

morn (the morn) tomorrow 215.22, 360.12

morning morning drink 91.6, 225.32, 330.14

mosses peat-bogs, moorland allocated to tenants for cutting fuel 218.8

mousquetaire *French* musketeer 51.33

mousted powdered 185.23

moveables for 94.17 and 360.42 see note to 94.17

muckle see **mickle**

muir moor 218.8

muir-cock moor-cock, male red grouse 321.36

muir-fowl moor-fowl, red grouse 121.23

mulct fine, exact a penalty 153.11

mummery play-acting, ridiculous ceremony 348.40

mumming adoption of a disguise to take part in a play or ceremony 187.19

munt mount 201.8

muscadel strong sweet wine made from muscat or similar grape 121.20

mutchkin quarter of a Scots pint (three quarters of an Imperial pint, 0.43 litres) 200.27

muzzle opening of barrel of a gun 287.2; mouth, nozzle 332.43

myrmidons see note to 127.36

mysell, mysel myself 92.18 etc.

na no 93.21 etc.; not 127.23 etc.

nae no 94.7 etc.; not 154.20 etc.

naebody nobody 314.33

naething, naithing nothing
164.3, 215.10, 314.30, 321.16

naig nag, horse 159.6, 159.16, 201.14

nane none 161.21

napry household linen, esp. table
linen 121.24

natheless nevertheless 159.16

nean *Cumbrian* none 298.10

neb nose 321.5

ne'er never 201.25; for 285.25 see
note

ne'er-do-good good-for-nothing
161.30

neight, neet *Cumbrian* night
298.12, 298.29

nice fastidious, over-particular 94.7

no not 53.4 etc.

nolt cattle, oxen 73.33, 77.36

nonjuring, non-juring for
48.15 and 167.33 see note to 48.15

non-juror for 173.22 see note to
48.15

noo *Cumbrian* now 298.10

nor than 285.29, 332.11

noteless unmarked, unnoticed 64.11

novelle any of a number of tales
making up a larger work, short
narrative(s) 15.15

nuncupative declared orally 217.18

o' of 67.7 etc.

obfuscate darken, obscure 70.23

objurgation severe rebuke,
scolding 57.29

oblectation delight, enjoyment 57.26

obsidional relating to a siege
266.24 (see note)

oich oh 91.35, 92.22

onnor honour 32.36

ony any 153.25 etc.

orderly, orderly-men non-commissioned officer(s) or pri-
vate(s) who attend(s) on superior officers to carry orders or
messages 235.30, 278.39, 278.39

ordinary *heraldry* device on a
shield or coat-of-arms 67.32, 255.20

orra occasional 43.7 (see note)

or before 218.5

o't of it 155.30 etc.

ou, ow *exclamation* oh 200.34,
314.22, 314.25, 320.23

out oh 93.2, 94.12

outfield outlying land of farm 218.8

outrecuidance self-conceit,
arrogance 78.24

outsight see note to 77.36–37

ower over 52.4 etc.; too, overmuch
164.4, 314.9, 335.25

Oxonian see note to 12.26

paction bargain, agreement 326.40

paley somewhat pale 43.38

palinode recantation 67.25

pall fine or rich cloth 5.1

pallet rough bed, mattress 87.43

pan hollow at the side of the lock
which holds the priming in a gun
287.2; for 129.19 see note

pang pack, stuff 320.42

pannel for 332.23 see note

paranomasia wordplay based on
words which sound alike 68.2

paretaria see note to 266.26

park enclosed piece of land, field,
tract of land connected with a
country house 18.41 etc.

park-dike field-wall 186.32

parole word of honour given by a
freed prisoner that he will return
to custody 253.37 etc.

parridge porridge 359.21 (see note)

partarre level area with ornamental flower-beds 42.1, 63.32

partizan adherent, supporter
48.23 etc.; member of a party of
irregular troops 213.21, 301.6

passant *heraldry* walking and looking ahead 9.15 (see note to
9.14–15) etc.

pat put 359.23

patch small piece of black silk worn on
the face for adornment 25.25

patent *adjective* protected by letters
patent, patented 40.19

patent *noun* for 100.24 etc. see
note to 100.24

patriarchal for 78.30 etc. see note
to 78.30

patrick partridge 332.32

pawnies turkey-cocks, peacocks
121.23

peach inform against, betray 31.20

pease pea plant 36.34

pease-straw stalks and foliage of
the pea plant, as used as bedding
for animals 238.36

peccadillo petty sin 326.26

peculium *Latin* private funds 216.30

pedigree genealogical tree or table 21.31, 324.8 (see note); ancestry, descent 78.17, 201.31.

peel-house small tower or fortified dwelling 212.9

pelisse fur cloak, cloak trimmed or lined with fur 5.9

pellitory see note to 266.26

pendicle small piece of ground subsidiary to a larger holding, portion of a larger farm let separately 218.12

penetralia *Latin* innermost parts 183.32

periwig wig 48.4, 61.21, 214.39

perquisition investigation, inquiry 80.19

persecutive persecutory, relating to persecution 182.6

pertinents *Scots law* adjuncts belonging to an estate 218.12

pet offence, slight 283.3

pharisaical resembling the Pharisees in assuming an outward show of spiritual pride and superiority 158.22

pharmacopeia collection or stock of drugs 125.28

philabeg *Gaelic fèileadh-beag* kilt 219.28

phrenesiac frenetic, delirious 224.15

physiognomia *Latin* physiognomy, facial appearance 214.6

piaffe *equestrian* step with a high, slow, showy action; (of a rider) ride a horse in this manner 289.11

pibroch piece of bagpipe music 82.18 etc.

pica a size of type 31.10 (see note)

picquetted tethered to a stake 237.17

pier-glass large mirror 213.40, 215.36

pingled troubled, harassed 127.22

pinners (cap with) long flaps on either side 215.42

pis-aller makeshift expedient, last resort 25.44, 252.30

pit put 242.24

placeman person who is appointed to office in return for political support, a yes-man 10.39

plack small copper coin usually valued at 4 pennies Scots (0.14p), 'a very small amount' 187.1, 218.5, 248.3, 332.35

plaid, plaidy long rectangle of

twilled woollen cloth worn as outer garment 51.9 etc.; wearer of plaid, Highlander 255.39, 298.39, 308.27

plaid-men Highlanders 298.27

pledge toast 43.22 (see note to 43.21–22)

plenipotentiary person invested with authority, delegate 80.10

plenishing for 77.37 and 94.9 see note to 77.36–37

plough-sock ploughshare 255.19

plover lapwing 121.22

ploy trick, piece of fun 321.5

pole-axe axe-blade attached to either a long or short handle, battle-axe 228.42

portal gateway, entrance 37.19, 199.34, 350.20

portmanteau travelling-bag, case 153.17 etc.

post *adverb* with relays of horses 278.34 (see note), 303.20, 311.15, 312.25

post *noun* express messenger 8.6 (see note), 331.43

post-boy driver, postilion 222.3, 222.5

post-chaise carriage hired from stage to stage, or drawn by horses so hired 26.22

postern (door) back or private door 112.17

post-horse horse kept for hire at a post-house or inn 221.40, 315.2

post-road road on which a series of post-houses was established, road on which mail was carried 230.38

potation drink, consumption of alcohol 57.12

pottage soup, porridge 359.20 (see note)

pottingar apothecary, druggist 121.26

poulerying see note to 298.11

pownie pony 242.29

powter poke, rummage 320.27

prandium *Latin* meal, lunch 46.5

pratty see **pretty**

preceese precise 159.14

preceesely precisely 152.39

preceptor teacher, instructor 13.4, 13.13, 63.10

predilection partiality, predisposition 6.23, 148.31, 245.21, 268.23

prelacy church government by

bishops 161.1

prelatic pertaining to prelacy or episcopacy 71.38

prelatist supporter of church government by bishops 66.7, 150.21 (see note), 185.25, 188.13

prelected lectured, discoursed 213.3

premonish forewarn, advise beforehand 219.20

presbytery the Presbyterian system; the ecclesiastical court above the Kirk Session and below the Synod 161.5, 161.7 (see note to 161.6–7), 179.35, 213.20

press crowd 162.30, 227.19, 248.21, cupboard 190.18; for 306.25 see note

presumptive for 6.20 and 14.22 see note to 6.20

pretty, pratty *used of men* fine, brave, gallant 87.25 etc.

primate head, superior 320.14

princeps *Latin* first, original 28.33 (see note to 28.32–33)

privilegiate privileged 217.18

professing making open profession of religious beliefs 184.26

professor person making profession of an art or science, public teacher 125.17, 159.27; one who makes open profession of religious faith 159.22

proner praise, extol 263.30

propone put forward, state 78.19

prosapia *Latin* lineage 78.19, 357.39

protocol see note to 255.2–3

provost-marshal, provost-martial military officer in charge of discipline 248.41, 288.24, 305.10

psalmody psalm-singing 219.4

pshaw exclamation expressing contempt, impatience, or disgust 6.36, 23.26, 278.26

public house, inn 152.31, 155.31, 159.31

puir poor 159.16 etc.

punctilio point of conduct, formality 55.38, 213.13

pund pound 94.28 (see note)

quaggy boggy, soft 82.35

quarter-master military officer responsible for quarters and supplies 200.41, 200.42, 203.13

quarter-sessions see notes to 23.20 and 165.11

quarto sheets of paper folded into four leaves 129.17

quasi *Latin* as if, virtually 53.17, 67.40

quean girl, unmarried young woman 313.29; impudent woman, hussy 332.29

quire choir 187.20

quodlibet *Latin* scholastic argument or exercise 68.10

quoit flat disc of stone or metal for throwing as a game 279.28 (see note), 279.29

quondam former 211.21, 284.28

rampant *heraldry* rearing up 37.6, 49.1, 49.8, 338.1

ranting noisy, boisterous, merry 160.42, 162.19

rapscallion rascal, scamp 305.4

rattle-pated rattle-headed, shallow and noisy 312.8

ream *noun* quantity of paper, normally 480 sheets 30.24

ream *verb* froth, bubble to the brim 51.16

receipt recipe 24.11

reckoning bill, account 50.30 etc.

recognosce reconnoitre 324.25 (see note)

redd separate (combatants), put an end to (fighting) 272.23, 332.9

reduction *Scots law* rescinding of a deed, annulment 359.11

reek smoke, steam 243.23, 332.42

reel¹ lively dance for couples facing each other 146.30

reel² small cylinder 324.12 (see note)

reformado see note to 227.17

regardless heedless 216.12

reif robbery 77.34

reises small branches of trees, brushwood 286.7

reiver robber, raider 74.16

remark observe, take notice of 132.8 etc.

rencontre chance meeting, encounter 11.18, 299.26; duel 67.13, 134.39

repine feel discontent, complain 156.38, 323.22

resiling see note to 331.29–30

reverend worthy of respect 177.13; reverent, deeply respectful 360.5

rheum see note to 170.41

ribband ribbon 53.25 (see note), 303.38

riggs land, ploughed fields 337.36

rin run 219.5, 242.28

rive tear 218.23 (see note to 218.22–23)

robe-de-chambre *French* dressing-gown 298.22

roe roe-deer 57.40 etc.

rokelay short cloak worn by women 51.9, 233.13

romaunt romance 128.5

rood linear measurement, varying from 6 to 8 yards (approx. 6 metres) 353.24

rotunda round-shaped building 39.8

route for 5.2 and 125.37 see note to 5.2

row roll, wrap 219.35

rowel sharp-pointed wheel on spurs 286.36

roynish see note to 41.43

rubrick passage written in red or otherwise distinguished in lettering; guiding direction 27.22

rudas cantankerous, rough-mannered 155.36

rude rough, unrefined, primitive, uncouth 19.21 etc.

ruffled decorated with frills 42.4, 199.3

rugging tugging, seizing for oneself 218.22 (see note to 218.22–23)

runt old cow due for slaughter 51.25

runthereout vagabond, roving person 285.26

sable black 5.41 etc.

sae so 95.7 etc.; for 335.26 see note to 335.26–27

sain bless 64.22

sair *adjective* severe, grievous 314.3, 320.39

sair *adverb* severely, greatly 314.25 etc.

salam salutation, manner of saluting 304.43

salient *heraldry* leaping 49.9

sall shall 199.3

saltation dancing, leaping 147.3

saltier-wise *heraldry* diagonally in the form of a cross 255.10

sang song 323.36, 359.3, 359.3

sapient wise, remarkable for wisdom 162.43 (see note)

sark shirt 199.3

Sasenach, Sassenagh, Sassenach *Scots from Gaelic* Saxon, English, lowland Scots 91.43 etc.; for 189.17 see note

sashed fitted with panes of glass 39.34, 182.18

saumon salmon 321.16

saut salt 321.36

scarted see note to 327.9–10

scathed damaged, blasted 81.39

scathless without harm 53.19

schellum scoundrel, villain 356.25

scion offshoot, descendant 8.35, 45.27

scoup bound, leap 355.36

screen head-scarf, shawl 152.43

scutcheon *heraldry* shield-shaped surface with armorial bearings 9.13; for 269.6 see note

seannachie *Gaelic seanachaidh* tradition bearer, teller of Gaelic heroic legends 78.20

second-sight, for 204.37 and 209.36 see note to 87.10

sectary member of a dissenting sect 30.20, 31.6

sedan-chair covered chair usually for one and carried on two poles 125.37

seer one who has the power of second sight, visionary 87.9, 87.12, 236.32

sell self 155.18

sensorium seat of sensation in the brain 303.3

sept tribe, clan 56.8, 78.18, 99.3, 230.9

sepulture burial 300.10

servitor lawyer's apprentice or clerk 332.3

setting for 146.39 and 195.7 see notes

sexagenary sexagenarian, sixty-year-old 224.13

shanks legs 225.22

sha'n't shall not 306.13

she *Gaelic English* for 127.22 etc. see note to 127.22–23

shibboleth test-word, password 30.32 (see note)

shilpit thin, insipid 52.23

shogh see note to 95.22

shoon shoes 146.24

shouther shoulder 314.5

shrewd severe, hard 46.18

shute shoot 321.7

shuttle instrument used in weaving for passing the thread of the weft across the cloth between the threads of the warp 255.19

sic, sick such 153.25 etc.

siccan such 162.33 etc.

sign make a sign by moving the hand 64.22

sike rivulet (usually dry in summer) 81.18

siller silver, money 201.14, 217.5, 332.29

sirs God preserve us 40.24 (see note), 72.23

sizes assizes, sessions of the criminal court of a country 38.9

skene-occle for 155.19 and 155.20 see note to 155.19

skiff small light boat 85.22, 88.37

slae sloe (fruit of the blackthorn) 61.14

slapdash hastily, carelessly 359.28

slash'd having vertical slits to show a contrasting lining 41.1

slouched see note to 305.6

slug bullet, shot 52.13, 82.8; for 305.2 see note

sma' small 186.36, 187.16, 331.29 (see note to 331.29–30)

smearing-house shed used for treating sheep by the application of a tar-and-grease compound 231.28

smoky suspicious 259.8

snafle simple form of bridle-bit 242.28

sneck see note to 210.20

snood ribbon tied round the forehead and under the hair at the back, worn particularly by young unmarried women 90.8 (see note)

socci *Latin* slippers 246.6

solecism incongruity, impropriety 16.34, 55.43

sooth truth 118.42, 204.37

sopite put to rest, settle 67.27

sornar, sorner vagabond, one who quarters himself upon others, sponger 73.37, 77.43

sort come to agreement 95.5; feed and litter 243.26

southern native of the south, Englishman 111.40

southland southern, from the south 185.7, 294.19

southron southerner(s), English

82.6, 356.9

sowens dish made of oat husks and meal steeped in water and fermented 161.13

spak spoke 314.12

spanker fast-going horse 201.24

spavined halting, lame 50.29

speerings news, information 160.7

spence inner apartment for storage etc. 85.42

spindle instrument used in spinning to twist the fibres into thread 35.3

spiry tapering up like a spire, pointed 63.35

spleuchan *Gaelic spliùchan* pouch for tobacco, leather purse 155.11

sprack lively, animated 224.17

sprechery plunder, pickings 213.38

spuilzie plunder, spoliation 73.37, 323.30; illegal seizure of another's goods 332.34; booty, spoil 243.27

spung rob 233.9

square-rigged *nautical* having yards and sails placed across the masts in contrast to fore and aft 235.40

stane stone 225.15

state statement, account 261.13

steading farm 186.33

steak-raid see note to 120.4

stick[1] hesitate, scruple 173.25

stick[2] stab 272.22

stieve rigid, inflexible 322.14

stile see note to 358.39

stint restrict 106.14

stinted undeveloped, undersized 228.19

stirk young bullock 74.42, 91.42

stirrup-cup see note to 50.24

stoor stern, grim, sturdy 215.37

stot bullock 51.25, 74.42

stoup beaker, tankard 79.41, 95.20 (see note to 95.18–20), 154.15 (see note)

stouth-reef theft by force (typically in a dwelling-house) 78.1

strae straw 320.42

strath broad river valley 64.1 etc.

strathspey Scottish dance, slower than a reel 91.31, 312.19

streek stretch 161.9

stripe strip, shred 28.5

stud horses belonging to one

owner 129.7

subaltern *adjective* subordinate 260.19, 279.25

subaltern *noun* junior officer 34.4

sublunary existing beneath the moon, earthly, temporal 53.12, 157.31, 200.29

substitute for 320.5 see note

supporter *heraldry* figure on each side of a shield, apparently supporting it 37.7 (see note to 37.6–7)

supremacy system which recognises the sovereign as the supreme head of the church 161.2

swingeing huge, immense 299.2

swuir swore 321.9

sybil prophetess, witch 35.3, 190.6

syboe young or spring onion 146.22

symposion *Greek* meeting over food or drink for conversation and discussion 55.41

symptomatic constituting a symptom of a disease, as applied to a secondary disease arising from a primary one 190.41

synod body of ministers and elders, constituting the ecclesiastical court next above the presbytery 65.23, 161.6 (see note to 161.6–7), 173.38

ta *Gaelic English* the 83.36 etc.

tacksman see note to 103.6

ta'en taken 314.7 etc.

taiglit tired, weary 83.37 etc.

tail retinue or entourage of a Highland chieftain 81.9, 81.10, 95.28

taillie deed of entail 47.4 (see note)

taishatr *Gaelic taibhsear* visionary, one who possesses the faculty of second-sight 87.12, 236.35

tak take 154.14 etc.

talbot large hunting hound, with long hanging ears and heavy jaws; heraldic representation of such 357.16, 357.18 (see note)

tan-pit pit containing the liquor in which hides are placed in tanning 36.29

tappit see note to 51.15

targed see note to 214.27

target, targe small round shield 79.14 etc.

tat *Gaelic English* that 83.37 etc.

tauld told 242.23, 314.6

taxt assessed, laid down 246.25

tearing violent, reckless 215.25

teil devil 155.16 (see note)

telt *Gaelic English* told 154.36

tem *Gaelic English* them 152.32

termagant violent, quarrelsome woman 162.25

thae these 320.39, 335.25, 356.24

theft-boot see note to 74.27

thir these 201.8

thof though 258.41

thoft thought 32.34

thraw twist, wrench 243.26

threepit insisted 321.8

throstle-cock male song-thrush 66.32, 66.36, 66.40

through-ganging thoroughgoing, full of energy or 'go' 201.27

tiend tenth part of the produce of the land collected for the support of religion 218.10

Tighearnach *Gaelic Tighearna* Lord, chieftain 127.21, 155.37

till't to it 93.14

tinchel ring of hunters driving together deer by closing in on them 123.2

tint lost 242.20

tippet band of cloth attached to a hood, scarf; hangman's noose 201.18 (see note to 201.17–18)

tirrivie fit of temper, tantrum 351.25

tocherless without a dowry 337.40

toft homestead 218.8

toime *Cumbrian* time 298.28

torrid hot in temper, ardent 214.5

town, toun country estate, house 43.5, 43.15; town 155.19

toy linen or wool cap with flat crown worn by elderly women 51.9

tracasserie *French* bickering, chicanery 266.16

tract track, way 174.43, 196.7, 239.21

treble the highest part in a musical composition, the third or soprano part 35.8

tree three 83.36, 289.38 (see note)

trencher plate, platter 321.36

trepanned ensnared, inveigled 256.39

trews for 95.7 etc. see note to 96.7

trindling rolling, trundling 215.40

trot-cosy kind of cloak with a hood, worn when travelling in cold weather 157.38

troth abbreviation of 'by my troth',

in truth 92.16 etc.

trow trust, believe 186.7, 186.13, 325.10

truckle submit, yield meanly or obsequiously 135.16

trudge for 202.36 see note

trysting-tree see note to 324.35–36

tuilzie fight, brawl 314.12, 321.11

tun-bellied rounded like a tun, barrel-shaped 38.15

turnspit see notes to 48.14 and 215.40

tutelar serving as a guardian or patron 193.38, 356.9

twa two 42.26 etc.

two-penny weak ale or beer sold at two pence the Scots pint 330.10

tyke dog 92.14, 357.18 (see note)

tyro beginner, novice 212.6

umwhile former, late 47.3

uncanny hard, severe 332.9

unco extraordinary, awful 267.29; very 313.40

uncouth rough, unfrequented 318.33

unction earnestness, appreciation 95.42; for 308.6 see note

unexperienced not furnished with, or taught by, experience 33.30, 248.10

unkenn'd unknown 95.5

unsonsy luckless, hapless 318.38; ill-omened, associated with evil powers 335.23

unsublimed unelevated, un-tutored in the aesthetics of the sublime 117.17

unsurmountable incapable of being overcome, insurmountable 193.14

untill to, unto 46.34

unwonted unaccustomed, un-usual 146.19

unwrung see note to 222.5–6

usquebaugh *Gaelic uisge-beatha* whisky 29.40, 79.42, 117.22

vaiselle *French* plate and dishes 121.24

vantage advantage, position of opportunity 235.10

vassal feudal subordinate 18.30 etc.

vassalage condition of feudal sub-ordination and allegiance 126.35

vera very 201.7, 201.7, 201.12, 215.10

vertu see note to 361.16

viands food, provisions 330.12

vice *Latin* in place of 134.5

vicinage vicinity, neighbourhood 44.34, 74.18

videlicet namely 281.27

vidette mounted sentinel placed in advance of an army to observe the movements of the enemy 184.16, 234.26

vilipend disparage, rate lowly, 62.6, 77.43, 358.4

virago overbearing woman, scold 161.4

vis-à-vis *French* face-to-face, opposite 216.8, 303.31

visitant (supernatural) visitor 295.13

vivers food, victuals 214.16

vocalic rich in vowels 111.35

voluntary musical piece played or sung spontaneously 223.12

wa' wall 61.8, 225.15, 359.39

wad would 52.15 etc.

wadna wouldn't 164.3 etc.

wadset for 103.6 and 216.38 see note to 103.6

wain wagon 225.27

wainscot wooden panelling 8.29

wainscotted having wood panel-ling lining 46.21, 274.25

walise valise, travelling case suit-able for strapping to a saddle 162.35, 225.27

wan won 201.28

wanchancy unlucky, dangerous 319.39

wappen-brief *German* document awarding heraldic emblem 49.12

ware¹ waste, spend 93.21, 162.18

ware² were 186.8

warming-pan long-handled pan of metal to contain hot coals, used for warming beds 75.9

warrandice guarantee 332.17

warrant bet, be sure, guarantee 93.27 (see note) etc.

waur worse 248.3

wax grow, increase 146.9

weal welfare, well-being 64.42

wee little 83.36, 155.18, 242.27, 359.10

weeds clothes, garments 18.28, 216.3, 336.5

weel well 127.23 etc.

weel-favoured, well-far'd, weel-fa'rd, weel fa'rd well-favoured, good-looking 161.29, 215.11, 313.42, 314.30

weise aim, shoot 285.31

wend betake oneself 165.13

westlander one from the west of Scotland 188.41

westland-man man from the west of Scotland 175.31

wha, whae who 160.34 etc.

whan when 313.43

whare where 153.19

whey watery part of milk which remains after separation of the curd 94.42, 339.40

whiles sometimes, occasionally 313.38, 320.40, 321.1, 336.23

whilk which 52.44 etc.

whilome once, formerly 330.17

whin see note to 327.9–10

whingeing whining, whimpering 160.33, 161.21

whirligig child's spinning-toy 284.6

whisht hush, (keep) quiet 160.41, 359.39

whit bit 29.23, 279.16, 279.16

white-iron see note to 314.35

wi' with 52.13 etc.

wight human being, person 39.17, 40.34 (see note), 200.31

winding-sheet sheet in which a corpse is wrapped for burial, shroud 236.33 (see note)

winna won't 216.1 etc.

winsome attractive in appearance, handsome 161.20

wire-wove see note to 6.4

withers see note to 222.5–6

wold open country, upland plain 64.33

wont for 254.29 see note to 254.28–29

wot know 160.35, 160.36, 266.24, 325.7

wrang wrong 244.34, 332.33

wreath drift, coil 204.3, 238.11

writer lawyer, solicitor 359.27

wrongous wrongful 332.26

wrought worked 42.26

wuss wish, trust 164.6

wyvern *heraldry* winged dragon with eagle's feet and serpent's tail 17.22

yate gate 351.22

ye you 45.31 etc.

yere your 157.42 etc.

yeresell yourself 285.31

yon yonder, that 84.22 etc.

PENGUIN CLASSICS

IVANHOE
WALTER SCOTT

'Fight on, brave knights! Man dies, but glory lives!'

Banished from England for seeking to marry against his father's wishes, Ivanhoe
joins Richard the Lion Heart on a crusade in the Holy Land. On his return, his
passionate desire is to be reunited with the beautiful but forbidden lady Rowena,
but he soon finds himself playing a more dangerous game as he is drawn into a
bitter power struggle between the noble King Richard and his evil and scheming
brother John. The first of Scott's novels to address a purely English subject,
Ivanhoe is set in a highly romanticized medieval world of tournaments and sieges,
chivalry and adventure, where dispossessed Saxons are pitted against their Norman
overlords, and where the historical and fictional seamlessly merge.

This volume is based on the acclaimed Edinburgh Edition of the Waverley
Novels whose first edition was drawn from Scott's original texts. It contains an
introduction that examines Scott's use of history in the light of contemporary ideas,
a chronology, bibliography, glossary and extensive notes.

'It remains one of the most exciting stories in the language' A. N. Wilson

Edited with an introduction by Graham Tulloch

PENGUIN CLASSICS

EMMA
JANE AUSTEN

> 'I never have been in love; it is not my way, or my nature;
> and I do not think I ever shall'

Beautiful, clever, rich – and single – Emma Woodhouse is perfectly content with her life and sees no need for either love or marriage. Nothing, however, delights her more than interfering in the romantic lives of others. But when she ignores the warnings of her good friend Mr Knightley and attempts to arrange a suitable match for her protégée Harriet Smith, her carefully laid plans soon unravel and have consequences that she never expected. With its imperfect but charming heroine and its witty and subtle exploration of relationships, *Emma* is often seen as Jane Austen's most flawless work.

This edition includes a new chronology and additional suggestions for further reading.

'A masterpiece ... the fusing of moral consideration and human drama achieves perfect pitch' Carol Shields

'These modern editions are to be strongly recommended for their scrupulous texts, informative notes and helpful introductions'
Brian Southam, The Jane Austen Society

Edited with an introduction and notes by Fiona Stafford

PENGUIN CLASSICS

LADY SUSAN/ THE WATSONS/ SANDITON
JANE AUSTEN

'She has poured forth her tender tale of love in vain
and exposed herself forever to the contempt of the whole world'

These three short works show Jane Austen experimenting with a variety of different literary styles, from melodrama to satire, and exploring a range of social classes and settings. The early epistolary novel *Lady Susan* depicts an unscrupulous coquette, toying with the affections of several men. In contrast, *The Watsons* is a delightful fragment, whose spirited heroine, Emma Watson, finds her marriage opportunities restricted by poverty and pride. Written in the last months of Austen's life, the uncompleted novel *Sanditon* is set in a newly established seaside resort, with a glorious cast of hypochondriacs and speculators, and shows the author contemplating a changing society with a mixture of scepticism and amusement.

Margaret Drabble's introduction examines these three works in the context of Jane Austen's major novels and her life, and discusses the social background of her fiction. This edition features a new chronology.

'In it [*Sanditon*] she exploits her greatest gifts, her management of dialogue and her skill with monologue. The book feels open and modern ... as vigorous and inventive as her earlier work' Carol Shields

Edited with an introduction and notes by Margaret Drabble

PENGUIN CLASSICS

MANSFIELD PARK
JANE AUSTEN

'We have all been more or less to blame ... everyone of us, excepting Fanny'

Taken from the poverty of her parents' home, Fanny Price is brought up with her rich cousins at Mansfield Park, acutely aware of her humble rank and with only her cousin Edmund as an ally. During her uncle's absence in Antigua, Mary Crawford and her brother Henry arrive in the neighbourhood, bringing with them London glamour and a reckless taste for flirtation. As her female cousins vie for Henry's attention, and even Edmund falls for Mary's dazzling charms, only Fanny remains doubtful about their influence and finds herself more isolated than ever. A subtle examination of social position and moral integrity, *Mansfield Park* is one of Jane Austen's most profound works.

This edition is based, for the first time since its original publication, on the first edition of 1814. It includes a new chronology, additional suggestions for further reading and the original Penguin Classics introduction by Tony Tanner.

'These modern editions are to be strongly recommended for their scrupulous texts, informative notes and helpful introductions'
Brian Southam, the Jane Austen Society

Edited with an introduction by Kathryn Sutherland

PENGUIN CLASSICS

NORTHANGER ABBEY
JANE AUSTEN

**'What have you been judging from? … Dearest Miss Morland, what ideas
have you been admitting?'**

During an eventful season at Bath, young, naive Catherine Morland experiences
fashionable society for the first time. She is delighted with her new acquaintances:
flirtatious Isabella, who introduces Catherine to the joys of Gothic romances, and
sophisticated Henry and Eleanor Tilney, who invite her to their father's house,
Northanger Abbey. There, influenced by novels of horror and intrigue, Catherine
comes to imagine terrible crimes committed by General Tilney, risking the loss of
Henry's affection, and must learn the difference between fiction and reality, false
friends and true. With its broad comedy and irrepressible heroine, *Northanger
Abbey* is the most youthful and optimistic of Jane Austen's works.

This edition is based on the first edition of 1818, and includes a new chronology
and additional suggestions for further reading.

'These modern editions are to be strongly recommended for their scrupulous texts,
informative notes and helpful introductions' Brian Southam, the Jane Austen
Society

Edited with an introduction by Marilyn Butler

PENGUIN CLASSICS

PERSUASION
JANE AUSTEN

> 'She had been forced into prudence in her youth,
> she learned romance as she grew older'

At twenty-seven, Anne Elliot is no longer young and has few romantic prospects. Eight years earlier, she had been persuaded by her friend Lady Russell to break off her engagement to Frederick Wentworth, a handsome naval captain with neither fortune nor rank. What happens when they encounter each other again is movingly told in Jane Austen's last completed novel. Set in the fashionable societies of Lyme Regis and Bath, *Persuasion* is a brilliant satire of vanity and pretension, but, above all, it is a love story tinged with the heartache of missed opportunities.

In her introduction, Gillian Beer discusses Austen's portrayal of the double-edged nature of persuasion and the clash between old and new worlds. This edition also includes a new chronology and full textual notes.

'These modern editions are to be strongly recommended for their scrupulous texts, informative notes and helpful introductions'
Brian Southam, The Jane Austen Society

Edited with an introduction and notes by Gillian Beer

PENGUIN CLASSICS

PRIDE AND PREJUDICE
JANE AUSTEN

'Vanity, not love, has been my folly'

When Elizabeth Bennet first meets eligible bachelor Fitzwilliam Darcy, she thinks him arrogant and conceited; he is indifferent to her good looks and lively mind. When she later discovers that Darcy has involved himself in the troubled relationship between his friend Bingley and her beloved sister Jane, she is determined to dislike him more than ever. In the sparkling comedy of manners that follows, Jane Austen shows the folly of judging by first impressions and superbly evokes the friendships, gossip and snobberies of provincial eighteenth-century middle-class life.

This edition also includes a new chronology, additional suggestions for further reading, and the original Penguin Classics introduction by Tony Tanner.

'*Pride and Prejudice* has always been the most popular of Jane Austen's books ... with its good humoured comedy, its sunny heroine, its dream denouement'
Claire Tomalin

'These modern editions are to be strongly recommended for their scrupulous texts, informative notes and helpful introductions'
Brian Southam, The Jane Austen Society

Edited by Vivien Jones with an introduction by Tony Tanner

PENGUIN CLASSICS

SENSE AND SENSIBILITY
JANE AUSTEN

> 'The more I know of the world the more am I convinced that
> I shall never see a man whom I can really love. I require so much!'

Marianne Dashwood wears her heart on her sleeve, and when she falls in love with the dashing but unsuitable John Willoughby she ignores her sister Elinor's warning that her impulsive behaviour leaves her open to gossip and innuendo. Meanwhile Elinor, always sensitive to social convention, is struggling to conceal her own romantic disappointment, even from those closest to her. Through their parallel experience of love – and its threatened loss – the sisters learn that sense must mix with sensibility if they are to find personal happiness in a society where status and money govern the rules of love.

This edition also includes explanatory notes, textual variants between first and second edition, and Tony Tanner's introduction to the original Penguin Classics edition.

'These modern editions are to be strongly recommended for their scrupulous texts, informative notes and helpful introductions'
Brian Southam, The Jane Austen Society

Edited with an introduction by Ros Ballaster

PENGUIN CLASSICS

THE PRIVATE MEMOIRS AND CONFESSIONS OF A JUSTIFIED SINNER JAMES HOGG

'My life has been a life of trouble and turmoil; of change and vicissitude;
of anger and exultation; of sorrow and of vengeance'

Robert Colwan, a clergyman's son, is so confident of his salvation as one of
the Lord's elect that he comes to look on himself as a man apart, unhindered
by considerations of mere earthly law. Through Robert's own unforgettable
account, we follow the strange and sinful life into which he is led by a devilish
doppelgänger – a life that will finally lead him to murder. Steeped in the folkloric
superstitions and theological traditions of eighteenth-century Scotland, this
macabre and haunting novel is a devastating portrayal of the stages by which the
human spirit can descend into darkness.

Based on the first edition of 1824, John Wain's text incorporates key revisions from
the 1837 edition to provide the most accurate possible version of this complex
and rewarding work. In his introduction, he illuminates the novel's historical
background of religious and political controversy.

'Astounding' André Gide

Edited with an introduction by John Wain

PENGUIN CLASSICS

BARCHESTER TOWERS
ANTHONY TROLLOPE

> 'I never saw anything like you clergymen …
> you are always thinking of fighting each other'

After the death of old Dr Grantly, a bitter struggle begins over who will succeed him as Bishop of Barchester. And when the decision is finally made to appoint the evangelical Dr Proudie, rather than the son of the old bishop, Archdeacon Grantly, resentment and suspicion threaten to cause deep divisions within the diocese. Trollope's masterly depiction of the plotting and back-stabbing that ensues lies at the heart of one of the most vivid and comic of his Barsetshire novels, peopled by such very different figures as the saintly Warden of Hiram's Hospital, Septimus Harding, the ineffectual but well-meaning new bishop and his terrifying wife, and the oily chaplain Mr Slope who has designs both on Mr Harding's daughter and the fascinating would-be femme fatale Signora Vesey-Neroni.

This is the second volume of Trollope's Chronicles of Barsetshire. In his introduction, Robin Gilmour examines the novel's political and social background and Trollope's concern with changes occurring in society. This edition also includes a preface by J. K. Galbraith.

Edited with an introduction and notes by Robin Gilmour
Preface by J. K. Galbraith

PENGUIN CLASSICS

CLARISSA, *OR* THE HISTORY OF A YOUNG LADY
SAMUEL RICHARDSON

'Oh thou savage-hearted monster!
What work hast thou made in one guilty hour, for a whole age of repentance!'

Pressured by her unscrupulous family to marry a wealthy man she detests, Clarissa Harlowe flees with the witty and debonair Robert Lovelace and places herself under his protection. It soon transpires, however, that Lovelace is an untrustworthy rake whose vague promises of marriage are accompanied by unwelcome and increasingly brutal sexual advances. And yet, Clarissa finds his charm alluring, her scrupulous sense of virtue tinged with unconfessed desire. Told through a complex series of interweaving letters, *Clarissa* is a richly ambiguous study of a fatally attracted couple and a work of astonishing power and immediacy. A huge success when it first appeared in 1747, it remains one of the greatest of all European novels.

In his introduction, Angus Ross examines characterization, the epistolary style, the role of the family and the position of women in *Clarissa*. This edition also includes a chronology, suggestions for further reading, tables of letters, notes, a glossary and an appendix on the music for the 'Ode to Wisdom'.

'The first book in the world for the knowledge it displays of the human heart'
Samuel Johnson

Edited with an introduction and notes by Angus Ross

THE STORY OF PENGUIN CLASSICS

Before 1946 ... 'Classics' are mainly the domain of academics and students; readable editions for everyone else are almost unheard of. This all changes when a little-known classicist, E. V. Rieu, presents Penguin founder Allen Lane with the translation of Homer's *Odyssey* that he has been working on in his spare time.

1946 Penguin Classics debuts with *The Odyssey*, which promptly sells three million copies. Suddenly, classics are no longer for the privileged few.

1950s Rieu, now series editor, turns to professional writers for the best modern, readable translations, including Dorothy L. Sayers's *Inferno* and Robert Graves's unexpurgated *Twelve Caesars*.

1960s The Classics are given the distinctive black covers that have remained a constant throughout the life of the series. Rieu retires in 1964, hailing the Penguin Classics list as 'the greatest educative force of the twentieth century.'

1970s A new generation of translators swells the Penguin Classics ranks, introducing readers of English to classics of world literature from more than twenty languages. The list grows to encompass more history, philosophy, science, religion and politics.

1980s The Penguin American Library launches with titles such as *Uncle Tom's Cabin*, and joins forces with Penguin Classics to provide the most comprehensive library of world literature available from any paperback publisher.

1990s The launch of Penguin Audiobooks brings the classics to a listening audience for the first time, and in 1999 the worldwide launch of the Penguin Classics website extends their reach to the global online community.

The 21st Century Penguin Classics are completely redesigned for the first time in nearly twenty years. This world-famous series now consists of more than 1300 titles, making the widest range of the best books ever written available to millions – and constantly redefining what makes a 'classic'.

The Odyssey continues ...

The best books ever written

PENGUIN ⟨🐧⟩ CLASSICS

SINCE 1946

Find out more at www.penguinclassics.com

PENGUIN CLASSICS

PAMELA
SAMUEL RICHARDSON

'I cannot be patient, I cannot be passive, when my virtue is in danger'

Fifteen-year-old Pamela Andrews, alone and unprotected, is relentlessly pursued by her dead mistress's son. Although she is attracted to young Mr B., she holds out against his demands and threats of abduction and rape, determined to defend her virginity and abide by her own moral standards. Psychologically acute in its investigations of sex, freedom and power, Richardson's first novel caused a sensation when it was first published, with its depiction of a servant heroine who dares to assert herself. Richly comic and full of lively scenes and descriptions, *Pamela* contains a diverse cast of characters, ranging from the vulgar and malevolent Mrs Jewkes to the aggressive but awkward country squire who serves this unusual love story as both its villain and its hero.

This edition incorporates all the revisions made by Richardson in his lifetime. Margaret A. Doody's introduction discusses the genre of epistolary novels, and examines characterization, the role of women and class differences in *Pamela*.

Edited by Peter Sabor with an introduction by Margaret A. Doody